ACKNOWLEDGMENT

This book is dedicated to Nancy, my wife, and to my four daughters: Susan and Janice, in Texas and Oregon, and Zwenle and Yasmin in the Philippines.

I could not have formulated a novel from the several years of research without the patience and encouragement of my wife, the guidance and critiques of my twin brother, Jack, and the hope of a legacy for my daughters and granddaughters.

Look to the future but never forget the past

We are a reflection of history

If we forget our past, if we ignore it, we are nothing

PREFACE

For the first time in modern history, a small Asian nation humbled a giant European empire. This devastating war in Manchuria was a lesson, unfortunately, that western nations failed to heed.

Ignore history and mistakes will be repeated. America misjudged the power of her enemies and ignored two previous sneak naval attacks by Japan: against China in 1894 and Russia in 1904. In 1941, America suffered a similar surprise attack. It should not have happened.

If a nation is less than vigilant, scoffs at enemy ability, enters a war divided by internal dissension, and lacks the will to sacrifice to win, then the seeds of defeat will already have been sown. Japan never really won the Russo-Japanese War of 1904-5 as much as Russia lost it for the above reasons. Japan had not planned on a long war, for which she was unprepared economically. Her goal was for a short war from which she could gain some territory or concessions. Victorious in 1905, though embittered by the terms of the peace treaty, Japan rashly began a long range plan to conquer and control the Pacific basin. In 1941, it was America that was caught unprepared. May it never happen again.

I have endeavored to write about the war from a romantic viewpoint that would offer more than a raw historical account. In this I hope I have balanced the true events with a multi-faceted human story that may very well have occurred, and which proposes that the autumn of the Victorian Era was both more adventurous and less staid than its contemporary society projected.

CONTENTS

ILLUSTRATIONS

CAST OF CHARACTERS

Alesandrov, Baron Viktor Alexeivitch		*Russian army Cossack captain*
Alexeiev, Eugene	Admiral	Russian Far East Viceroy
An-an, (Chao Li)		*Wife of Ellis Rogers*
Ariko, Jiro	Major	*Japanese army spy master*
Berezovsky, Marina		*Port Arthur merchant-trader*
Bezobrazov, Alexander		Russian financial clique head
Bigelow,	Commander	English naval observer
Chen, Hsiuh Yang	Captain	*Chinese junk owner*
Ch'in, Sheng		*Golden Pavilion owner*
Chevier, Claudette		*French nurse*
Crown	Captain	Russian naval officer
Esley, Philip		*English spy, Port Arthur*
Fairborne, Nigel	Commander	*English naval observer*
Feng		*Ariko's hired assassin*
Fock	Major General	Russian army, Port Arthur
Gaszcyhnska, Olga		*Sylvia Levinsky's mother*
Grippenberg, Oscar	Lt. General	2nd Manchurian Army
Gromov	Colonel	Russian army officer, Yalu river
Grozsky, Levi		*Russian student dissident*
Hata, Jiro	Captain	*Japanese destroyer commander*
Horikoshi, Rikyu	General	*Japanese intelligence officer*
Kamamura	Vice Admiral	Japanese navy

Khostoff	Colonel	Port Arthur fortress commander
Kim, (Ok-hum)		*Korean prostitute*
Komura	Baron	Japanese peace negotiator
Kondratenko, Roman Isidorovitch		Port Arthur Chief of Staff
Kuroki	General	Japanese First Army
Kuropatkin, Alexei Nicholaevitch		Russian Lt. General
Lebedeff, Arkady	*Inspector*	*Okhrana secret service*
Levinski, Sylvia		*Russian spy for Japan*
Linievitch	Lt. General	Russian army, Manchuria
Loong, Master		*Marina's agent*
Makharoff	Vice Admiral	Russian navy, Port Arthur
Newins, Wicks		*Reuters journalist*
Nojine, E.K.		Port Arthur journalist
Nozoe, Bungaku	*Lieutenant*	*Japanese jail commander*
Okazaka, Keizo	*Captain*	*Japanese navy, Sasebo*
Oku	General	Japanese Second Army
Owada, Shigeru	Colonel	Japanese army
Oyama	General	Japanese commander in chief
Packenham	Captain	British naval observer
Petrusha	Colonel	Port Arthur provost marshal
Plum Blossom Hu	*Clerk*	*British Shanghai consulate*
Rennenkampf	General	Russian army, Manchuria
Ri, (Man-choi)		*Korean prostitute*
Rogers, Ellis	*Captain*	*U.S. Army agent*
Romanov, Alexandra		German born Czarina
Romanov, Nicholas II		Russian Czar

Romanov, Cyril	Grand Duke	Czar's cousin
Rudnev	Captain	Commander, cruiser *Variag*
Ryokitsu, Arima	Commander	Blockship archtect
Samsonov	General	1st Manchurian Army
Sarnichev	Captain	Cruiser *Boyarin*
Sato, Nobihuro	*Lieutenant*	*Japanese torpedo boat cmdr.*
Scott, Harry	*Taipan*	*Hong Kong boat builder*
Smirnoff, Konstantine	Lt. General	Port Arthur fortress commander
Starck, Oscar V.	Admiral	Port Arthur naval commander
Stoessel, Anatole	General	Port Arthur military governor
Tanaka, Ikura		*Wife of Capt. Tanaka*
Tanaka, Tomoru	*Captain*	*Japanese army*
Tanaka, Yukio		*Daughter of Capt. Tanaka*
Tang		*Dalny family*
Tea Flower (Ti)		*Shanghai tavern hostess*
Tikobara, Hesibo	Captain	Japanese destroyer leader
Togo, Heihachiro	Vice Admiral	Japanese fleet commander
Ukhtomski	Prince	Rear Admiral under Makharoff
Uryu	Rear Admiral	Invasion fleet commander
Von Streich, Rupert	*Uberleutnant*	*Austrian army observer*
Von Waldersee	Field Marshal	China Expedition commander
Witgeft	Vice Admiral	Russian Navy, Port Arthur
Witte, Sergei	Count	Peace Conference leader

Xi (Liu Xi)		*Alesandrov's ex-mistress*
Yatskov, Mikhail	*Lieutenant*	*Chemulpo Russian guard*
Yin-lin		*Marina's servant girl*
Yoo, Rak-hoon		*Korean wagon driver*
Zasulich	General	Russian army-Yalu river
Zieman, Solomon	*Doctor*	*Mukden hospital surgeon*

NOTE: The italicized names indicate either a fictional character or a character whose name has been purposely changed in the interest of family privacy.

PLACES AND OBJECTS

AI-ho	Manchurian river
Akashi	Japanese cruiser
Akasuka	Japanese destroyer
Akitsushima	Japanese cruiser
Amur	Manchurian river
Antung	Yalu river town
Asahi	Japanese battleship
Boyarin	Russian cruiser
Bohai Bay	bay between Dalny and Chefu
Canton (Guangzhou)	Chinese city
Chefu	north China seaport
Chemulpo (Inchon)	Korean seaport
Chiyo Maru	Japanese mine ship
Chiyoda	Japanese cruiser
Chulienchang	Manchurian town
Dalny (Dalien)	Liaotung peninsula port city
Elliot Islands	island group east of Port Arthur
Far East Lumber Co.	Korean lumber enterprise (Russian)
Fuji	Japanese battleship
Fukien (Fujian)	Chinese province
Golden Hill	Port Arthur hill
Golden Pavilion	Shanghai tavern
Harbin	Manchurian capital
Hunhutze	Manchurian bandits
Kasuga	Japanese cruiser

Kasumio	Japanese destroyer
Koryets	Russian gunboat
Kuroki	Commander, Japanese 1st. Army
Kwantung	Peninsula surrounding Port Arthur
Liaotishan	Port Arthur headland
Liaotung (Liaodong)	Peninsula above Port Arthur
Liaoyang	Manchurian town and battle
Lindsay	Island off Korean west coast
Manjour	Captain Crown's vessel
Mokoku Maru	lead blockship
Monalpo	Korean seaport
Mukden (Shenyang)	Manchurian city
Mokoku Maru	leading blockship
Naniwa	Japanese invasion flagship
Nanshan	Manchurian town, battle
Novy Kry	Port Arthur newspaper
Okhrana	Russian secret police
Pallada	Russian heavy cruiser
Panmunjon	Korean town
Pascal	French warship
Peking (Beijing)	Chinese capital
Petropavlovsk	Russian battleship
Pitzuwo	Manchurian coastal town
Pobieda	Russian battleship
Port Arthur (Lushun)	Russian naval base
Pushkin Street	main Port Arthur street
Retvisan	Russian battleship
Rockingham Globe	fictitious English newspaper

Sasebo	Japanese naval base
Seoul	Korean capital
Shantung (Shandong)	Chinese peninsula/province
Shimonoseki	Japanese straits/city
Shimose	Japanese gunpowder
Shinome	Japanese destroyer
Shirakuma	Japanese destroyer
Silny	Russian destroyer
Steresguschy	Russian destroyer
Sumsky	Russian dragoon regiment
Taku (Tanggu)	North China port town
Talien Bay	Bay around Dalny
Talienwan	town near Hand Bay
Tientsin (Tianjin)	North China city
Tsesarevitch	Russian battleship
Tsingtao (Qingdao)	ex-German colony
Ujina	Hiroshima port
Variag	Russian light cruiser
Vicksburg	U.S. cruiser
Wei-hai-wei	British naval station
Wiju	Yalu river town
Yadsuma	Japanese destroyer
Yalu	border river, Korea/Manchuria
Yenesei	Russian mine sweeper

APPROXIMATE DISTANCES IN MILES IN 1905

Dalny to Harbin	436
Dalny to Talienwan	50
Dalny to Pitzuwo	60
Harbin to St Petersburg	6000
Liaoyang to Mukden	40
Mukden to Yalu	40
Mukden to Harbin	190
Nanshan to Liaoyang	60
Port Arthur to Dalny	35
Port Arthur to Mukden	271
Port Arthur to Harbin	461
Pyongyang to Panmunjon	90
Pyongyang to Yalu	100
Seoul to Pyongyang	35

PROLOGUE

In January the Japanese war fleet had lain hidden at anchorage in the Elliot Island group northeast of the Manchurian port of Port Arthur. During the first week of February the ships weighed anchor and steamed south toward China's north coast, while ostensibly on winter manuevers. At the end of that week the fleet had begun to move away from the vicinity of the British naval station at Wei-hai-wei on China's coast. Instead of steaming back along its announced northeast course toward Lindsay Island, the flagship, His Imperial Japanese Majesty's battleship (HIJMS) *Asahi*, had changed direction to lead the attack fleet due north toward Port Arthur's giant Russian naval base at the southern tip of Manchuria's Kwantung peninsula.

Southward in Bohai Bay, the commander of a Japanese torpedo boat tore open the envelope containing his secret orders. The dim early morning light caused him to squint in order to read the small typed words. Dated Sunday, February 7, 1904, the message read:

On this date destroy any foreign vessel bound for Port Arthur regardless of its flag. Halt your patrol at 1800 hours and return to rendezvous point.

Lieutenant Nobihuro Sato knew the meaning of the message. WAR!

Sato could hardly contain his excitement now that the die was cast. He rubbed his hands with glee, relishing the prospect of humbling the barbaric Russians. At long last Japan would teach a lesson to the western world.

He smacked his fist against the nearby bulkhead, raised his arms in triumph and shouted to the wind: *No more tolerance of insults or second class treatment. No more broken promises. Japan will seize Korea and then Manchuria. In time all China will fall to Japan. Perhaps even Siberia.*

In his eyes the future belonged to the land of the Rising Sun. Inevitably, the entire Pacific Ocean would belong to Japan.

The torpedo boat continued to cruise the bay, positioning itself midway between the north China coastal province of Shantung and Port Arthur. Under a gray sky the Japanese craft ploughed easily through the rough waters of the Yellow Sea. It's steam engine functioned smoothly, responding as capably as the British shipyards had intended. Sato hoped that Japan would soon have its own flourishing shipbuilding facilities, and if the war lasted long enough, perhaps he would be rewarded with command of a new destroyer, perhaps even a mighty cruiser.

Maintaining his balance on the rising and falling deck, Sato continued to scan the horizon through his binoculars as the day wore on uneventfully. He saw nothing aft and nothing to port or starboard. Ahead to the south loomed a dirty grey wall of fog that stretched from the leaden surface of the sea to blot out the southern sky. In the late afternoon, as the sun descended lower in the west, Sato steered his craft toward the curtain of fog. *Then he saw it!*

A dark blob had emerged slowly from the impenetrable veil of fog. He focused his glass on the object—a large black Chinese junk riding the water under full sail and headed north by northwest toward Port Arthur. The junk's three masts carried full lanteen sails that stretched tightly in the brisk breeze. The junk bore no flag or name. Except for four figures, the deck seemed deserted. Riding low in the water and obviously heavily laden, the vessel lumbered along with surprising ease.

Sato had been briefed before departing from the imperial naval base at Sasebo, Japan. "Open your orders at 0500 hours on the seventh," his commander had instructed. "Once you read your orders, maintain wireless silence. It is imperative that no foreign vessels identify or know the position of any ship of His Majesty's Imperial Japanese Navy."

The sighting of the large junk prompted Sato to ring the bell to alert his engineering officer below. "Full speed ahead," he shouted through the mouthpiece of the telegraph. Excitedly, he ordered his deck officer to ready the forward cannon. "Battle stations! Prepare to fire." Responding to the command, the gunners quickly fell into the rhythm of their long-practiced routine.

Sato fretted impatiently while the six-man gun crew scrambled to remove the canvas cover of the three-inch deck gun and hurried to rip off the top of an ammunition crate.

"Hurry! Hurry!" he yelled, "Prepare to fire."

Gloating with savage anticipation, he targeted his victim. "I have you now, you bastard!" This was one prey that he was hell-bent on blasting out of the water.

Sato glared at his gunnery officer. Patience not being one of his virtues, he drummed his fingers nervously. "Hurry," he shouted again. Crewmen slid crates of shells along the polished wooden deck. The gunners quickly slammed a shell into the breech of the forward deck gun. Sato raised his hand to signal the firing command.

The large black junk innocently pulled away from the fog bank. Oblivious to any danger, and partially blinded by the rays of the late afternoon sun, now beginning to dip to the surface of the sea, a Chinese crewman gripped the ship's wheel. Another crewman stood nearby.

The owner and captain, Chen Hsiuh Yang, stood forward near the starboard railing, conversing with his passenger, an American army officer dressed in mufti.

The American gazed apprehensively at the dark, frigid waters of the wintery Yellow Sea. The cheerless expanse of water reminded him of earlier hard lessons learned during his three years of life aboard commercial sailing ships: stay alert because in death there is a finality that is irreversible. He tempered the warning with the fatalism: *if it happens, it happens*, a saying that helped sooth apprehension of the unknown. Nevertheless, his survivor's zest for life overrode any tendency to slide passively into oblivion. He would fight to survive as he always had in the past.

The American, a lean, young infantry first lieutenant, eyed the sky. Speaking in fluent Mandarin Chinese, he observed to the captain, "It's good to feel the sun." The salt-heavy wintery front blowing down from Siberia had hidden the sun all day. Now, breaking through the high overcast, the rays of the sun gave a brief sparkle to the sullen waters of the bay and brightened the cheerless gloom of the harsh February day.

Moments later a sudden quickening wind rippled the water with white caps. "Looks like snow—maybe tonight, Chen." Lieutenant Ellis Rogers addressed the captain by his surname without benefit of title, a familiarity derived from long years of friendship. Shivering slightly, Rogers pulled up the collar of his padded Chinese coat and jammed his western campaign hat down tighter.

He suddenly froze as his eye caught the flash of fire in the distance. "Chen, look out...!" Both men ducked as the whistle of a hurtling projectile broke the afternoon silence. The shell exploded two hundred yards aft of the fan tail. Terrified by the noise of the explosion and the accompanying upward column of water, the Chinese helmsman abandoned the wheel and fled in panic. He raced with the other crewman toward the ladder extending below the deck. Chen yelled at them to stop. "Get back on deck, you cowards." Seeing his order ignored, he dashed aft to grasp the wheel, spinning it hard to port. The port railing of the turning boat dipped dangerously low, sending green seawater pouring over the gunnels.

Chen clung to the wheel, barely keeping a foothold on the tipping deck. Thrown off balance, the American thudded against the corner of a deck crate, sending a sickening stab of pain through his rib cage. As soon as he could recover his breath, he scrambled to his feet and hobbled toward Chen. The captain waved him aside, shouting, "Check below."

Rogers rubbed his side to ease the throbbing pain, then limped below to check on the bewildered crewmen. He raised his hand to quiet the babble of frightened voices and cautioned the men to stay calm until summoned by the captain. Brushing past the men, he stepped over the scattered mess of their interrupted meal that lay strewn on the lower deck. At his bunk he retrieved his army orders and passport, already stuffed in an oilskin pouch. He pushed a revolver and a scabbered knife into his belt before returning topside.

Back on the upper deck he looked over his shoulder toward the northeast. A small warship was slowly closing the distance. It flew no flag. Possibly a gunboat or torpedo craft, he surmised. Maybe Russian, maybe Japanese? Who else would menace the shipping lanes of the Yellow Sea so arrogantly?

At the helm, Chen strove to bring his craft about into a more southerly direction, trying to regain the cover of the thick bank of fog that had impeded his passage all afternoon, but now offered a welcome sanctuary. He could see that the faster warship was steadily gaining.

"We need the smoke pots," he shouted to the American "Take the wheel. I'll get the crew."

Rogers did not hear him at first; he was too absorbed in readying two life rings, loosely lashing their short lines to the railing. Before the two preservers went overboard, Chen left the wheel and ran back to Rogers, holding out his hand for the revolver in Rogers' belt.

Chen pointed to the wheel, making a zig-zag motion with one hand, then moved forward to the hatch opening. He yelled for the crew to come on deck. No one responded to his order. Descending the ladder far enough to show the revolver, he jerked his thumb upward. "Now," he shouted, "Back on deck!" The frightened crewmen moved toward him.

Rogers gripped the wheel as the reluctant crewmen gathered to crouch near a crate at the foot of the mast. Chen threw open the crate cover and pointed to the dirty clay pots inside. "Light the pots," he ordered. "Get them into the water. Quick!"

The frigid wind cut through the light clothing of the shivering men as they hastened to escape the captain's wrath. They scooped up the discolored clay pots filled with dirty oil and kerosene. The pots were attached to rough wood tubs that served as small rafts. The crewmen uncapped the pots, lit the black contents and lowered a pot onto the sea surface each time the junk's course zig-zagged. Soon, a pall of dense black smoke began to rise from the sea. Pushed by the bitterly cold siberian wind, the smoke spread like a dirty curtain behind the fleeing junk.

By the time Lieutenant Sato realized what was taking place, his target was already partially obscured. He no longer hesitated in his decision.

Momentarily, he had worried that his eagerness to destroy the Chinaman might be rash. What if the explosion of a shell would somehow alert the enemy fleet? Japanese Fleet Admiral Heihachiro Togo had stressed the necessity of surprise most emphatically. *Nothing,* he had emphasized, *nothing should expose the presence of Japan's navy.*

Sato considered a choice of ramming the junk, a collision that might damage his own ship, or the alternative of continuing to shell the fleeing Chinaman. He had to act fast. If the junk escaped and returned to the port of Chefu, the wireless station there would surely alert Port Arthur. Twice he slammed his fist against a bulkhead, biting his lip in frustration. *What should he do?* He muttered to himself, "You are the captain. Make a decision. Right or wrong, just make a decision!"

The Chinaman had become too tempting a target. Impetuously Sato made up his mind, raised his hand, and gave the order to fire a second shell. The gunnery officer hesitated. Sato glared at the officer. "Move. What are you waiting for?" he shouted. The gunners quickly slammed a second shell into the breech of the deck gun. Sato dropped his hand to signal the firing command. The loud whistle of the incoming shell caused Rogers and Chen to duck low. The explosive tore out a section of the starboard rail, splattering a shower of wood fragments through the air before crashing into the sea. The junk rocked violently from the impact. Both life rings had vanished with the railing.

A headless body lay sprawled on the deck, its legs jerking spasmodically in a gushing tide of blood. It was the luckless helmsman. Acting quickly, Chen pointed the revolver at the other crewmen, motioning them to push the body overboard and sluice the blood with a bucket of sea water.

"Damn, they have the range now," Rogers growled. "We don't have much time."

Both men eyed the fog bank, still disappointingly remote. The speedier warship continued to gain. Looking back, Rogers could see its gun crew gathered about the deck gun. The warship crept ever closer. The brief sun had almost disappeared. In the dimming light of the dying afternoon, the fog bank seemed hopelessly out of reach.

"Come on, come on," Rogers muttered, feeling himself pushing against the mast as if to aid their flight. Looking across the endless expanse of cold gray sea, he swallowed hard. Except for the enemy ship, not a sign of life appeared on the horizon. *Was this the way it would end?* The chance for survival in the icy water would be slim. A man might last fifteen minutes at most before slipping beneath the surface of the cruel sea. His chest constricted and he swallowed again to overcome the dryness of his mouth. The knot in his stomach tightened. Aside from the fear and the helpless anonimity of such a fate, what most bothered him most was his unfullfilled mission. He dreaded its failure. In a matter of seconds he and the junk could disappear forever.

Rogers shook his head to clear away the cobwebs of worry and doubt. He moved forward stiffly, his side still throbbing with pain. Searching the sea, he realized the warship had suddenly disappeared from view behind the smoke line. Ahead, he could see a narrow rim of calmer water bordering the wall of fog. They were almost into it, but the wind had diminished, not unusual near a fog bank.

With the wind abaft, Chen's usually impassive face hid his worry. "We need more speed," he said. The wind hummed through the taut shrouds, but more canvas was needed in the downwind passage. He and Rogers looked at the sail locker with a single thought.

"Good idea, we can do it" Rogers said. Benefitted with past experience, he leaped into action. He threw open the lid of the sail locker and shouted for the crew to help him pull out the large spread of canvas to arrange it on the deck. With their help, he began to hoist the sail slightly and quickly snapped hooks in place. Then he fastened a long length of line at each bottom corner of the canvas that hung limp against the mast. "Now pull the lines," he ordered as he hoisted the sail ever higher. He spoke firmly, trying not to panic the agitated crew. "Hold on to something and brace yourselves—and keep quiet. When I signal, play out the lines. When I say 'stop,' hold the lines steady. Easy as it goes." The shivering men understood.

Playing out the lines, they struggled to hold the lines as the wind buffetted the large, flapping sheet of canvas. They followed his directions, until the optimum wind pocket filled the large makeshift spinnaker. Chen smiled in amusement. What he wouldn't give to see the face of the enemy skipper looking at the spectacle of a sloop-rigged junk.

"Don't tie the lines; just keep that same tension or slack off when I say so," Rogers ordered. He thanked God for Chen's newly designed unorthodox keel. Junks were usually keel-less, but Chen's craft had one and it was even adjustable. The speed of the Chinese craft quickened perceptibly. The crew succeeded in pulling the billowing sail taut. The boxy hull tipped dangerously until a proper tension of the lines determined a safe heeling of the boat. Fortunately the sharp wind held steady, easing the fear that quirky gusts might spell disaster. Reassured, Rogers finally directed the crewmen to loop the lines around deck cleats to alleviate their struggle. The junk strained like a wild hound on a leash as the wind pushed against the pocketed canvas. The smashed deck rode barely free of the rushing water. Sea water boiled past the partially submerged port railing as a brisk, steady wind continued to aid the junk's flight.

Still at the wheel, Chen continued to glance over his shoulder at the smoke screen while easing the junk slightly more southward. The roomy but cumbersome and boxy hull continued to move with unusual smoothness through the choppy sea, now thick with whitecaps. He decided to abandon the zig-zag manuever to maintain a straight course in pursuit of the fog bank.

Moments passed. No one spoke in the mounting tension. Only the sound of creaking timbers, and water slapping against the hull broke the eerie silence. The red orb of a dippng sun dropped below the horizon.

Chen looked over his shoulder. His voice broke the stillness, "It is Japanese," he announced. "Definitely a torpedo boat."

Rogers looked back to see the warship emerging from the wall of smoke. It seemed closer than ever and continued to close the separation relentlessly. Rogers knew in his heart that it would be impossible for the warship to miss a target so close. So did Captain Chen.

Chen spun the wheel abruptly, banking hard to starboard just as the scream of a third shell broke the strained silence. Bits of wood tore into the sea. An acrid cloud of yellow smoke rose from the deck, mingling with a shower of sea water that drenched the wounded boat and its sprawling crew. Part of the aft port deck and railing had disappeared. Rogers rolled off his back, struggling to stand, wondering if he was hit. Miraculously he was not, nor were any of the others. Pretty good shooting, Rogers thought, almost in reluctant admiration. He scrambled to his feet, steeling himself for another explosion.

Then he looked up, surprised to see Chen standing fully erect at the wheel, his face covered with a devilish grin. The captain raised his fist in a triumphant salute. His form faded from sight as the junk slid silently into a cold world of impenetrable fog.

Quiet seconds trailed into minutes. Both men listened intently, hidden within the dense gray cover of fog. Chen slowly and silently eased his craft farther to starboard, seeking to come about to resume a northwesterly course. The spinnaker became a jib as they gradually headed into the wind. Rogers hissed to get the attention of the half-hidden crewmen. He signalled the change of course and motioned for them to slacken the lines to compensate for the wind shift, and then, once about, to tighten the lines again.

In the awesome silence, all heard the churning noise of the torpedo boat's screw as the fog-shrouded Japanese craft passed close by on a southwesterly course. The noise gradually faded until there was again utter silence.

"They took our bait," Chen whispered to the American. "Now is our best chance to jump ahead before they realize we may have turned back north."

By now, the fog was so thick that Rogers could no longer see the bow of the junk. He could barely make out the figures of the ghostly crew crouching close by. In a low voice he instructed them to hold on to each other if they had to, but not to slacken the lines. "Stay quiet and hold steady." The junk headed into the wind, heeling gracefully in response. Then he heard Chen call softly, "Take the wheel for a minute, Ellis. I'm going below."

The captain groped his way below deck to douse the overhead lantern in the crew's mess. He took care to extinguish the coals in the crew's brazier. From below he could hear the occasional slap of shroud lines breaking the silence, accompanied by the soft thud of seawater boiling past the speeding

Chen's voyage from Chepu to Dalny

Tsar Nicholas II

The Emperor (Mikado) of Japan

hull. Like a ghost ship, the junk pressed northward, disregarding any dangers that might lay hidden in the soupy fog. When he came back on deck, Chen brought warmer garments for the shivering crew. The winter bone-chilling air temperature hovered near 20 degrees F.

For over an hour the course of the boat remained unchanged. The icy wind continued to hold steady, permitting the crew to become more relaxed as they mastered control of the large auxiliary sail. Rogers peered at the dial of his pocket compass. Coming close to Chen's side he wordlessly pointed in the direction of Port Arthur. The Captain shook his head.

"No. We will try Dalny instead. We were attacked so something must be happening over there." He inclined his head toward the Russian naval base.

Another hour passed, then, suddenly, the boat slid out of the cover of fog into the inky blackness of the night. A light snowfall had commenced, elevating the temperature slightly. An hour later, without warning, the moon broke through the overcast for a brief period. Both men saw a line of warships dead ahead, dimly silhouetted against the northern horizon and crossing perpendicular to their course. From the size and shapes of the hulls, they recognized a large four-funneled armored battleship, flanked slightly astern by two three-funneled cruisers and preceded by a vanguard of four smaller destroyers. The warship flotilla showed no lights and moved straight westward toward Port Arthur.

Suddenly, one of the destroyers broke away from the flotilla and started to turn south. "Damn," Rogers muttered. "What now?"

But as quickly as it had appeared, the moon was blotted out again by the cloud cover. If the junk had been spotted, no movement of attack came from the warships. Those aboard the junk breathed a sigh of relief. For three more hours, the junk stayed on a slower but more direct northerly course. Time sped by fast.

A scant few minutes before midnight, all on board heard the far off rumble of cannon fire. Several flickering lights shone faintly on the western horizon. "Searchlights. Port Arthur," Chen muttered. The blue light of a Russian starshell traced through the sky, followed by another and then another.

"Just our bad luck to be in the way," Rogers observed. "It could have been worse. Somebody is getting clobbered over there."

Chen agreed. "It is my guess that the Japanese just hit Port Arthur. No wonder they were running without lights. I hope the Russians had no warships at Dalny port for the Japanese to attack, or we are heading into more trouble. But I doubt the Japanese would be so stupid to make such an attack on the naval base with a split force. They would more likely throw their full might against Port Arthur. We will soon find out. Tomorrow could be dangerous."

Rogers wondered if the U.S. War Department realized the untenability of his position. Under orders to proceed to Manchuria, he had wandered into a hornet's nest of trouble. He found himself thinking that it must have been far safer for him in Peking four years ago. As bad as the China siege had been, the Boxers in those days lacked the modern firepower of Japan and Russia, allies then and now enemies.

As unruffled as ever, Chen said: "We should reach Dalny by early morning. In another hour, we will lower the auxiliary sail. We do not want to arrive before dawn. So let's hope they left Dalny alone."

CHAPTER ONE

Lt. Nobihuro Sato cursed when he realized he had lost the slippery junk. He glanced at his pocket watch and cursed again. He was not going to arrive at the rendezvous point in time. He knew how little tolerance for mistakes Admiral Togo had. Sato's scowl deepened, accentuating the natural cruelty of his mouth.

The farewell fete at Sasebo base in Japan two days earlier had not disclosed the hour of attack. Amid the many full glasses of champagne and loud shouts of "banzai," the attack force had only been told that the Mikado's government had chosen war. Japan would crush the stupid Russians in a surprise attack as Japan had done to China ten years earlier. Why give the enemy a warning? That was weak western thinking and stupid reasoning. And Sunday was a good day to attack a Christian nation. Sunday at midnight would be the ultimate surprise.

Sato longed to be in the vanguard of the attack, to cover himself with glory. Instead, he had been assigned to flanking duty to support those who would teach the barbaric Russians a long overdue lesson. He had been disappointed when all the new torpedoes were given to the attack destroyers. His older "yellow cigars" had been polished till they gleamed and the torpedo tubes stood greased and ready. But Sato knew inwardly that the prime targets would be the Russian battleships, and that meant the torpedo destroyers would reap the glory. Well, perhaps his time would come—there was still the Russian Far Eastern Fleet at Vladivostok to be destroyed. Reluctantly, he called off the chase and headed north by northwest. With visions of glorious combat filling his mind, yet sobered by apprehension for his tardy rendezvous contact, he hurried to rejoin Admiral Togo's fleet.

Aboard HIJMS *Asahi*, eighteen destroyer captains sat at a long table facing Fleet Admiral Heihachiro Togo, who occupied a chair just away from the center of the table. Stationed behind the admiral were his chief of staff and several flag lieutenants. The audience of destroyer officers, with pencils poised above the notebooks the admiral had provided, listened intently for Togo to commence speaking. A hush fell over those occupying the crowded room as Togo looked up to address his audience.

One of the officers, Destroyer Captain Jiro Hata of Flotilla One, regarded Togo with a mixture of impatience and resentment. He did not like his leader. Hata itched for action, not a lecture. He had no doubt that the admiral had chosen correctly those who would lead the attack against the Russian Pacific Fleet, but scrutinizing Togo's short, squat, unimpressive figure, Hata sneered. The European appearance of Togo's face seemed particularly bothersome. Watching the large, white moustache shielding a perpetual scowl, and the short figure assuming the habitual stance of arms akimbo and palms planted firmly against hips, Hata almost shook his head in annoyance.

Even though Hata knew that Togo could not help his western face, the sneer mirrored the seething contempt Hata had for all caucasians. Togo's countenance painfully reminded Hata of one of the small number of caucasians aboard the *Asahi*. All were English naval observers, and the one who particularly irked Hata was the British Admiralty's special expert in torpedo warfare, Commander Nigel Fairborne. It galled Hata that the Japanese navy still entertained advice from foreign naval experts, even if the British had organized and trained Japan's navy for the past twenty years. Togo had lived and trained in Australia and England for several years. He spoke the English language well. But Hata believed that Japan was now fully capable of fighting a modern naval war without foreign guidance. The surprise victory over China's fleet ten years earlier should have proven that.

Hata avoided the English officers. He considered Fairborne to be the most supercilious ass he had ever met. Besides, the British officer's undisguised interest in young Japanese mess attendants was already a prime topic of shipboard gossip.

Fairborne stood in the rear of the crowded room, joined by two senior British officers, Captain Packenham and Commander Bigelow. Hata dared to stare at Fairborne, wondering why the Brit had the effrontery to attend the briefing. Admiral Togo's opening words jerked Hata to attention.

In his usual concise way, wasting few words and speaking slowly, Togo addressed his audience.

"Gentlemen, this very night at midnight, we will attack the Russian Pacific squadron at both Port Arthur and Dalny. I leave it to the Division Commanders to select the exact time after they have selected the point of attack. Your ships have been divided into two flotillas. Flotilla One, comprised of ten destroyers, will attack Port Arthur. Our information is that certainly all the battleships are in the roadstead at Port Arthur. But we have learned recently, however, that some smaller ships, perhaps even a cruiser or two, may be at Dalny, so Flotilla Two, with eight destroyers, will make a thorough reconnaissance there and strike if necessary."

Hata could hardly keep from laughing at the long faces of the men of Flotilla Two. What a disappointment for the poor devils, he thought; they know the glory and prizes are at Port Arthur, not Dalny. How nice that he was in the first flotilla. He sat gloating with smug triumph until the thought crossed his mind that there might not be any enemy warships at Dalny. The division of Togo's destroyer force began to trouble him.

After a momentary pause, the admiral held up his copy of a distributed map. "Each has before him a map of the Port Arthur roadstead and a map of the Bay of Talien and its port of Dalny. You can see exactly the places at Port Arthur where the enemy's ships are anchored. We have obtained these data from secret information given by Major Ariko, an army intelligence officer who is recently in Port Arthur in disguise. According to his information, it is more than probable that you will take the enemy completely off guard, for it appears that they do not expect the outbreak of hostilities for several days yet."

Hata wondered if the admiral, in spite of his words, was completely assured of Ariko's veracity. Hata had never liked Ariko and often referred to him as a "sneaky little bastard." Hata had little patience for any espionage agent. Their clandestine methods offended him. Also, typical of the prevailing interservice rivalry, he disliked cooperating so closely with the imperial army. He questioned why Togo would confer so closely with the army when this was clearly a naval battle plan.

Togo's next words startled him. "This will be a destroyer strike only. The rest of the fleet will be kept in reserve to support the invasion of Korea." Hata squirmed apprehensively. *No cruisers or battleships? What was this, a suicide mission? Well, so be it.* He had always resolved to lay down his life for his country as valiantly as possible. Dying for Japan was his most cherished dream. But the possibility of failure troubled him.

Togo pressed on, emphasizing the need for caution. The Russians, so he had been informed by Ariko, had conducted periodic mock destroyer strikes in their defensive training. Togo doubted that such preparedness would pose a great problem. He purposely failed to mention Ariko's information that Russian Admiral Starck was hosting a banquet for key officers at the admiral's home this very night. Togo did not want to lead his men to think the operation would be too easy with the absence of enemy officers aboard the Russian battleships.

Addressing his two flotilla commanders, Togo said, "I want, notwithstanding, to bring the following points to your notice: let the object of attack by each of you be the battleships. If by chance you meet with cruisers, try to avoid them as much as possible; only attack them if their searchlights find you and you are seriously threatened."

Hata fought to keep from shaking his head in disbelief. That strategy, he wanted to shout, would not deter him from an attack. If he encountered a large armored enemy cruiser, he would strike at once. The admiral was too conservative. Japan, unlike Russia, had no reserve fleet. So why not even the odds?

Togo cautioned the assembled group: "I need hardly remind you of the necessity of absolute invisibility of your ships. You must have your lights extinguishd or properly screened. Remind your engineers always to have their fires well banked and not to jeopardize the attack by letting sparks come up the funnel. Also check the steam pressure at the moment of attack. Maximum speed should only be reached at the time of attack or when discovered by the enemy, and let me remind you that the attack must be delivered with the greatest energy possible, because, gentlemen, we are at war, and only he who acts fearlessly can hope for success. Your duty, gentlemen, is very simple. Show yourselves worthy of the confidence which I place in you and of which I am responsible to His Majesty, The Mikado."

Admiral Togo rose to his feet, quickly followed by his audience. "I hope that we shall all meet again when your mission has been accomplished. If any of you has to die, his is the greater glory, that of having sacrificed his life for the greatness of Japan, and history will place him forever among its heroes."

Hata joined the others in a resounding cheer for the Mikado. But disappointment gripped him when he saw the admiral signal the head steward to serve each officer a glass of champagne. It had always irritated him to see Togo indulge in what Hata considered another stupid German naval custom. But he joined in the toast and drank to the success of their enterprise and stood in line to shake the admiral's hand. He detected no animosity on Togo's countenance when he shook the extended hand. Apparently the admiral had chosen to ignore the earlier unfortunate collision of Hata's ship with another destroyer. Though the damage was slight, Hata had received the full brunt of Togo's wrath. Few officers ever relaxed under the admiral's command because of his acid tongue and unrelenting discipline of subordinates.

The men of Flotilla One enjoyed the congratulations of fellow officers, then departed to gather in the cabin of the Division Commander's ship for last minute detailed instructions. Hata was furious to see Fairborne in the cabin.

"Why are you here, commander?" he snarled.

The Division commander interrupted to order all to come to attention.

"Commanders Bigelow and Fairborne are present under orders of Admiral Togo," he said. "They are both torpedo experts, as you should know. They will advise us on any torpedo problems and will report to the admiral, as interested neutrals, of possible future changes that might be advisable."

Hata thoroughly disliked his division commander because of the man's aloofness and excessive caution—an unmarried man who droned on and on, boringly repetitious in his instructions. He never seemed to know when to shut up, continuing long after making his point. Hata squirmed in his seat. Couldn't the man appreciate the sixteen bitterly cold days of tedious practice his men had just endured in the wintery waters of the Yellow Sea? *Dammit, Flotilla One was ready and eager to go into battle, not listen to a lecture.*

Hata objected at once to the commander's order to fit all torpedoes with the new net cutters. "We don't know if the net cutters will work any better than the old ones. The torpedoes always run badly with the net cutters attached. Besides, the stupid Russians are probably too lazy to have their torpedo nets in place."

The leader ignored Hata's impertinence. "If the nets are in place, we will have to rely on the cutters. Therefore, it will be necessary to get as close as possible when we attack. You each have your allotted position for attack; don't forget that from the moment the signal comes to separate, each of you will work independently. I should not have to remind you that under no circumstances will your ship, even though heavily damaged, fall into the hands of the enemy. Discharge your torpedoes with effect; everything else is secondary. If you are not rendered *hors de combat*, get out of sight at once and reload with the spare torpedoes. No shot must miss—remember, the enemy ships are anchored targets."

Hata shifted uncomfortably as the commander's monotonous voice labored on about the necessary chain of command, how to manuever in action, how to command the shipboard personnel. Seeing Hata's lip curl, the commander cautioned the men not to continue firing too hastily or too long because of the danger of damaging each other. Hata ground his teeth in anger at the obvious reference to his earlier collision. He glared at his commander.

His leader looked back with pity. If it were not for Hata's proven bravery and skill, the commander would seek his transfer at once. *The impatient and arrogant bastard*, the commander thought, though his facial expression did not change. Some day Hata would get his comeuppance. He was almost as insufferable as his cousin, torpedo boat commander Sato.

Enjoying the expression on Hata's face at the news, the commander made a surprise announcement: "Commanders Bigelow and Fairborne have courageously offered their services." He bowed to the Britons. "Mr. Bigelow will join me on the *Kasumio*. Mr. Fairborne will accompany Captain Hata."

Hata, his face flushed with rage, objected vociferously. "Sir, I do not want to be burdened with someone who is not Japanese. I do not want interference with my duties. I and my crew are fully capable of launching the attack that we have trained long and hard to do. It is our right to perform our mission unencumbered—for the glory of Japan and the emperor."

The commander, stifling a smile, cut him short. "I have spoken. There will be no change to the assignment. This briefing is now adjourned."

At last, back aboard his own ship, Hata tried to ignore Fairborne's presence, not speaking to him directly and ordering a junior deck officer to show Fairborne to his quarters. But Fairborne refused to be waved aside, insisting on accompanying the angry captain. Hata made a final inspection to ensure the readiness of his two torpedo tubes, checking that the torpedoes were charged with compressed air to regulation pressure, that the net cutters were in place, and, finally, that the torpedo safety pins were removed. He could not forget the ignominy suffered in the war with China when two other destroyer captains had fired their torpedoes without first removing the pins.

Hata arranged for the proper signals to be used in case the telegraph to the engine room broke down. He received assurance from his always reliable engineering officer that lumps of carefully selected coal lay piled in readiness on the stokehold plates. The deck crew also had waxed the wooden upper deck so the ammunition cases could slide easily, and the crew also made sure that all watertight doors functioned properly.

As the evening shadows lengthened, Hata ordered a special dinner for his men and reluctantly gave the command, "Pipe all hands to dinner." He often resented the language and European customs the Japanese had adopted.

He was aware that Fairborne had joined him to say, "Jolly good show, Captain. We have a saying in the royal navy: 'With a full stomach one works badly, but one fights all the better for it!'" Hata refused to acknowledge Fairborne's pleasantry.

The appointed hour of departure arrived. With the steam up and the circulators throbbing, Hata forgot any apprehension he may have had for the coming battle. Now he waited eagerly for action and impatiently strained to hear the commander's whistle. From that moment on, he vowed, he would not leave the ship's bridge. That was also Fairborne's intention.

The destroyers followed the commander's lead ship *Kasumio* on a mostly western course, soon vanishing into the darkness of the frigid night. The temperature had dropped back down to 20 degrees, and a light snowfall had commmenced. The ten-destroyer formation ploughed through the choppy sea, arrayed in three groups. Hata's unit of four destroyers led the way, followed by a second group of four. A last group of two brought up the rear. Fairborne broke the silence by offering his opinion that the last group might be lagging too far behind. Hata only glared at him.

Hata estimated it would take two and one-half hours to travel the forty miles to Port Arthur, longer if the commander continued to maintain half speed. Fortunately, the cautious leader soon whistled for speed increased to 20 knots.

Hata ordered his lieutenant to issue sidearms to the crew and to make sure the pistols were loaded. They would need the weapons in case they could board an enemy ship. Like his shipmates, Hata believed the Russians only responded defensively in battle, and were so ignorant they obeyed orders like automatons. He regarded their Russian Orthodox religion with contempt. All Christians, he knew, feared death and, even now, the enemy probably knelt for their heathen Sunday evening prayers, asking their god for protection. His lip curled in a contemptuous sneer. *Forget your prayers, Russians, tonight we decide who lives.*

Information from secret agent Major Ariko had indicated the enemy torpedoes rusted from months of neglect, and that the slothful Russian gunners suffered from lack of practice. The Japanese expected their own frenzy of training to overwhelm the enemy. He took pride in the enthusiasm of his crew who just as impatiently awaited the coming clash.

Two days ago, his men had departed from Japan's west coast Sasebo base amid the cheers of joyous relatives and friends. The celebrating civilian crowd had waved their little red sun flags, sung to the martial tunes of the military bands, tossed flowers in the wake of the ships and sent the fleet on its way with full expectations of a stunning victory over the despised foreigners.

Russia's counter proposal to Japanese demands for an answer to their note of January 13, in which Japan had disavowed any designs on Manchuria and had requested a like pledge from Russia in regard to Korea, had reached Tokyo on February 3. The Japanese government purposely sat on the counter proposal for four days while it ordered full military mobilization and sent orders to Admiral Togo "to destroy the Russian fleet." Troopships were loaded and sent to invade Korea. On Sunday, February 7,

Town and Harbor of Port Arthur

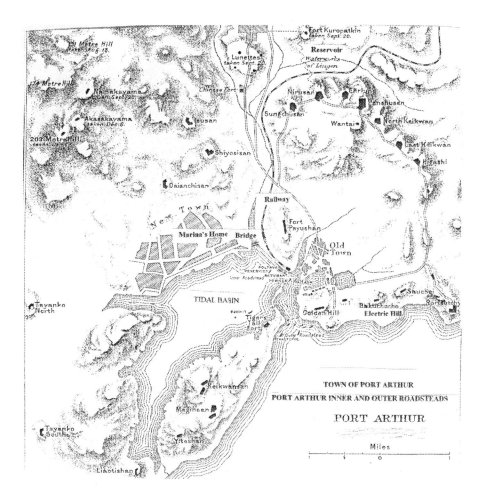

Togo had moved in for a midnight strike against Port Arthur as Japan's other force, the invasion fleet, moved into Korean waters.

It had occurred to Hata that if Sasebo's civilians knew war was imminent, then surely the Russians shared the knowledge and might be on guard. But it mattered little to him. Trailing black clouds of smoke, the destroyer flotilla crept closer to Port Arthur, running without lights and in complete wireless silence. The Russian port, named for British Lieutenant William Arthur in 1860, lay fully bathed in bright shore lights when the flotilla arrived at the outer roadstead.

The Japanese destroyer commander blew two whistles for the "separate" signal. Hata manuevered to follow the lead ship which had targeted the Russian battleship *Tsesarevitch.* The battleship was aptly named, he mused. Too bad he could not have first shot at the "Czar's Son" to start the destruction of the Romanoff navy.

Hata had orders to penetrate farther into the roadstead to attack the second target, the Russian picket ship *Pallada*, actually a heavy cruiser, whose searchlights illuminated the roadstead. The *Pallada's* lights, sweeping across the water, could betray the presence of the Japanese destroyers before their torpedoes struck. The Russian cruiser had to be eliminated at once.

Hata's pilot informed him that the tide flowed outward, which meant that the picket ship would face seaward with forward lookouts on duty who would be more vigilant than usual. The situation called for extreme caution. At the last council of war, it had been agreed that the destroyers would not employ the usual red and white signal given by all ships desirous of entering the Russian harbor.

Just outside the roadstead, the Japanese flotilla spotted two Russian patrol destroyers.

"They have seen us," Fairborne muttered.

"We will bluff it," said Hata, surprised that he was answering the Englishman.

Suddenly the two Japanese destroyers in the rear group collided in the darkness. One was seriously crippled, but could still proceed at a slower speed. For some inexplicable reason one of them gave the red and white entry signal. The game was up. Hata immediately ordered "Full speed ahead!"

The destroyer strained and quivered with the increased speed of 30 knots. Hata's heart beat furiously as dreams of glory danced before him. Cold salt spray splashed in his face and a rush of adrenalin shot through his veins. His ship charged toward the Russian picket cruiser, now only 300 yards dead ahead. Below deck, the torpedo man gripped the firing lever.

"Damn the *Akasuka!*"

Hata swore as Captain Hesibo Tikobara's destroyer loomed out of the darkness on collision course with Hata's port bow and driving hard toward the *Pallada.* The *Akasuka* had also targeted the cruiser. Hata veered off to avoid a collision.

Only 200 yards away and closing fast, Hata became aware that there was a great deal of commotion aboard the Russian cruiser. Where was the surprise? The Russian crewmen were *not* sleeping peacefully below in their hammocks. They were busily rushing to load the deck guns. They must have been sleeping beside the guns! And smoke pouring from the funnels? That meant the boilers were lit. The *Pallada* could easily weigh anchor and move out to challenge the smaller Japanese destroyers. There was no time to delay the attack.

Less than 100 yards from the *Pallada*, just as the Russian cruiser opened fire, the rival destroyer *Akasuka* discharged its two torpedoes. Hata saw a great column of water rise abaft the torpedoed Russian cruiser's bridge. Feeling little pity, he realized the Russian engine room stokers must have suffered heavy casualties.

The guns of other Russian ships began to pound away. Hata had to admit grudgingly that the enemy had cleared their guns with surprising rapidity, bathing the sea with exploding projectiles and blinding searchlights. The secrecy of the attack had ended.

Hata swiftly altered course to dodge the relentless searchlights. He was sure that the commander's *Kasumio* had discharged its two torpedoes, but he had seen no explosion from the Russian battleship *Tsesarevitch*. As he dashed past the huge ship, Hata saw two torpedoes hung up in the *Tsesarevitch's* torpedo nets, their propellers churning the water below. The nets, suspended from booms projecting out horizontally from the Russian ship, **were** in place and performing well.

He glanced at Fairborne. The Englishman, perfectly calm and expressionless, looked intently at the unexploded torpedoes, hanging helplessly like limp sausages. "It's the faulty net cutters, I dare say," Fairborne said.

Another Japanese destroyer, the *Shinonome*, narrowly missed Hata's ship, crossing his bow in a furious dash toward the battleship. A gigantic explosion rocked the Russian and lit up the night sky. Off his starboard bow, Hata saw another Japanese destroyer, the *Shirakuma*, limping slowly toward the torpedoed *Tsesarevitch*. The *Shirakuma*, crippled by the earlier collision in the roadstead, could only muster fourteen knots, but steadily maintained its course. The guns of the battleship *Tsesarevitch* mercilessly raked the *Shirakuma* with shellfire. An immense cloud of steam boiled upward from the riddled destroyer's deck. In seconds, one of its boilers burst, bringing the ship to a stop. Its stern began to settle in the water.

Both Hata and Fairborne spotted a third torpedo hanging on the Tsesarevitch's net.

Speaking calmly, Fairborne suggested to Hata that it might be prudent to change tactics and attack the battleship's bow or stern, both of which were unprotected by a torpedo net. Hata agreed and, without speaking, changed the course of his ship.

"Captain," he heard Fairborne say, "you were right. Why not remove the net cutters?"

Hata nodded. *To hell with the admiral's orders.* He shouted an order through the speaking tube as Fairborne hurried below to implement the command. The torpedomen pulled the torpedoes from their tubes and removed the cumbersome net cutters. Fairborne motioned for them to slap on more grease before reinserting the torpedoes. Hata hastened to manuever his ship aft of the stricken battleship. At the very moment the torpedo operator stood poised for the order to press the levers, the *Tsesarevitch's* searchlights engulfed Hata's ship. Coming in close, he dismissed the danger, still believing the Russians would be too stupid and too slow to raise or lower their gunsights. He pressed on, but immediately was blinded by the sea spray thrown up by near misses from exploding shells. Fearing a collision, he swerved away, but not before shells bursting overhead tore holes in the deck of his destroyer.

Hata barely escaped past the battleship when he heard a tremendous jarring blast and saw the *Tsesarevitch* showered midship by a high column of seawater. Still, the battleship, again torpedoed, continued to pound Hata's destroyer.

A 15 cm. shell tore through one wall of Hata's conning tower, exploding upon contact with the opposite wall. Another 15 cm. shell pierced the bow, killing a petty officer and two men. Water flooded the bow compartment. The funnel was so full of holes from 4.7 cm. shells that it looked like a black pedestal of swiss cheese. The severed mast sprawled on the destroyer's deck. Another 4.7cm. shell penetrated the hull, barely missed the engine room and exploded in the coal bunkers.

From below, Fairborne shouted through the speaking tube that seawater was seeping into the torpedo room "The torpedoes are ready," he yelled.

Amid the confusion of bursting shells, Hata's ship managed to duck out of the glare of searchlights and join the destroyer *Yadsuma*, speeding toward the pride of the Russian fleet, the new battleship *Retvisan*. Both Japanese destroyers, Hata's and the *Yadsuma*, aimed for the unprotected bow of the behemoth.

"Fire one torpedo," Hata ordered. But his torpedo and one from the *Yadsuma* missed. Fairborne helped the torpedomen ready a second pair of torpedoes as Hata altered course to attack the stern of the *Retvisan*. Again came the command, "Fire torpedo."

The missile struck with a thundering explosion, literally lifting the battleship from the sea.

Retvisan's undaunted gunners did not pause. Setting the sea afire with exploding shells, their missiles and searchlights lit up the Japanese destroyers as well as the Russian ships. Hata acknowleded reluctantly that the Russian gunners did not frighten easily and operated with considerable skill and courage. He was fast gaining new respect for the enemy.

Hata realized that his ship was in peril of being blown out of the water. Having lost the element of surprise, he could not evade the superior firepower of the Russian capital ships which now targeted him with increasing accuracy. If he were to fight another day for the glory of Japan, he would have to save his ship. The screeching whistle of the enemy shells, the explosive concussion of near misses, had caused him to become disoriented and no longer effective. He could not see any of the other destroyers, so he reluctantly gave the command to break off the action and run for the open sea. He escaped into the darkness, reducing speed to prevent water pressure in the flooded bow compartment from bursting a bulkhead. He wondered why there had been no counter fire from the shore batteries. Street lights burned brightly; the town seemed not to have received any alarm, which made him wonder who was in charge of the port garrison.

Once out of the roadstead, he saw his commander's destroyer signal "Recall." Unable to answer because of damage, Hata fired a rocket in response and proceeded to limp forward at a slow six-knot speed. Below the main deck his crew struggled to close the holes in the punctured hull.

Bypassing the telegraph, which had been blown away, Hata shouted down to his lieutenant to stay below to assist the engineer, "Get those shores, plugs, and wedges in action at once. Get that floodwater stopped."

The destroyer's hull had settled too much already. The bow was lower by two feet and the damage to the hull was too large to close with the wadding and fearnought on hand, so Fairborne ordered the engine room crewmen to use their canvas hammocks with the timbers. The upraised propeller screw had begun to churn air. By pumping water into an aft compartment to make the ship more horizontal, the screw was able to bite into the water to keep the ship moving. Gradually, the shellhole was closed enough to enable the pumps to control the inrush of seawater.

Except for the lost *Shirakuma,* the destroyers gathered about their commander's ship, and together all slowly beat their way through the darkness and light snowfall toward the Elliot Islands. All the destroyers had suffered damage; three were badly crippled. Anxious faces kept looking back at the enemy base, perplexed and yet heartened that the Russians had not given pursuit. Evidently the surprise blow had caused extreme confusion. Even one fast Russian cruiser could have inflicted terrible destruction on the damaged and slow moving destroyer flotilla.

Safely anchored inside the shelter of the Elliots, the destroyer crews awaited the presence of Admiral Togo. He arrived at dawn and at once took the wounded aboard his flagship. The exhausted surgeon of the flotilla now joined the team of surgeons preparing to operate in the *Asahi's* sickbay. Their grisly task was aided by clear and calm morning weather.

Hata, sobered by his ordeal, swallowed his pride and thanked Fairborne for his assistance. It was not easy for him to do so. Hata was heartbroken over the damage to his ship, knowing that he would have to spend valuable time at the home shipyards. He would never acknowledge that Fairborne had probably saved the ship. He was too busy bemoaning his bad luck, angry that he might miss future glorious action against the enemy, action that held the promise of quick promotion.

Fairborne congratulated Hata for his bravery and skill in torpedoing a battleship, assuring him that he would soon be back in action, and thanking Hata for sharing the excitement and success of the battle. Both men agreed that no mention of the net cutter removal was needed.

While awaiting the arrival of the admiral, Fairborne and Hata somehow began to converse, finding it easier as their talk progressed. Although not agreeing completely on Japan's strategy, the two did find much common ground in their discussion.

"Quite frankly, old boy," Fairborne had confided, "we British do not find your surprise strike against Port Arthur to be sporting, but if you impede the Russians in their advance toward India and Afghanistan, you'll do us a great favor."

Hata expressed surprise. "This isn't a cricket game," he protested. "What is wrong about hitting the enemy when he least expects it? The Russians have more capital ships than we do. And a reserve fleet. We needed to cripple their advantage. Nothing is fair in war."

"Then why didn't you use your battleships and cruisers to pound the inner harbor and town while the torpedo destroyers did their work in the outer roadstead? And why not use all your destroyers against the base. Why split the destroyer flotillas?" Fairborne asked.

"I imagine that the admiral was reluctant to gamble with the capital ships as long as the Russians outnumber us. We could not afford to be too reckless. Not until we are stronger," Hata answered.

"But Japanese ships have visited Port Arthur previously. You know that the large ships in the inner harbor cannot come out when the tide is low. And with that narrow entrance, the battleships can only emerge one at a time. Attacking the naval base when the tide is out was a splendid idea. But why not destroy the base as well as the fleet. Begging your pardon, but isn't the purpose of a battle to throw in all resources in a daring bid for victory?"

"You think Togo was too cautious?" Hata asked.

"Who knows. Only time will tell. I do think that he placed too much reliance on torpedoes. I say that because it is supposed to be my expertise. Frankly, I don't consider twenty torpedoes to be sufficient for destruction of an enemy fleet. Now you will have to slug it out with the Russians, and that could be costly. This could be a long war. Can your nation afford that?"

"We will win," said Hata. Fairborne admired his defiance, but wondered if the Japanese realized how expensive wars could be. A protracted war could bankrupt Japan.

Togo visited each destroyer to express his gratitude. He seemed oblivious that not only had he lost a destroyer, but none of the three torpedoed Russian ships had gone to the bottom. When Togo visited Hata's ship, he barely acknowledged Fairborne and became visibly irked upon being reminded by the brash Hata that the Russsian torpedo nets **had** been in place, that the net cutters had all failed to work, and partial success came only by attacking the bow and stern of two battleships—a ploy that usually did not work. Togo stomped off the deck of the destroyer. He did not like to confront unpleasaant news.

Hata watched Togo's departure with scorn, thinking correctly that in spite of the partial success of the raid, Togo probably would still soon be a world renowned hero. Hata had to admit how smashing the attack could have been if the old man had better employed the destroyers of Flotilla Two, and if shallow draft torpedo boats had succeeded in penetrating the inner roadstead where the bulk of the Russian ships lay anchored. Hata believed that undoubtedly the outcome would have been the early end of the Russian Pacific Fleet.

Hata also realized that the chance for further surprise attacks had vanished and that Russia would strike back with her larger navy. In spite of the frantic efforts of British shipyards to deliver warships to Japan, Russia still possessed a greater number of battleships. The task ahead would not be easy for Japan.

He moved against the railing of the ship's bridge to look back at the anchored Japanese fleet. From the black smoke pouring up the funnels of the battleships, he knew that the fleet prepared to weigh anchor to proceed to a point off the Manchurian coast to bombard Port Arthur. Russian coastal guns would prevent the fleet from coming in much closer than five miles off

Admiral Togo and General Nogi

Vice-Admiral Togo

ADMIRAL TOGO ON BATTLESHIP WITH ARMS AKIMBO

GENERAL BARON NOGI

shore. If the crippled Russian fleet did not come out to challenge the barrage, Togo would have to devise yet another strategy to lure them from the naval base. Hata prayed for his own return in time to participate in the final battle. With heavy heart he looked east toward Japan, dreading the forced inactivity at the Sasebo shipyard. Maybe he could convince the navy to put him aboard another warship while his destroyer was in drydock.

Within the large, semi-hidden harbor at the Elliot Islands, Fleet Admiral Togo watched the departing destroyers of Flotilla One. Making slow progress, two light cruisers towed those destroyers most heavily damaged. With a scowl on his face and arms characteristically akimbo, Togo damned Major Ariko for his faulty intelligence about the absence of torpedo nets, the diversion of Russian warships to Dalny, and the supposed lack of preparedness by the Russian gun crews. The story about absentee naval officers attending a dinner party at Admiral Starck's home must have been false also.

Aboard HIJMS *Asahi*, Togo's staff had listened to the uncoded wireless reports coming from the commander of Destroyer Flotilla One. The messages proudly boasted of victory. *Three Russian battleships torpedoed!*

Having returned to the admiral's flagship, Fairborne uncorked a bottle of Madeira and knocked back a stiff portion. He sat for a while in the dim light of his cabin, wondering what Lydia, his wife, was doing back in Sasebo. Probably enjoying the public baths. He wished he could escape his cramped quarters and relax among the nudity of the baths. Fairborne did not know that his wife had left Japan to go to Korea.

A soft knock at his door interrupted his reverie. Two more short, quick knocks followed. He knew the signal. Rising to his feet, he ushered in the simpering youthful mess attendant.

CHAPTER TWO

The port of Dalny marked the southeastern end of the Kwantung peninsula, and was slightly northeast from Port Arthur, roughly forty miles distant by railroad. Chen had reckoned correctly that the attackers would concentrate on the naval base. Luck was with him. The junk had successfully eluded the small squadron of destroyers sent by Admiral Togo to menace Dalny, arriving just after the Japanese squadron steamed away from the harbor.

The junk cleared the breakwater at dawn to search for a berth at the crowded quay. Chen manuevered his craft with some difficulty into the busy commercial port, now crowded more than ever with fleeing civilians—an exodus of utter turmoil. The telegraph at Port Arthur had conveyed news of the sneak attack. Refugees fleeing from the naval base, and many occupants of Dalny, desperately bid for the services of boat captains to take them from the peninsula. Enough smaller craft had commenced leaving the harbor so that Chen successfully found a space to secure his boat.

Chen wasted no time. With the dock lines quickly tied, he paid the restless crew, arranged for coolie laborers to handle the cargo, sent an emmisary to the harbor master with the appropriate bribe to facilitate movement of his cargo, and, all the while, kept questioning the curious on-lookers and harbor workers about the situation at Port Arthur. News had traveled fast. Chen and Rogers learned some of the details of the surprise midnight attack on the anchored Russian naval fleet. The excited crowd agreed that Japan and Russia were now definitely at war.

As soon as he had gleaned sufficient information, Chen turned to Rogers, saying, "Ellis, I know that it is important for you to go to the base as soon as possible. Don't delay on my account. You can still board the early train."

"But I want to help," Rogers protested.

Chen would have none of it. "We can take up the remainder of our business in a week or two. Now that you are up here, get established; we can resume old ties later." Chen genuinely regretted Rogers' departure, but guessed correctly the urgency of his mission.

"The cargo handlers are here," Chen added. "The shipment goes to the warehouse while I make arrangements with the merchants. I am well known here. Except for the trouble at the base, it will be business as usual."

"But the dead man and the hull damage?"

"Do not worry about Quan. If he has a family, I will give them his money. The authorities do not want to be bothered about his death. And if the rest of the crew fail to return, I can find many more men available; there always are. So be on your way. I will be very busy disposing of my cargo." Chen winked. "You know how it is, especially in wartime. There will be a good profit."

Rogers knew that Chen's operation promised success. The large black junk was cumbersome in appearance, but looks could be deceiving. The junk was really quite fast. It was not chopped off so severely square at the stern, and it did not ride as high on the water as most boxy junks did. A curious observer would have noted that the main lanteen sail was larger, eighteen feet along the bottom, with balsa batten boards extending outward from the mast. Rogers also recognized the danger of wartime confiscation. He did not want to concern himself since he was unaware of the full extent of the cargo. He had no doubt that the junk carried goods that would be delivered intact to the merchants of the town, no matter their content or how rigid the inspection. Chen was a crafty trader who knew all the tricks and how much cumshaw to dispense for guaranteed delivery to the commercial district.

Chen grasped Rogers' hand and cut short the words of gratitude. "Don't thank me. It is always good to have you aboard. But it is best you leave quickly before this place faces martial law. We can talk when I return at the end of the month." He shooed Rogers away, then called after him. "Where will you be staying?"

"At the residence of Mademoiselle Marina Berezovsky." Rogers saw the look of puzzled surprise. Odd! "Do you know her?" he asked.

Chen ignored the question. "Give her my regards," he called back, then turned to resume negotiations with the motley crowd gathered on the dock.

Rogers proceeded along the modern dock, shaking his head at the persistent offers of help from the coolies who tried to accompany him. It had surprised him that Chen knew Berezovsky. How strange! Perhaps he should have mentioned her name sooner. And Alesandrov's name as well. But Chen never pried nor gossiped. Still, it was careless of him that he had not thought to inform Chen fully of his travel arrangements.

His close friend, Captain Baron Viktor Alesandrov of the Russian Army, had spoken so little about Mademoiselle Berezovsky. That was odd too, so uncharacteristic of the Russian who was always so full of praise for the women he knew. Rogers hoped that he would find the lady friendly. He had no idea what she looked like, but knowing Viktor, she must be very attractive. He looked forward to a happy visit as Viktor's guest. Their long overdue reunion the previous month had been immensely gratifying.

As he walked up the incline of the cobbled street toward the customs post, deep in thought about Chen and Alesandrov, glimpses of the past flashed through his mind. He remembered his first encounter with junk captain Chen Hsiuh Wang eight years earlier in Shanghai. The wily mariner had offered shelter to a frightened sixteen-year old youth who had just jumped ship to escape from a brutal and sadistic shipmaster. Rogers smiled at the contrast between his own naivete then and the maturity the past few years had bestowed on him.

He would always remain greatful for Chen's succor when Rogers had jumped ship in Shanghai. Chen had arranged a working passage for him to Singapore, where Rogers had succeeded in signing on a British freighter bound for London. He had remained with the ship which had gone on to deliver a cargo to the West Indies. But by the time the ship stopped over in Havana, Rogers could no longer stomach the wretched hardships of sea life. He had declined the skipper's offer of advancement. Three years at sea were enough.

So he had stayed on in Havana, only to be caught up inadvertently in an adventure with the Cuban underground. That seemingly innocent flirtation had pushed him into America's war with Spain and the beginning of his unplanned military career. After that short war, the American army had shipped him to Manila for the Philippine Insurrection, and then to China for the Boxer Rebellion. He had renewed his ties with Chen during the Boxer conflict. That was almost four years ago. Their friendship had blossomed with the years. Chen always seemed to be there for him, becoming almost a father figure. Chen had also watched out for Rogers' secret wife, An-an, during Rogers' stint at a war college in the States the past year. The man's help had been invaluable. Surely, Chen must know about his relationship with An-an. The thought of her in Hong Kong made Rogers wonder again why she had not written since his return from the States.

At the harbor gate, Rogers presented his papers to the port authorities. The harried officials led him into a crowded waiting room, looked at his foreign clothing, briefly scanned his valise, and passed him through with instructions to report to the police station. They seemed almost relieved to be rid of him.

Military patrols twice halted him. "Your papers, please," they demanded, forming a ring around him and unshouldering their obsolete model 1878 Berdan rifles. As always the weapons carried the ever-present two-foot long triangular bayonet.

He surrendered his documents, explaining he was on his way to the nearby police station. He patiently shrugged off their truculent rudeness which he believed was a possible reaction to the outbreak of war and the unfamiliarity of these Siberian peasants with strange foreigners.

He easily found the police station by walking toward a nearby crowd. Inside the station, he could sense the obvious tension between the civilian personnel and their new military overseers. Soldiers had relegated the police to a subordinate role. The station commander, an army major, scanned the passport and noted approvingly that Rogers was American, not English or German. Russians increasingly distrusted most other Europeans because the foreign press had rooted so loudly for Japan. He asked if Rogers was a war correspondent. Shaking his head, Rogers proffered his military papers.

"*Amerikan, da?*" the major asked.

"*Konyeshna,* of course," Rogers replied, wishing he was fluent in Russian. "I am a friend of Captain Baron Alesandrov of the Don Cossacks, and I would be most pleased to tell him how cooperative his fellow officers are in Dalny."

Fudging the truth, he added, "I am to be assigned to General Kondratenko's headquarters as a military observer. Meanwhile, I report to Captain Alesandrov in Port Arthur. I shall be staying at the residence of Mademoiselle Berezovsky."

Upon hearing her name, the officer's attitude quickly changed. Officiously, he reached for a stamp marked URGENT. Rogers displayed a silver U.S. dollar. "I have no further use for this; perhaps you would accept it as a souvenir from my country?"

The major picked up another stamp, adding the words OFFICIAL—DO NOT DELAY.

The scene within the town reflected chaotic confusion. Civilians, mostly Chinese and Russian, milled about, eagerly seeking the latest news. Armed military patrols in their heavy, dark woolen greatcoats and their fur astrakhan hats, their knee-high black leather boots clomping in unison, marched up and down the streets, going nowhere in particular, but occasionally stopping suspicious looking civilians and closely checking all shops bearing name signs with Japanese characters. These shops were empty. Rogers later learned that all Japanese civilians had departed the previous day.

"They even took their furniture and pets," one irate merchant said. "That meant they would not return. We should have suspected something."

The angry townspeople all agreed that the Japanese would be punished severely for the sneak attack on the Imperial Russian fleet and that the war would crush the foolish enemy and would only last three months at the most.

Dalny's modernity surprised Rogers. The Russian government had spent millions of rubles developing the town into a major prosperous seaport, complete with fine brick buildings facing the broad tree-lined main thoroughfare. It wore a comfortable look of middle class elegance. The dockyards were busy and merchants and tradesmen prospered. The predominantly Chinese population secretly admitted that Russian officialdom treated them better than had the corrupt Manchu government.

Chen had mentioned at the quay that repairs on his boat would be no problem since large numbers of Baltic craftsmen worked in the local modern shipyard. "They are good mechanics," he said. "You will never know that the hull was damaged. Before, they reshaped the keel to my own design, and you know how well it functioned last night."

Chen had frowned at the memory of the shelling. "I promise the Japanese will pay for the repairs. They will need the use of boats like mine if they try to invade the peninsula. It will cost them dearly." He shrugged. "Anyway, if the war goes badly, I can always go south. Shanghai and Hong Kong are both booming."

"I am staying for the long haul," Rogers had said. "I hope you do too, my friend. I'd like to see you squeeze all the yen you can out of the Japanese navy. They scared the hell out of me last night." He preferred to believe that a good entrepreneur like Chen would probably profit handsomely from blockade running. He could see the direction in which the war was headed.

Wary of more military patrols with their arrogant and brusque demands to see his papers, Rogers hired a ricksha to carry him the short distance to the train station. He chose a porter who knew the way through back alleys to bypass the czarist officials, hoping to arrive at the station in time for the early train to Port Arthur.

His ricksha passed gangs of coolies transporting artillery shells, two to a sling, up the hill to the coastal defense guns. Dalny, part of the defense grid, was, in fact, weakly defended, because most of the government money had been squandered on civil works. Rogers made a mental note of the size of the artillery shells, thinking they might be inadequate against large, well armored ships.

Troops manned several check-points around the rail station. They halted and searched suspicious looking orientals. Although most of the Han natives wore baggy peasant trousers, tied off at the knee and ankle, and loose cotton blouses beneath quilted cotton winter coats, and braided their hair with the traditional queue, the patrols made them state their name and occupation, noting carefully their accent. Soldiers pulled out of line and marched off those who resembled Koreans or Japanese.

Approaching the train station, Rogers heard the traditional three bells signalling departure of a train. The locomotive, just arrived from Port Arthur, prepared to make a quick Monday morning turn-around because of the emergency at the naval base. Frightened hordes of passengers had disembarked from the train. Most were orientals, except for a few Russian women and children. All hastened to leave the station to go to the boats in the harbor.

The day continued bitterly cold as the northern sun failed to penetrate the thick, gloomy overcast. Rogers was glad that he had brought his quilted Chinese coat to ward off the chill. He rushed to purchase his ticket and boarded the train at once. It did not surprise him that he occupied the car alone. Few passengers had boarded for the return journey to the base.

He leaned back in his seat and stretched his legs, exhausted from the lack of sleep and the stress of the night voyage. Almost at once he began to nod as sleep fast overcame him.

A sudden movement jolted him awake. Someone had tugged at the valise at his side. He sat erect and looked around in time to see the blurred outline of a man rushing toward the exit. Blinking his eyes rapidly to rid them of sleep, Rogers leaped to his feet and ran to the train steps. Leaning out into the frigid air, he saw an oriental man running toward the side of the station building. The man glanced back furtively for a moment, then disappeared. His face was familiar, too familiar.

Rogers cut short his impulse to pursue the man, realizing the difficulty of finding him in the crowd. Returning to his seat, he felt relieved to find his valise undisturbed. Patting his waist belt and pockets, he could find nothing missing. He fretted that he could not remember where he had seen the familiar face before. It had to be someone from the recent past. The ferocious hatred he had seen on the face was disturbing. It was no help that the stranger wore the loose pajama-like garments and pill-box hat of a Chinese business man. Rogers sensed something else foreign about him. He sat down, took a deep breath, and forced himself to relax.

The locomotive lurched forward, sending a cloud of steam to envelope the windows of the car. It slowly labored to leave the station to begin the journey to a junction, some thirty miles northwest. At the junction the train would turn due south to the naval port.

Bone weary, aching with fatigue, Rogers now knew that sleep would be difficult. He clutched the valise to his chest, closed his eyes against the weak glare of the overhead lamp, and settled back to let the thoughts race through his mind. The many events of the past twenty-four hours competed for his attention, but the anticipation of meeting Captain Alesandrov in Port Arthur was uppermost.

It would be good to see Viktor Alesandrov again. He reflected back to the Shanghai business the previous month, and the happy New Year Eve reunion with the Russian officer. In spite of his fatigue, that particular past memory rapidly monopolized his consciousness. He wondered what had happened to Alesandrov on that New Year's night.

He kept nodding, continually interrupted by the jerking motion of the train. He was alone in the car and grateful for that; he needed to rest. He was anxious to arrive in Port Arthur to learn the true state of affairs there. Previous ominous news reports from Japan had ignored the Mikado's mobilization, but had described the break in diplomatic relations with Russia. Now that war clouds seemingly had gathered beyond salvation, did the gods of war plan further separation for him and An-an? He hoped a letter from her would reach him at the port.

As for Mademoiselle Berezovsky and her relationship with Alesandrov, he hoped his presence would not interfere with Viktor's arrangement. Knowing him, there had to be a liaison of a personal nature with the woman.

The train chugged northwest toward the junction with the main line. Under wintery skies the countryside lay barren and desolate with little snow as usual, but silent and bitterly cold. The land would be green and fertile with the coming of spring. But for now, little sign of life could be seen as the train skirted tiny hamlets whose occupants huddled indoors to avoid the mind-numbing siberian wind.

The train from Dalny ground to a halt at the drab rail terminal at Port Arthur. The few tired passengers aboard climbed down stiffly from the train into the wintery grayness of the late morning. The terminal, hardly more than a bare platform, seemed as ugly as that part of the town surrounding it. A thin sprinkling of snow lay on the ground, ruffled by the artic breeze flowing down from the upper reaches of the Manchurian peninsula. It was a dark day, but the faint corona of the sun, struggling to penetrate the heavy overcast, gave promise of a brighter afternoon. As the cold mist dispelled, the ghostly, cheerless town began to lose some of its gloominess. The American took a deep breath, sighing heavily, disappointed, yet wondering if perhaps some beauty of scenery might lay hidden elsewhere in the harsh vista. He shivered and looked around.

Coming into a strange town, as stark as Port Arthur, added to the misgivings he felt about his presence there. With no definite purpose for his foray northward other than to fulfill his promised visit to Captain Viktor Alesandrov, he could only hope that his mentor, Uncle Steve, would not be disappointed. Still, the certainty of war favored a busy schedule. He might be hard pressed to cope with the pressures of forthcoming combat, his neutrality, and his cloudy assignment with Uncle Steve's office. He was in a position that would have to be defined as the larger picture of the Port Arthur attack unfolded.

Maybe a letter from An-an would arrive soon to reassure him.

A sizeable crowd of out-bound passengers, bundled in winter garments, had grouped on the paved platform. Gathered at the end of a stone storage building, a group of ricksha porters had begun to move toward the few arriving passengers.

Rogers shivered slightly, set his valise on the ground, and stretched to ease his stiff muscles. Clad in his thick, padded Chinese coat, army-issue khaki trousers, and appearing taller because of his western-style American campaign hat, he thrust his hands into his coat pockets for warmth and hunched his shoulders against the cold. Looking around, he scanned the fortified heights behind the station and looked to his left at the prominent high and barren hill that rose above the town, a brown, rounded height inappropriately termed Golden Hill.

Facing south beyond the hill, he could see the docks of the inner harbor and the navy yard. From where he stood, and on to the north, a depressing cluster of shacks and shops called Old Town gave shelter to the large oriental populace. Behind Old Town, pressing against the ancient wall, was an older Chinese community, usually referred to as China Town. Off to the west, New Town, peopled by members of the Russian colony, rose on higher ground, a short distance from the dirty waters of the tidal basin. Commercial shops and some larger buildings defined the nearest edge of New Town, backed by stone residences, some plain, some fancy, climbing the higher ground beyond.

The American officer noticed a wizened old Chinaman watching him intently as if attempting to get his attention. He sighed again, picked up his valise, and prepared himself to face more Russian officialdom at the check-point close by. He debated whether to report at once to the local police station or first seek a hotel room. His uncertainty stemmed from his belief that he faced a great deal more discouraging delay as a result of the night attack on the Russian fleet. He was even unsure about his welcome at the Berezovsky home. The town looked deserted now, but soon would be stirring. The offices of the Viceroy, army generals, navy admirals, and Foreign Office bureaucrats would undoubtedly compete to control the situation, or else seek to escape whatever blame might follow. The historic reluctance of so many Russian field officers to accept responsibility was already known to Rogers. In the days ahead, he would witness the full extent of that flawed mentality.

A violent explosion broke the morning stillness. Even before he saw the destruction, Rogers ducked instinctively. His automatic reflex to the jarring blast came from past experience. Before his eyes, a building on the southern edge of Old Town disintegrated, accompanied by a flash of orange fire in the midst of an ascending plume of gray-black smoke. A moment later the piercing sound of a second nine-inch naval shell arced through the cold morning sky to smash another building. Hunks of stones, shattered timbers, and dark blobs that could have been broken bodies or random debris flew skyward.

The silent streets came alive as frantic mothers ran screaming from the shops and houses with their children, running in terror down the narrow streets or retreating back into the dubious safety of the flimsy buildings to crouch in the dark interiors, crying with uncontrollable fright.

He felt a hand plucking at his sleeve. It was the old man who had been watching him and was now at his side, trying to get his attention. Before he could respond to the man, the ancient one said, "I am Master Loong. You come with me. We leave now. Not safe here. Japanese kill you. Come, we go."

When he saw Rogers hesitate, the old Chinaman insisted, "Fine rady wait fo you. Missee Maleena."

Rogers almost smiled at the asian pronunciation of the letters r and l. He knew the old one surely meant *Marina*. Seeing recognition lighting the American's face, the old man snapped an order to halt a fleeing ricksha porter. He hurriedly climbed into the conveyance, motioning for Rogers to follow. Rogers no longer hesitated. The high-pitched screech of a third shell drowned the babble of voices in the station yard. The shell exploded off across the tidal creek, near the approach to New Town.

The ricksha porter needed no prodding. He dashed forward with the older passenger shouting directions. He carried them northward through the streets, running toward higher ground beyond Golden Hill. Looking up at the heights, Rogers saw a large crowd of curious townspeople gathered on the hill, straining for a better look at the outer roadstead and its crippled ships. He turned to the old man, pointed at the crowd, and shook his head. The ancient one nodded in agreement and called out a second command. In obeyance, the porter rounded the base of the hill and finally halted at the far northern side where the abandoned husk of an old fortification offered relative safety.

With no well defined targets, the Japanese continued to loft their shells haphazardly, hoping to strike the naval craft anchored out of sight in the inner harbor. The shells came in from the southwest horizon. The crowd stood its ground in foolhardy fascination, watching the enemy projectiles explode indiscriminately. Fired from a distance of five miles, the naval shells exploded randomly throughout Old Town. Buildings disappeared in a blast of fire and dirty smoke. Some of the shells splashed harmlessly in the shallow reaches of the inner roadstead.

Just as Rogers pondered the seeming lack of retaliation from the port's defenses, two Russian destroyers dashed from the harbor, and some of the heavy guns of the anchored Russian battleships opened up. Apparently punished by some hits on the Japanese fleet, the enemy cannonade began to slacken and soon ceased.

The old man ordered the porter to return to Old Town. The ricksha crossed through the town, passed the railway station at the foot of Fort Payushan, then proceeded westward across the narrow tidal basin bridge to New Town. The porter struggled up the incline toward a large residence that sat about half way up the sloping height.

The main building of the home sat back behind a high gated wall. Several smaller wooden buildings, also behind the wall, shielded the main structure from the narrow fronting roadway. These were occupied in the oriental fashion by servants and tradesmen. Some were storage sheds, worker's shops, and outdoor food preparation centers. The large two-story brick residence, set back from the smaller buildings, was the living quarters of Marina Berezovsky and her occasional guests.

* * * * * * * * *

Marina Berezovsky resided alone. Her parents no longer lived and she had never married. No one seemed to know the full source of her income, although all recognized her success in the mercantile trade. Imported merchandise and many scarce items came to her from the sampans and junks plying the coastal water of the Yellow Sea. If goods were in short supply, Marina always seemed to have them in her warehouse. Merchants of both Old Town and New Town depended on her and sought her business even though she always demanded cash payments. She drove hard bargains in her dealings with the merchants, but her own payments were prompt and she paid also in cash. All conceded she dealt fairly and honestly.

She was Eurasian, the only daughter of a Russian engineer and a Chinese mother. Her father had been a man of importance, active in building both the Trans-Siberian Railway and the Manchurian bound Chinese Eastern Railway. The father had married a Tsingtao beauty whose mercantile family had profitted from German traders moving into the Shantung peninsula. The marriage, a happy one for the many years it endured, had produced a beautiful, solitary child whose upbringing, though strict, was full of love and benvolence.

Marina enjoyed the best of two worlds. The product of dual cultures, endowed with facial features that were neither completely slavic nor oriental, she received full acceptance in both the european and asian communities. Unspoiled, always adored by her now deceased parents, and ever quick to learn, she had harvested the art of trading from her mother, and considerable political acumen from her father. The Russian colony at Port Arthur had earlier granted her equality because of the power held by her father. The wealth she had accumulated through her parents and her expanding business had continued to assure her social status.

The woman's beauty had attracted the attention of Russian officers at the naval base, both maritime and military, but she did not encourage suitors. She actively attended many social functions, especially the military balls. Though too busy to attend all the many social teas, she did faithfully participate in all charity drives. In spite of her relative reserve, she was genuinely liked by the Russian women of the base, who applauded her generosity and kindness, especially that shown to their children. And the Chinese townspeople smiled on her with pride for her successful business skills.

To many she was somewhat of a mystery woman. No one seemed to know the full source of her political influence. There were rumors that her father had been a close confidant of Sergei Witte, the fabled architect behind the Russian rail system that extended from Russia across Siberia to the Pacific shore at Vladivostok, and also south through Manchuria from Harbin to Port Arthur. But Witte was no longer the powerful Minister of Finance, having fallen from favor at the imperial court in St Petersburg. Nicholas II, Czar of all the Russias, both jealous and insecure, had feared and resented the power wielded by Witte. Finally, in 1903, the Czar had deposed the minister. Still, Witte's influence seemed to prevail; he had friends in the military, he had unlimited access to French bankers, and his wife, though resented as a Jewess, maintained close ties with the House of Rothschild. Witte patiently bided his time to regain his power at the royal court. Vague rumors of Marina's ties to Witte persisted among the Chinese residents of Port Arthur.

In any event, Marina's place in the society of the port remained secure. Her income and connections in Russia, though obscure, continued undiminished, and the loyalty of those who courted her attention endured.

She did not invite gossip, except for her associaton with Captain Baron Viktor Alesandrov.

The baron had quickly sought her favor as soon as he had arrived in Port Arthur. The ladies of the garrison were ecstatic about Grand Duke Cyril's friend, the handsome Cossack officer from Vladivostok, but he had devoted all his attention to Mdme. Berezovsky, and, in due time, became her house guest. If a romance did exist between them, they were at least discrete. She had discouraged any appearance of a liaison, and her servants had refused to add to idle gossip. The two were close friends, but how close was anyone's guess. Both disdained comment to suspicious hints. Both kept their relationship private and avoided scandal.

Marina had at first regarded Alesandrov with lingering suspicion, having heard rumors of an alleged disastrous affair at the Czar's court in St Petersburg. But, eventually, she succumbed to Alesandrov's overwhelming charm, not because she was sexually lonely, but because she genuinely liked him and his marvelous companionship. She became the secret envy of the local Russian women, both married and unmarried. In fact all, except for a few insecure and jealous husbands, enjoyed the company of Alesandrov and his inestimable grace. He lent much needed gaiety to the drabness of Port Arthur's garrison life.

Alesandrov was not a callous rogue with an overactive libido. He simply viewed his role on earth as a duty to enjoy life to the fullest and to share his happiness with others. It was his nature. He was an irrepressible optimist and it was an unhappy person who could not or did not relish his company and his exuberant love of life. He was at peace with himself, uncomplicated, thankful for his active libido and serenely grateful to God for sharing His handiwork of Adam's rib.

In answer to the tinkling bell, a woman servant appeared at the gate. The ancient Master Loong spoke to her briefly. She pushed the gate open for him and Rogers. They walked between the outer buildings flanking the broad interior garden which reposed under a canopy of graceful trees. The park-like setting, filled with carefully trimmed bushes and hedges, and sprinkled with beds of dormant but normally colorful flowers, was an exotic contrast to the stark plainness of Old Town. The garden breathed a relaxing peacefulness for all in its presence.

The servant ushered them through the entrance hall and into a large paneled reception room on the ground floor. The woman who came forward to greet Rogers was so strikingly beautiful that her appearance almost took away his breath. She was not at all what he had expected. Some people find others so bewitchingly attractive that they discover themselves spellbound at first sight. That was the effect of Marina on Rogers. He saw the glossy black hair with highlights of auburn, the smooth alabaster skin with a touch of color. He could not help staring at the large jade-green eyes with only a hint of oriental lid, the small but decidely european nose, the high slavic cheek bones, and the ripe, full, sensuous mouth that was the focal point of her beauty.

Almost helpless to hide his emotions, Rogers drank in her appearance. Straying from her face, his attention took in the full bosom, the long legs and shapely hips, the trim, soft belly beneath her gown. *I have been away from my wife too long,* he thought. Fearful of staring, yet entranced by the glamour and mystery of the Orient that she invoked, he reluctantly forced himself to look into her eyes. Speaking apologetically, he said,

"Mademoiselle Berezovsky, I regret my untimely entrance. I had no idea that I would arrive in the midst of a war. I'm afraid I may be intruding." He addressed her in Chinese, having forgotten whether she spoke or understood English. He had expected to greet Viktor, but guessed that he was occupied at the harbor.

She smiled and answered in perfect English. "You are my most welcome and honored guest. Please be seated and call me Marina. I am so happy that Master Loong found you."

She turned to thank the ancient one who quietly excused himself, bowing to both as he departed, his mission accomplished.

Marina seated herself opposite Rogers and tried to set him at ease as they exchanged pleasantries. She controlled the conversation, while studying her guest. He looked younger than Viktor's description of him. Probably 24 or 25, she guessed. Hazel eyes and brown-red hair with a slight wave, a fair but tanned complexion that set off the high forehead and hazel eyes that were so large they almost bulged. Trimly built, of average height with strong shoulders and back. Not handsome, but nice looking with strong well-chisled features. There was something about the frank look on the face of this good friend of Viktor that she found both comfortable and reassuring—and strangely tinged with excitement. It was her belief that she would find his presence enjoyable.

She continued, "I went early on the hill this morning with the others, curious to see what had happened last night. I left at once when the first shell struck." Noting that her guest seemed a little tired and distracted, she rang a tiny bell. A summoned servant entered to set a tray of sweet cakes and a samover of green tea on the small table before her. Marina poured the tea and continued,

"Perhaps we should have anticipated the attack last night. None knew that it would be such a surprise. We thought the Japanese would be more civilized. I suppose that sounds naive." She arched her eyebrows.

Rogers helped himself to the proffered cake and tea, but did not reply. What was civilized about war? Innocent civilians had just been blown apart in the town. The Japanese had their own concept of the western rules of war, having ignored the Sunday holiday and the midnight hour.

Marina wished her guest would relax more. He seemed uneasy, as if he wanted to drink in her femininity, but was shyly wary of offending her. She liked his interest. Marina was comfortable with her beauty, humble in spite of it, yet thankful for the possession. It gave her added assurance in her dealings with others. And if men sometimes stared, well, she was used to that. She took his admiration of her face and figure as a compliment, grateful that he found her so attractive. Women could enjoy that kind of power.

She liked his manner and humility, finding him refreshingly different from the Czarist officers of the base. She wasn't sure why a difference existed, but sensed it had something to do with the rumored American respect for women. Although he was not in full uniform, she could see that he was not bulkily built like so many of her slavic countrymen, nor was he a large man like her father. Average height and average looks. Probably eight years younger than she. But he exuded an honesty and frankness that intrigued her and caused her to accept him at once.

Viktor's glowing description of the man who had once saved his life, the soldier with whom he had campaigned so closely in the Boxer War, had already helped pave the way for her acceptance of Rogers.

She recalled Viktor relating the story of a youthful Chinese student-intrepreter, a girl named An-an, who had been with them in the war. Marina was curious to know more about the girl; that story with its unexplained details and vague ending still piqued her interest. Studying the face of her guest, Marina tried to fathom why An-an's unknown image aroused her sexual curiosity. She knew from Viktor that Rogers had shared a tent with his female assistant.

Anticipating the question about Viktor, Marina quickly informed Rogers, "It will be a disappointment for both you and Viktor that he is not here to greet you. I am devastated that he is gone. General Stoessel sent him to Korea last week, but I am certain he will return very soon."

Now that war had erupted, she worried about Viktor's welfare. No news had come from Korea in two days. Since the Japanese controlled the wireless stations in Korea, it was apparent to everyone why Russian messages were so long delayed. So be it. Her own pipeline of information should produce results with the arrival of one of her supply boats on the morrow. She shared Rogers' disappointment at Viktor's absence.

"But please enjoy your stay here in the meantime. Viktor will be so happy that you came and will want you to remain here as my guest. I will be your guide."

Her next remarks surprised Rogers. "You will want to know the political situation at our base. I can tell you frankly that matters are not good. If you like, I can take you to the harbor tomorrow. It is not good today. The navy is bringing the wounded ashore, and the increased security is not yet well organized."

She had become aware of the glazed look in his eyes and how wearily he slumped in his chair. "When did you last sleep?" she asked. He told her that it had been two days ago, but protested when she insisted that he needed a nap. She persisted, "Let me show you to your room so you can refresh yourself."

He surrendered to her admonitions on the promise that she would awaken him later in the afternoon. The stairway was not the usual overly steep asian structure. It slanted upward at a gradual and comfortable angle with a midway landing. He followed her up the stairs in silence, guiltily annoyed with himself for his awareness of her sexuality. He realized it was not her fault that he was bothered. He caught a faint whiff of her perfume while engrossed in silent wonder at the ripe fullness and marvelous movement of her hips. Leading the way, she smiled to herself, sensing he was watching her movements.

Marina led him to the bedrooms on the second floor. At his door, she turned to let him pass, almost brushing against him. She liked the twinge of excitement that the proximity of their bodies brought. If only Viktor could be with her tonight!

"I will send a servant to you at once," she said, smiling at his shyness. "Please sleep well. We will talk later, after dinner tonight. And please call me Marina."

He requested the eager and pretty servant girl to bring a basin of hot water when he awakened so he could shave and wash. She wanted to fetch it at once, but he was too weary. The need for sleep began to overpower and dull his senses. The girl seemed reluctant to leave, lingering to show him the wash basin, the pitcher of cold water, the chamber pot, and pulling back the top bed blankets, and offering to bring a warming pan for the cold sheets. She was a flirtatious little thing, eager to capture his attention, anxious for his approval, and asking repeatedly what she could do to make him comfortable.

"I am called Yin-lin," she said, pausing at the door as if waiting for him to change his mind. He walked to the door, touched her hand lightly and thanked her before pushing her through the doorway.

He hurried to sponge his face, hands, and crotch, undressed and threw himself on the bed, pulling the blankets up to his chin. He collapsed into a deep sleep immediately.

Undisturbed, he slept until six-thirty in the evening. Darkness had arrived and the icy winter chill of the night had enveloped Port Arthur. Emerging from a dream-free sleep, he heard the light knock on the bedroom door. Before he could respond, the door opened and Yin-lin entered, carrying a lighted oil lamp. Caught unaware, he jerked his knees upward to hide the nocturnal bulge beneath his blanket, but not before she noticed. Smiling, she set the lantern on the table and left the room. He started to arise from the bed, impelled to relieve himself in the chamber pot, when Yin-lin reentered with a basin of steaming hot water.

"Tell mademoiselle I will come downstairs immediately," he told her impatiently.

Sensing his need, she left at once, rolling her eyes as she passed through the doorway.

He bathed, shaved off the stubble of beard, and donned clean undergarments before hurrying down the stairs to the dining salon. Marina had changed into woolen lounging pajamas, comfortably warm and casual, presenting a sight he had never seen before, so shockingly unconventional for the era and his country.

"In my home we do not need always to be formal," she said half apologetically. "Come, I know you must be hungry."

After a dinner of steamed vegetables, rice, and the fabled Dalny shrimp, they conversed until nine in the evening, during which time she briefed him on various cultural and geographic topics of interest, avoided asking him questions, and was gratified that he did not pry into her own personal life. She could explain certain things to him later.

"We will have time to become better acquainted," she promised. "Tomorrow, I will tell you about the personages who manage this base, and you must tell me a little about yourself. I want you to make this your home." He arose as she did. "We will be busy tomorrow so we should retire early," she said. He knew it was the Chinese custom to arise at dawn.

Before they started up the stairs, she handed him a small goblet of red wine, assuring him that it would help him sleep. At the head of the stairs, as he thanked her profusely for the soothing meal, she pointed out her bedroom nearby and bade him goodnight. Impulsively, she reached for his hand and expressed her gratitude for his past favors for Viktor.

He assured her he would rest comfortably and needed nothing more than additional sleep. Pointedly, she reminded him of the freezing February weather, saying she was concerned that he would sleep warmly. "I will have Yin-lin prepare more warmth for your comfort."

Searching his face for approval, she paused for a moment before adding, "Yin-lin is my gift to you for warmth and happiness. Viktor wanted it that way. Goodnight."

Rogers entered his room, puzzled. What did she mean, he wondered?

He sat on the edge of the bed to remove his guest slippers, realizing that the room was indeed cold. He shrugged. He had been cold before; he could adjust. But he would discover how wrong he was to think that Manchuria was no colder than most places.

He had no sooner crept into bed, when a knock at the door alerted him that Yin-lin had entered. She wore cloth slippers and a loose but warm robe. He caught a glimpse of bare flesh as her robe briefly parted when she approached the bed. She stood before him wordlessly, watching his face for approval. Then he understood what Marina had meant.

"No, no," he protested. Rising from the bed, he led her to the door, seeking to hide his embarrassment. "Please go to your mistress," he said. "You are very kind. Good night and sleep well." He closed the door and turned away, feeling very awkward and foolish and wondering if there could have been a more graceful way to express his rejection.

Yin-lin's availability puzzled him. Was she indeed a gift? From Viktor? This was a game that Viktor Alesandrov understood and enjoyed and considered a normal function of life. But was it Viktor's idea? If not, did Marina know Yin-lin had offered herself? Could it be Marina's thought—or was it Viktor's—that a sexually satiated guest would be less attracted to Marina? Should he feel offended or grateful?

Yin-lin returned to Marina's chamber. "He did not want me," she wailed. Marina hugged her, wiped away the tears, and led her to the bed. The two shared their body warmth and were soon fast asleep, shielded from the frigid night.

Rogers was now fully awake and tossing restlessly from the encounter with pretty, little Yin-lin and his suspicion of Alesandrov's role. Viktor, ah Viktor! How disappointing not to find him here. What a noble friend, and yet, such an enigma at times. For the next hour and a half, Rogers lay with eyes closed, but with a mind that raced in high gear to review in detail his recent rendezvous with Alesandrov on New Year's Eve in Shanghai.

CHAPTER THREE

Captain Baron Viktor Alexeivitch Alesandrov had come to Shanghai aboard the Russian cruiser *Variag* as a member of a mission sent to negotiate with Chinese businessmen. The Russian mission had sought to open channels of trade, particularly for food products from northern Chinese ports in the event of damage to the South Manchurian Railway, the single track line that ran south from its union at Harbin with the Chinese Eastern Railway. The rail line was the land lifeline for Port Arthur.

Alesandrov had learned with pleasure that his young American comrade from the Boxer campaign was in the city. The two had arranged to celebrate the western New Year Eve at their favorite tavern, the Golden Pavilion, so they could reminisce about their China adventures three and one-half years earlier during the international rescue of the beleagured foreign legations in Peking. What a shame, he thought, that they had lost touch in those years.

When Rogers had entered the already crowded and noisy Shanghai tavern, he saw that Alesandrov had typically commandeered the best table and sat comfortably with the tavern's prettiest Chinese hostess. So like his Russian comrade! The girl was tall, like so many of the northern Chinese, and was Han, not Manchu. Her delicate features, enhanced by a generous application of rouge, mascara, and lipstick, gave her a theatrical and comely appearance. The tight silk gown clung to a shapely and sensuous figure.

Rogers remembered how Alesandrov had beckoned him over to the table. "Ellis, my dear friend, the years have been kind to you." He had stood to embrace his American friend, noting that Rogers seemed as shy and serious as ever, still a little hesitant around women, but the most sincere and trustworthy companion one could wish for. He had promised never to forget this comrade who had saved his life that day in the battle for the railway station in Tientsin, China.

"Hello, Viktor. Happy New Year!" Rogers saw that Alesandrov had changed little. As always, he admired and envied the tall Russian's handsome features and his ebullient charm—forever the polished gentleman officer with impeccable manners learned so well at the Czar's court.

Turning to the hostess, Alesandrov had said, "Tea Flower, my friend and I need to discuss private matters. Would you excuse us for a little while, my dear?" He had risen to shoo the girl gently from the table. She left reluctantly, but not before Alesandrov had pressed a banknote into her hand.

"You sure pick them, Viktor. Still on that regimen of yogurt and boiled cabbage?" Both had laughed at the reference to an alleged source of sexual vigor.

"Better than your Chinese ginseng," Alesandrov had retorted. When they were comfortably seated, he had leaned forward to confide to Rogers, "Actually she chose me; I intend to find out why."

Two bottles of an excellent vintage of champagne sat on the table. Rogers knew that he was in for a night of drinking. If there was one thing the Russian enjoyed even more than the company of women, it was good champagne. It seemed to agree with him equally as well as did attractive women.

Rogers knew that Alesandrov was an unabashed but charming womanizer who had never kept secret his appetite for appreciative women. The women were equally attracted to him. They thrilled to the blonde good looks of the tall officer with his guardsman moustache, trimmed in the British style. His courtly deference toward women, his fluent command of languages and his skill on the dance floor had made him always welcome at diplomatic balls.

When Alesandrov had filled two glasses, his uniform sleeve caught Rogers' attention. In a joking tone, the American had asked, "Where is that resplendent red and blue hussar uniform, Vicktor? I expected you would dress for the occasion." The Russian had always been a bit of a dandy.

Alesandrov had self consciously smoothed the silver trim on the front of his immaculate black Cossack uniform. "That is a long story," he had said. A shadow of saddness had flitted across his usually jovial face. "Want to hear about it? The night is young."

Rogers had recognized that the Russian felt compelled to talk, believing that here was a close Amercan friend with whom he could finally unburden some of the pain of his recent past. Alesandrov had signalled for another bottle of champagne before launching into his tale.

As Rogers had surmised, it was his friend's libido that had brought on trouble, causing Alesandrov's career to stumble badly.

Rogers had strained to listen above the din of noise in the tavern.

"…and it came at a time when I was out of favor with the Czar's wife. She was always difficult to please, and it was ever easy for her to turn against a friend when gossip came to her attention. She listened too much to the daily court gossip. You know how I enjoy the ladies. Well, the Czarina seemed to resent the attention her court attendants gave me. Most of the women who waited on her were married. But you can understand how compliant women, especially some married women, can be. One particularly favored me. Unfortunately, her husband was my colonel in the Sumsky Dragoons."

Alesandrov had paused to sip his champagne, shaking his head in dismay at the memory of his former life. "How I miss my regiment. We were really the Czar's favorite regiment, not the Imperial Guards, as they thought. We had such a glorious life in St Petersburg: the theater, the night clubs, the fashionable restaurants; it was all so civilized there." He had paused again, half closing his eyes in remembrance of past glories. After a moment, he had sighed and continued.

"The affair, I am afraid, became so torrid that it was carelessly conducted. My fault, really. As women do, the dear thing gossiped about our lovemaking, and how enjoyable it was, compared to the colonel. I grant you, he is a bit of a stuffed shirt."

Alesandrov had topped off his glass and had raised it in mock salute to a fond memory.

"Actually, she is a distant cousin of mine. I thought of it more as a family obligation, a learning experience, if you will. She was so innocent and so eager to learn. Such a ravishing adornment and wonderful pupil, always so ecstatic when we were together. A little on the plump side, but, my, my, Ellis, such *joie de vivre*. The spark between her legs became a raging bonfire as her passion grew and grew.

When the affair was exposed, the colonel did not challenge me to a duel. He did worse; he went to the Czarina. Because of her, I was banished from my coveted elite regiment and transferred to Vladivostok. So there I was in that Siberian hell-hole on the Pacific coast, thousands of miles from St Petersburg, away from my love, my friends, my comrades, my wonderful social life. This dismal port was such a terrible fate. But I have always tried not to be bitter. The entire affair was my fault because I started it. And like the biblical Job, I was made to suffer.

The simultaneous transfer to the Don Cossacks was, I confess, a blow to my ego. Yes, I know, Cossack regiments are the backbone of our cavalry, but they can be so provincial. And in eastern Siberia—Ellis, you cannot imagine how bleak life can be in a frontier outpost."

Rogers had understood his friend's pain. Victor could not tolerate a monastic existence. Maybe it was in his background. He had seldom mentioned his parents and did not seem to have a warm and loving family. From what little Rogers had gleaned from past conversations, Viktor had always yearned for his father's love and approval. The father appeared to be a rigid, retired military officer of high rank who was incapable of sharing emotions with his son, an only child. And the mother, who almost never entered the conversation, seemed to resent the son. There had been no warm, maternal love for her offspring. Perhaps that would explain Viktor's lifelong need for female companionship.

The parents slept apart and never engaged in outward signs of affection. Their conversations, while never quarrelsome, were always strictly polite and correct, lacking zest or humor. As a boy, Alesandrov had wondered if his father knew other women or if his mother was unhappy in her marriage.

The youth had been chosen by the family for a military career. Spoiled by female relatives, particularly an aunt and a governess, both of whom had initiated him in the mysteries and pleasures of sex, Alesandrov's slavic libido had never lost its appetite.

Alesandrov had refilled his glass and had continued to describe his loneliness at the distant ice-bound port. Except for a couple of married women, whom he had wisely chosen not to pursue, he had found the Russian women at Vladivostok to be as frigid as the winter weather. Worse, fellow officer had greeted him with suspicion and had not included him in social events.

So he had thrown himself into his duties with renewed fervor. In time, his exemplary behavior and devotion to work had gradually won the praise of the port's officer corps. Although not close to Alesandrov, the other Cossack officers had begun to treat him with respect. Alesandrov had continued to keep to himself. No one had inquired about his off-duty pursuits.

Alesandrov had compensated for his carnal urges by covertly frequenting one particular red-light establishment, whose madam had willingly cooperated. Her oriental prostitutes, imported for the enjoyment of the garrison, were considered to be unworthy of his rank and social position. Since he could not properly associate with them, he had devised extraordinary means of deception to hide his frequent visits.

He had found to his delight that the oriental whores assuaged his loneliness very well. They were not only more hygienic than those in Russia, but were more talented and innovative in their practices of sexual gratification. They were a cure for relaxing his inner torment.

He had told Rogers, "Ellis, can you imagine me learning new tricks? I had never experienced such innovative positions and with multiple partners. There was the *butterfly*, the *bicycle*, and many more." He leaned forward and said in confidence, "You know, Ellis, the female is really the stronger of the human species. We men delude ourselves with our belief of masculine sexual superiority." He had smiled at the fond memory of past encounters and the grateful balm they had provided for his maddening loneliness.

"Drink up, old chap," he had advised Rogers, trying to offer more champagne. "Remember those terribly hot August days on the march to Peking, after we had knocked out the forts at Taku and pushed past the gates of Tientsin? Living like dogs in the heat and stench along the river, sleeping in soiled clothes for days, with seldom any good water to drink or use for bathing. Thank God for that atrocious Chinese red wine in our canteens. It kept us healthy. We should savor moments like this.

By the way, what ever happened to the little Chinese girl, what was her name, Li-li, no An-an? I really liked her. I could see she adored you. We could all see that. You should have kept her. I never did reveal to you that I guessed her identity before you did." Alesandrov had referred to the girl's masquerade as a young man in order to serve as an army scout with Rogers.

"Later," Rogers had dodged, "It is your story for the moment." He had wondered later if he should have divulged the truth about An-an and her loot of the Viceroy's sycee, and the recovery of more of the marble-sized silver nuggets from buried loot that the regiment of Welsh Fusiliers had failed to retrieve. And should he have told his friend where Liu Xi, the Peking governor's concubine was? He had recognized that Alesandrov had had little choice in abandoning her. He had resolved to mention it at some other time.

Alesandrov had emptied his glass, had signalled his hostess to fetch another bottle and had urged Rogers to drink in memory of past adventures. The girl had hurried forward from the group of comely hostesses lounging at the bar. She had moved gracefully in the tight Chinese gown, slit up the sides to reveal shapely legs. The high collar of her dress had framed the pale skin of her neck. When she had set down the bottle of cold champagne, Alesandrov had patted her hand. Rogers had observed her fingers close over the crumpled ruble notes.

Rogers had glanced around the room at the other celebrants, mostly Europeans, civilian and military. A few prosperous Chinese merchants were sitting impassively at adjacent tables. Their traditional New Year celebration would come on the last day of their twelfth month, almost thirty days away. Meanwhile they had surveyed with amusement the raucous antics of the western barbarians.

Alesandrov had preferred to enjoy the New Year in the tradition of the western Gregorian calendar, choosing to ignore his country's Justinian calendar which lagged the western New Year by thirteen days.

He had asked a question, interrupting Rogers' smiling approval of the undulating movement of the hostess's hips retreating to the bar. "Am I boring you or would you like to hear the rest of the story?"

"No, no, please continue. How did you get out of Siberia, Viktor?"

Alesandrov had shrugged. "My deplorable exile terminated just short of one year. Being a distant relative of the royal family had its compensations. Although the Czarina wanted me out of sight..." He looked around the room carefully, then said in a lower voice. "The Russian people do not like the German ways of the Czarina. She still speaks bad Russian."

Pausing then to take a long sip of the champagne, rolling it over his tongue, savoring the vintage like a Frenchman with a grand prix taste, Alesandrov had continued. "I wrote discretely to the Czar's uncle, Grand Duke Cyril. He's with the fleet up in Manchuria, you know. Thus it was my good fortune to secure an assignment at Port Arthur. It may not be St Petersburg, but it is a happy change. Soon you will meet Mademoiselle Berezovsky. She has been such a wonderful boon to my existence at the naval base."

Rogers had chosen not to pursue the matter of Marina. Time enough for that later. He had wanted to question his friend about Port Arthur, that naval bastion that so tormented the Japanese because it controlled the approaches to Manchuria and poised like a torpedo at Japan's shipping in the Yellow Sea. Everyone had recognized that Japan would have seized neighboring

Korea long ago were it not for Russia's possession of the port and naval base.

Having noted that Rogers was out of uniform, Alesandrov had paused to ask about his business in Shanghai.

"Still a junior lieutenant, Ellis?"

"No. In recognition of my gallant exploits against the Boxers, I was promoted two years later to first lieutenant." He had laughed worriedly. "Now I'm possibly up for captain, but I may get an assignment that I won't like."

Alesandrov had raised his glass in salute, saying sarcastically, "You should have my problems. Anyway, here is to our American hero and the slow rewards of democracy."

Rogers had leaned forward to speak quietly. "I can't tell you why I'm in Shanghai, Viktor. I came here two months ago—it's a long story. Part of it has to do with the Empress Dowager. As you know, the bitch is back on the Celestial Throne, charming the diplomatic community as if she was never a part of the Boxer atrocities. My country will keep more military presence at the legation from now on. It is up to the U.S. Marines to keep an eye on her."

"Secret assignment?" Alesandrov had probed.

"Not really, Viktor. Not what you think. Sort of a roving job for the army. We can talk about it more in a better place. Unlike the English and Germans, be assured that I'm on your side."

He had preferred not to discuss the reason for his past slow promotion. Certainly his youth had been a deterrent, and he was not a West Pointer. The business in the Philippines had largely ended, although the treacherous Moslem Moros in some of the southern islands still continued their atrocities. His three and one-half years in China had been a proving ground, years that he would always cherish for many reasons.

It had been his knowledge of the cultures and politics of the Far East, as well as his proficiency in Mandarin, that had made Rogers the perfect agent for the War Department. The military chiefs in Washington had preferred to cloak him with a low rank, recognizing his usefulness in penetrating the veil of diplomatic deceit that the State Department persisted in practicing. Neither State nor War trusted each other. The War Department still recognized the need to modernize in the era of Europe's imperialistic expansionism. And, worse, China had continued to slide further into decadence, presenting an alarming target for dismemberment by European rivals.

The Mikado's surprise triumph over China, almost ten years earlier, had now made Japan a military force to be reckoned with. Tragically, none of the European royal houses had foreseen the true extent of Japan's power or her hatred of western culture.

So the War Office had seen in Rogers a dependable reporter for the asiatic scene. As a junior officer, he had stayed out of the limelight and passed relatively unnoticed by the State Department. His brief military career had proven his honesty and devotion to duty, and his flexibility in matters concerning weaponry. In short, he could be trusted to pass on vital information that stuffy armchair militarists so often disdained to notice.

The Department knew he had a close friend in the Russian army, one who had cooperated so well with American forces in north China. It had seemed logical that a trusted American observer could operate behind the scenes in the coming clash between Russia and Japan. State still clearly favored Japan. But it did not pass unnoticed in the War Department that Japan had feverishly embarked on a program to build its war machine.

Japanese officers diligently studied in British and German war colleges. And English shipyards worked overtime to supply warships to Japan's growing navy.

The men of the State Department may have scoffed at the danger, but it had worried the American military planners. Men of Rogers' caliber could make timely reports independent of military observers assigned to State Department legations.

Alesandrov had interrupted his friend's reverie. "I will not ask questions, Ellis. I am only happy we could reunite after almost four years. I value our friendship. When we separated before, I hoped that someday we could meet again to enjoy just such an occasion as this. Come, let us have dinner. The evening is ours. More champagne? Let me fill your glass."

"Do you plan to be in Shanghai long?" Rogers had inquired.

"No, Our business is almost finished. I will be leaving soon for Port Arthur, probably in a day or two. I was hoping that perhaps you could visit me. My friend Marina would put you up. I'd like to show you the progress we have made at the naval base. We Russians may have been rough on the natives earlier, but we are rather proud of our civilizing influence, I'm happy to say."

It had been the perfect opening for Rogers. "I wouldn't mind seeing Manchuria. I have the time to spare—if it could be arranged."

"By all means, come to Port Arthur," Alesandrov had implored. "I can be your guide. Bring your uniform. Marina would be delighted to meet you. I know you will like her."

"*What luck*," Rogers had thought. "It is a tempting offer, am I welcome, Viktor?"

Alesandrov had understood his meaning. "Of course. As an American military officer and my guest, there will be no problem. Submit the request.

I will manage the bureaucracy at my end. Better yet, get yourself assigned as an observer for our spring manuevers."

"You are sure?"

"Absolutely. I will inform Admiral Starck at the base. Fine chap. I know the family well. As for General Stoessel—you remember him from the Boxer Campaign. He is still as difficult as ever. Not that I like the bastard; you know how stubborn Balts can be. But I try to cooperate. I arranged for him to acquire a Chinese slave girl to join his household." He winked. "Let us just say that he is indebted to me for such a pretty servant. He will not object, I'm sure. He should be grateful for the way you found a way through the Tartar Wall at Peking."

Rogers had not been so sure that Stoessel would be any more likable or friendly than in the past.

"When would be a good time?"

"Why not the first or second week of February—by your calendar. The ice should be starting to melt by then. Later, we can ride the train up to Harbin, then over to the Maritime Provinces. Hunting should be excellent. We might even see a Siberian tiger. Real man killers."

Alesandrov had again refilled both glasses, while quickly glancing at his hostess who reclined against the bar. He had seemed to know she had read the note passed with the rubles. The note had read:

Do not join another table. Come to my table after our dinner. I want to see you tonight.

He had turned to Rogers. "So it is settled. I will be expecting you no later than mid-February. Now let us enjoy the dinner. And tell me all about your adventures after I left Peking. What happened when you caught our expedition's nominal commander, that fat Prussian pig, Field Marshal Count von Waldersee, diddling a Chinese prostitute on the Empress Dowager's own sacred bed. It is a wonder you were not cashiered—or did you use that incident to your own advantage?"

Rogers laughed. His close friendship with the Russian had evolved from the intense rivalry of the various foreign divisions of the international expeditionary army to be first ito breach the stout gates of Peking's Tartar Wall. The fierce fighting at the coastal Taku forts at the start of the campaign, and the overland march to rescue the city of Tientsin had fostered mutual respect. Their friendship had blossomed and transcended the enormous suspicions the Russian army held for their military allies. Russia viewed north China as it anticipated hegemony.

Rogers drank cautiously as the conversation grew more serious.

"Russia needs your goods," Alesandrov warned, "but my government resents your commercial interference."

"That is a double-edged sword," Rogers quickly protested. "The American business community is equally unhappy about the Czar's restrictions on open and free trading in Manchuria."

"Meaning?"

"Meaning that Russian bureaucracy prevents my country from enjoying its share of Manchurian trade."

There had followed a strained silence, finally broken by Rogers. "Let's not quarrel. Leave it to Wall Street and the Czar's quartermaster."

Alesandrov could not resist one last jab, "Just what I meant about your State Department."

As the conversation had continued, Rogers had tried to ignore a party of noisy German officers who had begun to shout loud beer-laden songs. At another table, English and Belgian consular workers were toasting each other into early inebriation. The music of the tavern owner, what there was of it, was scarcely audible over the loud conversations. The scratching of the gramaphone's dull needle against the record grooves mercifully could not compete with the shouting voices. Several of the hostesses had begun to drift across the floor to join various tables.

The jollity had continued with both men regaling each other with stories from the past, while enjoying the dinner of excellent Peking duck, lacquered with both pineapple and orange sauces and garnished with yams and the best mountain rice from the southern provinces.

Rogers recalled how the hostess had waited impatiently at the bar for permission to rejoin them. The inkeeper had already signified his assent. Tea Flower had not taken her eyes off the blonde Cossack, occasionally passing the tip of her tongue over her lower lip as she caught his eye, and provacatively crossing and uncrossing her legs to reveal a glimpse of a white thigh.

Alesandrov had pulled an envelope from his pocket, studied it for a moment, then had set it down before Rogers. Rogers had seen it was blank. He had wondered why his Russian friend was so deliberate about the movement. He was told, "Open it, but keep it flat on the table top."

Rogers had opened the envelope and had drawn out a piece of paper covered with notes, spreading it on the table top. Puzzled, he had looked at Alesandrov who was unsmiling.

"What I'm doing is for a purpose, Ellis, so please play along. While we talk, I'm going to draw you a quick map of the Port Arthur area so you will have no difficulty finding me." Alesandrov had produced a pen, reached across and had begun to sketch on the blank back of the paper. Rogers had observed his friend's reticence whenever a waiter or hostess approached the table.

"Ever been to Japan, Ellis?"

Rogers had nodded. "Only for a couple of days. Hard workers, those people. They unloaded their part of our cargo very fast. That was several years ago. I was only a young cabin boy then. I didn't get ashore."

"Too bad, Ellis. It is a very tidy country with clean people. The women, bless them, are wonderfully docile and compliant. I do not care too much for the men—too polite and too reserved, around me, anyway. I loved the public baths. It is so pleasurable to soak in the steaming hot water while a naked girl massages your arms and back. How can I describe the relaxation? Later, when I received the full massage on the table, I'm afraid that I misbehaved. It was difficult not to?" He had laughed uproariously. "The girls tried to be coy, but they were giggling and staring. The caucasian advantage in penis size, I guess. It was all so flattering. I suppose I received special treatment, amends perhaps, for the attempted assassination of the Czar much earlier on his first and only visit there. The Japanese had been so mortified. The Czar had received a nasty sword cut on his forehead. He never liked them after that. Now, he refers to them as 'little tailless monkeys.'"

Rogers had watched his friend draw while talking. He thought back to his close friendship with the Japanese army officer, Lieutenant Tomoru Tanaka, wondering if he was still teaching in Hiroshima. Alesandrov's frank distrust of the Japanese had always made Rogers a little uncomfortable. He had shifted the conversation.

"How about Korea?" he had asked.

"Not as clean as Japan," Alesandrov had responded, "but their girls are good, very enthusiastic. You can buy a slave girl there almost as cheaply as in China; she is yours for life. But the Koreans are not too stable. Sometimes they have a mean streak that can be most unsettling. I prefer the Chinese character, the ones we know, not the Manchus up north. Speaking of the Chinese, now that we have discussed private matters, let us bring Tea Flower back to the table."

He had finished the sketch and had asked Rogers to memorize it, while he had pointed out certain features in regard to the railway from Dalny to the naval base, the site of Marina's house, and the general layout of Old Town and New Town. He had done this with deliberate flourishes and emphatic hand motions. Then he had replaced the paper into the envelope and had slowly returned it to the breast pocket of his tunic.

Rogers had seen the tavern proprietor, Ch'in Sheng, beckon to Alesandrov's hostess. He had spoken to her through the barred window of the cash cage. Tea Flower had shaken her head. Ch'in Sheng had not raised his voice, but had hissed at her angrily, clutching one of the bars of the window.

With the waiter hurriedly clearing the dishes from the table, Alesandrov had beckoned to his hostess. Both had stood as she had approachd, and Alesandrov had gallantly pulled out a chair to seat her. He had ordered refreshments for her and had filled the empty glasses with champagne. Noticing that Rogers still carefully sipped his drink, he had joked, "It is wise to be cautious, Ellis. Russians are often like Irishmen. They drink until they are drunk." Alesandrov, however, seemed unfazed by the amount he had imbibed.

Alesandrov had continued to entertain his friend with lurid tales of St Petersburg cafe society. He had playfully teased the hostess, who had giggled as if she had understood his double entendres. Both men had further bemused her by practicing funny Chinese idioms.

At midnight, all had stood to toast the New Year. The tavern had rocked from the noisy celebration. Chinese patrons, reserved in the presence of westerners, had smiled bemusedly at the clownish behavior of the caucasian barbarians. Wine and beer had flowed freely amidst the babble of multiple foreign tongues, interspersed with the high-pitched Chinese dialect, producing a bedlam of deafening noise.

Ch'in Sheng, the owner, had remained unsmiling in his cash cage, undoubtedly anticipating his profit and wishing the night would go on forever.

When the crowd had resumed sitting, Alesandrov had leaned across the table to speak earnestly. "Ellis, let Tea Flower call for her friend. She wants me to stay, and I don't want you to be lonely tonight."

Thinking back to that night, Rogers remembered thanking his friend for his consideration, but had tried to beg off, saying he had other plans. He recalled the painful feeling of sadness and loneliness that had crept over him as he thought back to other New Year celebrations in Havana, Singapore, Manila and other foreign ports. This night had come to an end for him as he saw the images of the happy, laughing children of Mindanao that crowded his mind. He still missed the families there, the shy young people and the gracious, hospitable elders. And memories of his long absent mother in Montana, and the surrogates parents he had acquired in Chicago filled his thoughts. Suddenly he wanted to be with An-an. He longed to be with her in Hong Kong, to hold her tightly against his body, to caress her and tell her how much he loved and missed her. He couldn't imagine having another woman in his life. He was almost tempted to tell Viktor that he had married An-an.

Whether it was the din of noise in the tavern, the abundance of champagne, or the late hour, he felt a pressing need to escape into the night. His aching desire for An-an made everything else seem tawdry and disloyal.

He knew that Alesandrov had seen his sadness and was sure that he understood. Viktor would not insist that Rogers stay because he had always thought that Americans were often so infuriatingly puritannical. He had once told Rogers that no one was going to live forever—that a soldier's career especially denied longevity. "My God," he had said, "who wanted to die aged and bitter in an old soldier's home? *Live for today! Have fun! Enjoy women!*"

They had settled the bill with the proprietor. Each had expressed gratitude for the reunion, and Rogers had given his oath that he would come to Manchuria. Shaking hands in farewell, Alesandrov had said, "In case we do not chance to meet again before I leave Shanghai, I will be awaiting your visit. Just check with the harbor police for directions. Au revoir until next month, old friend."

Outside, in the street fronting the tavern, the doorman had hailed a ricksha. Though the night was dark and the street scarcely lit by the few small oil lanterns on the building, Rogers had been startled to catch a glimpse of a man he knew from the past to be a Japanese secret agent. The shadowy figure, whom Rogers recognized as Major Ariko, had quickly ducked into the recess of a darkened doorway directly across the street.

Summoned by the doorman's sharp handclap, the ricksha porter had loomed out of the darkness. Mounting the conveyance, Rogers had pretended not to see the faint outline of Ariko skulking in the shadows. He had left, wondering if Alesandrov would be all right, knowing there was no love lost between the two. And he remembered Ariko's past hatred of himself.

Even though Russia and Japan had acted as allies during the China campaign, Ariko had never cooperated. Now, with strained relations over Manchuria, the Japanese had become increasingly bellicose. Reluctantly, Rogers had given his command to the porter and had leaned back for the bouncing ride on the narrow cobbled street. The ricksha porter had sped away in a fast dogtrot, his strong peasant legs churning, and the muscled flesh of arms and back soon glistening with sweat.

Several blocks from the tavern, Rogers had ordered the porter to halt. He was worried. Recalling Ariko's ill-concealed contempt for all caucasians and the open arrogance toward Americans, particularly himself, he had acted on impulse and had ordered the Chinaman to pull the ricksha back to the tavern, instructing the porter to approach it from a side street. At the nearest corner, he had dismounted, motioned for the Chinaman to wait, and had walked to the edge of the building. Carefully he had peered around the corner and had looked down the street.

A Chinese girl, barely covered by a white shift, had appeared at the tavern's upstairs window. It was Tea Flower. Through an opened window, she had tossed a coin-weighted piece of paper to the waiting agent below. Ariko had caught the paper, pocketed it and had disappeared into the night. Before closing the window, Tea Flower had glanced toward the end of the street where Rogers stood. He had pulled back, uncertain if she had seen him. Against his better judgment, he had returned to the ricksha.

The next day, Rogers had learned with certainty that Alesandrov had left the city, none the worse for wear.

Tea Flower had returned to the bed, troubled by her deed and concerned about the man at the end of the street. Plagued by guilt, she shook Alesandrov and confessed. His reaction shocked her. Instead of anger, he held her lovingly in his arms, kissing her bare neck and shoulders, and teasing her hardening nipples with his lips.

"Why?" she asked.

"Because you acted as I planned. Regardless of your motive, you cooperated with my scheme perfectly."

She pulled back in amazement. "You knew that I would betray you? After we made love?"

He shrugged. "You were well paid?" She did not deny it.

"Your boss threatened you, did he not? My government has known about Major Ariko and Ch'in Sheng for a long time. Trouble is, we could never catch Ariko with his hand in the cash box, my dear. Besides, our Viceroy Alexeiev is always reluctant to antagonize the Japanese government for fear of retaliation. So I decided to supply Ariko with misinformation. We knew that your boss, Ch'in Sheng, works for the Japanese. And we were certain that Ariko would contact you because of your obvious popularity here. It was a perfect opportunity. The little fart stayed out of sight tonight because he knew I would recognize him."

She squirmed as his smooth hand traced a path across the soft skin of her belly. "Are you unhappy with me for using you?" he asked.

"Not if you forgive me." She arched her back, aroused by his touch, but her eyes reflected her worry. "What will happen to me? I am afraid of this man."

"Nothing should happen." he told her. "He will not suspect that you were part of my plot.

He will blame me or perhaps Ch'in Sheng. Your boss took the bait when I mentioned that I wanted the best table and your company because I planned to impress an old friend from another government. That I wanted privacy to discuss plans for improvement of the Port Arthur harbor."

She clung to him, hoping he would understand. "Ch'in ordered me to take the envelope from your pocket and pass it to Major Ariko—after you passed out."

"Did you really think that I was drunk?" he asked. He snorted, "I do not get drunk. But, of course, they did not know that." He searched her face closely, then asked gently, "Did I act like a drunken peasant when we made love?"

She shook her head, clasping him tightly. Quite the opposite, she thought. This man was slow and deliberate in his approach, a gentle but tireless lover, leading her at all times and purposely holding back to permit her to climax first.

"I am still afraid," she said, crowding against him and locking one leg around his waist.

He looked at her gravely. "Do not breath a word of this to anyone. Continue to play along with Ch'in. But from now on you must cooperate with our side. Understand? Good. Now here is my plan."

"Can we talk later?" she asked, grateful that she was in the good graces of this handsome Cossack whose virility she had admired all evening. She grasped his hand and pushed it lower.

"Love me again," she implored.

"Of course," he assented. "We have all night to discuss our arrangement..."

She cut off his words, covering his mouth with hers.

Early in the following month, Rogers had boarded a train to go north to the small port of Chefu, directly across from the Manchurian peninsula. He had contacted Chen, who had happened to be loading a cargo there, and had arranged for transportation to Port Arthur. Chen had expressed delight to have the company of his young friend on the short voyage across the Bay of Bohai. The two could talk for hours about past adventures. Rogers was soon to discover ghosts from Chen's past that would influence his stay with Alesandrov's friend, Marina Berezovsky.

Rogers had received instructions from American Army Intelligence in Shanghai to find out why so many Japanese nationals had been seen leaving the Kwantung and Liaotung Peninsulas. British steamers had reported an unusually large number of Japanese families departing with house pets and furniture. That had suggested a permanent relocation for whatever reason. Perhaps it meant war?

CHAPTER FOUR

The Japanese cruiser *Akashi* weighed anchor at Lindsay Island and departed for the west coast of Korea where she joined the invasion fleet off Chemulpo harbor. The same intelligence from Major Ariko that had been given to Admiral Togo was relayed by *Akashi* to the invasion flagship. Knowledge that the Russian Pacific Fleet was still berthed at Port Arthur came as a relief to the cruisers escorting the vulnerable Japanese troop transports.

Viktor Alesandrov had reached the Korean port of Chemulpo on February 4. He had arrived on the light cruiser *Variag*, an American-built warship that was part of Russia's Pacific Fleet. The warship, though modern, was in poor shape because of neglectful maintenance of the engine boilers. The money for maintenance had been corruptly diverted for another use.

General Stoessel, military commander of Port Arthur's army garrison, had assigned Alesandrov a mission to investigate the readiness of the military guard at the Russian post in Chemulpo, the Korean seaport for the capital city of Seoul. The port, sometimes called Inchon by the Japanese, hosted several foreign warships on hand to "show the flag" and to protect their nationals.

The various foreign governments took care to avoid embroilment in the Russian-Japanese quarrel. Most of the foreign powers faulted Russia for being the big bully. Japan had won enthusiastic sympathy and support in her role of the underdog, while carefully concealing her preparation for a massive naval assault on the Czar's eastern fleet.

Captain Rudnev of the *Variag* received Alesandrov's warm thanks for his hospitality in the short voyage from Port Arthur. Alesandrov hurried ashore to implement his task. As he had suspected, the guard commander, Lt. Mikhail Yatskov, had not done his job. Yatskov, a political graduate of Moscow's top military academy, was overweight, lazy, and openly discontented with his post. After four days of quarreling with the slovenly officer, who refused to take advice or correctly follow procedures, Alesandrov went aboard the other Russian warship in the harbor, the gunboat *Koreets,* to write his report for General Stoessel, and to prepare for the return voyage across the Yellow Sea to Port Arthur. He steadied himself for a harsh trip, for the weather had turned stormy, and the old gunboat did not handle well in rough waters. Unknown to the Russians, the Japanese cruiser *Chiyoda* had slipped out of the harbor at midnight and had headed south to rendezvous with the Japanese invasion fleet.

The morning of February 8 found Captain Rudnev as embarrassed and frustrated as ever because of his inability to find out what transpired in the Far East, particularly at Port Arthur. He knew that war drums were beating and that the Mikado's men were up to something, yet the Russians in Korea continued to flounder in the dark, unable to contact their garrisons in Manchuria.

All operators at the few wireless stations in Korea were now Japanese. They were no more cooperative than their arrogant military signal corps officers. With a lot of apologies, ever present smiles and excuses, and promises to look into the delay of transmitting Russian messages, they gave toothy grins and politely bobbed their heads, but failed to produce a solution.

Ignorant of the attack on Port Arthur, Rudnev abandoned use of the telegraph station and angrily ordered the gunboat *Koreets* to go at once to Port Arthur to ascertain the true situation. Was war imminent or not? What was rumor or fact? What was really happening?

That afternoon, the small Russian gunboat with Alesandrov aboard lifted anchor and departed on the rising tide. Alesandrov was grateful to be leaving Korea; he had never liked the country. He looked forward to being with Marina again. Perhaps Rogers had arrived. If he had, Marina would be happy to entertain him. Rogers was probably having glandular turmoil watching Marina walk around. Well, Yin-lin would calm him and reduce the swelling. He smiled at his crude humor.

The *Koreets* had hardly emerged from the harbor when she was menaced by two approaching Japanese torpedo boats. The combative Japanese closed in for an obvious attack. The *Koreets* took evasive action, firing a warning shot from her bow gun. To the delight of the Russian crew, one of the torpedo boats ran aground on a mud bank. The other torpedo boat swerved away when the Russian gunboat fired a second shell to discourage its pursuer, before turning sharply to return to Chemulpo harbor.

Seaward, framed against the southern horizon, a Japanese armada of five cruisers, six more torpedo boats and three troop transports steamed toward the harbor. Alesandrov knew he was witnessing the start of the invasion of Korea.

For the rest of the afternoon, the *Koreets* and the *Variag* lay anchored among the other foreign warships and watched helplessly as a parade of Korean sampans ferried ashore units of the Japanese First Army. The well executed landing proceeded into the night without interference and was completed by three o'clock in the morning. Captain Rudnev did not disclose to his crew members that his orders were to remain in Chemulpo and not interfere with any Japanese attempt to land troops absent a war declaration. The Russian government had decided not to oppose a Japanese invasion as long as the Japanese army did not march farther north then the 38th parallel.

At daybreak, still unaware of the attack on Port Arthur, Rudnev received a terse but polite dispatch from Japanese Rear Admiral Uryu of the convoy flagship *Naniwa*, The note, written in English, caused Rudnev to flush with anger. He handed the note to his executive officer, and turned to Alesandrov who had transferred aboard the previous evening.

"It is bad news," he told Alesandrov. "The Japanese want to fight. We must be at war!"

The executive officer passed the note to Alesandrov. It read:

> *Sir: As hostilities exist between the Government of Japan and the Government of Russia at present, I respectfully demand you to leave the port of Chemulpo with the force under your command before the noon (today) of the ninth of February 1904. Otherwise, I should be obliged to fight against you in the port. I have the honor to be Sir, you most obedient servant.*
>
> *S. Uryu, Rear Admiral.*

Rudnev resigned himself to the inevitable. He assembled his officers and told them, "We are outnumbered and outgunned. This ship can only operate at half speed because of the condition of the boilers. We don't have much chance against such a large enemy force. **But we will not surrender our ships.**"

He responded to Alesandrov's protest of Japan's blatant violation of Korean neutrality, "We cannot remain in the harbor and endanger the foreign ships. They will have received a similar note from Admiral Uryu, probably advising them also to leave the harbor. The cruiser *Chiyoda* came in this morning, no doubt to deliver this warning."

He ordered his aide, "Sound the general assembly."

To those officers and men who could hear him, Rudnev announced, "Let us put our trust in God and go bravely into battle for the Czar and for the Motherland—hurrah!" The loud responsive cheers of his crew caused tears to well up in his eyes.

Flag signals sent to the *Koreets* informed its crew of the decision to go down fighting. The cooks hurried to prepare a large meal. The officers and crew donned their best uniforms and manned their battle stations. The ship's band played the national anthem "God Save the Czar" as both Russian vessels steamed slowly past the foreign warships in the harbor, whose decks were lined with cheering sailors applauding the bravery of those on their way to meet their destiny outside the harbor.

With the *Koreets* in its wake, the *Variag* passed into the open sea to face the blocking Japanese flotilla. Under a sullen sky pressing against the leaden sea, Alesandrov watched the line of enemy warships slowly steaming ahead. Too bad we did not engage their transports yesterday, he thought. We could have taken a lot of them with us.

Rudnev, busy with the same thought, knew that the *Variag's* twelve six-inch guns were no match for the thirty-six possessed by the Japanese fleet, and certainly the enemy's four larger eight-inch guns could easily out-range him. The guns on the old *Koreets* were too obsolete to be effective. "We'll do what damage we can," he said to no one in particular.

The Japanese commenced firing at once. Before it could close the range, the *Variag* was hit. The first enemy eight-inch shell struck the upper deck, blowing to pieces the range finder and the mishipman who manned it.

Rudnev was never able thereafter to find the effective range. The unequal battle continued for one and one-half hours, leaving the forward decks a fiery shambles, and the steering gear smashed. Rudnev lay wounded on the bloody deck. Alesandrov suffered two broken ribs when an explosion had hurled him against a stanchion. His damaged rib cage hampered his efforts to aid Rudnev, but he was able finally to drag himself to Rudnev's side and pull him to safety. Each movement caused excrutiating pain, and each breath he took almost doubled him over in agony.

The executive officer got the *Variag* turned around to return to the harbor in spite of a gaping hole at the waterline that made the ship list on the port side. Miraculously, the gunboat *Koreets* had suffered no hits. Two hours after leaving Chemulpo, the two Russian warships limped back into the harbor. Thirty-one of the *Variag*'s crew were dead and ninety-one seriously wounded on its blood splattered decks. A distress flag went up as the anchors dropped.

"Stay with me until we get the casualties transferred," Rudnev asked Alesandrov.

At once the British, French, and Italian warships sent their doctors to assist the casualties. The bandaged wounded were hoisted by slings to the sampans below and transported to the foreign ships's sick bays. Only the captain of the warship U.S.S. *Vicksburg* refused assistance.

In spite of the pain of his injury, Alesandrov remained behind to assist in the scuttling of the *Variag*. Moving slowly to avoid the crippling pain that knifed into his lungs with every breath, Alesandrov helped two able bodied seamen open the Kingston valves of the damaged cruiser.

Abandoning the *Variag* and moving on to the gunboat Koreets, they joined the captain, whose crewmen had planted dynamite charges in the engine room. Finally, the Russian lifeboat moved away as Alesandrov and the others watched the destroyer *Variag* slowly vanish into the depths of the harbor, carrying its cargo of shattered dead. Moments later, from a safe distance, the dynamite party exploded the charges on the *Koreets*, sending it to also to a watery grave.

Doctors aboard the French warship *Pascal* bound Alesandrov's broken ribs. The bandages held the bones in place, but did little to ease the throbbing pain. A pretty French volunteer nurse assisted the doctors. She was on board as a passenger, having been brought aboard earlier from the French mission in Chemulpo, out of concern for her safety.

Claudette Chevier had served in a French hospital in Shanghai for one year. Departing aboard a Japanese passenger steamer from that city's port, she was on her way to Tokyo when the ship's British captain was directed by wireless to go at once to Korea. The diverted passengers had to disembark in Chemulpo to await a French ship outbound for Marseilles. The Japanese passenger ship had then steamed on to Korea's east coast to serve as a troop transport.

Unluckily, Miss Chevier happened to be in Seoul on a shopping spree when the French steamer had arrived in Chemulpo to take on the waiting passengers. Having missed her ship, the nurse came back from Seoul to Chemulpo to seek another passage home. French marines had brought her to the warship *Pascal* after the arrival of Captain Uryu's warning note.

The day after her invaluable assistance with the Russian wounded, Claudette Chevier had returned to visit Alesandrov in the sick ward. His actions, while being bandaged, had been so flirtatious that she felt compelled to explore why she found his manner so exciting. When she had bound the bandage around his bare, muscular torso, he had grasped her hand, pressed it against his belly, stared into her eyes, and murmured in perfect Parisian French that only she could assuage his torment. She had not experienced such a groin teasing sensation since leaving Marseilles.

For the next two days she continued to give him special attention; each time her heart had fluttered wildly as the words he whispered in her ear bedeviled her composure. She found excuses to spend more time at his bedside. On the fourth day he proposed a plan. She said no at first, then soon began to soften under his spell and by nightfall had agreed. The plan was for them to escape to Seoul and gradually make their way north to Russian-held territory across the Yalu river. He would pose as a French doctor recovering from a robbery and attack by Korean bandits, which would explain his loss of identifying French documents.

Under the pretext of returning to Seoul to retrieve valuable misplaced possessions, Claudette persuaded a gullible young French ensign, standing watch, to send her ashore on the warship's steam cutter. Alesandrov, she said, would act as her escort. The Russian left a sealed note to be opened and read later by the ship's captain. In the note, the pair thanked the captain for his care and generosity and promised to return the favor someday. Alesandrov wrote that he and Claudette would not return and he hoped the captain would understand with true gallic spirit that theirs was an affair of the heart.

Once ashore, they were able to hire a conveyance for the journey into Seoul. The rough ride, however, had belatedly convinced Alesandrov that his injury would not easily tolerate the journey northward, and that the harsh winter passage across the mountains might endanger the French woman's life. He convinced himself that he could survive the pain and hardship better on his own. It would be too much of a mad adventure for her.

"I want you to return to Chemulpo, Claudette. I was foolish to put your life in peril. Arrange passage on the first steamer returning the Russian sailors to Europe. I have learned that the Japanese government has consented to parole the wounded men on their word that they would no longer participate in the war. Those who refuse will be incarcerated in a prisoner of war camp in Japan. Neither option is agreeable to me." He knew that the lazy Yatskoff would accept.

Claudette had vehemently objected to his change of plan, insisting that she intended to remain with him, no matter the cost. He said no, believing that he could trade on the Korean dislike of the Japanese to aid his escape, but only if he traveled alone. She fell silent, sure that she could change his mind by morning. Their night together was a wonderful experience for her. At the inn in Seoul, she lived a night of unforgettable rapture in his arms. Overcoming his pain and sub-standard posture, and with his patient guidance, she pleasured him in a variety of ways. She was more determined than ever not to let him leave her.

Her world crashed the following morning. As they breakfasted in the inn, a squad of Japanese soldiers entered the dining room and arrested Alesandrov. Before they led him away from the table, he succeeded in pressing into her lap the pouch containing his valuables and money. The squad led him outside to the officer in charge. His heart sank at the sight of the master spy, Major Jiro Ariko.

Claudette tried in vain to find him, inquiring at all Japanese army and police posts. Her search the following day was no more successful. On the third day the Japanese informed her that Alesandrov had "disappeared." His location and fate were unknown. They ordered her to return to Chemulpo on February fifteen. She vowed to continue her search, but a week later, discouraged, although refusing to give up hope, she sailed to Dalny to offer her services to the Russian army.

Lydia Fairborne had been restless ever since her husband, Commander Nigel Fairborne, had sailed from Sasebo, Japan with Admiral Togo's fleet. Bored with her existence in Sasebo, she had gone to Korea, hoping to be closer to the social adventures that were sure to come in a neutral country that was the focal point of military intrigue. The outbreak of hostilities had curtailed her movements, but had also alerted her to the arrest of her friend and past amour, Alesandrov, knowledge which she had gained through her contacts with the Japanese bureaucracy. Because of her husband's service as an advisor aboard Admiral Togo's flagship, Mrs. Fairborne enjoyed privileged access to certain Japanese naval officers, men who lusted to sleep with caucasian women who were rumored to have different anatomically positioned genitalia, a myth that always caused much mirth when Japanese men exchanged bawdy jokes.

When Mrs. Fairborne heard mention of the captured Russian officer, she immediately concocted a plan for his release—or escape. Of all the men whom the lusty Lydia Fairborne had favored during her husband's long absences at sea, one man stood out among the rest. She could never forget Alesandrov. She had first flirted with him at a diplomatic ball in Tokyo. As usual, her husband had seemed indifferent; he and Lydia having agreed long before that their marriage could be an open arrangement. Even later, when a fellow officer had hinted to Nigel Fairborne that his wife was too often in the company of Alesandrov, Nigel had chosen to ignore the affair. Lydia happily immersed herself in erotic gratification with the Russian.

Commander Fairborne preferred the company of men, showing haughty indifference to women at social events. Lydia had always disliked the way he chose to make love to her, opting for a choice of orifices and positioning that she found degrading. Rather than endanger his career by their estrangement, they had agreed to their unique arrangement. In time, Mrs.

Fairborne's sexual freedom had given her enough experience to recognize those partners who excelled in performance. Becoming bolder, even aggressive, in choosing a partner, she had become a borderline nymphomaniac. Alesandrov was a boon to her restless sexuality.

Both the Fairbornes enjoyed the public baths in Japan. There were some Japanese men among the families at the baths, however, whom Lydia disliked. She told her husband that he was too carelessly friendly with these men, who seemed to share her husband's preferences.

"But they are the elite," he had protested. "They are some of the Fleet's finest officers."

"I know what they are," she had sneered. "They are afraid of women, unable to satisfy them, and perverse in strange ways. Why would you keep company with them?"

She warned, "Don't be so obvious. When you are here with your wife, at least keep up appearances. Act the part of a dutiful husband. Keep your assignations more discrete. You must not jeopardize your career."

She loved Nigel in spite of his sexual orientation, and she knew how much his career meant to him. She had tried to keep her own lovers out of sight when he was home on leave, which was increasingly infrequent. She did not want him to become the butt of cruel jokes and gossip.

Most Japanese men at the public baths were always dutifully polite and professed disinterest in her body, but she knew that their eyes drank in every detail of her nakedness. Japanese women envied her large breasts and long, unbowed legs, and wanted to look into her gray-green eyes and touch her blonde hair. She in turn secretly envied their thick forest of jet-black pubic hair and thought her own thin blonde delta did not provide an adequate screen. Otherwise, she enjoyed the beauty of her body, often admiring it in her full-length mirror. She wished that Nigel would lust for her as other men did, but she realized that he would never change. Boyhood habits that he had adopted at Eton were too deeply engrained.

As soon as Lydia Fairborne had learned where Viktor Alesandrov was incarcerated, she had hurried to the shabby building that served as a jail. The jail commander admitted to her brusquely that the Russian officer was in the building, but still under interrogation and could not be seen. She demanded, pleaded, and cajoled to little avail. Lieutenant Bungaku Nozoe was adamant in his refusal.

"He is a spy," he said. "My orders are to deny him contact with anyone. He is under sentence of execution. We have put him in Cell Four." Lydia did not know that "four" in Japanese sounded like the word for death.

Lydia returned in the afternoon with a request from the British authorities that she be allowed to see a member of the Russian royal family for humanitarian reasons. Nozoe sneered at the note, but reluctantly bowed to international pressure and consented to let her see the prisoner for ten minutes only.

He escorted her to the cold, cramped cell. Alesandrov lay on the dirty floor, bleeding and half-conscious with swollen lips, blackened and puffed eyes, and a trickle of blood seeping from a smashed nose. His shirt was off, showing the rib cage to be no longer bandaged and the flesh a blue-purple mass. Her heart skipped a beat when he seemed not to be breathing.

Nozoe growled an order. One of the two Korean guards lifted a bucket of water from the corridor floor, entered the cell, and threw part of the contents onto Alesandrov's face. The prisoner sputtered, rolling his head from side to side, emitting low groans. When the rest of the water hit his face, he shuddered, then opened his eyelids. Seeing Lydia through pain-misted eyes, he managed a weak grin.

Nozoe dismissed Lydia's protest, saying that the Russian had been injured trying to escape. It was plain to Lydia that Alesandrov had been brutally tortured. She was furious. Within an hour she appeared at the headquarters of Colonel Shigeru Owada. Identifying herself, she insisted that Alesandrov be moved to a hospital for better care.

Colonel Owada pondered her request and finally decided that the angry woman knew too many government bureaucrats. The best course in his judgment would be to acquiesce, get the Russian treated, then returned to his cell and readied for transfer to Japan where he could be kept safely out of sight. And "accidentally" die in captivity.

Lydia hired a wagon and driver. She had the driver take her to the red light district. Through a scar-faced pimp, she hired two young and strong ex-farm girls who had been forced by impoverished parents to go to the city to earn money as prostitutes. Once alone with the two girls, Lydia explained her plan to Kim Ok-hum and Ri Man-chol and promised to pay well. Having gained their confidence, she arranged to meet them at the dilapidated Korean hospital that same afternoon. Then she visited a chemist.

At the jail she presented her hospital pass to the angry jail commander. He ordered the two Korean guards to help carry Alesandrov to the horse-drawn wagon outside. They thrust him roughly onto the wooden bed of the wagon, squatting beside him, and motioning Lydia to sit beside the driver. Before obeying, Lydia covered Alesandrov with his torn, dirty white uniform blouse and a blanket she had brought.

The wagon halted at the rear of the hospital, a single story ramshackle building that was more of a clinic. The guards half carried, half supported Alesandrov and took him to an empty rear room. Lydia pressed money into the driver's hand and ordered him to wait for her return.

"Help me and there will be more money," she said.

She searched for a doctor at the front of the hospital, while secretly signalling to the two waiting Korean prostitutes. While the doctor attended to Alesandrov, she took the two girls to an empty room across the hall from where Alesandrov lay, and quickly outlined her plan, telling them to entertain the guards while she stood watch in the hall.

"Keep them busy while I take the Russian outside." She showed them the bottle in her bag and explained that it was a drug she would use on the guards while they were distracted. Showing them how the drug worked, she told them, "Start undressing. I will talk to the doctor and tell him we are not to be disturbed in this room until he is through with my friend."

The three waited patiently while the doctor tended to Alesandrov. When she heard the doctor protesting loudly in the hall, she left the room and was immediately accosted by Lieutenant Nozoe who had suddenly appeared on the scene and was now jabbing his finger into the doctor's chest and telling him the Russian was not to be registered as a patient and that he, Nozoe, was in charge.

"Why are you here?" she demanded. "Don't you trust your guards?"

"I don't trust you," he snarled, pushing her aside and crossing the hall. "Who is in this room with you?"

He threw open the door, then turned to leer at Lydia. "These are street women. Why did you bring them here? Are they for you or the Russian?"

Lydia stood her ground. "They are my paid helpers, regardless of their profession."

He did not believe her. He looked at Ri who had already removed her upper garment. "I can use your helpers. Go to the doctor and your lover. My guards will stay with you. Go."

He closed the door behind her, pulled his pistol from its holster, and shouted for Ri and Kim to remove all their clothing. With her ear pressed to the door, Lydia could hear him berating the frightened women. When the prostitutes were naked, Nozoe unbuttoned his trousers, threatened them with his pistol, and demanded they both kneel before him. The Japanese officer reveled in his power. Already his mind had leaped ahead to the English woman. When he was through with the whores, he would manage to dispose of the doctor and the Russian, and have his soldiers stand guard while he had his way with the demanding English bitch. There were so many ways he could concoct the story of her fate.

Lydia removed the bottle and a thick cloth from her handbag. She cracked open the door and peeked inside. Nozoe stood with his back half turned to the door, his naked buttocks thrusting forward as he rocked back on his heels. His eyes were closed and the pistol hung loosely in his hand. Lydia poured half the contents of the bottle onto the cloth and slid silently into the room. Signalling to Kim and Ri, she held up one forefinger for a moment, then, with compressed lips, punched one fist against the palm of her other hand. NOW!

Ri immediately bit down hard with all the force her jaws could muster. Kim slammed her hand against Nozoe's groin as Lydia knocked the pistol from his paralyzed hand. Kim added to his agony by grasping his scrotum and twisting fiercely. With his mouth hanging slack and unable to speak, Nozoe dropped to his knees, holding his bleeding member with both hands, gulping air frantically to catch his breath. Lydia pushed behind him and pressed the saturated cloth against his face. His struggles grew feebler, then ceased and he fell backward unconscious. Lydia looked down at his contorted face, then for good measure kicked her foot into his groin. His face began to turn blue.

The three women tied him with the cord Lydia had taken from her handbag. Satisfied that he was securely bound and asleep, Lydia crossed the hall to Alesandrov's room. Ri and Kim waited outside with Lydia's cloth and bottle. The odor of the ether mingled with the antiseptic smell of the corridor. Brushing past the startled guards and ignoring their insolent stares, Lydia rushed to Alesandrov's side.

"Are you all right? Can you stand now?" she asked.

Alesandrov raised his head and nodded. He motioned with his eyes to the two rifles the guards had stacked against the wall. She leaned forward to kiss him, pressing his hand to her bodice so he could feel the hidden weapon. She saw the recognition in his eyes, then moved behind him and ordered the guards to help him to his feet.

The two guards looked at each other and laughed derisively. Lydia called out for Ri and Kim to come into the room to help with Alesandrov. The distraction gave her time to bring forth the pistol. She trained the weapon on the two surprised guards and repeated her order. At first dizzy and unsteady, Alesandrov accepted their reluctant aid. Lydia stood off to one side with the pointed pistol. In a moment, Alesandrov's head cleared. Suddenly, he lifted his hands from their shoulders, stepped back, and raising his hands, brought their heads together with a loud, sickening crack. Both guards crumpled to their knees, momentarily stunned. Alesandrov reached for the pistol, stepped behind the men and dealt each a hard blow to the head, just behind the ear.

Ri and Kim held the cloth to the faces of both men while Lydia tied them with more cord from her bag. She took off their belts and yanked their trousers down to their ankles.

Both of the strong girls supported Alesandrov. The four made their way to the rear entrance. Lydia flashed her pass at the bewildered entrance attendant. She ordered her driver to proceed to a safe house she had previously rented on the northern outskirts of Seoul.

For three days she stayed with Alesandrov, nursing him with the help of Ri and Kim. When he had gained enough strength to travel, she paid the girls to take him in the wagon to Panmunjon and hide him until he was able to leave for the Russian border. She knew she dared not stay away from her hotel any longer. Before returning to the center of Seoul, she promised to visit Alesandrov in Panmunjon as soon as she could get away.

Lydia never came to Panmunjon. She found her husband waiting for her in an agitated state of mind. He had arrived the day before. "Where have you been?" he asked. "The police were here at the hotel, asking for you."

Major Ariko had ordered the Korean jailors be shot. His superiors had countermanded the order because the men had readily confessed and had revealed Nozoe's carelessness. Ariko now knew of Lydia's involvement, but realized he could not touch her. He was furious. He had tried to lodge a protest at the British Consulate, only to be run off by British marines. Offers of bribes had failed. *Damn the British!*

Ariko had cornered the Korean pimp who had provided Lydia with the two prostitutes. The man did not know the names of the girls or the location of their villages. He only knew them by presumably assumed names of Ri and Kim. Like Lydia Fairborne, they had disappeared with the Russian. Meanwhile, Ariko had another troubling problem.

At First Army headquarters in Seoul, General Rikyu Horikoshi fought to control his composure. His temper had reached the boiling point. He clenched his jaw and continued to drumbeat his fingers on the surface of his desk.

Major Jiro Ariko stood before the general's desk, shifting from one foot to the other. Nervous and uncomfortable, he dreaded what was coming from the Chief of Intelligence for the Imperial First Army. He feared it had something to do with the false information that the hostess at the Golden Pavilion tavern in Shanghai had retrieved from the pocket of the drunken Russian officer, information about the positions of the Russian battleships at Port Arthur, the lack of submarine nets, the unreadiness of the Russian crews, and the presence of enemy warships at Dalny, most of which had turned out to be fatally misleading intelligence.

Ariko was certain he would still be in Port Arthur were it not for the American who had recognized him on the morning train at the Dalny station. *Curse the luck.* He vowed to kill both the American and the bar hostess at the Golden Pavilion. What was her name, Tea Flower?

Meanwhile, he had to find and deal with the British woman, Lydia Fairborne. To hell with the role of her husband. Another naval bastard. Regardless of her British citizenship, he swore he would track her down to the end of the earth. No damn woman could ever dare to rob him of a prisoner as valuable as the Russian Alesandrov. The woman had cursed him with bad luck. What was it with these contemptible females? The thought of members of what he considered to be such a subservient sex caused him to flush with anger.

The sound of General Horikolshi's voice quickly snapped him back to reality.

Through tightened lips, the general hissed, "Major Ariko, I have received a directive from Admiral Togo. He is exceedingly unhappy about information his intelligence officers received from you. Admiral Togo informed our headquarters that because of your faulty report, he was unable to punish effectively the Russians at Port Arthur." The general paused to control his wrath. "The admiral demands that you have no further contact with Naval Intelligence."

Horikoshi sat silently for a moment as if carefully choosing his words. Ignoring the valuable but often erratic intelligence received previously from Ariko, and mindful of his personal dislike of the man, Horikoshi, with flushed face, continued.

"From now on, Major, you will work only on behalf of the Japanese army. Do I make myself clear?" He slammed his fist on the desk top and exploded, "You fuck up once more, Ariko, and I'll have your head. Now get back to Manchuria. Dismissed."

CHAPTER FIVE

In the morning, Rogers noticed that Yin-lin stayed out of sight. He was unaware of her hurt at his rejection, and her shame that Marina had found the incident of the night so humorous. Neither he nor Marina mentioned Yin-lin, but twice he caught Marina studying him with more than casual interest. His host seemed warmer and more relaxed.

Marina was delighted that his weariness had passed. At the morning meal, she proposed that they tour the harbor together—after she had brought him to General Stoessel's headquarters.

When both were ready, and the sun was high in the sky with its rays spreading downward onto the bare brown mountainside of Golden Hill, Marina ordered the one-horse carriage prepared. In the cold morning air, she offered Rogers a pair of Viktor's mittens and covered their legs with a warm lap robe. Her driver guided the carriage down the slope toward the naval base. The carriage detoured to stop in front of an impressive Chinese establishment, a large two-story brick godown crowded with tradesmen clamoring for supplies, all eager to hoard for the future. The godown or warehouse carried everything imaginable, from food to hardware.

"This is my office," Marina explained. "I have business to conduct with some of my retailers this morning. My driver will take you to army headquarters. When you are finished reporting to General Stoessel, come back here for me. Then we can go to the shipyard." She excused herself and vanished into the interior of the building.

Along the route to the administration building, the carriage passed several work crews laboring to recover bodies from some smashed houses. Not since the siege at Tientsin had Rogers seen such destruction that the

121

large guns of Togo's battleships had caused. One of the large naval shells had exploded into the house of the local jeweler, a Jewish family named Berman. The bodies of the three members of the family and their Chinese amah were unrecognizable heaps of bloody flesh. Farther on, a crowd of sailors had gathered near a Russian hall, converted from an old Chinese theater. The building was reserved for social events for local officials. A tea house attached to the side of the hall served Russian vodka instead of the vile Chinese vodka.

In the general's office anteroom, Rogers thought back to his earlier encounters with Stoessel three and one-half years earlier. He wondered if General Anatole Mikhailovitch Stoessel would remember him and the friction of those days. Some of those incidents had not been happy. Stoessel was cooperative only when it suited Russian interests. The man's monumental ego and reluctance to cooperate with the allies of the international army marching toward Peking at that time had made Rogers' duties considerably more difficult than necessary. Thank goodness for his aide, An-an, and her Russian language and liaison skills, and also Alesandrov's cooperation! Stoessel had never acknowledged Rogers' credit for diverting the Russian vanguard into Peking via the Tartar Wall's sewer gate, a tactic that had saved a great many Russian lives.

Rogers looked up to see a pretty Chinese girl leave Stoessel's office and walk hurriedly down the hall. The sentry at Stoessel's office door did not change expression while intently watching the young girl walk past Rogers.

Rogers wondered why the girl, dressed as a domestic, was at headquarters. Remembering Viktor's remarks about a servant girl he had procured for the general, Rogers reasoned that might explain her presence in the general's office. The girl did not look happy.

He waited patiently for the better part of an hour. Finally, a Russian sub lieutenant emerged with Rogers' papers. Speaking in halting English, interspersed with French, the young officer apologized, "I am very sorry. The general is too busy to see you now..." The officer paused, embarassed. "Perhaps another..."

"I understand," Rogers interrupted, attempting to smooth the awkwardness. "Of course, with the emergency at the naval base, and all...I only wanted to make my presence in Port Arthur known. By the way, any word from Captain Alesandrov?"

The Russian lieutenant shook his head negatively and retreated into Stoessel's office.

"How was your reception?" Marina asked.

"The general was too busy. I did not see him, but at least he knows I am on base."

She gave him a tight little smile. "You do not like General Stoessel?" She raised her hand to halt his protest. "Viktor talked to me about the past. He is hardly Viktor's favorite either."

Rogers was impressed by her perception, yet curious and guarded when she said, "Please let us be open with each other—as few secrets as possible." He nodded, intending to pursue that. Wasn't that part of his job?

Marina was soon ready and they left for the navy yard.

On the street fronting the shipyard, the provost marshal and his four guards flagged Marina's carriage to halt. The provost, Colonel Petrusha, demanded to see Rogers' papers and raised his hand to cut off Marina's protests. He ignored her explanation that Rogers was a house guest and was awaiting the return of his friend, Captain Alesandrov.

Speaking to Rogers in French, the provost demanded, "What is the purpose of your visit?"

He glared at Marina who again had started to speak. "Mademoiselle will please remain silent while I question this man."

Rogers bristled at the provost's rudeness. At that moment, another carriage drew abreast. An elderly lady in the carriage leaned out to hail Marina. "Good morning, my dear. I am so happy to see you are safe after that awful attack yesterday."

"Hello, and my best wishes to you and the family, Madame Starck. May I introduce you to Viktor's friend, American Lieutenant Ellis Rogers."

Rogers doffed his hat in salute.

"Will you be staying long, Lieutenant?"

"I am uncertain, now," he replied. "I hope I can be of some assistance and not be in the way. Events have taken a terrible turn."

"Please enjoy your stay." The admiral's wife was in a hurry, waved goodbye, and prompted her driver to go off to the admiral's office. Very cheerful lady, considering the crisis here, Rogers thought. Her husband's career is in jeopardy. He will be blamed for Russia's losses.

Colonel Petrusha reluctantly returned Rogers' papers, saluted and stepped back. Before the carriage could proceed, he reminded Marina, "You must obey the martial law, Mdme Berezovsky."

"I am not the enemy," she flared. "Do I or my friend look Japanese?" She urged her driver to go on.

"Perhaps I should not have displayed anger; I suppose Colonel Petrusha is just doing his duty," Marina said. "But he distrusts everyone, especially all foreigners, particularly the British and Germans. He's not even nice to the French who are supposed to be our friends. I just don't like his attitude toward women."

Rogers had met men like Petrusha before. Ramrod stiff, truculent and unbending, taking their job too seriously; such men saw no shades of gray, only black and white.

"He does not like anyone who is not military. He has never had a friendly word for me or any woman. He'll do his job, but he promises to be an unpleasant martinet," Marina warned.

The gate of the naval yard was closed and heavily guarded. They sat in the carriage watching the scene as a noisy crowd of relatives and friends milled about seeking news of casualties.

Rogers wondered how his countrymen would react if American soil was hit by a surprise naval assault, and an American city bombed. Would there be as much panic and turmoil? He remembered the fear of American coastal cities six years ago when the missing Spanish fleet was rumored to be headed for New York rather than Cuba. Fear can bring an ugly scene.

Questioning some of the workers entering and leaving the entrance to the shipyard, Marina learned of Russian progress and relayed the developments to Rogers.

Steam cutters began to arrive at the pier to discharge cargoes of broken bodies, mostly engine room personnel from the torpedoed battleships. There was no effort to cover the dead. The wounded were taken into the pier warehouse for more attention, then transported to an already crowded hospital.

"They are bringing in the last of the bodies," Marina informed Rogers. "And they have towed in one of the damaged battleships from the outer harbor. I understand it is the *Tsesarevich.* We don't have a drydock for battleships, only for cruisers or smaller vessels.

"What about the dead?" he asked. "Will there be a formal ceremony? Or will there be time with the Japanese fleet standing offshore?"

"No ceremony. We can't; the ground is too frozen. Burial will have to wait until the thaw in spring." Both could both see the burned and mangled bodies being lifted from the stretchers and laid out in a long row on the pier Marina said that the bodies would be moved as soon as relatives at the gate could enter to identify the remains. "The dead will be marked and taken to one of our government ice houses and kept there until spring." He knew that meant that the dead would lay preserved on blocks of ice under a thick layer of sawdust. Large square blocks of ice were usually cut from the frozen river every week and covered in sawdust-filled icehouses until needed for use in warm summer weather.

Rogers had seen many such scenes before. Not so for Marina. The presence of weeping relatives touched her deeply, and the sight of the torn bodies had almost unnerved her.

"We are not needed here," Rogers told her. "We should leave."

Marina agreed. "They will bring in the cruiser *Pallada* this afternoon. I don't want to see any more bodies." She looked up at the sky. "The weather is bad. Let us go to my factory. I need to issue some more orders, then we can go home." She placed her hand on his arm, a gesture that caused his heart to race. "I need your advice. This war is new to me and I need to make plans for the next few months."

He nodded in agreement and thought to himself, you should plan for the next few years. Wars have such a nasty way of perpetuating themselves. All the while he wondered where Marina had gained so much of her information.

Marina's carriage pushed through the crowd with difficulty. While passing through a section of Old Town, Marina pointed to a narrow, seemingly deserted alley and warned him to beware of the place. "Soldiers and sailors come here to drink and be entertained." she said. "The authorities think the Japanese have planted spies there to learn secrets from the men."

Rogers said he did not quite understand. Marina looked at him quizzically. "It is the street of brothels. It looks quiet now, but will come alive after dark. The provost would like to shut the place down, but is afraid the garrison men will riot if denied access. The place acts like a safety valve for lonely men who can turn violent if their urges are repressed."

Rogers was aware that his cheeks burned. "Don't worry, I don't go to such places." He glanced at Marina and thought she had an amused and unbelieving little smile. Then in a moment she sighed and visibly brightened and looked relieved. They rode on in silence.

At Marina's godown, Rogers was startled to encounter the same young and pretty maid whom he had seen at General Stoessel's headquarters. There was no recognition on her face as she passed him. He had told Marina that he would look around the warehouse while waiting for her to negotiate with some customers. He had rounded a corner to see the girl walking toward him. She had hurriedly brushed past and turned to enter a door behind the order counter.

When Marina joined him several minutes later, he mentioned that he had recognized a servant girl whom he had seen earlier at the general's office. "There must be a mistake," Marina declared, avoiding eye contact, "None of my people would be there."

She led him to a small tastefully decorated office room behind the counter where she motioned to a comfortable chair and ordered a pot of hot tea. "We can talk here undisturbed," she told him. "I want to ask you some questions." She studied him briefly before continuing.

"As Viktor's friend and guest, I wish to confide in you. I am sure you will agree that a war declaration will inevitably follow the Japanese midnight attack and the morning barrage yesterday. There have been no official announcements yet; however, I have put out some feelers. A supply boat will be coming in tonight with a cargo from Korea, and the latest news. If the boat is delayed by the Japanese fleet, the crew will send a carrier pigeon ashore with a message—an arrangement I made earlier. The bird is from my pigeon loft."

"Is the cargo also yours?"

She nodded affirmatively. "You have had lots of experience in war zones. Can you help me decide what I should best do in case we are blockaded? I mean, what kinds of materials should I lay in—for my factory?"

He watched her expression before answering, wondering what he might be getting himself into. He decided that she was sincere, and, because of Viktor, he should help her.

"I don't know what the garrison has stockpiled already, thus what critical shortages might arise in case of a blockade or long war," he said. "I do know that similar situations produce a shortage of fuel for one thing. I saw a mountain of coal piled near Fort Payushan, but the navy will probably need it. Cooking oil, candles, kerosene, and certainly rice may become dear. You could probably profit from a good supply of personal items such as needles and thread, shaving cream and brushes, tooth powder. and the better grades of soap. Writing materials will be needed and, certainly, wearing apparel for the civilians. I see you already have a large supply of cloth. You will see the early signs of shortages before long. If you have a good supplier, you will profit. Usually the local merchants cannot afford to store a large inventory beforehand. Try to find a way to store perishables: eggs, vegetables, bread, sugar and flour.

She jotted down notes as he spoke. "Tobacco, candy, liquor?"

"By all means," he agreed. "And playing cards. The nights will be long and lonely."

"I can recommend a good blockade runner," he volunteered. "Try Captain Chen."

"I know him well," she said. "He is very daring, but the Russians are suspicious of him."

Rogers did not pursue the matter. Something about her answer made him curious. She spoke as if she knew Chen intimately. Funny that Chen had never mentioned her. If the Russians were suspicious of Chen, would Marina be suspect also by her own people?

He changed the topic. "Tell me what happened here night before last?"

Marina described the surprise midnight attack on the base. "I had returned from the dinner reception at Madame Starck's home. I came home early because the naval officers had orders to be back on their ships by ten o'clock. At one or two minutes before the midnight hour, we were awakened by the sound of cannon from the sea. I think most of the townpeople thought it was a practice exercise. But the sound of explosions was only from seaward and not from the forts behind us. I ran to the window and looked north toward the forts. They showed no activity. There were no bugle calls or any kind of alarm. Everyone was caught by surprise. Then I saw the flashes of cannon fire out to sea, and I heard the Russian battleships firing their big guns, and then I saw a tremendous explosion from a ship that had been hit, and searchlights were lighting up the sky. I knew it had to be an attack, not a practice drill. Finally soldiers began arriving from the forts, and the shipyard became crowded and confused. The battle was very short—really over before most of us realized what had happened."

There had been an awkward moment during the conversation when she had insisted he leave the chair to sit beside her on the sofa. In positioning himself, his knee had touched hers accidentally. "Sorry," he had muttered, his cheeks burning. He wasn't sure if he was embarrassed at his clumsiness or from the thrill of touching her leg. Being so close to this beautiful woman had Rogers growing increasingly restless, and concerned about An-an.

Why hadn't she written? Each day he had hoped to hear from her. It had been so long and still no letters. If the war had not started, he would be tempted to ask Chen to sail south to Hong Kong to check on her.

Marina and Rogers talked long into the afternoon, enjoying the warm and cozy ambiance of her office. It surprised him to learn how knowledgeable she was about the international crisis, especially that in Europe. The Russians worried about the very real threat of invasion from Germany, and a Baltic Sea attack by England.

Marina talked at length about the strength of the Russian naval base, the forts on the heights above the harbor, and the supply lines into Port Arthur, both land and sea. They agreed that the railroad link from Russian strongholds in Siberia was overlong and precarious. Rogers told her that there was not a fort in existence that could not be overthrown. He also reminded her that the willingness of the Japanese to sacrifice thousands of men to win an objective was something he had seen up close. "And," he added, "both sides have to worry about the loyalty of the natives here, This is really Chinese land and the natives here have little incentive to take sides in this war."

As they prepared to leave the factory to return to her home, she warned him not to become too friendly with foreigners residing in Port Arthur, especially the English and Germans.

He inquired, "Do you think Japanese spies have been at work? Or do you suspect the British of aiding the Japanese? Or perhaps the attack was caused by a Russian error of judgment?"

Marina answered, *"Kto vinoval!* Who is to blame? Everyone will be blaming everyone else. The local Japanese were watched very closely. Someone else must have informed the Japanese government about conditions of readiness at our base. Why did Japanese warships enter Russian waters on Sunday night? How did the Japanese know the position of our battleships, and where our picket destroyers were? Why was the attack staged when the tide was out so that the battleships in the inner harbor could not leave? How did the Japanese ships know so well the route into the harbor? Someone must have informed the Japanese. Who else but the neutral British?"

Rogers shrugged. "I find it hard to believe the British would do such a thing."

"Perfidious Albion." Marina exclaimed. "Anything to stop the Russian bear."

* * * * * * * * *

Back in the first week of February, the British naval authorities at their naval station of Wei-hai-wei, usually referred to as"Way Highway," had wondered why the Russians had ignored signs of Japanese mobilization and the increased activity at Sasebo. Surely the Czar's people knew of the Japanese cancellation of army leaves and the call up of reserve units. The

Japanese had tried to keep secret the crowded troop trains converging on the port of Sasebo. But surely so much activity in Japan could not have gone unnoticed.

Rogers knew that England, as Japan's ally, because of the Anglo-Japanese Treaty of 1902, had cooperated closely with the Japanese navy. British trainers and observers rode with the Japanese fleet, while a flurry of British fleet manuevers in the North Sea kept the Russian Baltic Fleet off guard. A week before the attack on Port Arthur, Commander Nigel Fairborne had confided to his wife Lydia, in an unguarded moment, that a British merchant ship, with Japanese pilots aboard, had marked a course from the Elliot Islands to Port Arthur.

On February 3, while Rogers had been en route to Chefu to seek out Chen for a passage to Port Arthur, the Russian government had sent a telegraphic counter proposal to Tokyo in answer to Japanese demands to know the intentions of the Czar relative to Korea and Manchuria. Whether by design or by accident, the Russian note was delayed in Tokyo for four days. On February 4, an imperial conference in Tokyo had debated the possibility of war and the chances of victory for Japan. The following day, Japan broke diplomatic relations with Russia and recalled her minister from St Petersburg. Finally on February 7, the Russian peace note had arrived at the Mikado's palace, but Admiral Togo and his fleet were already passing through the night toward Port Arthur.

Rogers was not aware that two days after the Port Arthur attack, Marina had come into possession of a note given to Yin-lin by her pretty friend in Admiral Alexeiev's household. The note from the Czar had reached the viceroy/admiral, Eugene Alexeiev, one week prior to the attack. The brief message had informed Alexeiev that it was in the best interests of the Russian government that Japan start the war.

"...Let them begin hostilities. Thus the world will view Japan as the aggressor and not blame Russia."

* * * * * * * * *

During the evening meal, as he sat across the table from Marina, she had asked him, "Have you heard the news? One of our light cruisers, the *Novik,* went out to challenge the Japanese fleet. It steamed within 300 yards of their battle line and launched a torpedo, which missed. The *Novik* took a couple of shell bursts, but escaped and is now docked for repairs."

"That took a lot of courage," Rogers said, but was thinking to himself that it was too bad the entire Russian fleet did not leave anchorage and go forth to slug it out with Admiral Togo. The Russians could absorb several losses; the Japanese could not.

He told Marina, "Since the Japanese have no reserve fleet, no navy except the one that is out there, I think they would turn tail and run for Japan if too many of their capital ships were damaged. Russia still has three other fleets besides the one in Port Arthur."

"You forget that the Vladivostok Far Eastern Fleet is ice bound," said Marina. "The Black Sea Fleet cannot go through the Bosphorus into the Mediterranean because of the restrictive treaty with Turkey. That leaves the Baltic Fleet, which is needed for home defense, and, in any event, is too far from here."

"What about the coast defense guns here?"

"I am not sure about them." Marina answered. "They drove off the Japanese ships yesterday, but, I'm told, many of them were shut down in order to save money last year. The guns have to be degreased, cleaned, and test-fired. And laying mine fields off the coast is not going well."

"Why is that?"

"That is more bad news that I heard from Master Loong. There was a terrible accident yesterday. Admiral Starck sent our best mine layer, the *Yenesei*, toward Dalny to mine Talien Bay. The sea was rough and caused one of the mines to break loose and hit the *Yenesei*'s keel. The explosion killed the captain and 92 sailors."

Rogers thought he remembered hearing a large distant explosion.

Marina continued, "Admiral Starck sent some destroyers out to aid the *Yenesei*. One of our better modern cruisers, the *Boyarin* ran into one of the *Yenesei*'s mines. The chart of the minefield was lost with the *Yenesei* and now no one knows where the mines are."

"How badly hurt was the *Boyarin?*"

"Enough to cause the captain to order her abandoned. She was still afloat. He ordered her to be torpedoed by one of our destroyers so the Japanese could not capture her. The other ships's first torpedo jammed in the tube, and the second torpedo missed."

"That sounds suspicious. Maybe the other captain did not want to torpedo a cruiser that still may have looked recoverable." He wondered how Loong had gained so much censored news for his employer.

Marina thought Rogers was too skeptical. But she agreed that things weren't going well. "The *Boyarin* is still afloat. Something will have to be done about her tomorrow. I hope they can bring her into the harbor."

After the evening meal, Rogers retired early in order to start writing his report to American army intelligence in Shanghai. He made good progress and hoped the report was not too long or detailed. There was so much to relate.

A strong storm came up that evening to pelt Port Arthur with heavy rain. Rogers speculated that a storm of any magnitude would further endanger the *Boyarin.*

He paused in his writing to reflect on how much he enjoyed staying with Marina, in spite of the war and the lack of news about Viktor. He missed An-an terribly and felt a little guilty about his growing attraction for Marina. She was certainly one fine woman to look at. Her figure and graceful body movements would excite lust in any man.

He doubted he would soon finish his long report to army intelligence in Shanghai. Maybe he was dwelling too much on details. Pushing the report aside, he started a short letter to An-an. It had been weeks since he had received any news from her. When Chen slipped through the Japanese blockade, he could carry the letter and the army report to Chefu.

Loud voices downstairs disturbed his concentration. He could hear women crying. Throwing on a robe, he hurried down the stairs. Marina was in the arms of Yin-lin, sobbing distraughtly. Near the door, holding a pigeon, stood Master Loong, the old man who had met Rogers upon his arrival at the train station. Loong held out a note which was written in Chinese.

Rogers read the message:

Captain Viktor Alesandrov wounded. Recovering aboard French warship Pascal. Russian ships Variag and Koreets destroyed. Russian guard contingent at Chemulpo overcome and captured. Japanese invasion troops have landed and seized Seoul.

In the morning, while breakfasting, Marina and Rogers learned from Master Loong the news of Japan's formal declaration of war. Loong related that Admiral Starck had immediately sent *Yenesei's* sister ship, *Amur*, to continue the mine laying in Talien Bay. The stricken cruiser *Boyarin* was boarded and her valuable silver table service removed after an inspection showed the hull to be fatally damaged and the ship doomed to sink momentarily. Already a court martial had been called to try *Boyarin's* captain for abandoning his ship.

Later in the day, Loong imparted more news. The Russian government had chosen Admiral Eugene Alexeiev to stay on as viceroy. General Stoessel would continue as military commander of the port and the surrounding Kwantung Peninsula. And a General Smirnoff would come from Warsaw to assume command of the hill forts and defense works of Port Arthur.

Rogers' curiosity finally boiled over. With uncharacteristic bluntness, he asked Marina, "Where does your friend get all this information?"

Marina smiled and told him that Loong had a source employed at the port's newspaper, the *Novy Kry*, and the newspaper had a source at the admiral's headquarters. She wondered how much more she should tell Rogers. Apparently, he already suspected Stoessel's maid. "Ellis, you will learn that few secrets escape notice in this town."

Rogers spent the rest of the day trying to assure Marina that Viktor Alesandrov was on a neutral warship, safe from capture, and, undoubtedly, was mending from superficial wounds as fast as possible. His efforts to cheer her were not too successful.

Yin-lin, meanwhile, continued her flirtatioous overtures, provoking him more than once with suggestive movements of her body. He tried to ignore the way she pulled her robe tighter to accentuate her firm buttocks and moved her hand sensuously across her bosom and belly, whenever she caught his eye. He could imagine the heat of her loins and wondered if he could hold back if exposed to the sight of her nakedness, which she almost revealed by occasionally letting her robe slip open.

What a damn little tease. Someone should pound her little butt.

CHAPTER SIX

Although the week of inactivity in Panmunjon gave Alesandrov added opportunity to recover, he was increasingly bothered by his lack of exercise and amusement, and the presence of the two Korean girls. He continued to mend fast and no longer felt so weak and helpless. But he was bored by the inactivity, and it was mainly the girls who made him so restless. He found himself watching Kim and Ri with renewed interest each day, surprised at how increasingly desirable and attractive they had become. It reminded him of the old tale about the libidinous Eskimo stranded for days on an ice floe, and how much he had begun to admire the sexual allure of visiting seals.

Alesandrov watched how the girls braided their hair each morning after bathing. His inward energy reviving, he looked forward to their bathing ritual. Even with their backs turned, he could not fail to see more of their bodies than they intended to reveal.

His energy became a torment when they bathed him. Unable any longer to control his growing tumescence, he gave up trying. He noticed that the girls pretended not to notice, but twice he had heard them giggling about it in the next room.

Lydia had been gone for over a week. She had not returned as promised. In another week he believed he would be strong enough to leave Panmunjon. He had paid a messenger to carry a note to Lydia, begging for her presence and expressing his need to hold her in his arms. *When could she return? Why the delay? He did not want to leave without seeing her once again.*

The Korean girls secretly welcomed his increasing arousals, recognizing them as a sign of fast and healthy recovery. Soon he would leave them.

Both had developed a growing fondness for the Russian officer and regretted the approaching day of his departure.

Alesandrov continued to fret. *Still no word from Lydia. Wasn't she still in Seoul? Had his message to her been lost?*

On one particular day, at the end of the second week since his escape from Seoul, Alesandrov had surrendered to his physical need, abandoning all effort to curb his desire. He begged the girls for relief, finally convincing them that Lydia would not want him to suffer. Explaining his relationship with her and assuring them she would understand, perhaps even thank them for their services, Alesandrov even promised to buy each a small farm if they used their expertise to calm his nerves.

"I cannot sleep," he complained. "I am irritable and restless. I toss and turn and I have little appetite for food. Have pity. My chest will not heal if I cannot rest quietly."

Ri whispered to Kim, "Look at him. His member is so strong. I will agree to help him if you can make him comfortable."

The girls undressed as he had implored, letting him fondle their bodies and noting how the touching of their bodies made his desperate desire more acute than ever. Ri sat naked astride Alesandrov's loins, taking care not to touch or put pressure on his injured chest. She raised and lowered herself gently with slow and measured movements. He lay on his back, eyes closed, head cradled in Kim's warm lap where her robe had parted. Kim carefully massaged his neck and shoulders while watching with amusement Ri's flushed face and labored breathing, and her failing effort to appear unhurried and calm. Ri avoided Kim's eyes, wishing the girl would not watch her so closely as she struggled to control her own galloping passion. She rose and fell in her rocking motion, now concerned that she would be first to reach the high plateau of release she wanted him to experience.

Ri paused momentarily to help him control his rapid breathing. His ribs were still too tender for deep breaths. Slowly she resumed her rising and falling motions, wishing she could wipe the smirk off Kim's face, and her look of anticipation. It was no longer funny. Ri averted her eyes from Kim's eager expression of urgency and looked down at Alesandrov's closed eyes and pursed lips, and heard his low groans of pleasure. His responding upward thrusts signalled a growing approach to release. Ri moaned at her own inexorable plunge toward completion. Suddenly she lost her struggle to hold back and, with a strangled cry of passion, surrendered to a shuddering climax. She cried aloud again and again as the wave of pleasure crested and engulfed her senses. Ri half opened her eyes to see Alesandrov arching his back amid three short groans of relief. Kim cradled his head in the heat of her lap, dabbing at the beads of perspiration on his forehead. Ri withdrew and began massaging his belly to calm his paroxysms.

The three slept together that night and at dawn Kim took her turn. Although barely awake, Alesandrov was ready, and this time did not seem to be in pain from the effort.

Two days later, after a morning bath, Alesandrov persuaded them to assist so he could arise from bed and take a few steps. He gingerly leaned on the two girls with an arm around each shoulder, each hand cupping a soft breast, and took a few hesitating steps.

With rapid progress, he soon could walk unassisted. For the remainder of the week, the women shared him during the night, amazed at his stamina and the result of their therapy. They insisted on assuming the dominant position in order not to aggravate his rib cage. By the end of the week, magically recovering, he sang, he joked, and outwardly blossomed before their eyes.

On the weekend, a messenger brought a package from Lydia. It contained warm clothing for his journey: mittens, fur cap, stout boots, a rubber poncho and a long quilted Chinese overcoat. The package also included presents and money for Ri and Kim. A brief note told him that Lydia could not leave Seoul, that she and Nigel, who had returned, were too closely watched by the Japanese military police.

Lydia did not go into detail about their Seoul hospital incident, only mentioning that Japanese intelligence agents had interrogated the clinic doctor and the two Korean guards. The guards had blurted out that Lt. Nozoe had been found in a private room previously occupied by two Korean prostitutes. His trousers had been down around his knees and his bloodied private parts bore testimony to some kind of masochistic ritual.

Armed with money, clothing, weapons and a new will to survive, Alesandrov prepared to leave at the end of the month of March. Already he worried that he had lost too much valuable time. The Japanese would be moving north toward the Manchurian border. A small Japanese cavalry patrol had already recently penetrated Panmunjon, asking questions and searching houses. Subsequent patrols could begin a more thorough search.

"Go back to your families," he told Kim and Ri. "Stay with them until I have someone bring money for your land. Start looking for a farm. If the war expands, there will be a good market for your produce. And, as property owners, you will have no trouble finding good husbands."

Their farewell was tearful. Both girls promised somehow to contact Lydia in Seoul, pledging to carefully avoid Japanese army patrols and police. He left at dawn, hidden in a farmer's wagon beneath a warm robe. Kim and Ri stood in the doorway, watching the wagon fade in the distance until it disappeared over the rise of a low hill.

It was the worst of times for Alesandrov to go north through Korea. The low 200-meter high hills north of the Imjin river lay frozen and desolate under a hard crust of March ice and snow. Traveling farther north over the mountainous terrain, practically devoid of roads, was a hardship even in summer. In winter, travel promised to be a herculean effort through country infested with bandits. It was in his favor that the weather would probably delay the northward advance of the Japanese army until the spring thaw in April.

Alesandrov believed he carried sufficient gold and silver coins to buy the attention of the most avaricious Korean peasant. He counted on small gifts and trinkets in his pack to bolster his rapport with the females of peasant families. The revolver and knife that Lydia Fairborne had left with Kim and Ri were now safely in his pocket.

* * * * * * * * * *

A copy of the revealing telegram from Czar Nicholas II to Viceroy Alexeiev, slipped to Yin-lin by Alexeiev's maid, had angered Marina with the suggestion that Viktor had been sacrificed so shamelessly. *What a stupid way to begin a war. Giving the enemy such a huge advantage by purposely permitting them the first strike was insane. If Japan did not seem concerned by world opinion, why should Russia?*

Marina had seen her guest frown a couple of times as if puzzled by her activities. She resolved to be more careful. If the young American officer was suspicious, then others might also wonder, especially the provost Petrusha, who was undoubtedly on Stoessel's side. How much longer could she hide the role of both Stoessel's and Alexeiev's maids from Rogers? She must warn the viceroy's girl to be even more cautious.

In the privacy of her room, Marina wrote a short note in ink to an imaginary aunt in Russia. She wrote on paper with double-spaced lines and wide margins. Then she dipped another pen in a small bottle filled with milk and a colorless acid, and wrote in the empty spaces between the lines of ink. When finished, she held the paper up to the light. Satisfied there was no evidence of a second message, Marina placed the letter in an envelope and sealed it. The recipient would know how to heat the paper to bring forth the hidden message. She addressed the envelope to the same aunt, but had secretly placed another name under the letter's salutation. *The name was Witte.*

Rogers had been with her for one week when Marina received a message one morning from a blockade runner. The message told her that Viktor Alesandrov had disappeared from Seoul after being captured by Japanese intelligence agents in Chemulpo. It was enough to send her crying into Rogers' arms. He did his best to sooth her, promising to inquire through his army and American state department channels.

"How did you learn this?" he asked her.

"Your friend, Chen, slipped through the blockade last night. He had made a quick run to Chemulpo for a load of Korean hides. We'll all need more shoes and boots soon."

The mention of boots reminded Rogers of the foul smelling leather tannery located outside the Chinese wall beyond the old Chinese village that he had briefly visited. Large vats, filled with urine and animal feces, contained piles of Korean and Manchurian animal hides. The Russian guards used convict labor to tend the odoriferous vats that yielded surprisingly supple and smooth finished leather.

It troubled Rogers that Chen had not contacted him. But Marina, noting his frown, quickly assured him of Chen's greeting and expression of regret.

"He said to my messenger that he would return to see you in four more days. He had to leave before dawn to avoid Japanese destroyer patrols." Rogers now began to wonder about Chen's relationship with Marina. *Was he an employee or something closer?*

* * * * * * * * *

Admiral Togo's strategy changed when he realized that he could not risk damage to his battleships and cruisers from Port Arthur's shore batteries. Finding it impossible for his heavier ships to approach closer to the harbor mouth to attack the anchored Russian fleet, and aware that the Russians were in no hurry to emerge from the harbor, Togo determined to block any later attempt of the Russians to dash out for a quick escape to Vladivostok or to conduct a raid on shipping in Japanese coastal waters. Blockage of the channel became Togo's prime goal. The narrow channel was a problem for the Russian battleships, which had to steam singlely outward to reach the outer roadstead. A few well positioned sacrificial Japanese ships could block the inner channel and bottle up the Russian fleet in the inner harbor.

Admiral Togo had no difficulty choosing officers to lead the suggested blockship force. Everyone had volunteered at first. But as the date for implementing the strike approached, some volunteers began to keep a lower profile in their declining enthusiasm for what all now generally regarded as a suicide mission.

At a recent officer's gathering, Togo had hinted that he had finally selected the officer volunteers. He praised their bravery and hinted that those officers chosen might consider bringing certain enlisted men whose dash and bravery were undisputed, but whose past troublesome behavior might be an excuse for elimination. The officers missed the irony of the remark—except for Lt. Nobihuro Sato and his cousin Captain Jiro Hata. Sato wondered if he was targeted for failing to reach the rendezvous point at the designated hour after futilely pursuing that cursed black Chinese junk. And Hata, still smarting from the lack of recognition for his bravery in the attack on Russia's battleships at Port Arthur, suspected that Admiral Togo wanted to rid himself of more annoying criticism from a junior officer.

* * * * * * * * *

The harsh winter in St Petersburg exacerbated the despondency of the young female revolutionary. Confined indoors by the weather, she had ample time to recall her sad youth.

Sylvia Levinski blamed Sergei Witte for the death of her father. Years earlier, when she was a child, Witte was a railway administrator. Through his negligence, a Russian troop train had derailed and crashed into a ravine. Some of Witte's construction workers had forgotten to replace a rail that had been removed for repair. Many soldiers had died. Several innocent rail workers were subsequently executed. One was her father.

The father had dreamed as a boy of a career in the Russian army. Because he was a Jew, he had been rejected. He became a minor railway construction supervisor. Although blameless for the accident, he was nevertheless singled out for execution. Sylvia's mother, a gentile and a Polish intellectual, had thus been forced to raise Sylvia in near poverty.

Under Czar Alexander III, Witte had been sentenced to prison for the railway mishap, but soon after came to St. Petersburg to work on a new government tariff code. His expertise with numbers and his ability to undercut rivals eventually elevated him to the post of Minister of Transport.

It was this kind of inconsistency that puzzled the foreign community associated with the Czar's Court.

Witte later rose quickly to the important post of Minister of Finance and continued to wield great influence under the succeeding Czar, Nicholas II. But recently Witte had fallen out of grace with the Czar and had lost his post. Realistically, Witte still had a faithful following and it was rumored that he enjoyed close contacts with certain people in Port Arthur.

Olga Graszcynska had succeeded in enrolling her daughter Sylvia in a Moscow university, using her maiden name for Sylvia's school documents. After graduation with honors, Sylvia had returned to the name of her father and did not let her surname of Levinski hamper her activities.

An academically brilliant but quarrelsome student, she had attracted a loyal following of rebellious classmates who were drawn to the same socialist theories she espoused. She hated Russia's Romanoff rulers, blaming them equally for her father's death and for her subordinate rank in society. And she knew the history of Cossack barbarity against Jews during Russia's periodic pogroms. After leaving the university, she had organized an underground newspaper and had continued to plot against the Czarist government with her fellow dissidents.

Sylvia had read the defamatory "The Protocols of the Elders of Zion"— writings that her group recognized as anti-Jewish propaganda authored by the Czar's secret police, the Okhrana. She did not realize how rapidly the scurrilous accusations of a Jewish plot to rule the world would spread throughout Europe. The fabricated hoax would be believed and be used by the Czar to incite more bloody pogroms. Long after gullible Christians ceased persecuting Jews, Moslem clerics would continue to spread the lie.

Sylvia's rival for leadership among the dissidents had been an equally unhappy Jewish ex-student, Levi Grozsky. He had taunted her, "You are not orthodox and you are only half a Jew. All you want to do is argue. You are only half Russian and like most Polacks, you can't be trusted. You forget you are only a woman."

"Your mother was a gypsy whore," Sylvia had countered. "That is why you are so dark, even for a southern Russian." Aware that she had found a chink in his abrasive armor, Sylvia continued to spread the lie. When later she had betrayed Grozsky to the secret police, Sylvia had regained leadership among the students. With the declaration of war against Japan, Sylvia's antiwar group had increased its activities and propaganda, cranking out inflammatory leaflets that urged opposition to the unpopular war. Troops en route to Manchuria were given leaflets advising desertion.

Unknown to her group, Sylvia had been contacted by an official of the Japanese embassy in St. Petersburg before the war broke out. She had agreed to become an espionage agent for the Japanese government, relaying her information to the Japanese through a friendly source in the British consulate in Warsaw.

* * * * * * * * *

In the city of Hiroshima, Japan, Ikura Tanaka brought the sealed government envelope to her husband. Bowing to him, she held out the official envelope and stood by humbly as he read the message. A feeling of fear gripped her heart. After reading the letter, young Professor Tanaka sighed heavily, then handed the paper to his wife.

Ikura read the message. Looking up with teary eyes, she cried out, "Why? Why this just as we are starting to enjoy a good life?"

"The Emperor has called," Tanaka reminded her. "We have known that we are at war for almost one month. The call up of my reserve class was inevitable." He wanted to blame the Russians, but knew inwardly who had really started the war. He had cheered the news of the attack on Port Arthur as loudly as everyone else. Ikura re-read the message.

Captain Tomoru Tanaka,

You are commanded to appear for military duty for the duration of the war with Imperial Russia. Report at once to your regimental commander.

"How much time do we have?" Ikura asked.

"Today is Thursday, March the second. I'll have to leave no later than Saturday. Tomorrow, I must spend most of the day at the school to arrange for a substitute and prepare the necessary papers." He realized guiltily that he should have anticipated that necessity sooner.

Ikura bowed her head and shuffled off to pack his clothes. She pressed his uniform, shined his boots, and even polished his sword and brass. She laid out his toothbrush and shaving kit. When finished, Ikura retired to a corner and wept silently, wondering how she would provide for herself and their three-year old daughter, Yukio.

Bravely striving to control her emotions, Ikura prepared one of Tomoru's favorite dishes as a farewell gift: Japanese noodles cooked the way he liked them—chilled. She used the sashimuzsu method, adding a cup of water each time the pot's contents boiled. The nutty-flavored buckwheat soba pasta cooked slower and thoroughly. She rinsed the soba afterwards in cold water and chilled it further with chips of ice. The family ate slowly, sharing their sorrow in silence.

Professor Tanaka had dreaded the call to arms for the class of '96. He did not want to leave his family just as he and Ikura were beginning to save money to enjoy the comfortable life that his new professorship promised to provide.

Four years earlier, during the Boxer Rebellion in China, a younger Lieutenant Tanaka had welcomed the comraderie of military life and the adventures of the China campaign. Today was different. He had a family that was precious to him. And a return to the scenes of horror that he had seen in war-torn China held little attraction.

He had argued with some of his colleagues at the college. "It is always this way in every country," Tanaka had complained. "The drums beat, the flags wave, and the women cheer their sons and husbands marching bravely off to war. It is a grand parade that never ends in anything but misery and death."

His shocked colleagues had argued that he was defeatist and unpatriotic.

"I have witnessed war," Tanaka had protested. "I know what it is to come home to console the widows and orphans. No one wins in a war."

"But we must stop the Russians. Soon they will claim all of Manchuria. And we must seize Korea before they do."

"And be forced to give it up as we had to do with Port Arthur in 1895?" Tanaka questioned.

"Well, we destroyed the Chinese navy in one day. Even if taking Port Arthur cost a lot of lives, we captured it quickly. We'll take it again, and this time we will keep it and not let the Europeans tell us we have to give it up. We'll take the whole of Manchuria and keep it too," they argued. "We will seize their Manchurian railway, their mines, their timber reserves."

Tanaka did not share the feeling of others that the war would be easy or short, and that even if there were setbacks, Japan would still gain some territory in a peace settlement. Defeat was not likely, his friends stressed.

The government had always preached that Japan had never lost a war, and the gods would continue to favor the nation of the rising sun.

The young history professor was not so sure. He had served alongside Russian regiments in China and had seen firsthand the dedication of the Russian soldiers and their ability to endure severe hardships. It was true that like his colleagues he had resented Russia's steady encroachment into Manchuria and her obvious designs on Korea. Russia had not kept her promise to leave Manchuria and was stalling, not only about Manchuria, but about responding to Japanese peace proposals. Still, Tanaka's historical studies had convinced him that Japan's treasury and stockpile of food could not sustain a protracted conflict. War would be a gamble at best.

The professor's love for Ikura and little Yukio offset any residual desire for glory on the battlefield. He now lived in peaceful harmony with his family. Life was good, and his young, growing career held much promise for the future. What if he returned crippled or even blinded? What would his family do if he did not survive the war?

Tanaka's studies had given him a broader vision than that embraced by the Japanese military and their narrow emphasis on the chivalric code of the samurai, a code that stressed loyalty, courage, and honor. He knew that several of the older senior officers of the army, as samurai, had once worn padded armor and carried axes and spears. Had they really adjusted to a code of civilized behavior?

Tanaka recognized the admiration of western nations for Japan's fast entry into the industrial arena of the nineteenth century. The emperor's advisors had counseled, "If you can't compete with the enemy, emulate him." So in the 1870's Japan had embarked on a mad race to catch up with the western world. With a Prussian-trained army and an English-trained navy, Japan was now ready to seek her own overseas empire. Tanaka worried that Japan's friends might begin to resent her global ambitions.

He held the sobbing Ikura in his arms. Even little Yukio cried at the thought of his absence. That night, Ikura moved their sleeping mats closer together. When her final chores were finished and Yukio lay fast asleep, Ikura dropped her robe and slid naked against her husband. They made love as if there were no tomorrow. Ikura had never denied her husband anything on the marital bed, and this night she was exceptionally attentive. Finding joy together, both refused to dwell on the sadness that the morrow might bring.

* * * * * * * * *

Rogers had excused himself early to retire to the privacy of his bedroom in order to work on his report to army intelligence in Shanghai. Marina understood, but was reluctant to see him go up the stairs. She suggested that he could write with a clearer head early in the morning. That was the time she intended to write a letter to the French consulate in Seoul, seeking information about the missing Viktor Alesandrov.

"We should have heard some news by now," she complained. "Why could he not have sought asylum in a foreign consulate?"

"He must have been hiding or trying to reach the border," Rogers said.

Marina shook her head. "If the Japanese had him, I would know by now."

Rogers was almost tempted to ask how she would know. There were a lot of questions about Marina's activities that made him curious.

"Please stay for a glass of wine with me," she implored. "I need to talk tonight. It has been a long, troubling day." He was flattered by her attention and felt so close to her by this time that he agreed, but added, "Let me try to finish the report to my superiors; I am almost finished. If I could be excused for just one-half hour, I promise to stop the work and return. I would love a glass of wine and a chance to relax."

She made a pouting expression, then brightened and agreed. "Promise?"

He trudged up the stairs. *You've put off writing your report too long. Get to it.* Pausing at the mid-landing, he looked back. She was still watching and smiled up at him.

Marina called to Yin-lin, "Please prepare some hot water. I need to bathe."

Yin-lin boiled the water, then called to a muscular houseman to carry the large container up to Marina's bed chamber. She poured the water into a small portable tub, added cooling water, and tested the temperature. Satisfied, she helped Marina disrobe.

Marina sat on the board stretched across the top of the tub, while the girl poured water on her torso. She sighed contentedly as the warm water cascaded down her body. Yin-lin soaped and rinsed Marina's back, then expertly kneaded the tired shoulder and back muscles. Yin-lin had been well trained in the art of massage. The maid soaped the front of Marina in loving strokes, causing her mistress to stir restlessly. Marina looked quizically at Yin-lin, wondering whether to object, yet enjoying the sensation.

"Mistress has wonderful body." Yin-lin again soaped Marina's breasts in loving strokes. "You like the American?"

"Yes. Do you?"

"Of course. He a real gentleman."

"Please rinse me, Yin-lin, or I may stay here forever."

Yin-lin poured the warm water, then, throwing the towel across Marina's back and shoulders, used one end of the towel to dry Marina's breasts and belly.

"Yin-lin, stop it!"

The girl laughed and continued the sensuous drying ritual. Marina relaxed. Warm and comfortable, she looked down at her swelling breasts and hardened nipples. "You are a naughty girl, Yin-lin. Now help me dress."

Donning a light woolen bed gown and a warm robe, Marina thrust her feet into a pair of fur-lined slippers.

"The lieutenant and I wish to discuss some matters. Please see that we are not disturbed. We will have some of the new wine and some cakes. Please see if he is ready."

Yin -lin had quickly disrobed and had slipped into the tub. Drying after sharing the water, she threw on a loose robe and timidly knocked on Rogers' door.

"Yes?" he called out. When there was no answer, he rose to open the door. Yin-lin stood with her robe slightly askew, looking at at him hungrily.

"Mistress ask if you finish?" Yin-lin had much to learn yet from Marina's English lessons.

"I have," he answered. "I'll be right down." Before she turned away, he reached for her hand apologetically. "You are a lovely girl, Yin-lin. Can we just be friends?"

She nodded and turned to pad down the stairs to the parlor, her eyes glistening from unleashed tears.

Rogers joined Marina shortly, remarking that he had completed his report finally. "I wrote fast—I'm glad it is done," he told her. "I hope I did not keep you waiting."

He was surprised at the daring informality of her clothing. *What the heck, it is her home.* Purposely avoiding her gaze, and trying to relax in her presence, lest she think he was staring, he took the proffered glass of wine. *Jesus! Did Viktor appreciate what he had here?*

The wine, served chilled as he liked it, relaxed his stiffness in her presence. Her knee touched his as she reached to give him the wine glass. He did not draw away. Sitting close together for the first time on the couch in her home, he remarked about the loose talk that seemed to prevail throughout the town.

She agreed. "The people talk far too much. Gossip is easy to pick up— as is news of the war, and much of it is false or propaganda. For instance, I help support a restaurant that delivers food to shipyard workers at the base. My delivery servants report much news to me that the enemy would love to have."

Their conversation veered back to the top commander in Port Arthur. Rogers was trying to pinpoint the proper chain of command, a task that would have been easy had Alesandrov been present. But again Marina surprised him.

"The Viceroy, Admiral Alexeiev, is not a warrior. He should be in St Petersburg sitting at a desk. He's a difficult man for others to work with— doesn't delegate authority easily." Marina saw his shocked look and continued. "I know this from someone associated with his household, or rather Yin-lin, does."

So that was the connection! He had seen Yin-lin conversing with a visitor, a comely girl, whom one of the male garden workers had identified as Alexeiev's servant. *Good lord, first Stoessel's household, now also that of Admiral Alexeiev!*

"Are your servants trustworthy?" he asked.

"Of that I am certain," she replied. "Many in my house have been with me for years. They would tell me of anyone suspicious. I treat everyone fairly and I find them all very loyal."

"I sense that you are not a great fan of the admiral," he said.

"What does that mean?"

"I mean that he must not be favored by you."

"Oh that. No, I dislike what he is doing to Admiral Starck. He is blaming the success of the Japanese fleet's attack all on Admiral Starck. It is Alexeiev who exposed the battleships in the outer harbor, then ordered them not to drape their torpedo nets because he feared it might offend the Japanese."

"He must have known the Japanese were up to something, and, perhaps, ordered the battleships placed outside the channel so they would be battle ready," Rogers surmised.

Marina objected. "I have heard all the talk among the navy crews. If that were so, why did none of our ships have steam up and not be ready to pursue? We were caught unready. Now Mrs. Starck informs me that her husband will have to accept the blame in exchange that his pension not be endangered. The Starck family will have to return to Russia as soon as Makharoff, arrives here."

"Who?"

"Admiral Makharoff. He is said to be the best leader in the Russian navy. But he will still have to report to Alexeiev, who is so incompetent. By the way, did you know that Alexeiev is the bastard son of our former Czar, Alexander II?"

"No, I didn't."

"And General Stoessel?" Rogers was curious about Marina's feelings toward that official. "Oh him. You must know that I don't like the man.

That Kaiser-type moustache and his short, trimmed beard. Ugh! It seems to me that he holds his head up as if he despised those standing before him. Such arrogance! I don't trust his wife either; she strongly influences her husband."

"Now, now, Marina." He laughed with her, amused that she shared his dislike of Stoessel.

"I hope Port Arthur does not suffer from his leadership," he said. Then he related to her how, earlier in China, Stoessel had retreated without informing the American marine vanguard marching to relieve the besieged foreign Concessions at Tientsin.

"That was four years ago. Maybe he has changed, but I doubt it. There was also a time, almost a month later back then, when he arrived hours late to attack Tientsin's east gate. And before that he withdrew from Tientsin's vital railroad station without informing the Allies. Then he flubbed his unilateral attack on Tientsin's East Arsenal, and had to be rescued. He doesn't work well with other countries."

"We are alone now, with few friends and no allies," Marina observed. "He'll have to stand and fight. I wish your president Roosevelt and the Hearst newspapers were not so pro-Japanese."

"I wish you were right," Rogers agreed. "But while Stoessel puts others at risk, he has little stamina for going on the attack, and never, I've noticed, does he accept blame when things go wrong. It is always the other person's fault." He chose to ignore her remark about President Theodore Roosevelt.

"You really don't like Stoessel either, do you?" Marina asked.

"Well," Rogers said, "Maybe he bruised my ego. He never has given me the time of day. Always claims to be too busy to see me."

Rogers mentioned Master Loong. It had always intrigued him that the ancient one had known of his arrival day and time in Port Arthur. Evidently the old man was a pigeon fancier. He had seen Loong carrying a pigeon more than once.

"Master Loong is older than my father was," Marina said. "He is an invaluable aide for me. Everyone thinks he is a harmless old man, so no one questions his presence. There are few things he ever misses."

Rogers had seen Master Loong escort several mysterious callers to Marina's house, but he chose not to question the man's status.

The conversation turned more intimate as Marina half turned toward him, resting her arm on the back of the sofa and tucking one leg under her, distracting him with the way her light robe tightened to outline the shapely limb. Since coming into her home, Rogers no longer felt like a stranger and increasingly had grown more comfortable around her. And she had made it clear that she wanted him to stay on as her guest and friend. Wise in the ways of the East, he had refrained from mentioning lodging money, because he knew it would be insulting to his host.

"Viktor will return soon, I know it," she confided. "He would want you to be here to help me."

"I enjoy your hospitality." He leaned daringly close. Without flinching, Marina gazed at him with a half smile that seemed almost sensuous. "I don't want to overstay my welcome, Marina, but, to quote an old Chinese saying, visitors are like fish—after three days they begin to stink."

She laughed and playfully slapped his shoulder. The touch sent a stab of pleasure shooting through his groin. He tried to be serious.

"How well do you know our friend Chen?" he asked.

She paused momentarily as if carefully framing her answer. "He and my mother were distant relatives, actually second cousins. Mama had cared for him briefly when he was a very young boy in this big house. So you could say he is my cousin, though he seems like an uncle." Rogers recalled the odd way Chen had looked at him in Dalny when mention was first made of Marina. *Cousins? Everyone in China had multiple cousins, not one or two like in America. She spoke as if the relationship was very close. Why had Chen never mentioned Marina?*

"I had no idea that Chen is such a friend."

"Yes," she said. "He helped you, and he has helped me. He is one of the strongest and bravest men I have known." Rogers could not have agreed more. Her eyes became dreamy. "Whenever I need help, I go to him. He is so much like my father."

"I have few intimate women friends," Marina confided. "Too many women gossip and carry tales. It is true that my parents left me this home and my land, and a sum of money. But I have built up what I have by myself. My father lost much money in failed railroad bonds. It is a long story that only Viktor knows. I have an old family friend in Russia who gives me very good financial advice. That too is another story. Out here in the Orient, I am very much by myself. That is one reason I was attracted to Viktor."

"You seem to be a successful business woman," he noted, wondering if Viktor was part of her commercial business.

"I try to be fair in business. I am strict. I may charge high interest to discourage accounts payable, but I seldom foreclose, and that is a lesson not lost on others. I offer no credit to customers in my factory, because credit to the public means such customers will avoid coming to see me if debt is owing. Or seeking credit will become a habit that will soon cause anger when further credit is refused. It is not worth the ill feeling it creates." There was a moment's silence, then she half smiled and dropped a bombshell.

"How is Xi?"

Rogers was struck speechless by her question. He started to stammer a lame response. She helped put him at ease. "I know about her, Ellis. Viktor did not tell me, Chen did. He thought I might be hurt by my attraction to Viktor. I know that Chen took her to Hongkong. I am told that she is now betrothed to a Scottish shipbuilder."

Rogers wondered how much Chen had told her. Did Marina know that Chen had also taken An-an to Hongkong with Xi? That the two women were close friends?

"Chen said that Xi is a marvelously beautiful woman. Did you like her?"

Rogers spread his hands and tilted his head. With raised eyebrow, he replied, "Yes to both."

"I know that Viktor slept with her," Marina said.

Rogers began to be even more uncomfortable, wondering in what direction her frankness was leading. He did not respond. Hell yes, Viktor had slept with that exotic, hot woman, the concubine of the Governor of Peking. Rogers had helped rescue her from raping Russian soldiers, had saved her life when she lay in the Tungchow road with two broken legs after the soldiers had thrown her out a second story window of her house perched above the road. But it was Viktor who had ordered an army doctor to repair her legs. It was Viktor who had weaned her back to health and had cared for her. And it was Viktor who had pounded the mattress with her for almost one year.

"It would be unlike Viktor to be monogamous," Marina reasoned. She sighed. "Women in the Orient, and possibly in much of Europe, know that men have mistresses. I can accept that if the man is unmarried. I know that Viktor has known other women, maybe many. It is the nature of the beast called man."

Rogers disagreed. Why was the man always solely blamed? What about love and the chemistry between two people? Sure Alesandrov was lusty, but women threw themselves at him. Women enticed him shamelessly. He was the one pursued.

"You are probably wondering about Viktor and me?"

"No," he answered truthfully. It was none of his business. He glanced at Marina who sat beside him, looking so desirable, knowing instinctively that she must be more than a match for his friend.

"Why did he send Xi away?" Marina asked.

"He was called back to St Petersburg. He could not take her. An officer in the Sumsky Dragoons could never have an Asian for a lover or a wife. He would have had to leave the military and his friends at the Court.

It was sad. I know she loved him. He had saved her life. When they parted, she was devastated. It was easier for Viktor. He does not like to be around unhappy people, especially women."

Marina bit her lip. The silence was broken when she said, "Chen would not talk about you or your friend An-an. Isn't that her name? Is she pretty? Tell me about her."

It irked Rogers slightly that Marina had again asked about An-an. He had not dared to tell the army that he had married her against regulations and without permission. He wasn't sure if even Chen knew; he had not inquired about her. Chen did not discuss such things without an invitation. Was Marina testing him? Could he trust her to keep silent? And could not Marina know that he was not like Viktor?

He did not reply, only nodded his head affirmatively. As much as Marina's sensuality appealed to him, he would never betray Viktor. *Or would he?* It was tempting to sit so close to this intriguing woman. Rogers avoided a direct answer.

"When the Empress Dowager returned from exile to assume power in Peking, An-an went south with Chen. The Chinese ruler behaved herself only because of foreign presence. But everyone could read the handwriting—knew it was time to think of leaving Peking. If the Allies were so stupid to let her return, she might regain full power—then let her enemies beware.

An-an could never relax. When I was ordered to the States, we agreed she should go to a British protectorate. The Crown Colony seemed best."

He did not tell Marina that the move had been solely his idea, that he had persuaded An-an to sell her construction business and to go to HongKong to wait for him. But when he had returned to China from staff school in the States, the army had prevented a trip to HongKong so he could stay with An-an. It was almost like a plot against him, almost like the army knew he had a secret. The War Department seemed determined to use him shamelessly as their agent, ignoring his need to be with An-an. As soon as she could she had rushed up to Shanghai to meet him clandestinely.

Like so many oriental woman, An-an was completely faithful. He had sensed she had been a little unsure at first about Xi, realizing how sensuous Xi was. The two women had shared a bed during their travel and she had seen Xi naked and had envied her body. But she liked Xi, and the two had become firm friends when Viktor left.

How much could he tell Marina? How much a sexual and loving woman An-an was? How much he missed her? After the short three days in Shanghai with An-an upon his return from the States, the army had transferred him north to suffer the tortures of loneliness and unwilling celibacy.

The army was completely uncaring. He was theirs to use in China. As soldiers often said, if the army wanted him to have a woman, they would have issued him one! He had seen members of other armies tossed into oblivion in far off foreign posts. Would that be his fate? Denied promotion, denied a family, denied leave? There were times when he struggled against disloyal disappointment and bitterness. If only An-an could be with him! Could Marina truly understand how desperately lonely he was?

After a second glass of wine and another hour of conversation, Rogers hated to part company with Marina, but recognized the hour grew late.

"You will stay on in my home, will you not?" Marina asked. "We needed to talk like this."

"Yes," he answered. "But I am sure we will hear from Viktor soon. Try to be strong."

Marina had followed him up the stairs to the bedrooms. When he turned at his door to bid her goodnight, she embraced him and kissed him lightly on the cheek, murmuring something about the good wine and the welcome talk he had shared with her. Later, he realized how shocked and stupid he must have appeared. But Marina had gazed at him with her big soulful eyes and looked as if she might kiss him again. As he stiffened to pull back, she whispered, "Your presence has brightened my home. With Viktor away, I need someone to keep me company in this big house." Then she turned and was gone.

He crept into bed, unsure of her show of affection, uncertain how to accept it. In the night, he dreamed of making love. His rampant hormones brought him erotic fantasies of pleasure with his wife. *God, how he needed An-an!*

Marina, feeling more sentimental than she liked, asked Yin-lin to share her bed again. She began to cry. So did Yin-lin. Marina was at a loss to explain her emotional state. Was it Rogers and his comforting presence?

Or the wine and the late hour? "Why am I so sad and lonely, yet so happy?" she asked herself. "Why am I so vulnerable, so restless?"

Aware that Yin-lin was crying softly, Marina wrapped her arms around the girl and held her closely. The girl was more like a sister than a servant. Yin-lin turned to face Marina and the two embraced and soon fell asleep, each dreaming of the young American.

Dawn was just breaking when Rogers swung his legs out of bed and rose to his feet. He splashed water on his face, dried, then pulled on his trousers. He hoped he had not overslept. The wine had lulled him into such a restful sleep. People in the Orient rose before the light of day. Surely, others were up.

The sudden cracking explosion shook the house, knocking a glass of water to the floor, and cracking his door ajar a few inches. A brilliant light flashed through his room. He threw open his door as he heard women scream. Yin-lin ran past his door, clutching a short towel that barely covered her nakedness, her face contorted with fear.

He ran after the girl, grabbing her at the head of the stairs, telling her to be calm and to stay with Marina. She trembled in his arms and began to sob hysterically. Marina appeared at the door of her bedroom with the light of the room piercing the gown to silhouette her figure. He shoved Yin-lin toward Marina, shouting that he would go down to see what had happened. Before he reached the mid-landing, another explosive kraak sounded, this time more distant, from the direction of Old Town. *Navy shells!* He knew the sound.

Sprinting back up the stairs, he shouted to Marina to get dressed quickly and come downstairs. "Put on a coat and shoes," he yelled. "It is cold outside." He grabbed his own coat and boots and ran back down the stairs, taking two steps at a time.

In the yard outside, terrified servants had gathered in the cold morning air. Looking across the river, he saw flames and smoke shooting skyward from Old Town and the neighboring Chinese community, close to the Chinese wall. He did not need to look seaward to know who was lobbing the shells.

It was a naked feeling to be so exposed in the open. But the women would be safer out of the house. His brain reeled in anticipation of further havoc. Of course, a bomb-proof! He cursed himself for not having suggested a bomb shelter for Marina's household. The Russian defense guns were now firing from emplacements on Golden Hill and Electric Hill. He shouted to the servants to hide in Marina's concrete-walled storage house, and when Marina and Yin-lin appeared, he hustled them inside also. Absent a direct hit on the flimsy roof, at least the walls offered some protection. Marina held his hand and clung to his side. He put his arm around Yin-lin and pulled her close to stop her uncontrollable shaking.

Fortunately, the shells no longer hit New Town, but continued to pound the outer old Chinese settlements. Rogers helped Marina restore calm and order among the servants until the shelling finally stopped.

"We must construct a safety chamber at once," he cautioned. "Give me the men and tools; I know how to do it. We can start today."

Yin-lin had seemed reluctant to withdraw from the protective arm around her shoulder. And Marina had looked at him with unabashed pride at the way he had taken charge. An hour later, when the subject came up, she embraced him with gratitude and kissed both his cheeks, hesitating as if tempted to kiss his lips. He was glad she had not realized the throbbing sensation in the pit of his belly. *Or had she?*

CHAPTER SEVEN

On February 13, while impatiently waiting in Sasebo for final repairs on his destroyer, Captain Jiro Hata gloated at the news of the naval bombardment of Port Arthur the previous day. The base radio had indicated extensive damage to Old Town and the Chinese settlement farther inland. The shelling had been indiscriminate and designed to spread terror among the civilian populace. But the news also worried Hata, who feared the Russian port might be pounded into submission before his destroyer was readied for more combat.

Standing high on a catwalk on the upper drydock framework with his cousin, Lieutenant Nobihuro Sato, Hata voiced his concern. Pointing down to the cluttered deck of his ship, he complained about the slowness of the repairs. "I wish the Mikado would enlarge this yard. It is taking forever to fix the damage to my ship."

His cousin sought to calm him. "Remember how severely damaged your destroyer was? The shipwrights have worked around the clock," he reminded Hata. "I am certain you will be ready to join the blockship convoy. After the noble work you did in the initial attack against the Russian battleships, the admiral will surely want you to lead the expedition that we have volunteered for."

"I hope you are right," Hata groused. "Otherwise, everybody will win the glory before we do."

Sato smiled at his cousin's concern. He wished he could have shared Hata's bravery. What a glorious adventure that surprise midnight attack on the Czarist fleet must have been! The cowardly Russians evidently had been shocked into inaction, afraid to venture out of the port.

Sato had eagerly volunteered for the blockship duty, hoping to redeem the honor lost when he had chased that miserable black Chinese junk the night of the Port Arthur attack, and had arrived one hour late at the rendezvous island. If it had not been for the needs of the war, he guessed that Togo would have hung him out to dry.

The loss of the command of his torpedo boat had galled him. But Togo, for some reason, had relented and had assigned him to command the lead blockship. No matter that the *Mokoko Maru,* an old coastal freighter, would be scuttled and sunk in Port Arthur's harbor entrance. If he succeeded in blocking the channel at the upper tip of the Tiger Tail peninsula, he would bottle up the Russian fleet for months.

Neither man spoke of death, almost a certainty in such a suicidal venture. They had pushed their way past hundreds of others to win a place in the blockship venture. Both counted on a success that would ensure their place forever in Japan's glorious history.

The blockships, five old but sturdy steamers from Japan's dwindling maritime fleet, had been well prepared: all excess gear stripped, their hulls painted black and loaded with heavy stones and sacks of cement to make them sink quickly. They lay at anchor, manned by exuberant crewmen and ready to sail. If the February storms abated, the convoy could launch its surprise blockage in a few more days. Hata paced nervously. If only his destroyer could be readied in time!

The shrill steam whistle at the harbor entrance pierced the din of hammered rivets. The cousins turned to see two brand new armored light cruisers entering Sasebo harbor. "Those are the *Nisshin* and *Kasuga* that we have waited so long for," Hata said. "I hope they are bringing our spare parts."

The two warships, constructed at the Clyde Works in Scotland, had just arrived from Singapore with English crews. Originally intended for the Argentine navy, they had been diverted to Japan to become a welcome addition to the Mikado's navy.

One more week and I will be ready, Hata promised himself.

On February 21, the Japanese blockship convoy sailed from Sasebo, escorted by five destroyers. With fourteen-member crews, the blockships enjoyed the protection of the destroyer escort on an uneventful run northward to the Elliot Islands. The seas ran cold but calm under a depressingly gray overcast.

Final preparations went forward at the island group. Below decks, the crews placed dynamite cartridges to be ignited by electricity. Admiral Togo conferred with naval Commander Arima Ryokitsu, the architect of the plan. Sato and the other blockship commanders received instructions and maps, as did Hata aboard his readied destroyer.

Finally, the weather cleared on February 24. The departure from the Elliots was late, almost too late. But the convoy pushed on, finally arriving off Port Arthur at 3:00 AM. Sato saw the twinkling pre-dawn lights of the town and the sweeping harbor searchlights. He saw no sign of patrolling Russian picket ships.

The peaceful scene quickly changed. Four searchlights on Tiger Tail peninsula picked up the Japanese steamers, but failed to see the five escort destroyers lagging behind in the darkness.

Colonel Khostoff, the senior fortress commander, visiting from Fort Payushan, stood on the deck of the grounded battleship *Retvisan* with the deck officer. Watching the approaching vessels, he remarked to the naval officer, "Something is wrong. They are coming in too fast and are aligned five abreast in a row. Don't the fools know the rules?"

The port had anticipated the momentary arrival of some supply ships. But steamers had always entered the narrow channel in a single file and at slower speeds with a whistled alert signal. And flying flags and markers. With no flags and newly painted shiny black hulls, the ships looked suspicious, even from a distance.

Retvisan's gun crews chose to take no chances. Responding to the command "Fire One," they sent a shell splashing into the sea, just ahead of Sato's blockship. In the ensuing absence of recognition signals or frantic alarm sirens from the approaching ships, the second order followed: "Fire Two."

All five blockships were now bathed in the glare of several searchlights. As if they were ghosts in the night, five Japanese destroyers suddenly darted from behind the blockships and swerved around to attack the battleship. *Retvisan's* guns, joined by coast defense guns from the heights above the port, began rapid fire.

In spite of the still unrepaired 20 x 40 foot gash in her hull, the battleship operated well as a stationery gun platform, setting the channel ablaze with exploding shells. Sato's blockship, hit and unable to be steered properly, floundered helplessly. The *Mokoko Maru* finally limped to the east side of the channel and sank. The other four shell-damaged blockships, confused by Sato's erroneous turn to starboard, followed and were scuttled, but too far to seaward in the channel.

A Russian shell smashed into a second sinking blockship, obliberating its crew. Other Japanese crews scrambled into the small boats that had been towed behind the blockships and paddled madly out to sea in the darkness to be rescued by the Japanese destroyers. Most were saved, but some tow boats lost the race and their occupants were taken prisoner.

One man who escaped capture was Sato. He had pulled himself from the sea to crawl into one damaged tow boat, and lay hidden and shivering in four inches of icy water in the bottom of the boat. The towboat, soon lost from sight in the darkness, drifted away with the outgoing tide.

Sato passed in and out of consciousness, shivering uncontrollably all that day and into the night. Exhausted and numbed and too much in shock to care, his hypothermia made him delusional. He dreamed he strolled the bloody deck of a large black Chinese junk he had captured and had vengefully slaughtered its crew, including the stocky Chinese captain and the foreign officer on board.

Approaching the Japanese torpedo boat, which had trained its deck cannon on the Chinese craft, the black junk drew closer. The Chinaman flew a white parley flag. Most of its crew stood peacefully in a knot on the deck. The Chinese captain shouted across the water that he carried an injured Japanese naval officer whom he had rescued from the sea. Would the torpedo boat relieve him of his passenger?

The transfer of the unconscious man, warmly bundled in a wool blanket, and reeking strongly of sake and some unknown spicy substance, was quickly accomplished, along with a large bag of rice and a half case of sake. The Japanese commander thanked the junk commander for the rescue and the gift. He sent a note of introduction and commendation for future use by the Chinese captain, who professed to carry supplies to the Japanese First Army in north Korea.

"It never hurts to befriend the enemy," Chen told his crew. "Now let us go away fast. The price of my cargo just doubled."

Chen's ship, once out of sight, changed course for the Russian garrison at the Manchurian port of Pitzuwo.

In the light of day in Port Arthur, Admiral Alexeiev, without a close examination, thought the five partially submerged Japanese blockships were sunken armored warships. Early that day, he had telegraphed his jubilant news to the Czar. Four hours later, he learned the truth and shamefacedly had to send a second telegram.

That same morning, the Japanese destroyers and blockship survivors arrived at the Elliot group. Captain Hata soon learned how badly his destroyer had been damaged by enemy shells.

A directive from Togo's flagship angered Hata. Aside from news that his cousin Sato was missing, Hata grew more enraged when told he would have to return to Sasebo for repairs on his destroyer. His angry protests met with stony silence from his division commander. There was little love lost between the two in any event.

"Go to Sasebo at once," the commander ordered. *Hata was becoming a real pain in the ass.* The commander enjoyed the look on Hata's face when he told him that Togo would also insist the blockship attempt be repeated.

Hata had entertained little faith in the operation previously. Failure of success made him even more disgusted. *How in the name of the Mikado are we expected to block the harbor? The Russians will be more alert than ever.*

The ignominious tow by a coal collier back to Sasebo was made even more humiliating when the tow line broke repeatedly. By the time of arrival at the repair yard, Hata fumed to his first lieutenant, "I feel disgusted with this lousy operation." The prospect of two weeks or more of forced idleness during repairs made him openly rebellious.

At Sasebo he cursed workers for earlier shoddy repairs. He paced the area all day, growling and muttering threats, and was on everyone's back over the slightest infraction. Hata became the most hated naval officer at the base.

The only alleviation to his temperment came with the appearance of his cousin Sato. While visiting him at the hospital, both agreed that Sato had to be one tough and lucky survivalist. They took delight in deriding Togo's operation of the sea war. Things were moving too slowly for them. The Russians were far from knocked out or even seriously hurt.

The cousins also noted how so much of the truth had been suppressed. "The public is only told of our glorious victories," Sato complained. "The truth about our casualties and the hits our ships have taken are never revealed."

Failure of the first blockship attempt had not deterred Togo. He immediately ordered a second blockship expedition. The hunt for suitable but expendable merchant steamers began.

Rogers had guessed Togo's tactic. He told Marina, "I am sure the Japanese will return. It is their only hope to bottle up the Russian fleet."

Marina was annoyed. "Why does not our brave admiral send ships out to drive off the Japanese?"

Rogers tried to hazard a guess for Alexeiev's reluctance. "This is the era of battleships. Each side gauges their strength on the number of battleships on hand. The Russians already have had two battleships and one heavy cruiser knocked out of action. Until more battle craft arrive from Europe, Alexeiev will not want to jeopardize his remaining capital ships. He'll continue to fight defensively."

"That is wrong," Marina protested. "Are we supposed to sit here and let the Japs shell us at will?"

Rogers sympathized with her. It had always been his belief that letting the enemy initiate an attack was a flawed strategy. *Give the initiative to the enemy and he will decide the conduct of the war.* He told her to be patient, though he was worried that stressful days lay ahead.

"At least we will soon have the safety of the bomb proof," he reminded her. "It could be worse. Your naval officers are now better organized to repulse the enemy fleet. In fact, Togo has to prevent Russian warships from sneaking out to bomb Japan's coast. Soon the ice will be melting enough to let the fleet at Vladivostok sortie out to harass Japanese troop convoys and merchant ships, maybe even join up with the fleet here."

Marina shook her head. "If I know Admiral Alexeiev, he will sit back and let Togo scheme for a way to keep us blockaded. You are right. Russians are so defense minded."

"That may be true among your leaders. But yesterday in Old Town, I witnessed near clashes between army and navy personnel over your navy's inactivity. The soldiers are taunting the sailors. Colonel Petrusha has his hands full keeping order. We'll just have to keep on our toes. It will possibly take the Japanese a good month to organize more blockships. And they will have to be more daring next time. Meanwhile Togo will not sit idle. He may try another strategy."

"Like what?"

"Like doing what your navy is doing—lay mines outside the harbor."

* * * * * * * * *

The foreign correspondent for an English newspaper, of which Russian intelligence had never heard nor bothered to check, claimed to be a member of landed gentry near the Welsh border. He seemed to have plenty of money to spend—what he called his generous expense account—and freely bought drinks for junior officers in the drinking establishments on the main street.

"The Esleys are of a privileged class," he boasted, thus establishing his preference for the company of officers rather than enlisted men. But one thing Philip Esley quickly discovered was the lack of bonding between navy and army offficers. *Damn near as bad as in Japan,* he thought. He did not understand that his narrowed audience was the result of the different military schools the men had attended in Russia. Another problem was the general lack of knowledge among Russian officers for the reasons for the war, and the likely plan for holding off the enemy. Senior officers shared little knowledge with junior officers.

Holding off the enemy! The idea astonished Esley. No plan for attacking the Japanese? No daring naval assaults against the Japanese homeland? No large scale movement of a large army from Russia to Manchuria? Were the Russians just going to sit back and wait, meanwhile scoffing at the Japanese threat?

The common Russian attitude seemed to be, as Rogers had also observed, "We do as we are told. We will crush them if they try to attack our forts, the little tail-less monkeys."

. Utter contempt and lack of respect for the enemy. "The Japs are no challenge," he was told. "We will swat them like the little piss ants they are."

The army garrison, and even Russian sailors, had noticed the absence of aggressive Russian plans. Admiral Alexeiev seemed in no hurry to venture forth to smite the enemy. He had issued orders that Russian ships could go no farther than one day's voyage from the port. General Stoessel also waffled and refused to share his plans with other officers—except von

173

Essen, a real toady for Stoessel. Von Essen was even more stubborn and pigheaded than most other Balts, and extremely disliked by the bulk of the garrison. Both Stoessel and von Essen in turn despised Alexeiev. They resented his authority and coveted his rank as viceroy.

Provost Colonel Petrusha had his eye on Esley. So did Rogers. "I am not comfortable in the company of the English newsman," he told Marina. "He's in his cups most of the time."

Rogers did not like drunks. Many could be highly entertaining, full of marvelous and witty jokes and stories, but the same jokes and repeated stories often grew stale after while. When drunks sensed that their performance was no longer appreciated, their wit became personal and insulting. It did not do much good to punch them out; they always claimed later not to remember their obnoxious words or actions.

Rogers had accepted the offer of a beer from Esley one afternoon, hoping to learn news about old friends—British officers from the China Expedition. Esley seemed surprisingly ignorant about that topic. Rogers should have been warned by the man's drinking habits. Not only did Esley drink too fast; he drank too much at one sitting. Two swallows and he had emptied his glass of beer.

Finally, bleary-eyed and unsteady after continuous jokes that turned increasingly raunchy, Esley became resentful of the American who continued to turn a deaf ear to Esley's humor. He began to make fun of Rogers. "Ho, ho, *Yankeeey*. Dum te dum, dum te dum."

"Please don't refer to me as a Yankee. I'm not from the American northeast; I'm from the west." Rogers should have gotten up and walked away, but he was too polite. He was fast tiring of the Englishman.

"Ho, ho! Yankee Doodle Dandy." Esley tucked his hands in his armpits and crowed, flapping his arms like chicken wings. When Rogers failed to laugh at the crude insult, Esley stumbled to a table, where he picked up a napkin, formed it like a tricorn hat and slapped it on top of Roger's head, crowing "Yankee Doodle Dandy." Rogers threw off the hat and turned away.

Esley, slobbering and reeling, clutched the back of Rogers' shirt. That was too much. Rogers turned and shoved Esley backward. The drunk stumbled and fell against a table, which collapsed, sending him sprawling.

Rogers apologized to the bartender. "I will leave and wait outside for a short period." Stepping away from Esley he told him, "Be smart and don't get up."

Rogers tarried outside the tavern for five minutes. When Esley did not appear, Rogers left, vowing to avoid the man in the future.

When Colonel Petrusha learned of the incident, he radioed a message to the English consul in Chefu.

Please advise validity of Mr. Philip Esley as foreign correspondent of the Rockingham Globe.

The English consul tossed the telegram to one side. He had enough to do without chasing such trivial requests. His sympathies were with Japan. Why should he cooperate with the Russians?

Esley began to hang out at Port Arthur's newspaper, the *Novy Kry*, He concentrated on a Russian newsman named Nojine, trying to ingratiate himself with gifts of vodka and promises of favorable copy to be sent to English newspapers. Nojine, busy with his duties and his attempt to record a faithful journal of daily events in the besieged port, tried to cope with Esley's pestering presence with little success. The Englishman was too tenacious.

Marina told Rogers about Admiral Makharoff, the new Pacific Fleet commander. "He is rated as the best and most aggressive officer in our navy. He arrived today and has taken over from Admiral Starck. Makharoff is very good, a wizard at organization and training, and is aggressive in war."

Rogers had guessed correctly about Togo's intentions. Angry at Ariko's faulty information on February 7, angry at the failure of the torpedo net cutters, and now angry at his inability to penetrate Port Arthur's inner harbor, Togo had decided that if the blockships failed to close the Russian harbor, then the Japanese would sow mines throughout the waters outside the naval base. Also, while waiting for the second blockship attempt, he would pound the town and shipyard with indirect naval fire. He would accomplish this by using destroyers to approach the harbor to direct high angle fire from the cruisers and battleships sitting safely far out to sea. Togo ordered the bombardment to commence at 10:00AM on March 10.

Hata was ordered to leave Sasebo with his patched up destroyer to join the First Destroyer Division. The First and Second Destroyer Divisions had orders to place mines in the roadstead during the night before the Japanese fleet bombardment commenced.

Hata wondered if Togo knew what the hell he was doing. Hata's division had received orders not to approach Port Arthur by hugging the Liautishan coast, but to charge directly into the mouth of the roadstead. Nice try, Hata thought. Somehow he had to find the roadstead in the dark, dash in with a load of mines, and hope he could escape the fate of Russia's best minelayer, *Yenessei*, which had been blown up by one of its own mines with the loss of the skipper and ninety men. None of Hata's crew had laid mines before.

Under the cover of a dark night, with calm seas, Hata, half guessing, found the roadstead. The Russians were waiting. Russsian searchlights picked up the Japanese destroyers and the shelling started. The Japanese crews worked in the dark, trying to ignore the Russian shells and searchlights. Without prior knowledge or practice, fearful of an imminent explosion, and hopeful that the mines were placed at a correct depth, and the mine anchors were holding, the Japanese labored through the night, completing the work by 5:00 AM.

Two of Division One's destroyers, *Shinonome* and *Usugumo,* had sustained damage from the Russian shells. In the faint morning light, Destroyer Division One was limping out to sea, when it heard firing from the direction of the Liautishan cliffs. Concluding that Destroyer Division Two had tangled with Russian destroyers, Division One received orders to create a diversion by turning back to fire into Old Town.

Almost at once, Hata saw two Russian destroyers coming in from the sea, trying to gain the safety of Port Arthur's inner roadstead. One of the Russian ships seemed to be crippled. Hata's destroyer manuevered a wide circle in order to cut off the retreating Russian ships.

Unable to escape from Hata, the crippled Russian destroyer turned to fight. Hata ordered his gunners to concentrate on the enemy's largest gun, a three incher, or more correctly a 7.5 cm cannon. By the time Hata's excellent markmanship had knocked out the larger gun, the two ships had closed to within a 300-foot separation. Hata's guns began to demolish the Russian's smaller 4.7cm cannons. Clouds of steam boiled upward from the stricken Russian ship. Dead and wounded lay everywhere on her torn deck, and some Russians had started to abandon ship.

Hata steamed even closer, his men shooting the Russian sailors in the water.

177

"Prepare to board."

Hata screamed the order at the top of his voice. Armed Japanese crewmen waved cutlasses and revolvers and threw hook-ropes to pull the ships together. The deck of the Russian ship was littered with mutilated bodies: heads, feet, entrails lay everywhere. Two wounded Russian sailors in the water surrendered; others swimmers refused.

Hata's men clambered aboard the Russian vessel. A quick count of the dead on the deck revealed a number of missing Russian sailors.

One of Hata's petty officers rushed up with news that the stern hatchway was closed. "I think the Russians are below trying to blow up the ship, sir."

"Follow me," Hata ordered, and ran toward the hatch. The cover was forced open and Hata's senior petty officer climbed below. Shots rang out. Two bullets narrowly missed Hata's head. The boarding party ran down the passageway to force open the door at the far end. The senior petty officer, leading the way, dashed inside to have his head blown off. Hata dodged the cutlass blows of the Russian commander. He warded off the blows and struck back with his own cutlass, felling the Russian officer. All other Russians in the compartment were shot until two wounded survivors surrendered. On the deck of the compartment, several dynamite cartridges and even two mines cluttered the bloody space.

"The Russian is sinking, sir. Hurry topside!" The shouted warning interrupted Hata's search for papers in the compartment desk. He grabbed some documents and a Russian flag and hurried up the ladder.

The Russian ship listed at a dangerous angle. Hata could see that his own ship was being pulled over by the sinking Russian ship. The Japanese frantically cut the thick hawsers holding the vessels together. The freed Russian destroyer quickly heeled over and sank.

Looking back toward the harbor, Hata saw that the other Russian destroyer had eluded capture and was vanishing into the harbor entrance. Hata also saw a larger Russian destroyer, which he recognized from her funnels to be the *Novik,* emerging from the harbor. The ship flew the flag of Admiral Makharoff. Other Russian destroyers followed the *Novik.* Hata's destroyer fled and was saved by the concentrated shellfire from Japanese cruisers, which soon forced the pursuing Russians to turn and retreat.

Hata's ship was a mess and again needed extensive repairs. Reluctantly, Destroyer Division One steamed back to Sasebo, Japan.

At the end of the month, Hata once again said goodbye to his cousin Sato, who seemed to have recovered well at the base hospital. Plans for a second blockship attempt against Port Arthur were underway, but far from completed. "I hope the old man knows what he is doing this time," Hata said. The two usually referred to Admiral Togo as "the old man."

Sato was more charitable. "He has to try something—anything to please the armchair admirals in Tokyo."

Hata promised to return soon to see his cousin. Meanwhile, he had begged for duty aboard another ship while his destroyer underwent repairs, and his prayers had been answered. An ailing gunnery officer had left a battleship, creating a vacancy that gave Hata a chance to escape the boredom of the repair yard. The balttleship commander had accepted Hata's application for a temporary transfer, so Hata gratefully reported for duty, commanding the aft gun on the battleship *Fuji.*

Almost immediately, Hata clashed with the commander. Like many battleship men, Hata's new superior had a haughty and dismissive attitude toward destroyer officers. He clearly regarded them as inferior, and that was hard for Hata to stomach.

Stubbornly determined to prove his worth, Hata worked tirelessly with his gun crew until the heavy aft gun performed flawlessly. The crew was fast, almost too fast. Hata wanted the gun barrel sponged after each practice shot and kept insisting to his gunners, "If there are remnants of the gunpowder bags still burning in the breech, opening the breech too soon could cause a large flame to shoot out. Somebody will be badly burned." He could see from the crew's expressions that they doubted his warning. Also, he was unaware of a small crack that had appeared on the gun barrel.

Hata was surprised to see both Commanders Fairborne and Bigelow on board; he had not been advised at that instant that *Fuji* was scheduled to lead a concentrated bombardment of Port Arthur.

Togo ordered the battleships *Fuji* and *Yashima* to anchor under cover of the Liautishan cliffs to hit Port Arthur with high angle fire. Togo's other ships would stand well off the coast to act as spotters to radio gunnery corrections to the two battleships.

Entering Pigeon Bay, Commander Fairborne remarked to Bigelow that he thought *Fuji* was coming too close to land. "The admiral should realize by now how accurately the Russian coast batteries can shoot."

Hata had complained at first, speculating that the high angle fire was too hard on the guns, and especially the gear and deck that had to absorb the downward shock. But it worked. Safely sheltered from Russian cruisers and destroyers in the harbor, the two Japanese battleships fired a brace of shells over the cliffs. A quick wireless message told *Fuji* that the shells had successfully landed in the town, but the angle of fire needed to be shifted laterally.

A second brace of shells met with more success, but again a further lateral shift was ordered. The battleship's gunners were delighted at the success of finding their target. More wireless messages came from Togo's spotters.

Suddenly, a bracket of Russian 30 cm shells splashed into the sea close by. Hata ignored the danger.

He made his gunners sponge the barrel. A third shell was inserted into the breech. Before Hata could give the command to fire, a shrill whistle, followed by a loud roar, drowned out all communication. Hata was enveloped in thick yellow smoke and a blast of hot air that hurled his body aft.

The large Russian shell had struck the deck somewhere between the aft gun turret and the midship marker. The downward plunge of the shell had missed the gun barbette, but had smashed a large hole in the upper deck and had exploded on the lower deck, killing twelve men below. Blood and brains smeared the lower deck bulkheads.

Learning of the damage to the battleship, Togo halted the operation. The Japanese marveled at the Russian accuracy, correctly acknowledging it to be the result of improved training ordered by Russian Admiral Makharoff. What the Japanese did not know was that the Russians had intercepted the Japanese wireless messages.

Hata woke up in the ship's infirmary. "You are all right—just banged your head," the ship's surgeon assured him. Too woozy to walk, Hata rested with an ice bag on his head, until his strength returned.

On the second deck, seamen gathered the body parts and sewed them in a sack. Weighted with lead, the bag was lowered into the sea.

The crew now realized that the ship was listing noticeably to port. The Russian shell had continued on below to punch a hole in the ship's side below the waterline. Not discovered until an hour after the explosion, the inrushing torrent of water was finally contained by closed water tight compartment doors.

Togo ordered the battleship to return to Sasebo for repairs. Hata cursed the luck of *Fuji.* Faced with more shipyard idleness, he wondered if the ship was jinxed. Or was it him?

Commander Fairborne took advantage of the repair period to board a steamer headed north to Seoul. He arrived barely in time to find Lydia who had planned to depart for Tokyo.

* * * * * * * * *

Major Jiro Ariko had vowed to follow Lydia Fairborne to the ends of the earth to extract revenge for Alesandrov's escape from Seoul. He blamed her for the entire botched mess. He blamed Rogers even more for forcing him out of the Kwantung Peninsula. If not for the American, Ariko was certain he could have slipped back into Port Arthur to establish a firm base for espionage. It angered the Japanese officer that his cover had been blown by Rogers at the Dalny rail station. Still, he knew that Rogers might have recognized him in time even if he had not done so immediately on the train. He had never liked Rogers, even when America and Japan were allies in the China war. Now that Japan was fighting a "white" nation, Ariko despised Rogers more than ever.

The main object of Ariko's wrath, however, was the hostess at the Golden Pavilion tavern in Shanghai. The information she had stolen from the Russian officer had been so false that Ariko knew that his career was forever compromised. He marked the hostess for death and vowed to do the deed himself as soon as a lull in his duties at the front permitted. The hostess, whom he learned was called Tea Flower, had to have been part of a Russian plot, and Ariko swore vengeance on her.

Ariko had some agents in Port Arthur, but had planned to be on hand himself to assess the extent of the damage to the Russian battleships. He had also planned to establish a system to signal the Japanese fleet from land, to direct fleet gunfire, and to sabotage the base infrastructure.

Now he was forced to rely on the asian cook in Admiral Alexeiev's kitchen. The young cook, actually a Korean who had lived in Manchuria for years, looked as Mongolian as the natives and easily passed as a local native.

Another agent was an English newsman who had ostensibly arrived in Port Arthur to report on the coming conflict. Money, already aided by the man's thirst for beer and Scotch whiskey, and his rabid hatred for all things Russian, had bought his allegiance.

A few months earlier, the Englishman had been blunt with Ariko. "If I am to work with you, I expect to be paid a handsome retainer."

"What would it take to buy your loyalty?" Ariko had asked.

The Englishman had named a ridiculously high sum which Ariko had readily agreed to pay.

I should have asked for more, Philip Esley had silently complained.

Lastly, the departing staff of the Japanese Ambassador in St. Petersburg had alerted Ariko to the possiblility of employing a young, rebellious university graduate student in Russia, who headed an underground cell of anti-Czarist socialists. Ariko was informed that the student, a half-Jewish woman, had strong sympathies for Poland, a province that Russia could not afford to ignore or trust.

Ariko, now confined to his base in eastern Manchuria, could only set up an operation near Pitzuwo. The town was targeted as a likely invasion port for the Japanese army. He had to be careful in Pitzuwo to maintain a low profile while trying to pose as a Korean businessman. The local Chinese, he confirmed, hated the Japanese almost as much as they resented the Russian presence. The Japanese massacre of peninsula residents ten years earlier in the Chinese War of 1894 still burned deep in their memories.

After a week of travel along rough Korean mountain roads, the driver of the small wagon had rebelled against further travel. Yoo Rak-hoon had not planned to come so far north. But the promise of more money had persuaded him, against his better judgment, to stay on his uncharted course. Yoo was sure that he had erred in undertaking such a crazy journey. The money offer had been good, but how much farther north was he supposed to take the mad Russian? Every day Yoo's protests had met with menacing silence from his passenger, who lay doubled up in the bed of the wagon, grimacing with pain from the rough jolting.

The Russian had paid him a small sum of money a few times, with a promise of much more when the journey ended. And aside from impatient looks, the Russian had not verbally threatened him, but had pushed his coat aside a couple of times to reveal a revolver in his belt.

Yoo continued to follow the directions of his prone passenger, who often seemed to stare up at the sky, test the wind with a wetted finger, and study the evening stars. The weather was still bitterly cold, especially at night. The imminent end of winter in March meant that ice would soon be melting, but Korea had its own unpredictable sort of March. The cessation of snowfall often signalled drier but even colder air blowing in off the Sea of Japan. Yoo worried about a possible unseasonable snowstorm and the growing absence of civilized settlements.

They had not seen a farmhouse for two days. Another range of hills loomed ahead. Yoo turned to voice a protest, but the stubborn Russian this time made a fist and jabbed a finger to point ahead. Yoo gritted his teeth. Tonight, somehow, he would get rid of the foreigner. Perhaps when the man stopped to relieve his bladder, then Yoo would gallop off, hoping a bullet would not hit his back.

The driver crested a steep incline, pausing at the top to look down toward a narrow pass. A small hamlet below drew his attention. The sight of a group of mounted men, clustered near the small huts, made Yoo's decision final. He pointed to the riders and shook his head at the Russian, making it plain that he refused to proceed farther.

The Russian argued, tossed a few coins to the driver, and protested Yoo's obstinance. No amount of persuasion, bribe, or threat, however, could change Yoo's mind. Finally the Russian drew his revolver. Yoo cringed at the sight of the weapon. He motioned for the Russian to dismount. The ploy to bolt and run did not succeed because the passenger waved for Woo to get down first.

Yoo unhitched the horse as directed, but then panicked and ran down the hill toward the huts. Rounding a curve in the road, he looked back to see the Russian astride the horse, urging the beast off the road to detour around the hamlet. That was the last time Yoo Rak-hoon saw his horse or the Russian.

* * * * * * * * *

Grey daylight prodded Alesandrov awake at 5:00 AM. He awoke with a dull headache, having slept in a sitting position that had cramped his neck. He had not dared to lie prone in the darkness among the trees. The isolated

185

stand of trees had offered some protection from the wind whipping across the open fields of the snow covered valley. He leaned back against the tree trunk. The eerie quiet among the trees put him on edge.

The wagon horse stood tethered to a nearby tree, its head hanging low from exhaustion and the cold. The animal would somehow have to be fed, but how? His own supply of food was almost gone; he had none to spare for the horse.

Alesandrov had eluded his bandit pursuers for the past four days, riding northward parallel to the range of hills off to his left. Each day seemed an endless repetition of the preceding day. The cold siberian wind would pick up at 3:00 in the afternoon. One and a half hours later, the day would end with the wind weakened, and the cold dry air beginning to assault his aching body. The winter sun would slip below the ridge and night quickly close around him, making it difficult to decide where to seek shelter.

He had used his rubber poncho to help shield his body from the wet snow by day and as a ground cover at night. The bear fat used to waterproof his boots was gone. His knapsack lay nearby containing spare socks that were no longer dry. His last crusts of bread, and a flask of water lay within. He had added a little vodka to keep the liquid from freezing. *Thank God, diahhrea had not yet seized his gut.*

He knew the horse was almost finished. Should he sacrifice a bullet to put the animal out of its misery and carve some flesh for food from its carcass, or turn the animal loose to fend for itself? The snow was too deep for the horse to be of further use to him. A hard crust blanketed the snow,

Alesandrov's escape path through Korea

STALKING SIBERIAN TIGER

making each step a slow painful process as the horse had struggled to pull each leg from the binding clutch of snow and ice. The horse's legs bled from contact with the sharp ice crust that cut like jagged glass.

It was so cold. He jammed his hands in his armpits to try to stop the convulsive shivering of his body and the chattering of his teeth. Inside the double pair of gloves, his hands were sore and bleeding. He ran his tongue over painfully cracked lips, then closed his eyes, trying to think, trying to plan a course for the day.

He had left the rice country of Seoul to journey into the red-dirt hills north of the city. After Panmunjon, more hills. There had been no comfortable position in the wagon, scant room to lie down. He had tried to sit away from the side of the wagon to avoid the jolting punishment from the rutted road. The cold of the weather seemed to aggravate the pain in his injured ribs, undoing the recuperation he had enjoyed at Panmunjon with Ri and Kim.

At first the driver had found shelter for them in the scattered villages, where miserable small huts clustered around an open area from which trails and roads branched off in multiple directions like wagon wheel spokes. The villages and people grew increasingly dirty, miserable and scarce as he traveled north. He did not like or trust the flea-ridden villagers and sensed they liked him even less.

He had twice spotted a distant whitish-orange beast with black markings that he recognized from his hunting days as a snow tiger. Each time, fumbling for his belt, he had felt the comforting bulge of his revolver. Alesandrov hoped that the sparse coating of thin oil on the metal parts would not freeze.

It was now the third week of March and it seemed like years since he had slipped out of Panmunjon in the wagon. Kim and Ri were the only kind memories he had of the place. Knowing what he had endured on this journey, his original plan in Seoul to come north with the French nurse, Claudette Chevier, now seemed ludicrous. She would never have survived such a foolhardy ordeal. He was sure, though, that his sense of direction was correct, but fatigue and pain made him often despair of reaching the Yalu beyond the endless 600-foot high hills that seemed to stretch on forever.

Almost nodding off into sleep, Alesandrov shook himself awake. The eastern sky began to burst into bright patterns of oranges and reds. The day promised sunshine, but little warmth. The sun's yellow glare against the snow would be blinding—another day of squinting his eyes to ward off snow blindness. Pushing himself to his feet, he gathered his knapsack, took the reins of the horse and stumbled off across the field for yet another day of torturous walking. With ten more degrees of cold, the crust on the snow might have been strong enough to support his weight. But, like the horse, he struggled with each step to pull his legs free from the grip of the snow, sometimes stumbling and pitching forward to cut his wrists on the sharp ice crust.

At the end of the day he came to another stand of trees clumped at the foot of the mountain. All afternoon he had struggled to cross the valley, then had proceeded north on flat ground. A sixth sense told him he had gone far enough north. Tomorrow he vowed to turn west across the hills and take his chances on emerging north of the confluence of the Ai-ho and Yalu rivers, safely close to the Manchurian border. And he would abandon the horse in the morning.

He looked behind at the weary animal. It had followed him even after he had stopped leading it by the reins—as if he was its only hope for food.

He had half expected the horse to drop in its tracks. Its head hung so low its muzzzle barely cleared the top of the snow.

When he had seen the trees ahead, he had pressed on to escape the numbing wind and failing daylight. In the gloom of the tree shelter, he tied the reins of the unresisting horse to a tree, scooped out a hollow in the snow at the base of a nearby tree, spread his rubber poncho on the ground and hunkered down for the night.

He looked at the horse. A white frost had gathered on its nose and mane. With its head pointed north toward the moaning wind, it stood dejectedly on trembling legs, nearing collapse.

Shortly before midnight, Alesandrov awoke to the sound of the horse snorting in terror, pulling in agitation against the leather restraint. It took Alesandrov a minute or two to gather his senses and realize the danger. A pair of yellow eyes glared from the inky darkness. With his heart racing, Alesandrov struggled to get to his feet. Before he could move away from the tree, a huge, snarling mass flew through the air to land on the horse's back. The animal screamed a second before it was knocked off its feet and its neck snapped. In the dim light of the cloud-covered moon, Alesandrov saw the unmistakable black stripes and pale white-orange coat of the giant cat. It was the same Siberian tiger he had seen in the distance before stealing the Korean's horse.

Growling and hissing, the cat tore savagely at the horse's throat. It was the largest tiger he had ever seen, easily weighing 700 pounds, apparently driven south by the record severe winter.

He found himself floundering madly through the snow, terrified as he ran from the trees. It was only later after fatigue pitched him forward into the snow that he realized he had abandoned his poncho and knapsack. Too late!

Gasping for breath, he struggled to his feet and scrambled toward the rise of ground at the base of the mountain. There had been very few times in his life when he had felt so nakedly helpless. Soon he stopped again and fell exhausted to his knees. Images of past lovers flashed through his mind: his Russian cousin, and Xi, Tea Flower, Marina, Claudette, Lydia, and countless others whose names he no longer remembered. The memories strengthened his resolve. "I won't give up," he muttered to himself. "I won't. I am not going to die on this damn mountain."

Marina stood with Rogers in the midst of a large group of workers. She admired the sturdiness of the shelter.

"I like it," she told him. "I feel safer now."

'Steel pipes, sacks of cement, heavy timbers, and rice sacks filled with sand littered the space behind her home. The pit of the shelter had been dug to a depth of eight feet. Four-inch thick rough wooden planks placed over the pit formed a stout roof. A layer of concrete, four inches thick, reinforced with 3/4 inch steel pipe, had been poured over the planks. Then three layers of sandbags had been added on the dried concrete. Another foot of dirt covered the sandbags. The rear of the roof slanted slightly upward for rain drainage, and provided a slit for air on the side facing the hill. The front entry was shielded by an offset barrier of sandbags.

"That should do it," said Rogers. "We'll add some floor mats, sleeping cots, blankets, water jugs, some waste buckets, and some aromatic candles. An hour or two inside should not be too uncomfortable."

After a few days leave in Seoul to rest and to file a report to his superiors, assessing the Japanese torpedo attack on the Russian fleet at Port

Arthur, British Commander Nigel Fairborne had questioned his wife before returning for duty with Admiral Togo.

"There is some talk about your acquaintance with a certain Russian officer. You must be very careful, my dear. The war has commenced, and I am assigned to the Japanese side. It would not do for you to be seen in the company of Japan's enemies."

Still smarting from her treatment by Ariko's men, Lydia had protested, "I like the Japanese people, but I detest their brutal army. Some of the Japanese officers can be so arrogant." She had pursed her lips, careful not to invite too many questions, wondering how much the British officials had been told by the Japanese. "What kind of idle gossip have you heard?"

Fairborne had shrugged, "I don't take stock in unproven rumors. It is only a hint from the Admiralty that this Russian officer is a spy."

"How could he be a spy when he is a uniformed belligerent?" Lydia had flared. "I know him from past diplomatic functions."

"Are you still in contact with him?"

"No," Lydia had answered. "I heard he escaped from custody after his arrest by the Japanese. He was in full uniform when captured. The Japanese should have treated him as a prisoner of war, not as a spy. They even tortured him."

"Where is he now?"

"How should I know? Probably hiding somewhere in Korea, maybe dead. Why do the military police watch us so closely?"

"I have protested the matter to the British Admiralty," her husband had assured her. "But I must not jeopardize my assignment with the Japanese Navy."

"We are British subjects and should be treated with the proper respect," Lydia had protested. "I don't like being followed and watched every minute."

"I will have it stopped," her husband had promised. "Just be careful meanwhile."

Before reporting for duty aboard Admiral Togo's flagship, Fairborne had tendered his report to his British superiors, detailing the naval actions and stressing the partial success of the surprise midnight attack on Port Arthur. He had blamed Togo for over-reliance on torpedoes. But Fairborne was careful not to minimize the importance of torpedoes as effective weapons. After all, torpedoes were his area of expertise, and he believed in their growing importance in naval warfare. But, as he had pointed out, more torpedoes should have been used, more naval craft employed, and even a joint venture with land forces made part of the operation. The Russian fleet had been hurt, but was far from being destroyed. The bulk of the Russian warcraft was intact and able to strike back.

Lydia had been greatly relieved to learn that her assignation with Alesandrov had not been exposed in too much detail. Perhaps the British Admiralty had preferred not to hinder Nigel's valuable duties with her recklessness. With Nigel gone, Lydia had planned to leave Seoul, a city she had grown to dislike intensely. She had resolved to go to Tokyo. Her only regret was not to have told Nigel that she would leave and where she would go. She shrugged, sure that she could reestablish contact with him from Tokyo.

Life promised to be more exciting in Tokyo. Lydia had grown restless. Desirous of sex and disappointed by Nigel's inattention and poor performance, she endured erotic dreams of being surrounded by a phalanx of rampant penises pulsating with desire for her attention and gratification. Her maddening lubricity became a daily distracting occurrence.

CHAPTER EIGHT

After Nigel left Seoul, Lydia Fairborne made preparations to board a ship bound for Tokyo where she had several friends. She booked passage on a German steamer in early March.

On board as a fellow passenger, an Austrian junior army officer took more than casual interest in Fairborne's wife. He introduced himself, asked permission to join her at lunch, escorted her about the ship, and, by evening, had gained her confidence enough to sit with her for dinner.

Lydia enjoyed the overtures of the young blonde man, who had identified himself as a member of Austrian nobility. She flirtatiously made it easy for his attraction to blossom. He showered her with attention and compliments. After dinner, they danced in the ship's salon, where he held her daringly close. Dancing to the strains of a Strauss waltz, sipping too much champagne, and thoroughly enjoying herself, Lydia relaxed with the virile male companionship she had always coveted. Viktor was gone, perhaps forever. She still longed to be with him and could only hope he was safe. But if his absence was lengthy, she was certain he would seek another woman's arms; Viktor was too much like herself. Life went on.

Nigel's homecoming had been a predictable sexual disappointment. He had seemed more restless than ever, strangely anxious to return to duty, and more than ever tormented by her sexual apetite. In the end, he had left her with unfulfilled desire.

Her companion, Uberleutnant Rupert von Streich, charmed her with tales of Vienna, praised her beauty, and gazed at her with unabashed admiration. His adoration made her feel like the whole woman that Viktor had always so wonderfully excited.

At the end of the evening, back in her stateroom, still exhilarated by the excitement of the dance, Lydia undressed and, as she often did, stood naked before a mirror, admiring her figure. Happy again for the first time in days, she laughed recklessly and twirled in a pirouette, before slipping into a thin sleeping gown. She had scarcely settled on her pillow when two low knocks sounded at her door. Arising, Lydia donned a light robe over her thin sleeping gown and approached the door.

"Yes, who is it?"

"A friend has sent you an evening cocktail. May I leave it with you?" The voice, with an exaggerated accent, sounded familiar. She unlocked the door and opened it.

Von Streich stood in the passageway, holding a tray with two glasses and a bottle of orange liqueur. With a boyish grin and eyes sparkling with deviltry, he bowed low. Holding out the gift, he announced, "Compliments of an admirer. May I have Madame's permission to place it on the table?"

Lydia laughed. "You have little respect for my marriage," she giggled. "But come in and we'll share one last drink for the night. You are a naughty boy."

Why not, she told herself? Feeling giddy and recognizing the flush of arousement in her loins, she let her robe fall open to lay bare more of her cleavage and stood with the light of the lamp behind her, accentuating the outline of her body beneath the thin night garment.

One drink led to two. Gazing at him hungrily, she leaned forward to kiss him. His arms closed around her and his hand slipped lower.

Von Streich crept out of her cabin before dawn, a dazed and thoroughly exhausted young man who had met more than his match.

Later, he rendezvoued with Lydia for a late morning meal in the salon. He told her of his family in Vienna and of distant relatives in Hungary, and of his short military career and his present assignment to the Austrian embassy in Tokyo. In turn, Lydia related some of her experiences in Japan, hinting at her disappointing marriage, and stating that she was in no hurry to return to England. Not while her husband was posted in the Orient.

"Have you been to the public baths in Japan?" she asked. He had not; this was his first visit to Japan. He expressed a desire to go, especially with her.

"We have another night to enjoy," she told him. "You can hold me and kiss me." She lowered her voice to a whisper as the waiter approached their table. "I will undress and you will see me again. Perhaps, at the baths, you will also enjoy seeing the Japanese ladies? I know they will marvel at the blonde hair on your body." They both laughed as she continued to tease him. He reached across the table and put his hand over hers. She could sense, without proof of observance, how aroused he was, how hungrily he wanted to embrace her.

Gradually their talk turned to the war. He told her of his dislike for Russia, not the people, only the Czar's territorial ambitions. "We worry about the Russian bear and the expansion westward. Our neighbor may someday threaten our sovereignty."

"You should not worry," she told him. "Your Emperor and the German Kaiser are close allies, in fact cousins. The Czarina is also German. Most of the monarchs in Europe are of German blood, even in England. Surely you have the safety of blood ties and good neighbors."

"And your King Edward VII is also an uncle of the Czar and the Kaiser," von Streich reminded her. "But royal ambitions can cause even blood relatives to quarrel." His face took on a look of deep thought. After a moment, he startled her with a bold proposal. "Your monarch's family name is Saxe-Coburg-Gotha. Surely we are so closely united in blood and heritage that it would be good for both our countries to share knowledge about the Japanese. The West against the East, so to speak."

Lydia's hand, reaching beneath the starched white tablecloth, had begun to stray. "What are you suggesting?"

"Well, we of German blood distrust the orientals. When the Chinese murdered a couple of German missionaries a few years ago, we Austrians joined the allied effort to strike hard at the Chinese."

"I know." Lydia's hand squeezed him. "The murders were used as an excuse to seize a large chunk of north China territory. Now, at least they make good beer in Germany's Tsingtao."

"How about your Hong Kong territory?" he chided her.

"Let's not quibble. What do you have in mind?"

He pushed his enlarging member forward against her caressing hand. "Would it not be valuable if Austria and England knew what the Japanese are up to?"

"Certainly. But remember, my husband is posted with the Japanese navy. I have no quarrel with them. It is their army, I detest."

"Splendid. I may be very closely in touch with the Japanese army in the field. And you will be in Tokyo, or perhaps Sasebo with your husband. What if we compare notes?"

"You mean you want me to spy on the Japanese?"

He shrugged, "I would not call it that exactly. I could help you. And you could help me. And we both could help our countries."

"Let me think about it." She could feel his growing response to her touch. She squeezed again. His eyes glazed and his pursed mouth opened. She voiced a mutual thought, "Why talk about Japan? We are wasting the morning. Let us go to my cabin for awhile." She stood, smiling at his embarrassment as he struggled to rearrange his trousers so he could rise decently from his chair.

Lydia loved her husband dearly outside the bedroom. He could be wonderfully charming, courteous and kind, possessed of a quick mind and tolerant disposition. But in their bedroom chamber, she was completely turned off. The man seemed such a weakling in bed, whimpering for sympathy, wanting to cuddle possessively, to be treated like a small boy in need of a mother's indulgence.

She had tried to work with her husband, slowly and seductively slipping off her nightgown to display herself tantalizingly, jutting out her breasts, moistening a finger to tease her pubic mound. Only when she obeyed his request to turn her back and bend over to touch her toes did he seem to come alive. Then, seeing his arousal, if she turned to pounce on him and become the active partner, his libido rapidly died and he lost interest. If she lay on her back and displayed her shapely spread legs and flat stomach, he took little interest, seeming to shun her genitalia.

Until she turned her back. Then he became an insatiable monster, attacking her in a bestial performance that had no tenderness, no love, no sharing. It wasn't what she wanted. No amount of remonstrances or rejections or criticism deterred him until she would turn ferociously to face him and pummel him with her fists. Then he would plead for forgiveness and swear the usual promises to reform: "—inappropriate, entirely inappropriate, it was wrong, I am sorry."

"Why do you lie? Why do you continue to lie?" she always stormed.

She had told him in Seoul: "I have not always been a good or faithful wife. But I love you and want our marriage to endure. I can overlook all your faults except one. I recognize my own lust as I strive to understand your orientation. I have even allowed it occasionally. But then I feel like a victim of rape. Where is the joy and love, the mutual satisfaction? You are merely using me."

At the last minute, Captain Tomoru Tanaka had persuaded his regimental commander to delay Tanaka's departure for three more days. His position at the school had helped; also the army needed more time to clear the logjam of soldiers gathered in Sasebo.

Stragglers and last minute volunteers from Hiroshima and communities near Ujina had assembled in the Hiroshima city park before boarding Tanaka's train. As before, the city's populace sent the soldiers off to their questionable adventure with more display of waving flags and blare of martial music. The soldiers enjoyed the festive occasion, but Tanaka stayed away from the depot and dissuaded his family from going there. He wanted to spend every last minute at home with his family, having experienced the scene of farewell to troops before. How quickly people forget, he mused.

On Monday, dressed in his dark blue uniform and carrying a cardboard suitcase, he had boarded the train to travel south to the ferry landing at Shimonoseki. He had settled his affairs to the best of his ability, had given the family's meager savings to Ikura, and had borrowed as much money as possible. He had helped Ikura fill two large clay jars with rice and had persuaded a fellow professor, who owned part interest in a fishing boat, to provide the family with fresh fish, promising to settle the debt when he returned from the war.

On the first day of March the family had left their home along the Motoyasu-gawa river to visit the three hundred year-old Hiroshima-jo or Broad Island Castle. They had walked several blocks to share a picnic lunch in the Shukkei-en garden on the banks of the Kyo-bashi-gawa river.

Afterward, they crossed the city to the sea shore for a last outing until his return. The day was unseasonably warm. Delighted with the holiday, little Yukio skipped along the rocky beach, cavorting in the shallow reaches of the inland sea, gazing out at the numerous small islets to distant Shikoku island. At last, when the day had ended, the family bought a pail of Hiroshima's famed oysters to take home.

Tanaka had gone to the rail station alone after waving goodbye to Ikura and Yukio, bravely trying to appear happy before their eyes. The woman and her daughter could not hide their tears nor their sorrow, though they tried. The emotional farewell was too much for Tanaka. When they were out of sight, he ducked his head to hide the salty tears that wet his eyes.

The train ride south through southern Honshu to the straits at Shimonoseki was uneventful. Crossing the straits which separated the Sea of Japan from the Inland sea, another train carried him southwest through Kyushu to the naval base at Sasebo which lay just north of Nagasaki on the Sea of Japan.

At the railroad terminus in Sasebo, the station platform was crowded with troops pouring in from other parts of Japan. In early February, the Mikado had purposely shifted troops away from Sasebo in order to hide any hint of a military buildup. Many soldiers had been given leave to go to Tokyo or home as part of the concealment of mobilization. As an example, the Imperial Guards Division was kept idle near Hiroshima. Now the need for the charade no longer existed.

The Japanese government knew that foreign espionage agents would be attracted to the Sasebo naval base. Restrictions were increased, and foreign military attaches found themselves increasingly shut out of contact with army and navy headquarters.

Long lines of soldiers in heavy blue winter uniforms, white canvas gaiters, and high crowned hats embellished with a single metal star, crowded the raised concrete pavement on both sides of the tracks, a staging area that remained off limits even to Japanese civilians. Officers, carrying heavy swords at their sides and wearing leather puttees or spurred leather boots, quickly formed the soldiers into orderly ranks and strode down the aligned rows for a close inspection. They ordered the men to stack their rifles in upright pyramid bundles with the ends of the rifle barrels held in place with a loose loop of twine. The soldiers received more brief instructions, had their weapons inspected, and received rations before the officers marched them off to a city of tents that would provide temporary shelter before the troops boarded the transports in the harbor. Gradually squads became companies that grew into battalions and increased to regiments and finally divisions, until the full wartime strength of the Japanese First Army took shape.

Tanaka soon located his regimental colonel, and received his assignment. He learned he would command a company from Ujina and would serve in the Twelfth Division for duty in eastern Korea.

His colonel told him privately, "Keep this confidential, but we won't stay long in Korea. Just long enough to secure the southeastern areas, then we are destined for Manchuria, possibly the Yalu river border area. We'll sail for either Mosampo or Fusan on Korea's east coast."

The day of departure from Sasebo came sooner than expected. Surrounded by flanking destroyers and shepherded by two cruisers, the five troop transports lumbered northward over the rough water of the Japanese Sea.

Troops sprawled on the deck, relishing the late winter sunshine which sparkled off the water. For many it was a first time at sea and they found the experience exciting. Friendships quickly formed as groups in the same squads and platoons played games of cards and shared cigarettes and sweets. The men laughed and joked and spoke excitedly about the coming days of glory, all trying to guess their destination, and how they would kick the Russians all the way back across Siberia to the Ural Mountains. Sergeants gave daily lectures, exhorting the men to hate all Russians.

Ordered by his colonel to give further instructions in the use of their broad German-designed bayonet, Tanaka had repeated the standard drill, but had added, "The Russians are taller than you. Many are six feet. And their bayonets, though prone to snap sometimes, are two feet long. They are triangular and needle sharp. Your shorter height and shorter blades are a handicap. So you need to get in close at once to parrry their first thrust. Don't try to aim for the chest or the throat. Come in low and stab upward into their balls. Pierce their scrotum and your enemy will drop his guard or fall to his knees. Again, remember to aim low. The Russians believe the bayonet is the primary weapon, and they are good in its use. But you can be better."

Tanaka differed from his compatriots. At an earlier time in China, he had entertained the same notions now expressed by young officers in his division. Most were new to warfare. Four years ago he had gone into combat utterly unconcerned about death. He had told Rogers then that "fear of death" was unknown to the Japanese soldier, because his country's politicians and leaders had never mentioned it. Tanaka had not understood what Rogers meant by the expression and had blamed the concept on Rogers' "weak" religion.

"Why do your church people stress such an idea?" he had asked his American friend. "It is never on our minds."

Desire for glory had formerly pushed aside all thought of death for Tanaka. But subsequent exposure to combat, and the terrible death of comrades in China, had brought home to Tanaka the meaning of death. It wasn't what he wanted for himself—not with Ikura and Yukio waiting for him. So Captain Tomoru Tanaka, having plenty of time to think aboard the troop transport, determined to fight valiantly for his country, but not to sacrifice his life needlessly.

During the first night at sea, a storm gathered. The transports ploughed through rising waves covered with whitecaps. The strong winds and dropping temperatures kept most of the men in their hammocks below decks. As the storm intensified, the warm, fetid air in the cramped spaces in the hold soon forced many to go topside to line the railings with other miserable, retching soldiers. Not until the second night did the seas calm and the violent pitching of the ships' hulls subside to ease the torment of seasickness.

Tanaka found Korea a disappointment: he did not understand the language, did not like the appearance of the wretched people, and hated the thieving rascals at the port of Mosampo. And he found the countryside gloomy. The natives had stripped the hills long ago of trees for firewood. The denuded slopes made him long for the beauty of Hiroshima. Only with the warmer weather in the spring would the growth in the local rice fields emerge to bring a color of emerald green.

After a week, none too soon for him, Tanaka's division made way for arriving troops and marched overland to Seoul. In the capital city, Tanaka had acted as an interpreter for General Kuroki on an arranged visit to the palace of the Korean king, now a mere puppet on his throne. Accompanying English war correspondents had also appreciated Tanaka's skill at interpretation.

Dressed in his formal blue dress uniform, Tanaka had led the way behind the Korean Master of Ceremonies. The entourage entered a long but narrow carpeted reception room. At the far end of the room, standing on a dais raised three steps above the floor, and backed by a colorful hand painted screen, with a scene of beautiful flowers and ferns, the King and the Crown Prince waited. Off to their left, the tall, intelligent looking Chief Eunuch stood. He looked bored but alert, and appeared to be in charge of protocol.

Tanaka had told the correspondents to follow his lead. He moved behind the short, nervous Master of Ceremonies toward a long table in the center of the room. Stopping at the table, Tanaka made a low bow. Seeing the other guests follow his example, he made a signal for those behind him to go around the table in two split groups.

Thirty feet from the dais, Tanaka halted to make a second bow. Then making a final halt six feet from the King and his son, Tanaka made a third and longer obeisance to the King, and a shorter one to the Crown Prince.

The King smiled benevolently as the Master of Ceremonies, dressed in a richly decorated dark blue military uniform, gathered the cards of the westerners. He handed them to the unsmiling Chief Eunuch, who bowed and passed them to the Crown Prince.

The round-faced Crown Prince stood a head taller than his father. The royal pair and the Chief Eunuch were dressed in long flowing white robes, belted high with decorative sashes, and all wore a high, white conical hat.

Tanaka spoke to the Chief Eunuch in French and asked permission to translate in English the King's greeting. The ceremony was short, with Tanaka translating General Kuroki's Japanese greeting, the King's welcoming remarks in Korean, as passed on in French by the Chief Eunuch, and then the Eunuch's short speech in French. Watching him closely, Tanaka felt certain that official knew the English language.

After the brief ceremony, the royal pair disappeared out a side door. The guests were then served small powdered pastries with goblets of champagne, which had been placed on the long entry table.

Tanaka knew that the King was merely a figurehead, answerable to the Japanese occupation army. The Chief Eunuch had seemed overly officious and anxious to send the foreigners on their way. The press all thanked Tanaka for providing them with the opportunity to describe the royal court for their readers.

Tanaka returned to field duty, hoping his skills at the court would be appreciated enough to earn him a position at headquarters. His reluctance to face the hardships of combat had begun to bring him inner shame. But he kept thinking of Ikuro and little Yukio.

Watching the ever growing numbers of foreign correspondents arriving in Korea, Tanaka wondered if both armies might be too distracted by the journalists who were assembled to send dispatches from the front to hungry readers around the world. He was careful not to reveal that the First Army had orders to march north from Seoul to secure the Korean countryside along the way, and would finally converge on the upper end of the bay where the Yalu river emptied into the sea. Somewhere at the river, he was sure his division would try to outflank the enemy regiments farther upstream, especially near the confluence of the Yalu and Ai-ho rivers. Other following Japanese divisions would secure the lower reaches of the Yalu.

How the First Army planned to cross the Yalu was anyone's guess. Tanaka knew it would be a hazardous operation against the entrenched enemy. Thanks to one of Japan's secret agents, the First Army commander knew of the Russian concentration south of Mukden, and what it would take to smash through enemy defenses in order to seize vital roads and the rail line inland from the proposed landing across the Yalu.

Farther north in Korea, a small black dot struggled up the steep incline, moving slowly, leaving a trail of deep leg holes in the snow. The late season storm, which had persisted for three days, had dumped so much snow that the sides of the mountain and the flat valley below were an unblemished while mantle, solid in color except for an occasional outcropping of dark granite rock or an isolated clump of green conifer trees. The mountain, the valley, and the leaden sky shared an unbroken white expanse that seemed lost in time. Only the double line of track holes spoiled the spell of a beautiful painting of nature.

Several pairs of predator eyes on the valley plain looked up at the tracks. Steam rose from furry nostrils. A muzzle pointed skyward as the lead wolf howled. Others in the pack slowly followed the path of the dotted footmarks that moved upward from the valley floor.

A curtain of snow moved in from the east and began to blot out the tracks as the storm resumed from the previous day. The moving object disappeared from sight into a world of white on white, but the wolf pack easily picked up the spoor and followed silently.

Alesandrov breathed heavily and painfully. The deep wet snow clung to his legs, making climbing an agonizing effort. With each step he sank to his knees, laboriously pulling each leg free to take another step. Every breath brought a stab of pain to his injured ribs. Climbing the mountain had been sheer torture, made worse by the wind and the deep snow of the recurring storm. With the rising wind, snowflakes that had floated down like confetti, now bombarded him furiously.

He looked at the darkening sky. The afternoon was fleeting. He could not risk being caught in the open; he must find shelter before the evening shadows descended. Already tormenting frostbite had marred segments of his nose and ears and hands. Skin had peeled off his raw lips. Fatigue tempted him to lie down in the snow. If only he could rest for a time. But he dared not tarry, knowing sleep would overcome his senses and leave him frozen on the mountainside. Falling to his knees, he closed his eyes and slowly counted to ten. At the final count, struggling to catch his breath, his eyes opened to a blurred vision. Was he going snow-blind?

Far below in the valley, a Siberian tiger crouched silently in the shadow of the patch of trees at the foot of the mountain, also watching the slow progress of the traveler.

Alesandrov refused an impulse to give up. He forced himself to stand erect and resume his climb. The sudden unseasonable storm of the past few days had caught him woefully unprepared, and the tiger attack had narrowed his choices. Wet, cold and hungry and without matches, he had shunned the few shelters of trees and had looked instead for an outcropping of rock that he might use as a shield from the wind. His strength had evaporated. Further climbing for the remainder of the afternoon was impossible.

He began rolling snowballs into large round clumps of snow that he could barely lift but managed to place in a circular pattern on a flat and more level piece of ground at the base of a large rock. Gradually he placed a second ring of snow clumps slightly inward on top of the first ring until succeeding rings formed an inverted cone, built to the height of four feet. Dizzy from the labor and gasping with relief, he carefully closed the conical top of the structure with one last clump of snow.

After a short rest to catch his breath, he pushed a hole through the base of the shelter and crawled into the interior. Only partially closing off the crawl hole to leave an air passage, he was immediatly delighted at the warmth his body heat imparted to the enclosed room. It reminded him of the many similar snow houses he had built as a boy in Russia. Now he hoped that an overnight stay in this structure could save him from perishing during the night.

For a long time he sat in the small space, knees pulled up, head and arms resting on his knees. Several times he dozed off. He wondered if he dared to lie down in a more comfortable position. While shifting his weight, he discovered his revolver was missing. At first panicky, he decided to emerge from the shelter to look for the weapon. He found it just outside the entry hole, half covered with snow. Without thinking, he reached for the barrel, realizing too late that the skin of his hand was frozen to the metal. Unable to free his hand, he crawled back into the snow house. Breathless from the effort, he bunched more snow with his feet to close the hole. Then he placed the grip of the gun between his knees and waited in vain for his hand to pull free.

Drifting in and out of consciousness, Alesandrov emerged from a dream-like stupor, aware of a movement outside the shelter. He strained to listen, shaking his head in disbelief at his stupidity. The weapon, still glued to his hand, must have been pushed from his belt when he had first crawled inside. More shuffling movements outside caused him to tense. *Was it a low whimper he heard? There it was again!*

He snapped fully awake, sitting in the darkness, holding his breath to listen to the muffled sound outside, followed by a whining kind of growl and a scratching noise. Gritting his teeth, he clamped his knees tighter on the pistol grip and ripped his hand free, leaving much of the skin of his fingers and palm stuck to the barrel. Hurriedly, he picked up the gun by its walnut grip and tucked it into the warmth of his crotch. Plunging the injured hand into the snow, he was gratified to see the bleeding stop, although the fierce pain persisted.

His stiffened fingers of the other hand reached for the leather handle of the knife in his belt. He heard the low angry growl again. Then the partially blocked entry hole suddenly expanded inward. The plug of snow was followed by two furry feet and a snout pushing through the small icy entrance. Sharp, bared fangs of a grey wolf squirmed into view, the jaws snapping the air ferociously, red eyes glaring. The head of the maddened animal cleared the hole. Alesandrov scurried to rise to his knees, cursing as his gun dropped to the ground. He could not find it in the faint light. Using his left hand to pull the knife from its belt scabbard, he lashed out with the blade, slashing the animal across the nose. The wolf broke the silence of the night with frenzied howls, still lunging to push inside. Alesandrov slashed again, this time across the wolf's eyes. Wild with fear, he slashed again and again. Yelping with high-pitched shrieks of pain, the bloodied head pulled back. At once a tremendous ruckus outside rent the night air. The wolves were fighting. He could not see the scene of viscious snarling turmoil, but guessed the starving wolf pack had set upon their blinded companion, tearing him apart at the sight and scent of blood.

The cries and frenzied noise gradually faded. For the rest of the night he dozed off and on in spells. No further intrusion came and the darkness finally ended.

At daybreak, Alesandrov cautiously crept from the shelter of the snow house. The revolver was safely tucked into an inside pocket, warmed by his body. The snow had stopped. He looked around at the red smears and scattered tracks in the snow. The slaughtered wolf and the pack were nowhere in sight. As far as he could see in looking out over the white expanse, nothing but an endless field of packed snow came into view.

He hoped and prayed that the low mountain would be the last barrier he would have to cross. With no food and only snow to drink, he knew his strength could not last. He resolved to push on, but a nagging fear gripped his gut. What if he had misjudged the distance and direction? What if he was far from the border? How many more nights could he survive?

All day he toiled up the mountainside, pausing many times to catch his breath, but always forcing himself to press on. He could no longer afford the luxury of resting too long or sleeping at night. He had to continue on at the risk of collapsing unconscious in the snow.

Late in the afternoon, he finally cleared the crest of the mountain. Far away to the west, spread below him, he saw a wide ribbon of water snaking through a barren land of low, undulating brown hills. The day was too far gone for him to get off the western slope in daylight. But he resolved to keep moving if it took all night. Surely, he reasoned, the air would be warmer near the western river, because much of the shrubless and treeless river plain below showed only scattered patches of snow. Ugly though it was, the barren landscape offered renewed hope. Looking behind one last time at the frozen side of the mountain he had just climbed, he broke away from the icy wind blowing in off the distant eastern sea and started his western descent.

When Alesandrov at last came off the mountain to reach the Yalu, he quickly became aware of the width of the river, its frigid water and fast current. He stood on the shore, measuring the distance from the Korean mainland to the nearest island, and from that island to the next island. He faced three long, low islands cut from the river channel. The icy cold water was fairly shallow near the shore. He wondered if he had the stamina to swim across the river from island to island? Breaking the winter ice to

The swim across the Yalu River

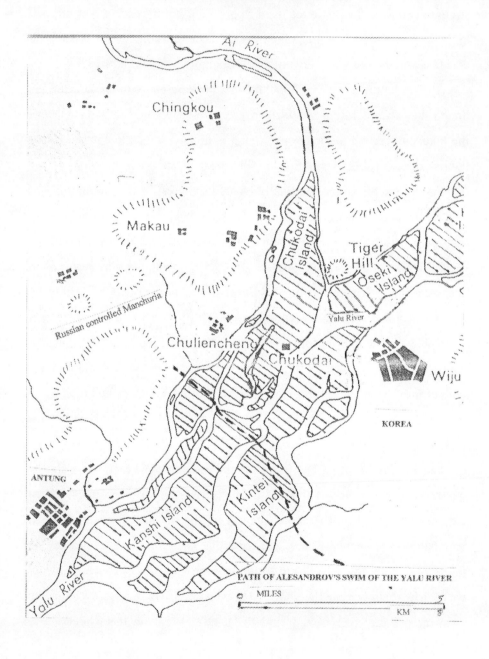

swim with other daring youths in Moscow's Neva river had been one thing. Braving the snow runoff of a siberian river in his enfeebled state was chancey at best.

Once across, surely he would find a Russian outpost or a calvalry patrol this close to the border. Making a decision, he rolled his padded greatcoat into a tight bundle, tied it on both ends and fastened it to his back, hoping it would act as a flotation aid.

He slowly waded far out into the water until he stood chest deep. Deciding he could withstand the water temperature, he braced himself, then struck out for the nearest island. The shock of the artic water made him dizzy and aware of how weak he really was. The current began to carry him downriver faster. Should he have gone farther up the river to allow for his drift in the current? Winded, cold, and desperate, he resisted an impulse to tread water and rest. He feared being swept past the island and struggled on, denying defeat. He kept moving. At the moment when he had almost surrendered in his despair of reaching land, his feet touched bottom and he waded ashore.

He crawled into the shelter of the low brush, gasping for breath, shaking violently from the cold, knowing he must press on. Reluctantly, he rose to his feet and stumbled across the narrow island. The effort helped warm his body slightly. Panting from the walk northward to the waist of the island, he again entered the icy river, shuddering from the cruel shock, and began swimming in deeper water to the middle and larger island. This time, his resolve to succeed made his crossing seem shorter, though no less painful.

He had to rest. He lay exhausted in the brush of the second island near the northern tip where the current had carried him, and closed his eyes to blot out reality. He lay longer than before until his breathing became less labored. Another island conquered and one more to go!

Alesandrov started to rise to his feet when he heard loud shouts and the splashing of water. He kept low and looked back at the river. Nothing. Then he looked farther upriver to see a small Japanese cavalry patrol splashing ashore on the island. Had they seen him? The twenty riders, wearing winter caps with ear flaps and swathed in fur-lined greatcoats, splashed ashore, making no effort to muffle their noise. Alesandrov suspected they were on a scouting foray of some sort. He watched as the patrol moved inland and wished he had gone farther south on the island. It was too late. But since the Japanese had not dispersed to search for him, he crawled farther from the shoreline and continued to lay prone in the low brush, guessing he was not an object of hunt.

Desperate to get warm, he began to scoop out a shallow basin in the sand. To hell with the patrol. He removed and unrolled the long greatcoat and was surprised to find it relatively dry.

A few minutes later, hearing no hoofbeats, he rose to peer ahead to his right. The patrol had crossed the island and the riders were already in the river swimming their mounts to the third island. He crouched in the brush and watched the riders move about the other island, sticking short pegs of wood with colored ribbons into the ground. Now he knew. It was a survey patrol placing markers for what he guessed would be future gun emplacements. So Japan was about to invade Manchuria!

He could go no farther; he had to rest. Swathed in his greatcoat, he huddled in the shallow depression. An hour later, he heard the hoofbeats of the returning Japanese cavalry clatter close by. As soon as the patrol was out of sight on the Korean mainland, Alesandrov rose to his knees and dug deeper into the sand for his makeshift shelter.

Shielded from the wind, he drifted in and out of a dream-like state as the hours passed. He thought of Marina, the comfort of her boudoir, their long conversations together. An image of flirtatious little Yin-lin came to mind. Should he have initiated her in the art of love? He thought how warm and tempting her body would be now, snuggled close to his freezing body.

He supposed that Lydia and her husband had fled from Seoul by this time. He'd like to kick Fairborne's butt for not satisfying his wife. But then who could keep up with that English woman? And what about Ellis Rogers? Had he ever arrived in Port Arthur? Was he still there? He hoped that Marina had welcomed Rogers. He was sure she had. Certainly, Rogers would be attracted to Marina. He suspected that his friend was tremendously attracted to asian women. He remembered how admiringly Rogers had looked at Xi in Peking.

Ah, passionate Xi! Guilt about his abandonment of her still troubled his thoughts. But what could he do? His career would have been terminated if he had stayed longer with her. What had to be done was done. He remembered the fate of a fellow officer at the military academy who had been cashiered for consorting with a gypsy—a beautiful cafe dancer, but still a gypsy. Painful? Yes. But Alesandrov resolved not to dwell on the unhappy ending of his own association. Life was too short. The good memory of loving Xi would stay with him forever.

And when he had come back to the Orient after his tumultuous life in St Petersburg, he had gone from the whores of Vladivostok to the arms of Marina. He wished he could establish a more permanent bond with Marina. That simply was not his nature. Marina had accepted him as he was, had not pressured him into a commitment, had been a wonderful lover, one of the best. He wondered if their relationship would always be so rewarding. Would he ever lose that restless urge to explore new frontiers of love, to seek other women; would he ever change?

If he could reach Russian lines, he resolved to send a message at once to Rogers in Port Arthur.

Late in the afternoon, rested, but still chilled to the bone, he walked across the island and began swimming to the third island. The icy water and his effort to survive were sheer agony. He walked across the island, through the trail of marker sticks to the far shore and struck out for the mainland. The distance from the island to the mainland was closer, so he made his last swim, pressing on in the belief that he was closing the long chapter on the nightmare journey from Panmunjon.

Twilight had approached when he saw riders swooping off the Manchurian hill on the mainland. He stopped and slumped resignedly, too weary and numb and stiff to run. His eyes blurred. Were they Hunhutse guerillas? He groped for his revolver.

Nearing the lone figure, the riders pulled up short.

Black Legs!

Alesandrov shouted the name a second time in Russian. The Chinese term for booted Russian soldiers expressed his relief. He made the sign of a cross and waved.

The Russian patrol stared in disbelief at the ragged figure waving at them and shouting in recognition of their insignia, "Fifth Siberian Rifles! Captain Alesandrov of the Don Cossacks."

The patrol lealder scowled momentarily, then chortled in disbelief and saluted. He leaned forward from the saddle and extended his hand. "I know you sir. We were together in the China Relief Expedition. You have lost a lot of weight. Didn' t recognize you with that beard. What in hell are you doing out here in the middle of nowhere? Doing a solitary patrol for the Czar?"

He stopped laughing and ordered the patrol to dismount to aid Alesandrov who had pitched forward face down in total collapse.

CHAPTER NINE

Von Streich's superiors, noting his dalliance with the English naval commander's wife, promptly ordered the Austrian officer to report to the headquarters of Japan's Fourth Army, which was assembling for embarkation to the mouth of the Yalu river in Korea. His orders introduced him as an accredited neutral military observer assigned to represent the Austro-Hungarian Empire.

Lydia soon grew restless in Tokyo. The capital was on a wartime footing with austerity measures in force. She did not want to stay in a city that was no longer as much fun. Longing for Alesandrov and lonely in the absence of von Streich, Lydia resolved to go to Sasebo to contact her husband. Either he could find her more comfortable quarters, or, perhaps, she could socialize with the wives of other English naval observers. Or she might even discover what the Japanese army planned, and be able to pass it on in some way to Port Arthur. *Damn the Japs!*

In Sasebo, after finding a scarce hotel room, Lydia learned that Nigel had mistakenly traveled to Seoul to see her. Their paths had crossed. Disappointed, she sent a message to the Seoul consulate and to the British embassy in Tokyo to inform her husband what hotel room she had engaged in Sasebo, telling him she would wait for his return.

Commander Fairborne, however, was delayed in Tokyo by the British Embassy, which wanted to debrief him thoroughly on Admiral Togo and the performance of the Japanese navy. The British Admiralty needed particular details that the Japanese Naval Office seemed increasingly reluctant to divulge. Except for its assigned naval observers, the Admiralty had begun to notice a growing reticence by Japanese admirals to be completely open about certain tactics, and equipment performance.

Lydia soon met a remarkably handsome Japanese naval captain who was assigned to shore duty. He was short, but his round, smooth, comely visage interested her. In a display of international hospitality, the captain offered to squire Lydia to certain social functions. She had acceded, not fully realizing the extent of Captain Keizo Okazaka's persistent devotion. Lydia found his school-boyish attention flattering and his ill-concealed lust amusing.

When he drank too much, she let him touch her, believing she could control his raging hormones, if he went too far. She tolerated his enamoration of her neck. She had heard that many Japanese men considered the feminine neck the prime object of beauty. The nape of Lydia's neck seemed to set Okazaka off. He lifted her hair to stare at her neck with undisguised admiration, murmuring words of praise, and stroking and brushing her neck with light, adoring kisses. Lydia was surprised—men usually sought to touch her breasts. Not Okazaka. He wanted her neck and he also wanted her feet. He begged to suck her toes, and when she agreed, she could sense his jerking climax.

Matching his intake of sake one night, she learned how easily he could become inebriated. Like most orientals, he had a low tolerance for alcohol. She served his sake warm in the Japanese fashion, but liked her own glass iced, a preference that horrified him. Aroused by this time, she loosened her blouse to lay bare the full display of her neck and shoulders. He ignored the accessibility of her ample breasts and went after the back of her neck, slavering like a puppy on a bone. When she finally pushed him away, he asked her to sit in a chair and remove her shoes and stockings. Sitting on the floor before her, with his eyes closed in rapture, he sucked on her toes.

After the third such encounter, impatient for her own needs, Lydia got up from the chair and removed her clothing. She lay on the bed and beckoned to him. He lay with her, fully clothed, except for his shoes, which he had removed at the door. He still wanted her feet, concentrating on her largest toe like a baby at a nipple. She finally got him to disrobe. He had a trim, pleasant body, although smaller than she liked. When she insisted on action, his performance too quickly terminated, much to her disappointment. Then, he resumed his attention to her feet and neck.

In ensuing days, Lydia began to discourage his slavish devotion, but Keizo Okazaka persisted. It was after attending a performance at a local theater, and back in the privacy of her room, that she learned about Captain Crown. She also learned about *shimose*. Captain Okazaka, hungry for her neck and toes, began to talk.

He related the story of Captain Crown while boasting about the prowess of the Japanese navy as well as his own important duties.

Crown, it appeared, was an old Etonian serving in the Czar's navy. He had been menaced in the Yellow Sea by an enemy cruiser, following Japan's Sunday night sneak attack on Port Arthur. Eluding the enemy warcraft, Crown had taken the Russian gunboat *Manjour* into Shanghai harbor. The Japanese task force, headed by the cruiser *Akitsushima*, lay in wait outside the harbor. When the Chinese government did not impound the *Manjour*, the Japanese cruiser threatened to come into the harbor after Crown. The Englishman stalled and bluffed for a considerable time, but the Chinese eventually invoked international law and neutralized the gunboat, repatriating the crew to Russia.

Except Crown.

Disguised as a British journalist, Crown brazenly boarded a merchant ship sailing for Sasebo. Japanese intelligence eventually caught up with

Crown, but seemed unsure about his true status. Was he an enemy ship captain or a neutral English national? Should he be imprisoned or treated as a war journalist?

Listening to the story, Lydia had a sudden thought. "Where is Crown now?" she asked.

"Residing in this very hotel," Okazaka answered. "The man is such a smooth rogue, even the English authorities are unsure how to handle him. We think he is a spy and we are watching him closely. Please be aware that he is more or less my responsibility, while he is in Sasebo."

Lydia raised her eyebrows. *So that was why Okazaka could be at the hotel so often!*

She interrupted Okazaka's love feast. When he came up for air, she asked him how it was possible for Togo's ships to fire into Port Arthur so accurately from a distance of nine miles offshore. "My husband could never tell me," she murmured.

"*Shimose*," he grunted. His eyes were glazed from the sake.

"What is that?"

Okazaka was beginning to fade. His words became slurred. She shook him. "Don't go to sleep. I want you to talk to me. Tell me about *shimose*."

He mumbled his explanation that *shimose* was the new secret Japanese gunpowder that so effectively increased the velocity of navy shells to enable the Mikado's navy to outrange the Russian guns.

"What does it look like? I'd like to see some. Bring me some tomorrow and I will let you stay for the night."

He promised.

* * * * * * * * *

Crown continued to enjoy his freedom. Though access to the naval base remained denied, he wandered freely about the streets of the town. He had glimpsed Lydia and made it a point to meet her. At their first afternoon tiffin, they shared tea and cakes.

"My husband will be here soon," she told him. "It is probably best that you not meet him, since he is with the Japanese navy. And it is best that we not share company too often."

Crown was quickly learning her true sympathies.

Okazaka had failed to bring her the powder sample as promised. So Lydia denied him her presence that next day. And the day after that. By the fourth day, the Japanese officer was desperate. "Why do you want the *shimose*?" he whined.

"I am gathering souvenirs. The war will be over some day and I want something to remember the glorious achievments of your navy. I have given you a souvenir, now reward me with a small bag."

"I must see you tonight?" he implored.

"Bring my present and we shall see."

Lydia received a one pound bag of the powder and endured Okazaka's fawning attention for one hour, then contrived to send him away.

She passed Crown's breakfast table the next morning and whispered to him not to join her. They sat apart in the dining room. When it was possible to do so, she caught his eye and nodded toward Okazaka's agent across the room. Crown gave her a look that indicated he understood.

When she finished eating, Lydia stood with her back to the Japanese agent. Blocking his view of her table, she deposited a small piece of paper under her tea saucer. Aware that Crown understood that the paper was meant for his eyes, she left the dining room. Before the waiter could clear the dishes, Crown rose and approached her table. Also blocking the view of the table, Crown deftly retrieved the note. Then he sat in Lydia's chair, faced the Japanese agent and stared insolently at the man until the uncomfortable agent stood up and made his exit.

Crown read Lydia's message: **Tonight at seven.**

That evening Crown went deliberately to a nearby restaurant for dinner. Lydia had the hotel staff send up her evening meal. At seven o'clock, a light knock prompted Lydia to open her door to Crown, who slid quickly into the room.

They sat together and reminisced about England for a pleasant length of time. While enjoying a glass of sherry, Crown advised her that he expected to be arrested and deported soon. "It is only a question of time," he said.

"Could you as a friend do a favor for me?" she asked. She told him about the bag of *shimose* and asked if he could take it with him, if he was deported.

"Of course," he agreed.

At nine o'clock, growing more relaxed and comfortable with each other, both were interrupted by the loud and repeated knocking on the door. Lydia motioned for Crown to stand behind the door as she cracked it open.

Captain Okazaka stood before her with an angry expression. "I need to see you at once."

Lydia stood her ground. "You cannot come in. It is late. I don't want to see you tonight."

"The Japanese officer insisted. "I must come in. I have something to tell you. It is about that Crown fellow." Okazaka had obviously been drinking.

Lydia flushed with anger. "It is late. I have told you no. Now go away."

Okazaka persisted. "Your husband's ship will arrive here day after tomorrow. What about our friendship? Do not deny me."

"If you are referring to what we have done together, take that up with Commander Fairborne. Now goodnight." She slammed the door shut.

Crown looked at her with a smirk on his face. He pursed his lips and squinted, then doubled over in silent laughter. Recovering, he held a finger to his lips, then stepped forward to embrace her.

"You are a wildcat," he whispered.

She liked the strong comfort of his arms. Feeling vulnerable, she nestled in his arms. In a moment they kissed. Crown was a large man and good looking in a rugged, outdoor way.

"We are undoubtedly being watched," he whispered. "In a few minutes, open the door to see if your Japanese friend has left. I don't want my presence to get you in trouble."

She understood and opened the door slightly to peer out. Okazaka was gone, but his resident agent lingered at the head of the stairs at the far end of the hallway.

Crown told her it was best he return to his room, but that he wanted to see her the next day. She nodded her agreement. "Wait here," she said. Leaving her door ajar, she walked down the hall toward the agent.

"Where is Captain Okazaka?" she asked.

The man looked at her with a blank expression, as if he did not understand English. Lydia pushed her way between him and the top of the stairs. With her back turned to the agent, she pulled a water glass from the pocket of her robe and let it fall down the stairs. The agent heard the thumping noise of the rolling glass and glimpsed a blank slip of paper. He glared at Lydia, then ran down the stairs to retrieve the glass.

Lydia turned to beckon to Crown, who scurried down the hall to his room. He blew a kiss to Lydia before closing his door.

Crown was arrested by naval intelligence agents pounding on his door early in the morning. He dressed, locked his door, and followed his escort to naval headquarters. His hearing took up most of the morning. By noon, his interrogators were so exasperated by his waffling and derisive sarcasm that they voted unanimously to expel him immediately from Japan. They ordered him to return to the hotel and prepare to board a departing steamer the next morning. Crown guessed the ship to be the same one scheduled to arrive with Lydia Fairborne's husband.

Okazaka sulked all day, tried to see Lydia that afternoon and again early in the evening, to no avail.

Lydia had thought about Crown all day. His presence had delighted her. She tried to think of a way to see him, but she knew she had to be cautious.

Crown sent her a sealed note late in the afternoon, saying he had to leave the next day. She resigned herself to never seeing him again and prepared to retire for the night. She had just removed her robe, donned a light nightgown and was getting into bed, when she heard a familiar tap on her door. It was Crown.

"What about the agent?" she asked, as Crown entered the room.

"I came from the water closet to find him loitering outside my door again, so I ran him down the stairs. He thought I might hit him." Crown pulled her against his body, marveling at her soft, warm femininity. "It has been so long since I was this close to a real woman," he told her.

With her loins warming to his touch, she threw her arms around his neck and kissed him hungrily. Crown impulsively lifted her upward. She wrapped her legs about his waist as he pushed up her night dress. The union was quickly and easily joined. Lydia laughed recklessly.

"What is that old saying—hoisted on one's own petard?"

The Japanese navy deposited Captain Crown aboard the departing German freighter with instructions for the skipper to carry Crown to Russian-held Newchwang, Manchuria. After disembarking at that port, Crown quickly boarded the train for nearby Port Arthur, but not before giving the bag of *shimose* to Russian intelligence for chemical evaluation in Russia.

Crown also brought important news to Admiral Makharoff in Port Arthur. He had not wasted his time in Sasebo. His daily walks about the town had given him access to porters, barbers, draymen, house servants and gossiping shipyard workers. The gleaning of information from Sasebo's streets had provided valuable details about Togo's proposed second blockship expedition.

With this information, Makharoff ordered a round-the-clock alert and beefed up the naval patrols outside the harbor. Knowing the Japanese penchant for midnight strikes, he ordered the destroyer *Silny* to follow a consistent criss-cross path at the mouth of the channel.

The admiral showed his gratitude by offering Crown a position on his staff.

* * * * * * * * * *

English journalist Philip Esley had leaked information to Ariko, and thence to Tokyo, about the failure of the blockships to close the entrance into the inner harbor. Togo's temper had flared at the information and had caused him to lash out at everyone. Togo did not take defeat lightly, especially when the politicians in Tokyo clamored for victories. The one great fear in Japanese military and naval circles was the possibility that the Russian fleet could break out of Port Arthur and go on a rampage against Japanese coastal cities, or, worse yet, upset Japan's plans for invasion of Manchuria by destroying troop transport convoys headed for Chemulpo and the Yalu river. If the Russian fleet would not come out to fight, the Japanese had to formulate another plan to bottle up the enemy fleet before reinforcements arrived from Vladivostok or from Europe.

A hurried conference with the blockship architect, Commander Arima Ryokitsu, convinced Togo that the blockship idea was still a sound manuever that merited a second chance. But there would be a few changes. Ryokitsu would lead the blockships in person. Larger, newer and faster steamers would be used as blockships, and this time the blockships would make a fast frontal charge directly into the harbor, instead of creeping around the Liaotishan cliffs. The same officers, but different crews, would man the steamers.

Four very serviceable civilian ships were gathered and brought to Sasebo where they were heavily loaded with stone ballast and sacks of cement. As before, the Japanese placed dynamite sticks in the depths of the holds, to be detonated by electric current.

General Stoessel's order preventing blockade runners from entering Port Arthur had also been disobeyed. A few German, British, and Chinese vessels continued to run the gauntlet of Togo's fleet and slip through to unload needed commodities. Occasionally, the Japanese succeeded in halting a blockade runner. European neutral ships were then subjected to a stern lecture and had their cargoes confiscated, but received no further punishment.

News came in and news went out from the port, and the local newspaper Novy Kry found an avid audience. Makharoff, the new base admiral, had arrived on March 10 and had made his presence immediately felt. Considered to be Russia's best and most innovative naval leader, the admiral had come from Russia's giant naval base at Kronstadt, had seen at once the problem in Port Arthur, and had rushed to correct the situation. Local training of the seamen had been vastly increased, incompetent admirals transferred, discipline tightened, and morale bolstered. Makharoff did not ask anyone to do that which he did not himself attempt. A man of science, he had been an artic explorer, had pioneered the naval ice breaker, and had established a formidable reputation in international naval circles. Even Togo had Makharoff's book aboard the Japanese flagship.

* * * * * * * * *

Unable to sleep, Rogers swung his feet out of bed at three in the morning. Restless and wide awake, he slipped on his shirt and trousers and a coat and wandered out onto Marina's upper story veranda. The night air was chilly, but less so than when he had arrived in Port Arthur over six weeks earlier. In a fortnight or more, the weather would start to warm slightly with the approach of spring. Maybe that was why he felt the restless need to do something. An early touch of spring fever, perhaps? Or was it his promotion?

Chen had delivered an official letter from Uncle Steve informing Rogers that he should pin on the set of the double bars of a captain that were attached to the letter. He suspected that the hasty raise in rank was possibly to make him more acceptable to the Russian staff officers in his capacity of a foreign army observer. Along with new orders, he now sought a way to absorb knowledge without arousing suspicions of espionage.

His stay with Marina had been most pleasant, but a nagging worry that he had failed to perform his mission adequately still troubled him. Being bottled up in the port by the Japanese fleet, which continued to parade daily up and down the coast, made Rogers yearn to break the stalemate, anything to make himself feel more useful.

Rogers also wanted to find out what had happened to Viktor Alesandrov. There had to be an answer to his friend's disappearance. Marina was more worried than she let on. He preferred to go south to a warmer climate, to be with An-an, to escape a war that he knew inwardly was going to be as ugly as any the world had ever seen. But he was on a mission, and he needed Alesandrov's help. Rogers sometimes wondered if it was loneliness that bothered him? *Or the presence of Marina?*

The bombproof had worked well. Short of a direct hit by Japan's largest naval shell, Marina and her household should be safe in the shelter. Others had seen his work and had begun to copy, ignoring General Stoessel's stupid directive that forbade such structures.

Normal life had continued in Port Arthur. The large and slightly unfinished hotel in the town had been converted into a hospital. The restaurants were crowded. Although the circus had ceased performing, General Stoessel had arranged some nightly orchestra concerts for the upper class. In order to prevent Russian sailors from imbibing too much of the bad Chinese vodka, he had converted a second Chinese establishment into a tea house.

Rogers' thoughts were interrupted when he heard someone open the windowed door to the veranda. Turning, he saw Marina, dressed in a warm robe, stepping into the night air. "I could not sleep," she said. "The night is ominous, as if something tragic is about to happen."

"It is very chilly out here," he told her. "Are you warm enough?" She replied in the affirmative.

She stood beside him, looking out over the town and the port. Few lights shown in the town, as ordered and enforced by Colonel Petrusha, the provost. The base was completely darkened, with no active searchlights. An uneasy hush hung over everything, but both knew that sentries faced the sea and stood alert.

"It is so quiet, almost peaceful," she murmured. She drew nearer, almost touching him. He could feel her warmth and envisioned the shape of the beguiling body that so intrigued him. A troubling ache gripped his groin.

"What is the date today, Marina? I am beginning to lose track of time."

"March 27," she answered. "It is late, almost half past three in the morning. Perhaps you should go back to bed."

He sighed and shook his head. "I've had too much rest already with so much inactivity."

He knew the tide was ebbing. Although Makharoff had increased naval coordination so that the entire Russian fleet could pass out of the narrow harbor channel in a record time of less than three hours, the twenty-foot tide, at its lowest point, kept the heavy battleships immobilized. And he knew that such knowledge was shared by the Japanese.

"Marina, I should be thinking about moving on. If I can take the train north to Mukden, I might be able to learn something about Viktor. Between Chen and me, some news might turn up. I owe it to you to at least look into his disappearance."

"I don't want you to leave." The determined firmness of her statement surprised him.

"Don't you worry about him?" Immediately he regretted his words.

"Of course I do." She looked hurt. "But I need you here to help me. Please. If Viktor is all right, he will surface somewhere. I am also seeking news. I know Viktor. He will let us know, when he can. We must be patient and hopeful."

"I know Viktor too. He is a fighter and survivor. But he is long overdue."

"Please stay," she pleaded. "I need your support and your strength. It is not that women are weak, but women need someone close by. It is lonely now that Stoessel has canceled so many social affairs. If you go, the house will be empty. I will miss you and be most unhappy."

He remained silent. She placed a hand over his. "Don't you long for company?" she asked.

She wondered if he had someone, a woman somewhere that he was faithful to. Surely he must find her, Marina, desirable. Why was he always so distant? She turned to face him.

"Ellis, I know that Viktor is not faithful, that he is not always loyal to me. I know about some of the others. He will never be satisfied with only one woman."

"Viktor is my friend," he said quietly. "I owe him."

She asked bluntly, "Do you have someone?"

He chose not to answer and stirred uncomfortably.

"Do you not get lonely?" she persisted.

"Marina, before you say any more—". His words were interrupted by the roar of cannon firing from the fort at the foot of Electric Hill.

* * * * * * * * *

The four Japanese blockship steamers, with escorting destroyers, had departed from the Elliots late at night on March 26. A light mist hung over the calm seas. At 2:30 AM all but two of the escorting destroyers had dropped away, leaving the blockships to proceed on ahead. One hour later, two miles out from the mainland, the blockships, steaming along in single file, were spotted by the signal station on Electric Hill. The fort opened fire at once.

The blockships continued on undaunted in the face of the cannonading until a Russian patrol ship, the destroyer *Silny,* charged toward the lead blockship. The *Chiyo Maru* inexcusably forgot its mission and swerved to ram the destroyer, just as the *Silny* torpedoed her. Blinded by searchlights and exploding shells, the other three blockships followed earlier instructions and turned with the crippled and sinking *Chiyo Maru.* With two officers dead, the second blockship detonated its dynamite charges and sank alongside the *Chiyo Maru.* The third blockship executed the same scuttling manuever. The fourth and last blockship took a torpedo hit just as its dynamite charges were about to be detonated. Lieutenant Sato and his dreams of glory vanished forever in a huge ball of fire.

Both of the escorting Japanese destroyers, arriving to rescue the blockship crews, fired on the *Silny,* crippling it with one torpedo.

But because of the the *Silny's* intervention, Togo's second blockship expedition had failed to close the harbor. Russian warships could still pass in and out of the harbor channel.

Fascinated by the scene, Rogers and Marina had watched the battle from the veranda. Then the firestorm had ended, the probing searchlight beams stopped sweeping in all directions, and the lights of the naval base and town began to dim. He took Marina's hand and led her inside.

"Goodnight, Marina." She kissed his cheek, then threw her arms about him and clung to him fiercely. It was all he could do to keep his hands off her. *What would Viktor think if he saw us?* Finally she released her hold and walked alone to her room.

CHAPTER TEN

Sylvia Levinski boarded the Trans-Siberian train early in March. To the annoyance of the baggage master, she transported three valises and two large and heavy steamer trunks. The baggage handlers attempted to protest the extent of her luggage, but were silenced by her intimidating refusal to explain her possessions, and by the way she dropped certain well known names in a threatening manner. Baggage space was tight because of the rush of goods to the war front. That did not deter Levinski. She warned the baggage handlers to exert special care, threatening them if any of her precious china and "perfume" bottles broke. The handlers did not remember small bottles of perfume giving off that kind of glassy clink. But they dared not argue too much even though they were curious about a woman going to a war zone with so many feminine articles.

Sylvia Levinski did not have the semitic thin lips, wide mouth, and aquiline nose of her paternal forbears. Actually, she was a rather handsome woman, if one could discount her perpetual grim look. She seldom smiled. If she had, she would have attracted a host of interested men. With her dark curly hair and exceedingly trim body, many men accepted her unsmiling manner as a challenge. Her well proportioned body usually drew admiring glances. She was not interested in using her body as a weapon or a pawn. Men held little interest for her. With the exception of her father's memory, which she revered, all other men represented a troubling threat. So Sylvia was constantly on her guard, although she could read men like a book and could easily turn on her charm as a weapon.

During the long, cold journey across the Ural mountains, she kept to herself, discouraging the conversation and company of fellow passengers.

She had demanded and had paid for both the top and bottom berths in her compartment, insisting she wanted no disturbances around her.

The train carried mainly troops and ordnance for the Manchurian theater of battle. Only two cars had been designated for civilian passengers on the outbound train. On the return journey from Siberia to Russia, the train would be less crowded with military personnel, except for the wounded in the Red Cross coaches, and would carry mostly civilians fleeing Port Arthur and the lower Liaotung peninsula.

The unfriendly aloofness of the woman caused resentment and rude staring, even among the other four female passengers. A couple of annoyed army officers, who had tried unsuccessfully to impose their presence upon her, bribed the conductor for information. The bribe produced only her name and home city of St Petersburg, all that he could glean.

One of the officers remarked, "Who does this woman think she is with her uppity airs?"

His companion agreed. "And why does she end her name with an i instead of a y? Is she Polish?"

The first long leg of the uncomfortable train ride across Siberia ended at the western shore of Lake Baikal. The lake, though frozen over solidly, did not have ice thick or strong enough to support the train safely. Efforts were currently underway to construct an extension of the line a short distance south of the lakeshore. Until the project was finished, the warm weather passengers had to disembark from the train and journey overland by wagon along the southern shore of the 100-mile long lake, the world's largest body of fresh water, to the terminus of the eastward line. Boarding another waiting train, the passengers could then resume the journey. It was the luck of Sylvia's fellow passengers that the ice was still strong enough to permit long lines of horse-drawn carts and sleighs to carry everyone across the surface of the long lake. During the arduous winter sleigh ride across the ice, Levinski had continued to act oblivious of her fellow pasengers.

The three-week train ride from St Petersburg had at last ended at Harbin, Manchuria. The city, capital of Russian Manchuria, was the junction of the Trans-Siberian Railway, which continued on to Vladivostok on the Pacific coast, and the Chinese-Eastern Railway, which went south to Port Arthur and Dalny. The southbound train was not scheduled to leave until the next day.

Amid the confusion of her arrival, a man dressed as an oriental porter, sidled up to Sylvia Levinski in the Harbin rail station and offered to transport her luggage to the hotel. During the negotiation, he revealed himself to be a Japanese army officer residing in Pitzuwo. "You don't need to know my name," he told her. The pseudo porter said this in rapid-fire Russian, adding that he would arrange for her luggage to be transferred to the southbound train the following morning. Acting as a guide on the ride to the hotel, the man told her not to try to contact him, that he would approach her later. "We may want you to go as far south as Mukden. It promises to be closer to the action. One of my agents there knows of a Russian proprietor who leaves soon for Moscow. He may sell his property cheaply. Use the money our embassy in St Petersburg gave you. Open a tavern of modest means, one that can attract off duty military men. We will provide you with adequate trained help. Prepare your intelligence notes. We expect you to inform us of all valuable conversations you overhear."

"Such as?"

"The arrival of new units, of course. Destination, if possible, of Russian battalions. Names and rank of their officers. All possible details of equipment and ordnances, especially numbers of machine guns, and calibers of artillery."

In the privacy of her hotel room, she unlocked all her luggage. The heaviest bulging metal steamer trunk held one-liter bottles of Smirnoff vodka. All the bottles appeared to be intact with no sign of leakage. The other trunk, sealed tightly like all her luggage, contained articles of clothing, and various tins of saleable food, and many printed revolutionary pamphlets. Two valises contained more clothing. Some of the clothing was wrapped tightly around three small bags of gold coins and several small bars of silver, as well as a few bundles of czarist rubles. The lighter valises contained various pieces of equipment: lengths of primer cord, two pistols, ammunition, two batteries, a small tin of black powder and some underwear.

A six-inch dagger lay in the bottom of her handbag.

Her student associates in Russia had urged her not to transport the outlawed objects so recklessly. The rebellious young woman had ignored the warning, believing her feminine wiles and the confusion of the war traffic would prevent close scrutiny by the officials. She would soon learn fear when confronted by the Okhrana, the Czar's secret police.

A short, thin man peeked through the small hole drilled in the wall separating Levinski's room from his. The shabbily dressed Siberian was more than a voyeur.

He had been on the train with the woman and had noticed the way she kept to herself, and had guarded her luggage. He had seen the elaborate seals on the luggage, and the size and weight of the trunks. The woman's aloofness had convinced him that she must be carrying something of great value. Aroused by his suspicion and greed, he had decided she would be an easy victim to rob. His clumsy attempt to rob her at the Lake Baikal detour had failed, so he had followed her to Harbin, determined to kill her if necessary and take her luggage. The Siberian had secured an empty hotel room adjacent to hers and had secretly drilled the tiny spy hole as he had in other hotel rooms before. He had engaged an associate, actually the hotel's night clerk, to make a key to fit Levinski's hotel door. But the night clerk had been foiled because the woman had insisted that the day clerk give her all available spare keys, compensating him with a substantial bribe and the promise to return the keys in the morning.

The Siberian knew that Levinski had engaged the room for only one night, but believed she would stay longer, thus giving the night clerk time to make a key copy. He remained glued to the peek hole, watching her open her luggage. The glimpse of some of the hidden ruble notes convinced him his efforts would be greatly rewarded. Somehow, during the next few hours, he must find a way to enter her room.

After she had retired for the night, he lay fully clothed on his bed, thinking and plotting and waiting in the dark. Suddenly aware of a spot of light behind the hole, he leaped from the bed and looked through the hole. He saw her in night clothing hurry from the room. He did not see her take a key or lock the door.

In seconds he was in the woman's room.

Levinski's bladder distress had forced her to rise hurriedly from her bed. The rough jolting train ride must have caused spasms in her bladder muscles. She reluctantly padded barefooted to the end of the hallway to the water closet. Glancing at her watch she saw it was 1:20 AM. In the small toilet room she wondered why she had not used the chamber pot placed beneath the bed. And she realized that her fatigue and confusion had caused her to forget to lock her door. She resolved to be more careful.

Hurrying back to the warmth of her bed, she was startled in opening the door to see the back of a stranger bending over her valises. He heard the door open and turned to pounce on her. His hand smothered her scream. He kicked her legs from under her and dragged her to the bed. Pushing his victim down on her back, he grasped a pillow to press on her head.

The pillow uncovered a six-inch dagger, which he did not see in time. She grasped the dagger and frantically plunged it into his side. The man cursed and groaned with pain.

"You Polish bitch!" Loosening his grip, he rolled off her and the bed and dropped to the floor. He tried to rise, but failed. Crawling blindly to the front wall, he collapsed beneath a window facing the street below.

A trickle of blood slipped over his lower lip and his eyes reflected the shock to his body. He said no more, faded into unconsciousness, and died in seconds.

Levinski stood over the body, dagger poised to strike. She knew he was dead when she felt the carotid artery of his neck. Not the kind to panic, she realized she must get rid of the corpse.

But how?

Although the man was thin and small, he was too heavy for her to pull from the room and down the corridor away from her door. Even if she could, she risked discovery with the noise. Drawing aside the window curtain, she looked down at the deserted street. The faint light from the street lamp barely penetrated the dark shadows of the thoroughfare. She lifted the bottom half of the double-hung window, shivering as the cold night air swept into the room.

She was able to pull the corpse to a sitting position, turning the body so the arms draped over the window ledge. Then she succeeded in pushing the upper half of the slender body onto the ledge. Pausing to catch her breath, she struggled to raise his legs and pushed against his feet until the body slid over the sill and plunged to the street below. Plummeting down the smooth face of the three-story building, the corpse landed with a sickening thump on the wooden sidewalk.

Levinski lowered the window, closed the curtain, then turned to search the room for blood stains. Only a small spot of blood showed on her night gown. The dagger blow had been low enough to pierce the man's vital organs to cause internal bleeding. She washed away the spot from her gown, tidied the room and packed her luggage, after laying out clean clothes. She dressed and lay on the bed, waiting for morning and trying to calm her racing heart.

It was almost five in the morning before her agitation subsided to permit her to fall asleep. Two hours later a loud rapping on the door awoke her.

"Who is it?" she finally answered.

"The police. Open the door. We want to talk to you at once."

With sleep-puffed eyes and tousled hair, Levinski timidly slid the bolt and opened the door.

In the hallway, behind two uniformed policemen, stood a crowd of people. The policemen, accompanied by an official in civilian clothes, pushed their way into the room before she could protest. She slammed the door to shut out the curious bystanders.

"What is this?" she demanded.

"I am Inspector Lebedeff. Were you alone all last night?"

"Of course. Why are you here?" Sylvia had no love for the Czarist police and was particularly resentful of the power such men held over women.

"A man was murdered last night. We think he was in this hotel. His body is beneath your window. Or did you not know that?"

She gave the official a hateful look. Following his pointing arm, she approached the window and looked below. The corpse lay face down on the planked walk, a pool of blood puddled beneath the broken head.

"I know nothing about this," she protested, drawing back from the window with a show of horror. In spite of their insistent questions, she maintained a lack of knowledge and angrily insisted they leave her alone. "You wake me up and insult me. I was on the train for more than three weeks before yesterday. After my first night in Harbin, you act like this. What makes you think he was in this hotel? And how did he die? Did someone shoot him in the head? Who is he?"

The police inspector stared at her quietly. Levinski realized she was talking too much.

"If he was murdered, do your duty and find the murderer," she shouted. "Now go. Talk to all those people in the hallway." She opened the door. The official and the two policemen looked at each other, then shrugged and left.

On the street, the inspector and the policemen watched the hospital wagon pick up the corpse. The inspector said to his assistants, "We don't know for sure that he was in the hotel. We know he was knifed, but from the condition of his head, he most probably fell or was pushed from some height."

He looked up at the face of the building. No visible sign of blood showed on the area below the woman's window and none below the window above the woman's room.

"I am suspicious," the inspector said. "The room above her is vacant. Someone told me that a crack of light beneath her door showed the woman's light was on late at night. We know she is one of several who arrived on the Trans-Siberian late yesterday."

One of the assistants spoke up. "The body does not appear to have been moved from somewhere else. Maybe he fell trying to climb through her window."

Lebedeff shot an impatient look at the police sergeant. "With a knife wound in his belly?"

Had the three more closely examined the window ledge, they would have noticed a tiny smear of blood on the outer bottom edge.

Levinski did not leave the hotel until she could follow her luggage being transported to the late morning train bound for Mukden. She wanted no further part of Harbin.

In an adjoining compartment, a Korean businessman sat alone. Dressed in a white native gown, with a tall stovepipe Korean hat atop his head, he reached up to feel the false straggily pointed beard and wispy moustache that adorned his face. Motioning to the conductor, he pressed a large denomination ruble note in his hand and requested that a sealed note be given to the sole Russian lady in the first compartment of the coach.

When she was sure that no one was watching, Levinski tore open the envelope and read its contents.

Please meet me in the rear *commode in ten minutes. Urgent. Use caution. Your Manchurian contact.*

She counted the minutes, then rose and walked casually back to the commode. The closet door was latched shut. She knocked. When the door opened, she pressed inside. She and the Korean businessman stood inches apart in the tiny space. He wasted no time.

"I am Major Ariko, Japanese Army Intelligence. I met you in Harbin. Go to Hotel Orient in Mukden. Your room is waiting. I will meet you there later."

She had to admit that his disguise was very good. He certainly did not look Japanese or military. Ariko cracked open the door, glanced about, then eased out. Sylvia waited a few more minutes, then followed. She walked forward to her compartment, unaware that Inspector Lebedeff sat in the rear rail coach reserved for Russian troops.

Mukden was a small city, but contained a war-swollen population of 150,000. Surrounded by an eleven mile long mud wall, and almost 190 miles south of Harbin, it was another railroad city, almost as drab as Harbin, but booming with the arrival of thousands of Russian troops. It was ten times the size of Port Arthur. With buildings under construction everywhere, Mukden seemed designated to be the staging area to counter the Japanese threat at the Yalu border.

Sylvia Levinski left the train, which then proceeded on south to Dalny and Port Arthur.

In her hotel room she waited for the faint one-two knock at the door. When she opened it, Ariko brushed past her. There was a moment of awkward silence as the two studied each other. He still wore the ridiculous high crowned native hat and false whiskers. She did not like the Japanese spymaster, noting the cruelty in his eyes and in the lines about the mouth of his expressionless face. She did not invite him to sit.

"I will be brief," he said. "You have enough vodka?" She nodded as he continued, "We have procured the shop for you. The owner decided to sell the storefront so he could return to Russia. He fears the war will reach him soon. I have engaged helpers so you can unpack tomorrow. Open your shop with few items. Start off modestly so you do not arouse suspicion. You can add to your stock as business improves."

243

She was anxious to get rid of him, sensing correctly that he did not like caucasians. "Anything else?"

"Yes, do you know anything about pigeons?"

Her lips curled. "I ate a few in my student days."

He ignored her sarcasm. "One of your helpers will feed and care for the birds. You, and only you, will receive and send the messages attached to the birds."

Apparently Ariko had decided not to use human couriers. His menacing tone of voice irritated her. She resented his patronizing manner.

"We think we know what happened in Harbin. Be more careful." Thin skinned as ever, Sylvia flushed and started to protest. He raised his hand to hush her. Stepping away from the door, he motioned for her to open it to check the hallway. Seeing no one outside, she opened the door fully for him. He left without further comment.

"Damn you," she muttered as he slipped out. "You impossible Jap toilet cleaner; this operation will cost you dearly."

In the days that followed, the citizens and troops of Mukden noticed the new business on the main street of the city. The owner had converted the old storefront into a small tavern. The business grew slowly as word spread about the comfortable but small establishment that served the best vodka, the Czar's state-sponsored Smirnoff, not the cheap local rot-gut Chinese vodka.

A sign soon went up proclaiming the tavern to be "Sylvia's Place."

She hired a six-foot four Mongolian wrestler as a bouncer, engaged a Siberian musical trio, and catered to young bored soldiers. She arranged for some appropriate food to be served for those who wanted light refreshments, and soon added good beer. If her customers wanted a full meal, they could go elsewhere. If they wanted a woman, the same held true. Sylvia recognized the danger women could present among quarrelsome military drinkers.

Always restless, she chose to act as hostess, wandering from table to table, picking up tidbits of gossip from soldiers whose tongues had been loosened by liquor. She hired only local young male Mongolians to serve her customers. As her profit grew, she ordered more cases of vodka from the Smirnoff factory in Russia.

The soldiers liked her trim looks and no-nonsense approach. Her severe, unsmiling countenance was misleading. She had a knack of drawing out information from homesick youths who learned to trust her. The military police and the state secret police did not bother her, recognizing that Sylvia's Place was one of few that did not have a boisterous atmosphere that might present a problem. Or so they thought. Sylvia became better acquainted with the Russian army and its plans than many of the Czarist officers.

One of her helpers cared for the pigeons in the loft behind the tavern. Early in the morning, while her helpers were busy cleaning the tavern, she would choose a pigeon, clip on the capsule containing the message, and send the bird on its way. Returning birds always seemed to arrive just before her evening guests congregated and while her helpers were busy with chores.

One day a plain clothes policeman entered the tavern. His presence unnerved Sylvia, but she pretended not to know him. When, finally, she could no longer avoid him, he asked if she did not remember him and the incident at the Harbin hotel.

"Why do you bother me?" she asked. "Have you not laid that case to rest?"

"We have not," Inspector Lebedeff answered. "We now know the victim was an ex-felon who had been accused of robbing hotel rooms. We arrested a hotel clerk who was caught copying room keys. We don't know if there was a connection between the two."

He studied her face. "We wonder what guest may have tempted the victim."

"I can't help you." Sylvia shrugged and started to walk away. "You solve your case."

"I will," he promised. "Have you read about Jean Valjean in *Les Miserables*? I'm like Inspector Javert."

"Good luck," she snapped. "Now if you will excuse me, I am busy."

He persisted. "Yours is an interesting establishment. You seem to have done well and it is only mid-April. You should prosper when summer arrives." Further efforts to prolong the conversation failed; she had already turned to leave. Lebedeff called after her, "*Dziekuje.*" If he had expected her to respond to his trick of using the Polish word for "thank you", he was disappointed.

He watched her abrupt departure. *You Jewish slut, I will be back.*

Sylvia never knew the many times he had journeyed to Mukden.

But she was sure she had not seen the last of Inspector Lebedeff.

* * * * * * * * * *

Rogers continued to chafe at his inactivity in Port Arthur. He toured the town, watched the repair of the damaged battleships at the basin, helped as much as he could at Marina's godown, and carefully avoided the provost and various foreign correspondents—Colonel Petrusha because he suspected the provost's suspicion of him, and the latter because most were such a hard-drinking bunch who would sell out their mothers in order to find a good story for their newspapers. Only a few were respected journalists that he liked. They too were watched closely by the provost.

But he kept his eyes and ears open to gossip and watched the work being done on the fortifications behind the town, work which he thought was sadly slow, too slow for the crisis he believed was imminent. The outer forts had only been half completed when Togo had made his surprise February attack. Frantic efforts to correct that shortcoming went forward under General Kondratenko. The naval improvements made by Admiral Makharoff were much more impressive. Fleet morale had reached a high point.

"I have learned from people at the base that Makharoff is furious because of the boarding of the destroyer *Steresguschi* and slaughter of its crew," Marina told Rogers. "If the Japanese come into the outer roadstead again, he will be ready and will go after them with cruisers and destroyers. If that does not scare them away, he will lead out the battleships too."

Rogers wondered about the delay. "Why not park a couple of battleships out there? If the tide is out, the navy won't have to wait for the larger warships to get out of the channel. Also, why not mine the outer roadstead except for a narrow channel through which Russian ships can pass. If Togo comes into the roadstead at night, he will hit the Russian mines."

"Sounds simple," Marina answered, "but our navy is worried about further damage to the capital ships. Our relative strengths are about equal now, so the admiral prefers to be cautious until more big ships arrive from Russia. As for mines, our mine layers are very scarce and few men are trained for such dangerous work."

'I wish I did not have to be so critical Marina, but the Japanese navy can only isolate the port, not capture it. That will have to be done by their army. Regardless of whether the enemy army can or can not land troops in Manchuria, sooner or later the Russian navy will have to slug it out with the Japanese. Your country cannot sit back and wait for the Japanese to make the first move." He believed that Marina agreed with him inwardly, but did not want to hear it from him. She had turned away without a response. He could understand her pride, so decided not to pursue the subject.

* * * * * * * * *

Fresh from attending the court martial of Sarnichev, *Boyarin's* captain, on charges of prematurely abandoning the damaged cruiser, Vice Admiral Makharoff rode to the office of the port's newspaper, *Novy Kry*. There he inquired of journalist Nojine why the paper had published reports of Japanese submarines laying offshore.

"The Japanese do not yet have submarines. Why are you spreading these false rumors?"

Nojine insisted, "We have the report on good authority from a reliable source." He was referring to Philip Esley's sworn statement. Esley professed to have received the news from the London *Times*. Actually the story had been passed along by the Japanese-friendly San Franciso *Chronicle,* which was in a guessing game with other newspapers. Both Tokyo and St Petersburg were avid readers of the London *Times*, not always reliable, but better than the others.

Makharoff left in a huff, vowing to round up the Englishman as soon as possible. It would not do to have false stories circulating among Russian service men. The admiral knew that England and America had one or two submarines, but the Russians had none yet ready, so it was absurd to credit the Japanese with submarines when they could not even build their own battleships.

With impish delight, the admiral decided to confuse the enemy. He instructed Captain Crown, who had just recently arrived in Port Arthur, to spread the story that Russia had contracted for German shipyards to build and deliver submarines for the Czar's navy in the Far East.

"Two can play the rumor game," he told Crown. "Now have the provost collar this fellow Esley."

* * * * * * * * * *

Commander Fairborne remarked to Captain Packenham that Russian forays from Port Arthur seemed to follow a predictable pattern. "Every day they leave the channel on the same course, go out to sea directly in the same direction, then turn, usually eastward, to follow the coast toward Dalny."

Packenham, one of the most cautious men Fairborne had ever met, and so worried about offending Togo that he had never ventured ashore since boarding the battleship months ago, replied that Togo had noticed the same thing and had a plan. "The Japanese know the areas that the Russians have mined. Togo is reasonably certain that the Russians do not know the exact locations of the Japanese mines since most of them have been laid at night. If Togo could lure the Russians to come out in pursuit and follow the same route as always, if he could persuade them to cross over Japanese mines laid on that route, he could be lucky."

Fairborne knew there were two big ifs. Suppose the weighted anchors had sunk in the soft mud below the surface, thus lowering the mines too deep to be effective? Or suppose the strong tide had dragged the mines to a different location? The Japanese mines were usually placed one foot below the surface of the sea—at low tide when it was safer for the Japanese to approach the harbor mouth. If the Russian battle wagons emerged at high tide, would the mines be anchored too deeply?

Hata supervised the laying of forty-eight heavy duty mines by the *Koryu Maru* in April. The four protective Japanese destroyers endured a night of storm tossed seas and torrents of rain during the hazardous operation. Hata despised the dangerous work as did his crew. One little slip and all would be blown to bits.

Aboard the cruiser *Diana*, Admiral Makharoff questioned his lookout, "Why so much activity out there tonight?" He referred to the lights that bobbed about offshore. The lookout assured him that the lights were undoubtedly Russian destroyers returning late from night reconnaisance.

In the murky light of dawn, two Russian destroyers approached the *Koryu Maru*, which had just completed its work. The Japanese opened fire when the Russian ships had approached within 300 feet. One of the Russian ships, the *Strashny*, was hit and sank. As Russian searchlights began sweeping across the water, the Japanese fired on the searchlights.

The gunfire noise alerted Marina and Rogers who arose from their beds to run out onto the veranda. They strained to see the activity in the far distance.

Russian cruisers weighed anchor to go after the Japanese destroyers. Flying the blue and white Russian navy flag, the cruisers *Diana, Bayan, Askhold and Novik* tore out to the open sea across the newly laid Japanese mines without incident. Watching, Makharoff ordered the waters surrounding the sunken Russian destroyer *Strashny* swept for mines. His order was never carried out.

Makharoff ordered his flag placed on the mast of the battleship *Petropavlovsk* and led the battleships *Poltava, Sevastapol, Pobieda and Peresvyet* in the wake of the cruisers. All turned southeast in pursuit of Hata's battle flotilla.

Japanese admiral Dewa, covering Hata's operation, saw the emerging Russian battleships follow their customary path toward the Japanese minefields. Before hurrying to join Dewa's cruiser, Togo's fleet also saw Makharoff's battle group pass over the minefields without harm.

Makharoff pursued Admiral Dewa for fifteen miles until the smoke smudges on the horizon told him that Togo's battleships had turned to engage the Russians. Makharoff ordered his lighter ships to return to the safety of the outer roadstead where the guns of the forts could offer protection. Being outnumbered, he followed with the battleships. Makharoff envisioned luring the Japanese back over the Russian minefields.

The tide had dropped when the Russians reached the roadstead. As Makharoff coursed over the hidden Japanese minefield, his scheme failed and his luck ran out.

Commander Fairborne, standing next to Captain Packenham and Admiral Togo on the bridge of the battleship *Mikasa*, had just remarked that Hata's mines may have been anchored too low, when it happened. On shore, Rogers watched the drama.

Marina had run back to Rogers' room to fetch his binoculars. From the veranda, she and Rogers saw the pursuing Japanese fleet begin to turn back in the face of the fort's guns. Then, before their eyes, the Russian flagship's bow suddenly rose high in the air as the *Petropavlovsk* hit an enemy mine.

The battleship halted dead in the water, and then a second mine exploded midships, igniting the ship's ammunition magazines. The massive secondary explosion broke the back of the huge ship, filling the air with a cloud of yellow smoke. A third explosion, caused by ruptured steam boilers, hid part of the battleship with a huge blanket of white smoke that intermingled with the yellow cloud.

Captain Crown lay on the bridge of the *Petropavlovsk*, his left leg blown off just below the knee. The stump of the leg was too numb to cause much pain, but was bleeding profusely. Crown, almost fainting from shock, saw Makharoff remove his overcoat and peaked hat, fall to his knees and clasp his hands in prayer.

With a mighty shudder, the broken battleship disappeared quickly below the surface, dragging most of the crew to a watery grave.

Togo turned to his officers who were shouting and applauding and shook his head. The admiral watched the scene quietly. His now silent staff removed their hats and bowed with respect. Later, at the Elliot islands, Togo ordered all the Japanese fleet's flags flown at half-mast.

The tragedy of the day had not ended. Picking her way carefully through the area in search of survivors, the Russian battleship *Pobieda* also hit a Japanese mine. Immediately, the surrounding Russian ships panicked and began firing into the water. Philip Esley's false rumors of Japanese submarines were now believed. When the indiscriminate firing finally stopped, the *Pobieda* limped back into the harbor. Her coal bunkers had absorbed much of the damage.

"I will visit the hospital this afternoon to wish Grand Duke Cyril a speedy recovery," Marina told Rogers. "He was pulled out of the water, semi-conscious, and burned rather severely. There were only 80 other survivors from the *Petropavlovsk*. 635 good men perished."

A pall of gloom descended over the Russian port. Makharoff's loss had shattered morale. His recognized ability, bravery, and reorganization had given the port a feeling of security and hope that most now feared was lost.

Many believed that the fall of Port Arthur was no longer so remote, that the fight was possibly lost with the irreplaceable admiral. Without his leadership, the Russian fleet appeared doomed. The best naval officers of the port, appointed to Makharoff's staff, had died with the admiral. The army, however, did not take such a pessimistic view. Although Alexeiev was down-hearted, General Stoessel shrugged off the loss, agreeing with fellow generals that the Russian navy would probably continue to be ineffective, but that the Japanese were not worthy opponents for the Russian army.

Marina was equally optimistic about the Russian army. But she worried constantly about Alesandrov and the lack of word from him.

The Russian doctor of the Mukden military hospital studied the unconscious officer's frost-bitten extremities. He had thawed the worst parts, the feet, with gradually reduced applications of snow. He had applied unguents, snipped off decayed flesh, and tenderly patted the feet and hands to increase circulation.

Black as a piece of coal, the smallest toe on the left foot had stubbornly refused to mend. On the third day of recuperation, as the Cossack officer began to show signs of awakening, the doctor made a final examination of the foot. Seeing there was no hope, he grasped the black toe and snapped it off.

CHAPTER ELEVEN

Someone was shaking him. Alesandrov awakened to a nagging pain in his left foot. Both feet and hands were bandaged and his face smeared with a greasy salve. Otherwise, he felt langurously relaxed and warm in the hospital bed.

He looked up at the medical man. The bearded doctor had pushed aside his white smock to reach for his vest watch. He held it up for Alesandrov to see. The time piece recorded dates as well as time.

"You have slept for three days," the doctor said. "It is time you woke up."

Alesandrov blinked uncomprehendingly. "Who are you? Where am I?"

"You are in Mukden, sir. I am Doctor Solomon Zieman." Alesandrov could see at once that Zieman was a Jew and thus only a contract doctor— attached to the Czar's army, but still a civilian not permitted to be an officer or a formal army medic because he was Jewish.

The doctor continued, "I could not save one of your frost-bitten toes. But you are healthy. We'll have you sitting up and about by tomorrow—if you can stay awake."

Alesandrov was relieved. Was he only missing one toe? If so, that was a small price to pay for survival. He pushed the memory of the freezing Korean nights and artic waters of the Yalu from his mind. He hoped he would never be so cold again.

"You were incoherent, but you kept repeating the names of several women," said the grinning doctor: "Marina, Lydia, someone called She, and something about a Flower—tea, I think. If they were cousins or sisters, you must have a very loving and close family. How wonderful. One name you mentioned consistently was Claudette. One of our nurses said that she thinks she knows who that is. I'll send in a nurse to tend to you."

Alesandrov had closed his eyes, trying to remember how he had arrived in Mukden. His mind was blank beyond his encounter with Sergeant Kholodov's patrol at the Yalu. He remembered the patrol but nothing after that.

When he opened his eyes, he saw a uniformed nurse enter the room. She wore a large red cross armband with a red cross emblem pinned on her cap. The nurse was crying as she approached the bed, gazing at him with tear-stained eyes.

"Don't you know me?"

"Nurse X," he pretended. "The one with the beautiful breasts."

"You beast. Have you forgotten me so soon?"

"Come closer. How can I know you, wearing all those clothes?" He held out his arms. "Come here. My God, Claudette, I thought I had lost you. Why are you here?"

Alesandrov tried to hide his own fragile emotion by joking. She understood his forced bravado. Men like him did not cry.

She hugged him with tears streaming from her eyes. "I did not want to return to France without you. I stayed to volunteer for service with your army, hoping to find you someday."

"Am I all in one piece, Claudette?" He seldom believed or trusted medical men.

"Yes, except for the toe. Thanks to the doctor, the frost bite was cured and you are mine again."

Doctor Zieman cracked the door open. "Stay with him nurse. Keep him awake so he will sleep tonight. We want to start his therapy tomorrow."

Why wait? She reached under the cover blanket and held him, feeling his firm cylinder of flesh pulsate with renewed life.

* * * * * * * * *

The news of Alesandrov's rescue reached Port Arthur by train, Marina was ecstatic, shouting to Rogers that Viktor was alive and recuperating from severe frostbite in a hospital in Mukden. She bubbled with excitement. "Now we can bring him home. Will you go after him, Ellis?"

He readily agreed, choosing not to spoil Marina's happiness. She obviously knew little about army regulations. He would go to Mukden at least to assess Viktor's condition. Here was his chance to get a change of scenery.

Marina knew that Rogers was restless, that he had been complaining for days that it was his duty to go north. She would no longer try to dissuade him from leaving. "Bring him back to me," she begged.

Rogers could see that the snows had melted and he knew the land battles might soon proceed with the end of winter. He was reluctant to leave Marina alone, wishing he could be more optimistic about Port Arthur's future. The Russians, as usual, were too smug about the war.

Marina asked if he thought there might be fighting near Mukden.

He told her, "The last time our friend Chen came in, he told me that the Japanese First Army has moved north from Seoul. He is sure the Japanese intend to cross the Yalu river border to enter Manchuria."

"If the Japanese do try to come into Manchuria, what will be your duties, Ellis?"

"You know that I am an accredited foreign army observer. Viktor can help me report on the war. I need to report to my superiors on various aspects of the conflict. I can't help or give advice; I can only observe and learn."

Her robe had parted slightly to reveal the thin silk night garment covering her body. The sight of her full breasts moving beneath the sheer fabric unnerved him. It was happening again. He remembered his schoolboy days when rampant hormones had created an embarassing crisis that had to be covered by a book held strategically in front of him when he was asked to stand to recite. *Please, Marina, don't do this to me.*

The train journey north to Mukden seemed to take forever. Planted fields of young kaoliang and corn covered the dusty plains west of the train rails. The low coastal hills on his right blocked a view of the eastern sea and formed a shallow valley for the railroad and the old Mandarin Road that curved tortuously parallel to the tracks. The train passed Kaiping and later Liaoyang. He knew that Mukden was still much farther up the line.

The train rolled into Mukden at the end of the 271 mile journey.

A hired rickksha carried Rogers to a large warehouse converted to house a makeshift army hospital. He entered the small room unannounced to see Viktor sitting up in bed with a pretty nurse hovering over him. The two did not notice him until he rapped on the open door.

Viktor was noticeably thinner. A touch of gray had appeared at his temples. He seemed unusually subdued. But when he saw Rogers, Alesandrov swung off the bed, knocking over a crutch, which he tried to hide as if embarassed by it. He hobbled toward Rogers, shouting with joy as the two embraced.

He introduced the nurse as Claudette. Rogers knew from her accent that she was French, possibly from the south of France. She looked young, pert

257

and friendly. He noticed how possessively she constantly fussed over his friend. Once he saw Viktor's hand caress her leg.

Viktor proposed a change from the room to a newly planted garden area. "The sun is shining today and spring is almost here. Why don't we sit outside. I can't seem to get enough warmth."

In the garden, when the nurse helped Alesandrov move his chair to face the sun, Rogers saw him make a biting motion toward her breast. She caught his head and buried his face in her bosom and kissed the top of his head. Rogers quickly looked the other way, pretending not to notice. He was preplexed. What was going on? These two acted like more than casual flirts—more like solid lovers, forced by the lack of privacy to grope each other openly.

Rogers sat across from Claudette. Pretty little lady, he thought. Very likable and unpretentious. Did she know about Marina? Would Viktor tell Marina? Rogers was puzzled and a little uncomfortable about the relationship. He was unaccustomed to such a public display of affection.

When the nurse returned to the ward to get a blanket for her patient, Rogers told Alesandrov, "Marina has been quite worried about you. She cried so much when she heard you were hurt. She never lost hope when you were reported missing. Have you written to her?"

"Only the message that I was here."

Rogers thought that his friend did not seem desperately anxious to hear news of Marina and Port Arthur. They talked of generalties for a time after Claudette returned with the blanket and then excused herself as if she understood that the two wanted to engage in man-talk.

"How do you like her, Ellis?"

"Your nurse is…"

"No, no, I mean Marina."

Rogers looked up to see Viktor eyeing him closely. It made him strangely uncomfortable.

"I can't say enough about the lady, Viktor. You are indeed fortunate to have such a wonderful woman for a friend."

"Her name is Marina, Ellis. And I know her well enough to know she would accept you as more than just a friend—mine or yours. She is a very caring and loving woman, well into her prime. Just how well did you come to know her?"

Rogers was irritated and wary. "Viktor, you know I do not talk much about the ladies. I'll tell you frankly, I could treasure such a woman. But I kept my place, Viktor. I value our friendship too much."

Alesandrov could see his friend was upset. "Please forgive me Ellis. I did not intend to pry. My apology, please. So much has happened since I was sent on the mission to Korea. So much that I've come to look at life differently. I would not have blamed you if you had fallen in love with her. And I would not have blamed Marina if she had turned to you. I had a close call in Korea, so petty jealousies don't trouble me as much anymore. Perhaps what happened in Korea has scarred me. It may take some time to be my old self again." He watched for some response from Roger. Hearing none, he continued.

"I used to doubt that I could ever devote my life to one woman, Ellis. I needed to share my love with so many others who were in need."

"With Claudette?"

"So you have noticed? She is like the mother I never loved. Fusses over me constantly. Says she has never been so gloriously happy. It's not just the sexual attraction. She loves me for what I am. It is that simple for her. Now I wonder if I will ever be able to leave her. For the first time in my life I have this wild urge to stay and protect her."

"But Marina loves you very much Viktor. I can't say that enough."

"Of course, of course. Tell me about her life now." Before Rogers could answer, Alesandrov said with an casual but serious look, "Have there been many changes for her with the onset of the war? Is she happy in Port Arthur?"

Rogers mulled that over in his mind. Had his friend really changed so much in such a short time? Where was the old light-hearted Viktor? He must have been through hell in Korea. Why all these questions?

"What about Yin-lin?"

"What about her, Viktor?"

"Did you?"

"Did I what? No, Viktor, I did not. How could I with Marina there?"

"I left word with Marina. How could you not?"

"Damn you, Viktor, so that was your idea?"

"Not really. I mentioned the possibility to Marina. Thought it would be good for both of you. Yin-lin and you, I mean. The girl needs a lover, Ellis. She is too close to Marina. Wants to share Marina's bed all the time. If Yin-lin went to you, Marina sent her, and Yin-lin wanted to go.

Marina is too good to the girl. Treats her like a kid sister."

"That is exactly the way I look at Yin-lin. She is like a kid sister," Rogers said. He decided to change the topic of conversation. "So what are your plans, Viktor? Are you going back to duty in Port Arthur?"

"I cannot leave now. My duty is here. Maybe later if I think I can stomach Stoessel. Some of the Cossack patrols have reported the Japs are massing near Antung. I know the terrain, so I believe rather that the enemy is secretly gathering farther north. They control Korea for the time being and they are cocky. I firmly believe they will soon strike at Manchuria.

Why else would they be sending so many army divisions north through Korea? What are your plans, Ellis?"

"I'd prefer to stay here to see what happens next month. The armies will be marching in May with the warm weather. If you want, I'll send a note to Marina saying you are still recuperating. She should be safe in Port Arthur, except for some occasional shelling by Togo's ships." He was disappointed that Viktor showed such little concern for Marina's welfare.

"Are you going to stay with the Russian army?" Alesandrov asked.

"Yes, too late to change now. I'd like to see our old friend, Tanaka, but I think I would rather see the war from the Russian side."

"Because of Marina?"

"Because of her *and* you, Viktor. That is why I am here."

Toward the end of the week, Alesandrov received permission to leave the ward for an outing away from the hospital. He proposed that he and Rogers have a drink at a tavern that had been recommended. "We need to drink to your promotion, Ellis, now that we are of equal rank. This tavern is a cozy spot, so I am told—it is called "Sylvia's Place."

Alesandrov could walk much better; the foot was tender but healing well. "I'll borrow some horses next week and we can ride out to some of the Cossack units," he told Rogers. "You should learn more about the new Russian army."

New? From his experience at Port Arthur, Rogers remembered seeing very little change or improvement since the old China adventure at Peking.

They entered the tavern and selected a table facing the entrance, an old habit both had adopted long ago for precautionary reasons. Both ordered vodka and soda with a preliminary chaser of straight vodka to see how good it was. Alesandrov began to reminisce.

"Ellis, I hate to dredge up the past so often. You have told me before about Xi. I am happy for her. She will make a wonderful wife. Two husbands, me, and now a third spouse. What kind of a man is he?"

"A good and successful businessman. Scotch and tight as hell with money, and has kind of a dour manner. But he is crazy about her. He has really put her on a pedestal. With her alone, he is generous and kind. She is fortunate to have such a good and caring husband."

"You have never mentioned little Li, your assistant from the Boxer days. What was her real name? An-an? I have been so forgetful lately. Where is she and what is she doing these days? I had always expected that you two would stay together. She was obviously so fond of you. How could you let her go?"

Rogers decided that it was time—for Marina's sake. "Can you keep a secret?"

"Try me." Alesandrov tossed down the shot of vodka. "Not bad. It is the real stuff all right.

If it is good for the Czar, it is good for us. But I wish the proprietor had some decent champagne. So what is the secret?"

"An-an and I are married, have been for a long time. It was a secret and private wedding by Reverend Babbitt in Peking. I trust that you, for several crucial reasons, will not tell anyone. She is in Hong Kong. The mail from there is bad. Haven't heard from her in weeks—actually months."

"You have my solemn promise." That is what Rogers liked about Viktor. Nothing more needed to be explained.

Rogers teased him. "Now, does that reassure you about Marina?"

"You are such a moralistic Baptist, Ellis. No wonder we run you people out of Russia."

"Not a Baptist. Maybe a Puritan. Twas the way I was raised."

"Not much fun for you Americans, Ellis. You miss a lot in life."

Rogers started to remind Viktor of all the trouble such morality avoided, but checked himself in time. He remembered Viktor's banishment to Siberia for transgressions of the flesh.

He had noticed that the tavern owner had approached their table a couple of times as if intent on listening to their conversation. She seemed particularly interested in what Alesandrov was saying. Viktor had noticed also, so both had lowered his voice each time she neared. Trim of figure and attractive with a dark gypsy-like appearance, she was identified by Alesandrov as Sylvia, the tavern owner.

"From what I have learned, she is kind of a mystery woman. No one knows why she came to Mukden, but she has prospered in this business. I am not attracted to her. I distrust women who are too serious and unhappy looking. I am guessing she is unhappy since she smiles so little. The customers, however, praise her."

"Does she know I am an American?"

"I am sure she does. Quite a few of the foreign news correspondents frequent this place, trying to pick up gossip. She must know all the uniforms."

"She seems Jewish. Not her face; something about her mannerisms." Rogers said.

Alesandrov nodded. "Maybe. I thought she had gypsy blood at first. If only she smiled."

"There is a gentleman off to my left, Viktor. Don't look now. His eyes have been piercing the back of your head since we came in."

"I know who you mean," Viktor said. "I sensed his presence early on. I remember him from Vladivostok. He is Inspector Arkady Lebedeff of the secret police."

"The Okhrana?"

"Yes. Everyone avoids him."

"Why is he here at the war front?"

"I don't know. Maybe he is after someone who comes in here. Or maybe because someone had been disseminating anti-war propaganda. I have seen one of the posters. The soldiers don't pay much attention, but that could change if things go badly for our side."

Alesandrov leaned back to study Rogers. With a sly smile he said, "So, Ellis, you are a married man. Does Marina know?"

"No. I have told no one but you. Please keep my secret, Viktor. I have my reasons."

"You have sworn me to silence. Now I must ask a favor of you. I need to be alone with Claudette. Can you get us a room? She and I are tied down at the hospital, and rooms are impossible to rent. It gets worse each day, I am told."

Rogers was saddened for Marina. He liked Claudette too much to blame her; evidently she did not know about Marina. What was he going to tell Marina when he returned to Port Arthur? He *was* going to return, was he not? Damn Viktor. Why did he have to make life so complicated?

"Take my room. Let me know when. I'll stay in the lobby for a few hours."

"Are you sure?"

"Yes, it is payback time for your kindness to An-an and me in Peking."

Alesandrov was visibly much happier when Rogers later met with him. The two had left Rogers' hotel to enjoy another beer at Sylvia's Place. As usual, Sylvia sought every excuse to approach their table, inquiring if there was anything she might do to make their stay enjoyable. Lebedeff was absent. Alesandrov impatiently waved the woman away from the table. Rogers inquired about the Russian chain of command.

"Tell me about the local field commanders, Viktor. I know that the commander-in-chief for Manchuria is Admiral Alexeiev."

"Well, the area commander is General Zasulich. From what I have learned—you know the generals never seem to want to keep the junior officers informed—he is dead certain that the Japs will invade at Antung, But, Ellis, I came in from Korea. I know that the enemy knows what Zasulich is thinking. Their intelligence is very good. They are not going to come ashore where they know he is waiting. They will strike across the river up around Wiju, about seven miles north of Antung, maybe even farther north if they find the area weakly defended.

The army commander for Manchuria is General Alexei Nicholaevitch Kuropatkin who was our Minister of War until the Czar sent him out here to take command of that part of Manchuria north of the Port Arthur peninsula. Stoessel still commands the immediate area around the port. Kuropatkin is fifty-six and hasn't seen a gun fired in anger in almost sixteen years. He is a bureaucrat, not a field commander. Worse, he has this morbid fear of failing, won't take chances, so he is locked in on defensive rather than offensive strategies. In addition, he has to take orders from Viceroy Alexeiev. We both know how inept the admiral is. What does a sailor know about land warfare?"

"Where is Kuropatkin now?" Rogers inquired.

"He has established his headquarters at Liaoyang. You came through there on the way up here. That is about 120 miles north of the southern Yalu terminus. What does that tell you about him, Ellis?"

"Sounds like he favors a strong defense line in the north rather than the south. But why would he stay on the defensive, waiting for the Japanese to come to him, even though he is outnumbered. A well entrenched southern defense line has the advantage of requiring fewer soldiers, I admit, but that still puts the ball in the enemy's court, especially so far south. Why do you think the Japanese will cross the Yalu around Wiju, Viktor?"

"Because that is where I crossed. That is where the islands are. The Japanese can throw up pontoon bridges from island to island and swarm across with heavy stuff, like artillery and transport wagons, Or they can hide artillery positions on the islands."

Rogers asked if the Japanese may have brought prefabricated pontoon bridges from Japan.

"They don't have to. I passed by the abandoned Russian lumber yards at Yongampo. Tons of good lumber there."

"Why are Russian lumber yards in Korea?"

"It is leased property of the Far East Lumber Company. That is the Bezobrazov clique's lumber concession."

Rogers had been informed of the group by Marina. A Russian conglomerate granted special favors by the Czar and the Viceroy, the group's investors were in conflict with Witte.

There was that name again. Marina seemed to know a lot about this man Witte who had pioneered the railroads into Manchuria.

Viktor told him, "That is why Witte's people, who are the railroad interests, lost out. Witte and Alexeiev clashed over monopoly rights in Manchuria and Korea. Witte did not want the military to become too powerful. He could forsee a time when the army and navy could seize control of the railroads and commercial establishments along the railroad line. Witte would lose his monopoly."

Rogers had asked Marina earlier if she thought the Czar and Alexeiev were profitting from the Manchurian venture. She had looked at him, smiled and answered, "Isn't that what it is all about?   Money and monopoly?"

He wondered if that was not the compelling force behind the Russo-Japanese quarrel—monopoly.   Shut out the other side's commercial competition.

So, it looked to Rogers like the Russians did not at the moment want a conflict in Korea, preferring to confine the war to Manchuria where they controlled the railroad supply lines extending back to Russia.   Clausewitz, the German military philosopher, had argued that the best offense is to create a bulge in the enemy's line; throw all one's strength against a certain point along the enemy line where the foe was stretched thin.   The Prussian trained Japanese army favored that strategy.   The philosophy was correct if the enemy was outnumbered.   And the Russians were.   Also, the wisdom of the world at the time favored the victor of the first battle.   Both Kuropatkin and his opposite number Oyama believed a first victory to be so psychologically paramount that both sides would prepare for the coming battle in carefully defined detail.

The problem was that the Russians were too scornful of Japanese ability to win.

* * * * * * * * * *

Sylvia continued to spread false rumors of Japanese transportation difficulties in Korea and of failed Japanese attempts to make landings around Port Arthur.   Foreign correspondents had witnessed the massing of Japanese troops of the First Army at the Korean port of Chemulpo, north of Seoul, and had predicted that the army would attack near the confluence of the Yalu and the sea.   Though not correct, the Russians believed it.   The

Japanese strategy was to attack the Russian regiments farther upstream, those who guarded the confluence of the Yalu and Ai-ho rivers. Other Japanese divisions, coming north by boat, would later secure the lower reaches of the Yalu. How the First Army planned to cross the Yalu was anyone's guess; Tanaka knew it would be a hazardous operation against the entrenched enemy. Thanks to Japanese secret agents, the Japanese army knew of the Russian concentration south of Mukden and what it would take to smash through Russian defenses in order to seize vital roads and the rail line inland from the proposed landing at the Yalu.

Japanese censors were so upset by the reckless reporting of attached foreign correspondents that they began to curb the movement of the newsmen. The Russians were unwisely much more generous in their treatment of the correspondents. So information flowed to the Japanese and rumors mounted.

Sylvia sent a message to Ariko informing him that the main strength of the Russian army waited near Antung, where the Japanese had crossed in the war against China ten years earlier. The overconfident Russian soldiers had told her, she said, that their trenches were exposed, shallow, and uncamouflaged because the Russians believed in mobility. Japanese agents, disguised as river fishermen, confirmed that the trenches were in full view of the Japanese side of the Yalu and that Russian artillery guns remained openly exposed in the corn fields. Russian overconfidence disdained earthen protection for the artillery.

Sylvia also informed Ariko that the river islands of Kyuri, Kintei and Oseki were lightly defended by Russia. And Japanese intelligence teams were delighted to learn that the Russians had characteristically dug their trenches on the Manchurian hillside instead of on flat terrain at the foot of the hills. Trenches on the face of the hill could be seen more easily than on the flat plains.

* * * * * * * * *

While constructing a southerly pontoon bridge that was never intended to be used, General Kuroki, commander of the Japanese First Army, began lobbing occasional shells across the river against Antung. Farther north he brought up portable pontoons weighing less than 100 pounds each, joined by light sheets of thin iron, all transported by Korean coolies. To hide this construction and the massing of three divisions of soldiers, Kuroki employed high movable screens of dry kaoliang and small trees. The Russians, concentrating all attention on Antung, failed to notice the shifting landscape.

During the night of April 29, under skies covered with rain clouds, General Kuroki successfully placed large artillery mortars in prepared camouflaged trenches on the islands. Kuroki had been a military attache during the Boer War and had observed how British army captain Percy Smith had used specially designed gun carriages to move heavy guns across unstable ground in the advance on Ladysmith.

The thought of the coming battle made Tanaka wonder if the Russian friend of the American officer, Rogers, with whom he had shared so many adventures in China, would be shooting at him. Tanaka and Alesandrov had been civil but cool to each other during their encounters in the Boxer Rebellion four years previously. They had little in common, but for Roger's sake had tolerated each other. Tanaka wondered where Rogers was now and whatever had happened to his pretty Chinese interpreter assistant, An-an.

He and Rogers had promised to keep in touch after the capture of Peking. Somehow, that pledge, like so many others, had faded with the years. Tanaka had endeavored to maintain his knowledge of Rogers' language because of the historical research necessitated by his teaching post at the college. He guessed that both armies would now be distracted by foreign news correspondents on hand to send dispatches from the front to hungry readers around the world. A comforting thought continued to remind Tanaka that his language skill might still earn him a place on the headquarter's staff.

On April 30 Tanaka was told to have his men carry three days rations and be ready to attack the next day.

On the night march along a narrow path parallel to the river, but well back out of sight of Russian patrols across the river, Tanaka reflected on the prospects for success in the coming battle. Although not as eager for battle as his enthusiastic, untried men, he relished the successful concealment of the Twelfth Division and the two support divisions in the rear. Thinking back to the long march north from Seoul, he remembered how well prepared the villages along the line of march had been. Advance commissary squads, protected by cavalry, had preceeded the infantry to provide shelter and hot meals. The infantry had arrived in the villages to find fires lit, food ready, and warm blankets. The Japanese wisely had purchased livestock and rice from Korean farmers at fair prices and had paid good wages to over 10,000 Korean coolies to collect and carry supplies for the army. Scouts had distributed diagrams detailing assigned quarters and had provided detailed maps of the roads and trails.

During that march, Tanaka had been surprised at how little the Japanese column was harrassed. He had cautioned his men not to talk to the news correspondents whose yellow journalism often provided important information to the enemy. By April 30 even the Russians were so exasperated by the press that they had moved all press correspondents north to Mukden.

While the Russians continued to ignore the movements of the Japanese army in Korea, Sylvia Levinski had done her best to throw the Russians off guard by spreading a rumor that the Japanese army was so bogged down on the muddy Korean roads that it would be late in May before they could mount an offensive. Even Russian General Rennenkampf had complacently moved his cavalry division back from the Yalu to conduct leisurely training manuevers.

Before Tanaka reached the crossing point on the Yalu, he thought back to earlier years in Korea. He remembered having been almost sent to Korea eight years ago when the Japanese army had unsuccessfully tried to seize control of the country before Russia did so. Arrogance on the part of certain Japanese generals and diplomats had alienated the Korean court.

The intrigue had reached such a shameful point that Tanaka had avoided teaching it at his university. The leading Japanese diplomat in Seoul had hired thugs to seize the troublesome Korean queen. The thugs had decapitated the queen, but had failed to kill the king, who had escaped to the Russian legation disguised as a woman. Under Russian protection, the king had issued a proclamation to have the queen's assassins cornered, decapitated and their heads delivered to him. After that threat, the Japanese had backed down and reluctantly agreed to a Russian demand that the king be restored to his throne. Tanaka was still incensed that his country, though not blameless, had been forced to accede to the Russian threat.

The blatant attempt by the Czar's friend, the Bezobrazov group, to harvest Korea's forests had also angered Tanaka. Japanese agents had reported the presence of Russian soldiers, disguised as forest rangers, to protect the Russian Far East Lumber Company. Japan knew how thoroughly the Czar and Bezobrazov profitted from the lumber venture.

The men of the Twelfth Division, with Tanaka in command of one company, crossed the river on a secretly constructed pontoon bridge and began groping their way in the misty darkness across cornfields and irrigation pools, past deserted farmhouses, feeling their way along as best they could while maintaining complete silence and showing no lights in the inky blackness.

When morning came and the fog had dispelled on May 1, the left flank of the Russian line awoke to the shocking sight of three divisions of blue coated enemy soldiers stretched along a six-mile front. The Japanese had crossed the Yalu and had circled north to prepare for a crossing of the adjoining Ai river in order to turn the lightly defended Russian left flank.

The Guards Division, and Tanaka with the Twelfth Division, watched the Second or Ujini Division ford the chest deep water of the Ai river. Japanese progress across the cold, fast water was painfully slow and the Japanese erred in following the strategy of their Prussian trainers by massing shoulder to shoulder in their frontal assault. The Russian counterfire caught the Japanese in the middle of the river and punished them with heavy casualties. The wounded drowned in the swift current, but enough struggling survivors finally reached the opposite bank to push the Russians back against the slopes of the hills. The sharp contrast of the dark blue Japanese uniforms against the yellow sand of the river plain caused more casualties until the order came to spread out and fire independently. With the order to launch a massive attack against the exposed Russian trenches, the three Japanese divisions advanced toward the slopes, while the hidden

Battle of the Yalu

BATTLE OF THE YALU RIVER

Japanese troops on the Yalu

7b General Zasulich (in white tunic) and his staff at the Battle of the Yalu

Cossack cavalry

mortars on the Yalu islands, which had remained silent, commenced firing shrapnel shells. Colonel Gromov's Russians were forced to abandon their trenches and retreat. Alesandrov begged to lead a force of Cossacks to scout the Japanese bridghead. General Zasulich denied the request.

The main Russian force around Antung to the south, faced with the threat of attack by two encircling Japanese divisions, started a withdrawal, believing that Gromov was protecting their left flank. In doing so they left the center of the Russian line exposed and under severe shrapnel fire from the Japanese guns on the islands. By 5:30 PM the Russians were in full retreat. Many surrendered. Most of the Russian artillery guns and machine guns had been abandoned. The battle was lost, with Russian casualties twice those of their enemy. Fleeing north, instead of entrenching in the mountains, the remnants of the Russian forces fell back toward Liaoyang.

Zasulich had held back his reserves behind Antung until too late. He had not committed his right flank, stubbornly believing the Japanese would attack there, and when Gromov folded, the Russian center lay exposed. The area south of Antung lay open for invasion by the Japanese. The road to Port Arthur also appeared to be abandoned by Kuropatkin. As Rogers noted, the Russians had demonstrated the folly of their failure to use offensive tactics. Korea and the lower Yalu river were now safely in Japanese hands.

General Oku and his Second Japanese Army immediately sailed from Korea to land at Pitzuwo to cut off Port Arthur, fifty miles to the south.

The Japanese had succeeded in invading Manchuria. It appeared to Rogers that Russia would be unable to evict them, at least for a long time. Alesandrov agreed with him that Port Arthur was essentially isolated beyond Russian aid. Japan's psycological victory in the war's first land battle shocked the European capitals. By scoffing at Japanese military prowess, and by failing to exercise strong leadership, the Russian generals had demonstrated to the world for the first time that an Asian nation could defeat an European world power. A Japanese victory in the war's first land battle was such a psychological feat that European capitals were stunned. Crowds in Tokyo were ecstatic. Crowds in St Petersburg could not believe the bad news and immediately turned against the Czar. Gloom descended on Port Arthur as well.

CHAPTER TWELVE

A clandestine radio set, operating in the open trade port of Chefu on the China coast, was in touch with the journalist Nojine at the Novy Kry newspaper in Port Arthur.

Lydia Fairborne's efforts to convey intelligence to Captain Crown had met with success when she was able to enlist the help of a disgruntled Irish mechanic and pipefitter aboard a mail ship plying the waters between Sasebo and the British naval station at Wei-hai-wei. Chefu was close to the British port.

Lydia's coded message had disclosed the formation of Togo's third blockship expedition and the intended date of attack. She also had warned of the impending landing of General Oku's Second Army at Pitzuwo, about sixty miles northeast of Dalny.

The engine room sailor's rabid hatred for the English made Lydia's money welcome recompense for his betrayal. The Irishman Donnelly did not want sex; he knew his place. Besides, he hated the English of all sexes. He had made an exception with Lydia because she paid so well. And she passed along an occasional bottle of good Irish whiskey to offset the dreadful warm sake the Japanese always favored.

The two had first met when Lydia had gone to the commercial dock to take possession of a package from von Streich. The enclosed gift was a beautiful figurine of flawless Austrian crystal. He had included a short letter to tell her that he was now attached to headquarters of the Japanese Fourth Army, preparing to ship out for the Manchurian peninsula.

He wrote recklessly of his desire for her: "—my dearest beloved, I close my eyes to see you as nature intended—standing naked before the altar of love. Like Venus, you bring to the surface my maddened passion. Oh that I might kiss the voluptuous crevices of your adorable body. I am tormented by your absence. I have only my erotic dreams to keep your image before my eyes. How agonizingly I suffer. Please pray to the Holy Virgin that we may soon be reunited so that I may lower myself onto your warmth and passion."

Lydia destroyed the foolhardy letter at once. She knew she must caution von Streich to be more circumspect. What if the letter fell into the wrong hands? Still, the note made her recall lovemaking that caused her to flush with desire. How could she contact him? Then Nigel's image threw a cold blanket of guilt on the thought.

Lydia was unaware of the death of Captain Crown. Japanese intelligence would soon remedy that omission.

* * * * * * * * *

Two days after Tanaka crossed the Yalu river, the Japanese navy tried to support the landing of General Oku's Second Army by making a third and last attempt to block the Port Arthur channel.

Marina had retired early the night of May 3 in order to start work in the morning on her flower beds, now that warmer weather had arrived. Before going to bed she had wandered onto her veranda to view the town and harbor below. She looked beyond the shallow river valley and the rail tracks that snaked along its length. Somewhere to the north she knew that Rogers and Alesandrov would be busy coping with the Japanese attack across the Yalu. She did not know that the battle had already ended so disastrously for Russia. The world would quickly realize that an tiny asian nation's army had humbled mighty Russia. Reports trickling in from the front had hinted at a retreat by Kuropatkin to a new defense line around Liaoyang. Did that mean, she wondered, that Port Arthur was in danger of attack by land? News of the setback might even cause a delay in the return of Ellis and Viktor. She hoped not. There seemed to be so much confusion about what had happened. As usual, both Stoessel and Alexeiev were tight lipped. News was sketchy and conflicting rumors swirled about the town. Her prayers that the quiet of the night would continue unbroken went unanswered.

At midnight she awoke to the sound of battle. An explosion in the distance sounded like a detonated mine. More noise and the glare of the searchlights drew her again to the veranda.

Togo's naval strength, now greater than ever with the death of Makharoff and the mining of the Russian battleships *Petropovlovsk and Pobieda,* still did not ease Togo's dread that the Port Arthur fleet might somehow escape the Japanese blockade. To assure the success of General Oku's landing on the Manchurian peninsula, Togo had received orders to make one last attempt to seal Port Arthur's channel. Under Lydia's watchful observance in Sasebo, Togo had gathered and equipped twelve freighters from Japan's shrinking merchant fleet. He had employed most of the same veteran officers of the previous two blockship strikes; only the crewmen were new. He had appointed Captain Hata to command the lead support destroyer.

"Block the enemy channel," he told Hata. In a menacing tone of voice, he stated flatly, "You will succeed." He might as well have added, "—or don't return." Hata knew the admiral's angry temperment was goaded by chronic rheumatism. Ships were always damp and wet.

Hata passed the word to his officers and crew. "This fireship will block the Russian fleet even if we all die." He saw the suicidal mission as his last chance to avenge the death of his cousin, Sato.

The plan was to have the blockships leave the Elliot group and approach the harbor on a zig-zag path. Togo realized that a direct approach from seaward would probably fail since the Russians were increasingly alert. So he positioned destroyers at so-called turning points to guide the freighters along a winding course.

Of the twelve blockships that departed from the Elliot group, four either broke down or were disabled by mines near the coast. Already Russian searchlights began probing the darkness. The eight remaining freighters followed the course marked by the positioned Japanese destroyers. The captains of the blockships had orders to proceed at full steam when they passed the last destroyer, which was Hata's.

But the Russians were on full alert. Their searchlights hunted for the blockships and the last two accompanying Japanese destroyers. One of the Japanese destroyers suddenly struck a mine and caught fire before sinking. Russian searchlights pinpointed the Japanese freighters and exposed them to intense bombardment from the shore batteries. Hata had just started to follow the freighters when a shell struck his destroyer, crippling the steering machinery. Issuing frantic orders to control the floundering destroyer, Hata saw only two blockships survive to enter the channel. Both sank, having failed to block the channel. Hata's doomed destroyer, blasted by shellfire from the forts and surrounded by approaching Russian destroyers, sank so rapidly that no one below deck survived. In the shallow water of the channel, Hata and five seamen climbed up into the destroyer's rigging. From his vantage point Hata could see that the approaching enemy ships barred hope of rescue. Vowing not to be taken prisoner, he ordered his men to follow and dove into the water.

The short swim across the narrow expanse of water brought the chilled men to the harbor's eastern shore. Hata led his men to hide behind a knoll, out of the glare of the searchlights. He hoped to get past the forts to make his way eastward toward Dalny.

It was too late. A Russian patrol had spotted them and closed in for the capture. Hata foolishly fired his revolver, but missed. When the Russians took cover, Hata and his party ran from behind the knoll just as a searchlight beam exposed them. The patrol's volley dropped three of the crew. Hata and the other two ran to hide behind a nearby embankment.

"They will kill us. We must surrender. The mission is over and has failed," one seaman whined. Hata saw the other seaman nod in agreement.

"No!" Hata shouted. "Stay with me. We will die for the Emperor."

"If we die, we are no good to our families. We must live to fight again," his men pleaded. They rose to step from behind their cover with their hands in the air. So did Hata. The patrol approached cautiously. When the Russians were close, Hata suddenly raised his weapon and killed both his men. He emptied the revolver at the patrol before a shot dropped him to the ground. As he struggled to rise, the Russians skewered him with repeated bayonet thrusts.

Tanaka's performance at the Yalu town of Chulienchang had so impressed General Kuroki's staff that they suggested he be sent to help the Second Army's landing at Pitzuwo and Talienwan. The bad weather and rough surf at Pitzuwo had stalled the landing operation, so Tanaka was sent farther south to Talienwan on Hand Bay. Talienwan was only about fifty miles by road from Dalny.

Two Japanese troopships had been cornered and sunk by three cruisers from Vladivostok. With the failure of the third blockship expedition, General Oku worried about landing all his divisions before the Russians attacked. He had orders to pinch off the narrow waist of land across the peninsula, a distance of only twenty miles from Pitzuwo to the west coast.

Forced to take command of the fleet, when Admiral Makharoff had died, Viceroy Admiral Alexeiev was more realistic than the army officers. He knew that the Japanese could invade Manchuria in the absence of opposition from Port Arthur. Although few military officers at the base had any confidence in Alexeiev's leadership, they would have had even less had they overheard his comments to his wife.

"I have little hope that our forts and land defenses can shut out the Japanese," he told her. "Start shipping some of our possessions to St Petersburg. Be diligent not to tip our hand. I do not intend to be trapped here if we are threatened with a land invasion."

When he learned the news of General Oku's successful landing at Pitzuwo, Alexeiev ordered a Red Cross train prepared. Accompanied by most of his staff, he fled Port Arthur. Marina dropped the bombshell on Chen. "Our glorious leader Alexeiev is gone," she announced. "Talk about rats deserting a sinking ship!"

"Where did the Viceroy go?"

"To Mukden. He claimed that the Czar ordered him to go there to check on Kuropatkin. The news coming down from the north does not sound encouraging. I'm so worried about Ellis and Viktor."

Chen chose not to worry her about the uncompleted Japanese landing at Pitzuwo. He was well aware of the obvious Japanese plans to push on south to Nanshan to cut off the Kwantung Peninsula at that narrow waist of land.

If successful, the operation would seal Port Arthur from further contact with the rest of Manchuria.

"Don't worry," Chen told Marina. "The harbor channel is still open. I will be back with news of the situation up north."

He embraced her in farewell. Marina was always surprised at his powerful arms and shoulders. Chen was now the father figure she had once had and so sorely missed. She longed for her parents and the past tranquility of the family household. Maturing, while buried in her business affairs, had left her little time for romance. Viktor was still the only man she had ever known intimately and longed for, filling a void in her life with his sensual exuberance and charm. He had introduced her to a form of pleasure that she had come to relish.

Chen had gradually emerged in a different form in her mind. She had never thought of him in sensual terms. When she had occasionally embraced him, she recognized the manliness and strength of this kind and amiable man. She had to remind herself that he was as young as he looked, only forty, too young to be thought of as a surrogate father and only eight years removed from her own age. How she loved and respected Chen, marveling at his patience and concern for her. That night, she wondered if Rogers' comforting presence had begun to arouse a latent interest in men other than Viktor. It troubled her, yet presented an interesting and exciting dilemma.

* * * * * * * * *

When Rogers reached his Mukden hotel after the Battle of the Yalu, the lobby lights were dim. The concierge barely acknowledged him and acted unhappy that he had to stand to reach for the room key.

"You have a visitor," he said and slumped back in his chair.

Rogers distrusted the concierge, having noted the man to be a surly lout who was almost too lazy to function as a human being. So he did not question the man. *It must be Viktor. Odd! Thought he was at Liaoyang.*

There was no light showing beneath his door. Quietly, he eased into the room, deciding not to disturb Viktor. Rogers decided he could sleep in the overstuffed chair. In seconds his eyes adjusted to the darkness. The head he saw on the pillow was not Viktor's; it was a woman's. For a fleeting moment his heart jumped with joy and he almost called out—An-an? Then he saw the head raise up and recognized Claudette.

She spoke dreamily. "Viktor?" He turned to tip-toe out of the room. "Come here, cheri," she called. "Come to me" She sat up in bed and he could see she was naked. She started to swing out of the bed, then stopped. "Is that you Viktor?" She raised the sheet to cover her breasts.

"I am sorry, Claudette. It's I—Ellis. I didn't mean to intrude. Thought you might have been at the hospital."

"Isn't Victor with you?"

"No. I guess he's not yet back from Liaoyang. But please stay where you are. I'll go to the lobby."

"Please don't go. I don't want to be here alone if Viktor is not with you."

"He'll be here in the morning, I'm sure."

"Please stay, Ellis. I'll feel safer. Please. You frightened me."

"OK—go back to sleep. I'll use the chair."

"No, it is too small. You can rest on half the bed." He hesitated and started to protest. She patted the nearest side of the bed. "Sit down. You must be as tired as I am. I did not recognize you wth the new moustache. Are you trying to make yourself look older, cheri?"

Grinning at her valid perception, he sat on the edge of the bed and removed his coat and boots.

"I am so weary," she murmured. "We have had little sleep or rest at the hospital. All the beds are in use. I didn't want to spend another night sleeping on the floor. Viktor was supposed to meet me here."

He could barely hear her as she spoke of the horde of wounded soldiers crowding the hospital's corridor floor, of the endless operations, the shortage of ether and morphine and bandages. "So many terrible head wounds from the enemy shrapnel. The cloth caps are no protection."

After a few sentences, her voice became almost a whisper and finally trailed off into silence. She was asleep. He pulled the blanket up around her neck and lay down on the bed after draping an extra army blanket over them. He too quickly fell asleep.

He dreamed that a naked Claudette had removed his clothing during the night and lay with her back nestled against his chest as one of his hands closed around her ample breast and the other hand cupped her vagina.

He awoke with a start. He was on his back, and Claudette lay facing the other way. Except for his coat and shoes, he was fully clothed and grateful for the warmth of the covering blanket. Claudette turned over as he pushed the blanket over her bare shoulders. In her sleep she flung an arm across his stomach. He thought he heard her whisper, "Viktor." He lay silently for awhile, listening to her heavy breathing. Still asleep, she moved closer and her hand reached down to hold him. He was surprised to discover that he was hard. Embarrassed, he debated how to avoid awakening her while trying to release her grip so he could slip out of bed. Deciding that it was best not to disturb her, he lay motionless for a time until sleep overtook him.

At dawn he arose, splashed some water on his face and stole silently from the room, leaving the key for her. Claudette had not stirred. He carefully closed and locked the door, grateful not to have awakened her.

Rogers sat at a table in Sylvia's Place enjoying a Chinese thousand-year egg and a bowl of hot cabbage soup. The morning sun was just piercing the gray overcast when Alesandrov entered.

"It's too bad we got separated. I was told you were here. I couldn't find Claudette. They are looking for her at the hospital."

"She is over at my hotel. Tell her to take the morning off. The poor woman is exhausted."

Alesandrov hurried away, speaking over his shoulder, "Thanks for helping her, Ellis. You are a dear friend."

Rogers gazed after his friend. *Yeah, sure, Viktor. Such a lucky bastard.*

Sylvia hesitatingly came to his table. "Can we serve you anything else?"

"No, thank you. Well, maybe another cup of tea."

"You are Americain, yes?" She spoke in French and was relieved he could understand her.

"Oui," he answered.

"Correspondent?"

"No, militaire. Observer for my government." He could see that Sylvia was fishing for information and was not sure what to say to him.

"Where did your handsome friend go?"

"Away." He refused to say where. Rogers noted a certain sadness in the young woman's manner. He had seen that kind of world weary sadness before. And he had also observed the hint of an inner toughness. Not one to have as an enemy, he thought, growing uncomfortable as she searched his face as if to read his thoughts. When she continued to ask questions, he decided to turn the tables by inquiring about her past. It worked. She became resentful at his questions and soon backed away from his table.

In the afternoon Rogers approached the Russian headquarters building. He pushed his way through the crowd. It seemed to him that most of the foreign photographers and correspondents had gathered at the building. He saw Alesandrov in the lobby. "How is Claudette?" he asked.

"Wonderful. She finally got up and went back to work. I tried to make her stay, but she has a strong sense of duty to her patients. The Red Cross does not have enough nurses, and the army has very few medical corpsmen. It is a terrible situation." He looked at Rogers with a sly grin. "The sleep worked wonders for her. She was all over me; said she had such wild dreams during the night."

Rogers hoped his face did not betray his embarrassment.

Alesandrov pulled him over to a secluded corner. "I just came from a staff meeting. The commanding general, Kuropatkin, is trying to set the record straight by publically blaming Zasulich for slugging it out with the Japanese at the Yalu. On the other hand Zasulich protested that he was only following orders, that he tried to avoid a full blown battle with Kuroki. Zasulich claims that his hand was forced when Colonel Gromov retreated without proper notification. Gromov will have a formal court martial tomorrow. Gromov is furious—doesn't want to be a scapegoat. Says he was hopelessly outnumbered and in danger of encirclement, and his men were cut to pieces by shrapnel shells fired from the river islands."

Alesandrov looked around cautiously, then spoke softly. "The men blame Kuropatkin for giving such vague orders. And they blame Zasulich for not being better prepared."

"Do you, Viktor?"

"Indeed I do. The Cossack regiments should have been used by Zasulich to reconnoiter. That is what the cavalry are for. I had begged permission to lead a troop to scout the enemy positions. I was told the enemy would never get across the river and that I was in no condition to return to duty. I swear on St. Michael's cross that I am as fit for duty as anyone out there."

Rogers had seldom seen his unflappable friend so angry. Viktor had changed so much.

"Ellis, we are going to suffer in this war if St Petersburg does not give us better generals. Our staff officers think we are not ready, that we should hold off large engagements with the enemy until more troops arrive from Russia. If our navy would act more aggressively, we could throw up a trench line across the peninsula and hold off Japan for years. Russia is so much more powerful and richer than Japan. I've been to Japan and I fail to see how those rice farmers should ever defeat us. They must be dreaming."

Rogers did not say so, but he had witnessed the lack of enthusiasm for the war by Russian soldiers. They stoically followed orders, but did not have the fire in their bellies that the soldiers of Nippon possessed.

Rogers was losing patience with Alesandrov. "Have you written to Marina, Viktor?"

"Not yet." Alesandrov saw the look on Rogers' face. "I have something better than a letter, Ellis. General Kuropatkin has answered a call from Port Arthur for more ammunition. He plans to send an ammo train down there tomorrow."

"The railway south of Liaoyang had been cut by the Japanese Second Army. How does he expect the train to get through Japanese lines?"

"He doesn't think the Japs control the rail line yet. We'll soon find out."

"We?"

The top Generals

The Generals

General Kuropatkin

Lieutenant-General Stoessel

Below, General Stoessel in
one of his heroic poses

1st Vice-Admiral Rozhestvensky

Below : Admiral Makarov, the
Russians' best admiral

M. V. Alekseev (1857–1918)

Above: Admiral Witgeft

Japanese General Oyama

General Nogi

"Yes, you and I. I volunteered us to go on the train with the Fifth Siberian Rifles. I thought it would be nice if we both visited Marina. You are coming, are you not?"

Rogers threw up his hands. "If you are game, so am I." Alesandrov never ceased to amaze him.

"I am spoiling for a fight with the Japanese, Ellis. Maybe it will help make up for what they put me through in Korea."

"Was it really so terrible, Viktor? Korea, I mean."

Alesandrov grinned, remembering the lively sex he had enjoyed with Ri and Kim. The two little devils were good, damn good. He had sent to Russia for the money he had promised them. He would get it to them somehow. Maybe Claudette and the French consulate could help.

"I can forgive and forget except for a certain enemy army major and the god-awful winter weather. It cost me some broken ribs and a toe. If I ever meet up with our friend Ariko, it will cost him a pair of balls jammed down his throat." Rogers knew his friend was serious.

The court martial of Colonel Gromov ended quickly. The three officer judges found him guilty of abandoning his assigned region of defense. Alexeiev, now in Mukden, had ordered unrealistically that no land in Manchuria be surrendered to the Japanese. The judges ignored the proof that Gromov's message to Zasulich, through no fault of his, had been delayed for several hours in the shifting tide of war.

Gromov was stripped of his rank and confined to quarters pending a formal sentence. The next morning he put a revolver barrel in his mouth and blew out his brains.

Russian infantry assembling for a defense

Japanese field artillery

Russian troops

The loaded ammunition train chuffed out of the Mukden station in the dawn darkness.

"This reminds me of our train run from Tientsin to the coast four years ago," Alesandrov remarked to his companion. Rogers had also been thinking of that wild ride through Boxer lines to seek help for beleagured Tientsin.

"Quite an adventure," he agreed. "Thanks to you and that English locomotive engineer, we succeeded."

"Just barely," said Alesandrov.

The speeding ammunition train passed through Liaoyang without incident. The rail line remained clear until a few miles short of the village of Nanshan. Japanese troops stood on the tracks and signalled for the train to halt. Under orders from the Siberian soldiers aboard, the train did not slow. It picked up speed and bore down on the Japanese transportation police, scattering them. Several shots fired at the train failed to slow its journey.

Rogers saw a startling transformation come over Alesandrov. "Now that I have been fired upon, I propose to abort this trip. First the navy at Chemulpo, now this. The Japanese infantry, having officially declared war on me, I now seek retribution."

Thinking that Alesandrov was joking, Rogers predicted that the train might have to stay in Port Arthur. There might not be a return.

"I think we will have a long visit with Marina," he said.

Alesandrov shook his head. "If the Russians still control Nanshan, I will get off there."

"You are not going on through to the port?" Rogers was amazed. "What about Marina?"

"Give her my love, Ellis. Give any excuse you can. I will come to her later. Right now, I am back in action. My country is at war. I know you will understand my motive."

Rogers tried to protest, but Alesandrov cut him off. "The war can't wait, Ellis. Marina can. Watch out for her and I will see you soon."

The train stopped very briefly at Nanshan. Rogers saw Captain Baron Viktor Alesandrov wave goodbye before disappearing into the crowd of Cossack cavalrymen.

There were no incidents for the remaining two-hour trip. Upon arrival in Port Arthur, the ammunition train was greeted by grateful fortress commanders.

Rogers engaged a ricksha to bring him to Marina's godown, guessing she would be there. She was.

Screaming with girlish delight, she flung her arms around him and kissed him on both cheeks before her amused employees. She looked around for Alesandrov, then, with tears in her eyes, she silently mouthed one word, "Where?"

It was probably one of the most awkward moments of his life. Assuring her that Viktor was all right, Rogers took Marina's hand and led her into the inner office.

"At the last minute, he couldn't come," he told her.

"Why not? Where is he? What has happened? Is he safe?" The words tumbled out in short bursts.

"He left the train at Nanshan. He said he would come here later."

"But why? Could the war not wait? I thought he was still convalescing. He has not written. Did he send a message?"

Rogers said no and tried his best to explain Viktor's decision. Marina was hurt and disappointed. "When will I see him again? I don't understand why he did not come with you." She began to cry as if her whole world had collapsed. Finally she dried her tears.

"I am sorry. I just cannot understand why he came so close and then turned away. Are you sure he said nothing else?" She had noted how much more mature Rogers' moustache made him look.

At her home that evening, Marina's disappointment began slowly to turn into anger. She was hurt and did not care who knew it. Rogers related to her his visit to Mukden and the recent events that had occurred. He took great care not to mention Claudette. Marina was understandably suspicious that she had not heard all the story. Her pouting silence made his efforts to converse more awkward than he liked. Marina felt betrayed and refused to accept Rogers' counseling. Deciding that Marina was going to have to resolve the problem by herself, he finally excused himself, pleading fatigue from the lengthy train ride.

When he saw her tear puffed eyes the next morning, he guessed that she must have cried all night. Rogers left her alone, opting not to give further advice. He had seen other similar cases of resentment by military wives, sweethearts, and dependents over the absence of their men. After a second day of awkward reserve, Marina seemed finally to have reached a decision to get on with her life, and matters returned to normal.

The desertion of Alexeiev had caused Marina to be as devastated as the rest of the garrison, but Rogers regarded the desertion less seriously. "Surely a new leader will emerge," he argued.

Marina was not hopeful. "The future does not look good. General Stoessel cannot be trusted to act responsibly for the army. If the Russian forces to the north cannot help us, who knows what will happen?"

Rogers argued. "This will pass."

"How would your country react if you lost your appointed leader?" Marina countered.

"If you mean our president," Rogers said, "it would indeed be a blow, but ours is a democracy where responsibility is more evenly spread. We lost our president three years ago. His promoters were crushed with grief and alarm, realizing that the new president, whom they called a damned reckless cowboy, was now in charge. Actually it was an improvement. President Roosevelt has turned out to be a strong leader who stands a very good chance of reelection."

While in Mukden, Rogers had learned of the death of Admiral Makharoff. He asked Marina about the admiral's successor, Vice Admiral Witgeft.

Marina shrugged. "Witgeft is now responsible for the fleet. He is untried and, by his own admission, is not a strong admiral. He is a land sailor. I am told that Admiral Skrydlov was sent as a replacement, but now cannot come down here on the train."

"Are you saying that Witgeft may be a poor leader?"

"I am contending that he has to prove himself. I don't think he wanted the leadership responsibility any more than Alexeiev did. If Alexeiev will not or cannot return, what is he doing in Mukden?"

Rogers threw up his hands in dismay. "He is a burr in everyone's saddle. It is unbelievable how much he and General Kuropatkin clash. Those two minds are diametrically opposite. Of course, being senior in rank, Alexeiev always wins the argument."

Marina reminded him, "Remember that Kuropatkin and Witte are firm allies. And that their opponent, Alexeiev, will do anything to help Bezobrazov and his clique retain control of the Far Eastern Lumber lands. If Kuropatkin wants to retreat, Alexeiev will surely resist any loss of land."

Rogers changed the topic. "Tell me about the blockship attempt that happened while I was gone. I heard mention of it at the train station yesterday."

"It was a Japanese disaster," Marina said. "I have heard an intelligence report that claims the Japanese lost 171 men. Only 63 were captured and 20 of them were wounded. Those who made it to shore refused to surrender and were killed. And the channel is still passable. Everyone talks about the bravery of the enemy to try such a suicidal mission."

Rogers wondered if Togo would make any more such blockship efforts after three failures. He chose to believe that Togo or his superiors in Tokyo would surely choose another tactic.

During the week, Chen came in on another successful blockade run. For the first time, he and Rogers and Marina relaxed in a three way conversation in which Rogers became aware of the bond between Chen and Marina. It seemed to be a strong platonic relationship that fitted the two comfortably. Their full commitment to each other still puzzled Rogers somewhat. He guessed it went way back in the family history. Chen made no mention of Alesandrov, nor did Marina.

Chen had mentioned the exodus of many merchants and their families from Dalny. "They are leaving for Chefu," he said. He named several acquaintances and told Marina that she might profit from the closeout sales of their merchandise.

Marina turned to Rogers and inquired if they could go to Dalny to hunt for bargains. "Would it be safe?"

"We'll see how things shape up next week," he said. Rogers felt uneasy about the reported landing of Japanese troops near Talienwan. Why weren't soldiers from Port Arthur sent inland to guard the railway and the eastern bays? Well, that was Stoessel for you. He'd keep everyone in Port Arthur to guard his little empire. If anyone went north, it would probably be General Fock, a fellow Balt. Rogers had not heard anything complimentary said of Fock's past performance.

Chen stayed in port for two days. Before leaving, he confided to Rogers. "I found out the name of the man who almost killed us before you and I came into Dalny from Chefu last February."

"You mean the captain of the torpedo boat that fired on us?"

"Yes. It was a Lieutenant Sato."

"How did you find out?"

"I inquired because I did not want him to check on the letter of marque the Japanese gave me after I rescued one of their men. I have even painted my boat a different color—teak brown."

Rogers gritted his teeth and muttered, "I'd like to confront him. The bastard really scared me that day."

Chen smiled. "We won't have to worry about him anymore. He was killed during the second blockship fight."

CHAPTER THIRTEEN

Rogers had given in to Marina's desire to go to Dalny, believing the change would do her good. The train ride passed pleasantly. It was good to get out of Port Arthur and view the countryside, now that Spring had arrived. It was almost like a holiday for both of them.

She sought to explain her situation. "The Tang family is one of my best customers, Ellis. They know I am coming to Dalny and have insisted that I be their guest. I really can't refuse. I wish they could have invited you, but you know how important appearances are in Chinese society. Tongues would wag."

Her discomfiture amused Rogers. He kept a straight face when he teased, "I'm disappointed, Marina. I hoped we could go out of town and do something wicked." When he saw that she took his words seriously and did not seem shocked, he hurried to assure her that he was only joking and that he had planned for them to take separate rooms at a hotel. He told her, "If your host's arrangement does not work out, I can still get you a room also— in case we have to stay an extra day or two."

"I'm sorry, Ellis. I didn't plan for us to stay in two different locations."

"No matter, Marina. You have much to do and I also. Who knows, maybe we will run into Chen. He is in and out of here all the time. I still don't see how he gets past the Japanese."

After a light breakfast alone at the hotel, Rogers met Marina in the morning and was introduced to the members of the Tang family. The father and mother of six children were shy and gracious in the oriental way. They bowed and nodded and bashfully sought to make him feel at home, while the smiling children hid behind their parents. "I told them you were a nice man and not a western devil," she teased. "They know you are a close friend of Chen."

Rogers declined the offer of food and excused himself as soon as convenient. He promised to meet Marina later in front of the big brick Russian Orthodox church near the waterfront.

While Marina was busily contacting departing merchants, Rogers toured the city and later even ventured into the northern back country. The waterfront was little changed. He was surprised at how few preparations for defense the Russians had made in the city. Surely the Japanese must appreciate how good the harbor facilities were. It was curious that they had chosen not to try to seize Dalny, landing instead farther north. Perhaps the Japanese wanted to avoid a naval battle so soon.

With good drydocks, the shipyards still hummed with activity in spite of the mixup with the Baltic ship workers who had recently arrived from Europe. The skilled craftsmen had been mistakenly routed to Port Arthur instead of Dalny. That was fortunate, especially since Stoessel would see to it that they remained in Port Arthur to repair the navy ships.

With Japan's Second Army landing only 60 miles northward, many local merchants had decided to vacate the city. They were selling their merchandise at a loss before sailing to Chefu aboard neutral ships. The Russians did not interfere and the Japanese navy let them pass through the quasi blockade.

Marina drove hard bargains for the available goods, buying only what merchandise she believed would bring a higher price later. She rented a vacant shop to store everything. Business was so good that she told Rogers she might want to stay for a third day.

"I will take you to dinner tonight," she told him. "I know a very good restaurant where we can relax, enjoy good music, and you can tell me finally about your past adventures and more about what happened up north in Mukden."

The restaurant was situated on a promontory overlooking the harbor. Flanking the entrance were large tanks of fresh fish and crustaceans: favorite species of fish, and prawns, squid, abalone, oysters, conch, sea slugs, clams.

At the end of the dinner, which was a relaxing success, Marina proposed they hire a carriage to take them for a tour of the harbor. He agreed. Both enjoyed the change from the rigidity of Port Arthur.

The slow-moving Mongolian pony pulled the two-wheeled carriage up and down the wide, sloping cobblestone streets of the commercial district, then ventured out into the bourgeoise suburbs. The Boston-like weather, partly sunny but cool under blowing clouds, carried the sharp smell of salt air and shrill cries of wheeling seagulls. The driver detoured on winding roads along the south Dalny cliffs, past boulder-strewn sandy beaches. Looking beyond the little rocky islands offshore, Rogers related again his and Chen's flight across the 100 mile stretch of Bohai Gulf from Chefu.

"We saw from a long distance some of the attack on Port Arthur," he told Marina. "I had no idea then that I was witnessing the start of a war or that I would soon meet someone like you. What a crazy chain of events."

A slight wind blowing off the sea had brought a chill in the air. "You must be cold," he told her. "I had better take you home." He asked for directions to her place. She hesitated as if reluctant to end the ride.

"It is early and such a shame to end the day." Then she startled him with a proposal that they go to his hotel. "Would that be wrong? I want to talk some more. It has been such a wonderful evening. Would you mind if we stay in Dalny one more day? We could return on the evening train tomorrow."

He hesitated, then agreed. He too did not want the evening to end. Besides, he wanted to talk to her more about Viktor and Chen. He wasn't sure what he wanted to say, only that he thought it time he interfered in a normally private matter. He would not have dared to bring up the subject in her house; the atmosphere in Dalny seemed more appropriate for privacy.

He gave the night clerk a large ruble note, then led Marina to the lift for a ride to the second floor of the hotel. He led her down the hall to the sparsely furnished room, fairly modern by Manchurian standards. Once inside, he took her coat and laid it on a chair. He sat on the bed and she sat beside him. After a moment of awkward silence, she walked around to the other side of the bed, removed her shoes, propped a pillow against the headframe and lay back against it.

"We don't have to keep up appearances," she said. "Why don't you get comfortable?"

He decided to follow suit. As he leaned back on his pillow, she closed her hand over his. "What should we talk about?"

"I know you are upset about Viktor," he said. "I didn't want to spoil the evening by bringing up the matter, but I think I have warned you before that he has changed. I am not sure that I understand what goes on in his mind, or how to describe it. He is not as happy and carefree as before. What happened in Korea has scarred him. He is obsessed by his need for vengeance against the Japanese for their treatment of him."

She had not changed expression or raised an objection, so he continued and told her about Viktor's toe and frostbite. He related some of their past adventures, carefully omitting any reference to Viktor's pursuit of women. He spoke of his profound admiration for Viktor's bravery and social grace. "I know he loves you very much, Marina. He will return, so you must be patient."

Marina did not reveal that she and Viktor had quarreled briefly before he had gone to Korea. He had accused her of becoming too possessive when she had teasingly inquired about his rumored affair with an officer's wife in Russia.

She squeezed Rogers' hand. "Please, let us talk about you. Tell me of your past." She gazed at him with fondness as if seeing him for the first time. She wanted to know more about this serious, reserved, and gentlemanly American, who could be so witty and self deprecating at times—who was so different and so easy to converse with. Other men seldom realized how important it was to a woman to feel safe and comfortable. She watched the coy smile on his lips and the sparkle in his eyes as humor sometimes entered the story he told.

He told her of his unhappy boyhood in Montana, of his stepfather's weakness and cruelty, and how he had run away at the age of ten, had been captured by renegade Indians, and had been rescued by a cavalry sergeant who later became his surrogate father at Fort Reilly. He told her of the few years he had lived in Chicago before leaving to serve on sailing ships for three years. He did not tell her of his step-sister, Desiree, and why he had left Chicago.

She knew the story of his first encounter with Chen in Shanghai. He told her more about his friendshp with Chen and about their later exciting adventures during the Boxer troubles around Tientsin. He briefly mentioned the war in Cuba, but very little of his service in the Philippines. That intrigued her.

"Did you have a girlfriend in the Philippines?" she asked.

He laughed and joked, "Many."

She persisted. "Are the girls there caring and loving?" His aloofness still puzzled her. She had seen his rejection of Yin-lin and his curious reserve with herself. Could he be a virgin? *Unlikely,*

"Socially, the Philippine islands are not quite as bad as China," he told her. "But the Spanish influence is still there. After almost 400 years of occupation, the Spaniards had taught the native men not to trust other men. All single women are closely guarded and protected and not permitted to be alone with a man without a chaperone present. It is a stifling custom that punishes women and creates jealousy and suspicion. Women are always pestered by would-be romeos."

"And China?"

"You know how it is in China, Marina. If you were not half Russian, you know how you would be treated. Women have few rights and a bleak future. China will someday have to give women equality and stop murdering unwanted female babies. Women are like chattel. You know that even in Port Arthur, if I wanted a woman, I could buy one easily. And I am not talking about prostitutes."

"Do you miss not being with a woman or having a girlfriend?"

"I'm with a woman now" She squeezed his hand. "Yes, of course. I often get lonely." He decided it was time to change the subject, fearing the talk was veering toward the subject of An-an.

"Tell me about Chen, Marina. I don't understand why he never mentioned you before."

"He has been like a father to me. Now that I am older, he is more like a brother. Chen is very protective, but does not interfere. He is really family."

"How does he feel about Viktor? Is there any resentment there?"

"I don't think so," she said. "He said very little at first, but has always been guarded about mentioning Viktor. Chen never preaches or offers unwanted advice, I know he wants me to be happy, no matter how he may feel about my relationship with Viktor."

No words were spoken for a few minutes as each mulled the conversation, Marina wanted to pierce his reserve, but wondered if she could match Rogers' honesty, especially if he asked her about Yin-lin. And she longed to embrace Rogers without feeling guilt or embarrassing him. They had talked about Viktor and Chen and she had not been completely forthcoming about either. Here, she was alone with Rogers in a strange hotel room, suddenly feeling very vulnerable and in need for someone to trust, to cuddle against, someone whose strong arms could comfort her, someone who could still make her feel both womanly and wanted. She moved closer to him so that their shoulders touched.

His next question surprised her. "Have you ever felt physically attracted to Chen? Do you really know how he feels about you?"

"I never thought about it that way." She was a little shocked. Had she missed something? Were Chen's feelings about her and Viktor that uncaring?

"Chen has never interfered in my relationship with Viktor. I was never aware that he might be much concerned until you mentioned it just now."

Chen had always been so reserved, even when she had embraced him. As if he were holding back? But he had never pushed her away; had always accepted her warmth and had never seemed in a hurry to release her, now that she thought about it.

"You are very close to your servant, I've noticed."

"Yes, Yin-lin is more than a handmaiden, almost like a younger sister. She also is very protective and knows every little secret that I have. She is sometimes daring when she bathes me or gives me a massage, and she asks too many questions about sex and making love with someone. She always wants to sleep with me and cuddle closely and tells me how much she admires my body and asks if I think she would be attractive to a man and what I think she should do to please a man. She embarrasses me sometimes, but I know she is only curious."

Rogers winced at the word "sex." That had always been such an unmentionable word in prudish America.

Marina did not speak of the few times she had awakened to find her breast wet or had to move Yin-lin's hand from her lower belly, or how the girl had pushed against her buttocks and moaned in her sleep. Marina had dismissed the incidents as the result of sensuous dreams by Yin-lin, and had ignored them because of her own need to share the bed with the girl's warmth on cold nights. Yin-lin seemed unable to keep her nightgown pushed down at night, and wanted to slip out her night clothes during hot summer nights, and to strip naked when she bathed Marina, or sit astride her when she massaged Marina's body. Marina regarded her servant as a free spirit with few inhibitions and accepted the girl's tomboyish absence of modesty.

Worried about the torment that might result from Yin-lin's sexual restlessness, Marina had finally presented her with an instrument purchased from a woman proprietor who dealt in sex toys. The object, beautifully crafted from ivory, had been astonishingly accurate in every phallic detail, so startingly lifelike with its ridges and veins that one had to touch it to be assured it was not the real thing it represented. Marina was never sure if the girl had utilized the instrument to calm her surging libido. She did not reveal this to Rogers. Why shock him?

Viktor had not resented Yin-lin's constant presence, often joking about what he would do to her beautiful little figure if she ever walked in on them. He had been unaware of the one embarrassing time when the girl had done just that, and Marina had signalled a threatening gesture over his shoulder to shoo her away, and then later had been subjected to many pestering questions about Viktor's body and the witnessed sex act. The girl's curiosity and hunger for detail were insatiable.

But Marina knew she had a devoted and priceless ally who would give her life to protect her mistress. Such loyalty was not easily found.

Marina became aware that Rogers had broken the silence to ask her a question, "Why are you so quiet? Are you ready to leave?"

She shook her head and pressed against him. "Can we talk a little longer before I go? I am so relaxed and happy for the first time in days. It is good that we could talk like this." She realized that even he had talked so daringly in more intimate detail, as if he were free of self imposed strictures that he may have had out of respect for her home.

"We don't need the light, do we?" Before he could answer, Marina arose and turned off the lamp and returned to the bed to kiss him lightly on the cheek. No further mention was made of Viktor.

Bathed in the faint moonlight seeping into the room, they talked late into the night. They talked openly and frankly, something they both felt was comfortable and long overdue, in spite of the odd and questionable setting.

"You have helped me overcome some of my fears and indecision," she said. "I apologize for my behavior lately. Although I still do not understand why, I realize that I cannot own another and that I am a coward if I fear losing someone so much. Life does not grant guarantees, and I must accept that."

She went on to speak of her childhood, her schooling, the oddity of her parent's biracial union, but also the benefits of two cultures. "I learned Chinese and Russian from my parents. I later became proficient in English; my parents did also, because of our trading business. The English traders first opened up the ports of China and have always led the way in our foreign commerce. More and more, English is replacing French as the international language."

In the dark quiet of the room, Marina dozed off briefly. She had not felt so relaxed in ages. During her short nap, her mind raced through unanswered questions. Rogers had accepted her as an equal at first sight, never once hesitating about her biracialty. But why had he not touched her? Did he not desire her? If it were Victor, he would be all over her, gentle but firm in his need for her body. Not Ellis. Maybe that was part of the attraction.

By now, in the twilight zone of her consciousness, her mind arrived at a conclusion: *Ellis had a hidden love!* She dreamed that she had confronted him, asking, "Who is she? Who is your lady friend?" And he had just smiled at her. She dreamed that she wanted to feel his hands on her body, to enjoy the wonderful things his hands could do. Was it wrong to desire that? To risk betraying Viktor—as she believed he had done so often to her?

She had come to the hotel with this young American officer, feeling no shame, harboring no preconceived notion of a seductive tryst. She could not explain her need to be alone with him—to explore his feelings, to try to understand his reluctance to touch her. She was not even sure if she would stop him if he did. It simply felt enjoyable to lay beside him, and she did not want it to end. So different from Port Arthur.

She emerged from her sleep to reach for him. He was awake and patted her hand.

Turning on his side to face her, he spoke softly, "I want to thank you, Marina, for trusting me and for being such a wonderful hostess the past four months. Regardless of what happens because of this war, I will tell you that meeting you has been an honor."

She moved against him and gave him the wettest and longest kiss he had experienced in months.

They awoke to the sound of gunfire in the darkened street below, followed by the sound of horse's hooves on the cobbled street, hoarse yells in a Mongolian dialect, and a scream of pain as a bullet found its mark. A window shattered below their room.

"Stay down," he warned Marina. Hunched low, he approached their window.

"Hunhutze," he yelled. "Get on the floor."

The Mongolian riders were firing at anything that moved in the darkness. A Siberian sentry lay on the street corner in a spreading pool of blood. Two other soldiers, dimly lit by the corner street lamp, crouched low to shoot at the bandits.

One of the riders dismounted and ran to a shop door to try to kick it in, searching for loot. He desisted when a bullet toppled his horse. Another rider pulled him to safety and the group cantered off into the night.

The clatter of hooves and the sound of rifle fire gradually faded. Marina clung to Rogers when they returned to the bed. "I don't want to leave, not now," she said. "The Tangs will understand." If they did not, Marina would have cared less. Even with no further interruption, she would not have left Rogers for any reason.

In the morning, Rogers went downstairs to learn that the raiders, Manchurian banditti called Hunhutzes, had attacked the sleeping city, undoubtedly prompted by the Japanese in a test of Dalny's defenses. Japan paid well for Hunhutze guerrilla harrassment.

"I have called for hot water," he told Marina. "You can bathe first. We have all day to finish our business. After breakfast, I'll get porters to send your merchandise to the rail station."

The incoming locomotive, arriving in the late afternoon, would have its freight cars uncoupled, then would be hooked up to the loaded waiting cars for the return passage to Port Arthur.

Marina disrobed in the small water closet that had a water spigot above the tiled floor. The drain in the middle of the floor carried away the warm bath water that she poured over her body. After dousing, soaping, and rinsing, she stood for a moment, debating whether to finish with an invigorating rinse of cold water. She filled the portable basin with cold water from the spigot and screamed as the icy water splashed over her.

"Is everything all right?" Rogers called out.

"Yes, I'll be out in a minute. That felt wonderful." She toweled and dressed and emerged to see him shaving at a wash basin on the dresser. His shirt was off. She looked admiringly at his muscled shoulders and trim waist. A knock at the door alerted them to the arrival of a porter carrying another large bucket of hot water. "Your turn, Ellis," she said.

Marina wished she had clean garments, but that could wait until they returned to Port Arthur that evening. She did not want to confront the Tangs. Rogers could collect her belongings and thank Mrs. Tang for her hospitality.

It took them most of the day to make final purchases and gather all items for shipment. Rogers noticed that Marina seemed happier than he had seen her in weeks, enjoying the leisurely final business transactions and later, the late afternoon chicken, fish, and pancit luncheon.

She nestled against him on the train seat and rested her head on his shoulder. Enjoying the clean freshness of her skin and hair, he let her nap as he listened to the clicking rumble of train wheels. Unseen by her, he had placed his revolver on the seat, alert to possible further Hunhutze trouble.

CHAPTER FOURTEEN

Marina joined Rogers on her veranda in the early evening of their return from Dalny. They watched the day vanish, with the setting sun disappearing behind the hills in the west. Both were in a pensive mood, especially Rogers. For the moment, he felt at peace with the world. It was a little different for Marina. Plagued by doubts about her growing fondness for the American, she wondered if she had done enough to reunite with her Russian lover. The interlude with Rogers had given her more happiness than she had experienced in weeks. Still, though she recognized Alesandrov's wandering eye, she refused to give up so easily. She had to try harder to see him. There had to be an explanation for his stay in Nanshan. In her heart, she suspected a rival for his affection. She could not explain her doubts; it was just a woman's intuition.

She moved closer to Rogers and placed her arm around his waist, not caring who saw them. Rogers had helped her loneliness, and the uncertainty of the life ahead made her want to enjoy his comforting presence while she could. He had helped her so much in Dalny, collecting her purchases, retrieving her luggage from the Tang home, and even now was providing a strong feeling of protection.

Yin-lin had been overly curious about the journey to Dalny, asking so many questions that Marina finally had to admonish her not to be so inquisitive. Marina believed rightly that Yin-lin lusted for the American and probably felt jealousy. Yin-lin did not know that she and Rogers had done nothing more than kiss passionately, but Yin-lin had to keep her place and not ask so many hinting questions.

Rogers watched the flickering lights of Old Town and the naval basin far below the home. The upper story veranda offered a panoramic view of the port and its bustling activity, of the darkening sea beyond Tiger Tail, and the range of low hills eastward toward Dalny. A strong smell of night blooming jasmine and the wonderful odor of newly blossoming calamondine trees wafted upward from the garden. The servants had retired for the evening and the fragant night air was now quiet and peaceful. He sighed. There would be no peace shortly. The middle of May was upon the land and the armies would soon clash with the onset of warmer spring weather. Good weather always meant the start of full scale warfare.

Marina squeezed his waist. "I have a favor to ask," she said. "Will you help me?"

"Of course."

"I refuse to give up on Viktor. Will you go north with Chen and bring him back to me? I must see him before the next battle. His relationship with the royal family and his recent injury could earn him a leave from duty. I know it in my heart."

"I can try, Marina. You know I want to help you and Viktor. Of course the railroad is blocked north of here, but I guess Chen and I can try to slip up there on his boat. The Japanese need him and should let him through."

Marina pressed against him. "I have already talked to Chen. I saw him this afternoon while you were writing your report. He does have goods to take to Nanshan."

Her directness amused him. "When does he plan to go?"

"Late tonight. Did you finish your report?"

He grinned. Women and their scheming ways! "Almost finished. I need another half hour at the desk. Being with you is making me lazy and restless." *Call it sexually horny,* he thought. *The sooner Viktor gets back with Marina, the better. I am running out of willpower.*

"You will go then? You are such a dear friend." She squeezed between him and the balustrade and gave him a warm kiss. He stifled a desire to let his hands explore her voluptuous body, to touch the full bosom, caress her thighs and kiss her naked body.

"You kiss so beautifully, Marina. How can I say no?" He broke away reluctantly, his concupisent groin throbbing madly. "I'll go to my room and finish the report. It won't take long to gather my things. Please send a servant to Chen to let him know I am coming. Oh—and see what is wrong with Yin-lin. She hasn't spoken to me since our return from Dalny this afternoon."

She promised, though she knew why Yin-lin pouted. "Hurry and maybe we can talk and rest together before you leave at midnight."

He completed his report by nine o'clock, sealed the envelope, applied his chop to the wax seal, and took the envelope downstairs to Marina's parlor desk. She was working on her correspondence and looked up as he approached.

"Here is my paper work. I'll leave it with you to forward to Shanghai. Now I can pack my things," he said, as he turned toward the stairs.

"Let me help you." He started to object. She pressed her finger against his lips and shook her head. "I want to. We have two hours."

Yin lin was standing outside Marina's bedroom door. They entered his room. Marina ignored the frown on Yin-lin's face and shut the door.

Rogers' report to U.S. Army headquarters in Shanghai was addressed to the man in charge of the office, a corpulent civilian who was code named "Uncle Steve." After four years, Rogers still had not learned the man's true name. Uncle Steve had been quite active in Shanghai in 1900 and 1901 during the Boxer Rebellion, but had avoided presence in the Orient after that, choosing to relay orders from his Washington office to subordinates in Shanghai. With the growing quarrel between Russia and Japan, he had returned to Shanghai where he had kept a tight rein on Rogers' career, repeatedly denying him leave and issuing vague promises about promotions and transfers. Rogers suspected he would have remained a second lieutenant if it had not been for the War Department's gratitude for services rendered in the capture of Peking and for completion of the Officer's Course in the States in 1902. Uncle Steve kept insisting that a low rank made Rogers less conspicuous and thus more valuable in his duties. But inquiries from other governments about honoring Rogers with foreign decorations had captured the Department's attention.

Rogers' subsequent promotion to Captain had come as a complete surprise so soon after his arrival in Port Arthur in the wake of his first report on Japan's surprise attack on the naval base. The terse telegram had instructed him to don the double shoulder bars and to follow the progress of the Russian army as an accredited army observer. Rogers often wondered if the promotion had anything to do with making him more acceptable at rank conscious Russian staff headquarters.

He had gone north to Manchuria, ostensibly to visit Viktor Alesandrov, but, in reality, to gain a foothold in Russian army circles. The outbreak of the war had made him overnight a valuable on-the-spot reporter of Russian war readiness.

The American press and public continued to root strongly for Japan's cause. The War Department was not as convinced as America's "yellow press" that a Japanese victory was that desirable or even attainable.

The lengthy second report that Rogers had dispatched to Shanghai had described the Russian blunders at the Battle of the Yalu. Rogers told of the contemptuous attitude of the Russian generals for the Japanese army, and the inability of the Russians to recognize how thoroughly they had been trounced at the Yalu river, and how little effort had been made to benefit from the lessons of the battle. He wrote:

"They (Russians) still refuse to conceal their artillery. They do not use their cavalry adequately to detect enemy movements. Senior officers do not confide in junior officers or often with each other." He had described at length how antiquated much of the Russian army had remained. "They manuever like they are still battling the Turks at Plevna. Similar to the Japanese, they tend to bunch up in close clusters to present the enemy with a good target. In the shallow trenches, the officers stand erect and unprotected close behind their prone enlisted men, as if demonstrating their bravado.

There are too few machine guns for the sergeants to operate. There is little peacetime firing practice, which makes the rifle infantryman a terrible marksman. The artillery crews are lazy and vulnerable. No gun pits are dug to hide the field pieces which are sited on flat, open ground and are completely unconcealed.

The Russian can be a good soldier, but is not permitted to act independently. Fire against the enemy is usually delivered in ordered volleys.

There seems to be a serious conflict of interest between the Viceroy and Kuropatkin, the area commander, thus conflicting orders given to subordinate commanders add to the confusion. Perhaps that is why unnecessary orders to retreat are too often given. Unprepared for the initial attacks, the Russians need to buy time, but they must stand firmer against the Japanese. As I mentioned previously, the inability of the Russian Pacific Fleet to challenge Admiral Togo has opened the way for the Japanese invasion of the Manchurian peninsula."

* * * * * * * * * *

Alesandrov was so busy helping to bolster Nanshan's uncompleted defenses that he had little time to pine for either Marina or Claudette. Although steadily fortified for ten years, much more work remained. Nanshan was the outpost guarding the approaches to Port Arthur and Dalny, thus most of the existing fortifications faced north. The Russians had not considered that the enemy might land south of Nanshan. The Japanese knew the terrain well. A Colonel Doi of the Japanese army, disguised as a coolie, had labored on Nanshan's fortifications.

Alesandrov was furious that General Kuropatkin had sent most of the cavalry mounts north and had ordered large numbers of Cossack troopers to man the newly dug trenches on the hillside. Cavalry were essential for reconnaisance. And only God seemed to know where the Japanese were and what they were up to.

General Kuropatkin had dismissed the Cossacks as "tired old men on little horses." How wrong and how degrading.

The trenches up on the slope were the work of Lt. Colonel Tretyakov, who had defied Stoessel's orders to keep the infantry trenches on flat ground at the foot of the Nanshan hill, a bare rounded eminence rising abruptly 600 feet above the river plain. Alesandrov's men worked steadily to pile sandbags above the forward lip of the trenches and lay double strands of barbed wire a few yards below them.

The arrival of the new improved model 1891 Mosin rifles had been a welcome gift. The .30 caliber weapon was 1 1/2 pounds lighter and 5 inches shorter than the existing obsolete Berdan rifles, and its 8-round clip of bullets using less fouling smokeless powder, was the latest improvement.

The fortification of Nanshan and the nearby village of Kinchau sat astride a narrow waist of land that divided Port Arthur's Kwantung Peninsula from the northern Liaotung Peninsula. This separation was barely two miles wide from coast to coast at high tide. Japan's Second Army had landed at Pitzuwo on the eastern shore of the peninsula, and now thirty more loaded Japanese transports discharged thousands of soldiers at Port Adams, fifteen miles to the west, across from Pitzuwo. The obvious Japanese strategy would be to squeeze off the lower Kwantung Peninsula, which was under General Stoessel's control.

Alesandrov struggled mightily not to limp in front of his men. The loss of a toe and patches of frostbitten flesh on his feet and legs still troubled him, especially at the end of a busy day. The healing process was progressing, though too slowly to suit him.

There were times when he could have used the services of a sword orderly or a batman, a serving man that his rank entitled him to have. In the past, he had avoided such employment because of his own meticulous standards of personal hygiene. Few Russian enlisted men used toothbrushes. The coarse dark bread they ate seemed to provide adequate dental care. But too few of the troops, many coarse peasants, had access to toilet paper. That offended Alesandrov. And he insisted on a daily bath, no matter how inconvenient. Unlike others, he used good German wool socks on his feet rather than the long strips of cloth the Russian soldiers wrapped around their feet for use inside their rough boots.

In spite of the pain in his extremities, he longed for a fight against the enemy—anything to dispel the lingering anger he harbored. The Russian defeat at the Yalu had rankled. He blamed General Zasulich and he also blamed Admiral Alexeiev's continuing interference with General Kuropatkin's command. Alexeiev had now departed from Port Arthur for good, but General Stoessel was still there and that was cause for worry about Marina—even though Claudette continued to occupy his thoughts more than ever.

Marina, ah Marina! What good times they had enjoyed together. She still had a few irritating inhibitions, but she had learned so much from him. Although not as innovative as Claudette, Marina was definitely an artist of the boudoir, a woman any man could appreciate.

He still wondered if she knew that Rogers was married? Had she asked? But that was Rogers' secret. Would it matter to Marina? Who knew? It had never been an obstacle for Alesandrov.

He rubbed his ankles which still swelled too much when he walked. He straightened up, conscious of the tug in his loins that told him he had been without a woman too long. Where was Claudette when he needed her? She still seemed to bring out a surprising loyalty in him. He wasn't that devoted to other women. Beautiful Marina was beginning to fade from his memory. He vowed to discuss her with Rogers. Something had to be settled.

* * * * * * * * * *

Chen's junk slipped into Society Bay or Nanshan Bay in the late morning hours of May 14. The voyage northward had been uneventful because Japan's navy had concentrated on the eastern side of the peninsula across from Society Bay. No one had bothered Chen in spite of the nearness of Japan's navy.

Within hours that day, Admiral Togo had suffered a heavy loss from Russian naval mines. The cruiser *Miyako* hit a mine off Talienwan port and was badly crippled. The following day, the fifteenth, Togo suffered grievous losses when the battleship *Hatsuse* struck a Russian mine and sank in minutes. The battleship *Yashima* tried to assist, but also struck a mine and sank a few hours later. Compounding the loss of the two battleships, the cruiser *Yoshino* and the gunboat *Oshima* were also lost in collisions. It was a black day for Japan.

For weeks afterwards Togo's crews believed Lydia Fairborne's planted rumor that Russian submarines had hit the battleships. Lydia knew that no Russian submarines operated in the Pacific but that such a false rumor would help inhibit Togo's movements. Tokyo withheld the loss from its people for months.

Lydia Fairborne had worked assiduously to impress the Japanese that Russia had submarines now present in Manchurian waters. But she had begun to realize that her espionage efforts against Japan's army were also a potent threat to the safety of her husband aboard a Japanese warship somewhere in these same waters. Commander Nigel Fairborne no longer served aboard Togo's flagship, having irritated Togo with frequent requests for leave to visit Lydia. Lydia was never sure what ship he was on. She began to worry about endangering Nigel's life.

The news of the Japanese battleship disaster had reached Port Arthur, giving Alexeiev's successor, Admiral Witgeft, the golden opportunity to challenge the weakened Japanese navy on more even terms. But Witgeft refused to venture forth from Port Arthur and the opportunity was soon lost.

Rogers bade goodbye to Chen and arranged to rendezvous with him within ten days. He had invited Chen to join him in Nanshan, but Chen had declined. Rogers could sense that Chen would be uncomfortable around Alesandrov.

Alesandrov was surprised to see Rogers arrive with an escort patrol of Cossacks. "I landed at Nanshan Bay, or Kinchau Bay, as the Chinese call it," Rogers explained. "It is impossible to come up by rail. The Japanese have definitely seized the tracks south of here so I sailed up with Chen."

"I am delighted to see you so soon," Alesandrov enthused. He waited for Rogers to give his reason for the trip.

Rogers came right to the point. "I won't prevaricate, Viktor. Marina wants you to come to Port Arthur."

"She sent you?"

"Well, in a way. But I needed to study the front up here so I could get a better feel for how the war is going. How *is* it going?"

"Not well. But first, about Marina. Doesn't she realize I am on duty here?"

"Well, you know how women are. They demand attention."

"Then give her some, Ellis. I'm busy up here." Rogers ignored the inference. Viktor seemed unduly irritable. Maybe he was not well.

"Let's have a beer, Viktor. You need to sit down."

After two gulps of the lukewarm Tsingtao beer, Alesandrov again protested that he could not leave Nanshan, something that Rogers had anticipated.

"I can't leave," Alesandrov repeated. "I am needed here. Marina must understand that. We are at war and the enemy continues to land troops on the peninsula. They will come after us here at Nanshan. We may be outnumbered, but they won't surprise us like they did at the Yalu. So, what are your plans? How long can you stay here?"

"It depends on the Japanese," Rogers answered. I really need to go up to Mukden. Maybe I can learn what Kuropatkin intends to do. Is he going to stand and fight or keep on ordering retreats? I hear that your viceroy Alexeiev wants him to attack. That he is not to surrender another inch of territory."

Alesandrov sniffed. "That would be good if we were not so outnumbered. We're getting new troops every day, but only in driblets. That single rail line across Siberia can only transport so many soldiers and supplies daily. The Japanese have shipped three armies already and are forming a fourth, maybe even a fifth. They have the sea lanes; we don't. He paused to finish the bottle of beer and sat brooding for a brief period.

"How is Marina?" *Finally you asked*, thought Rogers.

"What about Marina? She needs you Viktor. Can't you slip away for three or four days?"

"No. Please don't ask again. Dammit, tell her to sit on a cake of ice. I can't leave my post here. Don't think I am not hurting for a woman, Ellis, but I don't like being pushed into a corner. She'll just have to wait."

Rogers tried to sooth him. "Try to understand her point of view. She misses you terribly. You are only 40 miles apart. You know how women think!" Alesandrov shook his head.

That evening, after dinner in the officer's mess, Alesandrov made a startling request.

"I do worry about Marina, Ellis. But I also worry about Claudette, since she is farther away. She has not answered my letters, but then mail delivery is bad. If you are to join me for a couple of weeks—do I have that right—

can you slip up to Mukden and check on her? Her Russian is not that good and she is all alone in that seedy hotel. I worry about her."

Rogers asked bluntly, "Why is Claudette so much more a priority than Marina?"

Alesandrov shook his head in annoyance. "You don't know what I have there, Ellis. If you knew, you would understand."

"I'll certainly inquire about her. Any messages?"

Alesandrov said mischievously, "If you go to Mukden, just bring back Claudette. You know what I need." He arched his eyebrows, grinning.

Rogers had no legitimate reason to refuse. So he endured the long 100-mile train ride to Mukden, wondering to himself why he was so caught up in Alesandrov's love life. As much as he liked vivacious Claudette, he could not understand why Viktor did not relish every moment he could spend with Marina. What a woman! If it weren't for An-an, he would be tempted to move against Viktor. Viktor had known so many different women. So what made Claudette so special?

On May 16, Rogers arrived in Mukden, went to the hotel and found Claudette in bed with a woman, someone he disliked.

* * * * * * * * * *

It was inevitable that Claudette would encounter Sylvia Levinski. Sylvia had seen to that. The Polish woman had begun to spend some time at the hospital in hopes of garnering more information from wounded soldiers. Her meeting with Claudette was not really accidental. Sylvia had approached Claudette with conversations in French. She preyed on Claudette's loneliness and soon insisted that they become friends and that Claudette visit her establishment.

Time had passed slowly for the French nurse. In the absence of Rogers and Alesandrov, boredom began to torment Claudette. She desperately needed time away from the frenzied activity of the military hospital. She longed for female friendship. The other nurses at the hospital were Russian women who tended to shun her because she spoke limited Russian and was foreign. She could converse in French with Czarist officers who had been schooled in the language and who used French as well as German to hide their conversations from Russian enlisted men, many of whom were ill-versed even in Russian. It depended on what province they were from, since Russia was such a hodge-podge of nationalities: Poles, Czechs, Slovenes Balts, Finns, Bosnians. But Claudette was wary—the officers were men and men could easily misinterpret friendship.

Claudette found Sylvia's odd but passable French welcome and felt flattered by her attention. Their friendshp grew and finally she asked Sylvia to come to her hotel room for dinner and some woman talk. When Rogers and Alesandrov had departed from Mukden on the ammunition train, they had paid for the hotel room far in advance and had persuaded the hotel proprietor not to relinquish the room to anyone else but Claudette.

After the light meal and some wine, the two sat on the bed and relaxed. Sylvia seemed to know about Alesandrov. "Is he your lover?" she asked.

"*Mais oui.* I adore him."

"I can see why he wants you," Sylvia remarked. She told Claudette how much she admired her figure. "You have such full breasts. I am shaped more like a boy. As a nurse, would you look at my breasts and tell me if they are fully developed?" She removed her blouse without hesitation.

Although puzzled, Claudette complied. "Yes. While your breasts are smaller than mine, they are shapely and you have very pronounced nipples. Are they always so stiff?"

"Always. Please touch them and tell me they are normal."

Claudette felt Sylvia shiver as she felt the breast. "I think you are very healthy and normal."

"I am not so sure, Claudette. You are different. I am curious. You must excite your lover with such a full figure. How he must admire you. May I look at your bosom?"

Claudette thought the request odd, but obliged, taking off her blouse and pulling down the straps of her chemise and permitting Sylvia to touch her. The two women stood close together, bare breasted and feeling no embarrassment. Sylvia seemed a little agitated, breathing rapidly and slightly flushed with excitement. "You are so beautiful," she told Claudette. "Please sit on the bed and I will massage your shoulders and back like my dear mother used to do for me."

Claudette, weary from a hectic tour at the hospital, could scarcely believe the overwhelming gratification of Sylvia's nimble fingers kneading her tired and aching muscles so skillfully. Her day at the hospital had been so tiring. Sylvia ended the massage by having Claudette lay face down on the bed while she soothed her lower back. Claudette soon fell fast asleep. Sylvia placed a robe over Claudette's torso, set the door latch and quietly tiptoed out of the room.

After two days, Claudette came to the tavern and apologized. "I was not very hospitable. I must have been very tired to have fallen asleep so easily and to have slept so late. When I awoke the room was dark and you were gone. Will you forgive me?"

Ignoring the stares of the soldiers in the tavern, Sylvia embraced Claudette, kissed her lightly on the cheek and murmured, "I too missed your company. Can we visit soon?"

"Of course," Claudette said. "Can you come for dinner tonight? I'll have a meal sent to the room. I have a good wine. Please come and you can tell me about Poland and I'll tell you about southern France."

Later, like two schoolgirls, the two talked animatedly, thoroughly enjoying each other's company. Time slipped by rapidly.

An evening rain shower grew into a cold, heavy torrent, Claudette looked out the window at the pelting rain storm. "I did not realize the hour is so late. The weather is terrible, and there is a curfew. You may be stopped by the military police. Would you like to stay here tonight? I have a spare nightgown."

Claudette lay on the bed, drowsy from too much wine, trying to follow Sylvia's droning monologue. She could not keep her eyes open. Emerging from a short nap, she saw Sylvia propped up on one elbow, staring intently at her. Claudette made an embarrassed apology "I am sorry for my rudeness. I must prepare for bed." She arose, disrobed, and lathered herself lightly with perfumed soap at the wash basin. With her back turned to the bed, she rinsed with a washcloth, then powdered herself and put on her nightgown. After brushing her teeth, she pulled back the covers and crept between the cotton sheets, telling Sylvia that the chamber pot was beneath the bed on her side.

Now half awake, though feigning sleep, she watched Sylvia perform her ablutions, her trim boyish body standing nakedly and unhibitedly in full view. When finished, Sylvia switched off the light, picked up the nightgown and walked to the bed. She laid the gown across the rail of the four poster frame and slid naked under the covers. Claudette kept her eyes closed. Sylvia snuggled up close, kissed her goodnight on the cheek and the recess of her throat and whispered, "Pleasant dreams."

Claudette did not answer and drowsily drifted into a light sleep.

There were some things that happened during the night that both puzzled and perplexed Claudette. Once awakened and aware of Sylvia's movements, Claudette was torn between the need for an awkward protest or an angry confrontation that would embarass them both, or should she lay still as if asleep. Not wanting to create a scene or cause the loss of a new friendship, she chose the path of passivity, biting her lip to stifle a sound and forcing herself somewhat unsuccessfully to lay motionless as Sylvia moved up and down her body.

In the morning, Claudette pretended to have slept through the incident, making no mention of it. Sylvia gushed, "Thank you for the dinner and the evening. I slept soundly. It was the wine that relaxed me so much."

A knock on the door aroused Claudette. She rose from the bed, threw on her robe and approached the door, calling out, "Who is it?"

"It's I, Ellis." She recognized Roger's voice. Unthinking, she opened the door and flew into his arms. He hugged her, then his eyes opened in astonishment as he looked across the room at the bare shoulders of a woman in the bed. Claudette squealed with embarrassment and pushed him away from the door. She whispered, "It is an overnight guest. I'll get rid of her at once. Please wait out here for a couple of minutes while we dress. Please. Do you mind?"

Sylvia hurriedly dressed, saying, "I must go at once to the tavern." Embracing Claudette, she kissed her full on the mouth and was gone before Claudette could protest. Sylvia glared at Rogers in the corridor and brushed past him.

Claudette, still in her dressing gown, pulled him into the room, ignoring his hesitation, and continued to kiss him.

"Do you know her?" she asked Rogers. "The hour was so late and It was so stormy last night that I asked her to sleep here. I wish that I knew

you were coming, cherie. Oh, I am so glad to see you. Where is Viktor?"
She kissed him hungrily. "I missed both of you so much."

"I had no time to let you know," he apologized. "I hope that I am not
interfering."

"Where is Viktor?"

"I came alone. He could not leave. He asked me to look in on you and
tell you how much he loves and misses you. He is really quite concerned.
Are you on duty today?"

She nodded. "How long can you stay? Will you be here long? Is
Viktor well?"

He told her he had to interview some officers at General Kuropatkin's
headquarters, then return to Nanshan, "There will be fighting there very
soon, I'm afraid. The Japanese are marching toward Nanshan. I wish I
could tell you more. But Viktor is well."

"Give me a few minutes to put on my uniform, then we can go to the
hospital and have breakfast there. I refuse to hurry. The hospital can wait.
They have been working the nurses long hours without pity."

At the hospital dining area, they had breakfast. She introduced him to
some doctors and several envious nurses. He took his leave as soon as
possible because it was obvious that the staff was short handed and they
wanted her to report at once to her ward. She insisted that they have dinner
together and that he stay in her room for the night. She refused to take no
for an answer, so he agreed.

That afternoon, Dr. Zieman approached Claudette about Sylvia. "She is
here at the hospital more than I like," he complained. "I must warn you
about her." He held up his hand to halt her protest. "She is a Jew like me,
but she is also Polish. You would do well to be on your guard."

Claudette frowned. "How could she possibly be a threat?"

"Poles are untrustworthy and deceitful. We Russians know that. I know Poles and I know women. She does not like men. No one knows much about her and you can't trust her. Be careful. There is an Okhrana agent who has been watching her, and he has spoken to me."

Rogers spent the day introducing himself at staff headquarters, making discrete inquiries, trying to dispel the suspicions that the Russians had for foreign officers, especially the Germans and British. He tried to lay the groundwork for future cooperation.

He called for Claudette at the end of the day, escorting her back to the hotel. She was tired. "I did not sleep too soundly last night," she told him. "And my feet hurt from being on them all day." She seemed to anticipate his curiosity. "You are probably wondering about my guest of last night? You must know about Sylvia's Place?"

"It is none of my business, Claudette. But I was a little surprised to see her here."

"Well, she needed a place to sleep. This morning, I think she wanted to stay all day—not get out of bed. That is why she was not dressed."

"How well do you know her?"

"Not very well. We haven't been acquainted that long. What do you think of her?"

"Not a bad looking woman," he answered. "But I'm not sure what side she is on. She tried to listen to every word Viktor and I spoke in her tavern. We both noticed it—her curiosity, I mean."

"Maybe she was attracted to two handsome soldiers." He shook his head.

After a moment's silence she asked, "Why do you not think she likes soldiers, men that is?"

"Something about her. I could almost sense hatred when she looked at me. Was I interrupting something? I could see that she was naked in bed."

There was a long silence, broken finally by Claudette. "I need to talk to someone about this. Would it embarrass you if I did? I am confused." She ignored his hesitation. "I am a nurse, but I am a woman first, and it all took me by surprise. What do you think I should have done?" She proceeded to tell him about Sylvia's overtures during the night. "If it had been a man, I would have known how to manage it. I didn't know whether to stop her or pretend I was asleep. I am ashamed to say that I was very aroused. I've never been in that relationship before."

"Why not ask Viktor?"

"Oh, you know *him*, He'd probably laugh and treat it like a joke."

"Then it is your secret and mine and we will tell no one. Forget it ever happened. Just be careful about her. I think she can be a very mean person."

"Do you think she is a lesbian?"

"No, I don't. Since she did not ask you for anything, I suspect she just wanted attention from someone. I think she hates men, but that for the moment she was lonely and wanted you as a friend and someone she could be intimate with. She may only be a very sad and bitter woman who is crying out for affection from a world that has not treated her kindly." He looked around the room. "Do you have a spare blanket, Claudette?"

"You are sleeping on the bed, Ellis. I won't take no for an answer. And strip down to your underwear, so you don't wrinkle your uniform. You will sleep better. I see naked butts all day long. They all look alike."

"Mine is different."

"No, Viktor's is different. Please rub my feet before I fall asleep."

Afterward, he reached over and kissed her. Relaxed also, he struggled to stay awake on the soft mattress. "Feel better?"

She leaned over him and kissed him in return, then kissed him twice more. "French people like to kiss a lot. I hope you don't mind. It is nice to have someone in whom I can confide. I wish you were my brother."

His eyes were closed. "That might be incest," he muttered.

She giggled and snuggled closer. "For a serious person, you sometimes have a sense of humor. Why do I like to kiss you so much?" She opened her mouth and gave him a long kiss. "You have nice soft lips." She trailed her tongue along the length of his lower lip and stopped only when his heavy breathing told her he was fast asleep.

In the morning he departed reluctantly.

Claudette had kissed him repeatedly amid copious tears and told him what a dear friend he was and how comforting it was to have a man next to her at night and how safe she always felt in his presence and how good it was to be able to joke with him about life because he asked for nothing and respected her so much. "If it were not for Viktor, I would come after you," she told him. "You are such a gentleman, so loving and comforting."

She began to cry again. "Oh *cherie*, you can' t know how much I love him. Please don't let him get hurt. I don't want him to be at the hospital again. I almost lost him once."

"I hate to leave your wonderful company, Claudette. I'll assure Viktor you are safe and miss him terribly. You may not really know how much he dotes on you. He's changed a great deal."

She kissed him again. "We can't do this when Viktor is here, so kiss me. I have been so lonely. Kiss me passionately while you can. I won't seduce you." She pulled his head down closer and kissed him fiercely.

"How can you be so calm with me? Do you have a woman to care for you? Viktor won't tell me. I don't mean to tease you, but hug me tighter." After a moment, she released him and asked, "Can you stay another day? Can I see you tonight?"

"I don't know how long I will be in Mukden. I should leave today."

She melted in his arms. "Kiss me again."

He left shaking his head in wonder. How unlike an American woman she was. Such a free spirit! After being so close to Claudette, he longed to see Marina again and wondered how much longer he could keep his distance from her. Did these women think he was made of stone?

On the way to army headquarters, he passed Sylvia's Place. He knew she had seen him through the window as she turned hurriedly and left the dining room. He was tempted to enter the tavern and confront her, but realized that would be bullying and foolish. Claudette could manage her own affairs. He was immediately glad of his decision, because he spotted the Okhrana agent, Colonel Lebedeff, staring at the door through which Sylvia had just fled. Lebedeff sat in a far corner almost out of sight. Only two other tables were occupied at this early hour.

Colonel Lebedeff's mind had grown more suspicious each time he had seen Sylvia. This morning in particular, Lebedeff was troubled by the large number of pigeon cages he had seen behind the tavern from a vantage point high up in another building. He personally enjoyed eating the small pigeon eggs, but that was food the Chinese relished much more than the Russians. And Chinese did not frequent Sylvia's Place. So who could be eating all the eggs?

Why would she need so many pigeons?

Acting on impulse, he suddenly rose and walked toward the rear kitchen. The food preparation area and storage shelves for the vodka bottles covered the rear wall and almost masked the rear door. The outer door opened to a small dirt yard that contained a blood-stained wooden chopping block, an axe, and several empty vodka crates. The pigeon cages crowded the high rear stone wall at the property edge.

Sylvia stood before the cages holding one of the pigeons, her back half turned, Startled, she angrily asked what he wanted. "Are you spying on me?"

He smiled. "Why would I? It is curious that you should use such a word."

"What do you want?"

"I thought we could talk privately."

"Why?"

"I have some questions."

She turned as if hiding the pigeon.

"What is wrong with the bird?"

"It has an injured foot."

He moved toward her. "Let me see."

"Look if you must." She tossed the bird high in the air. Its spread wings rapidly carried it out of sight.

Lebedeff followed her back inside. She kept moving away from him, tending to her few customers. Finally he gave up and left, calling out, "I will be back."

Something about the injured bird troubled him. There had been a hint of brass as the bird soared. Surely not a metal splint?

* * * * * * * * *

331

Wincing occasionally with pain, Alesandrov continued to push himself and his men. The trenches on the slope of the hill needed to be deepened. There was a shortage of sandbags. Not all the machine guns had arrived. And now orders had arrived for a regiment to be sent to bolster the defenses of the adjacent village of Kinchau. He shook his head. That place was too vulnerable.

Rogers found him at the southern perimeter of Kinchau. Alesandrov did not seem to want to stop working. He barely greeted Rogers. "I didn't thnk you would be gone so long. What happened? And how is Claudette?"

"She is great company, Viktor. Sends her love—misses you terribly."

"Is she still at the hotel? Where did you stay?"

"I slept with her every night. The nights are cold up there." Alesandrov studied his laughing friend. Was the American telling another joke?

"Yeah, sure, Ellis. Nice story. Too bad you can't know how warm she sleeps. Tell me another lie." He was amused. Poor shy Ellis—he didn't know much about women. He loved his American friend dearly, but pitied his shyness and lack of experience with women. The poor lad was missing so much in life.

CHAPTER FIFTEEN

Captain Tomoru Tanaka knew that the men of his regiment marching towards Kinchau were obsessed with reaching Nanshan before the battle ended. The thunder they heard in the night was the sound of cannon. They marched with long strides, pressing eagerly onward though racked with thirst and fatigue. With their water bottles long since emptied, these sons of Yamato dreamed of sacrificing themselves on the altar of glory. They spoke to each other with joy and eagerness, their voices ringing with enthusiasm in their fever to fight for the emperor, to add glory to the history of their race. All anguished that they would reach the field of battle too late.

Returning transport coolies from the front were besieged with the question, "Is the fight still on?" Hurrying through the clouds of yellow dust, the soldiers struggled forward through villages and fields, tormented with dry, parched throats, hoping that the Russian defenders of Nanshan could hold out until their arrival.

Tanaka sighed with pity. His men could not begin to fathom the horrors of war. Had they been with him in the Boxer Uprising, or in the recent Yalu battle, they would have been sobered by the sights and sounds of war. But these men, innocent and not yet bloodied, would learn war soon enough.

In spite of strict censorship, the Tokyo newspapers had openly stated that the next battle would be fought at Nanshan. Ever suspicious of planted information, the Russians erred by chosing not to believe the Tokyo press.

The landing of Tanaka's regiment at Talienwan had been hazardous in the treacherous currents and mountainous waves whipped up by the strong northern winds. The scene had been chaotic as chartered Chinese junks had arrived with the troop transports and all had endeavored to put the men ashore. Small overloaded boats, strung together like beads on a necklace, were pulled behind steam launches, pitching and bobbing helplessly in the violent sea. Some men and animals had drowned, lost forever and pitied by their comrades for having died so ingloriously.

Later, when the storm had abated, Tanaka helped organize a pontoon bridge made with sampans lashed together and extended a few hundred yards out from the shore. The regiment landed, shouting with joy that they were on a peninsula about to become Japanese soil.

Contact with the Manchurian natives had been a disgusting experience for the soldiers. Stupid-looking old men smoking long-stemmed pipes, and joined by dirty-faced young boys, lined the shore, staring distrustfully at the Japanese. The filth and dirt of the Manchurian houses, the fearful smells, especially the overpowering odor of garlic, caused the soldiers to gag. The greedy natives seemed to be a race so obsessed with money that they would happily live in a pig pen if only their pockets held gold.

But the skill of the natives with horses and mules impressed the Nipponese. With no sticks or whips, the natives could herd the animals with only cries of "ata, ata" or "wo, wo" for right or left.

Before the regiment left for Nanshan, there had been a presentation of the regimental flag and an inspiring speech by the colonel. Following a pledge against any display of cowardice or disgrace, the men were excused to drink a last toast, cleanse their bodies, don clean uniforms, and say farewell prayers.

Unlike his men, Tanaka's heart was not in the imminent conflict. Proud of his patriotism, he winced with shame at his concern for self preservation, for his yearning to survive for Yuriko's sake. Ever since his departure from Japan, others had regarded him as too reserved, a cold fish, a man not exuberant about dying for the emperor, a man not bursting with *bushido,* the warrior spirit. After the battle at the Yalu, where he believed he had acted with valor, he had gone from the First to the Second Army to land at Pitzuwo, then had been sent farther south to Talienwan to aid more landings.

Now, moving toward Nanshan in Japan's effort to seize the narrow waist of land separating Port Arthur's Kwantung Peninsula from the upper Liaotung Peninsula, Tanaka had been ordered to go on alone, ahead of his marching company. He was wanted at Kinchau at once. A mounted army courier galloping south from Nanshan had met the marchers and had brought another mount for Tanaka to ride, and with orders to hasten on alone to General Oku's command post.

The general seemed possessed to impress the newsmen of the western press with Japan's military excellence. Tanaka's English speaking skills made him a wanted part of that effort.

At dawn on May 26, Tanaka had reached Kinchau just as the Russians abandoned the town. Severe Japanese losses during the night attack on the town had forced headquarters to throw Tanaka and all available officers at once into the battle for adjacent Nanshan. Still wet and cold from the downpour of rain during the night, Tanaka obeyed stoically.

At a brief council of war, Tanaka had been told that "our informant in Mukden reports that 4,000 men of the Fifth Siberian Rifle Regiment are defending Nanshan. They had been brought up from the naval base at Port Arthur. A General Fock from the base has a reserve force of 16,000, not yet committed. So far, we outnumber him. If we can seize the hill, our artillery will prevent General Fock from uniting with Kuropatkin's forces north of Nanshan. Port Arthur will then be completely cut off. Meanwhile, our Third Army under General Nogi is on the way from Japan to join us."

The Japanese barrage against Kinchau during the night had inflicted

Russian infantry at Kinchau Village

Russian infantry at Kinchau Village

Quarterdeck of the Japanese battleship *Asahi*

heavy casualties on the Russian defenders, who had held off the attackers until dawn. By the light of morning, fearing his men were depleting their ammunition, Lt. Colonel Tretyakov had ordered retreat. The unnecessary Russian evacuation of Kinchau reflected once again the unwillingness of Russian commanders to stubbornly stand and fight. The retreat was orderly. Early in the morning, just as Tanaka had arrived, Japanese artillery began to pound the Russian trenches at the foot of the Nanshan hill.

The Japanese had occupied Kinchau after the Russian evacuation. They had moved up their artillery and at 5:30AM shelled the Russian positions around the Nanshan hill. At 6:00AM, four Japanese gunboats in Nanshan Bay joined the barrage.

Tanaka rehearsed his orders: "Lead your men out the eastern edge of the town. Probe the enemy's defenses. The rest of the Tokyo Division will follow while the Osaka Division comes out the western part of the town toward the hill." Tanaka knew the battle plan in advance. It would be the typical Japanese employment of a two-punch attack—a frontal assault joined simultaneously by a flanking attack, something the Russians never seemed prepared to counter.

Rogers had joined Alesandrov at the second line of trenches on the side of the hill. "We are safer up here," Alesandrov told him. "That trench at the base of the hill will be hit first. And I pity our poor devils at the cannons. Look at our field guns, sitting out there in the open, exposed with no cover or concealment. Get ready to see some hot action when the enemy barrage lifts."

Red-eyed and weary from the strain of the Kinchau battle, Alesandrov yawned and stretched. "Last night in Kinchau was bad, but we held off the enemy. No reinforcements have arrived from the reserves. It looks like

Fock wants to save his division for Port Arthur. Maybe the general plans to fight to the last of the Fifth Siberians."

"What about the reserves?" Rogers asked.

Alesandrov answered, "Not only has Fock made no move to send up reinforcements from the reserve, he has even returned two regiments to Port Arthur. The man is mad!"

He told Rogers, "Colonel Tretyakov protested earlier to General Fock that placing the trenches on flat ground at the foot of the hill would make them less easily defended. Fock argued that the defenders on the face of the hill would be more exposed to enemy fire and that Russian bullets shot horizontally would be more effective. Can you imagine such reasoning?

Tretyakov argued that the hillside would be more difficult for the enemy to attack. It did no good to protest. Fock just walked away in anger, referring to Tretyakov as a "whiner."

Alesandrov knew the situation was grave when he saw the Japanese mass for a frontal assault. "They have ten times our number," he warned.

The concealed Japanese cannon quickly silenced the exposed Russian artillery. Those artillerymen, who could escape the punishing salvos, abandoned their guns and fled to the trenches. Alesandrov urged his men to stay calm, select their targets carefully, and fire independently. Fire by volleys had not worked well during the night.

The slaughter began at 9:00 AM. Tanaka groaned when the whistle blew for the banzai charge. With hundred of others in the First "Tokyo" Division, he rose and joined the shouting, and charged in close order against the Russian wire. As he dreaded, Russian machine guns beat back the first wave of attackers. Men fell dead and dying all around him. Two companies

Japanese suicide charge against Nanshan Hill

at the front of the charge were wiped out. Knocked off balance by his falling color sergeant, Tanaka hit the ground, then lay there, feigning death. The supporting Third "Nagoya" Division was pinned down by shellfire from the Russian gunboat *Bobr*, which had slipped into Hand Bay with three troop transports, shielded by Russian mines.

The Osaka Division, often referred to as the unlucky "Fourth," fared little better, dying by the hundreds during the sixteen hour battle that extended into the night. Tanaka lay still and watched pityingly as Russian snipers shot every moving wounded Japanese.

Foreign observers stationed with General Oku's staff watched the slaughter through field glasses as more waves of troops charged the hill. Astounded that men's lives could be spent so recklessly, some of the foreign observers protested the "Algerian tactic" that the French had used so effectively in north Africa was now stupidly wasteful in the face of machine guns and trenches protected by barbed wire.

"Is this the good training that von Moltke and his Prussians taught the Japanese army?" one of the British officers mocked the German observers. "Forcing men to charge shoulder to shoulder in a crowded mass against enemy machine guns is sheer suicide."

The second human wave at noon also had failed to reach the Russian trench. In the late afternoon, screaming "banzai, banzai," the doomed third wave charged madly forward until the merciless machine guns cut them to ribbons. Six more night charges failed as miserably. Aided by the distraction of the assaults, Tanaka was able to work his way back to the shore. By this time, the tide had receded so that a narrow strip of land on the side of the hill to the west lay open for the men of the Osaka Division to crowd around to reach the rear of the Russian line. On the eastern shore, the men of the Tokyo Division were not so fortunate with the dropping tide.

It had been a long and bloody day. Lightning split the skies to aid dynamo-powered Russian searchlights betray Tanaka's Tokyo Division men massed along the east banks of the bay. Wading in chest deep water, Tanaka led his men along the eastern strip of shoreline into the fire of the waiting Russian soldiers. The slippery mud bottom of the bay gave poor footing to the slowly wading Japanese. Those who were killed sank wordlessly. The wounded, unable to maintain their footing, drowned. One by one, Tanaka's men perished until the last man fell beneath the surface of the water.

Tanaka crawled out of the deeper water and lay shivering at the water's edge, his head pounding from the pain of a bullet that had knocked off his hat and creased his scalp. He choked on the salty water that threatened to filll his lungs. The screams and yells from his men had long ceased. Raising his head, he looked about. Except for several bodies floating nearby, his soldiers had vanished. He could hear rapid rifle fire coming from the western side of the hill, otherwise all was strangely quiet from the hill above. *Was he alive or dead?* He tried to crawl out of the shallow water, but his strength failed and he faded into merciful unconsciousness.

A panting runner ran forward to inform Alesandrov that the Osaka men on the western side of the hill had succeeded in outflanking the Russian defense. "They are behind the hill," the messenger gasped. "And General Fock has pulled out without notifying Colonel Tretyakov."

Alesandrov told Rogers to get out while he could. He told him that at last count he only had 26 survivors out of an original group of 250. The front had crumbled. Rogers lost sight of him in the withdrawal that at first was orderly, but soon became a disorganized rout. In the darkness, two confused Russian regiments began firing at each other. Men stumbling to the rear became separated and lost. Word spread that the Japanese had cut off the rear guard and the line of retreat. The panic and confusion grew. Fleeing horse drawn artillery caissons bolted down the road, scattering men right and left.

Alesandrov arrived at the Tafangshen rail station to find the station house crowded with officers resting on the floor. Wounded enlisted men, begging for water, lay on the ground around the station. Men searched the baggage cars at the siding for food, but could only find three wagon loads of bread, which they flavored with coarse salt and devoured. No other food was left behind. General Fock had selfishly ordered the two-wheeled kitchen carts to leave. Angry at Fock's abandonment, Colonel Tretyakov attempted to halt the panic by ordering a regimental band to play. The martial tune did help to alleviate some of the stress and slow the mad rush to the rear. Men began to fall into orderly ranks for the long walk southward.

Rogers was unable to make sense of the movement of the retreating Russians. Some headed south, some north. In the darkness, he finally trailed behind a group of Fifth Siberians, bypassing the Nankuanling rail station to move south through the low hills toward Dalny.

Coming in from the east from Talienwan, Tanaka's tardy regiment finally reached the battle scene. They crested a steep hill to look down at the rolling country below, with Kinchau on the right and the high mountain on the left. They saw the white cone-shaped field hospital tents being erected, and the pillars of white smoke rising skyward from the cremation fires. Members of the regiment paused silently to remove their hats and bow.

Piles of bodies, pieces of equipment, powder boxes, empty cartridge cases, torn uniforms, underwear, and gaiters littered the field. Bearers carried stretcher after stretcher to the tents, then returned for more casualties. Walking wounded covered with blood and mud, bearing red-stained bandages slowly approached the tents.

Shocked and disenchanted at the scene, the arriving regiment was ordered to aid the stretcher bearers in gathering the 4,000 Japanese corpses and to dig graves for almost 1400 Russian casualties. The reddened uniforms of their comrades had now darkened to purple blood, The faces of the dead had changed to blue with clotted hair and swollen eyelids, the faces staring upward with bared white teeth. The odor of the white smoke covering the piles of dead wafted across the now silent battlefield. After searching for numbers or names, the Japanese buried the Russian dead in shallow graves according to international Red Cross regulations, Few of the Russian dead carried identification for the Japanese to forward to Mukden. Some of the dead were buried with crosses or icons on their chest.

Some of Tanaka's regiment turned back from the silent battlefield, shame-faced and crestfallen that they had missed the battle. Others, sobered by the panorama, watched the growing number of wooden posts that marked the burial mounds of Russians.

At their designated bivouac area, Tanaka's regiment found two dozen wounded men, including one Russian, behind a farmhouse. The wounded had lain without water or rice or care for twenty hours, and now cried out in agony. Two rapidly lost color and began to breath faintly. Their eyes closed slowly and their lips stopped quivering as they died.

The fallen horses and mules received little attention from the few army veterinarians present. The dying gave a final neigh or snort, and all were left to rot as carrion for wolves and crows.

Warehouses and Russian living quarters revealed large supplies of winter clothing, food stuffs, and medicines. Russian searchlights that had harassed the Japanese were smashed in anger and piles of rockets were torched. The large number of Russian prisoners were marched off to Talienwan Bay for transport to Japan.

Tanaka remembered being carried on a stretcher along the narrow shoreline. He passed the remains of a brigade of Russian cavalry that had been surprised by Japanese coming around behind them from the west. With no avenue of escape, the cavalry had been driven into the sea to drown. The beach was covered with corpses of men and horses tossed ashore by the tide.

Rogers and several members of the Fifth Siberian Rifles straggled into Dalny in the late afternoon of June 28. Turmoil and chaos greeted them. The city was emptying fast. News of the Russian defeat at Nanshan had created panic among the people. Those who could afford to cross the Bohai Bay to mainland China were busily booking passage to Chefu. Others, less fortunate, had begun the long walk to Port Arthur. The mayor and 600 Russian citizens joined the trek because General Stoessel had forbidden use of the railroad.

General Fock's Russian military had made a half-hearted show of defending Dalny, but Stoessel had already ordered his divisions to destroy as much of the infrastructure as possible and desert the city in twenty-four hours. Fortunately or unfortunately, the army had failed to provide blasting powder to blow up the wharfs, rail tracks, and utility plants, so the city remained relatively intact, except for looting and pillaging by unrestrained Hunhutze predators. On the heels of the retreating Russians, bands of Hunhutzes swarmed into the city during the night and next day to burn and rob unmolested.

Rogers had rushed to the harbor to find Chen crowding panicky passengers onto his large junk. Anxious refugees jostled to bid against each other for passage, assuring a profitable voyage for Chen.

"Save room for the Tang family," Rogers called out.

"I already have," Chen answered. "Please tell them to hurry. I want to leave before dark. Are you coming?"

"No. I'll stay to help Marina."

Chen seemed relieved that Marina would not be abandoned. He jumped onto the dock for a quick private word with Rogers. "I will return in a couple of days. I think the Japanese, if they arrive soon, will permit more Chinese residents to leave with me. They will want to bring in their own people. Also, please tell her I will be watched more closely from now on, so she should plan on hard times." This was a warning that his blockade running days could be drawing to a close.

Rogers hurried to the Tang shop. It was a large structure with the family residence typically occupying the second floor above the shop. Chinese merchants preferred to devote all their time to running a business as close as possible to their abode, and to keep the home safely inconspicuous. The Tangs had wrapped all they could gather in large blankets and sheets and were ready to carry the bundles to the boat when Rogers arrived. He helped the father close the shutters and lock the doors, although sensing that the shop would probably be plundered in the absence of Russian police.

The Japanese were not feared as much as the local bandits, who would surely seek revenge against Russian authorities. As soon as Rogers had shepherded the Tang family to Chen's vessel and had waved goodbye to Chen, he pushed his way through the disappointed crowd left behind and walked toward the hotel where he had stayed with Marina. The memory of that night brought a smile to his face.

The hotel was shuttered and locked as were most of the surrounding local businesses. The citizenry had belatedly realized that Fock's military division would abandon the city without a fight. With the approach of darkness, an eerie silence fell over the once bustling community. Rogers was famished. He looked in vain for a open restaurant, but was able to buy only two boiled duck eggs from a street vendor. He found a place to sit, took a deep breath, and forced himself to relax.

Outside the hotel, Rogers watched the stream of refugees hurrying to vacate the city. Many were orientals. One man caught his attention. Though dressed as a Chinese businessman, the individual somehow seemed different. Perhaps it was the way he walked—almost like a soldier. There were other things about the man that seemed vaguely familiar. Was it the slightly different clothing? The man had an extraordinarily cruel face.

Suddenly, like a bolt out of the blue, it came to him. Of course! It was the same man who had tried to take his valise when Rogers had first boarded the train for Port Arthur immediately after his arrival in Dalny with Chen back on the eighth of February. Though dressed in disguise as a Chinaman, the man was Major Ariko, the Japanese army spymaster. Rogers knew it was Ariko because the face belonged to the shadowy figure who had retrieved the note from Viktor's hostess, Tea Flower, when she had tossed it from the upstairs room above the Golden Pavilion tavern the night of the New Year's Eve reunion with Alesandrov.

Four years previously in the Boxer conflict, Rogers had reason to believe Ariko despised him and wished him harm. Even though Japan was an ally, and Rogers had extremely close ties with the Japanese army, and with Lieutenant Tomoru Tanaka in particular, he had never trusted Ariko and had never let his guard down in the man's presence. He knew hatred when he saw it on someone's face. So what was Ariko doing in Dalny in disguise unless it was to pave the way for a Japanese occupation?

He ran toward Ariko who took off running. Rogers tried to jostle his way through the crowd, but it was no use. Some of the panicky crowd cursed him for seemingly trying to elbow his way to the head of the line. By the time Rogers pressed through the crowd, Ariko had disappeared.

The Hunhutzes took advantage of the absence of troops and police to loot and rob with little interference. They burned those shops and homes that were obviously Russian. Rogers helped several Russian officers organize army stragglers into a makeshift rear guard to defend the walking civilians on the road to Port Arthur. He was sure the Japanese would hurry to reach Dalny in a day or two to establish order in what remained of the city. The sky was aglow with the flames of burning buildings. Twice he had to shoot robbers who tried to attack the column of weary marching civilians. A long line of dejected people, led by the mayor, trudged toward Port Arthur, joined by soldiers who began to show more orderly discipline as they neared the neighboring forts. They brought with them a large herd of cattle that had been rounded up south of Nanshan.

The arriving refugees strained the facilities of the already crowded and damaged naval base. The Russian community formed aid societies to find housing for the homeless Russians. Saharoff, the ailing Dalny mayor, soon succumbed to what was probably pneumonia.

The Chinese refugees from Dalny were left to fend for themselves. Marina volunteered to provide canvas for makeshift tents. She organized the Chinese community, both in Old Town and the newer Chinatown, to furnish soup kitchens for the abandoned and desperate Chinese families.

Rogers was delayed in arriving because of helping Czarist officers. Several units of arriving battalions were refused entry into Port Arthur by

General Stoessel who was furious about the retreat. These turned away battalions were denied food and drink and forced to move to the eastern forts in the Green Hills line of defense.

Because the Chinese farmers traditionally believed that trees and grass were a hindrance to planted crops, the barren hillsides offered little nourishment to cattle and horses. In any event, the cattle were reserved for Russians and the Chinese refugees had to subsist on mule or horse meat.

CHAPTER SIXTEEN

When Rogers finally arrived at Marina's godown or warehouse one morning, tired, dirty and disheveled after the long trek from Dalny, he found her strangely reserved and distant. She greeted him but made no move to embrace or kiss him. Nor did she ask about Viktor. He told her that he had become separated from Alesandrov at Nanshan, but was sure that Viktor was safe. Her eyes were red from weeping and her face looked haggard. She had seen the returning troops and the crowd of people escaping Dalny and knew that the naval port and town of Port Arthur would be besieged by land as well as sea. All she had worked for now seemed to be collapsing. Rogers dismissed her coolness, blaming it on fatigue and disappointment. He tried to warn her.

"We are in it for the long haul," he told Marina. "There is no way out of here except by sea. Can you sell your business and home and leave now?"

"Who would buy? The Viceroy, Alexeiev, may have deserted this sinking ship, but the rest of us—the garrison and the townspeople are forbidden to leave. Have you read Stoessel's latest manifesto? Where would I go? This is my home. I am basically a Russian. Besides, I have an obligation to remain."

Rogers was not sure what obligation kept her there, but he knew she was resigned to her fate. With no escape, condemned to stay for the siege, he saw that dark days lay ahead as the Japanese noose tightened around Port Arthur. Like the others, she would have to endure the periodic shelling, and other hardships.

He was a little puzzled. She did not seem desperately anxious to leave, even if Chen could smuggle her out. Why?

349

Was her business a front for other activities? She had always seemed to be frank with him, but there had been some suspicious activities at her factory that he found troubling. Surely she could not be involved in the anti-Czarist movement? He'd never had a hint that her sympathies might lie with Japan. But what about China? She was half Chinese. Yet he refused to believe she would support the evil Empress Dowager. Nor would Chen! Could there be a latent power in China waiting to seize control of the government sometime in the future?   He had heard rumors of a revolutionary called Sun Yat-sen. No, if she was disloyal, it would be against the unpopular Czar, not her adopted country of Russia. If she was indeed guilty.

He remembered a past conversation in which she had discussed Sergei Witte. He had asked her why Witte had lost his post as the powerful Minister of Finance.

"Probably for three reasons," Marina had admitted. "Jealousy on the part of the Czar was certainly a factor last year. The Czar saw Witte's power and influence as a threat. Secondly, Witte may have increased taxation too much. The taxes, levied to support rapid industrialization throughout our empire, caused a small peasant revolt. He was blamed in Russia, but here in Manchuria and Siberia, we liked the prosperity brought by faster and better transportation. Also. the railroad created many new towns along its right of way. It was like the railroads opening up your American West."

"Why would Witte's enemies object to that?"

"Because they persuaded the Czar that the burden of repayment of large loans to foreign banks and investors caused a loss of Russian independence—that the House of Rothschild and the Bank of France held Russia captive. Witte's wife, Matilda, as you may know, is a Jewess."

"Are you saying that the Czar is firmly anti-Jewish?"

"Yes. Whenever he needs someone to blame for Russia's troubles, he kicks around the Jews with periodic pogroms."

Marina continued, "Thirdly, the military fears Witte because they know he wants to use the railroad for commercial development, not for the exclusive use of the military."

"Why can't control of the railroad help both the military and Witte?"

Marina shrugged. "Too many clashing personalities. The cabal of developers centered around the Bezobrazov Group to fight Witte. The cabal is aligned closely with the Czar and Alexeiev. They all profit handsomely."

"So how did you become involved?" Suspecting her friendship with Witte, he jumped ahead and guessed she was involved.

"Sergei Witte was my father's friend. My father constructed much of the Trans Siberian railroad and also the Chinese Eastern railroad coming south from Harbin."

"Does Witte know what is going on out here now that he is no longer Minister of Finance?" he asked.

"I see to it that he does."

Now Rogers understood. Her loyalty was to Russia *and* Witte.

She continued, "There were several reasons for the economic depression initially brought on by over speculation in railroad bonds. It was a world wide depression. Even America suffered. The depression still exists and will deepen. Let me give you some background. By 1901 Witte had urged removal of most of the 200,000 Russian troops in northern China and Manchuria. He believed the presence of so many Czarist soldiers would unnecessarily alienate the European powers and drag Japan into aggression against Korea. The Czar sided with the Bezobrazov cabal to insist on a strong Russian military presence in Manchuria. So Japan prepared for war to break the Russian economic monopoly and military strength in Manchuria."

Marina had not revealed how she maintained contact with Witte and his people in Russia. Nor did she explain her omission of the truth when Rogers had first arrived in the port.

Rogers shrugged off her continued coldness and blamed her depression on the tragic turn of events. He knew she would be worried about the probable losses to her business in the days ahead, and the bleak future she might face. What he did not realize was that her demeanor mainly reflected a strong feeling of guilt. Guilt that she had foolishly endangered his life by asking him to go to Nanshan for Viktor. Guilt also that she had been with Rogers in a Dalny hotel room in Viktor's absence. And worry about Viktor who might be dead or missing, but had strangely ignored writing to her again. She could not understand his aloofness.

After a brief morning meal, furnished by Yin-lin at the house, and a short nap thereafter, he walked to the parade ground by the navy yard where General Stoessel had ordered the surviving men of the Fifth Siberian Rifles to assemble.

Arrogant and mercurial as usual, Stoessel screamed at the ranks of soldiers, "You are a wretched, undisciplined corps of traitors, cowards and blackguards. I will try the lot of you by court martial. How dare you leave Kinchau. Don't you dare to show yourself in the town, lest your presence infect the whole garrison with your cowardice." Then, having been so ordered by Admiral Alexeiev, Stoessel reluctantly distributed sixty available Cross of St George medals to the wounded. There were not enough medals for all the wounded and none of the most deserving slightly wounded soldiers received any recognition. Three men, not wounded, received a medal. They were officer friends of the general and one was General Fock.

Rogers now felt uncomfortable in Marina's home, but she had insisted that he should remain. She warned him that their relationship had to cool, that God had singled her out for punishment, and that she deserved to lose Viktor. Rogers begged her not to feel so guilty. "Please don't turn religious on me, Marina. You believed that God is loving, kind, and forgiving. Now you say he is vindictive and you will go to hell. Well, hell is here and now, so blame me or the Japanese, not yourself. I am sorry to see you so unhappy."

In the days that followed, he wisely kept his distance and only tried to be helpful. He was hurting too, but kept his attitude cheerful at all times. He would have liked to live elsewhere, but there were no other quarters. Besides, he had promised Chen to look after Marina. Entering his room and glancing down the hall at her bedroom door became a painful reminder of her sensuality.

Marina went to the Orthodox Church and prayed for Alesandrov's safety. She prayed that he not be too lonely without her. *Poor Viktor, alone and without a woman all these weeks.* The thought tormented her.

Yin-lin was as helpful as always, but Marina did not know that the girl was approaching Rogers more than before, often coming into his room unannounced. It annoyed Rogers that Yin-lin was so careless in keeping her robe closed in his presence. It did not help curb his libido when her body was displayed so brazenly. He wanted to be close to Marina and it was an effort for him to remain so aloof. He could only hope that she would change in time and be happy again, and that Yin-lin would stop being such a pest.

Marina spent more time in her office at the godown. Rogers busied himself with written reports to Uncle Steve in Shanghai and increased his efforts to learn what was happening north of Nanshan. He firmly believed that Alesandrov was alive and well, and he made an effort to so convince Marina and help her all he could.

He did not want to leave the comforts of Marina's home. And he wanted, somehow, to reconcile with her. But how could he approach her if she continued to avoid him? Each passing day, his discomfort increased. He found himself lusting for her now that the reality of the loss of An-an had settled in. Twice he had impulsively decided to quit the house, only to weaken in the hope of an improving relationship with his host. She had her business to occupy her life; he had nothing except reports to write to Uncle Steve, and endless walks around the town and port. And always there was the reminder of his promise to Chen to look after Marina.

There were several hundred civilian laborers idled by the Japanese seizure of Dalny. Many were troublemakers who rebelled against army supervision. Sailors were also a problem. Given too much shore leave because of the blockade, they, like the laborers, drank vodka excessively and quarreled on the streets. The provost marshal, Colonel Petrusha, who should have been more diligent in searching for spies, spent far too much time harrassing the laborers, and still seemed unable to control their raucous behavior. German, French and Russian shop owners likewise ignored many of General Stoessel's edicts. Petrusha was simply stretched too thin to watch everyone.

In the week following Rogers' return to Port Arthur, a large brawl broke out in Old Town between the Siberian soldiers and Crimean sailors from the navy yard. The army men blamed the lack of navy support for the defeat at Kinchau and Nanshan. The soldier, who started the fight, shouted obscenities at a group of off-duty sailors, blaming Admiral Witgeft's unwillingness to venture from the harbor for permitting Japan's armies to land in Manchuria.

A bottle flew through the air and caught the soldier in the side of his head. Taverns along the street quickly emptied as the cursing men clashed. Before long the fight spread to the red light district. Colonel Petrusha, unable to contain the melee, called for help from garrisons of the hillside forts. General Smirnoff dispatched soldiers and by doing so clashed with Stoessel who told him that he, Stoessel, could handle the situation. Smirnoff, always at odds with Stoessel, reminded Stoessel that command of the forts and its defenders was his terrain.

"You may be governor of this Kwantung peninsula," he told Stoessel, "but I am the commandant, the authorized military commander." But Stoessel stubbornly insisted that he was in charge of Port Arthur and, militarily, he was senior to Smirnoff. This was a lie that Smirnoff would hear repeatedly and would never accept.

Stoessel truculently persisted, "You will remain commandant, but I shall run the fortress. Whether legal or not, it is my affair. I will answer for that."

Marina informed Rogers that Stoessel had continued to oppose all blockade runners. Rogers was incredulous. "He ordered that even though you are at war and these people are bringing in food and needed supplies? What idiocy!"

Marina agreed. "Yes. He actually refused permission for ship captains to unload their cargoes. I understand that General Smirnoff had to intervene, on behalf of the women in the port, to let a French captain unload a cargo of canned milk. Stoessel finally relented but told the captain never to come back."

Marina continued to profit handsomely because of the demand for her goods—enhanced by Chen's continued success in slipping past Japanese blockade vessels.

Yin-lin and Master Loong, through their contacts, kept Marina apprised of news from the northern front. Ever anxious to cozy up to Rogers, Yin-lin told him of the bitter quarreling in Port Arthur between Generals Stoessel and Smirnoff.

Shortly after his return, Rogers had chanced upon Philip Esley, still hanging around the Novy Kry newspaper office. He hardly recognized Esley. The Englishman had quickly crossed to the other side of the street upon seeing the approach of Rogers. He bore two black eyes, a taped broken nose and a wired broken jaw. He limped as if in great pain.

Rogers sought out the newsman, Nojine, at the newspaper office. During their conversation over a cup of tea at Saratov's restaurant, Rogers learned that a gang of angry Russian soldiers had set upon Esley and other foreigners, accusing them of passing information to Japanese spies. Esley had received the worst beating because of his past drunken and obnoxious behavior.

Nojine told Rogers, "The soldiers were arrested, but quickly released. They claimed to have seen Esley passing some papers to a blockade runner. Frankly, I wish he would stay away from our office. We have enough trouble from Colonel Petrusha."

"Petrusha is still in charge of base security?"

"More so than ever. What a tyrant! He questions everything we print. He wants to censor everything. So does Stoessel."

Nojine expressed his gratitude for the news of Nanshan that Rogers gave him. "I'll probably be threatened again for printing this."

"What I tell you is true," Rogers told him. "And all of it is well known to the Japanese and the West, so why should not the Russian town people know?"

"What are you free to tell me about matters that are not military?" Rogers asked Nojine.

"Not much. General Stoessel has curtailed most civic and social activities. In spite of damage from Japanese naval shells, morale remains high and, except for barroom brawls between army and navy men, the town is adjusting to war conditions and accepting the rationing of food supplies. By the way, are you still residing at Madame Berezovsky's home?" Without waiting for an answer, Nojine, after a moment of hesitation, said, "I can tell you in confidence that Colonel Petrusha still asks a lot of questions about her and who she knows in St Petersburg and Moscow."

"Why would he be suspicious of her?"

"I don't know," Nojine replied. "He certainly does not like her."

"And you?"

Nojine smiled. "Truthfully, we all love her."

Nojine asked about Alesandrov. Rogers replied, "I am sure he is with General Kuropatkin up around Liaoyang."

"Do you plan to go north to be with Kuropatkin?"

Rogers shook his head. "I don't see how anyone can get out of here now, except by navy craft. No, I'm stuck here like the rest, unless the war gets better for Russia."

Rogers wanted to contact Alesandrov, but knew that it would be impossible until the northern front stabilized. As soon as Chen helped solve the refugee problem, he surely would have an information pipeline to military activities north of Nanshan.

Meanwhile, Rogers continued to agonize over An-an's strange silence. He had sent frantic letters to her in Hong Kong, asking if she was all right and why hadn't she answered his many letters? Was she angry about something—like his long absence away from her? He was almost tempted to ask if she had found someone else. It was so unlike her to ignore him week after week, letter after letter. Of course, she would be busy with the demands of her import-export business, but why the long silence to her husband? A disappointing silence that was fast beginning to anger him. But, again, he weakened in trying to erase her memory.

During the month of June, both belligerents played catch-up. Dalny became the staging area for Nogi's Third Army, which, despite the stalemate, began probing attacks against Port Arthur's Green Hills defense line. The Russians had abandoned 300 rail cars in Dalny, but had saved their locomotives. Pending arrival of the narrow gauge engines ordered from America, the Japanese army employed gangs of Chinese coolies to push loaded freight cars along the wider gauge tracks favored by the Russians. Meanwhile, the Japanese started conversion of the tracks to narrow gauge.

When the news arrived that a naval squadron from Vladivostok had intercepted and sunk Japanese transports carrying the new train engines, the Japanese were devastated at the loss. They did not realize until later that, even worse, the sunken transports had carried siege guns to be used against the Russian forts. These massive cannon launched 500 pound shells that could smash the concrete forts. New cannon would now have to be manufactured in Japan, since none of the other large mortars there could be spared from Japan's coastal defense system. General Nogi faced the prospect of sacrificing thousands of his men in trying to storm the Russian defense grid that the siege mortars could have overcome.

The flirtatious Yin-lin confided to Rogers that there was trouble up north. General Stoessel had plagued Viceroy Alexeiev in Mukden with pleas for help. Alexeiev had ordered Kuropatkin to mount an offensive southward to recapture Nanshan and drive the Japanese army from Port

Arthur. Kuropatkin had argued in vain that he should stand fast at Liaoyang until more reinforcements arrived from Russia. Kuropatkin was convinced that an offensive southward would be futile and would expose his Manchurian army to flanking attacks from the Japanese. Although he knew he would eventually have to accede to the orders from Alexeiev and the Czar, Kuropatkin continued to stall. His half hearted obedience would greatly involve Viktor Alesandrov.

Both the Czar and Alexeiev had agreed that help should go to Stoessel, that it was important to keep the port intact until the Russian Baltic Fleet arrived. That was one thing that the Japanese dreaded most. Their navy would be outgunned if the Baltic Fleet linked up with both the Pacific Fleet at Port Arthur and the Far Eastern Fleet at Vladivostok. The Czar pressured Admiral Witgeft to use the Port Arthur fleet against Admiral Togo. Witgeft ran out of excuses to delay leaving the sanctuary of the port. Time was running out for him to avoid the Czar's orders to sally forth from the port, engage the enemy, and try to escape north to Vladivostok. Witgeft's lack of will to fight increasingly caused the townspeople of Port Arthur to deride the sailors for cowardice, and increased confrontations between the navy and the army in the streets.

Rogers learned that repairs had been completed on the battleship *Retvisan*, further adding to the pressure for Witgeft to fight.

* * * * * * * * *

On a couple of occasions Marina had awakened, troubled by her strained relationship with Rogers and made restless by the heat of the June nights and the nakedness of Yin-lin, who eschewed night clothing in the heat of the late spring season. It could be as hot in Port Arthur's summer as it was cold in the peninsula winter. Even if Marina had insisted on a night gown for Yin-lin, it would have been up around her neck by morning. Sleepless nights were becoming too common for Marina.

After two weeks of lonely torment, Marina came home one late evening, just ahead of the curfew. She had worked late at her factory as usual to avoid being alone with Rogers. This night, she decided that having Rogers' arms about her again would help start the healing process and perhaps help her decide what to do about Viktor. She had not heard from him since the return of Rogers. Yet, like Rogers, she was convinced Viktor was alive and safe.

The downstairs parlor was empty and silent. A small oil lantern illuminated the stairway. To conserve the supply of coal, Stoessel had decreed that the dynamos at the power station be shut down during the night. The navy yard had its own power supply from shipboard generators.

As she mounted the top steps of the stairway and turned past Rogers' door, she saw the door was ajar and heard the sound of voices in his room. She saw a fleeting glimpse of Rogers sitting on his bed clad only in his underwear. Yin-lin sat at the foot of the bed, her night robe askew enough to reveal one of her firm young breasts and part of the dark shadow on her lower belly. Rogers' voice was angry and he was almost shouting at Yin-lin. Marina hurried back to her bedroom, unwilling to face the pair and reluctant to show her jealousy. Sometime during the night, Yin-lin must have returned to the bed. In the morning she wore a smug smile that added further torment to Marina.

Marina blamed her own aloofness the past several days and did not fault Rogers for sleeping with the girl. Hurt and surprised at her jealousy, she now felt more abandoned than ever. Why had she ever allowed herself to grow so fond of Rogers? Why had she treated him so coldly? He had avoided her as much as she had kept her distance, and perhaps their bond was forever broken. Now her previous guilt turned to remorse and she blamed herself for what had happened. Why had she acted so foolishly?

Unable to contain her suspicions and jealousy, Marina had confronted Rogers soon thereafter. "I suppose it was inevitable that you would sleep with Yin-lin. Tell me, was she good?"

His bemused smile infuriated her. Speaking quietly, he asked, "Have you spoken to the girl?"

"No. But she knows I saw her in your room. It was almost as if she were teasing me. She admitted nothing; it was just the pleased look on her face later. I am not angry. I was surprised, that is all—but I guess I should not have been. Men are men!"

But Marina was angry that he would turn to someone other than herself. And she did not know whom to blame: herself, Yin-lin, or Ellis Rogers. It did not help that she remembered complying with Viktor's suggestion to offer her maid to Rogers when he had arrived in Port Arthur early in May. What had seemed awkward but otherwise acceptable then, did not seem all right now, because the American had brought a new dimension to her life. Their unfullfilled tryst in Dalny now made Yin-lin's presence in his room hurt like a betrayal.

Tormented by jealousy and stressed by trying to conceal her anguish, she fought to hold back the tears. She wanted Viktor and she also wanted her house guest, and now she felt rejected by both.

Rogers spoke quietly, "Marina, Yin-lin is your loyal handmaiden and friend. She can be a pest by coming into my room unannounced, but she is only seeking attention. I would not betray your trust and confidence in me."

He started to tell her how fond of her he was and how much he admired her as a woman and a friend, but she pulled back when he made a hesitant step toward her. She instantly regretted the motion, because he stopped, shrugged, and turned to leave the house. She heard him mutter, "I'm sorry—I wanted to tell you something." Stubborn false pride again prevented Marina from rushing after him.

Marina grew more lonely in the ensuing days. She fought an impulse to approach Rogers and continued to immerse herself in guilt. She asked herself if the relationship was really over. Had she lost Viktor and also now Ellis? He, Rogers, always seemed so cheerful and untroubled by her diffidence? His acceptance of her changed attitude bothered her most of all. She would have been more comfortable had he lashed out at her in denial about Yin-lin, or stormed out of her home or had argued with her. Instead, he lived life as if there was no tomorrow, showing her as much tender sympathy as he dared, and he continued to give her home the manly presence that it needed. Strength and kindness is what she needed and he supplied it patiently. But she refused to approach him.

Viktor would have never shown such understanding. He was too vain because adoring women had made him so. He would have told her to go fry ice and taken another mistress. Victor's sex drive was simply too great to lie dormant at the whims of one troubled woman.

Although she knew inwardly that she might be behaving unreasonably, and had no proof about his touching Yin-lin, she refused to confront the maid. Instead, Marina persisted in questioning Rogers about Viktor's baffling absence, dogging him with questions about Mukden, hinting that Viktor knew someone there and that Rogers was less than frank about Viktor's absence. Pressured in part by increasing shellfire damage to Port Arthur and the strain of the monotonous siege, Marina's suspicions mounted. She asked Rogers bluntly why he had separated from Chen and

Alesandrov to journey so far to Mukden. Chen had told her that he had seen little of Rogers in Nanshan, that the American had gone to Mukden for some reason. Chen thought it was something that Viktor had requested as a favor.

What kind of favor? What would be Viktor's interest in Mukden? Questions that she asked herself only increased her puzzlement. Were the three men holding back something from her? Rogers' answers had been slightly evasive. Why?

To make matters worse, Rogers had maintained his distance, playing her game of coolness. It caused her to become increasingly unsure of herself, almost panicky at the situation she had created—and was now too proud and stubborn to admit her blame.

One day she gave up on Chen who always avoided talking about other people. Confronting Rogers at her factory, she turned on him, saying that she believed he was avoiding her questions. "I don't believe you stayed with Viktor in Nanshan, that you were in Mukden all the time. What happened up there? Was there a girl?"

He seemed amused, saying, "There aren't many girls in Mukden, Marina. Some military wives and Red Cross nurses. Some prostitutes. It is a crowded military post now."

"You said before that Viktor was in a hospital there?"

"Yes, of course."

"And the nurses? Did you know them?"

"I met a few. They were always very busy."

"Was one of them a friend of Viktor's?"

Now Rogers knew that he was treading on dangerous ground. He could not afford to slip. "Let's just say one of them is my friend."

"A Russian woman?"

"Well, a nurse, but a Red Cross nurse."

"What is her name?"

"Why do you ask so many questions, Marina?"

"Because I want to know why Viktor has not returned to Port Arthur—why he has not written."

It was time to lie. Or bend the truth. He did not want to do either. Yet he wanted to protect Alesandrov's confidence in him. Christ! What a fix to be in!

"She is a French woman, a nurse. Viktor introduced her to me. I let her have my hotel room when I went to Nanshan with Viktor."

"Does she still have the room?"

"Yes."

"Is that where you stayed when you went back?"

"Yes. Look, Marina. She is just a friend. I only meant to do her a favor. I had business at army headquarters and I had no place to stay." So far no lies. He turned to leave.

She persisted. "Does Viktor know you slept with her?"

"Yes, I told him."

When he had gone, she sat puzzled. Why would Rogers be with another woman? If he was lonely, why would he choose a stranger when she wanted so much to be close to him? Did that explain his coldness toward her? If he preferred this French nurse, why so suddenly? What did this woman have to offer that she so guiltily was reluctant to surrender?

She sat dejected and unhappy for a long time, feeling saddened and rejected—and old and lonely. The shadows had gathered and it was past twilight when she stirred at last, wondering why she had stayed in her office so long. A sound of distant cannon fire drifted in from the eastern forts. She started to rise from her desk when Yin-lin appeared at the office door.

The girl told her, "I was worried. It is late. Is something wrong—you are crying?"

"No. I was just thinking about Viktor. No one knows where he is."

"Maybe he is in Mukden now. Maybe he had to go back to the hospital?"

A bombshell of understanding went off in Marina's head. So was that the answer? Viktor had recovered in a Mukden hospital after his journey through Korea. He was in the hospital for days, convalescing under the care of a nurse. Knowing Viktor, the nurse would have been the prettiest. Perhaps an intriguing foreigner? Someone with whom he could flirt outrageously. Someone he could take to a hotel. Ellis' hotel room? Would Ellis really turn his hotel room over to a newcomer when he left? That would be more like Viktor because of his association with the hospital staff.

So why had Ellis gone to Mukden in place of Viktor? Because he was free to travel when Viktor could not be spared from military duties? If Ellis had gone as a friend, that would be just like the American. So devoted to Viktor's friendship and so loyal. But it did not fit Ellis' image that he would lie to protect Viktor? Or that he would sleep with Viktor's amour. She began to have doubts about the story. Could it be that Ellis had merely been as reserved and trustworthy with this woman as he had been in Dalny with her?

The more she searched through the puzzle, the more Marina believed she had the correct answer. And the more she pondered, the more she distrusted Alesandrov. She had been unfair to Ellis and to herself. He had been a trusting friend and she had shut him out because of Viktor.

At her home, she told Yin-lin to bring a light dinner. She ran up the stairs to pound on Rogers' door to beg for his forgiveness. When there was no answer, she turned the door handle. The door opened to an empty room.

Rogers was gone and so were his things.

CHAPTER SEVENTEEN

In the weeks that followed his departure, Marina began to realize how much she had depended on Rogers and how much she missed him. She reluctantly forgave her maid and brought Yin-lin back to the bedroom. The house that had echoed with Rogers' laughter now stood silent and grim. This night she lay in bed with Yin-lin, listening to the girl's heavy breathing. No other sound reached her. The room down the hall where Rogers had slept so comfortingly nearby lay empty, perhaps deserted forever.

It bothered Marina that she needed Rogers more than apparently he needed her. The age factor also began to trouble her. In an era when men traditionally sought a female partner younger than themselves, Marina realized she was eight years older than Rogers. True, he was only twenty-four, but when he became her age, she'd be forty and on the downhill path. At least that was her reasoning. In all her innocence, she failed to understand that she was just beginning to reach her peak of sexual health at age thirty-two, and that the urge would hardly be diminishing several years later. In fact, due to many circumstances, it might even increase. Typical of so many well-bred oriental women, Marina could face the future scarcely showing her age. She would probably remain slender and trim and largely unwrinkled well into her dotage.

What she needed most was the challenge of a good man. She'd had it with fun-loving Viktor. Now, guiltily, she longed for it with this frank, calm, uncomplicated American. She missed his sandy-colored hair, gray-green eyes, and fair but tanned complexion. She longed for the closeness of his lean, trim body and the warmth it radiated. Tormented with loneliness, she remembered his tender kisses and gentle manner, and blushed, wondering how he would compare to Viktor's mad, unrestrained lovemaking.

His touch had been so slow and gentle. She thought of Dalny and wished she had known his body with more intimacy than the hesitant touching they had enjoyed at the hotel. What if their passion had been consumated? What if he had undressed her and made determined love instead of merely holding her in his sleep with one hand laying passively on her belly or across her chest? She had placed one leg over him during the night so knew that in his sleep he had been aroused. She had resisted the temptation to touch him to measure the full extent of his rigidity. Now, she regretted not daring to do so. Who knew what might have happened?

He had held her close and had kissed her in return for her first passionate overture, but had not explored her body. Only in his sleep had a hand strayed to her breast or belly. Would she have respected him less if they had dared to be intimate? She shook her head longingly in memory of their closeness.

Impulsively she turned against Yin-lin's back and hugged her. The night was hot and humid, and the girl was naked again. She closed her hand over Yin-lin's breast and pushed against the girl's hips, then timidly squeezed the breast, asking herself if this was the sensation a man would experience. The comforting closeness soon lulled her into a light sleep. Sometime later, Marina awoke to the torment of a hand gently riffling through her thick pubic forest. What was Yin-lin doing? Biting her lip to stifle a low moan, she pondered whether to slap the girl. Instead, she rolled over with her back to Yin-lin, feeling the furry warmth against her buttocks as Yin-lin pushed against her and again busied her hand.

Disturbed by her wetness, Marina arose, threw on a night robe, and strolled onto her veranda. The lights of the town below twinkled in the night. Under a black sky, a cruiser's searchlights swept across the dark waters of the channel entrance. Lonely and frustated, she sobbed and leaned against the low veranda wall. Tomorrow she resolved to send a message to Rogers. It would not be easy to locate him in the maze of fortifications in the hills where she was sure he had gone. But surely Master Loong could find him.

In the several weeks that had passed by, Marina had thought more and more about Rogers, finally admitting to herself that she was in love with him. His avoidance of an intimate relationship with her was, however, puzzling. He had always avoided her hints that he might have a secret lover. Once, weeks ago, he had countered by asking her pointedly if she ever intended to marry someday. She had answered, "It all depends. I would like to have a husband who is a loyal supporter and a good man."

"One who is romantic and tall, handsome and suave?" he had teased.

"No," she had replied. Her thoughts were of Viktor. "Someone who is not always looking at other women. He doesn't have to be handsome and tall, just faithful."

"Not even a good lover?" he had bantered.

She had laughed. "I can teach him what he needs to know." Stepping forward, she had kissed him, then had clung to him tightly.

He had tried, but had failed to release her grip. The nearness of her body must have tormented him. Out of the corner of her eye, she had seen Yin-lin watching. So had he.

"People will gossip," he had said. "Perhaps we should go inside."

But in the privacy of her parlor, he had resisted her overtures, as he had so many times before. Thinking back, she promised herself that she would force his hand if he ever pushed her away again. He might have used Viktor as an excuse before, but that romance was over. Viktor would never change, even if he survived the war. And who knew what the future held? Life was so uncertain in times of war. Even she might be a casualty of the intermittent bombardments by the Japanese fleet?

* * * * * * * * * *

Far to the south in Shanghai, a senior Chinese employee of the British administered Chinese Government Postal Service in Shanghai retrieved the letter from Hong Kong and hid it on his person. The envelope was addressed to Captain Ellis A. Rogers, US Vol., care of Her British Majesty's Consulate, Shanghai, and was marked "Attention Miss Plum Blossom Hu."

Four years previously, on his way to Peking during the Boxer troubles, Rogers had rescued a fourteen year old street prostitute from a sadistic pimp in Shanghai. She had called herself Plum Blossom. Before leaving the city, he had found employment for the girl at the British consulate, sending her money and using her as an intermediary to forward his sealed military reports to "Uncle Steve" in Manila. When the American War Department had later opened a branch office in Shanghai, Uncle Steve had agreed to continue Rogers' arrangement with Plum Blossom in order to keep the reports and mail from the scrutiny of the American State Department. Little Miss Hu had worked so diligently as an office housekeeper at the British consulate that the Consul General had elevated her to the position of junior clerk after two years.

When An-an had moved to Hong Kong, following the return to power of the Chinese Empress Dowager in Peking, Rogers had mailed his letters directly to An-an, but always from a British consulate mail-drop in north China. It had never occurred to him to use Plum Blossom's services for his personal mail. That was one of the worst mistakes he would ever make. His mail to An-an was re-routed through the Shanghai post office, and a British mail ship then carried it south to Hong Kong. Plum Blossom could have forwarded his mail via a safe and sealed diplomatic pouch.

Uncle Steve wanted all mail between Rogers and An-an intercepted by his agent at the Shanghai post office. How he had ever uncovered the truth about An-an was never discovered by Rogers. When Rogers' mail to Hong Kong had ceased arriving, An-an had desperately routed her letters to Plum Blossom, asking the girl for help in contacting Rogers. Her letters to Plum Blossom also had never arrived via the Shanghai post office.

Uncle Steve had a drawer full of Rogers' mail and he intended to keep it there. His reasoning was selfish. Rogers had married a Chinese national without army permission, which would have been denied anyway. Rogers was too valuable a field man to be distracted by an illegal wife who might want him to put his domestic life ahead of his clandestine military duties. He belonged to the War Department, and no distraction like a wife or girlfriend would be tolerated.

* * * * * * * * *

Tanaka was soon considered a "walking wounded" soldier and given light duty in Dalny during the rehabilitation of the port facilities and recovery of the city. General Nogi had arrived with reinforcements to take command of the Third Army. He had refused to reserve time to mourn for his elder son who had died at Nanshan, insisting that the war came first and that he would observe the period of mourning after the war.

Ten years earlier, the same General Nogi had seized Port Arthur in one day from the Chinese army and with only one regiment. The Chinese army had collapsed quickly. Any hope that Nogi may have had for a repeat performance was soon dashed when he reviewed the battles of the Yalu River and Nanshan. As difficult as those Japanese victories had been, the battle for Port Arthur promised to be even more demanding. Port Arthur had a garrison of 40 thousand soldiers and sailors. The place was ringed by interlocking forts and bolstered by the large cannon aboard the Russian ships in the harbor. Spies within the naval base had stressed the strength of the hill fortifications. And Nogi realized that his men would be facing multiple machine guns, carefully sited to cover the open areas fronting the trenches of the forts. He would soon learn how deadly those weapons could be.

Several days elapsed while the Japanese armies awaited shipments of ordnance from Japan. The enormous number of bullets and shells used to subdue Nanshan and Kinchau had shocked Japan's war planners. Would Japan be able to provide for its field armies in the future? The battlefield demands continued to exact an enormous unplanned expenditure. Of course this concern was secreted from the public, while Japan's financial giants sought more loans from friendly international bankers.

* * * * * * * * * *

Alesandrov and others who were cut off around Nanshan had retreated northward during the post battle confusion. Even if he could have retreated south with the bulk of General Fock's force, he would have refused to be bottled up in Dalny or Port Arthur. There would be no escape from the now growing Japanese Third Army that was designated to besiege the naval base. Japan's other three armies, the First, Second, and Fourth, would surely move north against General Kuropatkin and certainly try to prevent him from coming to the aid of Port Arthur. If Alesandrov was going to die, he wanted it to be on the plains of Manchuria where his Cossack cavalry could move freely, not in some stinking trench in the hills behind Port Arthur.

He longed for the front to stabilize so he could slip away to join Claudette in Mukden.

The disgruntled Russian soldiers, milling around Mukden, kept the army whorehouses busy—so busy that a time limit of five minutes was imposed on customers. The soldiers complained, but admitted that the price of three rubles was cheap. For the price of seventy-five cents, whose pent up desire lasted over five minutes anyway after months of celibacy?

At first, Sylvia saw the whorehouses as competition, but came to realize that they reduced the possibility of violent quarreling among frustated men who lacked such an outlet for their emotions. The cheap army beer dispensed to the soldiers was countered by her reduction in price. Sylvia competed by selling beer for one ruble per bottle to meet the army price of two rubles.

She hated Alesandrov because his presence kept Claudette away. She did not know that Alesandrov despised her as well and that Claudette wanted to avoid her. She hated Alesandrov for the image he protrayed: tall, handsome, self-assured—a man that Claudette could enjoy, but was denied to Sylvia. Yet, the few times she had encountered him, she imagined that his eyes undressed her. She wondered how much Claudette had told him of their night together in the hotel. It was a memory of intimacy that plagued Sylvia so much that it reinforced her determination to return to Russia. She began to devise a plan of escape from Ariko's insistent demands for information, and Lebedeff's annoying presence. Paramount, however, was her need to seek destruction of the Czarist army.

In the north, the Russian armies under Kuropatkin scranbled to strengthen their last line of retreat at Liaoyang. Contrary to General Kuropatkin's strategy, both the Czar and Viceroy Alexeiev continued to insist that Port Arthur was too valuable to lose and demanded that Kuropatkin strike southward to destroy Nogi's Third Army, now menacing the naval port.

Kuropatkin realized early on that he was outnumbered militarily and thus decided to delay as much as possible going on the offensive until the Russian buildup in Manchuria was completed. Then, and only then, would he feel safe to launch his attack southward against the advancing Japanese armies. The Russian buildup was slow because the three trains that traveled daily across Siberia could seldom attain a speed of more than six miles per hour on the single rail line.

Marina remembered discussing Kuropatkin's strategy with Rogers before he had left her. He had told her that he doubted that the Russian general would strike against the Japanese lines until the onset of winter, believing winter would be kinder to the Russians, and impede Japanese supply lines.

He had stated, "Kuropatkin believes there is a six months supply of food and coal in Port Arthur that should permit this town to hold out for that length of time. He's not going to risk his operations in the north just to appease the viceroy. The two men really seem to dislike each other."

Marina had agreed about the mutual distrust held by both men. She had told Rogers, "Kuropatkin was not a member of the Bezobrazov Group like Alexeiev. He was never in favor of the operations of the Far East Lumber Company that enabled Alexeiev, the Czar and others to grow rich exploiting timber reserves in Manchuria and Korea. Kuropatkin had visited Japan to talk to its leaders and he understood Japanese resentment of the Russian lumber company, which the Japanese viewed as a Russian excuse to stay permanently in Manchuria. Kuropatkin feared and warned that the Russian presence in Korea would cause a war."

"Was this before Alexeiev became viceroy?" Rogers had asked.

"Yes. And the quarrel worsened when Bezobrazov and his group persuaded the Czar to make Alexeiev the viceroy. It was not only this office that Kuropatkin coveted; it placed him under Alexeiev's command."

"Why?"

"Because," Marina had continued, "the office of viceroy is almost second in power to that of the Czar. It places all political and military control in the hands of one man in Manchuria. Kuropatkin at the time was Minister of War. He became so angry that he resigned his post, saying in essence that Admiral Alexeiev had no business administering army affairs, that he was a 'buffoon' who could not even ride a horse. Sergei Witte agreed and even used the same epithet. So Witte was removed from his office as Finance Minister."

Rogers had been a little confused and had asked, "You have mentioned Witte before. How does he fit into the picture, especially now that he is no longer in power?"

Marina had explained that Witte was still powerful in financial circles in Russia. "He was never in favor of placing the naval base here and all the money that was spent for the port. He preferred investments along his beloved railroad. He also clashed with Alexeiev and was as opposed to war with Japan as was Kuropatkin."

Rogers had wondered before why Marina was so defensive of Witte. The man had brought on a severe depression in Russia because of too rapid industrialization. He might also be blamed for squandering so much money to build up Dalny instead of bolstering Port Arthur's defense grid. The suspicion still lingered in his mind about how deeply Marina was involved with Witte.

Before Rogers had returned from Mukden, after visiting with Claudette, his eavesdropping at Kuropatkin's headquarters had convinced him that Kuropatkin was hopelessly defense-minded, that he would always wait for the Japanese to seize the initiative, that he was reactive rather than active.

He had overheard Kuropatkin protest that a Russian attack south from Liaoyang, or even Nanshan, would be foolhardy since the Japanese, with control of the sea lanes, could land an army in his rear or on one flank. "Let the garrison at Port Arthur hang on until we can begin to push the Japanese back south into the sea," Kuropatkin had argued.

But Alexeiev had convinced the Czar that Port Arthur should be aided, so Alexeiev had ordered Kuropatkin to mount an offensive toward Port Arthur by first recapturing Nanshan from the Japanese Second Army, instead of operating against the Japanese First and Fourth Armies in the Yalu river area. Rogers had since learned of the violent dialogue between Kuropatkin and Alexeiev just before the Nanshan battle. He had not known that Kuropatkin had lost the argument when the Czar had sided with Alexeiev.

* * * * * * * * * *

Marina brooded constantly about Roger's sudden departure. Her loneliness worsened in the weeks that followed. Her temper flared often, although she tried not to berate Yin-lin and her close servants. Most of her customers blamed her irritability on the stress of the blockade.

Her disposition was not aided by the knowledge that Colonel Petrusha had included her in his surveillance network. His Chinese agents spied on her at every opportunity. She was followed from her home to her warehouse and watched daily. Chen, too, was watched. Some of Petrusha's sympathetic operatives had approached Marina to warn her of their mission. She had rewarded their loyalty and had protested her innocence of being a foreign agent.

Lebedeff of the Okhrana had contacted Petrusha out of concern for so much leakage of information to the Japanese. The War Ministry in St Petersburg had given funds to Petrusha to engage civilian agents at the naval base. Petrusha watched the foreigners there, but was out of his league in matching wits with Ariko and his operatives.

Ariko was a master at espionage, which helped explain his hatred for Rogers and Alesandrov. And Ariko still vowed that when he could journey to Shanghai, he would personally kill the Chinese bitch who had given him the note of misinformation lifted from the Russian officer. Guilty or not, Ti Flower had to go, and Ariko wanted the pleasure of slitting her throat.

Another potential act of revenge for Ariko was the elimination of the wife of the British naval observer. Ariko could not forget that it was Lydia Fairborne who had rescued her Russian lover from the jail in Seoul. He had to delay in that matter because he no longer had such close ties with the Japanese Navy. Admiral Togo would no longer tolerate Ariko.

Ariko also wondered about Marina's loyalty to Russia. Much about the beautiful woman bothered him. But he had little success in bribing any of her employees to work for him.

Marina was solidly anti-Japanese, recognizing how little freedom she would enjoy if Nippon ruled Port Arthur. Under Petrusha's watchful eyes, Marina had begun to be shut out of the loop of social life at the naval base. With Rogers gone, and Alesandrov's fidelity in doubt, Marina shielded herself from the wearisome curfew by secluding herself in her home. In the absence of male company, she concentrated on how to gain more money, how to profit from the siege, what to do if the war dragged on, what her postwar moves might be, and, heaven forbid, what she should do if Russia lost the war.

One morning, unable to sleep, with a troubling and almost painful pressure in her stomach from what she blamed on lack of sex, she rose early, slipped on a light robe because of the June warmth, and ventured onto her veranda. As she passed through the doorway, she saw the ivory object that she had earlier gifted to Yin-lin. The naked ivory phallus lay bathed in a shaft of moonlight atop the dresser where Yin-lin had carelessly deposited it. Angered because she believed Yin-lin had placed it there deliberately to tease her, she resolved to confront the girl before the day ended.

Marina watched the rising sun vanish the night. The town below her home began to stir with activity. Fish and produce peddlers arrived at her gate with their wares. She stood for a long time watching the town come to life. Tears welled from her eyes as she heard the sounds of war in the far eastern distance. *Why had Viktor failed her. Where was Rogers? Why did she have to be so unhappy?*

Resolved to seek a solution, Marina had sent Master Loong to the hills to search for Rogers. After several days Marina had not suceeded in contacting Rogers. Master Loong had failed to gain permission to visit the outer Russian forts.

Rumors in the town had confirmed that an American observer officer was stationed at one of the eastern line of forts that supported the Green Hills defense line. Other rumors, planted by the English correspondent Esley and circulated by him, added to the growing doubt and confusion among the townspeople.

In the temporary lull in combat in the first part of July, General Kondratenko rushed to bolster the strength of the forts. The construction had little hope of being sufficient or timely.

Equally busy, General Nogi's Third Army built up reserve regiments, and stockpiled supplies for a coming offensive that promised a blood bath for both belligerents. Nogi had already received criticism for his lack of progress against the Russian forts around Port Arthur.

At mid-morning Marina sat Yin-lin down for a long talk and pointedly asked if the girl had gone to bed with the American. Yin-lin pursed her lips and rolled her eyes as if she recalled wonderful erotic memories. Marina saw through the facade and said angrily, "Captain Rogers would not say anything, so why do you pretend? You do not know him as a lover, and I want to know why you flirted with him. He is not interested in you and he did not like it when you came into his room half dressed."

Yin-lin started to protest her innocence.

"Don't deny it," Marina warned her. "I saw you sitting on his bed with your kiki showing." Yin-lin's lip curled. "Is mistress jealous?"

Marina fought to control her fury at the girl's impertinence. "Don't make me angry, Yin-lin. I am only trying to teach you good manners. If he wanted you, he would have told you so. I had Viktor, I thought, but I have grown very fond of the American, so, yes, I am concerned."

It was Yin-lin's turn to feel rejected., "Then you have slept with him, mistress?"

Marina exploded. "It is none of your business, girl. If I had you would not know it."

Marina stood and pointed to the door. "You have served me well, Yin-lin, and I love you. But you need to learn your place better. I want you to start sleeping in your own bedroom downstairs. The weather is too hot to share my bed with you."

Yin-lin began to cry. Marina added in dismissal, "I am an unhappy woman lately. Viktor may be gone forever. Perhaps he has found someone else. Now the American has disappeared and I am lonely. I want to sleep alone. We will talk later when I feel better."

Marina was still angry with herself for having asked Rogers weeks before to go north to look for Alesandrov. Would it have been better not to have learned of Viktor's infidelity? Why had she been so blind about Viktor?

What she had suspected previously and had overlooked was now a reality. Viktor had chosen someone else. He was not coming back. And now the American had disappeared.

Could she blame Rogers? He had risked his life to do her bidding—to search for Viktor. What if something bad had happened to him at Nanshan? What if he had died or been hurt?

And then when he had loyally returned to her, she had treated him cooly, had shunned his company, blaming him instead of Viktor. How could she have been so cruel and so blind? Now she was alone and had only herself to blame.

CHAPTER EIGHTEEN

The June days had passed by, both eventful and disappointing. News had filtered through Port Arthur that the viceroy had responded to Stoessel's appeal for help by ordering the northern armies to go south. But this rumor was only meant to bolster morale in the port. Kuropatkin had little intention of weakening his front by trying to "rescue" Stoessel.

Knowing from the intelligence garnered by Ariko and Sylvia Levinski that the Russians were playing a waiting game while building up reserves in the north, the Japanese First and Fourth Armies prepared to push northward along the western mountain range, while the Second Army marched easily along the flat land east of the mountains. Southward, the gathering Third Army began to form a land base to attack the Green Hills Line east of Port Arthur.

Captain Viktor Alesandrov was about to experience a long nightmare of combat as General Kuropatkin reluctantly sacrificed part of his army to appease the Czar's demand for a victory. Alesandrov had learned of the angry exchange between Alexeiev and Kuropatkin. He shared Kuropatkin's view that the northern Russian force was not yet ready to lash back at the Japanese. But he rode south with the cavalry of a Russian Balt, General Rennenkampf, in what he understood to be only a show of force with little hope or desire of reaching Nanshan. The cavalry cleaned out some Japanese-occupied villages. Alesandrov saw how effectively the Cossacks used their lances in their furious attacks. Personally, he placed little value in this weapon.

However, Rennenkampf soon had to withdraw his forces to avoid encirclement, the very Japanese tactic that Kuropatkin most dreaded. As ordered, Kuropatkin then chose another Balt, General Stakelberg, to advance south of Telissu, which was about twenty-five miles north of the last reported position of Oku's Second Army. Kuropatkin resented receiving army orders from a naval admiral, but had to obey his superior, the viceroy. He told Stakelberg to avoid a clash, if possible, because his real mission was not to conquer Nanshan, but to establish a defense line south of Telissu.

Privately, Viceroy Alexeiev had doubts that Port Arthur could be rescued or could hold out against the Japanese siege. But the Czar insisted that the naval port had to survive because of public opinion in Russia, and because the base would be needed to support the arrival of the Baltic Fleet— which the Czar in June had decided would be dispatched to the Yellow Sea.

In her Mukden tavern, Sylvia busied herself retrieving information from the vodka-loosened lips of her customers.

"We'll be gone a few days to study the Japanese defenses," a cavalry major told her, "then we'll be back for a good rest and some more of your superb vodka."

"I heard that some of the regiments would be going back to Nanshan," Sylvia probed. "And then to Port Arthur."

The major snorted, "Not likely. That would be suicidal. Our people will set up defenses around Telissu. That is the best we can do for the moment."

"You men are so brave," Sylvia gushed. "I hope your large army crushes the Japs. And I hope the artillery digs in and blows the Japs away."

"We don't need a whole army. We can roll up the Japs easily and we'll keep our artillery mobile to teach them a lesson."

Immediately Sylvia used her carrier pigeons to inform Ariko that Kuropatkin had no intention of bypassing Telissu to attack Nanshan and then march against Port Arthur. The Russian force would be small, she said, and would stay near Telissu with sited, unconcealed artillery. Sylvia exposed other details of the Russian movement, but could not warn the Japanese of the time of the attack.

Armed with this information, General Oku's divisions kept pushing forward, testing the Russian artillery positions by drawing their fire, and destroying many that were unconcealed. Having tested the Russian artillery, the Japanese soon learned most of the Russian gun positions and silenced them. The Japanese shelled the Russian troops, crowded shoulder to shoulder in shallow trenches, with deadly shrapnel fire. In spite of this punishment, the Russians still managed to close within 600 yards of the enemy trenches and fierce fighting ensued.

The Japanese began flanking movements around both sides of the Russian center. Alesandrov sent back couriers to report the flanking attempts. No telephone lines were in place, and heavy rain and the evening fog prevented use of the signalling heliographs. Stakelberg's lack of orders to some of his generals, and his confusing directions to others caused mass disorder. Russian reserves, rushed up by train, did not arrive in time. The day was a Chinese holiday, which further hampered the Russians because the Chinese coolies refused to work. Stakelberg should have won the battle, but having failed to make a general plan and by using bad judgment in choosing his positions, he failed to carry the day. Realizing he was outflanked, Stakelberg ordered a general retreat.

Disgusted with yet another Russian defeat, Alesandrov retreated with his Cossack troops. Morale suffered because the men had received only black bread and water for rations, and had experienced little sleep when the previous night's fog had rolled in. What was supposed to have been a holding action became a delaying movement of retreat.

Both sides suffered from the hot June weather that quickly made a change to summer wear mandatory. The Russians shed their long overcoats and fur astrakhans. The Japanese changed from blue wool to light khaki uniforms.

The remainder of June and the start of July saw the Russians continuing to retreat slowly back toward Liaoyang, pushed by the Japanese in a series of small battles, which the Japanese always won with superior tactics and inter-army cooperation.

* * * * * * * * *

The Pacific Fleet lay idle in Port Arthur. Fires in the boilers had been banked to preserve the shrinking supply of coal. Repairs on the damaged ships neared completion. Meanwhile, naval crews enjoyed too much shore liberty. Inevitably, they continued to clash with soldiers in the streets of the town.

Often townspeople joined in reviling and assaulting the sailors, blaming them for the defeats in the north and for cowardice in not engaging the blockading Japanese fleet. The provost, Petrusha, could hardly quell the altercations.

Admiral Witgeft was aware of the local sentiment, but he chose to ignore the taunts and jeers, and even the pleas that he smash the enemy blockade. He may have been dilatory and over cautious, but he was not the coward that the people labeled him. His was a fear of failure that was a common ailment among many of the naval officers who eschewed risk-taking and adventurous forays. Their fear of failure encouraged a defensive rather than offensive posture.

In her daily rides around the port, Marina had grown accustomed to the sight of the unguarded piles of coal, but she had noticed how they diminished. The hundreds of stacked wooden cases of vodka in the naval compound were another matter. Riflemen guarded the plentiful liquor and were rotated to discourage the temptation of theft.

Transactions in Port Arthur were increasingly handled by barter since most paper rubles had been burned purposely after a shell had damaged the Russo-Chinese Bank. Also much of the bank's supply of coins had been loaded aboard railway cars at the Quail Hill station near Old Town and transported to navy ships before the blockade became effective.

As casualties came down from the defense trenches in the hills, the authorities requisitioned the Nikodadze and Efimoff hotels for use as hospitals. Sartov's restaurant, the Viceregal Lodge and the Naval Club continued to attract crowds. Marina's warehouse supplied the Chinese restaurants of Old Town with ingredients for bird's nest soup and shark fin soup, but the harassment of the Japanese navy against native fishermen made supplies for that menu increasingly doubtful.

Philip Esley continued to drink as heavily as ever. Petrusha had jailed him twice on suspicion of espionage. For fear of alienating the foreign press journalists who might report unfavorably, the military authorities released him.

Yin-lin prayed to Kuan Yin, the goddess of fertility, for a lover.

The doctors at the hospitals began reporting an increasing number of venereal disease cases. Refugee women from Dalny were blamed. The hospitals filled with soldiers debilitated by syphilis and gonnorhea, and self-inflicted gunshot wounds.

Military morale plunged in the absence of a defining Russian victory.

Philip Esley walked through the gloom of night, carefully dodging the shafts of light emanating from the searchlights at the far end of the Tiger Tail peninsula. At the end of a path coursing through the rough rocks and pebbles near the edge of the water, he uttered a low whistle. Hearing nothing after several moments, he whistled again. Seconds later he heard the answering whistle, a long, low sound ending in two sharp, short notes. He waited until the searchlight's beam swept past him before he dashed forward to duck behind a large rock.

A small boat, masked by another large rock, rested in the shallow water of White Wolf Bay at the southern end of Tiger Tail. The seated figure of a Chinaman rose to step from the boat. Esley passed a wax-sealed envelope to the boatman with one hand, then grasped the bag of coins which the native hurriedly proffered. No words were spoken. Scrambling into the boat, the native quickly paddled away. Esley picked his way back to the mainland, treading carefully to avoid the two-man patrols that walked the long and lonely deserted stretch of shoreline.

The next day Esley spent money freely, buying drinks for men who had already drunk too much vodka. He listened to the gossip and rumors, tossed out a few comments likely to provoke an answer, and tried not to incite suspicion.

Hia next move was to walk to the Novy Kry. At the newspaper office, he sought the journalist Nojine, who tried without success to avoid him. Esley told Nojine that Admiral Witgeft planned to lead a squadron from the harbor on June 19 and would steam toward Dalny to catch Admiral Togo by surprise.

"Don't ask how I know," Esley warned. "I tell you this because you have been a friend."

Nojine raised an eyebrow, surprised that Esley dared to presume friendship after so many rebuffs. "How can I be sure your tip is reliable?" he asked.

"Have I ever been wrong?" Esley protested. "Watch, tomorrow. You'll see twice the number of coal barges usually sent out to the battleships. Notice how few men are granted shore leave in the morning. I am offering this to you freely. I have a good source among the Chinese that something exciting will happen."

Esley's news impressed Nojine the next morning. Indeed something was going on! Probing further, Nojine learned that Witgeft's artisans had completed repairs on the battleships *Retvissan* and *Sevastopol*. Nojine did not yet know that the Czar had just decided at last to send the Baltic Fleet from Russia to Vladivostok by way of Port Arthur.

Esley leaked both Witgeft's departure time and date, and also where Witgeft planned to anchor while assembling his armada. Nojine foolishly published this information in a special edition on the day of the departure. Although most copies were recalled by Petrusha, it was too late. Witgeft had to call off his foray. The incensed fleet admirals demanded that the Novy Kry be shut down for one month.

Two days transpired before Witgeft emerged from the port. His six battleships and four cruisers, one at a time, slowly threaded their way through the narrow channel to steam to the supposedly secret assembly area, which he belatedly discovered to be mined by the Japanese.

Admiral Togo had rushed back from the Sea of Japan where he had hunted in vain for the Vladivostok raiders who had sunk the Japanese steamers carrying the precious cargo of large siege mortars and railroad locomotives destined for Nogi's Third Army.

British Commander Nigel Fairborne stood on deck near the Japanese admiral and watched the telltale trail of black smoke on the horizon. Admiral Togo remarked to no one in particular, "The enemy is turning east to follow the coast." Fairborne watched as Togo gave orders for his ships to follow a parallel course to shadow the Russian line of ships. The two fleets sailed the same course eastward, eight miles apart.

Both Witgeft and Togo were edgy because each thought the other had numerical superiority. The waiting game continued until dusk when Togo courageously turned toward the Russian fleet. At that point, Witgeft lost his nerve and turned back toward Port Arthur, managing to enter the port unscathed. The coastal forts damaged several Japanese warships before Togo called off the chase.

In Mukden, Sylvia had been alerted to watch for an allegedly stolen Japanese battle order. On the day after Witgeft's return to anchorage in Port Arthur, the Japanese High Command had issued an order claiming that the forthcoming contest for Liaoyang would have to be postponed until after the rainy season, because Witgeft had proven capable of sallying forth from Port Arthur to endanger the Japanese supply line. The directive was a ploy to mislead the Russians. Sylvia made sure that Kuropatkin's headquarters received a copy of the intentionally misleading order.

Lulled by the planted order, Kuropatkin relaxed his hold on the mountain passes guarding Liaoyang and began shifting regiments elsewhere.

Without hesitating in their drive toward Liaoyang, the Japanese Fourth and First Armies maintained their momentum. On the same day of the order, Nogi's Third Army overran Port Arthur's outposts in a start of the land siege.

Moving along unguarded paths south of Telissu, the Japanese moved up toward pine-clad passes. While a center force faked a frontal assault, two other forces, wearing straw sandals instead of their heavy regulation boots, crept up the steep slopes on the left and right flanks of the Russian defenders. General Count Keller's men found themselves encircled by midday and began abandoning the passes guarding the Liao plain.

Alesandrov, perplexed by so many conflicting orders and the timidity of the Russian generals, remarked to his colonel, "We should have easily repulsed the Japanese and inflicted high casualties on them. For one week it has rained and those mountain trails were almost impassable for the Japanese to bring up supplies and ammunition. Why were the passes so unguarded? Keller gave up too easily. Now the way to Liaoyang lays open. Are we going to keep losing every battle?"

Alesandrov also blamed the Chinese natives who had refused to aid the Russians, fearing retaliation from the Japanese, whom they predicted would be the victors.

The popular and combative General Count Keller was killed a few months later, while trying to regain the passes.

* * * * * * * * *

Late in June, the Japanese Third Army finally launched its land attack against Port Arthur, forced to so do because the Russians on the hills behind the port could watch every enemy movement through telescopes. The attack was delayed two days because the Japanese believed that Chinese natives had informed the Russians of the timing of the offensive.

Tanaka sweated at night in the hot June weather. He had been marching silently with the men of his company since midnight. The late start sought to mislead the enemy of the Japanese advance. His men carried only two days supply of rations, so confident had General Nogi's Third Army headquarters been that the surprise night assault would succeed. Orders given to Tanaka and his fellow officers were for them to probe the eastern defense line of the enemy and to advance rapidly before the enemy could recover.

The faint moonlight starting to peek through the floating clouds, however, made the element of surprise dubious. Three hours had passed since the start of the march, which had left the flat valley below to wind up through the hills. As far as Tanaka knew, the sleeping Chinese villagers in the valley slept unaware of his departure into the inky darkness of the night. He had cautioned his men not to speak, to fold their tents quietly, douse the campfires, furl their battle flags, and bind the jaws of the horses and mules carrying canvas bags, ammunition and the light mountain cannon. Silently the men marched on, masked by the night, with only the silver star insignia on their blue hats, and their unsheathed bayonets glistening in the emerging moonlight.

Tanaka was glad to escape the boredom of garrison duty in Dalny. His countrymen had cleared the offshore mines, had restored order in the town, and had made Dalny the supply center for the Third Army. Two weeks ago, his regiment had bivouaced at the Chinese village of Pantou in the valley. The infestation of fleas and the overpowering odor of garlic in the requisitioned native houses had made sleeping outside more desirable.

Tents had finally arrived for shelter, but the awful clouds of flies robbed the men of rest during the day, pending the arrival of netting from Japan.

The Russians in the hills could look down on the Japanese encampment, but had seemed reluctant to shell the valley except sporadically, perhaps in order not to reveal their gun sites.

Tanaka's men had reached the bottom of a steep series of hills when a Russian patrol opened fire before fleeing. A Russian searchlight began sweeping across the rough terrain. Sensing increasing resistance, Tanaka ordered his men to dig in. Shallow trenches bolstered by dirt-filled bags created defensive breastworks. Scouts sent out to capture prisoners brought back two insolent and rude Siberian peasants, who seemed not to know the name of their general or even what location they presently occupied. Before the light of morning arrived, Tanaka ordered a rope stretched ahead parallel to his trench line. Anorther light rope was then tied perpendicular to the middle of the stretched rope. The other end of this rope led to a waiting Japanese patrol who could feel a tug on the rope if someone stumbled onto the stretched rope ahead. The waiting patrol could then rush forward to capture the hapless Russian scouts.

With the arrival of daylight, Russian machine guns began firing down at the Japanese trenches. The probing phase of the offensive had thus ceased. Orders came for Tanaka to strengthen and deepen his trenches. He was told that a general attack would occur in seven or eight days, as soon as reserve troops arrived from Dalny. The supply depot sent up more canvas bags.

Tanaka had his men dig the trench to a depth of four feet and a width of three feet. The excavcated dirt filled the canvas bags which the soldiers stacked above and about a foot forward of the outward trench edge, The one-foot lip permitted the men to sit or recline out of the way of traffic in the trench. At six-foot intervals the diggers left a four-inch space between two dirt bags along the next to last row of bags. These spaces served as loopholes for Tanaka's snipers.

A week transpired before Tanaka's regimental colonel alerted him of the assault against Kenzan Hill the next day. When the sun rose high in the sky, the soldiers dropped their heavy knapsacks and thick rolled-up wool overcoats. They placed a one-day ration of food in a sack which they tied to their back. Huddling in the trench to escape the whining bullets pelting from above, they smelled the foul odor of smokeless powder and listened to the noisy clatter of breech blocks of the little mountain cannon opening and closing as shells were loaded and empty ones ejected.

The men endured the hot, brutal sun from eight in the morning until three in the afternoon before the delayed order came to attack the perpendicular face of the mountain. During the long wait, Tanaka reminded his men to make the most of their marksmanship training.

"Fire carefully and deliberately. Make every shot count," he told them. He repeated the training poem taught earlier: "Pull the trigger as carefully and gently.

As the frost falls in the cold night."

The men repeated a cruder version of the poem: "Pull the trigger as carefully and gently.

As you would caress a woman's breast."

Facing shells fired from Russian gunboats in Takhe Bay, the Japanese struggled up the steep face of Kenzan Hill. Tanaka shouted, "Forward! Forward!" Yelling "Banzai" and singing the patriotic song "Kimi-ga-yo," Tanaka and his men scrambled upward among the rocks. Men fell back unconscious with a groan of "Ah-a" as they were hit. Clouds of dirt, and black and white smoke filled the grey sky. The Russians exploded small mines of black powder that failed to do much damage, but added to the hellish scene. Unable to halt the onslaught amidst a withering hail of bullets and the crash of shells, the Russian line wavered. Closing with the defenders in a bayonet duel that forced the Russian line to retreat, and their forward trenches to fall to the Japanese, Tanaka's men raised the sun flag with shouts of triumph. Exhilarated by their victory in forcing the Russians off the hill, the Japanese chased the Russians to the stronghold of Lingshuiho-tzu.

Tanaka sat wearily for a moment on a shattered rock amidst lingering clouds of smoke. The walking wounded helped the men of the hospital corps carry stretchers to the rear. Shells from the Russian gunboats still struck the hill occasionally.

As the day closed, the skies filled with thunder and lightning, followed by cold, pelting rain. Battles seemed often to be followed by stormy weather. Without shelter, the men huddled in miserable knots, regretting they had shed their overcoats. Throughout the night, they tried to improve the captured hilltop against an enemy counter attack.

General Stoessel ordered the retaking of Kenzan Hill, no matter the cost, deeming it too valuable to lose. From his position at Lingshuiho-tzu, Rogers watched as deadly Russian shrapnel struck the Japanese. Earth, rocks, and thick white and black smoke exploded upward. Closing to within a distance of 700 meters, and inspired by a drum and fife band, the Czarist soldiers shouted their usual "woolah" cry and charged. They forced their way into the Japanese camp before the surprised defenders fought them off. But the Russian counter attack eventually failed and the attackers were slaughtered by the aroused Japanese. Repeated attempts at the strongholds at Wangchi-tun, Maotao-kuo, and Antzu-ling also failed. The battle ended when both sides became so battered and exhausted that silence finally ensued.

In the days that followed the battle of Kenzan, now renamed Sword Hill, and battles at Waitou-shan and Shuangtingshan, both sides redressed for the summer weather. The Port Arthur defenders shed their dark blue overcoats and tall fur astrakhan hats for more sensible white forage caps, but retained their dark trousers and white blouses and high black boots. The Japanese Third Army continued to adopt lighter khaki uniforms and a lighter, lower crowned khaki hat.

Neither side completely trusted the Chinese natives who seemed willing to spy for whichever side paid most. Another troubling factor, as Tanaka soon discovered, came from Russian soldiers disguised as Chinese farmers. After losing some unsuspecting sentries, Tanaka issued an order in his sector to bar farmers from crossing the defense line. Two enemy soldiers in disguise were executed to discourage such activity.

With the month of July wearing on, the Japanese Third Army successfully pushed the Russian defenders back from the eastern defense perimeter toward the hill forts surrounding Port Arthur. Rogers teamed with a French and two British resident war correspondents to bribe a Chinese boat captain to carry their messages to Chefu on the north China coast. Rogers' message was always directed to Uncle Steve in Shanghai. Chen usually performed this duty for Rogers, but was not always available as the war in the north moved closer to Mukden.

Chen favored a Russian victory, but still carried supplies to the Japanese, both for the higher monetary reward and for the opportunity to glean information for Marina.

Following the short lull after Kenzan, the Russians hurried to stabilize the new defense line to which they had retreated west of the Green Hills sector.

Inspired by his history professor roots, Tanaka searched for but failed to find any trace of the graves of Japanese soldiers killed in the 1894 war with China, fought over this same ground.

To avoid a similar omission in the aftermath of the present battle, wooden marker poles located the fallen Japanese soldiers. The wooden marker bearing the name of the deceased was a square pole left in place for one year, then to be replaced by a stone marker.

Japanese battlefield surgeons removed the Adams apples of their dead. The ceremonial relics of flesh were preserved in small glass containers of alcohol to be sent to relatives in Japan, along with cremation boxes filled with ashes from the funeral pyres.

Japanese mortar attack in the Green Hills sector

CHAPTER NINETEEN

As much as Lydia Fairborne detested the Japanese army because of past insults, she now also began to hate the Mikado's navy, which she blamed for Nigel's difficulties. Worse, her own infidelity had been revealed to Nigel by Naval Commander Okazaka.

It had started when Nigel's heavy cruiser, the *Chiyoda,* had returned to Sasebo to have the heavy growth of barnacles scraped from her bottom, and for repair of her rear funnel which had been punctured by a Russian shell. Lydia was happy to have Nigel back again to relieve her loneliness. They had enjoyed each other's company, and his long absence from her had prompted him to perform sexually, although hardly as satisfactorily as she had hoped. She had succeeded in arousing him with attentive foreplay, but he had climaxed too quickly, leaving her unsatiated.

She had managed to relieve her own tensions in the privacy of her bath before returning to lay down with him to discuss their marriage, a talk that she believed was long overdue. To further encourage his attentiveness, she praised his performance. "See, Nigel," she informed him, "you can do it. I am proud of you. You can be a great lover, if you try."

"I do try," he insisted. "But, sometimes, I can't find enough interest or excitement. Maybe it is the war, or too much stress from ship duty."

"Do I pressure you too much?" she asked. "Maybe I ask too much of you."

He answered her question with a counter question that caught her completely off guard. "Do you have a lover?"

She momentarily lost her poise and could not answer. Finally, she asked, "Is this the time for confessions, Nigel?"

He turned on his side to face her. "No, Lydia, I have no wish to place guilt. I merely want to find a way that will help our marriage. Lately, I have begun to realize how fragile life is and I have come to know how much I need you. I was so happy to learn that my ship had to return to Sasebo."

She wondered if it was the war and the constant danger aboard the battle fleet that worried him, that made him realize the thin veneer of his mortality. She had inquired many times about his chance for a less hazardous assignment. Both had finally conceded that his opportunity for shore duty was slim.

"I am delighted you are here, Nigel." Without admitting her infidelity or accusing Nigel of attraction to men, she embraced him and said she too wanted to save the marriage. She tried to approach the matter delicately.

"I have hated your preferences before, Nigel. And you have overlooked the extent of my sexual need. We don't need to confess anything or make accusations. We have tried to accept our different desires, but we also need to make whatever changes are necessary to stay together. Let's not talk about separation or divorce. I am proud of you and I want you to love me and desire me and long for me when you are at sea. i want to find some way or method that will make our love stronger. Tell me what would really make you happy!"

He decided to confront Okazaka's charge. "We need to be frank, Lydia." He hesitated for several seconds, then plunged on. "A Japanese naval officer was on one of the berthing tugs that met our ship. He came aboard to meet me before I could leave. I don't quite know how to say this, Lydia, but he said he worked for Japanese Naval Intelligence—funny that I have not encountered him before—and he said that you were suspected of working for the Russian Okhrana."

"I don't," she said truthfully. She did not elaborate on the tips she had passed on to the Russian army. That had been voluntary, born of her strong dislike for Ariko and others who had tortured Viktor Alesandrov and had humiliated her in Korea. She worked for no one. So she decided to face the truth. *How much did Nigel know?*

"Who was this ass?" she asked.

"He introduced himself as Commander Okazaka."

Lydia felt a tug pulling her heart to the pit of her stomach. "What did he say?"

"He said that you had a lover, a British officer in the Russian Navy, a man who had been expelled from this city."

"Anything else?"

"No.

Lydia silently breathed a sigh of relief. So Okazaka had been silent about his pursuit of her. "Did you believe him?" she asked.

"It doesn't matter," Nigel answered. "Had we been alone in my quarters, I would have slapped his face. He could see how angry I was, so he excused himself, saluted, and walked away."

A long silence ensued as the Fairbornes struggled with their emotions. Finally Nigel told her, "I speak without rancor when I say that whatever has happened with you in the past is my fault. I don't intend to dwell on that or to listen to some pipsqueak. I have my heavy cross to bear and I hope you can forgive my past indiscretions." He raised his hand to silence her protest. "No, I have not been a good husband. Remember the scene at the hotel room in Tokyo?"

Lydia winced at the memory of that episode. Why would he bring that to her attention now? She had tried in vain to forgive him for the degradation she had felt that miserable night. Afterword she had resolved to put all that behind her.

He read her thoughts and insisted that she rethink the incident before commenting. Lydia recalled the day. She had planned a night of sexual fantasy with Nigel before he boarded ship the next day. It was a cold December day in Tokyo. She had shopped all day, after telling Nigel she would be at the baths and perhaps a fashion show or something, and would be home late.

She had shopped happily till late afternoon—had bought a present for Nigel—and later had relaxed nakedly in the steaming hot water of the public bath, enjoying the looks of envy from the Japanese women. She knew her figure excited interest from oriental women with smaller mammary glands. Lydia had always been happy with her body and not hesitant to expose it.

She remembered telling Nigel she would not be home until almost midnight, because she might attend a dance contest after the baths. But, on this night, she was so eager to give Nigel his present and then to make love with him that she decided to forego the dance presentation.

While soaking in the bath, Lydia had a devilish inspiration. She would bundle her clothing in her shopping bag, clad her nakedness with only her long, full-length coat, and wrap herself in her newly purchased lap robe for the short ride to the Imperial Hotel. Imagine Nigel's delighted surprise when she woud enter their room and open her coat. If that didn't arouse him, nothing else would.

She remembered in retrospect the curious look given her by the concierge before he gave her the room key and she entered the elevator. She had unlocked the door and entered the outer room. Nigel was not in his usual chair reading a novel by Proust. She had started to call out to him, then had decided to enter the bedroom to surprise him. What she saw was a profound shock.

Nigel lay on the bed naked, head to toe with a naked young Japanese man. The two were so engrossed in their activity that they failed to notice her. She had dropped her packages and had screamed loudly.

She had always wanted to banish the memory, only partially succeeding. "What could he give you that I couldn't" she had wailed later. "Why do you need men in your life?" Nigel had only muttered something about his loneliness in his student days at Eton. But now, with Nigel at her side, she wanted to forgive and forget. She too had experimented behind Nigel's back. So who was she to judge? At that time she had told him that they must start a new life. She insisted again.

"Whatever it takes to make us successful lovers, we must learn. We must break this cycle of distrust and deceit. What must I do for you?"

"I don't know," he said abjectedly. "Please help me in my temptations. Please lead."

"I'll find an answer," she swore. And she did.

Two months later, in the heat of mid-summer, after a tour with Admiral Togo, Nigel had returned to Sasebo. The couple had traveled to a cooler mountain resort, accompanied by a Japanese maid whom Lydia had introduced as Miyako. What Lydia had failed to reveal was that Miyako was training to be a courtesan—the kind that needed experience to capture a wealthy merchant. The young woman had agreed, as part of her training and for a price, to aid Lydia's scheme.

On their first night at the resort, Lydia had removed her clothing and had donned a loose robe which she left loosely tied. Nigel had been surprised to see Miyako dressed equally casually. His surprise grew when he saw Miyako stoop to kiss Lydia's cheek while combing her hair. Then he saw Lydia push aside the girl's robe to kiss her breast. He had felt his pulse quicken, but before he could question Lydia, she had asked him if he would mind if she and the girl disrobed—that she found the girl's body exciting, and that maybe he would also.

He watched the two embrace and kiss passionately. An invisible hand seemed to squeeze his gonads. Lydia watched him out of the corner of her eye and saw startled surprise, but no displeasure, only curiosity. Lydia took Miyako's hand and led her to Nigel. "Please join us, darling," she implored Nigel. "This is the present I want to share with you."

Both women had let their robes fall open. He watched them kiss open-mouthed. Lydia then caressed Nigel and glued her mouth to his. Reaching for his hand, she placed it on Miyako's breast, then whispered, "Let me undress you." She explored his middle to discover that he was indeed interested. With that, she and Miyako began removing his clothing.

"What did I tell you,:" Lydia exclaimed. "Isn't his member strong and beautiful? Isn't my husband a darling man?" Tenderly cupping his scrotum, she ran her tongue along his ear and whispered, "Let her stroke you."

Miyako slid her hand along his rigidity with measured strokes, then bent to kiss him.

"Now," Lydia gasped, "take me." She pulled him off his feet and wrapped her legs around him. "It's time, tiger. Love me."

In the few days that followed, Lydia had no difficulty exciting Nigel—as long as Miyako was with them. The presence of a second woman seemed to be the catalyst he needed. Both chose not to question why. Lydia was delighted with her experiment and happier than she had been in months. But she had to think about the future. Could she sustain his libido in the absence of Miyako? *Would a menage a trois always be necessary?* She finally asked him.

"Do you like to see us together? Miyako and I?"

"Yes, very much."

"Does she excite you? What if I let you have her?"

"I only want you," he murmured.

"Could you love another woman if I were not here?"

"No, I don't think I could."

"What if Miyako were not here. Just you and I?"

"I could fantasize. You could whisper things about the three of us."

"Will you stay away from men?"

"I promise. I swear I will."

"Today is our last day at the resort. Let's not waste time." She called to the girl. "Miyako, come here. We want you." She kissed him long and hard. "Let me do everything with Miyako only watching. Or she can caress me. Show us how good you are." *Could she share him with Miyako later? Why not wait and see?*

* * * * * * * * *

As with so many things in life, the happiness that Lydia and Nigel experienced in the presence of Miyako came to an end.

Lydia had agreed with her husband that she should leave Sasebo and the unwelcome harrassment of Commander Okazaka. She left when Nigel was recalled from leave with orders to join Togo. With Nigel's guidance, she moved to the British naval station at Wei-hai-wei on the north China coast near Chefu. Both swore to behave themselves and concentrate on the future, since the war had grown messier with time.

Nigel had told her before they parted, "There will be one or two more terrible naval battles since it is inevitable that the Russian and Japanese fleets will collide. I promise to be careful because I want to come back to you. You will wait for me?"

She promised and told him that when the war ended they would return to England to start a new life. Nigel was in line to inherit a baronet title from his father. The new Lord and Lady Fairborne would then survive quite nicely on their inherited estate in south England.

* * * * * * * * * *

Admiral Togo, having just ended a fruitless search for the Vladivostok raiders, had received intelligence reports from Sasebo—which passed along reports from Esley in Port Arthur—that increased activity in the Russian port suggested a change in plans by Russian Admiral Witgeft. Esley had based his alert on the recall of several naval guns from the ring of forts guarding the hills above Port Arthur. The cannon and many sailors had been relegated earlier to the forts since the Russian fleet lay idled in the harbor. Now the shifting of the men and guns back onto the ships seemed to hint an imminent departure by Witgeft from the harbor.

As Admiral Togo prepared to return to the Manchurian coast, Witgeft had received a final order from the Viceroy. Alexeiev had written: "I again reiterate my inflexible determination that you are to take the squadron out of Port Arthur."

Witgeft could stall no longer. He looked out the window of his office at the bright sunshine outside. Sadness cast a shadow on his face. In a dream the previous night, he had seen a vision of his death. The disturbing nightmare now seemed a tragic possibility.

The following day, Witgeft thought he had received a reprieve when a 4.7 cm enemy shell exploded amid the berthed ships of his fleet. A steel splinter wounded him in the leg. But the wound was slight and gave no excuse for him to tarry. Other Japanese shells struck the edge of Old Town and along the harbor quays. Witgeft and fellow admirals realized the danger all faced from land-based artillery that had targeted Port Arthur. Reluctantly, Witgeft gave orders for a fast dash to reach the relative safety of Vladivostok. During the buildup of steam in the fleet's boilers, Witgeft received a message from the Czar that repeated Alexeiev's insistence that the fleet leave at once.

Three days later, Witgeft led his fleet of six battleships, three cruisers, and eight destroyers out the dark, narrow channel and safely past the minefields into the open sea.

Marina had joined the farewell party at 4:30 in the morning to say goodbye to the admiral, who took his leave with a forboding salute to his assembled officers.

"Gentlemen, we shall meet in the next world."

Outside the harbor, one of the Russian destroyers turned away to hasten to Chefu with Witgeft's message to the Czar. Witgeft had written with considerable bitterness, "I personally, joined by a Conference of Flag Officers and Captains, and after taking into consideration all the local conditions, was adverse to this sortie which, in our opinion, cannot meet with success, and will hasten the capitulation of Port Arthur, which I have reported time after time to the Viceroy."

Witgeft was understandably pessimistic. Two of his battleships, *Persevyet* and *Retvizan* had been damaged previously by shell fire and had not been fully repaired. *Retvizan* was also slowed by 400 tons of water that had leaked through a patched hole in the hull. Two other battleships also suffered chronic mechanical problems.

Patrolling the sea off Round Island, the Japanese battleship *Mikasa* carried Nigel Fairborne toward the smoke smudge on the horizon that marked the presence of the Russian fleet. Togo's flagship *Mikasa* began aggressively to lead the attack. He noted the slow progress of the Russians, caused by mechanical problems on the Russian battleships *Tsesarevich* and *Pobieda.* Both Russsian ships finally stopped and signalled to Witgeft that they were "out of control." Now five miles apart from the enemy, Nigel could see that the Russians were outnumbered. Each side boasted six battleships, but the Japanese possessed eleven cruisers, seventeen attack destroyers, and twenty-nine torpedo boat destroyers.

Admiral Togo refrained from closing the distance too much for fear of losing any of his precious battleships. The gap gradually widened to six miles, but the *Mikasa* still suffered repeated hits. Togo, fearful of an escape by the Russians, who had begun to accelerate their speed, ordered his cruisers to attack. However, by 1PM, shellfire from the Russians forced the pursuing Japanese cruisers to retreat.

The duel continued in the exhausting afternoon heat until 4 PM, when the aging Russian battleship, *Poltava* faltered in speed, forcing the rest of the Russian fleet to slow also. *Mikasa* closed in for the kill, but was hit savagely by 12-inch shells from *Poltava.*

Nigel Fairborne fell victim to the cannonding and suffered severe shrapnel wounds. His torso and his extremities were pierced by red hot shards of steel. One fragment tore off one of his testicles. Mercifully, a loss of consciousness spared him the awful pain.

Almost two hours later, while Fairborne lay heavily sedated in *Mikasa*'s sickbay amid many other casualties, luck again favored Togo and saved him from the humiliation of a Russian escape to Vladivostok. With three of the Japanese battleships and one cruiser damaged, a lucky hit saved the day for Togo. A brace of 12-inch shells struck Witgeft's flagship *Tsesarevitch*. One shell knocked down the foremast. The other shell hit the starboard side of the conning tower and blew Witgeft and his entire staff to pieces.

None of the corpses were recognizable. All that remained of the admiral was a piece of his leg. The mangled corpse of the helmsman was pinned against the wheel by the roof of the collapsed conning tower thus jamming the steering gear. Mechanics rushed from below to free the steering mechanism from the roof and the corpse. *Tsesarvetch* circled helplessly, almost colliding with other Russian ships that blindly followed the erratic, uncontrollable flagship.

At this point, Prince Ukhtomski, aboard the battleship *Peresvyet,* hoisted the admiral's flag to assume command. Disobeying the Czar's orders, he turned back toward Port Arthur, signalling, "Follow me." *Peresvyet* and four other Russian battleships, accompanied by one cruiser and three destroyers, gained the safety of the harbor. *Tsesarevitch*, damaged by fifteen large shells, was escorted south to the German port of Kiaochow by three Russian destroyers, all to be interned there for the war's duration. The Russian cruiser *Diana* sailed to Saigon, French IndoChina to suffer internment by the French. Another cruiser, *Askold,* and one destroyer reached Shanghai for internment by the British. The cruiser *Novik* escaped to Sakhalin island where she fought two Japanese warships before her crew scuttled her.

Meanwhile, three Russian warships of the Vladivostok fleet, trying to come to the assistance of Witgeft, were intercepted. The Japanese cruisers sank one and damaged the other two.

From the shore at Chefu, Lydia witnessed a Japanese squadron coming into the harbor in pursuit of the Russian destroyer that had carried Witgeft's message to the Czar. Despite strong international and Chinese objections to the violation of Chinese neutrality, a Japanese landing party brazenly seized the Russian destroyer. That act quashed any sympathy Lydia and other townspeople may have held for Japan. The English at their neighboring naval station were equally appalled.

Prince Ukhtomski, considered second rate by fellow admirals, sufered the gibes and threats of an angry Port Arthur populace incensed by the Russian naval defeat.

By late August the food crisis in Port Arthur had become critical. Everyone had been put on half rations and that allotment was scheduled for a further cut the following month. Seeing her own food stocks dwindle, Marina persuaded Chen to travel to Shanghai for two purposes. One was to buy sacks of rice, a cherished staple that fetched high prices in the besieged town. Although the northern Chinese subsisted mainly on corn and wheat, a diet that produced taller people than those in the south of China, the northerners still longed for the luxury of rice. Another scarce item on the shopping list was electric fans. The townspeople suffered from the early summer heat that grew even more unbearable in August. Thus far, the enemy had not damaged the electric dynamo stations in the hills.

The other reason was disposal of the considerable amount of money that she had accumulated and hidden. She needed to safeguard it in a reputable bank.

Marina told Chen, "I've heard that our northern forces under Kuropatkin will mount a large offensive to drive the enemy south into the sea and to rescue us. I question if that is possible. It seems Kuropatkin hasn't won a battle yet. I don't trust our future here, so I am moving my money to a safer place."

Chen took a skeleton crew on the trip. He could hire more men in Shanghai if needed. He enjoyed good weather on the uneventful voyage southward and accomplished his task.

* * * * * * * * *

Major Ariko had such a burning hatred for those who had misled him in Shanghai in January that he decided to wait no longer to punish them. The first would be the tavern hostess at the Golden Pavilion who had given him the false information about the Russian Pacific Fleet in Port Arthur—what was her name? Ti Flower, that was it. And if the tavern owner, Ch'in Sheng, got in his way, he'd kill him too.

Ariko swore he would destroy the Russian officer, Alesandrov, and the American, Rogers, and the English woman, Fairborne who had foiled his vengeance in Seoul. If he could not accomplish the deed before the war ended, he swore to do it even in peace time.

But first, Ti Flower. Ariko sent word to agents in Shanghai to hire the most sadistic assassin available. "I want her to suffer," he ordered. "I want *kiao*."

This barbaric Chinese punishment of *kiao*, "The One Thousand Cuts," entailed slowly slicing pieces of flesh from the victim to produce a lingering and agonizing death. Ariko recalled how beautiful the hostess was. She would be unrecognizable when he was through with her.

Feng, the hired Chinese ruffian, decided to kidnap Ti Flower from the Shanghai tavern and bring her to a secluded warehouse on the Bund where he could perform his ritualistic murder. He chose to act alone.

The night he selected for the abduction was a night when Ti Flower was absent from her hostess duties. She had suffered a particularly troubling menstrual cycle and had secluded herself in order to rest as it concluded. Her period had depressed her. This was unusual for Ti Flower. She also found herself strangely bored witrh her duties. None of her customers had measured up to the excitement that she had enjoyed with the Russian officer the past New Year's Eve. How wonderful that evening had been for her. Since then she had longed to change her life, to escape from the tavern owner Ch'in Sheng and to be happy again—before her beauty faded and men no longer desired her.

She was alone in her quarters at the tavern, resting and thinking of the past when Feng stole into her room and brutally attacked her. He pounced on her before she could scream, savagely beating her face. He threw her limp body over his shoulder and escaped down a rear stairs.

Ti Flower, faintly aware of Feng's repeated threats, shouted in vain at the terrified ricksha porter. Feng continued to pummel her during the ride to the waterfront. He dragged her by the hair into a bare room in an old delapidated and vacant warehouse. A single light bulb hanging from a ceiling cord barely lit the stark concrete walls. A solitary bucket of water sat on the floor beneath the light.

Two lengths of small rope hung from ceiling hooks. Feng tied her right wrist to one cord, cursing as the semi-conscious woman slumped to the floor. He pushed her to a standing position, tightened the cord to support her weight, then decided one cord would be sufficient for his purpose. Maddened by her feeble struggles, he pounded her face with his fists until her knees buckled and her body sagged unresisting.

He drew the knife from his belt and cursed again because her long profuse hair was in the way of his first cut. Impatiently, he hacked off the long strands of hair until her bleeding face was exposed. Her eyes were almost closed from the repeated blows. Blood poured from her smashed nose and swollen lips. Sheng tore off her clothing and raised his knife.

First he would cut her face. His knife would cut a line around her skull just above her eyes. He would pull the skin of her face downward, then would cut off pieces of flesh while continuing to flay her. If she was still alive by the time he had slowly ripped off her skin down to her belly, he would cut her open to expose her entrails. Other unspeakable tortures would follow. Then he would cut her throat and remove her head only when life had fled her mutilated corpse.

He lifted a ladle of water from the bucket and threw the water on her battered face to revive her. She watched with horror as he raised the knife to make the first cut just above her left ear. Her face and chest were covered with blood and her shorn hair lay in a pile at her feet.

He made a small incision above her left ear. The sharp pain made her jerk her head to one side, causing him drop the slippery bloody knife. He smashed his fist against her face. When he bent to retrieve the knife, Ti Flower flailed with her legs, kicking him off balance. He fell to his knees, giving her an opportunity to kick his face. Reaching upward, he plunged his knife into her right thigh. Before he could rise, she dealt him another blow with her heel that knocked him forward on the floor. Another kick to the back of his neck momentarily rendered him helpless. Reaching with her free left hand, she pulled the knife from her leg, praying the bloody handle would not slip from her grasp. She cut loose her tied wrist as Feng struggled to rise from the floor. She kicked him in the belly to knock the wind from his lungs. Limping from the burning knife wound in her thigh, she unbolted and forced open the warehouse door and ran along the darkened quay outside. Naked and bloody and desperately seeking to escape, she fled alongside a row of moored boats.

Feng stumbled into the night, spitting blood and holding his broken nose. He saw the woman staggering ahead on the quay. Fog had rolled in to obscure his vision. Holding his knife, he ran toward her. Just before the fog hid her, he saw her turn toward a docked boat.

He groped his way through the enveloping fog to reach a line of boats tied to the quay. All but one were small boats that sat motionless in the water. The one large boat, a black junk, rocked slightly as if disturbed. He scrambled up the short ladder to the raised deck.

He saw her crouched in the shadows. She screamed as he lunged forward with the knife. A deckhand standing watch stepped out of the shadows to stop him, but Feng knocked him down. A shaft of light illuminated the deck as a cabin door opened. Ti Flower twisted away and ran toward the open door.

Chen had stepped forth onto the deck in response to the scream. He saw a naked figure with short hair fleeing toward him. In an instant he realized it was a woman. The bloody face was almost unrecognizable. Behind her, a man smeared with blood, advanced with a raised knife. The woman brushed past Chen. He saw his deckhand struggling to stand up. The man with the knife slashed at Chen who ducked. Stepping quickly to one side, Chen caught the arm, twisted it behind Feng's back and kicked his feet from under him. As Feng tried to rise, a belaying pin smashed against his skull. The deckhand hit him again and again. Chen helped his deck man throw Feng overboard. Unable to swim, the butcher sank like a rock into the dark water below.

Chen entered the cabin. Throwing a blanket around the crouching woman, he lifted her to one of the two cabin bunks. He motioned for the deckhand to leave. With the door closed, he began to examine her. In spite of her battered face, he could recognize the beauty of her figure. He had seen the knife wound on the inside of her naked thigh and now tried to staunch the flow of blood. He did his best to calm the hysterical woman, cleaning the blood from her face and pushing her broken nose into place. Her breathing became less rapid and her trembling slowed. With her face cleansed, Chen pushed aside the blanket to bathe her bloodied chest and belly, then bandaged the stab wound. He gave her a strong sedative and urged her to rest and sleep.

Chen left the cabin to instruct his helper to buy some medicine, giving him the money and telling him to roust the shopkeeper out of bed if necessary. To avoid any possible problem with the police, Chen cleaned the deck of stains. Rather than arouse any of the sleeping crew, he decided to stand watch himself until the deckhand returned. The fog had so completely shrouded the area that he doubted anyone would investigate. Enough moisture existed in the fog to wash away any drops of blood on the quay.

Chen now began to question who the woman was, and why some crazed madman had tried to kill her. And he asked himself what he should do with the woman. When she could talk rationally, he would ask her name and if she had kin. What if she had no one? Could he push her off his boat and leave her alone? He had planned to leave in the morning with the outgoing tide as soon as the fog lifted. He had not planned on any delay.

The presence of the strange woman and her nakedness brought forth a vision of Marina. For too many years, Chen had worshipped his pseudo cousin. He wondered if he would ever be able to tell her of his admiration. Would she always regard him as a father figure? Would he finish the rest of his life in lonely solitude? He did not avidly seek other women. Marina was the only one who had ever held his interest, except for a long dead wife.

Years earlier, the loss of a young wife had embittered Chen and had made him reluctant to chance such a tragedy again.

But he was a healthy man in his early forties, and there were often times when he wished for an end to his shyness with women. Only Marina had made him feel comfortable.

He had seen her happiness with Alesandrov. He had nothing against the Russian except a feeling of jealousy and envy. Envy that Alesandrov shared Marina's home and affection. Envy that the Russian's personality made him so sought after by the women of Port Arthur. Now Rogers was with Marina. His young friend no longer spoke of An-an. What had happened? Marina probably did not know about An-an unless Rogers had told her. Come to think of it, Rogers had not seemed overly happy lately.

Chen knew there would come a day when he no longer lived a life at sea. Where would he dwell? What would he do? He was making money now with the war. Lots of it. But that would end and then what? He shrugged off his gloomy thoughts. If only he could be like the young people and think of nothing but the present and not dwell on the future.

In a little less than an hour, the deckhand returned with an antibiotic, catgut sutures, a needle, iodine, and morphine. Chen chose not to awaken Ti Flower until shortly before daybreak. He gently shook her awake. She pulled the blanket tightly around her and looked at him groggily as he explained what he wanted to do for her knife wound, but first he had some questions for her to answer. When asked about her relatives, she explained that she was alone with no kin and was afraid to stay in Shanghai. She said that she was a hostess at the Golden Pavilion, but was never going to return there. Chen, asking for no further details, gave her a cup of hot tea to drink, while he prepared to dress her wound. She did not seem to be embarrassed when he opened the blanket covering her nakedness. Chen pretended not to be disturbed, although inwardly he was.

The wound was red and puffy, but did not seem to be infected. The bleeding had ceased.

"It is deep yet does not seem to have hit a leg bone," he told her. The cut was about six inches below her vagina. Luckily, the blade had missed the femoral artery. "I am going to clean it and then close the cut with stitches. I may hurt you so try to be brave, and please do not be shy."

Still relaxed from the sedation, she looked at him closely with a little smile. Such a kindly man and so considerate. "Are you the boat's doctor?"

He grinned, "Trust me." He warmed some water and bathed her legs. She continued to watch him with the same little half-smile. At least that part of the procedure was pleasurable. After drying her legs, he poured alcohol on the area, dried it and then painted the wound with iodine, warning her, "This may sting." He knew it would sting like Hades. He held her firmly as she arched her back in agony. He unfolded the slip of paper and poured the white powder on the wound. Then he administered the laudunum and held her like a child while it took effect. In a few minutes he threaded the catgut through the needle and as swiftly as possibly sutured the wound.

"You are a brave young lady," he told her. She took the cloth he offered and wiped her tears. He covered her with the blanket. His hand had become suddenly shaky. It had been years since he had seen such nudity and such a perfect body.

In the light of dawn, Chen cast off the mooring lines and left the quay. An hour later, safely out to sea, he turned the wheel over to his helmsman and returned to see Ti Flower. She was sleeping. Her pitiful face was still swollen and she would be bruised and sore for the next several days. If the wound failed to heal properly, he would stop at Tsingtao for a doctor's attention. Chen made her lie in bed for the remainder of the day. When awake, she followed every movement as he walked about the small cabin.

On the second day, she insisted on trying to walk. He lent her a pair of his lounging garments. By the third day, as they neared their destination, every muscle in her body still ached. The swelling of her lips and nose had subsided, but her eyes were frightfully blackened. Chen had explained to his men that he would stop at Chefu to discharge his passenger.

Ti Flower clung to him like a child when he picked her up in his arms and carried her off the junk to a waiting ricksha. She blew a kiss to the grinning crewmen and they clapped happily. Chen took her to the same Tang family that he had rescued from Dalny. He explained the situation to Mrs. Tang and paid for Ti Flower's lodging, promising to return in two weeks to check on her recovery.

At night, Chen slipped into the outer roadstead of the harbor at Port Arthur by hugging the western shoreline before rounding the lower tip of the Tiger Tail peninsula. He had memorized every meter of the harbor approach, so had no need to slow his entry. By raising his adjustable keel, something no other junk possessed, Chen could navigate the shallow water. The large red dragon he had painted on his mainsail was usually enough to grant him passage past the searchlights. Chen always took care to reward the searchlight crews.

CHAPTER TWENTY

Still suffering from his many wounds, but anxious to be with Lydia, Nigel Fairborne finally persuaded the hospital doctors in Sasebo to transfer him to Wei-hai-wei where his wife resided. He believed he would obtain a hospital discharge faster at the British station. The incessant chattering in Japanese by those around him, and the uncertain long term damage of his wounds, as well as the Japanese diet, had became a burden he wanted to escape.

The Japanese surgeons had patiently answered most of his persistent questions about his recovery, though typically without going into detail, while assuring him he would recover fully in time.

"What about my testicles?" Fairborne lamented. His scrotum was still heavily bandaged. An orderly had told him of his humiliating loss.

"Wound is healing," the doctor told him.

"Will I be a man again?"

"Yes. Lose one testicle. Only need one. Two balls better, but one will do. Just like kidneys. Be glad you not lose penis. Hee, hee," the doctor giggled.

Fairborne failed to see the humor. *What would happen to his manhood? Would Lydia reject him? Could he still perform,?* His bouts of depression did not make him a pleasant patient. What surprised him most was his lack of interest in the "feminine" hospital orderlies. He easily spotted the overtures of some of these young men and found them, for the first time, unappealing. Fairborne was unaware of his brain trauma.

The Japanese earlier, after a protracted delay, had alerted Lydia of Nigel's wounds and hospitalization, but the notice had been terse and devoid of detail. Her anxiety had only been alleviated when Nigel had arrived in Wei-hai-wei and she had been contacted by the medical staff of the small British hospital there. Nigel's British doctor permitted her to visit Nigel freely and had encouraged her to bring him cheer and love.

The doctor told her that Nigel needed distraction from his worry about sex and assured her that Nigel would be fine, but that his body was healing better than his mental condition.

"He suffered some rather extensive flesh wounds from shrapnel," the doctor advised her. "The Japanese doctors were good, so he will have very few noticeable scars. The trauma to his groin was severe and he lost a great deal of blood on board ship. We want to monitor him for a few more weeks to be sure the surgeons recovered all the metal fragments. Also, we need to wean him off the morphine dosage as his pain subsides."

"Will he be able to return to duty?"

"We believe so ultimately, but we will first recommend a few months of recuperation. You can help us aid his recovery. As soon as we have fully determined the extent of his head injury, we will discharge him to your care."

"What head injury? My husband did not mention that."

"He is not aware of it. His medical chart, transferred to us by the Japanese, reflected a blow to the forehead that caused temporary blindness. The Japanese doctors had to tap into his skull to drain internal bleeding. We are confident that he suffered no permanent damage, since his hearing and eyesight are again normal. He no longer has headaches and has a good appetite. A few more weeks-or months-down the road, he should be as good as new."

Lydia breathed a heavy sigh of relief. *Thank you God!* Then she aked, "What about his problem—you know—his genital area? He is so worried."

The doctor decided that Lydia was more modern than most women, so he spoke frankly.

"The left testicle was destroyed. That testicle is lower and thus helped protect the other one. The scrotum was sutured and has healed nicely. The torn flesh in his groin is coming along very well. As his wife, you need to reassure him when he is discharged to your care. Do you understand my meaning?"

Lydia understood fully. Nigel needed some tender female loving, and she could provide it better than anyone.

She visited Nigel everyday except for one day a week when she traveled to the nearby Chinese trade port at Chefu to shop. This was an excursion to help maintain her sanity. She did not like hospitals and she hated to see Nigel so worried and depressed. Lydia had reached under the bed cover to reassure herself that the penis, which lay nestled among the bandages, was indeed intact. When she had Nigel all to herself at the cottage, she would test his sexuality.

The shopping at Chefu was fun for her, and she soon found a Chinese restaurant that offered a congenial atmosphere and good meals. Conversations with the owner's wife led to a suggestion by the Chinese woman that a family friend very much wanted to meet Lydia.

One day, while enjoying luncheon in Chefu, Lydia had been approached by a Chinese merchant who had introduced himself as Mr. Tang and wondered if he might join her. At first hesitant, she soon discovered his reason when he mentioned he had business dealings in Dalny and Port Arthur, and said that she might have a common dislike for a certain

Japanese army officer. Her ears perked up at the mention of the man's name, "Ariko."

Tang made it clear that he had no love for Ariko who had seized his property in Dalny. He told Lydia that a Korean merchant had visited Tang's warehouse and had somehow stolen the keys to the warehouse gates and office. Tang was sure of this because the following day, when Tang and his family had fled the city, the Korean businessman had unlocked Tang's warehouse. When the Japanese army quickly occupied Dalny, the same Korean had changed into the uniform of a Japanese army major. Tang's neighbors in Dalny, still in touch with Tang, had heard the officer addressed as Major Ariko.

Tang had learned subsequently from the same neighbors that Ariko had questioned them about a Marina Berezovsky, whose name he had discovered on several receipts in Tang's office. Ariko had also asked for information on Marina's relationship to a Russian officer named Viktor Alesandrov, and an American called Rogers.

At the mention of Viktor's name, Lydia eagerly responded with questions about him.

Tang had shrugged, saying he was a good friend of Mdme. Berezovsky, but knew almost nothing about the Russian, except that the man had been a guest for some time at the Berezovsky home in Port Arthur. Tang had met the American, a Captain Rogers whom he described as a recent guest at the Berezovsky home.

What intrigued Lydia was that Tang hated Ariko as much as she did. He said he would do anything to thwart Ariko, even if he had to work for the Russians. Lydia believed she had found an ally. Of further interest to her was Tang's story of a young Chinese woman, an acquaintance of the Russian officer. The woman was recuperating in the Tang house from an attempted assassination perpetrated by one of Ariko's hired thugs. The young woman was from Shanghai, and had been brought to Chefu by a Chinese junk skipper.

"Recently?" Lydia asked. *Who was this "acquaintance?"*

"Very recently, about two weeks ago. Chen asked our family to help her recover from her wounds."

"Who?"

"Chen. I don't know his full name. Everyone calls him Chen. He goes to Shanghai several times a year to bring cargo to the north."

"Is the woman a good friend of this Chen?"

"I believe so; she must be. She also speaks well of this Russian, Alesandrov. She is a beautiful lady who was badly beaten by a thug in Shanghai."

"I must meet her. Can it be arranged?" Lydia's curiosity had begun to boil over. *This woman knew Viktor? Could Viktor be alive and safe?*

"Perhaps I can be of some help to you," she told Tang. "I will return to Chefu in ten days. May I come to your home to meet this lady?"

"Of course, please do."

Lydia and Tang talked further. She told him about her husband, but assured him that Nigel, though associated with the Japanese navy, was neutral, and that she preferred he not be involved for the time being. She said she did not plan to include him in her activities. Sensing that Tang understood her interest in forming some kind of agreement, she promised to explain later about her husband.

Ti Flower combed her hair. In Mrs. Tang's hand mirror, she could see that her hair, though still too short, had grown considerably in length and was no longer chopped in appearance. She combed her tresses with loving care while examining her image in the mirror. The swelling had disappeared from her face, and the purple and black marks were gone except for a faint trace of bluish pigment at the corners of her eyes. Her nose was as straight as before. The slight cut above her ear had healed. The only soreness on her body was the slow healing knife wound on her thigh.

The marvelous man who had rescued her had returned as promised and had seemed satisfied with the progress of her healing. When she had impulsively embraced and rewarded him with a kiss, he had stiffened with embarrassment, but had not pulled away. She had kissed him again when he left. That time he had relaxed and hugged her in return. She hoped she had smelled clean and fresh unlike the dirty, bloody mess of her naked body the night of her torture. Neither had mentioned the knife thrust into her thigh. She had assured him that all was well with her health. How embarrassingly close to her "kiki" the stab wound had been, especially when the Tangs had told her that Chen was no doctor and was not even married. Maybe one of the Tangs had informed him that she had healed. She recalled how Mrs. Tang had rolled her eyes and teased her when helping to remove the sutures.

She recalled how gentle and soft his hands had been when he had bathed her. She could have died from loss of blood, shock, or infection, were it not for the kind stranger. She owed her life to him. How could she ever repay the debt? She swore she would find a way somehow. After that first visit with Chen, the Tang's ten-year old daughter had revealed to her that she had heard the captain tell her father that Ti Flower was "a very pretty lady."

Ten days later, Lydia greeted Mrs. Tang at the modest, small house the Tang family occupied. The Tangs apologized for their lack of amenities. Lydia understood and praised them for so successfully starting a new life in Chefu.

"This war has caused so much suffering for the Chinese and Russians," Lyudia remarked. "Even the Japanese suffer. When I was in Tokyo, I saw much poverty. It will only get worse. Wars are so cruel."

She looked up to see Ti Flower enter the room. Lydia was startled to see the Chinese woman's beauty and obvious sensuality. With difficulty, she forced herself to refrain from asking at once the woman's connection with Viktor.

But, during the pleasant visit, she learned that Ti Flower had lost everything and had no prospects for the future. Obviously, the woman faced a bleak future. Whether it was pity, or curiosity, or friendliness, Lydia made a proposal that she never fully understood why, but one that would change her life and that of the young and pretty woman.

Lydia startled everyone by asking if Ti Flower would like to come to Wei-hai-wei to work for her. "My husband will soon come home from the hospital. I will need some help in caring for him. I can offer you a home and a modest income for some time. Please think about it."

Ti Flower expressed her gratitude, "I would love to help. I am fearful that I am too much of a burden in this crowded home." She ignored Mrs. Tang's show of protest. "I can never thank Mr. and Mrs. Tang enough for sheltering me, but I need to find a different life." She did not mention her subservient duties at the Golden Pavilion, or her dread of Ariko's vengeance. Instead, she turned to Lydia and confessed that she had briefly cooperated with Russian agents in Shanghai. Mr. Tang had already told her that Mrs. Fairborne was full of hatred for Ariko.

Lydia was impressed with the honesty and believed she was doing the right thing. She suggested that Ti Flower return that day with her to Wei-hai-wei.

In the few days that transpired before Nigel left the British hospital ward, Ti Flower and Lydia became knowledgeable about each other's past and their common interests. Both detested Ariko. Both favored a Russian victory. Both had a need for female companionship. And both had slept with Alesandrov.

Lydia found herself unresentful of Viktor's tryst with Ti Flower. Why not? She did not own him. And she could understand how Viktor could lust for the girl. She was beautiful, sensuous, and fast becoming a marvelous companion. Ti Flower, for her part, did not question Lydia's confessed infidelity. She sympathized with Lydia's sexual hunger, and she remembered all too well how desirable the Russian could be. Later, when she met Nigel, she saw the Englishman's shortcoming. But she liked him.

Nigel liked her attentiveness. He told Lydia how attractive the girl was, how much he enjoyed her presence. Lydia had seen his happy admiration of the girl's figure and had accepted that as a promising sign of Nigel's recovery.

"We promised to be honest with each other," she reminded him. "If she makes you hard, I want to know."

He started to protest. "What can I do," he whined. "I have only one bollox. I can't even take care of my wife."

"That is nonsense. Your bandages will come off next week, so you had better be ready."

Two days later, Nigel told Lydia, "Something has happened. For the first time in ages, I have no desire to be with men. In fact, the thought repels me. How could I have been so stupid before? Ugh!"

Lydia had already noticed his behavioral change and welcomed it.

At bedtime, she sat on the edge of the bed after removing her dress. When she bent to remove her stockings, she felt his hand trace a pattern across her back. She turned around to kiss him. "How you must have suffered when the shell hit," she sympathized.

"I don't remember much," he confessed. "There was this explosion. I felt myself thrown through the air and then all was black. I remember coming to for a moment. My eyes were full of blood and my head hurt terribly. I must have hit my head. My forehead was bleeding and my lap hurt like the devil. I remember trying to clear the blood from my eyes, and then my fingers were in my lap and I could smell burning flesh when I touched some hot metal in my leg. And then I woke up in a hospital with bandages all over, even my eyes, and I was tied to the bed and everything was dark and my head ached, oh so badly."

Lydia recalled the British doctor warning her that Nigel had suffered a severe prefrontal cortex injury that might alter his behavior. Could the blow to his forehead have caused him to change?

Ti Flower proved to be adept in her nursing duties. She fed Nigel at mealtime, made him as comfortable as possible, bathed his upper torso, and administered his medicine. She changed the dressing on his torso wounds and spread balm oil on the healed but tender flesh and scar tissue. One by one, the bandages lessened so that she could finally massage his body, taking care not to disturb his bandaged groin. Nigel loved the care and attention and relaxed happily in her presence, hoping that she could stay as long as possible with them.

When Lydia told her that she wanted to shorten her name to Ti, Ti Flower agreed. Lydia said that she had removed the last bandage and that Nigel's body was as normal as ever, except for a slight reduction in the size of his scrotum. "He is still afraid to let me touch his 'pouch.' Nigel can be such a baby sometimes."

Ti asked, "Have you—? You know."

Lydia laughed. "I will, and very soon—when he least expects it. The doctor told me not to wait much longer." Ti giggled with her.

Ti and Lydia occasionally journeyed to Chefu for a day's outing. On one such visit to theTang family, Lydia had an opportunity to ask Mr. Tang how difficult it would be to smuggle messages into Port Arthur.

Ti and Lydia enjoyed long daily talks about men, especially of Nigel and Alesandrov. Lydia had explained Nigel's past difficulties and had added some of her own sexual adventures, a sure sign that she trusted Ti. Their bond had grown so strong that the two could talk frankly about men: their strengths and weaknesses, their need for a woman, and what it took to please a man. Ti learned much about western culture, and Lydia profitted from Ti's frank descriptions of "innovative" sex.

"Your husband is a fine man, Lydia. I can understand why you love him so much."

Lydia embraced Ti and for the first time kissed her, telling her, "Nigel and I both like you very much Ti. I know that life has been cruel to you. I wish you could stay with us forever. I am so sick of this stupid war. I dread the day when Nigel will have to go back to the Japanese fleet."

"After the war, will you and your husband return to England?" Ti asked.

"Yes, Ti. We have a lovely home there. The countryside is so peaceful and beautiful. What about you?"

"We Asians try to enjoy life for the moment. Life is too uncertain to make too many future plans. I will search for a lover or a husband to support me. I don't want to go back to my old life."

* * * * * * * * * *

During the fighting in July, Rogers made a crude sketch of the immediate defense position he occupied, imagining it from the Japanese perspective—looking upward at the small unfinished, fortified blockhouse in which he stood. Crowded inside the blockhouse with him were a half dozen Russian officers. They eyed his work with some suspicion, but did not interfere. He sketched the hillside below the blockhouse. As he sketched, he looked from his loophole above the steep escarpment down at the deep Russian trench directly below the blockhouse—a ditch crowded with a mass of Russian infantrymen. Another trench, a very narrow one, branched off perpendicularly to join the blockhouse to the large ditch. Later, on the firing ledge of the large trench, Rogers watched the small figures of the Japanese on the slopes below. The Russian infantrymen were cautioned not to fire at the enemy digging a sap upward from the base of the hill.

"Let the fools dig," one of the officers told his men. "Let them bunch up, then we will hit them with grenades when they least expect it."

The sap was a shallow trench that each day had been progressively dug in a zig-zag pattern upward from the valley floor. Hour after hour, the Japanese engineers dug industriously in the hard, rocky earth. Late in the afternoon, under gathering evening shadows, Rogers noticed another sap being dug parallel to the existing one, and separated by about two hundred yards. He guessed it was dug to help distract some of the rifle fire from the heights, and that the two saps would eventually terminate at a strong connecting trench running parallel and just below the Russian breastworks. From the valley, the saps diverged outward from each other to progress up the hill. The zig-zag shape of the saps helped protect the digging work parties. The patient Japanese labored on the saps night and day, working under constant rifle and cannon fire. As the saps inched upward, the

Japanese returned the rifle fire and also employed their little mountain cannon. The saps were a form of trench warfare that seemed to Rogers to make more sense than Japanese General Nogi's mad frontal charges.

The Japanese worked feverishly to fill the cloth bags with the excavated soil, then piled the bags on the forward edge of the sap. At the foot of the escarpment, that steep incline that formed the front face of Russian fortifications, the Japanese would try to join the two saps with a deep trench that would be pushed outward from one sap to the other. Japanese troops massed in the saps, crouching low as they followed behind the engineers moving upward.

Sharpshooters among them countered the Russian fire, forcing the Russian defenders to keep their heads down.

Rogers believed that the Russians were over confident about their ability to disrupt the digging. He had heard the sounds of the sappers continuing to dig at night. There had been no letup in the engineer's activity. Each night, when an occasional Russian blue starshell lit up the dark hillside, it would reveal no enemy soldiers, but the saps would be farther up the hill.

Two weeks later in daylight, Rogers watched with pity as the Japanese assault team prepared to storm the escarpment from their forward parallel trench that had finally been dug to join the ends of the two saps. The parallel was so close to the Russian position that the crouching Japanese could only hold their rifles above their heads and shoot randomly toward the top of the escarpment.

All attempts by the Japanese infantry to leave the forward parallel in order to scale the escarpment failed. One by one, they were shot as they climbed out of the sheltering trench. The few who managed to reach the top of the escarpment were cut down as the Russians pressed their rifles through the loopholes to fire into the enemy bodies. A second attempt failed also in a repulse that left hundreds of dead and dying scattered along the face of the steep slope.

At daybreak, when the Japanese artillery began to shell the fortification, the Russians left their forward trench for the safety of trenches behind the concrete blockhouse. Many Japanese wounded, who had feigned death on the slopes, tried to escape the shells by dashing down the hill rather than wait for a less deadly attempt to leave in the dark of night. Many were shot as they ran for cover in small groups—some within yards of safety. When the shellfire abated, Russian riflemen returned to their forward trench at the top of the escarpment and cooly fired to pick off anyone who stirrred among the heaps of fallen enemy soldiers.

At the onset of darkness, the huge Japanese howitzers ceased firing, leaving the shelling to the smaller mountain cannon. The scene was illuminated by Russian searchlights and exploding blue starshells that exposed the battlefield on the barren hillside. A counter attack by the Russians failed. Though they overran the Japanese parallel, they were unable to drive the Japanese from their saps.

In the darkness, Japanese volunteers went out to assist the wounded, but did so under fire from men who had become too angry to respect the Red Cross rules.

Like moles, the Japanese extended their saps to bypass the blockhouse so they could attack other Russian strongpoints. Suffering terrible casualties, the Japanese steadily pushed their enemy back along the Green Hills sector.

By the third week of July, during a three day battle, the Japanese had forced the Russians to abandon their first defense line twelve miles north of Port Arthur. The Russians fell back to their second line of defense, now only six miles from the port. By the first of August, the Russians had retreated to their large concrete forts and the siege of those forts began.

The Japanese used their large siege mortars, launching shells now capable of smashing the concrete of the forts. They also then abandoned all restraint against shelling Port Arthur and began firing land based artillery shells into the town. Upon that occurance, Rogers deserted the forts to return to Port Arthur, desperately concerned about Marina's safety. Some of the townspeople fled to the hills to camp out, hoping to escape the large mortar shells.

Rogers was sick of the slaughter around the forts. He needed to find a way back into the town to send a report to Uncle Steve, but more importantly to have a bath, new food, and a change of clothes. He tried not to think of his reception at Marina's house. If she was still angry, so be it. He had to see her. He had to know her feelings and if she was safe. Even a glimpse of her would be a reward. Anything to escape the scenes of horror in the hills.

* * * * * * * * * *

On a hot late afternoon of early August, Marina stood in the partial shade of her seaward veranda. She saw the lone figure of a man slowly climbing the hill below her house. He was dressed in a Russian soldier's uniform, but was unarmed except for the pistol on his belt. He carried a large sack on his back and looked vaguely familiar.

She wondered what the soldier wanted. She was not alarmed. If it was bad news, an officer would have come to her home, The approaching man was not dressed as an officer. As the figure drew closer, her heart skipped a beat. The man had looked up at her and smiled. *It was Rogers.*

Screaming loudly with joy, Marina ran down the stairs and rushed outside into the street to throw herself on him. "I had to come back," he told her. "I could not help worrying about you since the Japanese army started shelling the town. I dressed this way to avoid being mistaken for an enemy soldier while coming through the hills."

She was still crying from joy and relief. He held her gently, shoo-shooing her sobs. "There, there, please don't cry."

"Why did you leave me?" she wailed. "It has been so lonely here—and so difficult without you. Why did you go to the front? This is not your war."

"I thought it best to leave," he said. "You were unhappy with me. It just became too awkward to impose on your hospitality." He would try to explain his army obligations later.

She pulled him closer. "Oh, Ellis, I was so confused. First Viktor, then you and some nurse, then you and Yin-lin. It was as if you did not like me. I wanted you to like me." He started to speak, but she continued. "I know Yin-lin lied about you, and I am sorry I reacted so badly because of Viktor."

"Forget all that," he told her softly. "Yin-lin is still a naughty little virgin, and my friendship with the nurse is strictly platonic. I wanted to tell you about…"

Marina interrupted. "I misjudged you. I know about Viktor and the nurse. I worked out the puzzle, and then I scolded Yin-lin. Why did you never come to me?"

He teased her. "Because I was afraid of you and your anger. I am only human, too." Then, more seriously, he explained, "I do like you Marina. More than you know. But I can't hurt you. I can never be someone you deserve. My life is confused and my career is too uncertain. And, yes, there is someone—or there was. I don't know what happened. I guess I am like you, disappointed, frustrated and lonely. I had to come back to see you."

He marveled at the softness of her body as she clung to him.

"Do you want to talk about it?" She took his hand and led him into the house.

"Not really," he answered. "I have a lot of hurt to get over. Maybe later. I'm at a point where I want to be selfish about my needs. Damn this war. Damn this suffering."

She led him up the stairs. He remembered how provacatively her hips had moved the first day she had met him and had walked ahead up the steps. The sensation was now being repeated. He ached to reach out to touch her, to feel the softness of her flesh.

"Marina, can you get me some bath water? Life is very primitive in the trenches. I must smell like a goat."

She led him into her room and pointed to a curtained enclosure on a small veranda outside a narrow door. "I had that added," she told him. "The weather has been so hot this summer. Enjoy the water. It is lukewarm and clean from the cistern on the roof. I will order some food for us and have it sent up to my room. You can wear one of my robes while I have your clothing laundered."

When she went downstairs, he undressed and showered in the veranda stall, enjoying the luxury of a soapy bath from something other than a bucket of water in a smelly trench. He had just toweled himself dry when he heard her enter the room. He wrapped the towel about his middle just as she reached through the curtain with a cotton robe, one that Viktor used to wear.

"I feel silly in this robe." he protested.

She laughed. "Are you squeaky clean?"

"I will be as soon as I shave." She handed him the basin. While he shaved, she sent his bag of dirty clothing downstairs. He had finished shaving when she returned carrying the food and some wine, having decided to keep the servants away.

They sat in the chairs placed before a low table, ate slowly, and talked for a long time. He enjoyed the cool air blown across a block of ice by the low fan on the table. Two ceiling fans also circulated the air. Twice she rose to fill his wine glass and each time she leaned over to kiss him. He couldn' t remember the last time he felt so relaxed and so full of desire.

"That was wonderful, Marina. No more wine, please, or I'll forget my manners." Filled with desire, he stood and embraced her. "Good lord, lady, you look and smell so good. You can't believe how much I missed you." He blushed. "I hope I'm not too bold, but it has been such a long time since I was close to you and so excited."

"Too long," she agreed, feeling his pressure. She walked across the room to her bed and lay down. Patting the pillow, she beckoned to him. "Remember our night in Dalny?"

He nodded, then approached the bed. She held out her arms. "Do you think you could kiss me?" she asked. "Really kiss me?" It was still light outside, but she had drawn the drapes.

He could feel the heat rising between them and realized he was losing control of his growing tumescence.

"Tell me you love me—please." She too was losing control. He told her he loved her. She searched his mouth with her tongue, then moved his hand to her breast. After more passionate groping, she rose from the bed and began to disrobe. He watched her teasing movements. When she stood naked beside the bed, he drank in the beauty of her body. It was all that he had envisioned and more than he had hoped for. She asked him to open his robe. "I want to see if I excite you." He reached up for her, but she pushed him back on the pillow.

He breathed with relief after freeing himself from the tight folds of the robe. She reached for his hand and begged him to explore her body, shuddering with a small climax as he did so. He reached up to kiss her hardened nipples. Sitting astride him and unable to restrain herself any longer, she mounted him and took the lead aggressively and shamelessly.

Later, she told him, "I lost my inhibitions when you left and I kept dreaming of you at night. I know I may be acting like a bitch in heat, but I don't care. I want to enjoy every moment of life I have left. I have waited too long for this. So, surprised? What else would you like to try?"

The room was dark and the passionate groans and cries had ceased when the exhausted pair finally slept.

At daybreak, he awoke to see her standing by the bed, looking down at him. He asked her if she was sore. She nodded, "A little, but no wonder; I was so passionate last night. Are you not tired?"

"Very," he admitted. "You are quite a tiger in bed."

"I learned a lot last night, Ellis. It was good not to have to be a formal lady for once. I shall always treasure the moment."

"Don't dress yet," he begged, "I want to look at your wonderful body. This is all like a dream that I hope never ends." He drank in her nakedness: the full bosom with prominent nipples and large aureoles, the surprisingly full pubic growth, the womanly but trim hips and strong shoulders, the spotless flesh.

Feeling his tumescence returning, he reached up to embrace her.

Rogers had not reveled in such good sex since his brief visit with An-an in Hong Kong two weeks before "Uncle Steve" had ordered him to go to

Manchuria. His memory of An-an came with considerable guilt. He wondered if he could ever love anyone as much as he still loved her. But she had abandoned him and the hurt lingered. If only he could escape the war and go to Hong Kong to look for her, to find out why their marriage had ended so disastrously. If she was still in Hong Kong. It was just not like An-an failing to write month after month, to ignore his many letters. Was she dead? The thought chilled him. Or had she cast him off like the missionary woman, Astrid, in Peking during the Boxer troubles—because he had placed duty to his country and allegiance to the army before his personal life?

He had been told once that the best way to get over someone was to get on on top of someone. Good advice, except that Marina liked the dominant position and the feeling of control and power it gave her.

But his feeling of guilt and doubt prevailed. What if there had been a horrible mistake and An-an was alive and wanted him back? Viktor had advised him long ago: "Don't ever confess to having an affair. Keep quiet and reform. The other person does not want to hear it, so why punish them? Don't even tell the priest because that kind of confession is not good for the soul."

For the moment, he simply wanted to escape the horrors of battle that he had experienced the past two months. He wanted to enjoy Marina's body with all the love and attention she showered on him. Almost eight months without a woman had made him selfish—and hungry.

Rogers' stay ended two weeks later in mid-August, shortly after the Battle of the Yellow Sea.

The Japanese land artillery had continued to shell Port Arthur in complete disregard of the civilian population. Rogers told Marina, "You must leave with Chen. Your life is in danger here." Chen had just arrived and would be a guest at the house after he had completed unloading the junk's cargo and had finished some minor repairs. He had slipped through the blockade, bringing machinery parts from a German warehouse in Chefu. He had also delivered a letter from Uncle Steve ordering Rogers to remain at the Russian network of forts guarding Port Arthur in order to gain valuable experience that might some day be useful for the harbor forts guarding the American west coast.

After reading his orders, Rogers made Marina pledge that she would prepare to leave the besieged port. He told her,

"The world doesn't know that the commanding general of this town and port thinks the chance for survival is slim. I think he will surrender the port when he has a good opportunity." Rogers based his belief on scraps of intelligence that Yin-lin and Master Loong had given to him. General Stoessel was clearly a cowardly grandstander who planned to survive.

"Who knows what will happen," Rogers cautioned. "Why not start trimming your inventory. Turn your assets into gold that can easily be concealed, either here or at your warehouse. You can leave the business with Master Loong and your foremen. And Yin-lin can help. When the fighting stops, you can return and start over."

Marina promised to start planning for a future departure. "We have so little time left," she told Rogers as she hugged him. "Chen will finish unloading and will stay here with us tomorrow night. Tonight may be our last night to be alone for awhile."

"Why are you so shy about Chen?" he asked her.

"He is family and does not suspect you have become my lover," she answered.

"Surely he knows about Viktor?"

"Yes, but he never approved. Sometimes he acts like my guardian. Would you want him to know about us?"

Rogers shook his head. He had seen how Chen sometimes looked so protectively at Marina. His manners around her smacked of more than familial fondness. Rogers had a gut feeling that Chen was in love with his younger cousin. Rogers had always been careful not to express his feelings about Marina in front of Chen; in fact, avoiding any reference to her that might be misconstrued. Chen never asked and Rogers never told.

Regardless of his own selfish feelings about Marina, Rogers agreed with her that their affair was best kept secret. Even if Chen suspected, he would never reproach his younger friend. But Chen was too decent a man for Rogers ever to want to lose his friendship or disappoint him. He and Chen went back a long way.

Rogers had briefed Marina on his orders from headquarters, but not the details. The U.S.War Department thought that he should join the garrisons of some of the forts and report back on their strengths, and how they coped with the Japanese assault. The Department was particularly interested in a comparison with the coastal batteries of Seattle and San Diego. Little thought seemed to be given to the danger that Rogers might face.

Marina and Rogers were resigned to his return to the front, both having recognized his duty. Their last night together was bittersweet, but as sensuous as both could hope for.

Later, as morning arrived, Rogers' thoughts turned briefly to An-an, and he made a quick assessment. Marina was a more mature lover. Her full figure and greater experience made their lovemaking always a rewarding experience that left him fully satiated and exhausted. An-an, however, was more aggressive and exciting, making every encounter seem as if it were her first. Her more athletic figure motivated a challenge in him that always produced his finest performance. He realized that such comparisons were unfair, because he believed that all sex was exciting and pleasing, and there was no such thing as a bad union. Some moments were just more memorable than others. Being with Marina would never be forgotten. Oddly, she had brought out a repressed longing for An-an that was overpowering.

He vowed that if he survived the siege, he would search the ends of the earth for the truth about An-an. There had to be an answer to her silence. But, oh God, how he missed her and could not hate her and would never forget her. She had saved his life in Peking during the battle for the Tartar Wall. He had married her against army regulations and because she meant more to him than life itself. But he needed Marina. He had no regrets. The time to deal with his betrayal would have to come later.

CHAPTER TWENTY-ONE

When Rogers reported to the commanding officer at West Panlung Fort on August 14, he quickly realized how much he had given up by leaving Marina. He missed the joy of her body, the freshly laundered bed sheets of her boudoir, the different foods from her kitchen, the laughter and good company of her servants and tradespeople in the peaceful surroundings of her home.

The visits to Marina's factory and the hectic activity of her business had made the war seem so remote—until he had seen the wounded brought down from the hills to the hospitals and heard the roar of battle to the east, a roar that grew nearer each week. Even the maddening edicts issued by Stoessel had been a novelty compared to the boredom of the trenches and the fort.

It had been hard to part with Marina. Both had recognized the possibility of never seeing each other again. "Come back to me, Ellis," she had begged. "Why can't we have a life together? Why can't this happiness go on forever? Why must you leave? Start a new life here. Stay and live with me."

He had tried to reason with her, to explain his army duties, his career obligations. "If I desert," he told her, "I will never be able to return home to America. And how can I be sure I'd be happy here? I have very little money."

Marina had reassured him that she had money, enough for both of them, that he could help her prosper in her business if he stayed. If he did not wish to stay, they could go somewhere else and start over. "Think how happy we could be. We'll have each other for the rest of our lives."

He had asked her about Viktor and had asked if she still loved him. What if Viktor came back to her? She had been adamant about the end of her relationship with Viktor, repeating several times that he had betrayed her, that their romance was irretrievably damaged and over. "It is finished," she had protested. "I suppose it had to happen sooner or later."

Still he had objected. In spite of the temptation to escape the dangers of the war, his sense of duty and patriotism prevailed. And the troubling reminder of An-an persisted. The ache for his wife was always there—overriding his anger at her silence.

He had warned Marina that her business might be permanently crippled, that Port Arthur could be blown into ruins. He predicted a bleak future for a destroyed town that would have to be rebuilt by the winning side, and that side might be too bankrupt to give much aid. He knew that the war could drag on for months, even years, but it would stop eventually as all wars did.

"Then take me with you. Stay in the army if you must, but let me stay with you," she had pleaded.

"I can't," he had told her. "As a Chinese citizen with dual Russian citizenship, I doubt that you could legally enter the United States. It would be difficult for you to stay with me or be accepted as my wife. You can't begin to comprehend the prejudice there. I hope my country will change some day. And I don't see how I could support you on army pay. And, as selfish as it may sound, I still need to complete my education."

"Then we will live in the Orient. If we leave Port Arthur, there are other places we can go to. There are other ways we can be happy. I need you. I don't want to be alone again."

He had wanted to ask her about Yin-lin, Master Loong, her servants. What would happen to them? Could she really be happy losing her home and business to start a new life in a new place among hostile strangers?

Would that not place too much of a strain on their love? But he kept silent, only asking that she be patient and continue to explore all the possibilities in his absence.

"I love you and I will return," he had assured her. "I have known so much happiness these past two weeks. I'm just trying to be realistic; I really don't mean to be a pessimist."

Every time he had raised doubts about their future, Marina had made love to him so overwhelmingly that he wondered why he was so hesitant. Was he stupid to question such a good thing? But there was always An-an's image to trouble him.

So he had said goodbye with all the emotion that such a parting could bring. He had returned to the hills and the horrors of war, asking himself why he was such a damn fool.

The Russian officers at West Panlung told him that they felt abandoned because the Czar's emphasis seemed to be on the northern front, and the war there had gone so badly.

"General Kuropatkin keeps retreating away from us. We don't understand why. The Czar's army has four and a half million soldiers. Japan only has about one million. Why can't the government send us some help, especially now that our fleet has been defeated and is back in port?"

Rogers did not state his belief that what the Russians really needed was a good military leader, or better yet, a superb general staff. As if they understood his silent thought, the officers told him that they had learned a month ago that the Manchurian commander, General Kuropatkin, had decided that Port Arthur did not need two competing generals of equal rank, so he had favored Lt. Gen. Smirnoff, the legitimate fortress commander.

Smirnoff had been told to remain and Lt. Gen. Stoessel had been ordered to board a fast destroyer to bring him northward.

Rogers was also surprised to learn that Stoessel had ignored the order, egotistically claiming he was senior in command in Port Arthur and, therefore, "I consider my presence here essential for the good of the Fatherland and our troops."

Furthermore, it had been Stoessel, influenced by his subordinate General Fock, who had failed to order a strong defense of the Green Hills line, thus permitting the Russian defense line now to be pushed back against the hill forts. The Japanese had lost 4000 men in the Green Hills sector, but had made a significant advance. They had lost another 1280 men in mopping up the inadequate defenses of Takushan and Siaogushan, known as Big Orphan and Little Orphan hills. This had been a high price to pay, but General Nogi did not seem overly concerned about the slaughter of his men.

The day before the arrival of Rogers at the fort, Nogi had sent up a photo observation balloon to find out why the Russian resistance was so strong. The balloon only remained aloft for half an hour because it was too good a target, and the Japanese officers aboard hated the contraption. Then Nogi sent a delegation under a white truce flag to offer a cease fire during which all non-combatants would be permitted to leave Port Arthur. The Russians had to refuse the offer, because the Japanese note had referred to the inevitable fall of the port and suggested a start of surrender negotiations.

A senior Russian officer, Colonel Tretyakov, soon to be a general, related to Rogers and others that release of the civilians would have strongly alleviated the food shortage, but that Stoessel had angrily called the note insolent and had refused to consider it. Smirnoff had reminded Stoessel that military etiquette called for a reply. And Stoessel had snorted, "Well, if an answer must go, let us send a blank piece of paper, or even write a joke on it."

Annoyed at Stoessel's crudeness, Smirnoff had composed an official answer, stating, "The honor and dignity of Russia do not allow overtures of any sort being made for a surrender." Stoessel had reluctantly signed the answer.

In his spare moments, Rogers sketched a crude map of the surrounding hills and the many defense fortifications that dotted the area north of the port. He included only the more important ones that he believed the Japanese would target in their advance westward from the Green Hills line. He believed that one vital need of the Japanese was to gain a height that would overlook the port and the battle fleet. There was such a height, Hill 203, he would later learn—a hill that General Nogi should have remembered from the war with China ten years earlier. The hill, 203 meters high, would become the most vital target of the Japanese siege army, but only after thousands of lives had been squandered.

* * * * * * * * *

CaptainTanaka led his men toward the hill called Takushan. The enemy artillery had pockmarked the ground so thoroughly that the march along narrow paths became impeded by a series of mud holes that the men stumbled into repeatedly. The incessant downpour of rain, combined with thick smoke from the battle ahead, slowed Tanaka's advance. When his company reached the Taku river, they found it nearly impassable with deep, muddy water overflowing the river banks. The men milled about reluctantly waiting for the order to jump into the rushing water. They were unwilling to risk drowning before clashing with the enemy. Engineers soon discovered that the river had been dammed by the Russians. They bravely swam into the water to breach the blockage.

Enemy machine guns opened up on Tanaka's company as it started to wade across. So many died under the Russian bullets that Tanaka could almost have crossed on a bridge of dead bodies. Pushing forward to reach the foot of the steep incline of Takushan, Tanaka and others tried to cut toe holds on the rocky face of the hill. Shrapnel and thrown rocks and timbers descended upon their heads. The steep terrain and the periodic glare from starshells and searchlights made progress too difficult. Tanaka was finally forced to halt the stalled night assault. While awaiting dawn, the company suffered many more casualties. With the first morning light, Tanaka looked back to see the bodies of his comrades scattered about the river banks.

His sergeant-major lay nearby, suffering an agonizing gut wound and begging others to shoot him. Then the guns of *Novik* and ten other Russian ships drew near on the coast and bombarded the Japanese infantry from the rear. The torment continued until 3 PM before supporting Japanese artillery drove away the Russian ships.

A message arrived from the brigade commander ordering, "The left wing will now storm Takushan, so your regiment will attack the north slope." Simultaneously, a message from the regimental left wing arrived urging joint action: "I hope your regiment also will join in this memorable assault and occupy Takushan with us."

The infantry rose and pressed forward in a scene from hell as they closed with the enemy amid the smoke of exploding shells. Dust and smoke half hid the scene of men bashing brains and bayoneting bowels. The Russians rolled large rocks down from above to crush the attackers. Russian batteries from the forts of Chikuan and Erhlung poured shells onto Takushan to cover the withdrawal of the retreating Russians. The Japanese had no time to rejoice at the sight of their Rising Sun flag waving on the mountain top, or to prepare for counter attacks. Large Russian shells commenced blasting the mountain top conquerors.

Tanaka ducked as a piece of a soldier's body slammed against the rock at his side. Behind him another shell shattered the bodies of twenty-six men grouped near the six captured Russian field guns.

His fellow officer, Lieutenant Kunio Segawa, lay dying from a shot in the abdomen. The man's brother, Captain Segawa, stepped near to give the lieutenant a drink of water. He told his brother that he had done well and asked if he had a last word. Kunio Segawa could only say, "Dear elder brother..." before he died. Some of the bystanders wept openly. Captain Segawa followed his brother in death two weeks later in a battle for East Fort Panlung, the next Japanese objective.

The next day, during a Russian counter attack, Tanaka's men surprised a body of seventy Siberians climbing a reverse slope and shot every one. It had always surprised Tanaka that the Russian soldier fought on when no hope of survival remained. He had once questioned a Russian sniper who had shot ten men from a nearby house after the battle of Nanshan had ended. The prisoner had answered the question of why he had fought on so stubbornly, replying, "We could not disobey the officer's command." Tanaka believed it stemmed from the ancient obedient relationship between Russian serf and landowner. Yet, the Russian soldiers at other times surrendered without shame, choosing, as Tanaka observed, "to live in shame rather than die in honor."

On the 18th of August, Tanaka reported for a new assignment at battalion headquarters. He said farewell to his assigned batman. Noting a small handmade box fastened to Takao's belt, he asked the purpose of the box. Takao grinned shyly and answered, "It is a coffin for my ashes if I die in the next battle."

The days were hot and the nights warm, permitting the men to sleep comfortably on the ground. Some officers had mats, but most slept on the grass. Tanaka rested, thinking of home and Ikura and little Yukio. He had looked long and lovingly at their photos before the day's light faded. There had been no mail from home since he had landed on the Manchurian shore, three and one-half months ago. He resolved to be patient and hoped that his family had received his letters. He always tried to write a cheerful letter every week, wondering each time if the letter would be preserved as his final one.

He remembered a letter shown to him by his lance corporal, Taketoshi Yamamoto. It was Yamamoto's last letter to his own family and had been sent with a lock of hair and some nail clippings. Yamamoto had written: "I am keeping my head on my shoulders, but I am filled with grief when I think of my dead comrades. Out of about 200 of our company, there are only 25 left. Fortunately or unfortunately, I am among this small number. But the life of man is only fifty years—unless I give up that life now, I may have no proper opportunity again. Sooner or later we all must die. I can die but once. My comrade was shot at my right hand. My officer's body was blown apart at my left, and I in the middle was untouched. I pinched myself, doubting whether it was a dream. My time for dying has not come yet. I must brace myself to avenge my comrades. Proud, impudent Russians; I will chastise them severely. Born a farmer's son, I shall yet be sung as a flower of the cherry tree—if I fight bravely and die on the battlefield instead of dying ignobly on a straw mat in some thatched hut. Banzai! I enter the death ground with a smile."

Yamamoto died three days later.

Tanaka stood on a hill overlooking the Russian western defense grid. The eastern outward defenses now rested in Japanese hands. As far as he could see, every prominance was covered with forts and trenches. Tanaka did not realize that he would be fighting in the fortified hills for four more months and that hundreds of thousands of men would die. Far to the north of the Manchurian peninsula, thousands more were dying.

Rogers had watched the Japanese assault on the Chikuan-shan fort that had begun at dawn. Japanese batteries had poured shells on the surrounding forts as well in an effort to destroy wire entanglements and trenches and concrete bunkers. Spherical shells shrieked through the air from both sides to burst with thundering explosions as the hellish scene unfolded. He saw the Japanese infantry begin to move forward cautiously. Bursting shells threw up clouds of smoke and dust, often obliberating the careful slow advance. The artillery exchange continued all day. When night fell, blue-white shafts of light arced through the sky over the valley below. The Japanese tried to use captured searchlights to find enemy gun emplacements, but the lack of sufficient electrical power made their efforts unproductive. Russian star rockets, fired at random, hung in the air like festive lanterns to illuminate the battlefield far better than searchlights. Rogers watched the Russian artillery concentrate on the muzzle flashes of the Japanese field guns, massed customarily around Japanese headquarters. The Japanese forces were finding the Chikuan fort area a hard nut to crack.

Tanaka dove to the ground as another star rocket burst overhead to illuminate the battlefield. "Don't move and keep still," he told his men. He could see some of the Russians on the parapet ahead making lewd finger and arm motions and dancing about as if unconcerned about enemy fire. It was another of those inexplicable scenes he had witnessed before.

Some participants in the folly of war seemed to live charmed lives. As with some of his fellow officers, standing erect in full sight of the enemy, waving their swords and defying death, so now these foolhardy Russians faced Japanese bullets that no matter however carefully aimed seemed to do no harm.

Tanaka, held in reserve with his company, crouched low while adjacent assault battalions rose with attached bayonets gleaming in the moonlight. They dashed forward with a roar of the war cry, *Banzai.* The heroic yells became fainter as Russian machine gun fire ripped into the charging ranks.

Unable to follow the assault troops, beaten back by the hail of bullets, cut off from communications from the rear, three companies fell back into the cover of a ravine. Tanaka and the others had no sooner entered the narrow opening of the ravine than a mine planted in the path exploded, blowing off the legs of Sergeant Ito. Instantly other soldiers hurled themselves from the path and against the sides of the ravine. Several died as mines purposely planted in the ravine walls exploded.

The survivors huddled in the ravine all the next day and night, unable to save the wounded and powerless to retreat. On the twenty-first of August, a runner from headquarters arrived in the darkness with orders for all three companies to launch a night assaault to break through the enemy wire entanglements. The Japanese had pounded the wire and the fort for three days, but the wire still halted the Japanese advance.

Tanaka, desperate to save his men, volunteered to go out with a few engineers in a suicide attempt to cut the wire. The men crawled forward without a whisper, feigning death whenever a star rocket burst overhead. They worked their way past scattered corpses to reach the line of wire.

Fortunately, a shell had cut the electrical circuit, so the wire was not charged. The men worked silently to cut a narrow opening, then sent back a corporal to report to the ravine group that the wire posts were still standing, but the wire had been cut.

The three companies successfully passed through the small breach to reach the rampart. They stood up to fire at the startled Russians who fled. But the triumph was short lived. Almost at once a strong Russian reinforcing detachment halted the panicky retreat and used their own machine gun fire to force their men forward. The Russian counter-attack surged back to the rampart, screaming *"Woolah, Woolah."* In the ensuing hand-to-hand struggle, both sides fought with bayonets, rifle butts, even bare fists.

"No retreat! No retreat!" Major Yoshinaga shouted, then fell with a bullet in his chest. Captain Okuba took command, but died also. Captain Matsuoka toppled over, unable to stand with part of his hip torn off. Lieutenant Miyake dropped, shot through both lungs. Captain Yanagawa, sword in hand, his face covered with blood, pressed against the rampart yelling "Charge!" He too fell and was bayoneted repeatedly.

The Japanese survivors fell back to the ravine, leaving behind mounds of their fallen comrades. Tanaka carried the secret maps entrusted to him by the dying Captain Matsuoka.

By the twenty-fourth, the survivors were pulled back from the Chikuan front to concentrate on the two forts at Panlung. Nogi's Third Army staff had sworn the foreign press corps to silence about the failed Chikuan attack. If the news had been leaked, the international bankers would have curtailed loans to the Japanese government.

* * * * * * * * *

448

In Port Arthur, the journalist Nojine had clashed with General Stoessel because of the unpopular reinstatement of General Fock, who had been relieved of command by General Smirnoff. Stoessel brought back his protege who continued to issue scathing criticism of the navy and other army officers. Stoessel accosted Nojine, whom he knew favored Smirnof, with the accusation, "You correspondents are liars. The one who pays most gets the truth."

Nojine wrote to friends of the Czar: "Port Arthur is enabled to hold out only by the efforts of Smirnoff and his excellent assistant Kondratenko. When I give you details, your hair will stand on end. Tell the Czar this, for it is absolutely necessary that Stoessel be removed."

Nojine sent the dispatch to Chefu for Lydia Fairborne to forward to Russia. The Russian consul at Chefu, unfortunately, intercepted the damaging note and destroyed it without revealing its contents. But the consul did inform Stoessel of Nojine's attempt to contact someone in Chefu and Russia. Stoessel shut down the newspaper for one month. And he continued to undermine Smirnoff's optimistic reports to the town populace by issuing his own pessimistic news releases. Morale in the town continued to decline.

Rogers received most of the news from Marina in letters she wrote, using Master Loong to deliver them. Loong risked his life more than once to find Rogers. Marina's news was often more depressing than Rogers liked. She told him of the disastrous defeat of Kuropatkin in the north at the vital junction of Tashihchiao, a defeat that had now opened the path to Liaoyang. She also imparted news that the Japanese Second and Fourth Armies had met and joined forces north of Tashihchiao at Haicheng. If the Russians could not stop the Japanese advance, the Second and Fourth

Armies would in two or three weeks meet and join Kuroki's First Army coming up from the Yalu. Then all three Japanese armies would attack Liaoyang, the gateway to Mukden. Thus scant hope remained for Port Arthur to receive help from General Kuropatkin.

Marina also notified him that a popular Port Arthur naval officer, Captain Wiren, had been promoted to Fleet Admiral over Admiral Prince Ukhtomski. Wiren had been told to take the Port Arthur fleet to Vladivostok, but had declined.

Marina wrote that shelling of the town had lessened, probably due to a temporary shortage of enemy shells. She also noted that many of the shells had failed to explode. "We gather these duds for reprocessing to be thrown back at the enemy."

Drunkeness, she told him, had continued unabated in spite of an increased restriction of vodka to the enlisted ranks. However, the officers suffered no such restrictions.

Food, though of a monotonous variety, was still in adequate supply. But, she added, "I fear that I may not be as clean and ready for you, because the water supply is now restricted to local water wells. The authorities think the Japanese may have poisoned the water supply at the waterworks, or soon will."

As he had predicted, Rogers now knew that the Japanese had decided to skirt the Chikuan stronghold and drive farther north and west to seize the Port Arthur water reservoirs. The twin forts of East and West Panlung, he believed, would be the next targets.

* * * * * * * * *

The Japanese infantry prepared a hurried course of training in preparation for their full-scale offensive set to commence on August 19. The engineer corps had lost so many trained men that the infantry now had to learn the work of demolishing the wire entanglements, mines and trenches. The engineers constructed imitation breastworks for practice. Members of each company were designated to go ahead of the troops to cut the barbed wire. Then other men would follow with saws to cut down the stakes holding the wire. Tanaka demonstrated how bamboo handles, attached to the iron handles of the cutters, could insulate the operator from the electrical current the Russians so often used to charge the barbed wire. He had seen how quickly the strong current could kill. But the ladders used to cross the simulated trenches were, he knew from experience, probably too short for the wide and deep enemy trenches.

Even though his field glasses revealed the Russian soldiers burying personnel mines, Tanaka remembered how difficult it was in the confusion of battle to memorize every location. Once located, the mines could be destroyed by cutting off the fuse.

Captain Tanaka was a member of the battalion ordered to seize the Waterworks Redoubt north of the railway. Not as confident as other officers that the redoubt seizure would be easy, Tanaka led the infantry up a wide ravine. His men moved quietly in a torrential rainstorm, wearing their straw sandals for a silent approach. Tanaka constantly urged the eager soldiers to proceed with more than usual caution and not rush the assault.

The Waterworks Redoubt attack was part of the Japanese effort to neutralize the Russian artillery protecting the line of forts. It was scheduled to precede by one day the massive offensive against all Russian forts. Russian intelligence knew of the scheduled frontal attack on the forts because the towns in Japan were flying celebratory flags in anticipation of an expected victory over the forts.

Russian engineers hurried to strengthen their defenses in front of the forts. They drove nails in carefully laid planks to impale the thin soles of the Japanese *tabi*. Lacking enough barbed wire, they strung old telegraph wire to trip the attackers. Some of the trip wire was also electrically charged. The forts had plenty of magnesium flares to back up the strategically placed searchlights. The searchlights were placed to coordinate with the machine guns to cover a plotted field of fire. This was formidable because the Russian army possessed ten machine guns for every one operated by the Japanese.

Tanaka realized he had walked into the first enemy trap when he heard one of his men yell with pain after stepping on one of the mud-buried planks. An upturned nail protruded from the top of the man's foot. A second later, he saw another man enveloped in a blue flash after grounding himself on an electrically charged wire. At once, a magnesium flare lit up the ravine, exposing Tanaka and his men to the merciless fire of waiting machine guns. Seventy-eight of the company died quickly. Only thirty escaped. The survivors hid in the rain and mud until morning. Again caught in the open in daylight, few made it back to safety. The dead would stay rotting on the field for one month.

In continuing bad weather, the full frontal assault on the East Panlung Fort opened the next night. Tanaka's decimated company had been rotated to the rear for replacements. He escaped the ordeal of others trapped before the East Panlung fort, watersoaked in the gullies and ravines, blinded by flares, slaughtered by arcs of machine gun fire, and torn by shrapnel. Rushing forward, the supporting Japanese artillery caissons had sliced through the bodies of their own dead and dying.

When morning arrived, Rogers looked toward East Panlung Fort, which had received the brunt of the assault. The ground fronting the fort lay strewn with bodies of the Japanese Ninth Division, many of the dead hanging grotesquely on the barbed wire. He saw men of Japan's Eleventh Division trying to leapfrog the several watercourses in front of the West Panlung Fort. The West Panlung garrison had supported the East Fort, but had received less of the assault.

Unable to move forward or back, the Japanese attack faltered. A temporary stalemate developed when the Russian fort's defenders lacked enough soldiers and sailors to counterattack. General Fock had refused Smirnoff's order to send up reserves, a stubborn stand that had caused Smirnoff to dismiss him.

Tanaka was ordered to move his reinforced company into the ground between the two Panlung forts. Crouching along the edge of a watercourse, he noticed how the Japanese assault had zeroed in on the East Fort while generally ignoring the supporting West Fort. It seemed to him that the western front was more vulnerable. Blowing his whistle, he ordered his company to dash forward up the northeast slope. The Japanese artillery crews, observing his movement, blasted the fort, giving Tanaka the opportunity to dig temporary fire pits. The Japanese artillery employed the newly arrived massive ll-inch mortar shells strong enought to crack open the concrete walls of the western fort, setting the interior on fire.

Rogers heard the yell for retreat and ran with the Russians to the rear exit to escape the spreading flames. With his ears ringing from the explosions and his mind dazed from the concussions and smoke, he fled with others, supported by covering fire from the old Chinese Wall, south of the two forts.

Tanaka signalled to the reserve units to renew the attack on the East Panlung Fort's south side, which now lacked help from its companion west fort.

A reserve regiment from Osaka failed miserably and retired in disgrace. Regulars of Japan's Seventh Regiment fought tenaciously to wrest control of the east fort. Although successful, the price they paid was high. At the evening roll call, only 200 of the Seventh's 1800 men answered.

Rogers joined the retreating Russian infantry to move up close to the stronghold of Wantai, known as Watcher's Tower, a prominance that overlooked the two captured Panlung forts. On August 24, he watched companies of Japanese infantry move out from the Panlung forts to assault Wantai.

* * * * * * * * *

Close to midnight, Tanaka and fellow officers filled their cups with water and drank a farewell toast. All were determined to die bravely. Many of the men were crying softly as they formed up to move out. The column moved away from the shelter of the river trees, passing an almost endless line of stretcher bearers bringing back the wounded from the Panlung forts.

The detachment reached a river on the far side of a hump-backed mountain. Groping blindly in the darkness, they threw themselves on the ground upon hearing voices ahead. Two scouts sent forward returned to report a long line of wounded up ahead. Tanaka soon passed the casualties lying along the river bank, groaning and breathing hard in misery.

Still unable to find the rendezvous point, the detachment finally located a staff officer who pointed in the proper direction. But after more repeated directions from others, the detachment could not find the right place and despaired of reaching the attack rendevous in time. Only fifteen minutes remained.

They came upon a body of engineers digging a sap. Following their instructions, Tanaka soon found the siege trenches. Passing beyond, across an open field, he quickly dropped to the ground to escape the glare of a searchlight. He looked at his watch and groaned when he saw it was a few minutes past 1 AM. Had the detachment failed and would now be disgraced?

Looking about, he realized the field lay strewn with corpses. Hearing the sound of distant firing, he led his men toward a narrow ravine which was crowded with dead and dying men. The ravine narrowed to such a small width that it became impossible to proceed without stepping over the wounded, crying for help and groaning with pain. There were no stretcher bearers and no medicine or bandages for those lying in heaps and piled against each other.

"Don't step on the corpses, but retrieve ammunition pouches from the dead," he told his men. It was impossible to avoid treading on the chests and heads of the prostrate men. A clatter of hoofs signalled the approach of artillery caissons which tore through the narrow tunnel, cutting to pieces those who lay in their path. Cursing, the detachment followed the artillery which had left a scene of broken swords and rifles, and a bloody jumbled mess of broken bones and torn flesh.

After a long wait at the far ravine exit, shadowy figures began to appear in the dark. Tanaka breathed a huge sigh of relief to see the main body of troops arriving. They had been delayed by troubling enemy searchlights.

The time had come. He stood in the midst of his non-commissioned officers, holding his cup of water. He knew his reprieve had expired and his death had to be near.

"Drink with me from this death cup," he told his men. "We go forward for the fourth time and surely we will all die together. I bid you farewell. Fight with all your might." Stripped down for the final assault, he had removed his shoes and wore only tabi socks. A towel was wrapped around his neck and a Japanese flag hung from the belt of his khaki uniform. He carried his sword, a water flask, and three hard biscuits, enough food for two days.

Passing through the opening in the wire and past the bodies of dead infantrymen and engineers, piled one upon another, caught in the barbed wire, some still grasping wire cutters, he climbed the slope of Panlung-shan, passing dark shadows that were not newly arrived replacements but corpses piled three and four deep. At the top of the mountain, he joined others of the "sure-death men."

Proceeding north and west from the Panlung sector, Tanaka marched with others of the Third Army for the assault on the Port Arthur waterworks around the fortifications of Wantai. Late at night on August 24, the Japanese artillery focused on Wantai's searchlights, hoping to spare the lives of the men crawling up the steep slopes. Under a moonless sky in the darkness of a night as black as ink, the Russians tormented Tanaka and others by switching off the lights momentarily to fool them into thinking the lights had been damaged by artillery shells. When the artillery fire shifted elsewhere, the Russians would turn on the lights again.

Two brigades ran out of ammunition trying to silence the Russian machine guns. Tanaka volunteered to lead a company to capture the deadly guns. He reached a point within five hundred yards of the Wantai ridge line before his decimated group was halted and pinned down. The two brigades in the rear, with replenished ammunition, tried to advance, but were stopped with heavy casualties. The stubborn Japanese refused to give up and kept advancing while the overheated barrels of the Russian water-cooled machine guns began to smoke. Thrown back repeatedly, the Japanese brigades regrouped at the lower slopes, leaving hundreds of their dead on the hillside, along with the survivors of Tanaka's company.

The Japanese started a rolling artillery barrage that crept forward, blanketing the hill with so much dust and smoke that Rogers could barely see below. He ducked low, every muscle tensed, as the barrage crept closer, exploding shells among both Russian and Japanese bodies. In the wake of the abruptly lifted barrage, the Japanese started another senseless charge, giving the Russian machine guns more fodder. Thousands of dead blanketed the hill before General Nogi finally called off the attack and ordered a regrouping at the East and West Panlung Forts.

Nogi had lost 18,000 men in the offensive to seize two forts and continued to lose as many as 100 men a day at other forts which were exposed to Wantai's battery in the higher hills.

Rogers wondered how the Japanese could absorb such losses. Their frontal charges had been so expensive that Japan could well win the battles, but lose the war. Even if they knocked out the machine gun nests and reached the foot of the Wantai fort, an enormous ditch, thirty feet wide and twenty-five feet deep would face the attackers.

For the next three weeks, Rogers watched both sides improve their positions while ignoring the corpses covering the hillside. Russian soldiers masked the smell of decaying flesh by hanging strips of cloth dipped in carbolic acid.

While awaiting reinforcements from Japan, Nogi occupied the weeks by initiating a training schedule. Nogi was already under much criticism from army headquarters, especially from General Kodama, who condemned the high number of Japanese casualties. Kodama was the brains behind Field Marshal Oyama, the newly appointed commander of the four armies in Manchuria. For the remainder of August and much of September, Nogi ordered a sap constructed that would zigzag upward to approach the Waterworks Redoubt, a suggestion from General Kodama who deplored so many Japanese casualties. But at the same time, Kodama warned, "You must hasten the fall of Port Arthur. We need the Third Army in norhern Manchuria."

The soldiers of Nippon hated digging the sap. It was hard, dirty and extremely boring work. Tanaka was as unenthusiastic as his men, but told them that the sap would probably keep them alive by curtailing casualties. Grumbling loudly, his men worked on for nineteen days of steady backbreaking labor, digging until the sap came within eighty yards of the Russian redoubt. Two Japanese soldiers, wearing steel armor around their heads and bodies, ran forward to look for mines. Both were blown apart by shells from the fort. An hour later, when darkness fell, the Japanese assault force jumped out of the sap and trotted forward. They made good progress, continuing the attack through the night until the Russians had to retire after losing 500 men.

Rogers attributed the success of the Japanese assault to another stupid order by Stoessel that had halted all unauthorized sorties against the sap. Stoessel's order said, "No more (such) attacks are to be made without my personal sanction." One young officer, who had led a brave but unsuccessful attack on the sap, was cashiered and transferred to another regiment in what Stoessel called a "pointless gallant act that cost the lives of five men for no purpose."

Stoessel's jealousy of Smirnoff and Kondratenko, the true commanders of the forts, continued unabated. They in turn seethed with anger at Stoessel's continuous interference.

* * * * * * * * * *

The bond betwen Nigel Fairborne and his amateur nurse, Ti, improved daily. At first reluctant to let her administer his care, because he wanted only Lydia's attention, Nigel soon began to realize the burden his injured body had placed on his wife. Before long, he developed trust in Ti and even welcomed the skill and attentive comfort of her care. From the beginning, he had admired Ti's figure, an admiration that rapidly grew into lust. He tried to hide his libidinous urge, but both Ti and Lydia soon noticed it.

Lydia knew what troubled Ti even before Ti came to her with a worried expression.

"You want to talk about Nigel, correct?"

"Yes," Ti replied. "Commander Fairborne has healed faster than I expected."

"We are friends, Ti. Call him Nigel. What happened?"

Ti hesitated, then plunged ahead without any niceties. "It is his cock. It stands up and crows when I enter the room every morning. I don't want you to be angry, but it is so noticeable."

"I'm more amused than annoyed," Lydia said. She had already told Ti about Nigel's previous sexual preferences. "It is a good sign, but what really arouses him, do you think?"

Ti was relieved not to face resentment. She told Lydia that she did not know why Nigel became so excited. She said she would notice the change immediately after she entered the room. Nigel would devour her with his

459

eyes, searching her face, studying her breasts, dwelling admiringly on the outline of her thighs and legs pressing against her gown. Ti was accustomed to that response in others, considering it quite normal and expected. But this man belonged to another woman, her employer, and that made Ti nervous.

"I pretend not to notice," she told Lydia. "And he is a perfect gentleman. But I thought you should know of his reaction."

Lydia was amused, but pretended to be puzzled. "This happens every day?" she asked.

"Yes, every day, and not just in the morning."

Lydia frowned. She thought she had taken ample care of Nigel since the bandages on his groin had been removed. Now, she wondered if his renewed and differently oriented appetite was a result of what Nigel's doctor had predicted might be a behavioral change resulting from his head injury. Had Nigel's brain been that rattled? Should she be upset or encouraged? Sex, though far infrequent, had been satisfactory with Nigel lately. She did not want that interrupted.

Lydia had a plan that she proposed would test Nigel's libido. She instructed Ti, "Enter his room at four this afternoon. Bring him a glass of lemonade. I will be right behind you. That time of the day is his low point in alertness. At home, he was usually taking a nap before dinner."

Nigel laid down a volume describing the official naval history of His Majesty's Fleet during the 19th century. The particular chapter of his attention had been boring. He closed his eyes for a moment, suddenly weary, then opened them when he heard a timid knock, followed by the entry of Ti carrying a tray with lemonade and cookies.

It happened beyond his control—a sudden surging erection that gave him an awakening alertness. The bulge had escaped the confinement of his pajamas. He shifted his legs to help conceal the protrusion and tried to concentrate on the far wall to hide his discomfiture. It was no use. His aroused blood coursed through every extremity. Nigel averted his gaze from Ti's bosom when she leaned forward to place the tray on the night stand. He ached to reach out to touch her. Suddenly Lydia had appeared beside the bed, smiling down at him. He looked up with surprise as she wordlessly snatched back the bed covers, then grasped his wrists before he could use his hands to cover his naked exposure.

Ti stood transfixed at the sight of the pulsing, red, swollen member. Even Lydia was surprised at his energy. She released his wrists, speaking over her shoulder to say, "Please leave us, Ti. I' ll be out in a moment." To Nigel, she said, "Is that for me, or is there something that I should know?"

"It is always for you. I can't help myself," Nigel pleaded. "It just happens. Help me, Lydia. I need relief." He tugged on her arm. "Please, please."

"Oh, all right. I am glad you need me. I will help you. But we need to talk about this." She could see he was desperately tense. "We must hurry." She knelt and moved down to kiss his body.

Dabbing at her lips with a towel, Lydia went to the door and called to Ti. Outside, she and Ti talked at length about Nigel. Lydia asked Ti if she was offended by Nigel's admiration, telling Ti that Nigel had grown fond of her and wanted Ti to stay as long as she could and hoped she was not angry because his body was so unruly. Ti answered that she was happy that Lydia was not angry and that she appreciated Nigel's interest. "But what should I do if he touches me?"

"He won't," Lydia assured her. "He's too proper an Englishman. But tell me if this continues. Perhaps we should be happy that he is so healthy. The three of us can discuss this as responsible adults. I hate to play games.

I just want my husband back sound and sane and ever more desirous of me. Are you certain that you don't mind?"

Ti laughed. She knew that Lydia knew of her past. "Did you calm him, Lydia?"

When Chen docked at the wharf at Chefu, the elder Tang was there to meet him. Chen inquired about Ti and was told that she had gone to Wei-hai-wei to work for an English couple. The Englishman, a naval officer, had been injured and was now recuperating under the care of his wife and with the help of Ti.

"The two women come to Chefu, usually every market day," Tang told Chen. "They seem to have a close relationship, and Ti is happy and has recovered from her injuries. She asked recently when you would arrive again, says she wants to see you."

"Why? Is she worried about anyone?"

"No, I think she has something to give you. I don't know what. She didn't say."

Against his better judgment, Chen lowered his guard and succumbed to Tang's suggestion that he take a load of produce to the British base.

Chen's inquiries at the base guardhouse led him to Lydia's cottage. Chen was sure that he had seen her somewhere before. She seemed most gracious, accepting him at once.

Lydia did not introduce him to her husband, pretending that Nigel was asleep. She was interested in Chen because of what Ti had told her of his pro-Russian sympathies. Perhaps here was a useful ally.

Chen was delighted at the transformation in Ti. She was beautiful and happy. More than ever, her appearance was a reward for his intervention at the wharf in Shanghai. The young woman seemed elated to see him.

Studying her, during the visit, Chen thought how nice it would have been to have had a family—perhaps a niece or daughter like Ti. He blushed at her open display of affection.

During their conversation, Ti asked Chen if he planned to return immediately to Chefu. When he answered in the affirmative, she impulsively proposed that he let her and Lydia accompany him on the short voyage. "He has such a beautiful boat," she gushed to Lydia. "It would be a nice adventure for you—and such a pleasant departure from the overland journey, especially in this heat."

Lydia agreed. Why not, she thought? Adventurous as ever, she said, "Nigel can get up and around on his own now. I can prepare his food so we can stay overnight with the Tang family if need be." She turned to Chen. "May we? If you can wait until tomorrow?"

"I would be delighted to have some company, ladies. I'll send a messenger when it is time to sail."

Chen welcomed the two women who met him at the dock late the next afternoon. He apologized for the tardy departure, but assured them that he had ample cabin room aboard for their comfort. He did not disclose that he had waited for a delayed light cargo of ammunition for the British-made Russian machine guns. With an unexpected lull in overseas commitments, the British army had surplus ammunition that they were willing to sell for a good price. French arms dealers in Chefu had previously approached Chen, but he distrusted them and was not anxious to draw more attention to his smuggling activities.

After dinner aboard the junk, and before they retired, Lydia surprised Chen by asking him if he knew a certain Russian officer named Viktor

Alesandrov. Ti had already told Lydia that Alesandrov was on his way to Port Arthur when she had met him in Shanghai.

Chen admitted that he had met Alesandrov as a guest at the home of a Mdme. Berezovsky in Port Arthur. He did not reveal details of his own friendship with Marina. Lydia asked just enough questions about Marina to satisfy her curiosity about Viktor's probable liaison with the Chinese-Russian woman. And Chen wondered how Lydia might have known Alesandrov, but, as usual, did not pry.

Chen showed the women their quarters. Their cabin adjoined his and both cabins were joined by a locked door. The women begged him not to lock the connecting door, saying they would feel safer if he was close by and available in an emergency.

At the midnight change of watch, Chen retired for the night. Lydia had heard Ti tossing restlessly in her bunk after they had discussed Chen earlier.

"Do you like him?" Ti had asked Lydia.

"Yes, indeed, very nice looking. He is so quiet and such a gentleman. He has a manner of strength and steadiness about him that is reassuring. Why don't you pursue him?"

Ti shook her head. "A sailor's wife is not for me. I do not like to be alone. But I owe him my life. I wish I could repay him."

"You will find a way, Ti. Goodnight. It is late."

Half an hour later, Lydia awoke to a kiss from Ti. Standing alongside her bunk, Ti bent down and kissed Lydia again. "I will be back later. I need to talk with Chen."

Lydia looked up with half-opened eyes and smiled. "Take your time, Ti. You have all night."

In the morning, Chen looked at the naked woman sleeping at his side. It had been years since he had enjoyed sex. It had been that long since he had even had sex. Ti had crept into his bunk as if it was the most natural thing in the world. She had excited him, made love to him, and taught him lovemaking that he'd never imagined possible. He now felt exhilerated despite the lack of sleep. He arose and dressed quietly, determined not to awaken Ti. He believed from her passionate cries that she must have enjoyed their coupling as much as he.

Lydia later said nothing to Ti except to ask the question, "Good?"

"Good," Ti agreed. She rolled her eyes, "Very good. He surprised me."

Lydia answered the knock at the door. She cracked open the door far enough to permit a bowing deckhand to push through two pails of fresh water. Lydia undressed and called to Ti, "Come on, join me. It is shower time. The drain pad is over here."

They took turns washing together under a spraying water pipe. They scrubbed each other with the rough salt-water soap and then enjoyed the rinse of cold fresh water as each poured the contents of the buckets on the other's body.

Lydia dried Ti's back and commented on the beauty of her body. *My, she thought, Chen must be a very happy man.*

When Chen sailed from Chefu, he had said farewell at the Tang residence, surprising everyone, including himself, by kissing Ti. It was a light kiss on the cheek, but, nevertheless, completely out of character for someone usually so taciturn. Looking out over the calm waters of the sea, Chen smiled at the memory and marveled at his boldness. How un-Chinese with such an open display of affection.

Chen crossed the Bay of Bohai in daylight. The few Japanese picket ships were absent, most called north to guard troopships. He had enjoyed good relations with the Japanese navy, but did not doubt that such coziness would decrease as the war spread. Smuggling to both sides had been lucrative so far, yet, like all changes in life, it surely would not last.

In Port Arthur, Marina told him that Master Loong could no longer carry her letters and messages to Rogers. The Japanese noose around the Russian forts had tightened, and the Chinese from the town were kept away from the forts, except to act as porters and stretcher bearers. Master Loong and others were banned. The Russians had discovered that someone in Port Arthur had organized a system of spying in which shepherds had used black goats in their flocks of white goats to indicate to the Japanese the number of men manning the forts. Each black goat was counted as an army battalion. For all the Russians knew, there may have been other revealing signals.

In the last letter from Marina, Rogers learned about the continuing Russian defeats in the north. The Russian army had retreated north of Liaoyang after its fall. Kuropatkin claimed to be mounting an offensive against the south, even as his army fell back to defend Mukden. Marina predicted that Kuropatkin's promised offensive would have to commence by early October to be effective, since both belligerents would go into winter quarters at the end of October.

As part of the buildup around Mukden, the Czar had ordered a second Manchurian Army to be formed and headed by General Oscar Grippenberg, independent of Kuropatkin's army.

Marina had informed Rogers that Hunhutze activity against the Russian railroad had increased with Japanese money and guidance. And that the long promised Baltic Fleet would soon leave Russia's Kronstadt base to come to the aid of the Pacific Fleet at Port Arthur. That voyage would take at least three months.

Rogers wondered if Alesandrov had survived so far. Marina had made no mention of him. She repeatedly insisted how much she missed and loved Rogers, Chen, she wrote, was helping her enormously.

Chen had surprised Marina by hugging her upon his return. Ever since his night with Ti, Chen had rediscovered the allure of sex. He felt like a young man again. With Alesandrov obviously out of the picture, from what little Yin-lin had told him, and with Rogers absent for weeks in the hill forts, Chen visited Marina's home more often. Because of his affair with Ti, and the renewed vigor it had brought, he drew closer to Marina, obeying her every whim, volunteering to run her errands, and promising to run the blockade more often. He bought her gifts. He procured scarce and expensive luxuries like butter, milk, eggs, fish, and meat that did not come from horses or mules.

Marina grew accustomed to his gentle bear hugs and the frequency of his visits. In Rogers' absence, she needed Chen's strength. As the month of September faded into October, she looked forward to Chen's presence, and had even pecked him on the cheek when he gave her his welcome gifts. She was beginning to regard Chen more as a close friend and less as a distant relative, and had begun to notice his masculinity more than before. But, sexually, she longed for Rogers and kept referring to him in conversations with Chen, even though she never disclosed their intimacy.

Marina dreaded the coming of winter with its cooler weather. She would be sleeping alone without Rogers' body warmth. Yin-lin had absented herself more, and Marina suspected there was something going on between her and Stoessel's pretty young maid. She knew the maid tolerated but hated Stoessel's control and avoided him at every opportunity. Luckily for the maid, the general's wife had begun occupying more of his time. But Madame Stoessel interfered far too much in military affairs.

The servants told Marina that Yin-lin and the maid were closeted for hours alone in Yin-lin's downstairs room, and the maid had stayed with Yin-lin several nights. Grumbling, they criticized Yin-lin for not performing many of her tasks.

The waning hot weather of September had brought misery to both combatants in the hills encircling Port Arthur. Flies by the millions bedeviled the soldiers. The rain and heat had spoiled much of the Japanese rice supply, causing a widespread outbreak of beri-beri, accompanied by dysentery. Typhoid was also a problem, brought on by desperate Japanese who drank water from streams that had collected waste from dead human bodies and defecating horses, and from kitchens located too close to the field hospitals where even the stretchers lay caked with dried blood and bloated black flies.

The Russian defenders in the forts were also too careless with proper sanitation. Scurvy and dysentery outbreaks occurred there. Also a proliferation of faulty Russian shells and time fuses that exploded prematurely caused an increase in suicides among the younger Czarist soldiers.

The ability of the large eleven inch, 500 pound Japanese mortar shells to crack the concrete walls of the forts had added to Russian pessimism. The Japanese had constructed a miniature railway to transport the heavy artillery shells from the ordnance depot to the howitzers.

In town, Marina sold her cement supplies at a good price. Stoessel had ignored his order against bomb shelters and had hastened to build one for his own use.

The heavy cruiser *Palla*da had tried to escape to Vladivostok. Escorted by two destroyers, she was intercepted by the Japanese who had been tipped off by the spy Esley. The damaged *Pallada* had limped back into Port

Arthur. She lay helpless under the guns of the Japanese whose artillery spotter on Namako-yama hill directed fire. He could not see the Russian fleet, but guessed their positions with considerable accuracy. The hospital ship *Mongolia* suffered a hit which the Russians protested to Tokyo via the French government.

At the end of summer, General Kodama, Oyama's chief of staff, was sent to confer with Nogi because of Nogi's slow progress against the forts and concern for his high casualty rate. Kodama decided against sacking Nogi for fear of what it might do to the morale of the Third Army. Nogi, equally unhappy, became reclusive and even suicidal. But he stayed on, enjoying good press from the foreign correspondents, who relished his occasional picnics served with champagne, caviar, sweets and good beer. The British press idolized him because of his approachability. So, following Kodama's firm suggestion, Nogi ordered more saps dug.

A Russian quartermaster officer had purchased several small tin boxes from Marina—the kind that usually held butter or processed meat. Master Loong later told her what the boxes were used for, and she had urged Chen to procure many more at Chefu. He returned with a large supply of the empty little tins, which the Russian army promptly took off her hands. From then on, she sold all that Chen could bring. The tins, she discovered, were converted into grenades. Filled with black powder and scrap bits of metal from the machine shops, the tin boxes were attached to a short fuse that could be quickly lit with a match. The grenades were so deadly and useful that three grenade factories were soon in operation in Port Arthur's Old Town.

Rogers had noted with interest how effective and useful the grenades were in operation against the Japanese saps. Machine gun fire and searchlights could pin down the Japanese, but the grenades not only rooted them out of the saps as they crouched in the shallow trenches, but could blast large gaps in the ranks of the charging Nipponese.

Rogers passed on this information to Uncle Steve in Shanghai. He also stressed the inevitability of future warfare that would encompass deep elaborate trenches with barbed wire entanglements and multiple machine gun emplacements. And he predicted that large concrete forts were increasingly vulnerable to powerful siege guns and in danger from gas attacks. Already the Russians had experimented with burning oil and other noxious fumes in attacking the enemy saps. The Japanese, he reasoned, could just as easily block the ventilation ports of supposedly impregnable large fortifications. Forts facing in one direction and with no rear defense could be bypassed by mobile forces.

Mobility was the key. He knew that automobiles were fast gaining acceptance in Europe. Perhaps they would replace cavalry. And suppose a way could be found to make them armored? The new flying machines also promised to become a potent weapon. Perhaps they might replace the need to always have to capture the high ground.

The Japanese armies continued to move closer to Mukden. Tashihchiao had fallen. Then Liaoyang. And in October there was the defeat of Russians at Shao Ho which laid bare the route to Mukden.

Profiles of Forts Nirusan and Hill 203

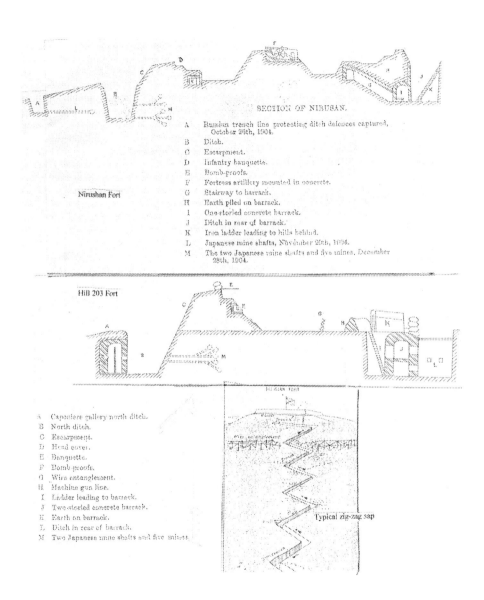

SECTION OF NIRUSAN.

Nirushan Fort

A   Russian trench line protecting ditch defences captured, October 26th, 1904.
B   Ditch.
C   Escarpment.
D   Infantry banquette.
E   Bomb-proofs.
F   Fortress artillery mounted in concrete.
G   Stairway to barrack.
H   Earth piled on barrack.
I   One-storied concrete barrack.
J   Ditch in rear of barrack.
K   Iron ladder leading to hills behind.
L   Japanese mine shafts, November 20th, 1904.
M   The two Japanese mine shafts and five mines, December 28th, 1904.

Hill 203 Fort

RUSSIAN FORT

A   Caponiere gallery north ditch.
B   North ditch.
C   Escarpment.
D   Head cover.
E   Banquette.
F   Bomb-proofs.
G   Wire entanglement.
H   Machine gun line.
I   Ladder leading to barrack.
J   Two-storied concrete barrack.
K   Earth on barrack.
L   Ditch in rear of barrack.
M   Two Japanese mine shafts and five mines.

Typical zig-zag sap

471

CHAPTER TWENTY-TWO

Deep in the bowels of Fort Nirusan, Rogers sat alone, ignored by the boisterous group of Russian soldiers gathered at an adjacent large rough wooden table. The soldiers had been drinking their daily allotment of vodka and were now exchanging bawdy jokes and talking about home, while eating their noon meal. The small mess hall lacked cleanliness and smelled strongly of unwashed human bodies. The crude manners and coarse, loud talk of the fort's defenders were difficult to ignore, but then Rogers had to remind himself that these men had been subjected to weeks of enemy attacks, the boredom of daily life in the forts, and the ever present imminence of death. Part of their behavior was a form of bravado to retain their sanity under such conditions. If men had to live under brutal conditions, it seemed natural that it would be reflected in their behavior. So Rogers tried to ignore the distracting noise.

He studied the rough sketch he had made of Fort Nirusan. Like most of the forts of Russian design, Nirusan featured frontal trenches below the fort, protected by a line of barbed wire. A huge trench had been dug farther back from the front trenches and was at the foot of a steep slope known as an escarpment. The escarpment rose almost vertically upward to the breastworks of the fort where riflemen manned sandbagged banquettes that had been loop-holed and covered with a protective layer of timber and dirt. Bombproofs or bomb shelters had been dug into the banquettes. In the middle of the fort, an artillery piece sat on a concrete base atop a large dirt prominance. Toward the rear of the fort, where the hillside continued upward behind the fort, the Russians had constructed a sloping stairway

Eleven inch mortar

SERIES OF SAPS LEADING TO FORT NIRUSAN

Japanese 11 inch mortar emplaced near Port Arthur

leading down to the subterranean barracks. Behind the barracks, a passageway opened into a wide and deep ditch in which an iron ladder had been placed to provide an escape route up the hillside. The position of the forts prevented attacking enemy troops from gaining the nearby top of the hill and presented a lesser target to enemy shelling than a hilltop position would.

The most dominate obstacle to enemy attack was the escarpment which rose steeply from the upper edge of the massive frontal ditch. Enemy soldiers could not scale the escarpment until they found a way to get across or out of the deep ditch that measured both a depth and width of forty feet. Russian soldiers defending the outer trenches could, if necessary, retreat from the outer trenches to the banquettes above the escarpment where they could fire down into the ditch and rake the face of the escarpment with machine gun fire. Those attackers who were tumbled into the ditch would be without cover from Russian grenades or hot oil poured on their heads.

Furthermore, concrete chambers called caponieres had been constructed at the corners of the four sided fortification. These corner chambers could defend one side of the fort should an adjoining side be overrun.

The Japanese could approach the outer trenches and the ditch with the use of saps that snaked upward from the valley floor. But getting out of their saps, across the ditch and up the face of the escarpment demonstrated repeatedly the heartbreaking folly of frontal assaults. The Japanese offensive at the end of September, and a subsequent one late in October, had resulted in such heavy loss of life that the Japanese planners realized they must find a way to fill the frontal ditch, preferably by blowing up the escarpment. To aid the dwindling supply of sappers, the Japanese army pressed more infantrymen into service to dig mine tunnels under the ditch and into the escarpment. The period from late October to late November were days of frenzied digging—by the Japanese to mine the ditch and slope, and by the Russians to dig counter tunnels to blow up their enemy.

Forts Nirusan and Shojusan were part of a four fort grid that guarded the western hills above Port Arthur. When Rogers joined the defenders of Nirusan, he had accompanied a handful of foreign army observers and newspaper correspondents who wanted to experience the attack on the hill forts. Few of the foreigners withstood life in the forts more than a week. Rogers stubbornly held out and now sat alone as the sole foreigner at Nirusan.

Before leaving the town of Port Arthur, Rogers had visited Nojine, the Russian newspaper man at the *Novy Kry* office. Nojine had confided that the Englishman, Philip Esley, had been asking a lot of questions about the hills. Nojine knew what Esley wanted to know—the importance of a hill above Nirusan known as Hill 203. This 203-meter high hill was adjacent to another important and slightly higher prominence called Hill 210, but only Hill 203 afforded an unimpeded view of the Russian fleet whose destruction was so important to the Japanese.

"Since the main objective of the Japanese all along has been the destruction of our fleet," Nojine explained, "the capture of Hill 203 would hasten that aim if they could install observers with cannon to fire down into the fleet ancnhorage."

"I take it that you mean possession of Hill 203 would give the Japanese an unobstructed view of the fleet?" Rogers asked.

"Yes," Nojine continued. "Hill 210 has a partially obstructed view. Only Hill 203 lays bare our entire fleet. It would be like shooting fish in a bucket. The Japanese have apparently forgotten about the view from atop Hill 203. Strange, because Nogi captured Port Arthur from the Chinese back in 1894. He should have remembered the hill since the Japanese were here for almost five years before France and Germany insisted they relinquish it to Russia."

Rogers wondered aloud if the Japanese could get past the western forts to seize Hill 203.

"I don't know," said Nojine. "But they got past the stronger eastern forts."

Rogers agreed, then added, "But look at the tremendous loss of life they suffered. My guess is that the Japanese are going to have to change strategies. Surely they cannot continue to absorb such large losses."

"They will have to do something," Nojine stated. "The Baltic Fleet is on the way to join us. Our Pacific Fleet may be bottled up for the present, but it is still strong and much of the damage has been repaired."

Now, days later, Rogers sat looking at his rough sketch and wondering when the blow would fall. The Japanese would have to act and fast. With winter coming, the northern front would stabilize. Both sides would suffer from the harsh weather. Could the Japanese outlast the Russians, he wondered?

Hill 203 had been initially attacked in September, but excessive casualties had caused the Japanese to abort the attack. Nirusan would have to fall first.

Chikuan, Wantai, and now Nirusan. General Kodama was screaming at Nogi to wrap up the siege of Port Arthur, yet complaining about the huge loss of life suffered by Nogi's divisions. Nirusan still stood in the way of Japanese domination of Hill 203. Frustated and impatient, Nogi gave the order for an all-out night assault on Nirusan. *Casualties be damned.*

The Russian machine guns mercilessly raked the advancing line of enemy assault troops. Captain Tanaka pushed his way through the piles of bodies, urging his company onward, remembering the words of his regimental commander, Colonel Aoki: "This battle is our great chance of serving our country. We must succeed. To be ready to die is not enough. What is expected of you is a determination not to fail to die. You are now a sure death detachment." The regiment's senior captain, now a brevet major, waved his sword, shouting "Banzai, Banzai, Forward!" The machine gun fire had piled bodies three and four feet deep, with the wounded buried beneath groaning piteously.

The attack had almost stalled when a Japanese bombardment ripped into the Russian skirmish trench below the Nirusan fort. The shells tore off heads, legs, arms. Trench boards and sandbags flew skyward. Rogers saw the Russians in the trenches falter, then begin a hurried retreat toward the fort. Sensing victory, the Japanese pushed on, but their numbers were now too few.

Suddenly, the senior captain fell, toppling heavily to the ground, his sword flung outward.

Tanaka ran to the captain's side, but it was no use. Corporal Ito knelt beside his captain, crying over his body. When the corporal saw Tanaka, he shouted that Tanaka was now in charge of the assault. Shocked at the sudden responsibility, Tanaka retrieved the secret map of Nirusan from the captain's belt and ordered two wounded men to carry the captain's body back to the aid station. Both men were struck down by bullets before they had gone far.

Shouting for Lt. Ninomiya to hold the platoons together, Tanaka called out, "Company forward." He pushed onward as if in a dream. "Keep the line together," Tanaka shouted again and again. The Nirusan fort stood out against the dark skyline. The gleam of massed bayonets lessened, making Tanaka aware that he was no longer surrounded by a company, only a handful of survivors.

Intermittent bursts of magnesium flares illuminated the piles of dead. As if struck by a giant club, Tanaka was suddenly knocked to the ground. A bursting shell had found its mark. Numb with shock, Tanaka struggled to rise. Disoriented, he felt his legs. They seemed to be all right. But one arm was numb. He saw his hand dangling at the wrist, almost severed and bleeding profusely. His vision was so blurred, he imagined he was looking up through water over his head. All his movements seemed to be choreographed in slow motion. He tasted blood and saw the front of his blouse soaked with it. Fumbling in his pouch for bandages. he found a large one to wrap around his wrist, tying it one-handed and by using his teeth. Then he fashioned a sling from the flag in his belt that he had vowed to plant on the Nirusan fort. He felt for his water flask, but a bullet had severed the strap holding it to his belt.

He struggled to his feet, aware that the cannonading had increased and the voices of his comrades had lessened. Flinching from the glare of rockets and noise of bursting grenades, he threw aside the scabbard of his sword and waved the naked blade to exhort his men to follow as he tried again to go up the steep slope of the hill. It was too late. Someone shouted "Counter Attack." He looked up to see Russians pouring over the top of the rampart. Tanaka's survivors began to fall back in the face of the viscious hand-to-hand attack. Steel rang against steel as bayonets clashed. A bullet broke Tanaka's blade. He went down from a blow to the head.

Private Kensuke Ono ran to Tanaka's side. Ono had been shot in one eye and bayoneted in his side. Still, he managed to place more bandages on

Tanaka's wrist while the blood from his head poured on Tanaka. "We will die together," Ono begged.

"No," Tanaka told him. "Go back to report on the attack."

Stubborn and blinded by the blood in his eyes, Ono kept saying, "I will stay and defend you." Tanaka ordered, "Go back and report on my death."

Ono reluctantly stood up and, though clearly disoriented, called back that he would fetch a stretcher.

Tanaka lay alone, weak from loss of blood, contemplating suicide to escape the disgrace of capture. The enemy began passing in front of the trench, shooting the Japanese wounded. A Russian soldier saw Tanaka move and fired a shot. Another Russian ran forward to bayonet Tanaka, but a handful of Japanese rose to run between him and Tanaka. All were shot down. An unknown Japanese officer ran up to the trench with sword raised high, yelling "Banzai." A Russian bullet knocked him off his feet to fall dead at Tanaka's side. The numbness had left Tanaka's head, leaving his eye and wrist throbbing with pain. He prayed for death to end his agony.

A salvo of Japanese percussion shells exploded, sending shards of hot steel cutting into the necks, backs and legs of men squirming face down in the torn earth. A soldier lying nearby with his face shredded by shrapnel begged to die, his wish mercifully granted as the color faded from his features and he slowly expired.

Two Japanese hospital orderlies crawled among the wounded and dying to bandage bleeding men. Tanaka saw a Russian officer pointing to a leg wound and making signs for help. One orderly took a bandage from his waist bag and bandaged the Russian. As soon as the orderly had finished, the Russian pulled out a pistol and shot him. Two Russians, passing among the wounded, grasped Tanaka's coat and pulled him upward, then released their hold of the blood-soaked coat, thinking Tanaka was dead.

Tanaka lay still, feigning death for what seemed an eternity. A short while later, a Japanese soldier, with his head bandaged, fell at Tanaka's side. He heard the man whisper, "Let me help you. We must go back." The bandaged man reached out to a nearby mortally wounded soldier who begged for water or to be shot. Before Tanaka's helper could pour water into the man's mouth, the wounded soldier raised his hands as if praying, "Namu-Amida-Butan, Namu-Amida-Butan." Then his voice faded and he drew his last breath.

The bandaged helper raised Tanaka's arm, pulled him onto his back and carried him out of the pile of dead, occasionally falling down to escape detection by the Russians who continued to fire at the moving wounded Japanese. Tanaka wondered if his rescuer was one of his men and asked his name.

"My name is Takesburo Kondo."

"What regiment?"

"The Kochi regiment."

Kondo carried Tanaka through the wire entanglements, then beckoned to another wounded man to aid him to carry Tanaka to the ravine. There they covered him with an overcoat. A shell fell nearby, throwing sand and pebbles onto Tanaka and other wounded men. Private Kondo persuaded four men with a stretcher to carry Tanaka back to the first aid station.

Tanaka struggled into consciousness and looked up to see two surgeons bending over him. "Surgeon Yasiu! and Surgeon Ando!" He knew them both. One held his good hand while the other stroked his forehead. One said, "We were told by Sgt. Sadaoka and others, who came in among the wounded, that you had been killed below the rampart at the fort."

Tanaka at Nirusan battlefield surgical station

As soon as he was properly bandaged, stretcher bearers came to carry him to the rear. As they picked him up, he saw the body of Major Uyemure lying off to his left. The major's servant was clinging to the body, crying inconsolably.

At the rear field station, surgeons walked among the rows of men brought back on stretchers or who had dragged themselves in. The surgeons turned over the men, examining them to seek those most seriously wounded for immediate surgery. One surgeon had the task of separating the hopeless cases. He would draw in his breath as if slurping hot soup. This time-saving sucking sound took the place of a formal statement which most surgeons disliked making. The wounded men knew the meaning of the sound. Resigned to their fate, they were given a final drink of sake laced with morphine, then carried to a special "death" tent.

Two tents were equipped for field surgical operations. Each tent had two operating tables. A stream of water mixed with disinfectant poured from an elevated barrel down a trough into a second barrel. Surgeons threw amputated limbs, flesh, entrails, bones and bullets into the lower trough. A pump constantly recirculated the water. A strainer in the second barrel retrieved the debris.

Surgical instruments lay in pans of antiseptic. Bandages were drawn from heated sealed glass or tin cases.

Burn cases were wrapped in oil soaked bandages.

Chinese coolies carried the wounded in carts from the field surgery station to a rail head for transportation via train to the Dalny hospital. Those scheduled for further operations or care in Japan were taken to the harbor at Dalny. The loading of the wounded onto the hospital ships crowding the harbor was delegated to the 8th Osaka Regiment which had been disgraced because of cowardice at the front.

In the weeks that followed, Tanaka mended reasonably well. He felt sorrow for the loss of the use of his eye and one hand, but counted himself lucky to have survived. While in the hospital in Dalny, he learned that the attack on Nirusan had failed and that a second and third attack had also failed, even more horribly. But repeated attacks coupled with the use of mines would at last overrun the mighty fortress and defeat the stubborn enemy.

A month later, discharged from the hospital and glad to have successfully endured the agonizing physical pain of his wounds, Tanaka refused to be invalided home. He volunteered for rear echelon duty in the port city. He dreaded returning home to Ikura and Yukio in his disabled condition, horrified at how they might confront his changed appearance. He threw himself into his duties to avoid self pity and fears of his future. Only at night when he was alone did the ghosts of battle return to plague his memory. Tanaka was strong and stubborn in his refusal to give up hope, and was reluctant to leave Manchuria until Port Arthur had fallen. He wrote encouraging letters home, careful not to reveal his injuries.

After his discharge from the hospital, he learned that his rescuer, Takesaburo Kondo, had been shot by a sniper near the forward first aid station.

Even though the Japanese attack on Fort Nirusan had failed, Rogers deemed it wise to move to a less threatened fort. He knew from the activity of sappers below Nirusan that it was only a matter of time before the attackers succeeded in breaching the escarpment. His mission for the War Department would be a failure if he lost his life needlessly. Being blown to bits held little appeal, and since there remained few lessons to be learned at the fort, he moved to Hill 203.

His choice was bad as he soon learned when he arrived at the hill's fortifications. The view that he enjoyed from the prominance made it very clear why Hill 203 would inevitably be the next target of Japan's Third Army. Far below, anchored in the calm, cold water of the tidal basin, five Russian battleships nestled undisturbed. Maintenance crews had successfully repaired the damaged ships. The ships were lightly manned, for the bulk of the crews had been sent to help man the trenches in the hills. Few naval officers had joined their men, preferring to enjoy the idle leisure of the tea houses and restaurants of the town. The admirals continued to refuse to leave the harbor, claiming they would be more effective against Togo by waiting for the arrival of the Czar's Baltic Fleet.

Rogers realized that the earlier blood bath at Hill 203, back in August, had convinced Nogi's superiors that different but slower methods to capture the port town had to be employed. The Japanese army accepted a more patient strategy. The expenditure of millions of dollars of ammunition, the terrible slaughter of their soldiers and the questionable result of incessant bombardment by heavy siege mortars made it apparent that Nogi's tactics had to be changed. The answer pointed to more mines to blow up the forts. There were 2000 men in the sapper corps at the start of the war. Now, not enough experienced men remained to build the mine tunnels. More and more untrained infantrymen were pressed into service for the work which proceeded too slowly and at high cost in lives.

Finally, near the end of the year on November 26, again hounded to complete the subjugation of Port Arthur, Nogi reverted to his old recklessness, employing bloody frontal assaults. He vowed to commit hari kari at the end of the war to atone for the deaths of so many thousands of his men and for the failures he had endured. But the capture of Hill 203 was his fixation, and he swore he would succeed in his goal, no matter the cost.

Following his retreat from Fort Nirusan to the fortifications at Hill 203, Roger watched the frantic Russian effort to strengthen Hill 203 against the coming Japanese attacks. Like similar forts, the Russian design featured a strong point near but not on the crest of the hill. Typically, the three downward looking sides of the fort faced the enemy with a huge frontal ditch. The bottom of the forward face of the ditch contained concealed subterannean concrete passageways or galleries that could be used to fire on any enemy soldiers who might gain access to the ditch. Men stationed in the galleries at alcoves in the gallery wall could protect the depths of the ditch. Like Fort Nirusan, strongholds called caponieres were located at the corners of the three-sided fort. Again, typically, the usual steep escarpment rising upward from the ditch was crested by sandbagged banquettes or protected platforms on which the defenders stood. Just under the banquettes, bombproof dugouts gave protection against artillery shells. The excavated interior of the fort was protected by a line of machine guns and barbed wire entanglements. Ladders behind the machine gun emplacements led down into two-story subterranean concrete barracks. The rear barracks windows faced out to a protective ditch. A wooden bridge across this ditch provided an escape route to the hillside behind the fort.

From late November to the beginning of December, Rogers watched the Russian defenders labor to widen the underground galleries to a width of nine feet and strengthen the walls of the caponieres to six feet of solid concrete. The walls were not reinforced with iron nor sufficiently aged for maximum strength. Rogers tested the concrete by scraping his fingernails across the surface. He could see that the concrete was curing too slowly in the cold, damp depths of the gallery interior.

More alcoves were added between the caponieres. The alcoves were separated by three feet of solid concrete so that each alcove could be defended separately.

By the end of November, the Japanese saps had finally reached a connecting parallel trench below the outer Russian trenches. From this parallel, the Japanese began to tunnel deep into the hillside beneath the Russian trench, galleries and caponieres to gain access to the 40-foot wide deep ditch at the foot of the escarpment. In turn, the Russians dug deeper with counter mines.

The ear splitting explosion of a huge eleven-inch mortar shell forced those on the hill to crouch low. When Rogers saw the damage inflicted on the concrete walls, he knew that the Japanese had a weapon that could systematically pulverize the fort. Not only was the concrete of poor quality and less than adequately cured, it's strength, even at best, was no match for the destructive huge mortar shells. Each explosion not only cracked and split the thick concrete, but also sent lethal chunks of stone cascading through the air. The defenders could only burrow deeper into the torn earth and ruined concrete to await the charge of Nipponese infantry. The incoming shells arrived at predictable time intervals and with such telltale loud whistles that the Russians usually had time to duck for cover. But that cover was fast disintegrating under the impact of the shells.

The Japanese attacked Hill 210 first, thinking its slightly higher elevation would give a better view of the harbor. The sap for Hill 210 was longer than usual in length and ran parallel to the upward length of the hill. In spite of enfilading Russian fire from the fortified slopes of Akasakayama on the eastern side of Hill 203, the lengthy Japanese sap succeeded in reaching the lower Russian trenches by November 27. A subsequent bayonet attack succeeding in giving the Japanese possession of the forward Russian trenches.

On December 1, the Japanese captured half of Hill 210's crest. But the irregularity of the hill blocked part of the view of the Russian fleet. That victory convinced the Japanese that the more desirable target should be Hill 203 where the view was unimpeded.

A lucky direct hit on the large cannon mounted inside the fortress at Hill 203 knocked it out. Rogers hunkered down with the fortification's survivors to await the final Japanese assault.

"We'll teach them a lesson this time," Lieutenant Harkoff growled. His men had rigged a ship's torpedo which they exploded the first of December, blowing up the Japanese tunnels and killing more than two dozen Japanese engineers. However, the enormous explosion also damaged the roof of the northwest caponiere, leaving a small hole that the Japanese discovered and began patiently enlarging to enable them to drop hand grenades through the hole and to rake the interior with machine gun fire. Further enlargement made it possible to drop sandbags into the interior. Volunteers struggled to enter the hole to stack the sandbags for protection against rifle fire from occupants of the alcoves. The number 6 alcove gave the most trouble to the Japanese, since its capture was thwarted by covering fire from alcoves 1 and 2.

A Japanese colonel told his men, "We need to push sandbags out from the northwest caponiere chamber to surround alcove 6 and isolate it. If we can do that, then we can dynamite the inner gallery wall to gain entrance into the ditch below the escarpment."

One lucky Japanese volunteer struggled to push a sandbag ahead of his body. A second man crawled forth to place his feet against those of the first man to enable them to push the sandbag closer to the alcoves. Tossed Japanese grenades tore apart the bodies of the alcove defenders and filled the alcove passageways with noxious fumes that asphyxiated the few Russian survivors.

Freed at last from the obstacle of the alcoves, the Japanese were now held up by sharpshooters firing from the southeast caponiere where Rogers huddled. He was surprised that the Japanese seemed to know that an escape passage led from this caponiere into the interior of the fort. There had been no such tunnel from the northeast caponiere. In spite of their casualties, the Japanese began throwing up a wall of sandbags, not only for protection but also to block off the northeast caponiere from its southeast neighbor. It was obvious to Rogers and his companions that the Japanese intended to build their wall to sufficient height to mount a small cannon that could blast the southeast caponiere.

Lt. Harkoff yelled to his sharpshooters, "Pin them down while we put up our own wall." He sent one of his men to fetch a small mountain cannon. The work on Harkoff's sandbag wall went slowly, too slowly, because the Japanese, having the advantage of starting sooner, were making faster progress on their own wall. The Japanese mounted their cannon first and blasted the Russian barrier, knocking down part of the wall. But Russian sharpshooters soon killed the men servicing the Japanese cannon.

Then Rogers witnessed an astonishing sight. A Japanese captain had flung himself over the top of his wall and was running toward the Russians. He had covered himself with several grenades which someone had lit. Smoke and flame erupted from several points on his body as he hurtled toward Harkoff and his men. Sharpshooter bullets hit him twice, but he stumbled on to fall against the Russian sandbag barrier. Harkoff and his men raced back toward the northeast caponiere chamber, but it was too late. The tremendous blast from the simultaneously exploding grenades blew the captain's body to bits and toppled the Russian wall. Harkoff and his men died in the explosion.

Rogers waited no longer. He retreated back above ground to the banquettes, knowing the Russians in the southeast caponiere could probably hold off the Japanese from more attacks, but the Japanese would use their cannon to prevent further interruption of their work behind the cover of their wall—work on mine tunnels they were now extending under the floor of the gallery.

Breaking through to the ditch at last, the Japanese tried to fill it with dirt, rubbish, sandbags, and even corn stalks brought up from farmhouses in the valley. That effort went too slowly, giving the Russians time to pour oil and rocks of sulphur onto the corn stalks, incinerating several of the soldiers aiding the engineers. The Japanese made the decision to continue a tunnel under the escarpment in order to blow it up to fill the ditch with dirt. Looking down into the ditch from the baguette above, Rogers watched the industrious Japanese engineers erect vertical wire screens to block Russian grenades being tossed down into the ditch. The Japanese positioned men with long poles holding water buckets to pour water on the lit fuses of the Russian grenades. After two days of waiting for completion of the mine tunnels, an impatient Japanese general sent a brigade of infantry into the ditch to assault the escarpment. Men of the 7th Hokkaido Division died in vain trying to claw their way up the steep escarpment wall above the ditch. The Japanese had attacked at night, though they disliked night combat. Groups of ten and twenty would reach the top of the escarpment only to be tumbled back down into the ditch by Russian machine gun fire. Silhouetted in the glare of star rockets and exploding shells, the Japanese threw themselves against the steep escarpment slope in vain.

Rogers could detect the sound of digging that had progressed past the escarpment into the fort's interior. At last the Japanese engineers finished digging three tunnels under the escarpment. Dynamite charges were placed and exploded, blowing tons of dirt to fill the ditch from the collapsd escarpment. Rogers abandoned the tumbled banquettes and retreated behind the line of machine guns near the rear of the fortification. When the Japanese brought up their mountain cannons to destroy the several machine guns, he scurried down the iron ladders into the subterranean barracks. He could hear the yells, curses, screams and explosions above as the two sides closed for a furious bayonet fight. The tall and burly Siberians usually had the advantage over the smaller Japanese who hurled themselves against the Russian bayonets repeatedly. The English style knife bayonet of the Japanese may have been much shorter than the three-foot triangular Russian blade, but the thin Russian blade too often bent or broke in the fray.

When Russian bodies and exploding grenades began to drop into the barracks, Rogers decided to save himself by dropping out of a lower window onto a makeshift bridge that crossed over the ditch behind the barracks. He scrambled up the rear hillside to a ravine that led him eastward toward the fortified slopes of the adjacent Akasakayama hillside. Behind him the fight for Hill 203 continued until the upper slopes were littered with dead and dying combatants.

Through the half darkness of the bitterly cold and waning night, Rogers passed through the long lines of walking wounded retreating from the steep slopes of Hill 203 to a lower fortification to the west of New Town. He skirted a bombardment of the northern edge of the town to continue on to Marina's factory in Old Town, hoping to reach it by late afternoon.

He walked silently across the hills and low ravines, sick at heart of the slaughter of the past few days, sick of the war itself, and despondent that his future seemed so bleak. He realized that he was too lonely and tired, too weary to care about the fighting, and disheartened that the battle for Port Arthur seemed to be ending so ingloriously.

He trudged on mile after mile, listening to the sound of battle from the hills above, trying not to visualize the senseless death of so many valiant soldiers of both armies. The last view that he had of the interior of the fort were the smashed bodies of the crew of the large gun that had taken a direct hit.

It is over, he kept mumbling to himself. The Japanese had taken Hill 203 and paid an awful price. But now they could bring up their heavy mortars and shell the five anchored Russian battleships at their leisure. With the warships in the harbor destroyed, there would be little incentive for either side to continue the battle, unless the Russians chose to continue to resist General Nogi, while hoping that Admiral Rodjestvensky would arrive with his seven battleships of the Baltic Fleet.

Even Marina's joyous welcome at her warehouse failed to banish his gloom. Her amorous advances relieved some of his tensions, but failed to restore his former enthusiasm for the defense of Port Arthur. He drank too much wine in a vain attempt to relax, only to became more sleepy and moody.

The following day, Marina told him that Yin-lin's friend had revealed that Stoessel's wife was packing trunks with kitchen utensils and some food as if preparing for a long journey. Also that Stoessel had dispatched a message to General Nogi's headquarters, without confering with the other general officers of the garrison.

Rogers had agreed that if Stoessel's maid was right, then, "I think Stoessel plans to surrender." He remembered bitterly of Stoessel's boast that he would die on the last fortified hill above Port Arthur.

As if they had received a hint of Stoessel's frame of mind, the officer corps gathered to assess their chances of survival with the fall of Hill 203. Some argued that the western line of forts were self-contained and did not rely on either the town or the naval base. Colonel Reiss protested with other defeatests that only 4,000 men were combat able. "We lack bandages for the wounded. There are 6,000 cases of scurvy in the hospitals."

One of the anti-Stoessel generals jumped up to argue that there had to be at least 26,000 soldiers and sailors, not counting over 1600 officers. Another general shouted:

"I gave General Stoessel my report that tons of food are still stored in the warehouses. And, there are lots more food stored aboard the ships in the harbor. I'd estimate we could eat at half rations at least another four months. After that, we still have almost 3,000 horses that could be eaten."

He was supported by other generals who argued that several isolated good, stout defense positions still held out in the eastern sector in spite of the loss of the abandoned eastern line of forts.

"So the loss of North Keikwansan, Nirusan, and Shojusan have gravely endangered us; we can still implement General Kondrachenko's proposal, bless his memory, that we break out of Port Arthur by attacking the eastern Japanese line, which has to be thinly held. We can break through and spike their heavy mortars. We can push on to occupy Dalny and destroy Japanese supply depots there. Even if we lose and have to surrender, let us do so at Dalny after hurting the Japanese there."

General Nogi read Stoessel's note delivered by the Russian couriers under a white flag of truce. He dictated an answer, stating a convenient time for the parley.

On January 2, at 1:20 PM, the first peace meeting was held with the Japanese insistence on an unconditional surrender. After a ten minute deliberation, a Russian note countered with several modifications to include provisions for all Russian soldiers and sailors to return to Russia, that the Russians be permitted to keep all remaining 1800 horses, and that the peace negotiations be delayed to allow for a reply from the Czar. The Russians further stated that no Russian law existed to give the Russians permission to return home on parole after promising not to serve again in the military.

General Nogi refused to grant parole to any but officers and civilians. All soldiers and sailors would have to surrender as prisoners of war. Furthermore, all horses would have to be surrendered and all personal property be left behind. The hospitals would remain unmolested. The sixty Japanese prisoners held by the Russians were be released at once.

The Russians deliberated for ten minutes, then asked, "Are the terms final?"

The Japanese reply was "Yes."

During the progress of the peace parley, the Russians burned their regimental colors. When asked about the size of the garrison, the Russian negotiator lied by saying only 4,000 men were physically able to march out. The Japanese knew that the true number was 1300 officers and 24,000 men, and that the Russians had four months provisions remaining, and plenty of ammunition.

Fires broke out throughout the town. Stoessel blamed the fires on 4,000 civilian ruffians and confessed that he had lost control of the rioters who were seizing stores of vodka and were looting shops. He requested General Nogi to forward a telegram to the Czar requesting that Russian officers be permitted to give their parole.

The Japanese agreed to send the telegram at 7:30 PM but insisted that the capitulation be signed by 8:45 PM. without further delay. After the signing, Stoessel and Nogi shook hands and praised each other. Stoessel claimed that he had always opposed the war, as had Alexeiev, and used several other excuses to shift blame from himself. He blamed the ignorance of the Russian people for the war because they had not understood the true character of the Japanese.

The next morning, Nogi handed Stoessel the Czar's reply telegram which read:

I allow each officer to profit by the reserved privilege to return to Russia under obligation not to serve or take part in the present war, or to share the destiny of their men. I thank you and your garrison for their gallant defense. Nicholas.

Nogi said his two sons had died in the war, one at Nanshan and the other on Hill 203, but he did not believe they had died in vain. He requested that a photograph be taken of both generals together. During the photo session, Stoessel presented his favorite horse to Nogi. Nogi declined the present, saying that all presents and booty belonged to the Japanese army.

When fires continued to rage throughout the town, Stoessel again requested that the Japanese help stop the burning and looting.

Stoessel and his staff were escorted in horse-drawn wagons to the rail head at Chorashi. Other officers, wearing light blue overcoats and wearing patent leather boots, marched to the village of Lahutse, thence the fifteen miles to Chorashi rail station to board the train. At Chorashi, Stoessel and his family tried to say goodbye to assembled Russian troops guarded by Japanese military police, but were shunned by soldiers who refused to shake his hand.

* * * * * * * * *

Philip Esley listened to the Chinese informant whom he had rewarded so well in the past. The man claimed he had information that he was sure Esley would pay to receive. He said that he had joined a coolie detail carrying ammunition from the waterfront to Fort Payushan. The boxes that he and his fellow laborers had carried were marked as machine gun ammunition manufactured by Vickers of England. He had heard one of the Russian guards carelessly confide to a companion that the ammunition had arrived from Chefu as part of a cargo of produce smuggled in by a junk.

"Whose junk?" Esley demanded.

The informant shrugged. He said he didn't know, only that it was a large brown junk that often slipped through the blockade. It had a large red dragon painted on its sail.

"How do you know that?"

Again a shrug of the shoulders. Then, pressured further, the man boasted that he had a cousin who had worked at the Berezovsky warehouse. "Sometimes my cousin could steal some of the produce stored there. Last week, he took two hen's eggs and a can of milk. He told me this because he was caught and discharged. He was very angry. Now his family will starve. My cousin told me that he had often seen many heavy boxes delivered, wrapped in produce sacks.

"How can you be sure it is this junk?" Esley persisted.

The man answered that he did not know of another large seagoing junk that had slipped through the blockade so often with fresh produce.

After learning this, Esley went to Marina's place and offered to pay a high price for a tin of butter and some good East India tea. He asked the naive clerk if the tea had recently arrived aboard a junk that had its mainsail adorned with a huge red dragon. When the clerk nodded, Esley asked, "That is Captain Chen's junk, yes?" Again the clerk nodded.

Esley quickly dropped the subject, completed his purchases and was careful to tip the clerk, telling him to keep the change.

That night Esley rowed across a narrow portion of the tidal basin, slipped past the abandoned fortifications and hooded searchlights, and patiently waited for the Chinese courier to arrive. He passed his notes, retrieved the bag of money, and vanished back into the dark night blanketing a surrendered naval port that awaited the arrival of Japanese occupation regiments from Dalny.

CHAPTER TWENTY-THREE

Chen sensed that something was wrong when he approached the Liaotishun headland outside Port Arthur. The voyage from Chefu had been uneventful, and the weather, though predictably cold, had not been stormy. Indeed, he had made good time, having experienced a steady head wind all the way. No fog or snow. Clear vision all the way.

But there were two Japanese torpedo boats now in his path, and that boded no good. Their searchlights were playing constantly across the water, directly ahead of his bow.

He was glad that he had safely deposited Marina's gold in Tsingtao's Chinese-German Bank. A last minute sixth sense had warned him to place the receipts for the gold in his shoe. He and Marina had decided early in December to start moving her money to a safer place. Even if Port Arthur could hold out for three or four more months, further catastrophic damage to the town was likely. Old Town had suffered extensive damage in the latest round of shelling. Fortunately, Marina's godown had miraculously escaped a direct hit, but the shells had been a wakeup call. After one particularly nasty bombardment, Marina had converted most of her remaining cash into gold that was then melted and pounded into thin sheets that could be taped to a human body and hidden under clothing.

Chen reasoned that if he altered course, he would only arouse suspicion. He made the decision to hold steady and bluff his way past the nearest patrol craft. His junk slid unchallenged past the first Japanese ship, but he saw it flash a signal to the fartherest warship. That approaching vessel moved to block his path, effectively boxing him between the two Japanese ships. A searchlight caught the junk, blinding Chen by its glare. A voice shouted through a megaphone for him to heave to and drop his anchor. He slackened his sails and obeyed quickly to avoid being fired on. The lead torpedo boat pulled alongside and the crew threw two lines for Chen and his crew to tie to the deck stanchions. The Japanese armed boarding party swarmed aboard the junk and leveled their handguns at Chen and his crew.

"I have a letter of marque," Chen protested.

"Be quiet," the naval lieutenant ordered. Pointing to the hatches, the officer told him to open all the covers, and snapped an order for his men to search Chen's cabin, the crew's quarters, and the deck cargo.

"Come with me," the lieutenant ordered. Pointing his weapon at Chen, he motioned for him to proceed ahead down the ladder.

Chen silently thanked the fates for depriving him of time to load contraband back in Tsingtao. He tried to explain that his cargo was only produce and canned goods destined for the hungry Chinese in Dalny, not Port Arthur. The officer sneered and ordered his men to rip open the crates, cut into the bales, and uncover everything in sight. The search was thorough and destructive. When they had finished, the boarding party ordered Chen to sail to Dalny. Chen obeyed, still preplexed about the halting of his boat. He had received no explanation, was puzzled by the increased patrol activity, and appeared to have been purposely targeted.

At the Dalny harbor, Chen was placed under arrest and taken to the Japanese military jail. He protested that he was a Chinese citizen and asked for a hearing. None was granted, even though he produced his letter of marque, which the jailors promptly tore into pieces. He soon learned that his boat had been impounded and taken to an offshore anchorage.

Chen was languishing in jail when news came of the surrender by Stoessel. Chen and others were released from custody. The Japanese were anxious to wind up affairs in Dalny in order to prepare for the immediate transfer of General Nogi's Third Army to the northern front. When Chen sought to recover his boat, the authorities brusquely dismissed him with the news that he no longer owned the junk, and that it would be turned over to the Japanese army.

Robbed of his money and all his possessions, Chen was forced to walk the long miles to Port Arthur.

* * * * * * * * *

Any hope that Marina may have held that her business would survive the surrender of the forts and the arrival of a new military administration was quickly dashed on January 5, when an army officer appeared at her godown and demanded her keys. He told her that her buildings and all her inventory were requisitioned for the Japanese army.

"Take my inventory, if you must, but not my buildings," she had protested. "I need to stay in business. I am a Chinese citizen."

"You also are a Russian citizen," she was informed. "Port Arthur now belongs to the Japanese. You are free to leave. It would be best if you did."

"But my home is here."

"Your home will be occupied by a Japanese army officer as his headquarters. You have three days to vacate. Russians are no longer welcome here. You must leave everything in place except your clothing. Otherwise, we will punish you."

That evening, Marina and Rogers busied themselves preparing to evacuate. She gathered her remaining cash, all her jewelry, photos of her parents, and the little clothing she could carry. The remaining gold was melted down that night in her outdoor oven, poured onto a smooth concrete surface and pounded into thin flat sheets. Her melted silver dollars and silver houseware were poured into a mold that Rogers had formed of clay. When completed the mold was a glorified breast support shaped into two cups and a wide framework that also formed a waist girdle.

She looked at it dubiously, "It is going to be too heavy, I fear."

Rogers grinned, "Better a backache than leave it to some Japanese officer. You'll need the money. Besides, you are going to look great with a padded belly and bosom. Just pretend to be pregnant. Since it is my invention, I'll claim fatherhood. I will push you in a wheelbarrow if you are weighted too heavily."

Marina appreciated the joke. "Just be sure you file down the rough edges on this thing."

With Rogers' help she tucked her breasts into the cups after padding her flesh with thick cloths. He showed her how he would fasten the hole in the back strap to a small metal stud on the strap. With an amused smile, she looked at her image in a mirror. "Not a bad fit. You should patent this. How did you guess my size so well?"

Rogers smiled. "I remember the good things in life. This will be heavy and uncomfortable, and you will need someone to unhook this device, but you'll have money to start a new life."

"*We* will have money," she corrected him.

He unhooked and removed the silver breast support and silver girdle. "We can leave this off for now. I'll have to pad your shoulders more. Just don't take deep breaths."

* * * * * * * * *

Chen slipped into the newer Chinese settlement by the Chinese Wall. It too had been badly damaged by the war. From there he made his way into the battered remains of Old Town. At Marina's godown he found a Japanese sentry posted at the entrance. A "closed" sign was nailed to the gate. The sentry eyed him with suspicion so Chen did not tarry. He rested a short period at the edge of Old Town, then crossed the small shell-pocked bridge to walk toward Marina's home on the hill above New Town.

Marina and Rogers fed him while listening to his story. Her heart sank when he told her he had lost his boat. "Don't worry," he told her. "I won't give up easily. I'll fight to get it back."

"And I will help you," Rogers assured him. Damn if he would let Chen lose everything.

The three plotted that night to forcibly seize Chen's boat, cut it loose to drift away with the outgoing tide, and once far enough out of the harbor, they would raise the sails and make a run for Chefu.

Rogers said, "If we can make it to Chefu, we can lie low there until we find a way to slip down the coast to friendlier territory." He wondered if he was jumping ahead too fast. Marina and Chen were no longer bound to north China, but he was, until replaced by Uncle Steve.

Before they retired for the night, Marina said, "An officer came by today to say the Japanese will arrive tomorrow afternoon. We'll leave early. I gave my spare money to the servants. I hope they can survive. I have burned my papers, but I left all the house furnishings in place. I wish I could burn everything."

Rogers awakened to the sound of Marina sliding into his bed. She snuggled against him for warmth. He guessed it must be near dawn. "Chen will hear us," he protested.

She told him that Chen had gone to look for Yin-lin. "He left early in the morning darkness. He said he could not sleep. I am worried about him. He is very angry about his boat."

"What about Yin-lin?"

"Later," she told him.

She began to caress his belly and playfully bit the back of his neck and whispered "This will be our last time alone in my home. We may not be together like this for awhile." He turned and pulled her against his body. She kissed him and said, "We will have to tell Chen about our love—if he has not already guessed it."

Chen later returned to have breakfast with them. He had found Yin-lin in bed with the abandoned servant girl of Stoessel's household. "She doesn't want to leave with us," he said.

The trio left shortly after dawn. First, they had to get by the Japanese army patrols on the road to Dalny. Rogers carried his service revolver and asked if Marina and Chen had any weapons that were not too obvious. "Chen has a dagger. He's very good at throwing it," Marina said. She showed him a small deringer she had tucked in her waistband. "It works well at close range."

Disguised as menial house servants, Marina and Chen walked silently behind Rogers. Marina had climbed out of the wheelbarrow as the three neared another army patrol checkpoint. She laughed, "I have so much gold wrapped around my legs and butt that I don't think I can walk very far. I weigh a ton."

Rogers grinned as he told her, out of earshot of Chen, "You are going to attract a lot of attention with those big tits. You really are top heavy." Marina poked him in the ribs, "Jealous? What do you want, a taste of silver?"

"Not if I risk breaking a tooth."

Chen and Rogers had taken turns pushing the wheelbarrow which carried Marina and their bundles of clothing and food. They thought it less suspicious if Marina walked past the Japanese check point, since the soldiers were searching all conveyances, even those of the Chinese since so many natives had worked as spies for the Russians. The Japanese army had halted foot traffic in and out of Port Arthur and was making sure that nothing valuable left the port after the wave of looting that had taken place following the surrender. The Japanese authorities were speedily restoring order following the civic unrest that Stoessel had admitted to Nogi he could not control.

At the checkpoint, after Rogers held up his pass, the bored guards waved him and Chen through, but held up Marina. They leered at her prominant bosom, and one of them started to reach out to touch her. Rogers angrily intervened while the other soldiers laughed. The guards eyed her thick waist and protruding buttocks.

Rogers demanded to know why they were stopping her. "Can't you see she is pregnant?" He thrust himself between Marina and the soldier. He did not realize that he had spoken English, but his protest was unmistakable. The soldier raised his rifle menacingly. He and Rogers stared at each other briefly, then Rogers pushed aside his unbuttoned coat to reveal his holstered revolver. The other two barricade guards pulled back warily.

Chen spoke in halting Japanese, "Master, perhaps we should ask for his officer." Rogers did not understand what Chen said, but both he and Chen saw the sudden change in the guard.

With a belligerant gesture, the guard pushed his weapon forward and barked, "Go! Go at once!"

"Hurry on ahead," Rogers told his companions. "I'll watch to make sure he doesn't shoot one of us in the back." He kept looking over his shoulder, conscious that he walked stiffly as if anticipating the shock of a bullet. Finally out of range, they stepped to the side of the road to rest and to permit a column of Russian prisoners of war to pass by. Armed Japanese guards, carrying their rolled red blankets on their back, prodded the prisoners on their way to Japanese prisons. The dejected Russian soldiers, muffled against the cold, but stripped of all possessions, passed by without a glance. Their boots were in poor condition and many wore Chinese clothing and Chinese sheepskin coats.

Farther down the road, Rogers spotted a small horse-drawn cart and persuaded the farmer to take money to carry them. He soon almost preferred walking and pushing the wheelbarrow rather than endure the rough, jolting ride on the rutted road. No more obstacles stood in their way until they reached Dalny.

The city was congested with military traffic. Long lines of Russian military prisoners were herded onto transports for the voyage to Japan. Russian civilians were retained for use as unpaid laborers, so that Japanese soldiers could be freed for duty in the north.

Finding a room for the night was impossible. They all wore warm clothing, but Rogers dreaded the thought of Marina spending a sleepless night in the open. And she needed a release from the heavy weight she carried. He left Chen and Marina at the waterfront to rest while he searched for shelter.

"Captain Rogers?" Startled, he turned to see a bandaged Japanese officer.

"Yes?" Then, in a flash of understanding, he recognized his old friend from the Boxer Rebellion. "My God, it is you! Tomoru Tanaka! Old friend, how are you?" He wanted to embrace his friend, but held out his hand instead, then quickly pulled his hand back, embarrassed. "Sorry Tom, I didn't realize." Tanaka's right arm and hand were heavily bandaged. His bandaged left arm was in a shoulder sling. A black patch covered his left eye.

Tanaka brushed aside the mumbled apology. He seemed unsure what to say. "Were you with our army?"

"No, Tom, I was ordered to stay with the Russians. My God, Tom, what you must have gone through. I'm so happy that you survived."

Tanaka shook his head sadly. "It is not over yet. The Third Corps will go north soon."

"Surely not you. You look pretty badly smashed, Tom. They won't put you in the trenches again. I would hope not."

Tanaka said he had to stay on as an interpreter. "I did not lose the eyeball, but the sight is gone. The right arm will be all right. The left arm is questionable. It is almost six centimeters shorter. I got this at Fort Nirushan." He spoke without bitterness.

Rogers winced. How could he ever reveal he was also there. "I am so sorry. At least you are alive."

"Are you going home now, Ellis?"

"I hope so. I'm going to slip on south, get warm, and look for someone." He saw Tanaka's questioning look. "It is An-an, Tom. She has disappeared. I don't know if she is alive or dead. I left her in Hong Kong a year ago. Nothing but silence since then."

He continued, "I tell you, old friend, your side has won a great victory, but what a terrible cost. If your country wins the war, will you go back to the university?"

Tanaka shrugged. "I hope they will let me come back. But I am half blind and probably crippled. Veterans will be plentiful and many will return healthy and sound. I want no pity. I fought for my country and did the best I could. I just want to go back to my family. I fear they are not healthy. Japan has suffered very much at home. Food is scarce." Rogers understood. He wished he could find the right words to say.

Tanaka continued, "Things are bad in Port Arthur?" Inwardly he knew they had to be. He saw Rogers nod. He added, "I will be sent there for the victory parade. They will need my English language knowledge. Then the rest of us will entrain for the northern front."

The two talked for a long time. Rogers finally realized the day was getting shorter. Already the sun had dipped over the western hills. He knew he must get back to Chen and Marina. There was still the task of finding a place to sleep and keep warm. He explained his predicament to Tanaka. "The couple are Chinese. Grand people. But his boat, a good-sized junk, has been impounded. He doesn't know why. Maybe some mistaken suspicion of smuggling. He had a letter of marque from your navy and had ferried supplies to the Japanese army in the north all year. It must be some kind of mixup."

They walked to the waterfront and he introduced his friend to Chen and Marina. "They are my best friends, Tom. I know it is the fortunes of war, but they are civilians who did not fight your army. They need to survive. If they could only go south, away from Manchuria."

"Take them with you, Ellis."

"I can't. They need transportation which I can't provide. We had planned to travel together and go to south China to get away from this war. Now the boat is gone."

Tanaka studied the woman, whom he thought was too big and too fat, but certainly had a very beautiful face. Obviously a half-breed, probably part Russian. Well, that was not her fault. He also noted the tenderness that

Rogers showed the woman. He could see the couple was cold. So was Rogers. He led them to a nearby shop. A Japanese sentry stood guard over the cluster of buildings. Tanaka spoke briefly to the sentry, then opened the shop door.

"This used to be a restaurant. The sentry said there was still some wood and charcoal in the kitchen. If you can sleep on the floor, perhaps you can light a fire to warm the kitchen. You will be safe here until morning. I will return early in the morning to see what can be done about the boat, but I think the matter is beyond my control. Point out the boat to me."

Tanaka looked out over the harbor water as Rogers pointed out the brown hull of Chen's boat. The craft was anchored in shallow water far away in a distant corner of the harbor. The junk was larger than Tanaka had anticipated. He recognized it as a sea-going craft.

"I am afraid that I cannot help much in this matter. I heard about this boat. The army has assigned it to the staff of an intelligence officer who will arrive to take possession tomorrow. It will be used up north as a sort of spy ship to watch for smugglers. She will fly a Chinese flag. I was told that she is fast and draws a shallow draft—excellent for coastal waters. The army will put Hunhutzes on board to man her."

"Could we go aboard for a quick look? There are some charts of the south coast that I will need. Just me and my Chinese friend. The woman can't travel well."

"Is she with child?"

"I believe so."

Tanaka persuaded a staff officer to loan him a small steam launch to take them to the junk. Two armed Japanese sailors accompanied them.

The junk was undisturbed, much to Chen's satisfaction. Aside from the missing cargo and the rubbish strewn around the lower deck, Chen noted that his craft was seaworthy. While Rogers was in the cabin searching for the charts, Tanaka confided to him, "Two of the Hunhutzes will go aboard this afternoon to get her ready, and will stay on board as guards."

Chen saw Rogers carrying the four rolled sea charts. When he passed Rogers, he winked. Then he mouthed a single word, "Tonight."

After they returned to the harbor quay, Tanaka made sure they remembered the location of the vacant shop where Marina waited. He excused himself, saying, "I must go to the hospital for treatment. Tomorrow, we can talk about the future."

As he said goodbye to Tanaka, Rogers inquired, "Just out of curiosity, who is the intelligence officer who will take control of the junk?"

Tanaka looked as if he did not want to answer. "It is a Major Ariko. Maybe you remember him from China?"

Rogers returned to Chen with a positive determination, "You damned right it's tonight. Before we go back to the restaurant, let's scout the harbor. We need to find a rowboat."

As twilight was descending, Chen and Rogers saw a rowboat carrying three Manchurian men row toward Chen's junk. Waiting patiently for forty minutes, Rogers and Chen saw a single occupant return with the rowboat. He beached the boat, laid the two oars in the sand, then overtuned the boat on top of the oars to hide them. *Careless*, Rogers thought. He saw the posted Japanese sentry still watching the beach from the higher ground above the seawall.

Chen glanced at the darkened sky and announced that there would be no moon that night, a cold night with a good cloud cover and a soft breeze. The sentry watched them as they walked to the restaurant.

Chen remarked that he worried about Marina. "With all that weight of metal, she will sink like an anchor if we are dumped in the water. We won't be able to save her."

"It is a risk we have to take," said Rogers. "Anyway, how could any of us swim ashore in this icy water? Let's think positive. I'm mad as hell. So are you. I'm ready to fight. Damn that rotten Ariko!"

As they neared the shop, Chen spoke quietly. "Ellis, Marina is very special to me. You and she are my only two friends. Promise that if anything happens to me, you will take care of her. I'll do the same for you."

Rogers agreed. "Thanks, old friend. And if you ever get to Hong Kong, find out if An-an is alive."

Marina lay on the floor, curled in a fetal position. The metal undergarments lay nearby, covered by a lap robe. Her face was pale. Rogers inquired, "Are you able to make it? You look so tired and weak." He leaned closer. "Will you be all right?"

Marina groaned. "I feel terrible. After what has happened these past few days, I am numb." She whispered, "It is near the end of my monthly period. Almost over. Bad timing. Don't tell Chen." She lay back wearily and looked up at him with a wan smile, her half closed eyes highlighted by dark circles. "Give me two hours of sleep, and I will be all right."

Rogers was not so sure. He lay down, trying to rest comfortably on the hard floor. Thank goodness the floor was wooden and not cold stone. He had no concern about waking on time with that kind of discomfort.

At three in the morning, they gathered their bundles and helped Marina dress. Rogers peered out the half opened restaurant door. "Come on, the sentry is gone." They crept furtively toward the beach. Rogers peeked around the corner of the building. "The other sentry must be gone too. I don't see anyone watching the beach."

The three descended the steps leading to the beach. Walking quietly across the sand, they found the rowboat and the oars beneath it. Rogers and Chen helped Marina into the rowboat. Before Chen could protest, Rogers motioned for him to be seated and handed him the two oars as he pushed the rowboat into deeper water. He winced at the shock of cold water flooding his boots.

"No more talking from here on," Chen warned. "We will row toward the starboard midships. I dropped a line over the side while we were out there this afternoon. If it is still in place, one of us can climb up to the deck. There should only be the two Hunhutzes on board. I don't have to tell you how treacherous they are. Show no mercy."

Chen and Rogers rowed in unison, paddling noiselessly across the harbor, praying they would not be challenged. Once past the cluster of boats moored near the shore, they breathed easier. No other obstacles remained in their path. Chen's junk floated alone about two hundred yards out from the shoreline.

"Let me go up first, Chen. If they have seen us, I'll use my revolver."

Chen shook his head. "Maybe. But if we are not spotted, I will go first and use my knife, if needed. The less noise, the better."

They guided the rowboat against the junk's hull, pushing with their hands to break the noise of contact. Chen silently pointed to the line dangling over the side, then pointed to himself. Rogers nodded in agreement. He held onto the rope as Chen pulled himself upward, the knife clamped between his teeth.

Chen peered over the gunnel. Seeing nothing, he climbed onto the deck. He crouched briefly in the dark to assure himself that no one was on deck. A faint lantern light showed beneath a cabin door. He shook the line to signal Marina to come aboard. He had prearranged for her to cling to the line while he pulled her upward.

Marina welcomed his powerful grasp as he pulled her over the top of the railing. She still clung to him after he released his hold, and was still hugging him when Rogers' head appeared at the railing. "That was scary. You are so strong," she whispered to Chen, finally releasing her hold. Rogers grinned. It pleased him to see Marina show some attention to Chen.

Now the three had only to subdue the two guards and they could be on their way to freedom—if they could pass out of the harbor unnoticed.

Chen motioned for Marina to stand to one side of the cabin entrance. Carefully he turned the handle and eased open the door. One Hunhutze sat at the table with his back to the door, eating noisily from an iron pot. The only light was from an oil lamp on the table.

Chen had barely stepped inside, when the man turned as if to speak to his companion. When he saw Chen, he hurled the pot. Chen ducked. The pot clanged against the door. Before Chen could straighten up, the man was on him in an instant, wielding a wicked knife. Chen stepped free and pushed his assailant away. The Hunhutze charged. Chen stepped to one side and drove his knife into the man's side. The blow floored the assailant. Chen stepped forward, reached down and cut the man's throat.

Rogers had heard the commotion and pushed into the cabin. "It's a mess," Chen growled. "Help me get him out of here. Grab his legs."

As quickly as possible, they threw the corpse onto the deck and brought Marina inside. Chen threw a couple of towels on the spilled food and blood.

Rogers started for the door. "We have to find the other one. You watch Marina and I will go below. He must be down there. We have to hurry."

He descended the wooden steps of the ladder as quietly as he could. The enclosed area below seemed darker than the black night on deck. At the foot of the ladder, Rogers paused, trying to accustom his eyes to the darkness. He listened for a sound, any sound, even heavy breathing. The silence was eerie. Long familiar with Chen's boat, he began to move away from the ladder.

A sudden weight struck his shoulder, pitching him to his knees. He instinctively rolled forward. Now he could hear the man's growl and sensed his nearness. He reached for the knife in his boot. Something whistled past his head.

The light from Chen's lantern broke the darkness. Chen stood at the head of the stairs, peering into the darkness. "Is he down there?"

"Yeah. He's here somewhere. Show me some light, but stay up there. This one is slippery. I'll find him." At that moment, a body crashed against him. A shaft of light from Chen's lantern caught the upraised Hunhutze knife. Rogers jammed the barrel of his revolver against the man's belly and fired. The explosion was muffled by the clothing and closeness of the man's body.

Chen scramblod down the ladder to catch the body as Rogers pushed it away. Chen buried the blade of his knife in the man's heart, then wordlessly mounted the ladder, pulling the corpse upward.

After the bodies had been weighted and eased over the side, Chen and Rogers cranked up the two anchors. Already the rowboat had drifted away with the ebbing tide. From long practice the two broke out the canvas and began hoisting the sails. The breeze caught the first sail and the junk began to slide forward. Chen ran inside the cabin to bring out Marina, who had started to clean the spilled food.

"We can get that cleaned later, Marina. We need you on the wheel."

"What will I do?" she asked, suddenly feeling helpless.

Chen placed her hands on the wheel and pointed to the eastern cape. "Just keep her pointed in that direction. I'll take over as soon as all the sails are up."

The junk began to move faster. Marina gripped the wheel tightly, marveling at the increased speed. She uttered a cry of fear as the junk began to tilt too far to port.

"Help her, Chen. I'll finish this for now."

Chen stood behind Marina, his hands over hers. "Watch how I move the wheel." He had pressed his body against her to help control her movements. She liked the sensation. He taught her a world of seamanship in the fifteen or twenty minutes that it took to get underway. When their course was finally set on a comfortable, controlled broad reach, he left her and helped Rogers finish the minor chores.

As the lights of the harbor began to fade from sight, he relinquished the wheel to Rogers and urged Marina to go into the cabin out of the cold wind. The rough water of the open sea soon increased the pitch and roll of the bow.

Marina thrilled to Chen's commanding presence. Clearly the master of his vessel, he told her to strip down to remove the gold plates and silver breast yoke. Tossing her a blanket, he winked as he brushed past her to return to the deck. Marina watched him leave. With renewed interest, she pursed her lips at the increased respect she felt for him. So different from the humble guest when he had visited her home.

At the first light of dawn, certain Japanese realized that the junk had disappeared from the harbor. It was a mystery that they never solved.

The voyage south to the China coast was long and nerve wracking and full of tension whenever they spotted smoke from a passing freighter or warship. But none challenged their passage.

"We can dock at Wei-hai-wei," Chen announced. "I don't trust Chefu. Someone there could alert the Japanese by radio. As a neutral boat, the British at Wei-hai-wei will respect our presence. The harbor master there knows this vessel and, with no published alarm, he will not question us. We can dock long enough to check the boat thoroughly, take on drinking water and some food, if the vendors outside the gates have some to sell. I want to make sure the boat can proceed down the coast into southern waters—at least as far as Tsingtao."

* * * * * * * * *

Tanaka awoke at dawn to the nagging pain of his shattered arm. Learning to cope with the one semi-useful arm and struggling to adapt to his blind eye, he fought the temptation of self pity. He desperately longed to go home to his wife and child. Something in her last letter seemed desperate and ominous. Was the media lying about conditions at the home front?

He was weary of the cruel war and had to fight his urge to escape, feeling a strong guilt at the thought of abandoning his comrades who had already sacrificed so much.

He walked to the waterfront, shivering slightly in the cold morning air. Standing on the rise above the quays, he looked out toward Chen's boat. It was gone.

He looked over at the beach. The rowboat was also missing. And there was no sentry stationed above the beach. Beyond the harbor, the horizon was void of any vessel. Turning away, he walked up the incline to the shop, which he found empty.

"How long have you been at your post?" he asked the sentry. "And whom did you relieve?"

"About one hour, sir. There was no one here when I arrived."

Tanaka walked on up the street, happy in spite of his pain. Even though these sentries were not formally posted with an officer of the guard, they had been preassigned for certain shifts as military police to guard designated areas against looting. He began to smile with smug satisfaction. If he had ever done any kind favor in his life, this was one to help heal the tragedy of the war. The presence of a rowboat with oars, placed conveniently near the water's edge, the absence of two sentries, and the visitation to the junk had not been accidental. He was reasonably sure that Rogers was armed. Perhaps the Chinese couple was also.

He had never liked that bastard Ariko. In a way, he was glad he had not mentioned to the Chinese woman that Ariko was also taking over her home.

CHAPTER TWENTY-FOUR

At Wei-hai-wei, Chen went ashore first to explain to the harbor master that he was on his way to Tsingtao and had two passengers aboard: a Chinese servant and an American officer. The port authority asked if the officer was Captain Ellis Rogers. Learning that it was, they said a telegram had come in four days ago for the American. They had held the telegram, not knowing where to forward it because of the collapse of Port Arthur.

Rogers recovered the unciphered telegram. It held no secrets. In the body of the message, the sender, Uncle Steve, had curtly ordered Rogers to go north at once to report to the headquarters of General Kuropatkin and to notify Shanghai at once upon his arrival. The message also indicated that future messages or instructions for Rogers would be sent via St. Petersburg. Rogers already knew that Uncle Steve would expect him to check with the British naval station rather than the less reliable Chefu wireless office. Since early August, Rogers had made an arrangement with the British that they would forward his messages with Chen.

Chen was not unknown at the British station, and was always welcomed because he carried the latest war news.

Rogers had to admit to himself that he had half expected such an order from the War Department. As usual, Uncle Steve had avoided his inquiries and seemed as determined as ever to keep Rogers at the Russian front. Rogers also knew that almost all American war observers and correspondents were stationed with the Japanese army. That would remain the status as long as American politicians favored a Japanese victory.

Rogers' reputation from the siege of Peking four years earlier was well known and appreciated at Wei-hai-wei. The military club and many ancillary privileges were his to enjoy, so he had little difficulty purchasing both a Webley revolver for Chen and an American flag for Chen's junk. He and Chen had decided to raise an old mainsail rather than the red dragon sail, and display an American flag to discourage any interception by a Japanese naval vessel.

Rogers arranged for the laundering of their clothes and borrowed a couple of Chinese servants to come aboard to clean the interior of the junk. Chen jettisoned as much disposable gear as possible, stripping the boat for the fast run to Shanghai and thence to Hong Kong, with a quick stop at Tsingtao to retrieve Marina's deposited gold from the Chinese-German Bank.

He had rejected a previous plan to hire additional crewmen at Chefu because of the possibility of a leak to the Japanese. Chen stubbornly assured Rogers that the good weather favored the first leg of the voyage with just himself and Marina aboard. He had designed the boat for handling by one man—himself. All he needed was someone to give him time for a short period of rest and sleep. Rogers had confidence in Chen's seamanship, but worried about the strain on Marina.

Marina shared more than Chen's disappointment that Rogers could not continue the voyage with them. She was devastated at the message from Uncle Steve. What had promised to be the start of a new adventure for her and the prolongation of Rogers' love had suddenly disintegrated. Even though Rogers promised to join them as soon as possible, she had a premonition that this was the start of a second romantic failure in her life. First Viktor, now Rogers. Coupled with the loss of her home and business, it was a bitter pill to swallow.

Chen was embarrassed by her emotional state. He saw Marina clutching Rogers, weeping distraughtly. Deciding it was best to leave the pair alone,

Chen announced that he had a last minute errand to run. He needed a tool from the base machine shop, and promised to return in two hours. He had never seen Marina so upset. Maybe Rogers could calm her. She certainly had grown fond of the American.

As soon as they were alone, Marina threw all caution to the wind. She wrapped her arms around Rogers and said tearfully, "I don't know how long the war will last, or when I can see you again, or what the future holds for us. I know that life is full of changes and this has to be one of the worst." She fought to control her sobs. "Ellis, what if we never meet again? I want you to make love to me before we leave in the morning. Love me as if we will never see each other again. Leave me with a happiness that I can always remember and cherish."

He tried to reassure her that his absence would only be temporary. but she drowned his protests with frantic kisses, asking him not to waste the short time they could enjoy together. Hungrily, she stripped off her garments and began unbuttoning his shirt and trousers. She overcame his initial reluctance by aggressively arousing him with her hands. He let her take the lead and was soon in the mood—enough to bring her the relaxation and joy she coveted and needed. Pausing only momentarily to catch their breath, they repeated their performance until they realized that the always prompt Chen would soon return. They were dressed and seated at the table sharing a glass of wine when Chen's footsteps on the deck announced his arrival.

Not many words were spoken that evening. Chen had decided to slip away from the station early in the morning in order to take advantage of the darkness.

He and Rogers slept badly and were awake at four. They both crept out of the cabin, choosing not to awaken Marina. Rogers assisted Chen to raise the anchor and hoist enough sail to get the junk underway. He shook hands silently, then pushed Chen's bow free of the dock. He knew that once underway, Chen would lash the wheel, raise the remaining sails, then set a course close enough to shore to elude Japanese patrol ships.

Rogers stood silently on the deserted quay, watching the Stars and Stripes fluttering from Chen's mast. After the junk was swallowed by the dark night, he felt more lonesome than he had in ages. All he could envision was Marina's soft, yielding nakedness. His heart ached at the thought of her absence—and the horrors of war to which he had to return. He tried not to think of the weeks, perhaps months, that would pass before their reunion. There was only one other woman who had brought him such peace and happiness. *What in God's name had happened to An-an?*

The cold Janauary weather began to pierce his jacket. Throwing back his shoulders and standing erect, he commenced walking toward the warmth of a nearby base galley. On the way, in the quiet time before daylight, he tried to solve some of the puzzles of the past eleven months. Life, he thought, could be so uncertain and cruel.

For three days Chen hugged the coast, ever wary of Japanese warships and occasionally halting briefly to rest, drifting in the open sea while adjusting the sails and helping Marina in various chores. At night he held a steady course hour after hour, giving himself little rest.

Although her heart ached for Rogers, the shipboard activity kept Marina occupied enough to take her mind off most of her sorrows. With some fresh food aboard and a clean boat, she quickly entered into the spirit of the adventure, relieving Chen at the wheel for short periods of time to permit him to lay nearby on a pad on the deck for a quick nap. He insisted on resting by the wheel while she steered, and made her sleep in the cabin at night so she could rest undisturbed. Luckily, the winter storms failed to develop.

When they came in sight of the German-controlled port of Tsingtao, Chen moored far out in the roadstead. Before leaving the boat, he checked and loaded Marina's derringer, her only weapon on board, except for his knife. He hailed a harbor sampan to ferry him ashore. Discovering that the sampan man's family owned a harbor store, Chen requested him to purchase a list of foodstuffs, including fresh meat, fish, eggs, bread, and assorted tins of food. He promised to pay a good price upon his return from the bank where he had deposited Marina's gold on earlier voyages. The deposits had been negotiated under joint names with right of withdrawal by one party. Marina trusted her cousin implicitly.

The teutonic efficiency at the Chinese-German Bank made the withdrawal easy. Chen succeeded in obtaining a good supply of British pound notes, several German marks, and two valises of gold bars. He kept his Webley revolver handy. On his return to the dock on a hired ricksha, Chen detoured to a gun shop to purchase a small but deadly Belgian pistol for Marina and a Mannlicher rifle for the boat.

Marina screamed with delight when she saw the groceries and her gold brought aboard. Chen paid the sampan pilot for the food, adding a generous tip. Chen did not reveal the contents of the valises and purposely lied that the junk was returning north to Tientsin's port near Taku. Then he immediately raised anchor and, once out of the harbor, turned south for Shanghai.

On the long run to Shanghai, Chen again drove himself mercilessly with little rest, ever mindful that the Japanese navy would look for him in the sea lanes. His luck held in the few days it took to reach his destination. Again, he moored far from shore during the one day and night he rested before going ashore into Shanghai to hire two reliable, experienced deckhands.

With water and fresh provisions and added help on board, Chen's junk left the harbor during the second night. He had barely cleared the harbor in the darkness when a Japanese light cruiser arrived. The cruiser received a chilly reception from the Chinese and British authorities who had lately begun to realize that British domination in the Yangtse valley might be endangered by Japan's growing power in the Orient, now that Port Arthur had fallen and the Russian Manchurian Army continued to retreat from disastrous military defeats.

With deck duties assumed by the two hired seamen, Chen and Marina now had time to enjoy sufficient sleep and rest. For safety, they shared one cabin, which caused Marina to realize how comfortable she felt in such close contact with Chen. He never violated her privacy or made advances or said anything, but she soon grew aware of his soulful looks and obvious strong feelings for her. Before they arrived at Hong Kong, a new relationship had developed between the pair. His commanding presence and strength helped assuage her loneliness and disappointment for the absence of Rogers. Chen's solicitude for her comfort and happiness was a welcome panacea. She began to resolve some of her doubts about sharing life with Chen for an extended period that might stretch into several weeks or even months. She thanked God for providing such a loyal protector.

The long calm days at sea afforded them much time to explore the past, to learn more about Chen's loss of his wife years earlier, and for her to ask questions about the missing An-an. She volunteered information about her relationship with Viktor Alesandrov, and they talked without shame about Rogers and Yin-lin and life in Port Arthur. She sensed that Chen suspected her intimacy with Rogers, but seemed not to mind. Both welcomed the new trust and sharing of their days together. She inquired timidly about his love life. He told her of his long celibacy, with the exception of the woman Ti Flower, who had seduced him in gratitude for saving her life. When she asked if the experience had been rewarding after so many lonely years, he confessed that it was such a pleasurable revelation that he hoped to find a wife and have children. Already he was prepared to leave the sea and settle down on land.

"I realized it was wrong not to live a full life after my wife died," he mused. "I have lost those years without a companion. Now I propose to change before it is too late. If I suffered, I have myself to blame. Since my encounter with Ti, I have been restless. I want a family."

Marina wanted to ask if he had anyone in mind or was looking for a particular kind of soulmate, but desisted when she saw how hungrtily he gazed at her. This was so unlike the Chen she had known for most of her life. Or had she really known him? This Ti person must have been quite a lover to change him so much.

He did not ask her what changes in life she might contemplate, believing it too personal. He had grown aware that she was concerned about her age. For a beautiful woman who had always been so successful and independent, Marina sometimes seemed unsure of how desirable she was. She was modestly wealthy, but humble. She could face old age in comfortable circumstances. With her health and beauty, she still seemed restless, as if searching for something in the future. He wished he were younger and not seventeen years beyond her age of thirty-two. The difference in age had always presented an insurmountable bar—at least in his consciousness.

The topic of conversation turned to An-an. Marina asked him to tell all he knew about the missing girl. She felt little twinges of envy when Chen praised the beauty and vitality of the girl. The high praise of An-an by Chen should not have bothered her, but it did. After all, that was the kind of partner that she should have known would be Rogers' choice.

She listened to Chen's story of An-an's student days in Peking, her subsequent salvation of her father after his dismissal at the university, the trauma of her kidnapping and torture by the Boxer viceroy in Tientsin, her experiences as a disguised cavalry scout for the American expeditionary force during the Rebellion, and how she and Rogers had fallen in love while working as a team to find a way to penetrate the infamous Tartar Wall.

"All who knew her loved her, including Viktor. Even the British Army had rewarded her with a medal for her services." Chen's voice broke momentarily. "Ellis' heart is broken by her loss. I promised I would try to find out what happened. I think she has died."

Marina was saddened but curious. "Why did you never tell me Ellis married her?"

"Because he was always secretive about it, since his army denied him permission for marriage to an Oriental. He did tell you he was married, did he not?"

"He did not say he was married until late this summer when he came in from the Green Hills Line. I had guessed as much for several reasons, but he never wanted to talk about it."

"He was hurt," Chen told her. "Very hurt."

On their last night at sea, while discussing Rogers, Chen abruptly asked her, "Do you love him, Marina?" He was surprised at his boldness. He was even more surprised at her reaction.

"Yes," she said. Her voice was soft and longing. "I love him as much as you do. I love you both." She stood and walked around the table to kiss him on the cheek. She held him close, her eyes wet with tears.

"Oh Chen, what will happen to us?" He held her as she sobbed, knowing she needed to release her emotions. He said nothing, only patted her shoulder and said, "We'll go on living like before, Marina. It is all part of life."

After their arrival in Hong Kong, Chen and Marina continued to reside on his boat while they toured the island so she could enjoy the points of interest. Both wanted to relax before making a decision about their future. Marina reveled in the orderly and peaceful atmosphere of the Crown Colony while shopping for clothing and much needed toiletries. The war in Manchuria seemed so far away with its devastation and death and unpleasant memories. Everything sacred to her in Port Arthur had been stolen, but that was the past. There was the future to consider. So she bravely pushed aside the bitterness of her loss and concentrated on making a new life.

It surprised her that Chen acted as if he were more at peace with himself and in no hurry to return to his smuggling forays. He seemed reluctant to distance himself from her and had suggested a couple of times that they stay close to each other in their new adventure. Although happy to have his strength and support, she began to wonder if she might be a burden to his freedom. She missed Rogers and sometimes wondered how much Chen knew about her affair with Rogers. She was sure he would never inquire.

She had deposited her gold in a British bank and had even offered money to Chen, which seemed to horrify him. He claimed to have saved a tidy sum, but never mentioned how much, only hinting that he hoped to start a new venture somewhere in south China. Hong Kong had continued to grow rapidly each year. It was such a novel and satisfying contrast to war ravaged Port Arthur that Marina did not want anything to interrupt what had come to be almost a radiant vacation. While she shopped and continued to recover from her past ordeal, Chen began renewing old ties within the business community and started to make inquiries about An-an.

In his search, Chen made the mistake of concentrating too much in the native quarter of the city, not realizing he would have had greater success in the commercial district. He did not know that An-an had a thriving import-export office. It was during this brief period that Chen met a Scottish taipan, a boat builder who had admired Chen's boat in the harbor. He had approached Chen to inquire about the hull design and obvious speed of the craft. Their talk led to a close bond that boat enthusiasts so often enjoy. The Scotchman gave Chen his business card and introduced himself as Harry Scott. Before their first talk ended, Scott accepted Chen's refusal to sell the junk, and graciously proposed a possible partnership in a business venture.

"You obviously know boats far better than any of my employees," Scott remarked. "You say you have no desire to lease or sell your craft. Would there be, perhaps, an opportunity for us to explore a way to throw some business to each other. You are in shipping and I am in construction. If you could help me in redesigning my commercial boats, I could refer some trading business your way. I know the right people among the British bankers here and several Portuguese in Macao and Chinese merchants upriver in Canton. And, I am selling more boats each year to the people in Formosa—or Taiwan as many now refer to it. I could offer you a commission for overseeing design aspects of my boat construction and for conducting sea trials. You could recommend my line of boats among the boat captains." The idea appealed to Chen. It would open the window of opportunity for him. And perhaps such a venture could include Marina.

During their second meeting, Scott proposed a business luncheon at the racetrack where he was a member. "Bring your business companion, what was the name? Mdme Berezovsky? I will bring my wife—she is northern Chinese—and we can discuss the possibilities of business."

Chen got the idea that Scott was anxious to cultivate a Chinese entrepreneur who could be useful among the close knit Chinese merchants who traditionally excluded foreigners or non-family members. Well, that was all right. He in turn could use some close ties among the Anglo crowd. Chen did not want to part with his sea-going junk, a craft that had always been so much a part of his life, but he also did not want to live long days at sea away from Marina. He told her about Scott's proposal and the offer of purchase.

"I would hate to see you part with your boat," she agreed. "You two have been together through so many adventures." She had already guessed Chen's plans to curtail his voyages and wondered what he really had in mind.

Chen admitted it would be like losing an old friend. "But she needs to work," he said. "She'll rot laying idle at some anchorage." After a brief moment of thought, he joked, "Why don't I lease her to you? That way we could both make a profit and still keep control." Noting the puzzled look on her face, he wondered if he was moving too fast. Marina had not indicated whether her plans included retirement or more mercantile ventures at which she was so good. After she thought carefully for a moment, her answer surprised him.

"That might be a way for me to start over again. I have the money. I need someone I can trust." He saw her hesitate. "I value our relationship, Chen. But partnerships can be dangerous to one or both. I would not want to lose your friendship because of any business problems."

"We don't have to decide now," he said. "I still need to find out about An-an."

"Yes," she responded, "And we should wait to hear from Ellis. I worry about him." She saw his smile and wondered if he understood how much she ached for Rogers. But what if they found An-an? Would she lose both Rogers and Chen? Would she find herself alone in a strange city? Suddenly the future began to look bleak. She asked Chen for more time.

"Not right away, Chen. Please have patience with me. I want to be very careful about my decisions. I need to learn more about this area and find a place to live."

"This boat is your home for as long as you wish," he told her. She reached for his hand and squeezed it.

"You are such a dear friend," she told him. "How can I ever repay you for saving my life?"

He looked at her so hungrily that she almost embraced him. It worried her that she was becoming such a sentimental part of his life. She could not forget Ellis and how much she longed for his arms around her.

She broke the awkward silence to tell him that she might look for a place in the New Territories or somewhere around the Pearl River estuary. "I'll not go back to Port Arthur," she said. "I can't live under Japanese domination. There is no place in Russia for me. All my life I have lived in north China and have seen it go steadily downhill under the Empress Dowager T'zu Hsi. Nothing will change there soon and I won't throw away years of my life wondering if the Russians, Japanese, or Germans will start another war. My home and business are gone. If I'm to start over, I want it to be in a more stable place. I think I can find that under the British. What about you, Chen?"

"I hate to lose touch with you, Marina. I can't tell you how much I enjoyed our voyage south together. Let's look together for Ellis' wife and after we have lunch Saturday with Mr. Scott, you or I can make a decision. I am going upriver to Canton with him tomorrow to examine some Chinese boats for possible resale. He wants to experience my 'expertise' as he calls it." He remembered the look Scott had given him when Chen had mentioned that he had a woman business partner, a half Russian companion. Scott had noticed Chen's enthusiasm when mentioning Marina and had wondered how close their business arrangement was.

"Will you be gone long?" Marina asked.

"Only a day, maybe two at the most. We'll go on one of his boats. On Saturday, as I said, he will have his wife along. He could help you, Marina. He is well known around Hong Kong."

Chen had a great sense of humor. He could laugh and joke with the best. But when doing business, he was very grave and controlled. He had one expression—his "business face" as Marina had chided him. Unlike so many Chinese who loved to gamble, Chen was careful with his money and emotions. Because of his inscrutable face when dealing with adversaries, he would have made a great gambler.

Marina was used to his impassive business expression, but was unprepared for the look on Chen's face when he saw Scott's wife. Marina had seen Chen's fleeting look of interest before when they had passed by comely maidens. Men were like that. She saw it as a sign of health. Mrs. Scott was indeed gorgeous but seemed to have completely floored Chen. He stared, mouth agape, eyes bulging, at a loss for words. Scott had noticed it also and had frowned. Marina had a momentary rush of resentment.

Neither Scott nor Marina had seen the look of panic on the face of Scott's wife.

Chen quickly recovered his composure, introduced Marina, then apologized. "I was startled," he said. "Mrs. Scott reminded me of a dear friend I lost in the seizure of Peking by the allied armies five years ago." He deliberately lied by adding, "She disappeared. Friends told me she had died, but for a long time I never lost hope. Forgive me, please, Mrs. Scott. The resemblance is uncanny."

"You say she died?" Scott asked suspiciously. "My wife is from Peking. Perhaps she knew her."

Larry Scott's wife was indeed Xi, whom Chen had brought from Peking to Hong Kong, together with An-an. Chen sensed that Scott did not know that his wife had once been the concubine of the Peking city governor.

Xi's worried expression relaxed upon hearing Chen's cover. They avoided looking at each other during the meal. Marina sensed the tension and hastened to speak Chinese with Xi. Scott's language skill was limited, so he ignored the chatter of the two women while conversing with Chen.

At the end of the meal, just before desert was served, Scott excused himself in order to retire to the bathroom. "Too much beer earlier. I'll be right back," he promised.

As soon as he left, Xi spoke to Chen. "You don't know me."

"That is right. I don't know you. Never saw you before." He leaned closer and hissed, "Where is An-an?"

"You haven't heard?"

"No. What happened?"

"We only have a few minutes," Xi said. She told Marina, "Chen will tell you everything. Chen old friend, thank you for not revealing me. Please keep my secret." She turned to Marina again and said, "Chen and I knew each other a few years ago in Peking. Can I come to the boat tomorrow? We can talk about An-an and the past."

"Of course," Chen exclaimed. "Is she alive?"

Scott neared the table. Seeing his approach, Xi smiled and leaned back. "Yes, she is alive. Sad and lonely, but very much alive."

Chen had never been as close to An-an as he had to Rogers. That was because Chen's presence in those past days had been too involved with commerce, leaving little time for socializing. Now it was different. Chen had retired from the sea. With Marina's money combined with his, he could afford to slow his activities.

He was eager to contact An-an for Rogers' sake. He hoped he could learn the reason for her long silence without undue embarrassment for both. So Chen let Xi arrange the meeting with himself and Marina, hoping the two women would bond and make his mission more comfortable.

Xi came early as Chen had expected she would. He had already explained the beautiful and sensuous Xi's past to Marina: her tragic and disappointing first marriage to a wealthy but weak young man whom his relatives had accused Xi of killing by her relentless sexual appetite. He related her equally unsatisfying concubinage with Peking's old and cruel governor, who gave her money and power, but no satisfying sex, and then her rescue by Rogers and An-an after Russian soldiers had attacked her during the war and thrown her out a second story window, and how Alesandrov had cared for her while her broken bones mended. Under probing from Marina, Chen had reluctantly related Xi's love affair with Alesandrov. Marina winced and thought *that is so like Viktor.*

Chen continued to tell how the Russian had abandoned Xi when he was called back to St Petersburg at the end of the Boxer Rebellion. And how Xi and An-an had become fast friends, and how he had offered to bring them both to Hong Kong when the old Empress Dowager's return had caused Rogers to be sent back to America to attend officer's school, and Alesandrov had been rotated to Russia. The two women had feared the old ruler's revenge after international diplomats turned their backs on the previous atrocities perpetrated against westerners with her encouragement.

Marina was intrigued by the story and had just asked for more details when Xi arrived. Xi was not alone. Marina knew at once from Chen's description that the young, slim and beautiful stranger with Xi was An-an. Her heart sank with a realization of the hopeless competition, and she suddenly felt old and unsure of herself. Like a rejected outsider.

There was no initial awkwardness for An-an who had flung herself on Chen, crying and hugging him and repeatedly asking, "Where is my husband? What happened to him? Please do not bring me bad news," she implored. Marina observed the scene with envy, marveling at Chen's compassion and how tenderly he sought to calm the hysterical young woman. Chen seemed so different with his arms around a woman. But Marina knew she did not own Chen or did she? Was she jealous?

Chen had confessed to Marina how Rogers had written repeatedly to An-an, at least once every week, and had sought in vain to find out why his letters were never answered, month after month. Now he was assuring An-an that her husband lived in daily danger, but was alive and well and terribly worried about her. He said that he and Marina had left him in Wei-hai-wei because of fresh orders for her husband to go immediately to northern Manchuria.

"But why have I not heard from him? It was exactly a year ago that he left to meet you in Chefu on his way to Port Arthur. I wrote to him

constantly. I began to believe that he had been hurt or had forgotten me."
She sobbed uncontrollably and embraced Chen.

Chen held her closely and patted her back. He agreed that something
was wrong and that all of them would search for answers about the missing
mail. He assured An-an that Rogers had complained of never receiving mail
from her, and he repeated that Rogers had written to her at least once a
week. "Your husband has missed you so much," he told her.

After An-an had become less agitated and distraught, Chen hurried to
introduce her to Marina. An-an apologized for being so emotional, but
Marina assured her that she understood. The afternoon passed fast though
somewhat awkwardly. The women sparred carefully and politely, not yet
sure of themselves. Chen, caught in the middle, tried his best to keep the
conversation going. He talked at length with Xi and An-an, bringing them
up to date on the events of the past year, while Marina served refreshments.
An-an watched Marina's movements, feeling uneasy and a little threatened.
The Eurasian woman was far too beautiful for An-an's peace of mind.

Before the visit ended, Marina drew An-an aside and proposed that they
meet alone as soon as possible. Marina wanted to have some questions
answered, and An-an was equally receptive to the idea. An-an insisted that
Marina come to her home alone in two days, saying that she hoped to be in a
happier mood by then. "I'd like to talk to you alone. As one woman to
another."

"I would like that," Marina agreed. "I will come."

On that day, while Chen conferred with Scott, Marina boarded a ricksha
sent by An-an. After the usual pleasantries, An-an came right to the point.
She wanted to know what Marina's relationship was with Chen. And with
Rogers. She knew how reticent Chen had always been to gossip. But Chen

had let it slip that Marina was her husband's landlady in Port Arthur. An-an wanted to know more.

"You must have known my husband very well this past year. You could tell me if anything is wrong. I still don't understand about our letters. It is weird, almost like some evil plot to keep us apart."

Marina agreed. "Let us be frank with each other. I'll start with the rendezvous your husband had with his friend, Viktor Alesandrov. Yes, Viktor was also my lover. Now that I know about Xi and Viktor, I'll tell you the whole story about Viktor, then we can talk about Ellis. Carefully omitting her affair with Rogers, Marina related in detail the events of the past year. She confessed her earlier feelings about Alesandrov and how she had turned against him when she learned that he had a French nurse in the Russian army as his latest lover. That she had grown very fond of Rogers who had been such a gentleman and friend when he was her guest. She talked about the siege of Port Arthur and the dark days that followed. She said she had lost touch with Alesandrov, but knew that Rogers would try to find him in north Manchuria. While Marina talked about Port Arthur, An-an studied her. She could envision how her husband might be tempted by Marina's full and sensuous body during long months of loneliness away from his wife. She tried to shake off her feeling of doubt and inferiority.

When An-an's turn to talk came, she told Marina about her past days with Rogers, first as his secret admirer during their life together as army scouts for the American regiments marching to relieve the Boxer siege of Peking. How they had lived and died together in that short war, then, with Alesandrov's help, had lived as man and wife before secretly marrying. She spoke briefly about Xi and Viktor and how tragic it had been for Xi when Viktor had been forced to leave her alone in China. An-an had comforted Xi and had insisted on bringing her to Hong Kong when Rogers had been recalled to the States. Xi had drawn much attention in the British colony and had been avidly pursued by the boat taipan Scott.

An-an continued her story, happy to unburden herself and to be able to confide in Marina. "Larry Scott helped her forget about Viktor. He made her happy and has been a wonderful husband, though a little possessive of her sometimes. I think you will find her a good friend if you stay in Hong Kong. Do you have any plans? Do you know if Chen does? He is such an interesting man. Has he ever talked to you about his past? Why he never remarried?"

Marina knew what An-an was hinting at. "Chen and I have shared so much these past several weeks. I have come to admire him in many ways. And he seems in his own shy manner to have some feelings for me. I see how he looks at me sometimes. We will probably work together in some enterprise since I was fortunate to escape with my money."

Before their meeting ended, both women believed they understood each other better. An-an decided to ask no further questions. And Marina, knowing she had lost Rogers, accepted life's decision. But she demanded one thing. "Go to your husband at once," she begged An-an.

"If you do nothing else, go to him. He needs you. Go at once." She hugged An-an. "I will give you the money. I will watch over your interests until you return. But go now. Wait no longer."

They cried together. An-an agreed that only by going north to Manchuria, could she ever learn what had happened to the letters and be reunited with her husband. She would leave at once and start with questions in Shanghai. If the Americans would not help her, then she would appeal to the British. She vowed to find the solution to the mystery of the missing letters before she left Shanghai. Beyond that city there was only Manchuria and the war zone.

Shanghai had to have some answers. If not, then Chefu or Dalny. Maybe the Japanese might help her. Marina had advised her to hurry to Dalny to find Tanaka and ask for his help to secure a travel pass to travel north through Manchuria. If that failed, she would somehow have to slip through the front lines into Russian-held territory. That could be formidable, but she was willing.

And somehow she would get through Japanese lines to find her husband. She was willing to face death in order to find her husband.

CHAPTER TWENTY-FIVE

When An-an's steamer arrived in Shanghai, she went at once to the British Consulate. She had prearranged with the ship's captain that she could stay aboard until the ship's departure. That relieved her of the stress of finding a place to stay for a few days.

The late winter weather had grown colder and nastier. She pulled up the collar of her coat and shivered as the ricksha pulled her through the bleak city streets.

At the consulate, a consular officer and a young female interpreter-clerk stood behind the counter. The officer said he knew of Rogers from past arrangements, and that any mail from Rogers that had arrived in the diplomatic pouch had been forwarded to an American agent in the city. He gave her the agent's address and also advised her to contact the American consulate. Beyond that he could offer no further advice.

The young female interpreter, who had stood by listening, surprised An-an by stopping her outside the consular reception room.

"I know your husband, Mrs. Rogers. I am Plum Blossom Hu. "Your husband helped me a few years ago. Did he ever speak of me?"

"Yes. Many times." She embraced the girl. "I am so happy to meet you at last. Can you help me? I have so many questions for you."

"Of course, Mrs. Rogers. What is wrong?"

"I haven't heard from my husband in over a year. He had told me that he would use this consulate to forward his mail to his superiors here in Shanghai instead of going through the American consulate. I wrote to you several times asking for help, but there was never an answer."

"That is odd," said Plum Blossom. "I never received any of your letters. We have received many letters from him this past year. Most were official reports to an American office now in this city. Recently, a few were for you, but I believe he mailed most of his letter directly to you rather than use the diplomatic pouch. I forwarded those letter that we received for you."

"By diplomatic pouch to Hong Kong?"

"No, through the Shanghai postal service."

An-an knew that Plum Blossom had asked Rogers to cease sending support money when the consulate had elevated her to the position of clerk-interpreter. He had agreed at first, then had recanted, telling Plum Blossom that he would insist on some remuneration to her as long as he found it necessary to depend on her to funnel his mail through the Britrish consulate to the local office of the American War Department. He had asked Uncle Steve to provide extra funds for this service. Plum Blossom had advised her superior of this service but found no objection as long as her loyalty remained with the British Crown. The British Foreign Office expected and often received small favors from the Americans in return.

Since the death of Queen Victoria, the British government had sought to improve relations with America after their error of supporting the Confederate government in the civil war against President Lincoln and the Union north. Years later, when America had defeated Spain, the British had conceded that the Caribbean seas could be better protected by the American navy, thus freeing the British to deal with the growing power of Germany and the troublesome attitude of the Russian Czar.

So Plum Blossom had faithfully sorted the mail in the diplomatic pouches and had carefully forwarded the sealed official mail from Rogers to Uncle Steve. She had trusted the Chinese government postal service, still administered by British civil servants, to deliver the personal mail from her friend and benefactor, Rogers.

Two days later, Lydia and Nigel brought Ti to the British consulate where they presented Ti as their ward and sought travel papers for her. An-an was there talking to Plum Blossom about the mystery of the missing mail. Plum Blossom excused herself to tend to the Fairbornes, who had an appointment. An-an watched the British couple and the pretty young Chinese woman with them. She overheard the man, a British naval officer in uniform, explain that he and his wife were returning home to England and would be accompanied by their ward, a Miss Ti Fairborne. Plum Blossom answered many of their questions, covered by her realm of knowledge, before ushering Nigel into the consular officer's room. While waiting for Nigel, Lydia and Ti began to converse with An-an and Plum Blossom. The polite topic of the weather led to idle conversation about the city of Shanghai, and then gradually became more intimate.

After mutual introductions, An-an explained that she was on her way to Manchuria to seek her husband who was an American army observer with the Russian forces. She mentioned that she had worked with the British army four years earlier during the Boxer troubles and was well acquainted with many career officers of the British Indian Army. And she said that she had met and worked with the high ranking officers Beatty and Jellicoe of the Royal Navy.

Lydia was fascinated with An-an's story and hastened to invite her to have luncheon as soon as she and Nigel concluded their business at the consulate. She told An-an that her husband had been serving also as an observer but with Admiral Togo on a Japanese battleship. Lydia gave An-

an hope by saying that perhaps Nigel could get her a letter of introduction that would enable her to pass through the Japanese lines around Mukden.

When Nigel emerged from the office, after making an appointment to return the papers he had been given by the vice consul to fill out at his leisure at the hotel, he was introduced to An-an and learned enough in a few minutes to also insist that she come with them for a luncheon.

At the restaurant, Nigel apologized to Ti and Lydia for dominating the conversation with An-an as he shared war stories with her. He mentioned that he knew of Rogers and had heard many complimentary things said about his assistance and cooperation with the British forces during the earlier international expedition's march on Tientsin and Peking.

"I came onto the scene shortly after the siege had been lifted at Peking, but I was busy with naval affairs and never had the opportunity to meet your husband at any of the officer's clubs. Pity. I would have liked that. Now that I remember, General Gaselee once mentioned medals given for meritorious service."

An-an blushed. "I received a medal. My husband was not permitted to accept his."

During this affable luncheon gathering, An-an dropped the name of Viktor Alesandrov. Nigel pretended not to have heard, and both Ti and Lydia exchanged wary looks, then quickly changed the topic of conversation.

Lydia drew An-an aside after the meal and expressed interest in meeting her again. She and Ti arranged for an afternoon tea at the end of the week at Lydia's hotel dining room "where the trio could engage in women's talk."

That evening, a runner carried a note from a Japanese secret agent posted outside the British consulate. The agent had followed Nigel's group to the hotel and had overheard some of the conversation and had noted the names of the party. The note was delivered to a Japanese army intelligence officer who had just arrived in Shanghai. The officer relished reading the note and sneered with delight at the names of the three women.

"Will that be all, sir?" the secret agent asked.

The officer gave money to the agent and waved him away. The agent bowed and murmured his gratitude: "Thank you, Major Ariko."

Alerted British counter intelligence agents and postal inspectors listened to the story told by An-an and Plum Blossom and were understandably concerned that a breech of classified information might exist. An investigative team started its probe without consulting with the Americans. Operatives placed within the postal service planted a bogus letter addressed to An-an in Hong Kong. Disappearance of the letter helped narrow the number of suspects. The team concentrated on those postal employees who might be sympathetic to the Russians or Japanese. They trailed suspects after work hours and were surprised to note that one Chinese man occasionally traveled to an American War Department office. He seemed to have money to spend, spoke passable English and had few acquaintances or friends, an obvious loner. So the investigative team began to focus on this postal supervisor named Nelson Ng, pronounced "Eng."

An informant working with the team said that he had been told to direct all letters bearing the names Chao or Rogers directly to Ng. When he had questioned the order, the informant had been angrily threatened by Ng to follow the procedure or be fired. British operatives followed Ng after work. He usually went directly home in an apparent unsuspicious routine.

Unknown to the investigators, Ng had indeed carried An-an's planted letter to his abode and had hidden it. He had taken no further action until a second letter showed up, this time addressed to Rogers' Chefu letter box via

Plum Blossom. Ng had taken the second letter home. Now he decided to take the two letters to Uncle Steve's office because he wanted the payoff money.

In his absence, the British team searched Ng's house, finding no proof of wrongdoing except for a concealed considerable amount of American dollars. Ng had always insisted on Chinese silver dollars, but had lately asked for U.S. dollars because he could get a better deal with the Chinese money changers.

"I'll wager that he has both letters on his person," the team leader said. His operatives had followed Ng to the U.S. War Department office and had permitted him to enter unmolested. But when he emerged, they halted him a short distance away and searched him. The letters were not on his person, but he carried several American silver dollars. They told Ng that some marked money was missing from the post office and all employees were subject to search. The team was now sure that they had the right man, but carefully avoided mentioning any missing mail to Ng. Their surveillance tightened.

A third fake letter, bearing a Russian postage stamp, was inserted in a mail bag on a British freighter newly arrived from Chefu. The letter, addressed to a Miss An-an Chao at a Hong Kong address, was brought by the mail sorter to Supervisor Ng. When he left work that day, Ng was stopped on the street and searched. The letter in Ng's pocket prompted the team leader to say, "We've got our man."

Under intensive questioning at police headquarters, Ng broke down and confessed that he intended to sell the letter to an American civilian who fitted Uncle Steve's description. Ng denied knowledge of the other missing letters, but the operatives knew better. They did not inform the Chinese government of the operation, but instead awaited word from the British

Foreign Office on how next to proceed. The Foreign Office chose not to confront Uncle Steve or the U.S. War Department, since the matter might become too messy and embarrassing for the Americans. The British wanted to mend relations with the Americans since the future pointed to increasing American strength in the Pacific and more trouble for the British in dealing with the German Kaiser. And the British recognized that Rogers' secret marriage might invite reprisals that would hurt his military career.

The final British decision was to imprison Ng for his actions, and let Rogers and An-an handle the matter, bolstered with a proposed affidavit from the British in case the American War Department officer tried to deny involvement or threaten Rogers. British Intelligence kept An-an informed, delighted at the chance to tweak Uncle Sam's nose a little.

The day before An-an was to meet for a final time with Lydia and Ti for a farewell luncheon, she gained an audience with Uncle Steve. He had granted permission for the meeting after reading her note that contained a veiled threat that she knew where her missing mail was and was on her way to confer with her husband in Manchuria. What happened during the stormy meeting was an unhappy and frustating esperience for An-a, and one that she would remember for a long time.

When an orderly escorted An-an into the small American War Department office, she almost gagged. The overpowering rancid stench of cigar smoke nauseated her. The fat, red-faced man in civilian clothing did not rise to greet her. Unsmiling and openly resentful, he sat silently, studying her expression.

An-an sensed his hostility during the long silence. Finally, she broke the tension by introducing herself as the wife of Captain Ellis Rogers. She saw no point in denying it any longer, believing she was protected by her knowledge about the letters.

"I know who you are," he answered rudely. "What do you want?"

An-an decided to forego further niceties. It was time to take off the gloves. In his case, rudeness was best met with rudeness. "I think you know why I am here." She had no idea what this man's title was or even his name, other than the code name *Uncle Steve*, which Ellis had given her.

The man exhaled a cloud of cigar smoke and blew it toward her face. "You'll have to be more explicit," he grunted.

She fanned away the naseous smoke and snapped, "I want my letters." Still there was no answer. She struggled to cope with his rude silence, but carcful not to endanger her husband's career. "If you do not wish to help me, I will tell you what I know." She tried to ignore the sneering smirk on his lips and another enormous cloud of the offensive smoke blown toward her. She persisted, "My husband does not know what I know. His letters to me were taken. My letters to him were taken. And I have proof that someone in this building has them. I want the letters returned and I want to know why they were taken. And I want to know where my husband is."

The man's face grew even redder with anger. He banged loudly on the desk. "How dare you come here with accusations. First, your husband, as you refer to him, is not legally married. We don't recognize you as his wife. And second, Captain Rogers has a sworn duty to obey army regulations which he has already violated. Thirdly, I cannot tell you where he is and neither he nor I can reveal his mission, even to you. I warn you not to jeopardize his career."

Uncle Steve wondered how much the woman knew. She did not seem to be intimidated by him. He wished he had been able to contact Ng to find out what had happened. If she knew the letters were missing and that they were in the building, then Ng may have talked. He grew more wary. Perhaps he should change his tactics and be more conciliatory. This woman could be trouble. She wasn't the usual meek and timid Chinese female civilian.

He tried again. "You say that some letters are missing and that you think they may be misplaced here somewhere. I presume that you have inquired at the post office?"

An-an continued to stare at him, refusing to soften her stand and play his game. He met her silence with another comment. "Well, you should explore all the options. I really have no obligation to assist you. Your private mail is of no concern of this office. We would like to help, for Captain Rogers' sake, however, we are very busy."

An-an insisted, "I want my letters and the captain's letters too," she said. "I will leave Shanghai as soon as I have them. If you won't tell me where he is, I will find him anyway. And I will tell him what has happened. Perhaps the British, who run the post office, can help me."

He clenched his jaw. *Damn the limeys. So that is who put this idea in her head!* He rose to his feet as if to signal the end of the interview. "I will start an inquiry about the letters you say are missing. I can't stop you from going to Manchuria, but I would advise strongly against it. Do not interfere with his duties or we will have to recall him and send him home to the States."

Home? Now she knew he was bluffing. This man had refused to give Ellis a leave countless times, had kept him in the Orient for years, had used him shamelessly in one dirty operation after another. She wanted to tell this fat pig that her husband would love to go home, except that he had no home in the States to go to. She bit her tongue and did not answer at once. She did not want to be separated from her husband. Still, this man needed her husband more than Ellis needed him. Regardless of how angry and disappointed she was, she took care not to burn her bridges behind her. She repeated, "All I want are my letters and my husband."

Uncle Steve motioned to the door and said in a more conciliatory manner. "If I find out anything in the next couple of days, I promise you will be notified. Meanwhile, please stay calm. Tell the front desk where we can contact you."

An-an turned to leave. She had to get the promised British affidavits and a letter asking for safe passage through Japanese lines. Perhaps Commmander Fairborne could use his influence. She departed, believing that Uncle Steve realized she knew too much. Surely he would give her what she wanted and hope that she would go away for good. She called for a ricksha to carry her to the British consulate. All she wanted were the letters and her husband.

* * * * * * * * *

Sylvia Levinski had grown concerned about the approach of the Japanese army. She had no desire to be caught up in the fighting. She had considered the war lost when Port Arthur fell to the Japanese. If the Russian army could not prevent the surrender of that naval base, then the army would only continue to retreat farther northward until it gave up all of Manchuria.

Reservists from the homeland, western Russia rather than Siberia, had begun to arrive at the Manchurian front in increasing numbers. Discontent for the unpopular war was spreading throughout Russia with the rise in taxation and the growing casualty lists.

At the end of January, Sylvia was still seething from the news that a peaceful civilian demonstration in St Petersburg had resulted in a massacre before the Winter Palace. Her socialist group had instigated the mass gathering, and several of them and others in the crowd had been killed by the Czarist police.

The news made her more than ever determined to escape from Ariko and Lebedeff and go to Russia. She believed the time had come for her to strike a fatal blow at the Czar by returning to help foment revolution.

She proposed to Ariko that she could be more useful in Russia agitating for civil unrest now that Japan seemed to be winning the war. To solve the problem of how she could close the tavern and leave without inciting suspicion, she proposed to Ariko that her fake death be staged. If Ariko could provide counterfeit identification papers and orders, she could slip away unnoticed with the staged death as a cover. She claimed she could attend to the details, further pleading that Colonel Lebedeff's constant surveillance continued to endanger her present work. But Ariko saw things differently. He was adamant that she stay. Sylvia may have wanted a change, but he was not yet ready to let her go. She had been useful and, as he saw it, she could continue her successful work by remaining in Manchuria. Although she had voiced her concern about Lebedeff's suspicions of her, Ariko suspected correctly that her dwindling interest in the war had more to do with self-preservation than worry about Lebedeff's nagging pursuit. There was no way that Ariko would relinquish control of Sylvia when victory over Russia loomed on the horizon. Even if Mukden fell, as he was confident that it would, there was still Harbin to overcome, more battles to be won, and, worse, the prospect that Japan's supply lines would become more fragile as the enemy retreated farther and farther northward.

Before leaving for Shanghai, he told Sylvia, "Soon Mukden will have to fall. Your work has been good and we continue to need your services to fool the enemy. You must remain in Mukden until the spring thaw." His eyes flashed with anger. "The Baltic Fleet was last seen at Madagascar. You cannot leave until that fleet comes here and we destroy it."

He could sense that Sylvia might no longer be trusted. If she feared Lebedeff so much, he knew that he could use the Okhrana officer as a threat to curb her. Before leaving her, he threatened, "I will provide false identification and travel documents soon, but don't try to leave without my consent or this Lebedeff man may learn more about you than would be healthy."

Ariko also realized that if Sylvia revealed the Japanese espionage operation, his own usefulness would be compromised. It could work both ways—so Sylvia had to be eliminated, but in a non-suspicious manner at a more opportune time.

Sylvia saw her chance for escape, when she discovered that Ariko had slipped away to the fallen fortress of Port Arthur. She worried about Lebedeff's constant surveillance of her tavern and she guessed correctly that Ariko had ordered his agents to watch her closely. In his absence, Sylvia again tried to visit the French nurse at the hospital. She needed something that Claudette could provide, but Claudette still avoided her.

With a desperate need to act before Ariko returned or Lebedeff arrested her, Sylvia managed to accost Doctor Solomon Zieman. She knew he was a Jew. From long practice, she could scrutinize any throng in St Petersburg and spot every Jew, no matter how well they might be dressed or in disguise. It wasn't their semitic features; it was their mannerisms, their passion for money, their sarcastic humor, their body movements. Although half Jewish, she admitted only to being Polish and had developed a dislike for Jews.

She blocked Zieman's path and came right to the point when he tried to say that he was too busy to talk to her. She cut him off curtly,

"I need a body, doctor—a cadaver of a woman about my size and age."

"Don't bother me with such nonsense, woman." He tried to push past her, but she blocked him again.

"Please leave my presence or I shall call a guard," he warned.

Sylvia held up her hand. "I too am a Jew," she said. She pulled at a gold chain on her neck to reveal a pendant bearing a Star of David emblem. Before he could protest, she added, "Your family lives in Kiev at 183 Danilov Street."

He halted in dismay. "How did you know that?"

Now that she had his attention, Sylvia took her time in explaining. "We live in troubled times, doctor. The Czar does not like Jews, even doctors serving Mother Russia. I can help protect your family."

Zieman recognized the veiled inference. "Are you trying to threaten me?"

Sylvia's lip curled. "I am trying to appeal to your Jewishness. But let's not play games, doctor. You surely have a spare corpse. Even an asian cadaver would serve my purpose."

"And what purpose is that?"

Sylvia hurried to tell him that she was in danger and had to return to St Petersburg as soon as possible. "I need to leave a body behind that would be mistaken for me. Never mind why." There was something about Sylvia's directness that warned Zieman that he should listen to her. He remained silent as she expounded further. At the conclusion of her argument, he realized that the woman would never take no for an answer and that she could cause considerable trouble if he refused.

She had hinted that she worked for the Okhrana and that it was only the Japanese she feared and wanted to deceive. With Mukden in danger of falling to the enemy, and chaos on the horizon, he reluctantly consented to help her. Bodies were plentiful. Several lay in a hospital ice house awaiting burial when the frozen ground thawed later in the spring.

"I will make it worth your while," she told him. "Wrap the body like a piece of merchandise. I will send servants to bring it to my tavern Saturday night."

Zieman knew he was playing with fire in agreeing to help her. He had disliked and distrusted her previously because she was Polish and he resented that province's anti-semitic prejudice, so often fanned by their dominant Roman Catholic Church. He watched her leave, cursing himself for his weakness and hoping he would soon see the last of her.

On her way out of the hospital, Sylvia darted into a dressing room and snatched two white nurse's gowns and caps and a blue nurse's cape. She hid them under her coat and walked away briskly. The harried staff was too busy preparing for a possible evacuation of the patients to question her movements.

CHAPTER TWENTY-SIX

In Shanghai, on the eve of the departure of the Fairbornes for England, Lydia proposed that she and Ti meet An-an not at Lydia's hotel dining room but in a private room at a small but reputable Chinese restaurant that was noted for the excellent cuisine of its star chef. It was not in the best of Shanghai's neighborhoods, but the three believed there was safety in numbers and they would face no problems. They arrived at the establishment in the early afternoon, happy to be out of the cold and early spring wind that blew off the China sea.

The dining room was small and cozy and located alone on the second floor of the restaurant. All other dining areas were on the ground floor. The trio wanted privacy and an undisturbed milieu so that they could have a memorable last gathering before all went their separate ways, perhaps never to meet again.

Engaged in giggling and happy conversation, they relived past events, confided secrets they would never have disclosed to a man, and promised to keep in close touch with each other for the rest of their lives. The three had adopted a close bond, similar to that enjoyed between An-an and Xi in Hong Kong. An-an noted the intimate relationship between Lydia and Ti and accepted it without question. She knew that Ti would be going to England with Lydia and Commander Fairborne. She guessed that there was more to the story than perceived, but was happy that Ti had a home to share with the Fairbornes.

The early dinner matched the reputation of the chef. Consisting mostly of seafood with excellent sauces, the meal was carried on large trays to their table. The waiters closed the dining room door and Lydia rose to lock it, then the women began to relax. An-an pushed aside the memory of her recent bitter encounter with Uncle Steve.

She chose not to bother Lydia and Ti with the story of that event, since she believed she needed more time to sort out her questions and primarily hurry to find her husband. She resolved to approach Commander Fairborne the next day to ask for his help. It would be a relief to leave her temporary seedy hotel room and board a freighter that could carry her northward to Manchuria. Together with Ellis Rogers, wherever he was, she believed they could resolve the matter of the stolen letters. For the moment, she urged herself to enjoy the happy gathering.

The laughter of the women was suddenly interrupted by a loud crash as the locked door was kicked in. The women looked up in startled surprise as intruders swarmed through the doorway. Seven men, none masked, rushed toward them. In a short few moments, the women were gagged and bound to their chairs. They recognized the leader of the gang immediately. The man they knew they should fear was the Japanese spy leader, Ariko.

Ariko had secured the hallway and had used other men to prevent anyone from coming up the stairs from the ground floor. Armed men had placed a closed sign on the front entrance and held the manager, kitchen staff and a few early guests hostage.

Ariko strutted before the struggling women and glared menacingly at them for several seconds. Finally, he spoke: "I have waited years for this moment. Now I will have my revenge." Sneering with smug satisfaction, he spoke first to An-an. "I never did like you or the American you were with in Peking. I hated you for being with him, but I hated him more because he was an arrogant westerner. Because of men like him, Japan was prevented from occupying the Philippines after the Spanish left." He spit on the floor. "The islands are rightfully ours. The Pacific is our ocean."

He walked toward An-an and removed the cloth band from her mouth. She spit out the wadded piece of cloth. "Make one scream," he threatened, "and I will cut your throat at once."

An-an squirmed to free herself from her bonds. Her lip curled as she said, "I know you from the expedition that freed the legations at Peking. The American and I kept our eyes on you because you always acted so unfriendly and different from your countrymen. They were honorable gentlemen. You were scum. I could always see the hatred on your face whenever I rode into the Japanese camp."

Ariko scoffed, "Well, I have you now. I failed to have your husband killed on the river boat when he first arrived in north China. I won't fail with you."

An-an remembered hearing her husband relate an attack made on him just upriver from the Taku forts on the Pei-ho river. How a Chinese mercenary had tried to cut his throat as he slept in the small deck cabin, and how the man had pushed a cobra snake through the porthole. Ellis had stated that he could never connect Ariko with that incident, but had always been suspicious because the hired mercenary was after the orders that he carried in a breast pocket.

Their friend Tanaka had told them during the campaign to ignore Ariko who was an intelligence agent who shunned combat and was universally disliked by his fellow Japanese.

Her husband had warned her to watch her back, explaining, "The man is sick. He hates anyone who is not Japanese. He has the mark of a murderer written all over him. Just stay away from him."

Staring at her tormentor, An-an was afraid, but not terrified like Ti. Ti was gasping for air, sure that her end had arrived. Standing before her, Ariko grasped her hair and pulled her head back and snarled, "You traitorous bitch. My career was almost ruined by that note you passed to me that night at the Golden Pavilion Tavern. I lost my assignment with Admiral Togo because of your deception."

Both Lydia and An-an knew the story of the note passed by Tea Flower, as she was then known, on that night just after the midnight hour of New Year's Eve one year ago. Ariko had been badly duped by Alesandrov, and Togo's surprise attack on the anchored Russian Fleet at Port Arthur had fallen far short of its intended goal. Since then, Ariko had seethed with anger as he imagined how the Russian must have gloated.

Ariko thought that his revenge had come when he had captured the injured Alesandrov at Seoul. He knew he should have killed the bastard at once instead of torturing and beating him half to death. Only Ariko's reassignment to Manchuria and the prominence of her husband had saved Lydia from Ariko's wrath.

He now lashed out at Lydia who sat staring at him with a look of cool contempt.

"And you," he stormed, "you robbed me of the chance to kill that Russian devil when you freed him from jail. You are no longer protected by your husband's position." He tore off Lydia's gag. "I want to hear you beg for mercy."

"Lydia smiled and used a favorite military epithet, "Up yours, you sod. When my husband and the Royal Navy get through with you, you'll wish you had never crossed me." Lydia's coarser side sprang forth, "You are pathetic, you little yellow dwarf."

Angry that his men had hear her insult, Ariko struck her face with his open hand. He turned abruptly to his followers and ordered them from the room. Locking the door behind them and now alone with the women, he unsheathed a knife and cut the rope binding An-an. "You are an ex-soldier, so I'll shoot you. Don't try anything." He stepped closer to Lydia and Ti, cutting their bonds also. "The knife is for you two. Slow and painful. I want you to suffer as I have." It surprised him that the women had not flinched. "I want all of you to beg for mercy."

The women did not back off, instead stepped forward one step. His arrogance made him careless. "He's too cocky, An-an thought. "He'll drop his guard. He may be good with a knife, but he's not a combat soldier and may be no good with a pistol."

An-an tried to draw attention away from the other two women by taunting Ariko, "Why are you not up at the front fighting the Russians instead of women. Are you not a man?"

Lydia had recovered from the blow to her face and cried out, "Our husbands will come after you if anything happens to us."

Ariko scoffed, "There are no witnesses. The restaurant people know better than to talk. No one will ever know what happened to you. Your husbands don't even know that you are here. You will disappear, but you will suffer first."

An-an continued to goad him, "Think again, smiley. One husband knows and the other soon will. I have been to the British consulate and I have conferred with them and an American War Department representative. Both know why I am in Shanghai and both know of your past behavior and threats. Your name will be the first mentioned if we are missing. You will not escape punishment or blame or retribution."

As they talked, the women had begun to edge away from each other in a circular pattern. Ariko was amused at the manuever and the obvious fear on their faces. He knew the women recognized the hopelessness of their plight and he believed they were only trying to escape. He was not concerned that he was alone with them. He enjoyed every minute of their anxiety. He had not unholstered his pistol and was recklessly disdainful about what the circling women might attempt. "Run for the door," he taunted. *It would be great sport to drop them like clay pigeons.*

Lydia screamed as she grabbed her purse and hurled it at him. It missed but served to distract him. He reached for his pistol and focused on her, giving An-an an opening. She sprang at his back, knocking him off balance. Grasping his tunic, she threw out her foot to trip him. If she had to die, she wanted to go down fighting. The two toppled against a table which collapsed, sending them sprawling beside the overturned table. Ariko's knife had fallen to the floor.

Another knife, a restaurant carving knife lay on the floor amid the spilled heap of food and dishes. Knives were not ordinarily present on a Chinese table, only chopsticks or, on a more affluent table setting, perhaps a large spoon or even a fork. The carving knife had arrived on the tray with the Peking duck. Ariko saw the knife and strained to reach it. He could not unholster his pistol because his body lay on one arm and An-an's weight pinned the other arm.

An-an also saw the shiny blade and struggled to break free. She flung an arm outward, barely touching the knife handle, but enough to flip it toward Lydia who had rushed forward to help her. Ti also ran toward the struggling pair on the floor. She scooped up the large pitcher of ice water from the floor and smashed it on Ariko's head. He had already struck An-an, pushing her off his other arm, and had almost regained a sitting position when the blow on the head knocked him prone. Before he could sit up again, this time with a drawn pistol, Lydia was on him like a tiger. Ariko dodged her and rolled onto his knees, pointing his pistol at the nearest target, Ti.

Ti tensed, awaiting the shock of the bullet. An-an was still trying to get to her feet and was too far to the side to help Ti. She flinched with horror, dreading the imminent explosion. Carving knife in hand, Lydia had regained her feet and threw herself forward to stab at Ariko's throat. He knocked aside the blade with his pistol hand and shoved Lydia to her knees. His pistol exploded with a roar. The bullet narrowly missed Lydia who struck again with the knife, not realizing that the dull point of the carving tool would barely penetrate Ariko's skin.

An-an and Ti rushed Ariko's blind side to distract him. He swung around to aim at them. Lydia, screaming in anguished frustration, scooped up the nearest object on the floor, a small lidless pot of curry sauce and paprika, and hurled it in Ariko's face. He blinked and involuntarily threw up his hands to rub his eyes, worsening the sting of the fiery condiment. His vision blinded, he gasped from the burning torment of the sauce and staggered in a circle.

Lydia again had retrieved the carving knife. This time, she lunged at the throat of the kneeling enemy, aiming for the side of his neck. The dull point of the carving knife barely nicked the muscle of his neck. She eluded Ariko's blinded clutch and darted behind him. Desperate with fear she raised the blade and slashed the sharp edge across his larynx. Choking on the blood that filled his throat, Ariko left an openng for her to repeat the slicing motion, this time the knife cut deeply into his carotid artery. He fell to his knees, throwing up his arm to ward off another cut. Blood gushed from his mouth. His curses began to fade to a choking, bubbly gurgle.

An-an clamped her hand on the pistol and threw herself forward. Before she could reach Ariko, she heard Lydia's savage scream and saw her grasp Ariko's hair to draw back his head for another savage slice. Ariko was through. His eyes glazed and his breathing faded as his life blood spewed forth. It was over.

For long moments afterward, the trio of hysterical women hugged each other, sobbing in wonder and relief at their escape. They ignored the pounding on the locked door.

Nigel Fairborne hurried to get Lydia and Ti out of Shanghai. He helped An-an by using his rank to secure a passage for her on a north-bound French freighter. Still shaken by their ordeal, the three women bade each other a tearful farewell.

An-an carried the letters she and Rogers had mailed to each other, Uncle Steve had produced them at the last minute with a denial of personal involvement and suggesting that a bureaucratic mixup beyond his control had misplaced the letters. He had delivered the letters to her hotel, wished her well on her journey and had even disclosed that Rogers was undoubtedly in Mukden.

An-an left at once, vowing she would never let the matter die so easily. If and when reunited with her husband, they would make Uncle Steve pay. Concealed on her person were certified letters of testimony from Nigel, the British consulate and Plum Blossom, and a certified copy of Ng's confession.

She could only hope she had not lost her husband and that she was not too late to find him. She prayed over and over that he would understand and forgive her long silence.

Uncle Steve posted a letter to Rogers, in answer to previous inquiries, trying to explain his lack of knowledge about any missing letters. Determined to foil An-an's search, he sent another letter to Mukden by regular mail, safe in the belief that the Japanese would probably intercept it before it reached Russian hands. In this letter, he hinted that An-an was a spy who spoke fluent Russian, knew Captain Viktor Alesandrov intimately, and traveled by passing herself off as the wife of an American military observer. Satisfied that she and the letters would be destroyed before she reached Russian lines, he relaxed. Who would miss a lone Chinese female traveler?

CHAPTER TWENTY-SEVEN

The French steamer, *Chevalier Rouge*, arrived in Dalny in the early morning hours of a cold April day. The Japanese army had done wonders in repairing war damage in the port city. The revitalized urban area bustled with Third Army troops boarding trains bound for the northern front. There was haste in moving the troops because of the need to throw fresh reserves into the battle for Mukden. The Japanese armies awaited an early spring thaw to begin the final assault on the city.

When An-an disembarked, she went immediately to staff headquarters of the Hiroshima regiment where Chen had advised her she could locate Captain Tanaka. Luckily Tanaka had not yet departed for the war front.

He had recognized her immediately and came forward to greet her. He bowed low and shook her hand. "You are prettier than ever and so feminine, even without your uniform." He laughingly referred to the British uniform coat she had worn while scouting for the American regiments in China during the Boxer Uprising. They had shared many adventures.

"What has it been? Four or five years, at least?" An-an averted her face to keep from staring at him. His disfiguring wounds shocked her. She hardly recognized Tanaka. It had been a long time since she had bade him farewell in Peking at the end of the China War. He was so thin and scarred and war damaged that she almost cried. Momentarily at a loss for words, she finally touched his arm and said, "Oh Tom, I am so sorry. How you must have suffered."

"Please don't pity me," he advised. He threw up his arms in dismissal. "I am still alive. What I need is the courage to go home."

"Go now," she implored. "How long has it been?"

559

"Fourteen months," he answered. "It seems like a lifetime."

"Don't wait, Tom. Ikura and Yukio want you home. If you don't have to stay, go back to them." They had talked about his wife and daughter so often in the past.

He shook his head. "Look at me. How can they accept me like this?"

"They will," she told him. "Believe me, they will and gladly. Go now. Don't wait to go home in an urn. Besides, from what I heard in Hong Kong, food is growing scarce in some parts of Japan. Your family needs you."

He shook his head again. "I can't. Not with so many buried here and so many others yet to die. It wouldn't be fair to them or to my emperor."

She saw that it was futile to argue. Changing the subject, she said, "I have not had breakfast, Tom. Is there a restaurant nearby where we can talk? I have a favor to ask of you."

Over luncheon at a newly opened Chinese restaurant, she told him her story and how desperately she needed to find her husband. "I hope I haven't lost him. So many terrible things have happened."

She told him about Chen and Marina. She already knew how Tanaka had aided them, so she told him of their arrival in Hong Kong. While they finished the meal, she told him of Ariko's death.

"It was a dreadful experience," she said, referring to Ariko's attack. "When I was sure he was dead, I confronted his henchmen with his pistol. With no leader, they panicked and ran away. The restaurant guests were sent home. The police came and took our statements. They took his body to the Japanese consulate and gave the excuse that some of his gang members had killed him. But the Japanese knew better. They hunted down and eliminated all of Ariko's gang. You can understand what a loss of face it was for the consulate. The British cooperated with the Japanese."

She told him about her life in Hong Kong and why her husband had been with the Russian army in Port Arthur. She made no mention of Alesandrov, although she was sure that he must be with her husband in Mukden.

She made little mention of Uncle Steve's betrayal, only that she now had all her missing mail, and how vital it was for her to find Rogers.

After hearing An-an's story, Tanaka told her of the series of battles that had see-sawed back and forth in Manchuria. He described the Japanese triumphs. "After our victories at Ulsan and Liaoyang, we needed to concentrate on conquering Mukden. With winter coming on early, we strove to win at Sha-ho in October. That was made more urgent when we learned that Russia's Baltic Fleet had started its journey in mid October. While the northern front stabilized during the winter stalemate, most of the fighting, probably the fiercest of the war, occurred in the hills behind Port Arthur. Our losses there were terrible during October, November and December. After Stoessel's surrender of Port Arthur on January 2, we hurried to build up the Third Army in order to help break the northern stalemate at Sandepu, which is about 36 miles southwest of Mukden. The battle for Mukden could start any day. I expect to come north in time for that battle." He sighed. "I wish I knew how much longer this war will last."

At the end of the meal, he promised to provide a rail pass for her travel toward the front. "But I would advise against such a journey. Our intelligence agents have warned of a coming large offensive by General Kuropatkin. You could be trapped up there. It will be difficult to get past our front line, anyway, and you would still have to get through the Russian line."

"I have to go," she insisted.

"Well, you might be able to hire a native to guide you on foot through the mountains to swing west past Mukden and come in from the north. Our army and theirs could shoot you as a spy. It will be terribly dangerous."

"I must go," she said simply. "I have no choice. It is a matter of life or death. I must find Ellis."

"I'll do what I can," he assured her. "There is a train leaving tomorrow. I'll get the pass for you. Please don't get caught. And watch out for the Siberian tigers."

He saw her at the train station the following morning. She wanted to hug him, but he maintained his rigid formality and bowed in farewell. Few words were spoken because of the curious military bystanders surrounding them.

An-an succeeded in reaching the town of Lamutan. But that was as far as she got by rail. Train travel from that point was restricted to military personnel because the area beyond was part of a stalemated battlefield. Both sides were gathering strength for the spring offensive. Unknown to An-an, Oyama's strategy was to deceive the Russian armies by pretending to marshall his forces for a strike both east and at the center of the Russian defense. Instead, he used Sylvia to spread false rumors that led the Russians to believe that Oyama had five full strength armies driving toward Mukden. In truth, the Fifth Army was hardly more than a division and a few battalions of reservists. And Nogi's Third Army had been moved from the rear to a position east of the Hun river.

Oyama's ploy worked. Thinking that the final Japanese drive toward Mukden would be east of the railway line, Kuropatkin withdrew forces from the west to concentrate on the east. Taking advantage of this misculation, Nogi led his Third Army in an westward arc around Mukden to try to cut the rail line leading north from Mukden. This also favored An-an's attempt to swing west and north of Mukden.

An-an refused to give up. She hired a guide to lead her through the mountain passes to the west, dodging Japanese patrols, and skirting Japanese front line outposts.

Getting across "no man's land" in the mountains was slow and dangerous for her. She had to contend with roving patrols, concealed snipers, hidden land mines, and the bitter mountain cold. The snow was dry on the eve of spring, the last cold spell before the snow would start to melt. An-an was grateful that the snow was dry and powdery. The crunch of wet snow underfoot would have been dangerously loud.

She learned to avoid certain areas where strands of wire festooned with chimes made of broken fragments of bottles or empty rusting tin cans stretched from tree to tree. Only a slight bump against the wires would alert those in the forward Japanese posts. She and her guide picked their way carefully past the wire to detour from Japanese outposts.

Disguised as a peasant woman, An-an made progress until the third day when her guide abandoned her. Before turning back he had indicated to her the northeast path she should take and had pointed to some far off landmarks she should aim for.

She traveled mostly at night to avoid any surprise encounters. Myriad stars overhead twinkled like gems on a necklace, but provided enough light to guide her path. She slept in short exhausted naps in clumps of bushes, always careful to walk backward in the snow to leave footprints to confuse military patrols. And always fear of the deadly Siberian tigers.

Her knuckles and cheeks were dry, red, and sorely chapped. Deviating from the serried ridges which ran northward, she had to plunge down each hillside and struggle across a flat plain to reach the next ridge. She studied the stars at night to ascertain directions, as Rogers had taught her to do.

Her last close encounter with the Japanese came when her fatigue caused her to brush against a wire hung with tin cans. She heard the whistle of a mortar shell, and threw herself headlong into the snow. Following the explosion of the shell, too close to be accidental, she lay still for a long time, banking on the hope that a patrol would not emerge until morning. She bunched snow around her body and almost screamed when her hand uncovered the long-dead fingers of a Russian soldier. Recoiling in horror, she began to slide cautiously across the snow to distance herself from the frozen corpse. Dreading another shell, she finally forced herself to stand and continue to wend her way through the trees. Vomit and blood along the trail indicated a group of pickets who must have fled north, coughing and spitting blood from long nights lying in the cold snow, always wet and sick.

At last, as morning neared, she came upon an abandoned outpost which she believed to be Russian. Faint footprints pointed to the north. Shortly before noon, she encountered a Cossack patrol. Addressing them in fluent Russian, An-an revealed her identity and asked permission to continue to Mukden, saying that she was traveling alone and had come through Japanese lines by the Hun river. She told them that her husband was a foreign observer attached to the Czar's army, and that she was also trying to contact Captain Viktor Alesandrov. "Could they help her?"

The patrol insisted on escorting her because of their suspicions that she might be a Japanese agent. Why would a Chinese woman, and a pretty one at that, be so conversant in the Russian language and be able to mount and ride a cavalry horse so easily?

Turning east, the patrol was nearing Mukden when shots in the distance to the south distracted them. "We have to leave," the patrol lieutenant told her. "You are on your own from this point. Turn the horse in when you reach the city and report to headquarters. They can help you find Captain Rogers. Give our name to Baron Alesandrov." He grinned and shouted as he rode away, "Try the hospital for the baron. He has a girlfriend there—a French nurse, Claudette."

* * * * * * * * * *

After dark, three of Sylvia's Manchurian servants appeared at a side door of the hospital where they waited patiently for the delivery promised to their employer. Sylvia had explained to them that the "bundle" they were to bring from the hospital was the carcass of a frozen hog that she had purchased from the hospital commissary. They had been cautioned not to disturb the wrapping of the bundle.

At the appointed hour, the unlocked side door opened and Dr. Zieman beckoned to them. They entered a small storage room. Zieman motioned to a bound bundle that lay on a table. Two narrow wooden boards were tied to the sides of the bundle to serve as carrying handles. Two of the servants grasped the boards and carried the wrapped object to a small cart that Sylvia had provided. The third servant gave Zieman a small box, bowed and hurried away. When they were out of sight, Zieman opened the box. Inside were two bottles of vodka, a small cloth bag containing a sizeable amount of ruble notes and coins, and a loaded revolver.

After her helpers had placed the bundle on a table in the tavern kitchen and had been dismissed, Sylvia unwrapped the army blankets and thin covering sheets of wool from around the corpse to reveal a young Chinese woman who had died of typhoid fever. The body carried the incipient odor of decay. She guessed that it had been thawing for a few hours from a frozen state. The sheet covered cadaver was curled in a tight fetal position that made its human form almost imperceptible.

Shuddering slightly, Sylvia sprinkled the corpse with kerosene and sawdust. She banked a low pile of sawdust on the floor around the table. Unsatisfied, she decided to place the body beneath the wooden table where it might burn more thoroughly. She pushed the corpse off the table onto the floor and started to pull the table over it when she cried out in alarm and began to curse. *Damn Zieman! How could he do this to me?*

Both feet of the body had come uncovered and the sight of them sent Sylvia into a frenzy. She saw the unmistakable "bound" feet of the Chinese corpse—feet that had been purposely crippled from years of binding with tight cloths that had pulled the toes and heel together to produce a severly high arch. Deformed feet were considered a mark of beauty by Chinese men who could enjoy the teetering steps of the owner and the sensual movement of the female posterior. The imprisoning custom was fast fading as Chinese women became more emancipated.

"Why couldn't the fool have given me the body of a Manchurian woman or a farmer's wife? Now what am I going to do?" she asked herself. Anyone who discovered the body, or what was left of it, would know it was not a caucasian foot. Even if the body were burned or charred beyond recognition, the foot bones would probably still be distinguishable.

She cursed Zieman again. The body could not be used. There was no alternative but to rush to the hospital and demand that Zieman produce another cadaver. But she had to burn the tavern that night. The place already reeked of kerosene and the floor was littered with sawdust and broken glass and the walls were bathed with tossed vodka. *What if Zieman refused her demand?*

Desperate for a solution and almost panicking from the lack of time, she dressed in one of the stolen nurse uniforms, quickly pulled on the blue cape, placed a small boning knife in her handbag, stepped out into the night and locked the door behind her. Almost sobbing with disappointment, she hurried along the street past sentries patrolling the streets to enforce the curfew. They respected her uniform and let her pass unchallenged.

Nearing the hospital, Sylvia heard a female voice call out to her in Russian. She halted and peered into the darkness. A figure approached her. Instead of a Russian face, she saw an oriental visage that spoke to her, "Excuse me, madam. Would you help me please? I am looking for the hospital. It is late and I must get off the street."

Sylvia did not respond to the query.

The voice continued, "My name is An-an Rogers. I am looking for my husband. Would you happen to know him? He is an American army officer attached to the Russian army."

After the initial shock, Sylvia's mind whirled with possibilities. She spoke slowly and deliberately. "Yes, I have met him. I was on my way to the hospital also. But you are right. We must be off the streets before the time gets later. Follow me and I will tell you how to contact your husband, but you will have to wait until daylight."

A sudden rain shower had begun to soak the streets. The two women hurried. Sylvia retraced her steps to the tavern.

Inside the building, Sylvia led An-an to the tiny bedroom, pointed to the small bed which she invited An-an to share. "Please don't come into the kitchen. The place stinks from fumigation by my helpers. They did not finish cleaning the floor, so I hope you can stand the odor. Nothing cleans a wooden floor like kerosene and sawdust, but they quit early and won't finish the task until morning—before I open for business."

An-an told Sylvia that she had stopped Sylvia because of the nurse's uniform. "I was trying to find the hospital because I have heard from a friend that there is a nurse named Claudette who knows my husband and also his best friend, a Russian army officer."

"Would that be a Cossack officer? If so, I know them both as customers."

"Yes, indeed. Oh, I am so happy that I met you."

Sylvia said, "I will take you to your husband and his Russian friend in the morning. You can stay here tonight if you don't mind sharing my small bed. There is no lodging in Mukden. The army has taken everything."

An-an was so tired and sleepy that she would have accepted a blanket and a place on the floor. She expressed her gratitude and began removing her shoes and dress. She hoped she could clean herself in the morning. Looking up, she saw Sylvia staring at her.

"You are very pretty," Sylvia told her.

Embarrassed, An-an flushed and turned her back. Sylvia eyed her hungrily, then turned to leave. She called out, "Don't wait for me. I will brew some tea for us and try to sweep up some of the kerosene-soaked sawdust. It has a bad smell because I have added a chemical to kill bugs and rodents. Please don't come into the kitchen."

When Sylvia returned, she found An-an fast asleep. At that moment, a sudden change came over the tavern owner.

An-an awoke to the overpowering odor of the kerosene and vodka. She was alone in bed. She could hear a noise in the adjoining kitchen. In spite of her exhaustion, the strong odor had awakened her. She sat up in bed until her head cleared a little, then swung her feet off the bed and stood up. She grimaced as her feet came into contact with a covering of kerosene and vodka-soaked sawdust. The bedroom floor was wet and slippery. She shuddered. *Something was wrong.* Groping her way in the pitch black darkness of the room, she found her clothing. She struggled into her dress, then sat down on the bed to pull on her shoes. Opening the bedroom door, she stumbled toward the light coming from the kitchen.

* * * * * * * * * *

Sylvia had spread a thick covering of sawdust all over the kitchen floor. After emptying bottle after bottle of vodka on the sawdust, she splashed the contents of the can of kerosene first on the walls, then on the naked corpse on the floor. Rushing to finish the task, she placed a path of newspapers on the floor—a trail that led to the front entrance. She had donned the nurse's garments and was fully dressed to meet the cold of the night. Humming a Russian lullaby, she picked up her packed valise, pulled a packet of matches from her pocket and headed for the front entrance.

Looking back as she stepped through the doorway, she saw An-an standing by the kitchen doorway, staring in disbelief. Sylvia pulled the door shut, and placed a key in the door, hesitating only long enough to crack the door open enough to drop a lighted match on the paper trail, then slammed the door shut and locked it.

Almost screaming with terror, An-an grabbed her coat and valise and rushed to the back entrance. The light in the kitchen had suddenly gone out, and flames were licking at the paper trail. An-an tripped over the cadaver and sprawled on the floor.

With a mighty whoosh, the tavern exploded in a massive fireball that defied all efforts to extinguish it. The explosion shredded the soaked walls, blew out the windows and doors and flattened the rear fence. An-an was propelled into the rear yard, saved from death and mutilation because the force of the blast had passed slightly above her prone body where she had fallen beside the cadaver. The awful heat of the fire forced her to rise from the brick-paved yard and stumble through the wrecked fence. She found herself on a street, fleeing the conflagration, running through the wet side streets toward what she hoped was the hospital. Almost hysterical and numbed by shock, she still clutched her purse and valise.

The army sentries and the curious crowd that gathered near the front of Sylvia's Place ignored the curfew to watch the flames devour the structure. The intensity of the inferno was shocking. With no ready supply of water nearby, soldiers and firemen and bystanders stood by helpless to halt the fire which reduced the tavern to a pile of ashes. A rumor spread through the crowd that that the tavern owner was missing and presumed to have perished in the flames.

An-an's intuition was correct. The hospital suddenly loomed up in the darkness. It was a large, ugly, sprawling building with an interior almost as dark as the cold night.

Once planned to be a hotel for Russian army officers, it had been converted to a hospital to accomodate the many wounded soldiers of the northern Manchurian campaign. Already overcrowded with the most seriously wounded of the battlefield casualties, the hospital faced a serious problem with its shortage of beds, staff, and medical supplies.

Stepped up schedules of train arrivals and departures had attempted to alleviate the overcrowding as the Russian army began evacuating increasing numbers of patients northward to Harbin. All in Mukden knew that the distant cannonading came from the start of a new Japanese offensive that had replaced the failed plan for a Russian drive to the south. Since the previous day, the glow on the horizon from Japanese artillery had drawn nearer. Extra train cars, attached to the Red Cross cars, carried staff officers and some civilians toward Harbin.

An-an's arrival in Mukden had coincided with the well executed start of an enormous Japanese offensive, now that General Oyama had his five armies moving from the south and east in a coordinated drive to capture Mukden. Again, the Russian armies had been caught unready and unable to ward off the onslaught.

The shortage of skilled surgeons and the overwhelming demands for their services had caused many of the staff, particularly Dr. Zieman, to spend most of the waking hours in the hospital dressing rooms, trying to snatch a few hours of sleep before the arrival of fresh casualties.

Zieman had fallen into an exhausted sleep in a chair in the small lobby. He was awakened by the shouting of a sentry at the front entrance. Curiosity at the sound of a woman's pleading voice caused Zieman to stand and walk toward the front door.

A young and pretty asian woman, bloodied and smudged with smoke and dirt, wearing a dress stained with blood from cuts on her arms, stood at the entrance pleading with the duty sentry to let her enter. She was soaked from the rain, still besmudged with soot and staring hysterically from some kind of shock.

Zieman interrupted the argument. "What is the matter?" he asked.

The sentry growled that the woman wanted to come into the hospital and he would not let her do so. "She says she has been in an accident— something about a fire—and is hurt and wants to see a doctor or one of the nurses. She is only a Chinese civilian."

Zieman interceded, His practiced eyes quickly scanned her appearance. "What is your name and where were you hurt?" he asked.

571

From his blood-stained white medical coat, An-an knew he must be a doctor. Throwing herself on his mercy, she said, "I am Mrs. Rogers, the wife of an American army observer here in Mukden. There has been an explosion. I think I am all right, but I need to come in out of the rain and get some medical attention for these cuts."

Zieman signalled for the guard to let her enter. He took her into a small side room for a quick examination, sponging off the cuts and applying a mild germicide. Aside from the supercial cuts and scraped knees and elbows, he could perceive no serious injuries. He informed her, "I will ask one of the nurses to help you clean yourself. We have no spare beds; many of the new patients are even sleeping on the floors of the corridors." He gestured toward the lobby. "You can use my chair. I'll sleep on one of the operating tables." Wearily, he turned to leave. "Goodnight. You can tell me in the morning. I must get some sleep." He saw the glow of a large fire a few blocks away and the sound of shouting people running toward the fire. Too weary to care, he left for one of the operating rooms.

In the morning he saw her coiled in the lobby chair, still soiled and still asleep. No nurse had tended to her. He decided not to awaken her, to let her rest, and have one of the morning shift nurses take care of her later. He was curious to hear her story, and he wondered if she might be the wife of the American officer he had seen so often with nurse Claudette's officer friend.

An-an awoke to a gentle shaking by a nurse. She had emerged from a nightmare in which she had seen a crazed nurse, engulfed in flames, crying out in suicidal terror, "What have I done?"

Stiff, sore, and headachy, and relieved to have the dream vanish, she could not at first remember where she was. Slowly recognition returned. Embarrassed by her appearance, she asked the nurse if there were some place where she could wash herself. The nurse nodded and pointed to a neaby water closet. "Pee in there. You can wash in the basin by the water spout. I'll get you a towel."

An-an stared after the retreating nurse. *The French accent. Could it be?*

At daybreak, Lebedeff examined the charred corpse which the firemen had pulled from the ashes of the tavern. Lebedeff called for an army surgeon to come look at the remains of the unrecognizable body. The surgeon concluded that it was a female body and was undoubtedly that of the tavern owner. Still intact around the upper vertebrae was a gold chain holding a Russian orthodox cross inscribed with the name, *Sylvia Levinski.*

Lebedeff began to harbor suspicions when he kicked through some of the rubble in the small rear yard and found the broken iron handle of the well pump. The fractured edge had not yet rusted. When he examined the well, he found a severed piece of rope that had held the well bucket used to raise water in case the well pump malfunctioned. No wonder the fire had burned out of control with no nearby supply of water.

Returning to the area that was once the kitchen, Lebedeff looked again at the body. At once, he was struck by the small size of the feet. He recalled the surgeon, asking him again if he had not noticed the odd shaped feet bones held together by charred flesh. The chagrined surgeon admitted that the feet must be those of an oriental, not a caucasian. Only a Chinese woman would have deformed "bound feet" like that, he told Lebedeff.

Lebedeff went at once to the office of the provost to sound an alert. Then he boarded the last evening train for Harbin.

Earlier, that same morning, the first departing train engine had chuffed northward toward Harbin, carrying cars filled with wounded soldiers. Two doctors, some medical corpsmen, and some Red Cross nurses tended to the men. One nurse was noticeably busy, moving about ceaselessly while avoiding conversation with the other attendants. The nurse was a stranger to the doctors, but they had accepted her as a welcome addition to the harried nurses.

At Harbin, this nurse inexplicably disappeared in the confusion of the crowded city.

Lebedeff arrived in Harbin where he had begun to interrogate train personnel about unusual passengers. When he learned about a reclusive woman, veiled, clad in black, and shunning contact with everyone, he was sure that Sylvia had survived the fire. A telegram sent to St. Petersburg, and also the detraining station at Lake Baikal, alerted Okhrana agents there to watch for the train's arrival.

An-an washed her soiled dress in the small wash basin. There was no soap, but she managed to erase most of the dirt and smoke smudges. When the nurse returned with the towel, An-an asked in Russian if she might borrow a hospital robe. The nurse, who had been looking at her closely, nodded and said, "You can borrow my robe."

The nurse went after the robe, wondering to herself how such a pretty and obviously culltured young Chinese woman happened to be injured and in such a remote military city as Mukden. A high ranking Russian officer's mistress? A local warlord's concubine? None of those labels seemed to fit. The woman was too self assured, and had too many western mannerisms, and was too comfortable with her nakedness.

An-an thanked the nurse for the garment. After a moment's silence, she asked the nurse in passable French, "Are you French?"

When the nurse nodded in the affirmative, An-an said, "Do you speak English? Is your name Claudette? If so, do you know a Russian officer named Viktor Alesandrov?"

The nurse laughed and said, "Mais oui, he is my amour."

An-an embraced her and began crying, "I am Ellis Rogers' wife. Can you help me, Claudette? Can you help me find Viktor and my husband?"

Three hours later, cleansed, fed, and bubbling with excitement from a long talk with Claudette, An-an followed her to the headquarters office of the Russian cavalry division.

She did not have to wait long for Alesandrov's arrival. He burst into the room to smother her with a mighty embrace. She suffered through his bear hugs, fond kisses and excited chatter of Russian as she repeatedly insisted, "My husband! Where is Ellis? Is he all right? Where is he?"

Her tall friend finally beamed down at her and answered, "He's fine. Angry, but fine. You have some explaining to do, my dear, so have a good story to tell him." He was well aware of Rogers' disappointment and hurt.

"Just take me to him. Please. I have so much to tell him. I'll tell you later."

The smile faded from Alesandrov's face. He told An-an, "As I said, he is in good health, but he has gone to Harbin on business. He was ordered to go there to meet a high ranking American observer. Something about a new assignment, I think in America."

* * * * * * * * * *

Rogers came to the Harbin train station in the hope that his friends, Viktor and Claudette, might be among the crowd arriving from Mukden. Each day had brought more and more staff officers and wounded army evacuees to the Manchurian capital. Rogers had seen the signs of a collapsing Russian defense and knew that unless the Russian generals changed their tactics and made a determined stand against the approaching enemy armies, Mukden would fall to Oyama's onslaught. He also knew that Viktor would insist on Claudette leaving Mukden early to escape more danger. She was a volunteer nurse and he had enough power to enable her to leave.

He recalled his last day in Mukden, sitting with Viktor in Sylvia's Place, brooding about the coming battle for Mukden. The Japanese armies were drawing ever closer and both Generals Kuropatkin and Linievich seemed unable or unwilling to stop them. It was the usual reluctance of Russian generals to be daring or innovative because their fear of failure and disgrace persisted.

The outward devotion for Claudette that Viktor always exhibited had brought back memories of Marina for Rogers. He wondered if he would ever see her again, or experience the passion of her body. Then, inevitably, the image of An-an would crowd out all other memories and his hurt and feeling of betrayal would be renewed. He wished some message from Hong Kong would come through from Marina and Chen. There had been no word from them. Had they uncovered any clue about An-an's disappearance and silence? Were they really searching? Or did they have bad news for him?

Even Uncle Steve's messages were infrequent.

He remembered sitting alone before Viktor's arrival—feeling depressed, lonely, and very weary of the war with the incessant cold weather, bad food, and constant defeatism. He needed a change. Maybe Uncle Steve was right in demanding that he go to Harbin. Maybe Mukden was doomed. Maybe even Harbin would soon follow the same path.

He had surrendered his hotel room to Viktor and Claudette. At the officers' barracks, he had slept uncomfortably on a rough wooden bunk. Most of the other foreign observers had departed for the safer Harbin. Several had deserted through Japanese lines to stay with the Japanese, as if they sensed the hopelessness of a Russian victory.

When Viktor had arrived, Rogers was cheered a little. Viktor was always such good company and refreshingly optimistic. Rogers, for months, had envied his friend's romance with Claudette. They were so obviously happy with each other. Victor seemed to offer Claudette a good refuge from the horrors of her hospital caseload and she, in turn, gave him the needed outlet for his galloping libido.

The two officer's had talked for the better part of an hour. Sylvia was not as hospitable as usual. Viktor had made a joke about her sullen attitude and had called her attention to the absence of champagne. She had merely shrugged and walked away without answering. Rogers had also noticed how her stock of beer and vodka had dwindled.

The last telegram that Rogers had received from Uncle Steve had demanded more information and analysis about the collapsing Russian front, and, uncharacteristically, had expressed gratitude for Rogers' good work in Mukden. Feeling the pressure of Uncle Steve's insistence for the truth about the Russian front, and for him to meet with a certain American colonel, an important military emmisary there, Rogers had departed for Harbin to seek an explanation for the troubling and continuing series of Czarist military defeats. The rebellious Russian soldiers, though cursing their officers, went stoically to their deaths day after day. If the riots and demonstrations on the home front continued, the unrest among the soldiers would surely worsen and there would be a military rebellion.

Claudette had told him about the alarming increase in self-inflicted wounds that had occurred. And suicides among untried junior officers, ordered to the front lines, had become painfully prevalent. To add to the woes of the Manchurian forces, the cream of the Russian army was still kept in western Russia to cope with open rebellion by segments of the civilian populace, and to safeguard Russia's western borders against German or English rivals.

At the Harbin train station, Rogers watched the unloading of stretchers from the rail cars. This was the face of war that disturbed him most. Men whose lives had been forever altered or even ruined lay on the stretchers, deposited in orderly rows on the crowded station platform. The few available nurses moved among the wounded, brushing away flies, offering a drink of water, and occasionally pulling a blanket over the face of those who had expired.

One of the nurses caught Rogers' attention. There was something familiar about the shape of her body, and her movements. When she had turned to look at him, he knew at once it was the owner of the tavern in Mukden. *So she had volunteered her services for the army? How noble! What had happened to her business, Sylvia's Place?* He started to approach her, though wary of the look of hatred on her face. A sudden call from out of the crowd distracted him.

"Rogers, I say there, Rogers!" He did not see anyone familiar at first in the crowd behind him, so thought the shout may have been for somebody else. When he turned back to look at Sylvia, she had disappeared. Then he realized that the shout must have been for him, since the language was

English and the accent definitely American. Looking again at the crowd, he spotted three officers clad in American uniforms. Two were young lieutenants; the third was a tall and erect bird colonel who beckoned to him. He approached the trio and saluted the colonel who had extended his hand. After greeting the colonel's aides, Rogers addressed the senior officer, "How good to see an American uniform from the Philippines."

In the past, the familiar colonel had chewed him out on a couple of occasions, but then he had been a stern taskmaster for all junior officers on Mindanao. Rogers thought of Uncle Ben Wallace. "How is the Tenth Cavalry, colonel?"

"Excellent. They could teach these people a thing or two." It was obvious to Rogers that the colonel saw a lot of flaws in the Russian command system. Unlike the American army that gave enlisted men considerable freedom of action in combat, the Russian commanders denied such independence to the Czarist soldier. And so did the Japanese command for its men.

The colonel explained that he was present with his team to study the collapsing Russian front. They had arrived only recently and reflected America's shifting sympathy for the Russian defeats. The colonel belonged to a school of advocates of "open warfare," favoring attack rather than defense movements. He had no love for wars of attrition or for stalemated trench warfare and hoped to understand the lessons to be learned from the Russian debacle. He had learned enough to appreciate the value of Rogers' information, which he now intended to extract. The team wanted to debrief Rogers as soon as possible before they left the Harbin area.

The colonel said, "We are leaving day after tomorrow to return to Korea. Your commander, General Arthur MacArthur is there to watch the Japanese system. Has his son, young Douglas, with him."

Rogers could sense that officers from the Philippines were arriving to observe the conflict in Manchuria now that the war approached a climax. He recalled MacArthur's son, a young lieutenant, who had always been overly ambitious and well protected by his father and politically active mother. Rogers could not help asking himself where had these Americans been when he had gone through the hell of the Port Arthur siege?

The colonel wanted to pick his brain and Rogers was happy to oblige. It was a joy to converse with kindred spirits. He unburdened himself at dinner that evening, describing the warfare at Port Arthur and the lessons he learned there. But he saw the expressions of doubt when he told of how well the civilian populace of the port, though discontented and often rebellious, had withstood the shelling of the town. "Civilians will endure an amazing amount of punishment without surrendering," he stressed. "Stubbornly besieging a city or town for weeks or months may not be the best strategy against courageous civilians." And though he knew that the colonel was a cavalryman, the favored branch of the military, he told him of the inevitable replacement of cavalry by observation balloons that could efficiently direct artillery fire, if used properly.

He saw more doubt when he described the Russian use of the deadly hand grenades to assault enemy positions, knowing that his own army favored the rifle and bayonet. He told the team how quickly the Japanese had converted the wide gauge Russian rail tracks to accomodate their own narrower gauge locomotives. "Rapid movement of troops is essential," he reminded the team. "If the rail system is lacking, then roads need to be properly built and maintained. Muddy quagmires will inhibit transportation, so I see the coming importance of motor vehicles, especially heavy trucks with good motor maintainence men."

He enlightened the colonel and his lieutenants with all that he knew. One of the aides jotted down rough but copious notes. The colonel seemed to be greatly impressed with the information. After sending the two lieutenants to the bar to inquire about American beer, he leaned closer and confided quietly, "I know why you are here, Rogers. I received a coded message from the War Department before I came up from Mindanao. Except for the Department representative in Shanghai, no one else knows. Just keep up the good work."

No more was said about Rogers' mission and there was no direct reference to Uncle Steve by name. The aides returned to say that the Russian supply of beer was limited and did not include any American brands.

The colonel concluded, "You will stay on to see this thing finished, I'm sure. I am going to recommend that you be assigned to any peace commission that may evolve in the next few weeks. As you probably may not know, the Japanese have advanced peace feelers. Their ambassador in Washington has approached President Roosevelt, requesting that he act as a mediator to end the war. The president is interested and I am sure that the Russians will agree. They will have to. You must have heard about their Baltic Fleet?"

When Rogers told the colonel that he had little knowledge of the Baltic Fleet, because the Russian staff was undoubtedly withholding such information in order not to upset troop morale, the senior officer proceeded to relate the naval news. How the Baltic Fleet had finally departed from Russia after months of delay and how, in an unready condition, had recklessly entered the North Sea where they had encountered a fleet of English fishing trawlers at night amid heavy fog. Thinking the trawlers were Japanese warships, the Russians had panicked and had fired on the trawlers, causing several English casualties. "That action was inexcusable," Rogers was told. "The English press clamored for a war declaration and demanded reparations. The Russians will have to pay.

Everything went wrong after that. The Fleet began to run out of coal in the Mediterranean; some of the warships broke down and had to be repaired. It was a long and slow voyage. After exiting the Suez Canal weeks later, the ships finally reached the French Indo-China coast. Meanwhile, the Japanese will have tracked every ship movement and are undoubtedly preparing a deadly welcome in the Japanese Sea. The Russians will have to charge right into the Tsushima Straits and be trapped and annihilated by the waiting Japanese fleet. Thousands of brave Russsian sailors will die—really in vain because Port Arthur has already fallen. The Baltic Fleet will be too late to be of any use. It is a disaster waiting to happen."

He shook his head in disgust. "If I didn't know better, I'd have to say the Russian high command wanted to lose this war. Sure the Japanese hit them first without warning, but even then it should not have been such a surprise. After the Pacific Fleet was so badly crippled at Port Arthur, the Russians admirals seemed to do everything wrong. They have always badly underestimated the Japanese and let them take the initiative in battle after battle. You don't win wars by letting your opponent take the iniative."

Rogers knew that weakness only too well. It was rewarding to hear someone else agree with him. Of course, the Japanese had committed blunders too, but they had fought as a unified army without the jealousies and command divisiveness of the Russian army. He did point out that Russia could still get its act together and have a chance to win the war. "If the Japanese keep stretching their supply lines, they will be lured ever deeper from Manchuria into Siberia and be hurt. Russia is still big and powerful and could still commit its European army into the eastern front."

The colonel did not think so, that it was too late. "Russia faces an internal revolution. The Czar's power is threatened and he may have to compromise with his people. The Russian population is as weary of war as the Japanese. Both belligerents should stop the war now."

Rogers remarked that the Japanese could declare a victory and demand that Russia pay for the war and give up some territory. "The Japanese soldiers will gladly die for their emperor and the Japanese people will accept the loss of so many soldiers if there is a final victory. On the other hand, Russia may still negotiate good peace terms. She can recover and get revenge at a later time."

The colonel nodded. "That is why we need your expertise at a peace table. Neither side should win overwhelmingly or else they will be at each other's throats a few years down the road. As I said, I will put you in for a transfer to stateside. When was your last leave?"

He was appalled at what he heard. "You have not had a leave in over five years? Why?"

Rogers shrugged and grinned. "I have a mentor in the War Department—in Shanghai. He thinks I am invaluable, I guess."

"Bullshit," the colonel exploded. "I'll look into that matter, even if I have to knock over some chairs in Washington." He was well acquainted with Washington politics and knew the influential Senator Warren very well. And Senator Warren carried great weight over the War Department promotion list.

CHAPTER TWENTY-EIGHT

A west bound train left Harbin late that night for the long journey across Siberia. Besides the loaded cars of even more wounded soldiers, the westerly train transported two cars loaded with military dependants fleeing Harbin, the next target of the Japanese armies if Mukden failed to halt the Japanese offensive. A black-clad and heavily veiled woman sat apart from the others, blocking her passenger seat with a large valise. Most of the passengers presumed she was the grieving widow of a recently killed senior military officer. They respected her privacy. At the train's first stop, several hours away from Harbin, the passengers returned from a visit to the station's primitive toilet facilities, and lined up for a chance to buy some bread and sausage from the local food counter. They had found the veiled woman's seat unoccupied. Most assumed she had moved to the second passenger car.

It had been "cold as hell," in Mukden at the end of February. At least that was the label used by Rogers to show his displeasure with the Manchurian weather. "If I ever go to a hot climate and complain," he told himself, "I don't deserve pity."

January, 1905 had been brutally cold; but the month of February had been worse. To add to the misery of the common soldier on both sides of the conflict, the Japanese high command had relentlessly persevered in their attacks. Traditionally, soldiers halted hostilities and went into winter quarters to await warmer spring weather. Not in this wretched war. The Russian commanders, numbed by indecision and lack of imagination, kept retreating as Oyama's men pursued the attack.

When Uncle Steve had directed Rogers to go north to Harbin, he feared, and much of the world had conceded, the likelihood that Mukden was doomed. He hated to leave Viktor and Claudette behind to face the coming battle. Viktor, though disgusted with Russian leadership and politics, and worried about Claudette's safety, loyally refused to go to Harbin with Rogers.

The loss of Liaoyang had been a blow from which Russia never recovered. Continuous retreats and the defeat at Sha Ho had obliberated any hope that Kuropatkin could rescue Port Arthur. The recall of Admiral Alexeiev to St Petersburg had relieved Kuropatkin of that official's constant meddling. But the dispatch of General Grippenberg to head the newly formed Second Manchurian Army was a bad error on the part of the Russian Czar. Grippenberg was untried and unready and a fatally weak choice.

At the end of January, following the Winter Palace massacre of civilians in St. Petersburg, the Czar had telegraphed Kuropatkin to start an offensive in order to prevent Nogi's Third Army from joining Oyama's four armies gathering before Mukden. Local rivers remained frozen in the brutal cold. Captured Japanese prisoners revealed that the Japanese were suffering from the elements as badly as the Russians. Oyama had even relaxed his uniform code to permit the Japanese soldiers to wear sensible Chinese quilted coats.

Alesandrov had been sent south with a 6,000-man cavalry and artillery group to try to disrupt Nogi's Third Army march north from the captured fortress of Port Arthur. The object of the Russian group was to cut the rail line and destroy stockpiled food and ammunition at Newchang. But the lack of forage for the horses in the devastated countryside slowed the march by two days, allowing the Japanese to prepare a strong defense. Three cavalry charges against the supply depot failed, and the Russians had to return to an area near Sandepu, a few miles north of Sha Ho and west of the Mandarin Road and the railroad.

Russian general Grippenberg had attacked Sandepu in the face of a howling blizzard. In spite of numerical superiority, he made a series of errors that enabled the Japanese to retain the village, which now effectively separated the two Russian army corps. Subsequently, Grippenberg and a corps commander, Stakelberg, were relieved of their commands. The toll of 20,000 Russian and 9,000 Japanese casualties left army hospitals unable to cope.

The London *Times* pointed out that the Russian soldiers had been told repeatedly that they would defeat the Japanese as soon as the enemy had been flushed from their mountain strongholds and forced to fight on the plains. That prophecy had rung hollow after Liaoyang, then Sha Ho, and later Sandepu. And now the crucial battle for Mukden loomed far to the north.

However, Japan's inability to crush Kuropatkin had put pressure on Oyama to achieve an overwhelming victory to end the war, or else the financial markets aiding Japan might dry up. And Oyama had begun to face a manpower shortage with continuing high casualties and lack of replacements from Japan's depleted army reserves.

Kuropatkin had continued to react rather than act. His deployment of forces convinced the Japanese that he would stay on the defensive in trying to protect Mukden. So Oyama had decided that the best strategy would be to lure Kuropatkin into a decisive battle on the Mukden plains. By using deception, he hoped to convince Kuropatkin that the Japanese planned to marshall their forces in the hills for an attack from the west in order to avoid the plains where superior Russian cannon and a larger cavalry force had gathered.

Oyama had played on Kuropatkin's self deception by using various means of misinformation to fool him. He had fed fake information to recognized spies such as the very effective Sylvia Levinski, Lydia Fairborne, and her one time lover, the Austrian officer, Uberleutnant Rupert von Streich, who was attached to Japan's Fourth Army.

The Russians moved large numbers of men from the plains to guard against an attack on Mukden from the hill country. At the end of February, the convergence of Oyama's five armies south and east of Mukden started the battle for Mukden. Superior use of Japanese artillery and successful flanking tactics continued to roll back the Russians in spite of their strong defensive trenches. Very little of the lessons learned the previous year seemed to have impressed the Russian generals. By the start of March, Rogers could tell by the hordes of wounded Russian soldiers, arriving by train from Mukden, that the fighting there had been both bitter and disastrous.

He absorbed as much of the scene as possible to add to his next report to Uncle Steve in Shanghai. But it was becoming tiresome to describe the continuous Russian defeats. And Russian censorship had become a burden. He had to be careful what he reported and even more cautious in dispatching his notes to Shanghai.

He had no choice but to live with the Russian army and suffer their same hardships. Occasionally, once a week, he could join scores of naked men crammed into a steaming bathhouse to wash away the grime of trench warfare. He quickly shed his puritannical aversion to seeing stark naked men soaping, scrubbing, and rinsing each other. The baths were wonderfully refreshing in spite of the aftermath of returning to the outside bitter winter weather and the stark barracks to continue the monotonous, animal-like existence.

In the past he had compared notes with an adventurous reporter named Wicks Newins, a Reuters correspondent with whom he had lived and died in the siege of the foreign legations of Peking almost five years earlier. The two enjoyed a special bond. Rogers was delighted to chance upon Newins at Russian headquarters where Newins, although working for a British news service, was tolerated because his copy usually favored the Russian side.

Newins was exuberant. "God in heaven, how glad I am to see an American face, old friend! This must be my lucky day. I had a miserable time getting here last week, and I have been getting a frosty reception since. These people are not only uncooperative, they are the unhappiest bunch I have ever seen."

"How did you get here?" Rogers asked. He wondered if Newins had arrived from Russia or had come in by way of the Harbin-Vladivostok railway.

"Neither," Newins replied, "I've been with the Japanese the last few months. I was cut off in the Russian retreat and rounded up by the Japanese at Liaoyang."

Rogers was astonished. "You mean you got back through the front lines without being shot?"

"It took a little money," Newins admitted. "Wait until Reuters gets my cost account." He proceeded to tell Rogers that he had not yet seen many foreign correspondents in Harbin. "There are a lot of them with the Japanese."

Rogers agreed that most western correspondents were with the Japanese army, because the world still favored a Japanese victory. Few newspapers wanted to follow a defeated belligerent. He finally asked the newsman why he had decided to link up with the Russians.

"Too many news people with the Japanese. We were all writing the same copy. But, frankly, my main gripe was how the Japs ignored us. It kept getting worse. We were always kept in the rear. We were not permitted to watch combat or view the front line. It did no good to complain. They tried to keep us all in the dark, even the foreign army people. So I decided to switch sides. Maybe I'll have better luck here."

Rogers warned, "If you want to get your ass shot off here, the Russians will be happy to oblige." He proposed that they get something to eat. "Then we can compare notes and I promise to fill you in on who's who in the Mukden-Harbin command."

Newins continued to list the press corps frustrations. "I remember there was one belligerant German army officer who told off the Japanese for refusing him permission to climb a hill to view the action in the valley. The Japanese liaison officer told the German, a Captain Hoffman, that the hill was off limits. Hoffman exploded, saying in essence, 'We trained your army and taught you everything. You are of the yellow race and uncivilized. Now, damn you, I will climb that hill.' But the Jap quietly told him, 'You are not going,' and walked away. Kind of dumb, because Hoffman thoroughly understands Russian mentality. He could have been useful to the Japanese.

There are some Americans there who are also miffed. One of them is from the Philippines. Maybe you know him? Captain Pershing?"

"Good Lord, yes. I was with him in Cuba and served under him on Mindanao. Black Jack Pershing. A soldiers's soldier—he's a career soldier who is going places some day."

"Why the name Black Jack?"

Rogers explained that it was because John Pershing served so long with his favorite troops, the Negro 10th U.S. Cavalry Regiment. "He chased

Indians with them at Wounded Knee, made Roosevelt's victory possible at Kettle Hill in Cuba while he, Pershing, charged up adjacent San Juan Hill. Down on Mindanao, the Filipinos love him because he is rough on the Moros. He speaks the Moro tongue, knows their culture inside and out, and how they use the Moslem religion as an excuse to kill Christian Filipinos. He learned early that you can never trust a Moro."

Newins said, "There are several free lance reporters also with the Japanese. One very interesting fellow is the writer Jack London. He's quite a story teller, especially when he is drunk."

"I agree," Rogers exclaimed. "I love his book, *The Sea Wolf.* Brought back some vivid memories of my life at sea, although some were not so pleasant."

Before the day ended, Rogers found a better place for Newins to stay. The journalist seemed to have a generous expense account and insisted that Rogers share his room. Rogers was glad to accept. Anything to escape the dismal, cold Russian barracks. The two spent hours reminiscing about the long ago siege in Peking, where Newins, a civilian volunteer, was in the thick of combat atop the Tartar Wall.

But bad thoughts crowded Rogers' mind when Newins inquired about An-an. "What ever happened to your Chinese lady friend?"

"I married her," Rogers countered. "With this war and all, it's been a long time since I have seen her." With that, he let the topic drop and changed the subject.

* * * * * * * * * *

The Battle of Mukden was hell for the civilians of Mukden. When the first enemy shells began to pound the inner defensive trenches outside the city, the panic stricken shopkeepers and civilian dependents clamored to escape the city's imminent destruction. The incessant bombardment, the loud explosions, the daily parade of mud splattered and bloodied soldiers retreating into the city, the piles of dead soldiers awaiting burial, the jammed hospital unable to receive more casualties, all completely unnerved even those experienced and battle hardened.

The crowds struggled for survival and clamored for escape northward. There were not enough trains to transport everyone, although ten trains a day were now in service for the Russian army. Civilians were beaten back as the army commandeered every spare rail car. After a week of battle, the defenders of Mukden bowed to the inevitable. Defenses crumbled, forcing Kuropatkin and his staff to order the city evacuated. The 190-mile retreat to Harbin began.

The army headquarters staff seemed to have forgotten the thousands of wounded soldiers in the hospital in their haste to depart the city. Alesandrov refused to leave without Claudette and An-an. And Claudette refused to leave those in her care who would be left to die of neglect. Alesandrov and other courageous officers piled hay into empty freight cars and stuffed as many casualties as possible into the makeshift railway wards. Using threats and even shooting some of the worst malingerers, they were able to attach the temporary hospital cars to departing locomotives. Alesandrov used his Cossacks to round up baggage wagons, throwing trunks, furniture, and household goods into the street to free space in the wagons for the remainder of the hospital patients. Those left behind were deemed too badly wounded to be moved, with others too hopelessly sick to survive.

Alesandrov refused to let Claudette and An-an out of his sight. With them at his side he drove one of the last loaded wagons to leave the city just ahead of entering Japanese cavalry patrols. Claudette listened helplessly to the moans and cries of the wounded patients being roughly jostled on the rutted, narrow road crowded with walking refugees. At periodic pauses along the escape route, Alesandrov and other wagons halted to disgorge their dead. Military convicts under heavy guard dug shallow graves to bury those who died along the way. The long winding procession finally reached Harbin days later. The Japanese, not wishing to destroy the historic and ancient city, occupied Mukden peacefully, and then their armies halted.

* * * * * * * * *

Amid the chaos of hordes of disoriented troops pushing into Harbin, Rogers faithfully continued writing dispatches to Uncle Steve, hoping that most of the mail would successfully reach Shanghai. The arrival of warmer weather had done little to dispel his gloom. Everywhere, czarist soldiers were refusing to fight. Desertions increased. Sullen arriving troop replacements reflected the anti-war riots sweeping throughout the homeland.

One day in June, while visiting Kuropatkin's headquarters, Rogers was approached by a junior officer from the Kiev regiment.

"Begging your pardon, sir, I have a message for you. Captain Alesandrov of the Don Cossacks asked me to find you. You can find him at the Muscovy restaurant—he has a surprise for you and would like to meet you there."

Rogers finally smiled. *So Viktor had gotten away from Mukden! How about Claudette?*

He hurried down the teeming thoroughfare toward the restaurant centered in the city near the train depot. He pushed through the mass of people and bullied his way to the front entrance, where he flashed some

592

ruble notes that enabled him to choose an empty table situated in a small curtained alcove. He tipped the head waiter to find Alesandrov, knowing he had to be in the building somewhere. While waiting, he ordered a bottle of champagne, and sat scowling at those who wanted to share the table. He could hear Alesandrov's name being called.

A sudden movement of the curtain parting caused him to look up. Viktor and Claudette crowded the entrance. Viktor had a mischievous grin on his face. When Rogers leaped to his feet to greet them, he received the shock of his life. Viktor stood aside to reveal a third person behind him. It was An-an.

She began to cry hysterically as she rushed toward him. Flinging her arms about her husband and clutching him fiercely, she called his name repeatedly: "Ellis, Ellis, oh Ellis."

Finding his voice at last, he murmured, "It's all right. Don't cry." He was a little embarrassed because people were staring. And a little annoyed with himself because he was so reserved. The wall that he had built around himself the past year and the shock of her appearance had numbed him. He struggled to find the myriad questions he had to ask.

Both blinded by emotion barely heard Viktor say, "We need to find quarters for the night, so please excuse us. We will catch up with you later."

Alone with An-an behind the curtain, Rogers patiently tried to calm her. It took considerable effort. She clung to him as if fearful he would disappear. At last her sobs subsided and she was able to tell him about the missing mail. She laid a package of her letters on the table. Slowly, she began to relate what had happened in Shanghai.

As she talked, he fought to control his anger. What he was hearing seemed inconceivable. His mood alternated between anger and disappointment. He might have killed Uncle Steve had he been present. At the end of the narration, he smashed his fist on the table top and swore that he was through. Through with the army, through with the war, through with the whole bloody business. His world had crashed and all he could think of was how to get out and to do so at once. He relented enough to assure An-an that, of course, his plans included her. "I'll get hold of myself," he promised. "I need some time to think."

He found Viktor and Claudette the next day—or rather they found him at headquarters where he was seeking a pass to Vladivostok. Viktor relayed the news that he had been ordered to entrain for Sevastopol to help quell the rioting populace. It was not a duty that he relished. He informed Rogers, "Of course, I'll insist that Claudette leave also. The unrest there is bad. And in Odessa, scores of civilians have been shot. Mutinous sailors have seized the battleship *Potemkin* and have taken her to Rumania."

When Alesandrov heard Rogers state his determination to resign his commission and board a ship in Vladivostok bound for Shanghai, he confided that he too might resign.

"I have been thinking about it lately. I would have to pull strings or ask for a reassignment or leave the country or something, but I could do it. There is little hope left; the war has to be almost over. The Czar must be discouraged. Everyone seems to be impotent and unable to make a decision. I am fast losing my patriotism." He breathed a deep sigh. "I tell you Ellis, I would love to stay for one good Russian victory. I would relish seeing Oyama's armies sucked into Siberia where they can be cut off and wiped out. They don't realize how big that place is. It is such a long way from their supply base in Korea." He sighed again. "Damn this country. The Japs can't keep winning. Let them have Manchuria. We'll slaughter them in Siberia."

Rogers agreed. "I too think the war is nearing an end. The Japanese can't push on much farther without endangering themselves. If your goverrnment commits a couple of well trained armies from eastern Europe, the tide will turn. The Japanese economy can't support the war another year. But the unrest in Russia is worsening and if it keeps up, Russia will have to sue for peace."

He asked Viktor, "If you do resign, what are your plans?"

"I don't know, Ellis. I have my land and my inheritance money. If Claudette is not happy in Russia, we'll find another country. Europe is a big place."

Few conversations with Alesandrov followed after that. Fate, as usual, intervened.

In the days that followed, before he and An-an could leave Harbin, they explored all their options. Both resolved to find a solution. Both agreed that they had to leave Harbin as soon as possible, even though the war was settling into a stalemate. First, he wired a message to Uncle Steve. The short and curt note stated his resignation from the army, and expressed anger at the way he had been treated, and that Uncle Steve could expect to see him soon.

* * * * * * * * * *

An-an had told him everything, so a few days later at the train depot, he was somewhat prepared when she had clutched his sleeve and cried out, "There she is! Over there! That crazy Russian woman from Mukden!"

He knew at once that she meant Sylvia Levinski. When he saw Levinski, he started to run toward her with An-an close behind. Sylvia was on the station platform across the tracks from where they had stood, screaming profanities at them. Rogers had leaped down from the platform and had started to run across the double set of tracks. He reached the opposite platform and drew his revolver when he saw the small pistol in her hand. He started to climb up on the platform. Sylvia fired a shot at him. The bullet missed him, striking sparks from the iron railing he had grasped. Ducking, he turned to An-an close behind him, and shouted for her to hide below the platform edge.

Panic-stricken bystanders screamed and ran in all directions. He raised his head to aim a shot at Sylvia just in time to see her reach into her bag and bring out a small bomb. He recognized the small black round iron ball with a short fuse protruding from the top. Before he could level his weapon to aim at her, she had already struck a match to light the bomb fuse. Trapped on the train tracks between the two platforms and with nowhere to hide, Rogers reached for An-an.

Sylvia tossed the bomb at them and ran toward the station house. Rogers leaped toward the sputtering fuse, scooped up the small bomb and flung it over the platform edge toward Sylvia. He pulled An-an close to him and tried to shield their bodies below the platform. The bomb exploded, sending shards of jagged metal and a cloud of black smoke into the air. When Rogers raised his head, Sylvia had disappeared. He turned to the sound of a loud shout and saw a man, whom he recognized as the Okhrana officer, Lebedeff, rushing toward him with drawn pistol.

But Sylvia had vanished and Lebedeff and his agents could not find her. Later he informed Rogers that earlier he had sealed all approaches to the St. Petersburg rail station when he had learned that a disguised woman fitting her description had boarded a north-bound train the day after the tavern fire in Mukden. A subsequent search for her all along the train depots of the Siberian railway and in St. Petersburg had produced no results. Now

Lebedeff realized that she must have disembarked somewhere outside of Harbin and perhaps again doubled back into the city to fool her pursuers. But where had she disappeared to now?

Smugly smiling after her escape in disguise from Harbin, Sylvia managed to elude the waiting Okhrana agents at Lake Baikal. Carrying only her purse containing money and a revolver, she vanished into the thick forest growth behind the Lake Baikal station. While in Harbin, she had contacted a rebellious group of Siberians who had furnished her with a map of the location of an "underground" farmhouse near the lake, promising that the army deserter occupants there would provide her with shelter for a month or two until she could resume her flight to Moscow.

She followed the path traced on a small map. The path was already becoming faint as the sun dipped over the horizon and late afternoon shadows made the dense forest darker than she liked. She made her way past wild rose bushes, patches of violets and buttercups, and tangling wild grape vines. Huge rhododendron bushes that had become trees hung over the path like a brilliant canopy. She breathed the clean fresh air, so different from Harbin's smoky atmosphere.

But her anxiety increased when she realized how dark the path had become. Fancied noises and ominous shadows caused her heart to palpitate wildly. She quickened her pace.

Ahead of her and off to the left, a huge Siberian tiger reared upward to sharpen his two-inch long claws on a conifer tree. Called Hu Lin, "The King," by local hunters, who had unsuccessfully sought him in the past, the giant cat began marking his territory on the tree and path with his urine. Hu Lin was hungry and restless.

The Tiger Hu Lin / New Hampshire Peace Conference

The Tiger Hu Lin

16b Official photograph celebrating the Treaty of Portsmouth. President Roosevelt is in the centre, with Witte on the extreme left. Baron Rosen stands between these two, while the small unhappy man with large ears is the Japanese plenipotentiary, Komura

Foresters in the area were now wary of the tiger after coming across the torn clothing and gnawed bones of two men who had been missing for weeks.

Unaware of invading the cat's territory, Sylvia hurried on, hoping to find the farmhouse before evening shadows closed in and she would be walking in total darkness. Once she looked back and thought she saw two gleaming yellow eyes. She stopped for a moment, then began to panic, She started to run, tripping over vines and lashed by hanging tree limbs. She dashed down the forested path, wrapped in a cloak of fear that engulfed her senses.

Out of the shadows the savage predator suddenly lunged forward and sprang on her back, its usual mode of attack. Before she could scream, the animal dug its hind claws into the back flesh of her legs, and sank its sharp fangs into her neck, severing her spine.

CHAPTER TWENTY-NINE

From Harbin, Rogers and An-an boarded a train to go east to Vladivostok. In that port city, now ice free, they took passage on an English freighter bound for Hong Kong with a stopover in Shanghai.

Rogers had wired Uncle Steve of his resignation from the army. Except for Viktor, he had not told anyone else of his intention and he had ignored the colonel's earlier order to prepare for duty at a forthcoming Peace Conference in America.

The voyage south was an opportunity for the couple to renew married bliss and for them to escape the war, to plan for the future, to plot monumental changes for their destiny, and primarily to erase the agony of the past year and a half.

In Shanghai, Uncle Steve read a telegram from the War Department ordering him to provide transportation for Rogers to come to the San Francisco Presidio. The Department had refused Rogers' resignation. Worse, it had ignored the fact that he had a wife. It had left it up to Uncle Steve to arrange the travel papers, insisting there be no delay for Rogers. He must leave at once for the United States west coast.

* * * * * * * * * *

Three days later, Rogers charged into Uncle Steve's office and stood at his desk, glaring down at the seated official. The corpulent civilian should have seen the warning signs. He looked up at Rogers with impatience and scolded him.

"I don't know why you dared to leave Harbin without permission. If this is about your missing mail, I warn you not to let your temper get the best of your judgment. I tried to explain to Miss Chao that the mixup was only a bureaucratic fumble. Now, what is bothering you and why are you here without permission?"

Rogers began to lose control. "She is my wife, damn you, and her name is Mrs. Rogers."

"Now, now. Don't be insubordinate. All right then, *Mrs. Rogers.*"

Uncle Steve exhaled a cloud of smoke from his cigar, then coughed up phlegm and expectorated into his ever-present spittoon. He wondered how tough he dared to be. "I don't like your attitude, soldier. What is this about a resignation? You are under my orders, so listen to what I have to say."

Rogers refused to be intimidated. Watching so many men die over the past several months had made him less impressed with rank and the Washington bureaucracy. He was so full of anger that it finally spilled over. Blinded by what had happened to An-an, he exploded. "Fuck you, you fat son of a bitch." He let loose with a string of uncharacteristic profanity. "After what you put my wife through, I ought to pull you from behind that desk and rip off your balls."

Uncle Steve flinched as Rogers moved forward. He was too speechless to answer. *Was this the same young and nervous junior officer he had interviewed and then sent to Peking five years ago? The young loyal and obedient soldier who had been at his beck and call since then?* He sputtered in protest, his face the color of rare cooked beet. The noxious cigar had fallen from his fat lips and lay smoldering on the desktop. He tried to speak, but Rogers cut him short. "Listen, damn you to hell. I am through with the army and I am through with you. I have resigned and there is not a damn thing you can do about it. Don't ever cross me or my wife again."

Momentarily cowed, Uncle Steve managed to speak, "I don't understand your attitude—your insolent insubordination."

Rogers ignored his protest and continued, bringing his anger slowly under control, "I don't want to hear any lies. I know the full story. The British know it. The Shanghai postal inspectors know it. Maybe the whole world should know it, especially the War Department."

Now subdued, Uncle Steve became almost humble. He had not expected such a violent confrontation and such threats. He began to realize that his own career might be on the line, that he was facing a serious problem. Who knew what this infuriated and rebellious young officer might say or do? Did he really know everything? Did his wife possess some kind of incriminating proof? If the British knew something, suppose they had talked?

Choosing to ignore the insults, he hurried to make amends. "Look, Rogers, there is no need to get nasty about all this. We can come to some kind of agreement. I promise that I will provide documents for you and your wife to travel to the States. She will need clearance from the State Department, a passport, travel papers, health certificate and so on. I can do all that and I will set that process in motion at once. For some reason the War Department has ordered that you come to the San Francisco Presidio at once." He still wondered why Rogers was in such demand for the forthcoming peace negotiations on the east coast. He did not know that President Roosevelt had accepted the Japanese request to mediate the peace conference and was scrambling to assemble a knowledgeable team of any good men who knew the Manchurian area—something that the State Department had failed to provide.

"I told you that I have resigned. To hell with you and the army. Just get my wife's papers ready. And mine too."

Uncle Steve said soothingly, "Your resignation was denied by the War Department. If you want to see America again, you must go at once to San Francisco. By the way, how well do you know Senator Warren?"

Although the question caught him off guard, Rogers' face did not betray his surprise. *Who was this Senator Warren?*

Not hearing an answer, the official pressed on, "I understand that Captain John Pershing also recommended you."

Again Rogers refused to comment.

"Look Rogers, put the good of your country ahead of your feelings. Reconsider your resignation request—which has been refused anyway. You could have a good future ahead. Talk this over with Mrs. Rogers. I will meet with both of you tomorrow and start preparing all the necessary documents for you and your wife."

Rogers rose to his feet and stood looking down at the florid civilian. "You really are scum." With that he turned abruptly and left, angrily slamming the door behind him.

At their Shanghai hotel that evening, he and An-an talked long into the night. At first she reiterated her offer that they could ignore America, live in Hong Kong, and stay happy the rest of their lives. But the more they talked, the more she realized that Hong Kong did not hold as much appeal as before.

She liked both Xi and Larry Scott and treasured their friendship, and knew that she would easily like Marina. However, Xi might make talk about Viktor Alesandrov too awkward. So would Marina for the same reason. And even more troubling was the close relationship between her husband Ellis and Marina. An-an had resolved earlier not to question him about his bond with Marina, if there was one. She swore not to permit jealousy to cripple her life. But the nagging suspicion, however slight, might make a Hong Kong domicile troubling in the future. Who knew what might result from such a close proximity to Marina. Perhaps a cross or careless word, a petty lover's quarrel, something that might be said in jest or spite. Why test a love that had already endured so much recent pain?

She had noticed how tenderly Marina had talked about Ellis and it had made her uncomfortable.

So she began to emphasize her desire to see America. She suggested that her husband might want to rethink his decision to resign his army commission—that the enemy was not the War Department, but its representative in Shanghai.

"You have a very good chance for advancement," she told him. "I don't think you really want to leave the army. Why don't we go to this Uncle Steve, whatever his name is, and make our own demands. He has pushed himself into a corner. So, we'll tell **him** what **we** want in exchange for cancelling your resignation. If he refuses—." She shrugged.

Rogers at last reluctantly agreed. He did want to keep his commission. He did want to go back to America to try to find his mother, and to show An-an his country. Even if he could not force the issue with Uncle Steve, there was always Hong Kong, as An-an had pointed out. But he silently vowed never to be cowed again by Uncle Steve.

The War Department official was tremendously relieved to see them the next day and gave them a cordial greeting, acting as if the previous day's unpleasantness had never happened. Rogers expressed himself at once, putting it bluntly, "If I choose not to resign from the army and agree to go to the States as ordered, what will you do for us? I want to hear a good offer—

or else we are gone." He was almost surprised at his boldness. His contempt for the official had given him resolute courage.

Uncle Steve hurried to answer, "I will do whatever it takes to get you to the States. I will provide passage for you both, pay all expenses, produce the necessary documents. I'll do it all. The only thing I ask is that you leave for the States at once and that any misunderstanding we had in the past be forgotten."

Both An-an and Rogers looked at each other. *Could they trust him?* Finally Rogers nodded and said, "O.K., you have a bargain. But we will never forget how you almost ruined our marriage, how my wife was almost assassinated in Shanghai while trying to find me, and how she nearly died trying to reach me in Mukden. No, that is unforgivable. But we can set it aside for now. Just get all our travel papers together and then keep out of our lives."

Uncle Steve agreed, asking, "Then you will report at once at the Presidio?"

"Yes. We'll see you in two days. That should give you enough time. Put me in for six months leave and have all my back pay ready."

Outside the office, he told An-an, "He had better not fail. Let's relax and do the sights. We can use the time in the next two days to pack and send the necessary telegrams to Hong Kong."

An-an wired Marina with an offer for her to take over the import-export business office, telling her that the office staff would assist in handling the details, and An-an would open a companion office in San Francisco, since that was where she was sure that Rogers would be posted. Chen's association with Larry Scott's boat business was doing well, but An-an knew that Marina, with so many years of business success, might refuse to remain idle. Hong Kong was expanding faster than anyone had dreamed, and opportunities abounded.

With the help of two tugboats, the P & O liner eased into its berth in Honolulu. The ship had stopped for refueling. While the black gang and stevedores brought the sacks of coal aboard from the coal barges, Rogers explained to An-an that the United States, like most countries with active navies, maintained supplies of coal at strategically located coaling stations. Since the refueling process would take most of the day, he suggested they visit the city's commercial area for last minute shopping and especially for passport photos, which Uncle Steve had not been able to provide in the short time before their departure from Shanghai. "No problem," he had advised them, "you can easily get them in Honolulu."

When they returned to the ship, an immigration officer at the gangplank asked for their papers. He was polite and deferential to Rogers, but eyed An-an with suspicion. Rogers proffered his papers, saying, "My wife and I are traveling on an army errand. The papers should be in order."

The immigration man studied the papers, then said, "I understand your orders, sir, but these documents say nothing about army orders for the lady."

"You mean my wife," Rogers corrected him. "I am on an important errand. Obviously my wife is with me and we are in a hurry."

"Do you have a marriage certificate?"

Rogers was fast getting annoyed. "You have it in your hand."

"Yes," the official argued, "but this paper is from a private civil wedding performed by some missionary in China. It has no stamps or seal. It is dated from a time when we were unofficially at war with China. I'm afraid it won't do. Where is her passport?"

Grinding his teeth in exasperation, Rogers produced the passport photos that they had bought that afternoon. "These are hers. We were assured by the War Department that the ship's captain, who has the passports, would be authorized to add these to her passport and seal them.

"That is very unusual. You say that the ship's captain has her passport?"

"Yes. He has ours in his safe. Army Intelligence delivered them to the captain before we left Shanghai. There was no time to get a decent photo."

"I understand that your passport is undoubtedly in order, sir, but the lady's passport would have been issued and delivered by our consulate in Shanghai. It is a State Department matter, outside the army's jurisdiction. This is all very confusing and unusual. Why did you not apply at the consulate?"

Rogers did not want to mention the trouble he had encountered at the Shanghai consulate a few years ago when he had first gone to north China. He had almost come to blows with the supercilious and officious young consulate clerk and his marine sergeant protector.

"I am not too welcome at the Shanghai consulate, a past misunderstanding."

"Well, I am afraid that we may have to detain your wife. You can understand, I hope, that a passport is needed to get you into the United States, not out of it. And you are now standing on American soil. Has your wife ever been to the United States?"

Rogers shook his head and heaved a big sigh. *Had Uncle Steve tricked them again?* He tried to reason. "Look, we'll be right back and bring the passports to you."

"Sorry, sir. The lady will have to stay here with me."

Rogers started to shove An-an up the gangplank, telling the man that the ship was a P&O liner, flying the British flag, and therefore not American soil, but his way was blocked and two other immigration guards had hurried forward in answer to a whistle call.

An-an pleaded with Rogers to go alone to fetch the passports while she waited. The guard gave his consent and Rogers hurried aboard.

He soon returned with the passports and was told that his, though old, was legal. Hers was not regulation. "I am sorry folks, but the lady, er, your wife, will have to appear at the immigration office in the morning. They are closed for now. But, don't worry. She should be able to get another passport processed without too much trouble."

"And how long will that take?"

The man was vague. "It should not take more than half a day."

Rogers threw up his hands. "But this ship leaves in the morning."

The man offered no sympathy. He reminded Rogers that if An-an tried to leave Honolulu, she would be arrested in San Francisco—that he would be wise to bring her to the office in the morning and they would do all within their power to expedite the process.

So Uncle Steve had failed them again! Was it done on purpose? Or maybe the couple had been too trusting about the War Department's ability to circumvent the State Department rules. Rogers sent a telegram to Shanghai demanding an explanation, then he sat down with An-an at a nearby restaurant to hatch a scheme to cure their dilemma.

At noon, tug boats nosed the P&O steamer out into the channel. As the ship neared Diamond Head, a fast steam cutter intercepted the ship, cutting across her bow and signalling that two passengers, who had missed the ship,

608

were ready to come aboard. The British captain, having met and talked previously with Rogers, agreed to oblige.

Safely on board, Rogers told An-an that the stubborn immigration official, unaware that they had left Honolulu, would soon miss them. "When we reach San Franciso, an army delegation from the Presidio will be waiting for us. I have requested that. I will take you to Chinatown where you can stay until I get this mixup straightened out." ·

An-an had already told him that she preferred to remain behind in Chinatown. He had explained that he did not expect to be in Portsmouth, New Hampshire too long.

"O.K. Then when the conference is over, I will return to the Presidio. Captain Pershing, who will be coming to the Presidio, had indicated that he wants me to join his staff for several months. For a mere captain, he is very influential in Washington." An-an asked him why Pershing had shown no resentment toward her race.

"He's not racially prejudiced. He has commanded a black cavalry regiment in combat and in peacetime, and he knows how good they are. That is why they call him Black Jack Pershing. Besides, he has had a *querida* in the Philippines during the fighting against the Moros on Mindanao. A very pretty lady. Maybe you remind him of her."

"What about the State Department?"

"Don't worry. The State Department Secretary will help us. The President will see to that. And until the matter is cleared up, you will be safe in Chinatown. I'll be back on a train from New Hampshire before State's idiots can bother us in San Francisco. It is all bureaucratic politics, so don't worry."

And so the long journey together that they had begun during the march on Peking with the China Expedition was nearing a successful ending. An-

an clung to his side as they watched the steady course of the British liner knifing through the blue-gray waters of the Pacific. A team of four dolphins led the way, endlessly crisscrossing the prow of the ship, barely avoiding the edge of the metal hull with each playful leap. An-an was fascinated by the scene. "Such happy creatures," she said. "It's a good omen. I believe they are welcoming us to your country. We must be as carefree and joyous as they seem to be. Surely God will keep us together for the rest of our journey through life."

Rogers agreed. "There will be ups and downs, and disappointment and discouragment at times. That is part of life. But so is happiness and just rewards. We have each other to share in the next great adventure, so let us make the most of it." He pulled her body close to his and kissed her tenderly. "To hell with Port Arthur and all the tragedy it represented. That's a distant memory we can move beyond." He raised an imaginary glass in a mock salute: "Here's to us. *Tian-qi zhen hao,* what a lovely day."

He pulled her closer. "Let's follow the dolphins."

THE END

EPILOGUE

An-an stayed safely and comfortably in San Francisco's Chinatown where city authorities had always wisely let the Chinese community manage their own civic and justice affairs.

Rogers attended the Peace Conference in Portsmouth, New Hampshire. There he met Sergei Witte, leader of the Russian peace delegation and soon to be made a count. The large and unkept Witte, unpopular and somewhat anti-American, changed course after listening to Rogers' advice.

Earlier, Marina, seething from loss of her home and business in Port Arthur, had contacted Witte to warn that a strong hand would be needed to resolve the differences between Japan and Russia. She believed that America could provide that strength if privy to how the war was fought. Rogers provided that information and persuaded Witte to hang tough and to court the American press with a publicity campaign. Witte, with renewed confidence, did and turned American public opinion in favor of Russia.

Japan's diplomats failed to follow suit and lost public favor by being too unyielding in their insistence that Russia pay for the war. In any successful arbitration both sides need to concede something. Russia gave up some land and hegemony in Korea. Stubbornly, Japan, although virtually ruined economically, yielded little. President Roosevelt had begun to fear Japan's growing naval ambitions, and worried about America's "achilles heel," the Philippines.

Witte returned home a hero to his defeated nation, bringing a face-saving treaty. Japanese diplomat Baron Komura, a Harvard graduate, returned to a bankrupt nation, scorned and vilified. Disappointed and furious crowds of Japanese civilians rioted in massive protests.

Hundreds of thousands of brave Japanese and Russian soldiers and sailors had died in a bloody and now almost forgotten war, but one that set the stage nine years later for the even more horrible conflict known as the Great War or World War I.

Viktor married Claudette and brought her to St Petersburg where he soon became disillusioned with the brutal treatment of dissident citizens by Cossack regiments angry at supposed betrayal during the war. He resigned his commission and moved Claudette to southern France after she became ill from the harsh Russian winter. He gave up his land and titles to become a French citizen and vintner, and proved to his neighbors that a Russian emigre could produce one of France's best champagnes. He corresponded often with Rogers and An-an and was reunited with Rogers during America's unfortunate invasion of northern Russia in 1919 during the Russian Revolution.

After her insane attack on Rogers and An-an in Harbin, Sylvia Levinski met her destiny in Siberia. Lebedeff closed his case after examining her purse and two booted legs, all that remained in that dark, forbidding forest.

Marina and Chen purchased An-an's business in Hong Kong. Their venture prospered as well as the association with Larry and Xi Scott's shipbuilding business. Marina was increasingly content with her marriage to Chen and his proof that some older men remain surprisingly virile.

Ti became a member of the Fairborne family on their estate in England. Her successful arrangement with Nigel and Lydia remained a mystery to others, but was, nonetheless, accepted in their liberal social circle. Fairborne and Captain Packenham made recomendations to the British Admiralty that led to the development of the new Dreadnought class of battleships. And Fairborne also advanced the theory that defective steel armor on Russian ships had contributed to Russian naval defeats. He predicted that someday metalurgists would prove the steel plates to have been too brittle to withstand the shock of Japanese naval shells.

The spy, Philip Esley, was rejected by the Japanese conquerors of Port Arthur. A hopeless drunk, he spent his last days in a British sanitorium and was protected by the British government.

Captain Tanaka was invalided home to Hiroshima to find his wife, Ikura, and daughter, Yukio, near starvation. He slowly began to rebuild his life. He was successful, through General Nogi's intercession, in regaining his employment as a university professor, in spite of his war injuries.

General Nogi became a postwar principal of a school. Remorseful, because of the terrible casualties of the Third Army at Port Arthur, he and his wife received their emperor's permission to commit hari kari a few years later.

Food riots erupted in Hiroshima and larger Japanese cities. Togo's flagship *Mikasa* mysteriously blew up in Sasebo harbor. The Japanese prime minister and his cabinet resigned. News that Russia had refused to pay the war debt brought on much bitterness which the Japanese militarists used to their advantage, vowing retribution and blaming the Treaty of Portsmouth and the western world for Japan's hardships.

President Theodore Roosevelt won the Nobel Peace Prize for his efforts in the Treaty of Portsmouth that ended the war.

Generals Kuropatkin and Viceroy Admiral Alexeiev had prominent roles in World War I. General Kuropatkin, commander of the largest army in history in 1905, later survived the Russian revolution to become a clerk and school teacher.

General Smirnoff testified against General Stoessel. Stoessel was courtmartialed and sentenced to be shot, but was later pardoned and survived for a career in World War I.

General Fock was courtmartialed for failure to support Tretyakov at Nanshan.

Generals Samsonov and Rennenkampf served Russia in World War I and were involved in the disastrous Russian defeat at Tannenberg. Samsonov committed suicide after that battle.

Novy Kry's E. K. Nojine returned to Russia to write a book about the Port Arthur siege.

Alexander Bezobrazov served as Russian Secretary of State, then retired to Switzerland.

Scuttled Russian battleships *Poltava* and *Peresviet* and the cruiser *Pallada* were refloatred to become part of the Japanese navy.

Port Arthur, renamed Lushun, is now a major Chinese submarine base. Dalny is a modern beach resort titled Dalian or Dairen. Chefu was renamed Yantai. Mukden is now Shenyang.

Rogers joined Pershing's team after the Peace Conference. He and An-an studied for college degrees until 1910, then transferred to the Mexican border where both experienced more adventures during the Mexican Revolution.

Lessons of history are too often ignored or forgotten. Japan won the First Sino-Japanese War of 1894 with its sneak attack on China's navy. Japan won the Russo-Japanese War of 1904-5 largely with its sneak attack on Russia's Pacific Fleet at Port Arthur. Japan won a big advantage over America with its sneak attack on America's Pacific Fleet at Pearl Harbor in 1941. And Japan persisted with a sneak attack on Darwin, Australia in 1942.

Unfortunately, on the eve of war in Europe, the lessons of trench warfare learned by European army observers on the heights above Port Arthur and on the plains and hills of Manchuria had largely been forgotten or ignored. By 1914 it was too late to remind the contentious crowned heads of Europe that, "those who ignore history are doomed to repeat it."

History is exciting and sometimes romantic. But history also involves humans who sacrifice their lives in loyal and dedicated service to their countries. History records conflicts between nation-states who struggle to gain power, often motivated by greed, economic opportunities, nationalism, even religion. In every generation former allies or enemies may reverse roles in a maddening cycle. In the end the citizens of nations endure catastrophic suffering and make the ultimate sacrifice. Thus history is repeated as succeeding generations continue to reject the lessons of their fathers. Because of this failure and the latent evil in human nature, it continues to be necessary for a nation to remain strong, well armed and vigilant.

THE END

Gene Denson

REFERENCES

Before Port Arthur in a Destroyer: The Personal Diary of a
   Japanese Naval
Officer by Hesibo Tikobara. Translated from Spanish by
   Captain R. Grant, D.S.
John Murray Press, London, 1907

Human Bullets: A Soldier's Story of Port Arthur by
   Captain Tadayoshi Sakurai
Translated by Masiyiro Honda and Alice M. Bacon
Tokyo Teibi, 1925 & Houghton Mifflin co., New York, 1907

Port Arthur: The Siege and Capitulation by Ellis Ashmead-Bartlett
W. Blackwood & Sons. Edinburgh &London, 1906

Port Arthur: Three Months with the Besiegers by Frederic Villiers
Longmans, Green and Co., London & New York, 1905

Red Sun Rising: The Siege of Port Arthur by Reginald Hargreaves
J.B. Lippincott Co. Pa. & New York, 1962

Russia Against Japan, 1904-1905 by J. N. Westwood
State University of New York Press. Albany, 1986

Russian Hussar: A Story of the Imperial Cavcalry, 1911-1920
   by Vladimir Littauer

The Illustrated History of the Russo-Japanese War by
    J. N. Westwood
Henry Regnery Company. Chicagto, 1973

The War of the Rising Sun and Tumbling Bear. A Military History
    of the Russo-Japanese War,1904-5 by R.M. Connaughton
Routledge Press, London, 1988

Tigers in the Snow by Peter Mathiessen
North Press, New York, 2000

Tsushima (Island of Donkey Ears) by A. Novikoff-Priboy
Translated by Eden and Cedar Paul
Alfred A. Knopf Press, New York

Windows on the River Neva: A Memoir by Paul Grabbe
Pomerica Press, Ltd. New York 1977

ABOUT THE AUTHOR

Gene Denson has always believed that the Russian-Japanese War of 1904-1905 should be more familiar to Americans because of its relationship to the Japanese-American War thirty-six years later, known to history as World War Two. He served in the U.S. Merchant Marine in this war and was briefly an artillery officer in the Korean War. He is a retired history professor who has been a communication engineer, areospace senior test engineer, Superior Court officer and security officer. He has lived in Asia and currently resides in Deltona, Florida with his wife Nancy. This novel, though it stands alone, is a sequel to his previous novel, *The Tartar Wall*, which dealt with the Boxer Rebellion in China. The author has a third book in work which will complete the trilogy story of his protagonist, Ellis Rogers, who represents events and characters involved in the author's own life...an affirmation of the testament that "truth is often stranger than fiction." And often more exciting.

Printed in the United States
1455200001B/133-153

9 781410 724458